RIFT

I0770022

aberrant
form
press

THOMAS
ASHER

RIFT

a novel

Published by Aberrant Form Press, LLC

First edition October 2025
Published in the United States by Aberrant Form Press, LLC.

Cover art created by Pablo Dominguez, © 2021
Illustrated plates by Steve White, © 2021 Thomas Asher
Appendix illustrations © 2021 by Frederic Wierum
Appendix illustrations © 2021 by Mark Witton
Appendix illustrations © 2025 by Rudolf Hima
All remaining illustrations © 2025 by Thomas Asher

Excerpts from THE MYTH OF SISYPHUS by Albert Camus, translated by Justin O'Brien, translation copyright ©1955, copyright renewed 1983 by Penguin Random House LLC. Used by permission of Alfred A. Knopf, an imprint of the Knopf Doubleday Publishing Group, a division of Penguin Random House LLC. All rights reserved.

www.tomashernovels.com/rift
www.facebook.com/tomashernovels • www.instagram.com/tomasherofficial

For Roger

"God does not play dice with the universe."

—Albert Einstein

HOMO SAPIENS

i.

Six men labored in single file across the Siberian tundra, plumes of white condensation rising into the crisp air from beneath their fur-lined hoods. Backpacks loaded with food, water, and gear bounced in synchrony to their cadence, while shouldered rifles glinted gold beneath the waning rays of a dying ember cresting a nearby mountainside. The company plodded along quietly in its shadow, their faces slathered in bag balm, gloves and boots lined with carbon-activated warmers.

Sy-raykuo—Kuo for short—was the man leading the expedition. A local Nganasan native, he guided the men across the unforgiving terrain, heading southwest along a hillside abutting the frozen Kheta River. He paused intermittently to survey the familiar route, squinting across drifts of powder that stretched beyond his perception—their ridges always bloomed pink beneath the Rayleigh during this time of day. But the primary object of Kuo's fixation was the silence in his ears, interrupted only by the snow crunching underfoot, the air cycling through his lungs. It was the silence that filled him with unease.

After decades of captive breeding and rewilding in the northeast, Northern Siberia was teeming with wildlife. *Eco-engineering,* the stewards called it. Since the program's inception, over two dozen new species thrived in the region. Among them, wisent bison, Yakutian horses, musk ox, Saiga antelope, reindeer, and elk all helped restore the ancient steppe grassland.

Once ungulate populations had stabilized, the stewards next introduced the Siberian tiger and the extirpated tundra wolf. These predators served a critical role in maintaining ecological balance as animal populations expanded west into the Taymyr Peninsula, and it was in the silent spaces that predators stalked.

Then there were the necrofauna.

Mammuthus asiaticus—or kalàja, according to the Nganasan people—were some of the first "de-extinct" species introduced to the region. Mammoths were hybrids of the extinct steppe mammoth and the functionally extinct Asian elephant. Before the Quaternary Extinction, these mega-herbivores had dominated Earth's ecosystems, shaping the soil beneath their feet. After their resurrection and repatriation to Siberia, the kalàja once again reigned supreme, restoring ancient grasslands that shielded the carbon-rich permafrost from the sun, thereby prolonging sequestration of the single largest carbon reservoir on Earth.

The Pleistocene Project was one of humanity's last efforts to mitigate runaway climate change, and the revival of the fading Asian elephant also served as a second chance for the species, its gene pool preserved within a new form. A phoenix from the ashes.

But most of the Samoyedic natives did not see it that way. Kalàja herds grew and migrated west, raiding and destroying native farmland along the way. In winter, they subsisted mainly on tree bark and lichen. Modern Siberian grasses, it turned out, did not sit well with the primitive gastrointestinal systems of mammoths. As their herds expanded, kalàja populations went unchecked, their sheer size exempting them from natural predation. Kuo's village was among those forced to ration food after herds decimated most of the crops before the last harvest.

Then came the plague: a novel strain of *Mycobacterium tuberculosis* that swept through several Samoyedic villages. This illness, the natives concluded, was caused by the spirit of the kalàja, punishing man for removing it from the realm of the dead. Because of this, the other dominant Samoyedic tribe, the Enets, outright refused to handle any part of a resurrected mammoth. To them, a tusk or pelt formed a vessel for the animal's spirit. When touched, possession took hold of the item's handler, exiling their soul to the realm of the dead.

The climbing death tolls brought the natives back to their roots, and a resurgence in ancient shamanistic ways helped restore balance. Kuo himself had trained in the shamanistic arts. Outside of leading expeditions, he was responsible for carrying out the last rites of the dead.

But it wasn't until a large outbreak of tuberculosis reached the city of Novosibirsk that the Russian government stepped in. Within months, the Ministry of Health oversaw a mass-vaccination campaign across the region. A year later, Minzdrav confirmed *Mammuthus asiaticus* as the primary reservoir for the disease—something the natives had known all along.

To control megafauna populations, the Ministry of Natural Resources and the Environment—Miniprody for short—introduced an international lottery system for trophy hunters to help cull the herds. The government employed the Nganasan people to sustain these hunts until a suitable predator could be introduced to the region.

For his part, Kuo facilitated sanctioned expeditions and ensured kills were legal and humane. Hunters came for the thrill and the photo op, but the animals stayed behind. They shipped the meat to Krasnoyarsk. Pelts went to non-native villages, ivory to Moscow. Nothing went to waste.

On this particular expedition, Kuo's group consisted of an American, an Australian, two Russians, and a Chinese man. He led them through a cluster of low-lying shrubs as they negotiated the hillside. Before long, the men rounded the crest, and the wind welcomed their arrival, rapping against the thick salves slathered on their faces. Kuo's elk-skin jacket shielded his core.

His callused eyelids fell and then rose again, and his gaze drifted down toward a boundless plain. At the edge of his purview, grazing woolly rhinos materialized alongside feral Yakutian horses, their shaggy hides rimmed in the soft glow of dusk. Beyond them loomed the faint blue outline of the vast Putarone Plateau, where the Russian gas giant Benzineft drilled deep into the Arctic soil. Around a kilometer to the south, a small, wooded area of snow-covered larch stood solitary in the golden light, and near the base of the hill on which Kuo and his men stood was a smattering of dusted boulders long ago deposited by ancient glaciers—now fading monoliths from a bygone era.

"You sure there's mammoths out here?" Julian Miller, the American, grunted. "We've been walkin' for almost four hours."

Miller was a dentist and infamously maligned trophy hunter back in the United States.

"Mammoth are most active at twilight," Kuo said in broken English. "We have only now entered kalàja territory."

Miller muttered something under his breath, but Kuo struggled to make it out through the man's thick Texas accent. Something about "experience." About not *needing* a guide.

This man is going to be trouble, he thought.

Already, he suspected Miller of forging his tuberculosis vaccination papers.

Miller seemed to be at odds with Logan Campbell, the Australian. Campbell, in turn, did not hide his disdain for Miller. Kuo suspected it had to do with Campbell being a professional trophy hunter; to him, the dentist was a mere hobbyist, a loudmouthed amateur.

The most respectful and quiet of the lot, Jian Oiao, was the CEO of a large computer tech company out of China. He had also placed the highest bid to secure a spot for the hunt and was the only man capable of using his financial clout to bypass the lottery altogether.

The two Russians rounded out the bunch—one joining in on the hunt, and the other sent by Miniprody to collect samples and facilitate an audit of the expedition. The deputy joining in on the excursion was Dimitri Borisyuk, Assistant to the Minister of the Central Body of Miniprody. Tagging along was his friend Timur Volkov, a well-connected bureaucrat from Moscow who had decided not to pass up an opportunity to take down a mammoth.

Kuo had been with worse groups. At least everyone could speak a common language, which happened to be English.

The men settled at the base of the hill, taking refuge beneath the shadows of the towering snow-covered henge that shielded them from the harsh wind. Kuo turned to face them.

"We set up camp here. Ready our gear. Then we hunt."

"'Bout gatdamn *time*," Miller growled.

Kuo ignored him, looking around at the other men. "Do not stray from group. Stick together."

"And if I need to take shits, comrade?" Volkov snorted in a heavy Russian accent.

Subdued chuckles came from all but Jian.

"Pair up and take shits-buddy," Kuo said, prompting laughter from all but the CEO.

Miller gave Jian, who was sitting quiet beside him, a playful nudge. "Hey, loosen up—Jon, is it?"

Jian looked up to meet his gaze with a composed expression, and the group fell into an uncomfortable silence. With a stone-cold stare, he responded, "Yes. Like Johnny Appleseed. And you are... Tex?"

"Jonny Boy makes joke!" Volkov erupted. He pointed at Miller with a grin. "From now on, comrade, you are Tex."

They finished setting up camp as the last rays of daylight fell behind the mountains. Kuo readied a drone to be sent up in the morning to locate the nearest mammoth herd. His limbs ached as he slipped into his insulated sleeping bag and fell heavily onto his pillow. The men were silent. Kuo faded from consciousness.

ii.

At first, Kuo wasn't sure what had startled him awake. His eyes shot open and darted around the blackened interior of the tent. As his vision adapted, he began to parse the outline of other human shapes sitting upright around him.

The others heard it too. Noises erupted a few dozen meters from the encampment.

Animal sounds. A struggle.

A trumpeting wail shattered the night air. Then silence fell once more.

Campbell reached for his rifle. "That's a bloody mammoth," he whispered as he motioned for the entrance, wearing nothing but a tank and underwear.

Kuo grabbed him by the shoulder. He sensed Campbell's eyes searing into him through the still blackness. *This is our opportunity,* the Australian's body language communicated. This behavior surprised Kuo; up to that point, Campbell hadn't struck him as impulsive. And now, he was going to run into an active situation in nothing but his bungies. Maybe he was more like Miller than Kuo had thought.

Kuo remained firm, shaking his head with a finger to his lips.

A chorus of growls broke the silence, returned by the resonant roar of the mammoth. It sounded like a juvenile.

"Tigers?" Miller whispered.

"Smilodons," Kuo said. "Entire pride of them." The rhythm of pulsing blood drummed in his ears. His breathing grew shallow.

Siberian tigers—*amba* to the Nganasan people—stayed away from mammoths. The big cats had been introduced to the region some years prior, but they were solitary, and they never pursued anything larger than a horse. Smilodons, though, were more akin to lions, employing coordinated pack-hunting tactics to take down larger prey. Encountering a smilodon pride was rare because their introduction to the region was so new. After a protracted captive breeding program, the government had phased in the smilodons to regulate mammoth and rhino populations.

Miniprody had its predator.

To the Nganasans, they were the aslan.

Of all the Siberian necrofauna, Kuo despised the aslan most. Like mammoths, the cats were not of this realm. But they were also not of this land—the Samoyedic land. Mammoths and woolly rhinos had roamed the Siberian plains over a million years prior, but large sabertooths had never stalked Eurasia. They were from the Americas. They did not belong in Siberia.

At least that means the herd is nearby.

The kalàja never strayed far from a fallen member, often lingering for days before moving on. Sometimes, they returned to mourn their dead after the aslan had finished feeding.

But until smilodon numbers went up, *Homo sapiens* stood in to cull the herds.

iii.

Dawn broke, casting shadows from the stony columns onto the green walls of the tent. Loud snores erupted from the Miniprody deputy's sleeping bag.

Sluggish at first, Kuo rose and rubbed the sleep from his eyes. His mind snapped into focus.

The smilodons… the mammoth.

After the men woke, Kuo led them out beyond the boulder field and onto the open plain. He spotted the carcass almost immediately, its shaggy brown fur ruffling in the light breeze beneath a dusting of snow. It had the square head of an Asian elephant, but the bulk and long tusks of a steppe mammoth. The fur was clumped together with ice and blood, and a frozen waterfall of black coagulum cascaded from a ragged stump that once formed a trunk. One of the legs was severed and missing.

As they drew near, a foul stench penetrated the air. The bureaucrat, Volkov, heaved.

Kuo turned to the deputy. "If your comrade can't stay quiet around mammoth scent, perhaps you should hang back," he whispered.

He kept watch for the rest of the herd.

They can't be far.

Borisyuk gave him a sour look and turned to Volkov, mumbling something in Russian. He turned back to Kuo.

"Here." The deputy handed him a collection kit. "I need two saliva sample. This one for blood. And this for hair."

Kuo took the kit and led the other men to the carcass, from which streaks of red snow trailed off toward the distant grouping of larch trees. Bloody paw prints marred the serenity of the fresh snowfall. The aslan seldom stuck by a kill for long. Instead, they would drag whatever they could carry back to their den or some nearby tree cover to feed.

But, Kuo thought, *there still might be scavengers.*

"It is subadult kalàja," he said, walking up to the animal. "Separated from the herd."

He was surprised there were no other animals around the mammoth. The smell had started to spread with the morning thaw and would soon draw other predators.

Kuo reached into his pocket and removed a surgical mask. He was leaning in to collect the samples when he spotted movement in his periphery. He jerked his head up, and his gaze fell on a pair of small amber eyes staring back at him about twenty meters from the carcass. The fox must have been standing there the whole time, its white coat blending seamlessly into its surroundings.

"Why's it hangin' back?" Miller said.

Then, without warning, a towering brown mass emerged from behind one of the boulders—a fully grown cow, the mother of the slain subadult. She bellowed a deafening rumble, kicking up jets of snow in her wake as she charged the men with astonishing speed.

There was no time to react. Kuo froze. His only hope was to stand his ground. If he fled, she would run him down. He waved to the others to do the same.

There was the click of a rifle loading.

"*Do not shoot!*" Kuo growled, keeping his eyes on the advancing beast. Even if someone managed to get a shot in, it wouldn't stop her before she trampled them to death. "You shoot, we are dead!"

The cow came straight at him in a herculean display of pure adrenaline and no sign of backing down. Ingots of packed snow fell from her hulking frame as her ears fanned outward.

Kuo did not flinch. His legs trembled like mad over the shaking earth. His heart, it seemed, had catapulted into his skull, pounding with ceaseless fury against its bony walls as another bellow rattled his bones.

This is it. This is how I leave this Earth.

Kuo was about to squeeze his eyes shut when the mammoth stopped several meters from where he stood. He sucked cold air through his teeth, nearly losing his composure as a horrifying groan swelled from her depths. She stared down her trunk at him, raked the ground with clubbed feet, then backed away slowly, her ears thrashing in agitation. But it wasn't over yet. Again, the mammoth charged, this time stopping within just a few meters. She appeared wary but was obviously trying hard to call his bluff, get him to flinch. But, after her third offensive, the mammoth yielded and turned away, trumpeting a refrain of mournful wails as she receded into the distance.

Kuo exhaled and turned toward the men. Against his request, they had run for cover.

"Line up," he said and started a head count.

Four men. He counted again. Still four.

The American was gone.

"Where is Miller?"

Campbell nodded toward the now-distant mammoth.

Kuo turned and squinted in the sunlight. "*Derr'mo.*"

Several hundred meters out, Miller was stalking close behind her, rifle in hand. The two of them headed east, then disappeared behind the crest of a snowdrift.

"*Son of bitches!*" Kuo pulled out a pair of binoculars and watched the plain beyond the sloping dune. A minute passed. The brown body of the mammoth emerged in the distance. He waited. Two minutes. Three. Five. Miller did not reappear.

A distant scream pierced the gentle breeze.

iv.

Snowflakes tumbled from the heavens. Kuo stayed low, raising his binoculars to scan the tree line from where he had last seen Miller. It was here that the American's footsteps stopped, met by those of a solitary aslan. A scuffle had taken place.

Kuo tracked a path through the blood-dappled snow that led to the gently swaying copse of larch and spotted a smilodon lazing under one of the trees. Her muscular tongue lapped something just beyond his view.

Grooming, he thought.

The aslan's bulky head bobbed atop a muscular neck with black spots that continued down her tawny coat. A long, bushy tail rose and fell behind her—a snow leopard trait, and a reminder of her forced existence, because Smilodon DNA had been hybridized with that of Central Asian snow leopards to help the big cats better adapt to the harsh steppe climate.

Kuo moved in closer. Again, he peered through the binoculars. Three cubs came into view, their fuzzy limbs writhing over each other as they gorged on their mother's milk. Kuo panned back to the bobbing head of the female. What he saw next forced him to wrench the binoculars away and hold back an onslaught of involuntary retching.

The mother smilo wasn't *grooming*; she was scraping the skin clean off a *human arm*.

Kuo gathered himself and looked again. The cat paused for a moment and stretched her mouth into a yawn, exposing two pearlescent canines that resembled large, recurved stakes. She repositioned the limb between her powerful forepaws, standing it upright. The pale blue fingers curled inward, the wrist limp. Her muscular tongue scraped against exposed connective tissue, lapping thick smears of blood onto its studded surface.

Kuo imagined the sensation of hundreds of barbed papillae grating against his flesh like sandpaper. His skin crawled.

More movement caught his eye. He panned the binoculars across the tree line and spotted two more adults, their patchy coats concealing them beneath the mottled underbrush. More movement. *At least two more. That makes at least five adults*—a pride of them, resting after a meal.

"What is it?" Borisyuk whispered beside him in Russian. He had decided to accompany Kuo, as this was now a government matter.

Kuo responded, also in Russian, and passed the binoculars. "Found Miller."

Borisyuk peered through the oculars. "Da...." He shook his head. "Fucking American." He turned back to Kuo. "This was not your fault. Was bound to happen. That is why we have them sign waiver."

Kuo shook his head. "I have capture crew nearby. I'll call them in to help me recover the body. Smilos will need to be put down."

"Nyet. Can't let you do that, comrade."

"Excuse me?"

Looking through the binoculars, Borisyuk responded in English, "These animal, they are protected. They are under jurisdiction of Miniprody."

Still in Russian, Kuo shot back. "They are *eating* a fucking *man* right in front of us. They will do this again. There is native village only a few kilometer from here. Are you telling me—"

"Not up for debate, Tavgi. Get your men. Make sure they use nonlethals."

Hot blood flushed Kuo's cheeks. The umbrella term "Tavgi" was an old Russian word for Siberian natives. In recent years, it had fallen back into use and was considered a modern slur. Borisyuk didn't give a shit about that village.

But the truth was more nuanced—the local tribes were at risk regardless of the attack on Miller. Kuo knew it, and so did the deputy. They also knew that *Smilodon fatalis* was hardwired to kill people; that human flesh was neither an acquired taste nor a preferred one for the big cats. Thousands of years ago, when smilodons cohabitated with man, they had evolved to recognize *Homo sapiens* as a threat—competition over limited resources. African lions did it with rival predators like hyenas. Smilodon was no different. Neither were ancient humans, who would not have hesitated to kill a cat on sight. *That*, Kuo knew, was the real reason the aslan had killed the American.

"*Call* your *men*." Borisyuk's words filled the frigid air with menace.

v.

Back at the camp, the men in the expedition huddled around a small fire, awaiting a substitute guide after Kuo's announcement that he would stay behind to help retrieve Miller's remains. Another local Nganasan had been assigned to the group, Kuo assured them, and was already en route.

No one spoke.

An hour passed, and the roar of an approaching snowmobile compelled the men to lift their heads.

The sled screamed into the campsite with two natives aboard, hauling a large wire cage on skis. The driver removed his helmet, followed by the passenger—Kuo's cousin, Numatsku. The driver, Dyamaku, was also a local shaman and a friend of Numatsku's.

Dyamaku approached Kuo and extended a handshake. "Kuo, good to see you," he said in Russian.

Numatsku came up behind him. "How many aslan?"

"Seven adult. Two male, five female. One with three cub."

"They have cub? How big?" Dyamaku said.

"Da. Still small. They have milk teeth."

"Good. We will take mother down last." Dyamaku turned and patted the wire cage. "Good thing we were hauling this. We will keep cub secure until mother's sedative fades and it is safe to nurse. Our tranq dosing would kill suckling cub five time over."

vi.

The falling snow contrasted against the gruesome scene framed behind the still thicket. Miller's body had been horrifically mauled, his abdominal cavity opened up into a hollow exenteration absent of viscera. Congealed blood pooled at the bottom around ropes of shredded muscle that sheathed the spinal column. His chewed face was devoid of any semblance of humanity, the nose, lips, and ears reduced to knotted stubs, the eye sockets nothing more than blood-filled voids. His lipless mouth gaped, his reddened teeth pried apart by a swollen tongue.

Beside the body, two incapacitated male aslan dozed, their reddened muzzles clotted with cruor. Mammoth remains—leg bones, fur, part of a trunk—were scattered nearby. Beneath Miller, the snow was stained deep crimson amid a flurry of brownish-red paw prints. A ragged length of intestine stretched to a fallen tree limb, where it had gotten snagged as the big cat dragged his corpse through the underbrush.

But the signature of a smilo kill was the presence of puncture wounds at the top of the victim's skull—two holes, each the width of a human thumb that pierced deep into the grey matter. Ambushed from behind. This was often how they found the bodies.

Bastard was dead before he even hit the ground.

Footsteps approached Kuo from behind.

"He deserves last rites," Dyamaku said in Russian as he and Numatsku entered the wood. The cubs cried for their mother from the cage.

Kuo spat. "He is not one of us. Not Nganasan."

"He is on Nganasan land. This is hallowed ground. His spirit has passed into realm of the dead on *our* land. Here it will remain long after the body is taken away."

"He is right, Kuo," Numatsku said. His expression betrayed fear. "We need to perform last rites."

"Fine." Kuo was growing impatient, but if he denied Miller last rites, he would never hear the end of it. "I will lead. I do not have drum, though."

"Not a problem." Numatsku walked to the sled parked at the edge of the tree line and reached into his gear bag. He pulled out an elk-skin tambourine, walked back over to Kuo, and handed it to him. "You can use mine."

vii.

The body was not to be disturbed until the séance had ended.

The three men built a small fire and encircled it among the slumbering cats. Kuo stared into the orange flames and breathed in. At his feet lay a piece of parchment adorned with a crude drawing of a circle bisected into quadrants. In the lower right was Miller, and in the lower left, the pride of aslan. The top two quadrants housed the moon and sun. Kuo's helping spirits, the kajkə, would come to rest in this circle after their task was complete.

Kuo pulled his ceremonial headband over his eyes, and everything fell into blackness. He let his mind drift. A gentle wind stirred, rapping his ears, and soon, the sound drowned out the wailing cubs. The scent of smoke hung heavy. The frigid January air numbed all remaining sensations. Shamans trained their minds to achieve sensory deprivation, which facilitated the spiritual journey into the realm of the dead.

Kuo's spirit stirred.

The séance had begun.

"*Dis. Ko-u ko-u ko-u...*" he chanted, calling on his helping spirits.

At first, Kuo took the form of an elk, then a swan, then the clouds on which the swan traveled. These were the first of the kajkə upon which he called. With their assistance, he beckoned Miller's spirit to the other side. His voice droned in rhythm with his body, swaying fore and aft on crossed legs. The beating of the drum had hold of him now.

It did not take long for Kuo to leave himself, and soon, he was levitating over the warm flames—above his men and the sleeping cats. Above the trees. Above the Earth.

Far below, he could still hear supporting chants from Numatsku and Dyamaku over the percussive rapping of the drum. They tethered him to the realm of the living. Without them, he might never find his way back. "*Ee-is, ee ee. O-uok o-uok o-uok. Ges. Oo-ok Oo-ok Oo-ok...*" they droned.

Something rushed past Kuo.

Miller.

It was done.

Kuo descended through the clouds and falling snow and re-entered his body. He and his men chanted together.

"*Hee-hei-hee! Hee-hei-hee! Hee-hei-hee! Hee-hei-hee...*"

Once more, Kuo smelled the stench of death.

RIFT

ONE

We roamed free among the wild elk
food aplenty
elk hide to keep our bodies warm.
I am no longer a master of elk.
I am no longer of this world.
I walk now among spirits,
they return the calls of the shaman.
You now walk the path to the other realm.
Go forward.

—Nganasan prayer

α | VECTOR ALPHA >

The sharp smell of diesel wormed into Jerome's sinuses, his kaffiyeh whipping alongside strands of long black hair as the Benz roared over cracked desert. Resembling a small jeep, these "safari wagons" held up best to the punishing environment of the Moroccan Sahara, and they were especially well suited for digs.

The harsh midday sun beamed into the roofless cabin as dust billowed past. Beside Jerome, the rolled-up burlap roofing swayed in tandem with the rocking chassis. A fine layer of ground grit coated every inch of the interior, where the console served as a makeshift field kit with dirt-riddled brushes and metal picks in its cupholders. Around the shifter, discarded fossil fragments bounced haphazardly in the shadow of a plastic retro Spinosaurus superglued to the dash. A rusted pickaxe leaned against a dented toolbox that rattled noisily under a two-person tent at his feet.

Jerome turned and nodded to two men in the back.

"How much farther?" he yelled over the rumble of the engine.

His guide, Ismail, turned away from the stretch of desert flying past, his eyes obscured behind a pair of red bootleg Ray-Bans. A scraggly black beard did little to mask his sunken cheeks. Beside Ismail sat one of the expedition's guards, Karim, whose head easily cleared the vehicle's roll bar. Six foot four and built like an ox, Karim made Ismail appear emaciated by comparison. Both men hailed from the nearby oasis town of Erfoud.

"Very close now," Ismail said with a heavy East Moroccan accent, then reached over the console to point past the windshield. "That hill, over there."

About a mile out, Jerome spotted a steep bluff rising from the shimmering sands. *The Gara Sbaa formation.* A limestone cap formed a white protuberance atop the fossil-rich red beds below, and a thick blue haze blanketed a large talus at its base. The formation stretched to the horizon, reflected in the heat haze along the desert floor.

Jerome figured the team could climb to the dig site in around twenty minutes and take the next day or two to prospect the area. He projected that it should take three weeks for quarrying and transport, assuming they found anything of value. But getting the fossils down from such a high spot in the middle of nowhere posed its own challenges.

Ahead of them, another safari wagon led the convoy. In the back seat, Jerome's postdoc Murphy "Murph" O'Brien stared ahead at the looming escarpment. Her red ponytail bobbed beneath a gray baseball cap. In the front, the expedition's leader, paleontologist Qadir Nassar, pored over field notes as he pointed the driver to their destination.

Throughout his career, Dr. Nassar had led many Saharan digs that unearthed countless North African fossils. Among his most famous finds were a new giant subspecies of the azhdarchid pterosaur, *Alanqa saharica*, and the most complete *Spinosaurus aegyptiacus* ever found. He had followed in the footsteps of his father, Nadeem Nassar, who was also a well-known Moroccan paleontologist. Qadir's mother was French, and the family had moved to the United States when he was a young boy, but it was here, in Morocco, that he appeared to be in his element.

Jerome returned to the men in the back seat. Karim disregarded the vehicle's other occupants, silently scanning the stone formations for threats. A long rifle leaned upright across his barreled chest, partially obscuring a red-and-yellow Royal Moroccan Army insignia. Every few minutes, his shoulder-mounted radio buzzed with chatter from a group of local desert nomads aiding the army in surveilling for fossil looters and Islamic insurgents looking for fresh hostages.

Jerome did his best to put this from his mind, to remind himself that this specimen was worth the risk. Recent Kem Kem finds out of this locality were among the most well-preserved, far exceeding the exquisite soft tissue remains isolated from T. rex fossils out of the Hell Creek Formation by his friend and colleague, Amara Schwartz. Good samples were already a rarity, and such finds played a critical role in his research.

Close behind, five more vehicles rounded out the convoy. The smell of gasoline fumes reminded Jerome of his childhood, before most governments phased out petroleum-guzzling cars, and before most supply lines suspended operations. He could barely make out the shapes of the remaining convoy through a trailing plume of brown dust. These vehicles housed Qadir's two graduate students, several local volunteers, and four more guards.

He peered out again across swaths of parched earth and imagined the vast river delta that flowed through the region almost a hundred million years ago, stretching north toward the Tethys Sea. Giant theropods like Spinosaurus and Carcharodontosaurus stalked these ancient Saharan estuaries, ruling over an impressive assemblage of crocodiles, pterosaurs, and car-sized fish.

But what made the Kem Kem so unique was that, despite harboring such large predatory fauna, herbivores were relatively rare. Save for a couple of sauropods, a thyreophoran tooth, and an isolated set of possible hadrosaur footprints, few such fossils had been found. This preponderance of carnivores was known as "Stromer's Riddle."[1]

Hell on Earth.

Even as recently as three thousand years ago, lush vegetation proliferated across the Sahara Desert to form an ecosystem that harbored a wide variety of vertebrates. Now, it was a wasteland.

How ironic that the Sahara holds the key to preserving life for the rest of us.

Riding through the barren desert was like traveling forward in time—a snapshot of the impending desolation to come. In the last decade, arboreal bird populations had plummeted worldwide, an anomaly referred to as the

---

1 See appendices for more information.

Mass Avian Extinction. To most experts, it marked the beginning of the Sixth Extinction. After the loss of hundreds of thousands of species due to climate change, local ecosystems began collapsing all over the planet. A runaway train on a collision course with life as everyone knew it.

And here Jerome was, digging up the past to try and save the future.

Jerome shouted back to Ismail again. "How do you get gas for these vehicles?"

Ismail shrugged. "Russia, mostly, I think."

Benzineft—the Russian petrol giant—was infamous for its recent drilling in the Arctic, a move that threatened to liberate vast stores of sequestered carbon into the atmosphere. International sanctions seemed to do little to halt the drilling.

This vehicle is probably powered by Arctic crude, Jerome thought, *while we're on a mission to prevent a mass-extinction event caused by runaway climate change.*

When they arrived at the site, Ismail pointed to a flat recess halfway up the rock face toward a limestone cap that loomed overhead like an ancient altar. Beneath it lay the Cenomanian–Turonian platform—and their dig site.

"That's where I found it," he said.

Getting up the rocky talus proved more difficult than Jerome had anticipated. The pile of loose rock shifted beneath his feet as he scrambled over piled stones. Rocks tumbled down the slope, interrupting the sound of labored breathing as stinging sweat seeped into his eyes. The shade of the looming precipice did little to stifle the suffocating heat.

Then came the vertical climb. Two of the locals fixed running ropes into cleats, then hung back at the wall base to belay the rest of the team as they scaled the rough sandstone. Jerome rounded the flat recess that Ismail had already prospected, close behind the younger and more agile Murph, who glided up the rock face with ease. Jerome heaved with his hands on his knees, but Murph was already at work. She procured a miniaturized portable CT scanner and waved it over the striated rock.

"Here," she said after a few hours of prospecting. "This looks like our site. At least two articulated skeletons. Theropods. No preliminary signs of osseous burrows." She was referring to boring beetle burrows formed in bones by the larvae of an ancient carrion beetle *Osteocallis mandibulus*. The presence of these tunneling structures spelled doom for Jerome's efforts, because such fossils always had poor soft tissue yields. Larval tunnels exposed osseous tissues to decay, and Jerome wanted to rule out their presence before extricating a specimen.

"Looks like multiple individuals, possibly theropods," Qadir said. "We'll cut around, take it back to Chicago as a slab. Looks like a couple years' worth of excavation once it's out of the ground."

For nearly a month, the team toiled in the blazing sun, excavating the reddish sandstone slab. Embedded inside the chunk of rock were four remarkably preserved skeletons, buried in a mudflow some ninety-five million years prior. It was the type of find his colleagues often referred to as a "fossil bonanza."

In the dig's final weeks, Jerome realized logistics had hardly been discussed.

"This thing has to weigh three tons," Murph said on one particularly hot day.

Jerome wiped his earth-caked hands onto his shorts and called Ismail over. "Let's arrange to get a flatbed trailer and heavy forklift out here. Maybe a crane. Who do I talk to about that?"

Ismail thought for a moment. "Erfoud Construction in town. They should have what you need."

Qadir shot a look over to Karim. The two men erupted into laughter.

Karim turned to Jerome, his rifle aimed at the ground. "Sahbi— brother Romey—you'll never get a lift up here. We have arranged for a chopper." He shook his head, flashing another grin at Qadir as he returned to his post, chuckling to himself.

Qadir stepped forward with a toothy smile and placed a hand on Jerome's shoulder. Through his dark sunglasses, Jerome regarded two piercing but kind green eyes.

"I have a good relationship with the Moroccan military," Qadir said, a subtle French accent betraying the American paleontologist's roots.

"Whatever I need on digs, I get. Just leave the logistics to me and work on that field tan of yours. We'll get your samples where they need to go. Good?"

Over the coming days, they plastered a field jacket around the slab and wedged beams underneath to form a reinforced pallet. As they cleaned up the site, packing away tents and gear in the baking sun, the faint percussive thumping of helicopter blades echoed in the distance. Jerome craned his neck toward the horizon and spotted the soft outline of a refurbished Chinook roaring toward them above the sandy dunes. He parsed remnants of faded USAF decal beneath a Moroccan Royal Air Force seal as the aircraft approached. The twin rotors cut through the air above the team as they secured the specimen to the rigging under the heat billowing from the chopper's exhaust vents. From there, it would be transported to the airport and await shipment to the United States.

The Veritas Protocol was becoming reality.

June 23, 2056, 10:04 — North American Paleontological Convention
Arie Crown Theater, McCormick Place Convention Center
Chicago, Illinois – United States of America

Beads of sweat formed on Jerome's forehead. Blazing stage lights. Blank stares. His eyes panned across the auditorium at an ocean of unfamiliar eyes.

Captive audience.

They knew Jerome, though—or "Romey," as he had come to be known in the paleontology world—as the leading paleogeneticist of his time. Yet he still felt disconnected—not entirely at home in either the paleo or molecular biology circles. A bit of a misfit in the science community. But he wasn't here to fit in. He was here to win over the minds of the masses, to bring them on board with his exciting discovery.

Someone's throat cleared. A ringtone shattered the ambience of shifting bodies, creaking chairs. Then a hushed apology.

While he had a propensity for it—so he'd been told—Jerome hated public speaking. Even so, he considered it a necessary evil. Investors didn't just come to you. You needed to go to them, and the public sphere proved an effective means to that end. Corporate America. Government officials with blank checks. It was all the same to Jerome.

Get on your knees. Kiss the ring. Suck it. Bite it. Whatever they want.

The glare of a reflection bloomed off his name badge. It caught the edge of his glasses and panned across his vision.

I wonder if the electricity powering those stage lights is carbon-neutral. A water bottle crinkled in someone's hand as if to mock him.

Win minds. Right.

Mutterings from the crowd broke Jerome from his momentary stupor, a languid sort of apathy. A pause the audience probably thought he worked into his talk for dramatic effect. He forced a smile, turned to face a colossal projection screen, and progressed to the next slide. *The big reveal.* The moment he'd been building up to…

…a slab of rock?

But *this* slab was special.

Jerome rubbed his hand over his thick, graying beard and inhaled. "This two-ton hunk of sandstone is known as UCR PC75, excavated on a Moroccan expedition led by Dr. Qadir Nassar in March of 2053," he said, pacing the stage with a laser pointer affixed to the screen. "Two years of painstaking excavation in our lab produced four exquisitely preserved specimens—a family of subadult *Deltadromeus agilis*—entombed in this section of an ancient mudflow dating ninety-five million years ago in what is now Northern Africa."

Another photo showed his team's progress one year in—they had chipped away most of the stone, uncovering a tangled mass of four partially excavated skeletons on top of a reinforced bench. A schematic of the slab's contents was draped over the specimen next to the then-postdoctoral fellow Murph, who loomed above it with her pneumatic Air Scribe in hand. Above her snarled red hair, vacuum hoses dangled into the frame as she peered through a dissecting microscope suspended from above. Probing tools, rotary drills, and various reagents lay scattered about the space, and a computer screen displayed a guided CT scan of the specimen.

Though elements of the photograph had been staged for the public eye, it was a typical field lab. Nothing extraordinary. Except that it *was* extraordinary, unique, *critical.* A mere PR photograph could not convey its significance—just serve as filler for unfamiliar eyes to gawk at while Jerome elaborated. Those same eyes now reflecting name badges draped around necks. Jerome wondered how many of those plastic sleeves would find their way from the convention's attendees to the Pacific trash heap, a floating shrine to man's assault on the natural world.

Jerome's hand felt clammy around the laser pointer. He looked out at the placid expressions of the audience members, their faces mirroring the auditorium's neutral tones.

Click.

The next slide drew a chorus of whispers from the audience. It was a 3D rendering of one of the skulls. Atop its snout, a pair of ornate dendritic crests fanned out at a steep angle, each fused to a prominent lacrimal horn. The first Deltadromeus skull ever recovered. And Jerome's team had unearthed *four*—all from UCR PC75.

"While PC75 sheds light on this enigmatic species, there is far more beneath the surface. We now believe Deltadromeus stuck to wooded areas and hunted in packs from birth, then opted for a solitary lifestyle beyond the forest once it reached adulthood. But these skulls give us a more complete picture of the dinosaur's phylogeny—which I will go into shortly." There was a collective muttering throughout the audience. The controversy around classifying *D. agilis* was nothing new. "These new findings are illuminating, to be sure, but they are not what make PC75 special. Not *really…*"

Next slide. A histologic cross-section of spongy bone consumed the screen. *Changing gears. A deeper dive, or maybe more of a fall… down the rabbit hole.* Time would tell. The audience stared, puzzled and mesmerized by the image of a lattice-like structure. *They don't know what they're looking at. Not yet.*

"And here, in this confocal image at 300 times magnification, you can appreciate capillary beds isolated from part of a demineralized femur of one of the specimens. These vessels are pliable—stretchy—as if the animal died only yesterday. Using new and existing methods, we have been able to identify elastin, tropomyosin, and the triple-helix of fibrillar type I collagen. With the use of mass spectrometry, we confirmed the existence of these proteins. Some of you may not be surprised by this because Dr. Schwartz at UNC-Chapel Hill described similar tissues in *Tyrannosaurus rex* fossils. So, not even these soft tissues are what make PC75 unique…"

A second, similar image appeared on the screen, also showing the microstructure of bone. Then a third.

"The first micrograph on the left is PC75, our Deltadromeus sample," Jerome said. "Next to it, we have the equally well-defined vasculature from Schwartz's *Tyrannosaurus rex* sample. The third is from an extant ostrich femur, two years after conducting a specialized preservation protocol using iron oxide. Schwartz and colleagues developed this technique to replicate a natural chemical pathway involving iron oxide that preserves tissues through deep time. Being that blood is rich in iron-containing hemoglobin, it is evident why such vascular networks—and their contents—tend to be among the best-preserved tissues via this pathway.

"Notice the remarkable state of each sample and their similarities to one another. The eagle-eyed among you may be able to discern the presence of both red and white blood cells in all three of these specimens. We also isolated a single osteoclast from PC75, not pictured here. Of particular interest to us is that all of these cells contained highly fragmentary nuclei…"

The next slide looked like a neon-green constellation against an obsidian backdrop. Jerome looked toward the captive crowd; an expectant silence hung in the air. To the untrained eye, it might have looked like an image of deep space from the new Orion probe en route to Mars.

Billionaires trying to terraform another planet when we can't even reverse our own damage here on Earth. Stupid.

Jerome cleared his intrusive thoughts and proceeded. "What we did *not* expect to find was remarkably intact chromatin—indicated here in green with a fluorescent histone stain. Histones are binding proteins that sequester and wind DNA, condensing it into chromosomes. We found chromatin in several of the nuclei of these cells." There was a collective gasp from the audience as he advanced to the next slide, and a new type of energy propagated through the collective. "The tricky part, though, is extraction and imaging. After all, the presence of histone and what appears to be chromatin does not mean intact, workable DNA. We needed to probe deeper. What comes next falls on the cusp of what modern science can achieve, but I am happy to say *we are there,* folks, and I am thrilled to share it with you here today."

A new image bled onto the screen. Many in the audience had leaned in, jaws agape, letting it sink in. They were looking at a scanning tunneling micrograph of deoxyribonucleic acid—*the DNA of a dinosaur.*

Jerome faced the crowd once more. No more aberrant ringtones. No crinkling plastic. No throats clearing.

Only silence.

β | ANTHROPOCENE>

The hum of jet engines oscillated against the shrill mechanics of adjusting airfoils, impelling Sung-ho Shin to look up from his phone. Silently, he gazed out into the gloom from the comfort of his private Gulfstream G850 as rain streamed across the oval window to muddy the hazy Chicago skyline. Had it not been for the bright green ribbons of algal blooms, Lake Michigan might not have been visible against the gray doldrums. Thousands of lights glimmered between the shore and the horizon, twinkling through the eddies rippling across the glass. Even through the swirling view, the city appeared dated, almost primitive compared to the sleek, modern aesthetic back in Seoul.

Shin inhaled. A red-hot disc reflected in the glass, framed by the crisp white of his open-collared shirt. His phone buzzed on his desk as wisps of white smoke billowed from his nostrils.

just got to the lecture... overslept

Great. Landing soon. Rain slowing things up, just waiting for the ok from air traffic control.

When you going to make contact?

already on it

How close can you get?

very

Good. Shin put his phone down and stamped out the cigarette. He rose from the seat and stretched, running his fingers through closely cropped jet-black hair. A gold watch with a diamond-studded face, still set to another time zone, reflected the dim light coming through the plane's portholes. A faint scent of expensive cologne punctuated by cheap tobacco followed him as he walked to the end of the mahogany-lined cabin.

Geun, his flight attendant, emerged from the galley entrance in a fitted gray suit that paired well with the Chicago gloom.

"Something I can get you, sir?"

Shin's arms fell to his sides, and he gave a bow.

"No, thank you, Geun. I need to stretch my legs."

As the CEO of the Korean biotech giant Mitogen, Shin found himself jittery at rest. There was only so much he could accomplish during the fourteen-hour flight from Seoul, and after an hour into circling O'Hare, he had grown irritable.

Torrential rains and high winds often clogged flights coming in and out of Chicago. Over the last two decades, altered weather patterns had impacted every stretch of the globe to varying degrees. Shin was taken aback by how much it incapacitated such an iconic American city.

So, here he was, stuck at ten thousand feet with a stocked bar and idle hands as ground crews worked to siphon water from the runway's overflowing aqueducts.

He walked over to the bar, picked up a whiskey glass, and poured a generous measure of Macallan 1926, neat. Swirled it under his nose, then took a healthy sip and let it sit under his tongue.

Stagnant, he thought. That was the word for a modern America dogged by storm surges, erratic weather patterns, and toxic algal blooms. The U.S. government's resistance to adapt to these changes made it an apt designation. Once the world leader in innovation, the U.S. was now getting left behind—falling into decay.

Shin swallowed.

Out with a whimper.

Mitogen's beginnings were humble, starting as a small, Korean-based pharmaceutical venture exploring novel therapeutics for mitochondrial diseases. In the first two years, Shin's research team had grown to nearly a hundred scientists, with two new divisions opening in the U.S. and Europe. But after almost a decade of intensive research and development, only one drug had gone to market. Six months later, it was recalled due to respiratory failure in a small number of patients. Two died.

Less than one percent. Almost zero, actually.

Shin relaxed his grip around his glass. Studied how the skin of his knuckles filled back in with color.

Less than one percent....

But the drug's side effects were so severe that it prompted the American FDA to step in. Other countries soon followed. Within months, Mitogen's American division filed for bankruptcy.

He breathed to restore his heart rate and took another sip.

Mitogen's first big break came in time. In 2047, a small independent study on Russian cosmonauts had revealed the drug's benefits in low gravity, and it was off to the races. It turned out that mitochondrial dysfunction was a driver of muscle atrophy, reduced bone density, and a laundry list of other ailments that had plagued astronauts for nearly a century. Even proto-colonists on Mars and the lunar surface suffered from the effects of mitochondrial dysfunction.[1] A year after the study, Mitogen was awarded grants by NASA, the European Space Agency, and Russia's Roscosmos to develop treatments for humans in microgravity.

With the influx of funds, the company started developing a "super mitochondrion," an artificial organelle with the ability to enhance, even *replace*, a host cell's innate respiratory functions. Shin's teams achieved this by genetically engineering *Rickettsia prowazekii*—an intracellular bacterium sharing a common ancestor with mitochondria. According to

---

1 See appendices for more information

endosymbiotic theory, one lineage of this common ancestor evolved to assimilate within eukaryotic cells billions of years ago, evolving into mitochondria while retaining a distinct genome separate from that of the cell.

Shin walked back to his seat, his nerves blunted enough to stay off his feet while turbulence threatened to jolt the aircraft without warning. He savored the aroma of his drink and lit another cigarette.

He sank into his seat, now deep in thought. Recalled the time one of his scientific teams discovered a way to reprogram rickettsial bacteria to assume the role of eukaryotic cellular respiration. *Artificial mitochondria.* Because of their shared heritage, Rickettsia made an ideal vector for Mitogen's novel method of mitochondrial replacement therapy, known as *mitotransfection.*[2]

Shin polished off his drink, then waved Geun over. Handed him the empty glass and nodded for another. He sensed himself growing impatient with the pilot. But he rarely expressed his displeasure with minor inconveniences, wanted his staff to feel valued. So, he merely sighed and ruminated while he waited for Geun to return.

He wavered on the edge of hebetude. Always fought against a buzz as if to flex his mental faculties. In college, he'd be ten shots deep, solving integrals and working out organic reactions at parties to show his peers he could outdo them under any circumstance. Now, he competed internally with himself. Fought torpor and ruminated on how overcoming the ailments of low gravity had just been the beginning for Mitogen. How his aspirations for the company's tech were far-reaching and ambitious. Mitotransfection was the way forward in seeking cures for a host of genetic disorders and most cancers, and—Shin believed—would one day enhance human physiology and *double* life expectancy.

But Mitogen's research up to this point had only gone as far as animal studies. Human trials in mitotransfection were still a long way off, driving Shin to seek ways to diversify and expand the company further. One such opportunity arose with the Russian-based Pleistocene Project, an eco-engineering initiative seeking to resurrect a host of ancient species that could regenerate the ancient Siberian steppe and sequester vast stores of carbon

---

2 See appendices for more information

dioxide in its soils. For decades, cloning ancient DNA posed a significant challenge because most of the embryos did not make it to term; those that did rarely survived more than forty-eight hours after birth. One reason for this had to do with mitonuclear compatibility.

Whiskey burbled into a fresh glass toward the rear of the cabin. Shin shifted in his seat.

The concept of mitonuclear compatibility was simple in theory: eukaryotic cells contained two sets of DNA—*cellular* DNA containing the genome of a given species, and *mitochondrial* DNA, or mtDNA, passed down maternally through each generation of that species. The relationship between the two dictated the development and survival of an organism's offspring. The concept seemed straightforward on the surface, but for decades, scientists had found it near-impossible to replicate in practice.

Geun severed his thoughts, extending another whiskey toward him. "Sir."

Shin took it and bowed his head with a smile. He sipped, gazed back out through the rain carving tributaries across the window, and slipped back into his thoughts.

The problem with cloning, he knew, was that surrogate mtDNA was genetically distinct for a given species. Since an extinct animal had no parents, a surrogate from another species was required. Consequently, a surrogate's mitochondria were typically incompatible with the cellular DNA of the implanted clone embryo, even among closely related species. Establishing mitonuclear compatibility was a necessity that had seemed unattainable until Mitogen changed the game with its proprietary mitotransfection technique. It was the missing piece that revolutionized cloning and resurrection science, and Shin held the patents.

So began the dawn of designer mitochondria.

The Pleistocene Project was proof that the technology worked—that its potential applications extended far beyond low-gravity prophylaxis. With human trials still far off, showcasing the technology in the cloning sphere brought much-needed publicity to Mitogen. Carrying out mitotransfection in other species allowed for a compelling proof-of-concept that drew the type of attention Shin figured could result in a push for novel human applications.

Mitogen's rise would ultimately secure the company's foothold in off-world biotech—the future of human augmentation that would forever transform life among the stars. He was certain of that. Grew more certain with each sip from his drink.

That was the long game.

After its work with Russia, Mitogen had received solicitations to help resurrect an array of extinct species like the thylacine, Steller's sea cow, and the recently extinguished orangutan. Most of these requests came from failing zoos still clinging to their long-expired relevance, whose interest in resurrection science seemed less about raising awareness of conservation and more about keeping the lights on. The truth, to Shin, was evident: most of these resurrected species had no habitat to return *to*. For them, there was nothing left to conserve.

Such novelties were a dead-end for Mitogen, so Shin had turned his attention to a new revival effort: *birds*. As avian species began disappearing at alarming rates across the planet, it became apparent just how critical they were to global ecosystems and how much humanity depended on their continued survival. Even off-world colonies relied on terrestrial ecosystems for food, medicine, and other resources.

But cloning birds posed a unique set of challenges. In mammals, the process was straightforward: remove the nuclear DNA of the host egg cell and replace it with that of the species to be cloned. Then, transfect the engineered mitochondria and implant the egg into a surrogate mother.

Birds were different. Their embryos gestated outside of the body in a large, hard-shelled egg. At its center, the microscopic nucleus sat obscured within an opaque yolk behind a mantle of translucent albumin.

Logistical challenges aside, successful avian cloning required specialized techniques beyond the scope of Mitogen's existing capabilities. But rather than spend money on ground-up R&D, Shin sought someone who *already* had the necessary experience: Jerome Powell.

As it turned out, Jerome had been conducting avian cloning experiments with ancient DNA in secret—*a likely effort*, Shin surmised as he finished his cigarette and stuffed it into an ashtray, *to shield the study from scrutiny under the Cartagena Protocol.*[3]

3 See appendices for more information

There was already international backlash over genetically engineered species from several Eastern European countries struggling to control the migration of Russian mammoths across their borders. Most officials in these regions authorized citizens to shoot the animals on sight. Some went as far as threatening to reopen the ivory trade with China. All initiated litigation against Russia and Mitogen.

Despite the obstacles, Shin knew Jerome's endeavor was rooted in a fundamental truth—that birds were disappearing at an alarming rate, and soon, humanity might follow. This truth, Shin knew, would ultimately bring sweeping policy reforms over LMOs—living modified organisms. As food chains began to fail, these same countries showing hostility toward de-extinction would be begging to ramp up genetic engineering efforts to avoid their impending collapse.

He kicked his glass back. Nodded to Geun for another.

By pushing the project along, Shin knew that not only would Mitogen eliminate its resurgent financial woes, but would also secure a critical role in the most ambitious rewilding effort in *history*. If the Pleistocene Project demonstrated the safety and efficacy of mitotransfection, the Great Avian Revival would pave the way for cornering a niche in wilding—perhaps even terraforming—the outer colonies.

"Sir, we're clear to land now," the pilot said in Korean over the cabin's intercom. "We'll be on the ground in five minutes." The mechanical whir of landing gear rumbled from the bowels of the fuselage.

Neat whisky in hand, Shin bowed his head to Geun for the third time. He glanced back down at his phone—*no new messages*.

No matter. Jerome was in play.

γ | DELTA RUNNER >

The crowd's silence was fleeting. Collective shock bubbled up into excitement as muttering panned through the auditorium. Jerome detected a few scoffs and chuckles, but most attendees seemed floored by the revelation: ancient DNA. *Dinosaur* DNA. No longer a Hollywood fantasy, but a tangible *reality*.

A door clicked open at the back of the auditorium. Few heads turned. Most eyes, though, remained fixated, unblinking, on Jerome. A familiar form passed beneath the glow of the exit sign and stole his gaze—it was Murph. Her ginger hair was arranged in the usual carefree bun, sprouts sticking out every which way. *Late, as usual.* Glasses rimmed her eyes, a rare look for her. *Thrown on in a rush. Face is pale, missing the usual makeup.* A handsome young Asian man accompanied her: athletic build, clean-cut. *That smooth talker she met at the bar last night. Or maybe it was the subtle Korean accent that won her over.*

She batted the man toward the opposite end of the auditorium before navigating to an obscure chair in the back. Jerome pretended not to notice, though he couldn't help but betray his amusement with a grin.

A restless voice erupted from the front row.

"You isolated dinosaur DNA?"

Lingered too long.

Jerome raised a hand over his eyes. He could begin to make out the face of a man of around fifty, arms folded across his chest, salt-and-pepper mustache twitching, brow furrowed. A pair of beady eyes winced at the projection screen from behind his rounded honey-brown spectacles.

Jerome smiled. "That is our claim, yes." His tone was measured, deliberate. "We have roughly seventy percent of the Deltadromeus genome."

A dull ache settled above his eye socket. Interruptions like this were something he was still learning to address.

Renewed murmuring started throughout the crowd, and the glow of screens bloomed on the faces of those eager to inform whichever social media network led the pecking order these days.

"But I will ask that you hold your questions until after the talk," he said, his pulse quickening.

He turned to face the projection screen, and silence restored itself within the crowd.

"All due respect, Dr. Powell, that's impossible."

Another interruption. *Same asshole.*

"DNA has, at best, a half-life of five hundred years. This fossil is *ninety-five million* years old."

Without a word, Jerome smiled and advanced the slide. The words *Hemoglobin: The Great Stabilizer* flashed in bold black lettering. He turned back to the man. "As the Russians would attest, that is not entirely true." Reserved laughter rose from the crowd. "The Siberian Pleistocene Project has shown that we can extract, sequence, and clone *million*-year-old DNA."

Jerome was, of course, referencing the de-extinct megafauna roaming northeast Siberia. Mammoths, for instance, were cloned from fragmentary DNA dating back almost two million years. Admittedly, these were not *actual* mammoths, only hybrids containing equal parts mammoth and Asian elephant DNA.

"But our team went further," he continued, "and we have shown it is possible to extract genetic material from species far, *far* older..."

"You mean to clone a dinosaur?" the man asked sardonically.

"No." Jerome peered at his feet, his head shaking. A voice inside him screamed. *This isn't a discussion.* Graying black locks fell onto his cheeks, and he pulled them back behind his ears. He wanted to choose his next words carefully. "These so-called 'de-extinction' projects have largely been unsuccessful in what they set out to do. For instance, the Pleistocene Project's objective is to revive the ancient Siberian steppe, generating vast grasslands not seen since the Ice Age. For millions of years, these grasses shielded the soil from the sun, keeping it cool beneath a layer of permafrost that acted as a carbon sink. After the disappearance of the mammoth, woodlands replaced these symbiotic grasses. Soils became more exposed, more susceptible to temperature extremes. Carbon stores have been inching to the surface ever since."

Another sweaty lock of hair grazed his cheek. He swept it back again, doing his best to conceal his agitation.

"While Russia's resurrected mammoths showed initial promise in restoring grasslands to the region, the symbiotic relationship they once shared with the land is no longer present. In fact, they are migrating large distances to find alternative food sources. Part of the reason has to do with their ancient physiology—we now know mammoth hybrids lack an enzyme needed for the efficient breakdown of polysaccharides in modern Eurasian bushgrasses. As a consequence, they have become an invasive species wherever they migrate, spreading disease and disrupting what is left of local ecosystems. To this day, their populations still go unchecked, despite the Russian government's efforts to control their numbers with the introduction of carnivorous megafauna and awarding permits to trophy hunters."

Jerome's gaze met the crowd once more. All eyes were on him. Though he had lost Murph in the glare of the lights, he imagined her stare burning into him, willing him not to go further off-script, to keep from making new enemies in the process. But it was already too late for that.

"In the last few years, scientists have observed an actual *decline* in the density of East Siberian bushgrasses, which defeats the purpose of the venture altogether. As global temperatures rise, the Siberian permafrost is once again exposed to temperature fluctuations, threatening to release billions of tons of sequestered carbon dioxide into our atmosphere. So, now we have two problems: the looming threat of a mass carbon dump that will further exacerbate runaway climate change, and a host of new invasive species we struggle to contain as they fan out across Eurasia. Eco-engineering endeavors like the Pleistocene Project have failed. They have done little to mitigate the ongoing climate crisis and have—in many cases—made things *worse*." Jerome paced briskly from one end of the large stage to the next, his arms waving through the air. He knew he was veering off message, but he couldn't stop. Knew he needed to find a way to loop back to what was important.

"If we can't even get this right with something as geologically recent as a mammoth, then what destruction would a ninety-five-million-year-old theropod leave in its wake? What would Deltadromeus even eat? Like Russia's mammoths, would it, too, lack critical digestive enzymes and adaptations to fit into the modern era? What diseases would a *dinosaur* be susceptible to? Would it, in turn, carry ancient plagues that could devastate surrounding wildlife, or even us? If there *were* a benefit to such a resurrection, would it be worth the *risk?* I don't believe that it would. We need a more focused approach when utilizing genetic engineering in our conservation efforts." Nearly out of breath, Jerome stopped and faced the mustached man again. "So, back to your point, Mister…"

"*Doctor.* Krentz."

"Apologies, Dr. Krentz… you are correct in pointing out that DNA *this* old defies modern convention. You are not the only one in the room who thinks this, I assure you. If we are not going to outright *clone* the animal, then does cracking its genome have any relevance in the conservation space? If not, why bother?" The question was rhetorical, but Jerome did not pause long enough to risk another interruption. Krentz, for now, had been silenced.

"The short answer is yes," he continued with a broad smile. "There is a role for fossil DNA. For starters, fDNA from animals like Deltadromeus provides unique insight into the evolutionary trajectory of modern avialans. We can run a novel sequence against a database and show how closely related *D. agilis* is to extant birds, like *Gallus* and ostrich. It also gives us a better sense of where to place Deltadromeus in the evolutionary tree.

"Until now, Deltadromeus was a mystery, with the most recent consensus placing the species within abelisauroidea, and more specifically the family noasauridae. The recent skull discoveries, however, are suggestive of coelurosaur morphology. Indeed, once we sequenced the genome of *D. agilis* and ran it through our database, we confirmed this to be true. We determined that Deltadromeus shares a more recent common ancestor with modern-day birds than initially thought. It is a megaraptoran tyrannosauroid, along with its synonyms *Australovenator* and *Aerosteon*, which fall under the same clade that gave rise to *Tyrannosaurus rex*, *Velociraptor*, and all modern birds."

Jerome's tongue grated the roof of his mouth like sandpaper. He took a swig of his water, his clammy fingers slipping over the plastic he so loathed.

"More importantly, we can learn a lot about how animals like Deltadromeus lived and how they adapted to their environments. This knowledge can inform us of the current state of our world. Give us clues on how to preserve our remaining bird species. Cretaceous coelurosaurs possessed adaptations we can study that enabled them to thrive in the carbon dioxide-rich, oxygen-depleted hothouse leading up to the Cenomanian–Turonian boundary and beyond.

"As today's atmospheric conditions begin to resemble those of that time, perhaps there are genetic modifications we can make to the most vulnerable avian species before it's too late, with coelurosaur DNA as our guide. Which brings us to the second point..."

The presentation remote slipped precariously in Jerome's sweaty palm. The silence was so stark that he could hear the buzzing of the stage lights overhead. Another slide flickered across thousands of unblinking eyes.

Several dozen bodies leaned forward, squinting at the presentation screen.

"To provide some context, let's look at where our extant coelurosaur friends—modern-day birds—sit today." Jerome progressed to a slide showing images of endangered and recently extinct birds. The Californian condor, a pair of albatrosses, a short-eared owl, and half a dozen hummingbirds saturated the projection screen in a spectrum of vivid splendor and beauty. Beauty that would soon fade from the Earth.

"Today, we are seeing mass avian die-offs across the globe," he continued. "While many species of amphibians are also seeing a sharp decline, the rate observed in birds has surpassed it by an order of magnitude. There are numerous factors for this, including loss of habitat and recent surges in diseases like West Nile Virus. However, the dominant driver behind this devastation appears to be a higher demand on thermoregulation, particularly in avian species with higher metabolic demands. This finding correlates with the rate of rising global temperatures."

Jerome proceeded to the next slide.

	LATE CRETACEOUS (OAE 2 95MA)	PRE-INDUSTRIAL	2020	2043	2100
atmospheric CO_2	900ppm	280ppm	410ppm	550ppm	750ppm
atmospheric O_2	13%	25%	21%	19%	14%
atm temperature (avg)	24°C	13.5°C	15°C	17.5°C	21°C

"This simplified table seeks to illustrate the rapid rate of atmospheric change observed since before the industrial revolution—as compared to the most recent hothouse conditions of the late Cretaceous, represented here in column one, which was marked by an oceanic anoxic event called OAE 2, around ninety-five million years ago.

"OAE 2, also known as the Bonarelli event and the Cenomanian–Turonian boundary event, was driven by a surge in methane venting from the ocean floor. This acidified the Earth's oceans and expelled carbon dioxide into the atmosphere to the tune of *nine hundred parts per million*. The result? A runaway greenhouse effect that increased the average atmospheric temperature to around twenty-four degrees Celsius. By contrast, today's average is seventeen point five degrees and climbing."

Jerome felt almost outside of himself, the words flowing from him with little forethought. "This was a mass extinction event, particularly in Earth's oceans, choking off oxygen for five hundred thousand years and wiping out *fifty* percent of all marine life. We can observe this same process unfolding today." His limbs hummed with warmth. Sweat slicked his face, but he paid it no heed. "Toxic algal blooms. Coral bleaching. Species of tropical fish disappearing—a primary food source and economic staple, slipping away year over year like sand through our fingers. Atmospheric carbon is rising exponentially, mirrored by climbing global temperatures. Even with our comparatively modest four-degree shift, it is not hard to understand why the Cretaceous Thermal Maximum was, far and away, *the most disruptive* atmospheric change in the last hundred million years." His higher consciousness observed from a distance, amused by his body's automation through his subconscious, like the act of driving and snapping out of deep rumination, only to realize he had no memory of the last ten miles. "And we are heading for a modern equivalent—the Anthropocene Thermal Maximum—accelerated by artificial carbon emissions."

Jerome's final point boomed over the PA.

You have arrived at your destination.

Few stirred in their seats. The *tap-tap* of fingers on screens ceased. Jerome had recaptured the minds of the audience.

Focus on the message.

He cleared his throat, then raised the water bottle to his lips and sipped. Wresting autonomy over his higher faculties, he metered his voice. "We have all witnessed the effects of four degrees, and yet we continue down the same path. Extreme weather events are no longer an exception, but the norm. Island nations are falling into economic ruin as rising sea levels breach their lands. In the summer months, the Arctic is devoid of ice, while currents are warming in the East Siberian Sea. The once-restored Siberian permafrost has all but disappeared, allowing tons of carbon to leach into the atmosphere. The ice caps, which have receded beyond critical levels, no longer sequester harmful methane stores generated by hydrothermal vents on the ocean floor. As the ice disappears, we see atmospheric carbon spike further. Methane is now venting from our oceans at a rate consistent with that of OAE 2. Meanwhile, oxygen levels are plummeting.

"How many of you flew to Chicago from the west coast? How many supercells did you watch on your screens at 30,000 feet as you navigated punishing turbulence over the Midwest? How many of you are here seeking temporary refuge from the wildfires in California and Oregon, have lost property to storm surges breaching sea walls in the Gulf, or wear respirators in your cities every day?"

Several dozen bodies shifted, many heads swiveled.

Jerome pressed.

"I fear we are fast approaching the point of no return. In a sense, we are already there, and if we are not careful, we will experience widescale ecological collapse in our lifetimes—*certainly* in our children's—an event the likes of which has never been witnessed by humanity. The Sixth Extinction."

The muffled echo of Jerome's digitized voice reverberated through the auditorium and faded. He was silent, staring at a sea of stoic faces. Sweat crept down his cheeks; his button-up shirt was starting to stick to his back.

"Natural selection cannot keep pace in the modern world. Adaptation takes time, and anthropogenic climate change is incompatible with this fundamental truth. It is incompatible with life." A lump swelled at the back of his throat. "Birds are the first domino to fall. They are the proverbial and literal canaries in the coal mine, and we would be wise to heed their warning."

Jerome panned his gaze over the crowd. *Looking for Murph.* Tried to ignore the sting of sweat on his back, the notion that the audience might be more distracted by his pit stains than his words.

He spotted her. She gave a nod of reassurance.

Jerome took a breath and turned his focus back to the message.

"So, I ask you this," he said. "Which domino are we? When will we fall?" This time, he did pause for effect, peering into the audience through the stinging sweat seeping into his eyes. "We are staring down the gun barrel of a mass extinction event. But I may have answers that could change our fate. We have the tools to fight extinction. If natural selection cannot keep up with the new demands placed on ecosystems, genetic engineering can provide some hope. We can, for instance, look at which genes allowed Deltadromeus to thrive in hothouse temperatures containing lower atmospheric oxygen. We can begin implementing those adaptations into modern birds within a matter of weeks."[1]

He swept his hair back again. His hand migrated to cup his face and wipe the sweat from his beard.

"We can help dwindling bird populations adapt to the changes affecting them *now*. We don't need to depend on the goodwill of humanity, corporations, or governments to reduce emissions. We don't need to depend on the Paris Accord, the Geneva Accord, or any other moral grandstanding

---

1 See appendices for more information on Jerome's fDNA extraction techniques

any longer, because we have the tools to create the necessary adaptations at will. We *can* act *now.* And we must."

The man with the honey spectacles leaned back, arms still folded over his chest, silent, perceptive.

"This is all overwhelming, I know," Jerome continued, trying unsuccessfully to clear his throat. "At times, it feels hopeless. So, I will leave you all with a message of hope in the midst of this, the crisis of our lifetimes. This block of sandstone, these skeletons, as you'll soon see, hold part of the key—not just for paleontology, but for all of us. We can reverse the tide. Give life a fighting chance."

Stillness fell upon expectant faces. The air felt electric. Alive.

Jerome filled his lungs.

"Until now, we have looked to the past to inform the present, to help us understand the origins of life… how we got here… where we might be headed. But now, we are situated at a pivotal moment when we can *bring* the past *into* the present. *With it, we can transform our future…* and we will."

δ | THE CARTAGENA PROTOCOL >

The hotel room fell into shadow as the sun bled into the Chicago skyline. Jerome gazed out at the city lights, lost in thought, reflecting on the keynote address he had delivered earlier that day. He wondered if he had generated any interest from would-be investors. The crowd seemed energized by the revelation that dinosaur genomes could be elucidated despite all modern conventions—less so by the tired droning of environmentalism. A persistent disquietude stirred within him. Had it been enough? Were his colleagues as excited by his discovery, and its implications, as he was?

On its own, a new fossil discovery always gave Jerome the same thrill. That feeling never grew old. He recalled the first time he'd experienced it, when he was around seven. He had been out exploring the edge of his neighborhood development, a sleepy Boston suburb tucked into one of the last remaining frontiers of the American northeast—an expanse of marshland, an ecosystem pushed into an ever-shrinking plot at the edge of an advancing human metastasis.

Over the years, the natural habitat had retracted, giving way to new homes and roadways, until all that remained was a narrow wetland beyond a chain-link fence. Jerome would find himself exploring the receding ecosystem throughout his childhood, his naivety shielding him from the reality of that place—from the inconvenient truth that his own existence contributed to its decay, had forced countless organisms into retreat. Into death. Annihilation.

On many of these expeditions, Jerome hunted for amphibians—toads, salamanders—which proved difficult to find one spring. He remembered one day from that year in particular. He had walked along the outer perimeter of the chain-link fence where water ponded under the shade of a lone birch. The knee-high water lay stagnant in the sweltering malaise of a suffocating natural order. Thick yellow swirls of pollen coalesced at the surface—an evolving fractal, a dynamic Rorschach blot that held more meaning now than it did then. As a child, it reminded him of lava.

The placid morass fanned out beyond Jerome's estimation, obscured by thick reeds that stretched toward a sparse copse awash with imposing cattails and gently swaying florets. On most jaunts, he liked to see how far he could navigate across mounds of rock and earth without slipping into the "hot magma" below. But on that day, along the base of the waterlogged birch, something caught Jerome's eye—a flurry of activity beneath the murky water. To get a better look, he had to break his cardinal rule.

He had to wade into the lava.

Jerome still remembered the warmth of the water, the soft silt squishing between his bare toes, the cloudless cerulean sky, the glaring May heat beneath the shade of the tree—a damp heat typically reserved for early July. The strangeness of the silent air that, in years prior, hummed with chirping frogs and singing birds. On that day, he only heard the dull roar of distant city traffic.

Ripples propagated out from him as he waded farther, and frothy yellow clumps of wet pollen caked onto his rolled jeans. Once he drew near, the frantic writhing of hundreds of tiny tadpoles materialized beneath the surface. Their tails thrashed, darting past one another around a clouded mass blanketed beneath a thin veneer of green algae. The object protruded through the murky water, with its bulk mostly obscured beneath the thick mud. A mossy, damp smell filled the air—the stench of simultaneous growth and rot. The tadpoles hit critical mass here, a writhing swarm, their oval mouths cupping the object. Glistening sunlight pierced the still leaves above, reflecting in Jerome's eyes.

With his advance, the tadpoles scattered away through the turbid water. He could make out a familiar shape—a small bone protruding from the muck. It looked like a dinosaur bone. In his excitement, he had recalled the wonder of visiting the Boston Museum of Science's dinosaur exhibit, where a simulated dig site allowed kids to unearth dinosaur bones like a real paleontologist. But this was real. And it was his own.

Later that year, Jerome assembled the skeleton for a school project, claiming he had found a baby Velociraptor. The size was not all that far off. He had even arranged the second toe to resemble a retractable claw and reconstructed the 'missing' teeth and tail vertebrae with clay. Never mind that *V. mongoliensis* got its name from the continent where it was found, way on the other side of the world in the middle of Eurasia. But no one told him otherwise, despite some questioning gazes from school staff.

Jerome later learned the skeleton belonged to an individual *Botaurus lentiginosus*—American bittern—a species of ground-dwelling heron once endemic to the northeastern United States. He recalled seeing one of the birds at dusk some summers prior during one of his excursions. The booming *pump-er-lunk* of its mating call had drawn him in. It was a beautiful bird, mottled brown down its back and cream-colored streaks along its underside. Distinctive black stripes extended lengthwise down each side of its long neck. Jerome recalled the peculiar pose it assumed as he approached—frozen against the backdrop of tall grass, its neck outstretched, beak aimed skyward. Deathly still as it blended into the surround.

Jerome also eventually realized his skeleton had been one of the last surviving individuals of *B. lentiginosus* in New England before the species went extinct by 2045. Multiple factors contributed to their demise: loss of habitat, disease, dwindling food sources. But the primary cause was thought to arise from metabolic distress brought on by increased thermoregulatory demand. As temperature averages climbed, the bird's range receded farther north, concentrating in northern Maine during the breeding season and eventually into Canada before fading away entirely. Higher demand for heat dissipation meant less energy for foraging, less energy for outcompeting new species, less energy for yet another migration, and ultimately less energy for breeding.

And *Botaurus* was not the only species. Many more disappeared each year.

The more Jerome learned about the changing world, the more he wanted to know. He wanted to know things like how, before the industrial revolution, the natural background extinction rate was around one extinction per million bird species annually. How, in 2023, it approached *one hundred* per million per year. And how, as of his keynote address, the figure hovered just shy of two thousand per million.

The loss of the American bittern had sparked something within Jerome. By the time he had learned of its extinction, he was well on his way to earning a Ph.D. in molecular paleontology with a focus in paleogenetics. For him, its demise landed particularly hard—far more than the growing list of other endangered and lost species. This time, it was personal. He had a direct connection. It struck him as odd the way people tended to care about something only when it affected them directly. Indeed, that was his experience with the American bittern. He was no exception. It dug at his core—the *finality* of extinction, the notion it could not be reversed.

But what if it could?

Leading up to his graduate thesis defense, Jerome had heard of such de-extinction endeavors. Efforts to repopulate the Earth with passenger pigeons and dodos (the latter having gone re-extinct on account of the modern house cat's affinity for chicks). Entire families of imperiled salamanders engineered to be resistant to a plague of chytrid fungus. Resurrected steppe mammoths, woolly rhinos, smilodons invading parts of Europe.

But what about the American bittern? What about the critical *keystone* species on the brink—those yet to be lost to a rapidly-changing climate?

A decade into his career, Jerome found a way to marry the world of the dead with that of the living.

Transforming the present with the past.

The discovery of fDNA had brought him the same thrill as the day he unearthed the remains of his first skeleton, even if it wasn't his first *authentic* fossil.

Now, his fossil discoveries—in particular fDNA and its sequencing— would revolutionize paleogenetics. But public opinion was a different matter.

For Jerome, retrieving and sequencing genetic remains from prehistoric fossils sparked something in him far beyond that original childhood wonder. The notion of implementing it into a living organism, further still. Keeping the latter from the public, still yet further—a welling urgency slowly bubbling to the surface. And he acted on it as if by instinct.

The American bittern *had* been resurrected. Or, rather, something like it.

From an ancient tomb embedded for millions of years in sandstone, Lazarus had come forth. And only Jerome and his colleagues knew of its existence—because they had created it.

It was his own.

Ring.

An orange radiance had consumed the sky beyond the silhouetted skyscrapers. Jerome's gaze left the Chicago lights and fell on the hotel room phone. He was now standing in the dark.

He thought back to the keynote and about the man who had interrupted the talk—almost derailed him. Murph walking in late with some guy she had met at the hotel bar. *Ring.* Now, a late-night phone call. Another in a series of intrusions. Affronts to his stream of consciousness, his only escape from the changing world.

Who would be calling at this hour?

Another ring. Jerome walked over to the receiver by the bed and raised it to his ear.

"Hello?" On the other end, there was only silence. "Hello?"

"Yes, Dr. Powell, I hope this is not bad time."

Jerome did not recognize the voice. The man sounded of middle age. He spoke with a distinctive Korean accent and broken but well-articulated English.

"Not at all," Jerome lied. "Who is this?" Again, he met silence. "Hello?"

"Dr. Powell, that is not important. Let me be brief. I am calling on behalf of my constituents at Mitogen to make offer. They wish to expand your research into other application. Worth your while. Will you be free to meet for dinner tomorrow evening?"

The man's tone carried a subtle urgency beneath its friendly veneer. Perhaps a cultural barrier was to blame, but the proposition made Jerome uneasy.

Mitogen was also a key player in the failed Pleistocene Project, which he had just publicly denounced. This was not the type of investor he sought.

"Sorry, but I am not interested."

Jerome went to hang up.

A single word erupted from the receiver. "*Lazarus.*"

A jolt shot through Jerome's chest, and he raised the phone back to his ear. "What?"

"*Botaurus lentiginosus.*"

"Where did you… Who are you?"

Project Lazarus. The name of Jerome's American bittern resurrection project—known only to him and those directly involved with it. It marked the beginning of the Veritas Protocol, his genetic engineering effort that would revive hundreds of bird species over the next fifteen years. If word got out, the project risked severe backlash, an international outcry. The EPA would shut him down. His career would be over.

Made an example of.

"Dr. Powell, are you familiar with Cartagena Protocol on Biosafety?"

Jerome's heart leaped into his throat. "Are you threatening me?"

"Not at all. I am merely suggesting that we can be of great mutual benefit."

"In what way?"

The Cartagena Protocol—an international agreement between the European Union, South America, and over a hundred other governments—limited the migration of genetically modified species across borders. The treaty had grown increasingly strict in recent years, particularly in Europe and Canada. Recently, tensions boiled with the invasion of Siberian mammoths into Poland and the Baltics—the most recent in a string of events sparking renewed rhetoric between Russia and the West.

Jerome needed time to convince the international community of the importance of relaxing restrictions to restore the global ecology. In the United States, he had only recently cleared FDA approval for his research. An application for eventual release and rewilding had been filed with the EPA, but approval could take *years*. The last thing he needed was for revived birds to be shot from the sky when they might one day cross international borders.

Managing public opinion—regardless of policy—needed to be carried out in time. *He needed time.* Needed the international community to know that, unlike the Pleistocene Project, Veritas was *critical* to preserving life as humanity knew it. Perhaps even to the continuation of humankind on Earth. If his efforts leaked prematurely, the project might be over before it started.

The voice on the other end of the line pulled him back into the moment. "Mitogen has representatives sitting on ethics board at European Commission. We understand this to be obstacle to your ultimate goal. We have a lot of influence, Dr. Powell. When Europe folds, others will follow." The man paused, perhaps waiting for a response. Jerome did not answer. "We are also aware that your bittern hatchling do not mature beyond forty-eight hour. We have answer to this, as well."

Jerome sat at the edge of the bed, consumed in darkness. He stared at his shadow on the wall, shrouded in the dull glow of buildings and endless streams of traffic blooming through the hotel window.

"And what do you want from me?"

"Meet my associate tomorrow for dinner. Your ride will arrive in front of hotel lobby at six o'clock p.m. Your postdoc, Murph, will be there with her new friend."

Click. The line went dead.

April 18, 2059 - Hybrid Genomics and Embryonics
Mitonuclear Genetic Technologies, U.S. Headquarters
Cambridge, Massachusetts – United States of America

ε | PAN AVES >

The high-pitched alarm of the sequencer blared from inside the lab. Dr. Amara Schwartz looked up from the soft glow of her computer screen. She rubbed her eyes.

DNA samples are ready.

Her office desk was something of an organized mess. In one corner was a literature backlog—recent journal publications arranged haphazardly beneath a half-full cup of tepid coffee. In the other, three pairs of reading glasses sat atop a pile of printed protocols scribbled with notes in red ink. The center of the desk hosted a fingerprint-covered laptop screen smothered in sticky notes alongside a medley of pens, paperclips, and hair ties to round out the aesthetic.

Amara preferred the tangibility of paper, the tactile feedback of writing in ink, of flipping a page. It tied her to the process. Made it more real, more intimate.

She lifted a soiled lab coat draped over the back of her chair. Each blemish had a story: stains of pink Tris buffer here, a spilled *E. coli* colony there. She remembered the day it came to her office, crisp white with her name embroidered in blue—"*Dr. Amara Schwartz, Ph.D.*"—beneath a once-vibrant green Mitogen logo. She reached into one of the pockets and pulled out a worn key badge. The photo was streaked and scratched—its faded ink now smeared like fingerpaint—although her white smile persisted through the wear like a fading Cheshire Cat's.

Despite appearances, Amara was meticulous with her research. Precise. Methodical. That was why, when Jerome Powell decided to move into the private sector, he had asked her to leave a comfortable tenure at UNC-Chapel Hill and join him in the Paleogenomics and Embryonics division at Mitogen's U.S. headquarters.

It will be every bit as rewarding as academia, Romey had promised, *with far better pay and less regulation. Less dependence on federal grants. Less oversight.*

He had been right. They were doing things at breakneck speed—*months*—that would have otherwise taken decades.

It helped that Mitogen's CEO, Dr. Shin, was adept at evading regulations, something he often discussed openly at board meetings. He achieved results by "building relationships" with heads of state, who, in turn, appointed Mitogen employees to high-up positions at regulatory agencies like the EPA and EFSA.[1] When necessary, he used his financial clout to wrangle leadership into submission by going after them in primary campaigns or influencing international policy on trade deals and sanctions.

But Shin's preferred tool was fear. He leveraged it with exacting ease to incite dissent among the EU's member states as the planet's ecosystems collapsed like a house of cards. The impact on the European economy was immeasurable, and at a time when Germany's austerity measures had already crippled countries like Italy and Greece.

Luck did the rest. The most significant continental recession in modern history, amid another refugee crisis out of northwest Africa and an openly opportunistic Russia, was enough to get the EU to ultimately fold. Once the dust settled, Mitogen's immunity from the Cartagena Protocol and a fresh, hand-picked appointee to the European Commission ushered in a new world order.

---

1 Environmental Protection Agency (U.S.) and European Food Safety Authority

Shin was hailed a hero.

But even *he* had his stakeholders to answer to.

Shin's investors especially wanted to know how Jerome and Amara's work on the Veritas Protocol could be applied to Mitogen's ultimate aim of cornering the market for off-Earth biotech. French energy juggernaut Hélatome was the most significant shareholder, with two investors on the board of trustees. In exchange for its contributions, the energy giant secured a five-year moratorium that saw its lunar mining colonies included in Mitogen's Phase III clinical trials for mitotransfection, while its competitors were excluded. This gave Hélatome a significant edge against other lunar colonies at the height of the helium mining wars. Its employees could work longer, faster, and more efficiently.

But if it helps our planet's collapsing ecosystems in the process, I'll tell them anything they want to hear.

Amara glanced around the office, eyes burning. All the other staff had gone home for the night. It was not uncommon for her to find herself alone, working late.

The office couch occasionally proved comfortable enough for a little shut-eye between shifts.

More than occasionally.

Already, she longed for the blanket and pillow stowed in the bottom drawer of her desk.

Not yet. Too much left to do.

She rubbed her eyes. Imagined the lab techs, interns, and other staff comfortably at home with their families. Even Romey was probably in bed with his wife.

Half-absent, she skimmed the talking points typed out on her laptop display.

She was slated to present at the next board of trustees meeting the following month. Her report detailed the latest developments in the Veritas Protocol's rewilding initiative and outlined the Powell Protocol for genetically engineering avian genomes with ancient DNA. A novel gene of the extinct coelurosaur *Deltadromeus agilis* appeared to demonstrate the most promise:

```
Plasmid Vector:
product | CRISPR-associated protein 17 (subtype IIB)/sgRNA/hRNA
complex
gene | Cas17
organism | Pyrococcus poseidus
domain | thermoautotrophican archaea

Insertion Sequence (hRNA) Product:
protein | Heat Shock Protein 70
gene | HSP70
organism | Deltadromeus agilis
domain | eukarya (kingdom: animalia, clade: dinosauria)
```

TARGET
Male and Female Primordial germ cells (PGCs) of *Botaurus stellaris*, Eurasian bittern.

PRODUCT
Generate reproductive chimeras (*B. stellaris*) to produce desired genetically engineered offspring: climate-tolerant *Botaurus powellus*, "de-extinct" American bittern.

AIM
» Part of Mitogen's larger rewilding initiative to restore local ecosystems.
» Future potential for wilding off-planet colonies, food independence
» Altered-G pharmaceuticals.
» Future potential for human applications in conjunction with enhanced mitotransfection.

She was in the process of outlining the steps by which selected *D. agilis* genes were inserted into the genome of a target species, like the American bittern, using CRISPR gene editing.[2] The technology had previously led to cures for a slew of Mendelian diseases like cystic fibrosis, sickle cell, and retinitis pigmentosa. The eradication of HIV and some cancers soon followed. Now, CRISPR was being used to clone and revive endangered and extinct animal populations in a last-ditch effort to rescue a hemorrhaging natural order.

For her part, Amara was investigating properties of various Deltadromeus genes after inserting them into *Botaurus stellaris* germ cell cultures to study how an engineered species of modern bird might adapt to environmental stressors. The results spoke for themselves. As Jerome had predicted, Cretaceous theropods like *Deltadromeus agilis* developed specific genetic adaptations to rising global temperatures during the Cenomanian and leading into the Turonian. Among dinosaurs, coelurosaurs in particular evolved to tolerate acute and variable temperature extremes. Deltadromeus, it seemed, could thermoregulate with startling efficiency in a way that most extant theropods—birds—simply could not.

---

2 See appendices for more information on CRISPR gene editing

Until now.

Botaurus stellaris, which had not yet faced extinction, ultimately had a higher purpose beyond the confines of a Petri dish—it had been selected as the surrogate species to revive its cousin through the Veritas Protocol's American Bittern Resurrection Initiative.

One of the keys to ensuring the project's success lay in a specific *D. agilis* gene locus encoding a novel heat shock protein called HSP70. While similar protein-encoding sequences were also isolated from Amara's *T. rex* samples, HSP70 in *D. agilis* was far more responsive to acute temperature fluctuations, in addition to extended periods of thermal stress. This finding corresponded to the environmental extremes the dinosaur would have faced during the second Oceanic Anoxic Event, something Jerome had also predicted.

Amara's findings suggested the animal had the ability to modulate heat dissipation by altering blood plasma volume and capillary vasodilation. In conjunction with this, increased mitochondrial density generated an incredibly efficient level of cellular respiration not seen in modern avialans. Even the remaining birds in the present-day tropics could not dissipate heat with such efficiency. HSP70, it turned out, directed an unprecedented up-regulation of mitochondrial division and replication in Deltadromeus that, to Amara, seemed near-impossible.

Jerome was right all along.

She hoped that this new gene, HSP70, would be the key to generating a unique generation of heat-tolerant hybrids. One that might enable the Veritas Protocol to finally enter its rewilding phase and re-introduce the bittern to North America.

In light of this milestone, Mitogen had received bids from governments across the globe seeking to restore lost ecosystems. Amara and Jerome's teams were already developing surrogate germ cell lines for African ostriches, New Zealand moa, and Cambodian giant ibis. In the United States, there were petitions for the resurrection of Californian condors, piping plovers, and over three dozen other species. Each passing day brought a fresh round of inquiries, and that was just for *birds*.

But Shin had set his sights much higher with HS134, a secretive subdivision under Synapsid Genomics.

Homo sapiens.

After animal trials had gone exceedingly well, the genetic engineering ethics board in Seoul fast-tracked Mitogen to begin human trials on its next generation of biological manipulation, coined "DNA hardening." For the first time, a fully developed person could manipulate their genetic makeup at will. Change it from one week to the next, if one so desired.

Amara tore herself from her computer screen, and the incessant blaring of the sequencer filtered back into her awareness. She stood from her chair, pulled her graying dreadlocks into a neat updo, and donned the hood of her ESD smocks. She gave herself a once-over in the mirror hanging on the lab entrance door, pretending not to notice the crow's feet at the corners of her eyes, and entered.

She made her way past slate benches of labware, picturing herself with straighter hair, maybe something a little more manageable. Maybe darker skin, after a lifetime of being told she wasn't "black enough." She scoffed at the depravity of it. Dissociated from her small role in the slippery slope toward a new age of "molecular eugenics."

Enhancements.

Veritas's bittern initiative was only the beginning.

TWO

"Lazarus, come out!"
He who was dead came out...

—John 11

| PEREZ >

91 years after Jerome's keynote

Full white clouds drifted overhead. They looked almost natural, tumbling clockwise along unseen convection currents as they passed over the clean lines of the geodesics above. Clouds inside the dome formed by adiabatic cooling—a typical condensation pattern seen in nature—and contributed to a self-contained water cycle.

Forecast calls for rain tomorrow, Camila Perez thought as she returned her focus to the dead bird at her feet. A field of blood-red amaryllis, native to sub-Saharan Africa, was in full bloom all around her, the petals as motionless as the carcass they partially obscured.

The bird's feathers were splayed, toes curled into rigor mortis. Impact splatter speckled its striped breast plumage.

Shaking her head, Perez crouched and scooped the bird into a specimen bag. There was an unnatural way the head dangled from its crushed neck, rotating like a wilted flower petal, its shattered beak painted deep scarlet.

"¡Ay! Another one," she mumbled to herself.

She waved her wrist over the animal's neck, where its chip was located, and her helmet's heads-up display projected a digital ID onto her visor. She puffed aside a few strands of black hair and read the analysis.

African cuckoo, *Cuculus gularis*. Male. Specimen **AR04736**. Heart rate: indeterminate. Metabolic rate: indeterminate. Status: deceased.

Over the last year, Perez had inherited the role of ARC's "bird coroner." The causes of death were almost always the same—diffuse internal bleeding, cerebral contusions and swelling, fractured skulls and fractured cervical vertebrae secondary to high-velocity impact.

Her bangs fell back over her eyes. *One of these days,* she thought, *I might remember to tie my hair back before I suit up.* Beads of sweat erupted across her brow, caught by a pair of prominent eyebrows that shielded her olive eyes from the onslaught of perspiration. The whir of her environmental suit's internal climate control hummed into action, punctuated by an electrical smell that caused a strange sensory dissonance with her surroundings.

She wondered to herself whether she would ever know the scent of forests and fields of flowers.

Specimen bag in hand, Perez continued on foot along the dome's western perimeter. The amaryllises dotted the surrounding grassland, spreading into a nearby vale of vibrant leopard orchids bisected by a sparkling river. Golden pollen granules ascended lazily into the still air as miniature drones swooped in and out of vivid stellates, their wings shimmering in the filtered sunlight. They were the ARC's pollinators, a stand-in for the extinct East African honeybee.

Perez looked far off, wincing through the soft radiance. Her visor's UV polarizer was malfunctioning again. Around a kilometer out, a small tree-covered mountain basked in the crisp morning dew. Farther beyond, the far end of the dome's carapace formed a pale blue backdrop. Beyond it, she made out the faint outline of the Saharan Atlas Mountains, along which the dome was nestled.

She was still in awe of this place most days, the sheer size of it, what science had *achieved.*

Like the clouds, the interior mountain at the center of the dome looked quite natural. Lush green forest surrounded its base, the tree line extending two-thirds of the way up. But Mount Qalil was far from typical; it was *hollow*. The mountain's interior had been excavated and reinforced to conceal the dome's "lung" deep within, with Qalil's expansive cavern doubling as a roosting habitat for desert long-eared bats. Based on the stillness around Perez, it was evident that the mountain was dormant at the moment.

Perez turned and continued through thick flowers and bushgrass. The muffled sound of rushing water grew in her ears; as she neared ARC's southern perimeter, she came to a large moat running along its circumference. The water flowed clockwise, feeding a small system of branching rivulets that snaked throughout the dome, one of which circumscribed Qalil's western flank. Perez craned her neck and began to scan sections of the dome's sloping carapace across the outer bank. Each geodesic was only a few centimeters thick but stood two stories high. Thousands of these hexagonal panels interlocked to form a honeycombed spherical array that stretched kilometers in every direction.

Her eye caught something about six panels up. Squinting, she could see a tiny red smear on its inner surface.

"Athena, three times magnification," she said. Her HUD outlined a segment of her visual field and expanded it. She made out a tuft of feathers embedded within a ribbon of caked blood. "Photograph that."

As Perez suspected, the bird had flown straight into the dome's barrier. She shook her head again.

Just like the rest.

Perez returned her field of view to standard and peered through the translucent barrier, into the desert beyond the ARC. The abrupt transition from lush sub-Saharan greenery to the barren wasteland outside always jarred her. In some ways, the Sahara reminded her of home, its frequent sandstorms reminiscent of the dust storms that rose from Spain's own desertification.

Off in the distance, a muddled-looking EDEN loomed like a mountainous dewdrop in the hazy desert air. Its north end engulfed the lower third of Djebel Aïssa, the largest mountain in the Saharan Atlas. It also vaulted over Aïn Ouerka, a small lake at Aïssa's base. Along with NEBO to the east, these domes formed part of SANCTUM's network of sanctuaries scattered across Europe and parts of North Africa—territories of the United European Federation.

SANCTUM—*the Settlement and Advancement of Nature and Colonisation beyond Terrestrial Utilization Modalities*—began as a joint venture between the European government and biotech giant Mitogen in 2064. Now, it fell primarily under the jurisdiction of a unified Europe that had coalesced out of the European Union before Perez was born. The ARC served as a proving ground for self-sustainable off-world colonisation, but it also doubled as a nature preserve—one of few such closed ecosystems in the world.

Part of Perez's research centered around ways to generate thriving ecosystems on Mars and beyond. The ARC was a small step toward terraforming the Red Planet and establishing prosperous colonies on other worlds—perhaps one day even protoplanets in the asteroid belt like 4-Vesta and Ceres. But Perez's passion remained on Earth: the bleak prospect of preserving the ninety percent of endangered plant and animal species slated for extinction in the next twenty years. ARC-Algeria, in particular, was focused primarily on sub-Saharan ecosystems.

Growing up amid the height of the Anthropocene Thermal Maximum had left a profound impact on Perez. Birds were among the first to be almost wiped out in the wild, then fishes and corals as the oceans warmed and acidified with bicarbonate. Most modern conservation focused on genetically altering wildlife, even *people*, to adapt to temperature extremes and plummeting atmospheric oxygen. But the biggest offender—habitat loss—posed a far more significant challenge. One by one, entire species were lost, relegated to some "resurrection" list. But the problem was no longer bringing back viable species—it was *sustaining* them in a world bereft of a home. A sanctuary.

The Sixth Extinction marched on.

As a girl, Perez remembered her parents hosting refugees trying to escape coastal flooding in Cataluña and Valencia. Other parts of Europe had suffered far worse.

Dwindling resources, though, posed the most imminent threat to European society. The Federation's justice system was the first to address this issue by moving the incarcerated to low-orbit prisoner colonies, often referred to as "gaols."

Resource waste mitigation.

Going to the gaols was a life sentence. No one ever came back. Many suspected that food and supply shipments to the prisons were so erratic and infrequent that the incarcerated simply starved.

But hunger was not exclusive to the gaols. Rations were tight across the UEF, especially in Perez's home province of Spain, which suffered some of the worst human rights offenses under Federalist rule. She remembered when Uncle Diego went to the gaols. He had stolen bread to feed his family. After his disappearance, the Federation processed his two boys—Perez's cousins—into the foster network. She never saw them again.

When she was little, Perez's mother often invoked Uncle Diego to warn her she might one day land herself in a gaol because of her strong-willed and outspoken nature, a characteristic her father admired.

"If they take me, they take me," she had joked once at the dinner table as she probed a slab of roasted pork. Her cheeks puffed out, tongue darting in and out in exaggerated fashion. *"¡Puaj!"* The early makings of a budding vegetarian. "I would prefer to die if that happens."

"Camila, do not say these things!" her mother had snapped.

Perez remembered the worry in Mamá's eyes, wrinkled at their corners, the furrowing of her brow. Inevitably, Mamá always broke down after an outburst.

"I do not know what I would do if I ever lost you, Camilita mía." Mamá's hard stare would break eventually, soften, her eyes glossed and far away. Then came the obligatory sigh, and it was back to business. "Now, eat your food. You know it is not easy to come by good meat. And you are so *thin*. You need to eat, chavala."

"Pero—"

"Speak *English*, Camilita." Mamá straightened in her chair, her expression glum. "We have talked of this. We do not need any more trouble from school."

Perez tilted her head back and forth, pretending to ignore her mother. "Que si no sé qué, qué si no sé cuánto," she grumbled.

Papá laid down his fork, his expression stern, jaw muscles twitching.

"Camila, that is enough from you. You heard Mamá." His voice commanded attention. One could not avoid looking directly at Papá when he spoke. "We speak English. That is the end of it."

Perez turned her lips down and puffed her cheeks. "But I want patatas. And you and Mamá *always* talk Spanish without me. Why do we *always*—"

"*Camila…*"

Like Mamá, Papá softened, but he did not break his tone. "Osito, if you upset your mother *one more time*… I shall take you to the gaols myself!" He stood and lunged at her playfully, extending two curled fingers toward her like *T. rex* claws. Perez was too young to know it at that time, but Papá was scared. And so was Mamá.

"¡Aye, Papá! ¡No, no me envíes a las gaols!" She squealed as he scooped her in his arms.

Mamá appealed for calm. "Enough now, you two. No one is going to the gaols today. Please sit and eat your food before it goes cold."

Perez also remembered when the threat of the gaols turned real.

She was maybe nine or ten the first time the UEF Ministry of Intelligence dispatched agents to her home. They had accused her father of conspiring with Spanish guerillas disaffected by Spain's induction into the Federation. Papá swore up and down that they hosted only refugees in need, that no talk of apostasy ever fell on his or his wife's ears. Perez remembered when they isolated her in her tiny bedroom, questioning her for hours, trying to get her to turn on Papá, even though he was telling the truth.

Since the uprising, it was common knowledge Spanish citizens disproportionately filled the gaols—a government-sanctioned reprisal of sorts. There was no evidence her father, Adrián Perez, ever conspired with the Castellano Rebeldes, and a conviction never materialized. Still, Perez remembered the cold fear at the prospect of being taken from her parents, like her cousins from Uncle Diego. She imagined Mamá and Papá's sunken faces and pale, starving bodies riddled with bruises from countless beatings, their souls broken, deprived of human contact. Clothes soiled with their own blood and filth. She wasn't sure what went on in the orbiting prisons, but she imagined it might have been something along those lines.

In the face of what her family had endured, Perez's determination carried her far in her career, and she gained widespread respect in the field of veterinary research. After obtaining her Doctorate in Veterinary Medicine, she completed her Ph.D. in ecology and evolutionary biology. She was a standout in conservation and population studies, which led to her employment as Head of Animal Research on SANCTUM-Algeria's ARC initiative.

But despite her accomplishments, Perez was haunted by a persistent underlying shame. One the Federation—*the Father of all of Europe*—instilled in her from the outset. It was a potent control tactic, shame. *Shame* for the rebellion that happened before she was born, one she never espoused. *Shame* for being Spanish. *Shame* for not speaking English at school. *Shame* for being born—being *alive*. For consuming precious resources.

Shame.

But more than that, she felt regret. *Regret* she did not know enough to fight harder back then, to overcome that sense of guilt fostered inside her. *Regret* she had lost much of her ability to speak her native tongue. *Regret* she had let the Father *win*.

Fuck the Father.

A renewed sense of awareness brought the soft hum of her suit, the dampened rush of the moat, back to her ears. Her gaze tracked EDEN's smooth outline as it caught the morning sun. Specimen bag in hand, she broke away and started back across the field toward a waiting rover.

"Athena, add *Cuculus gularis* to the aviary log." Her voice cracked as she spoke. "We have another species flying into the hex panels."

A soft female voice came over her earpiece. "Yes, Dr. Perez, I will log a request for a species transfer to the trapping team. Which aviary would you prefer?"

"Acacia… and be sure to have the transfer team set up mock nests. This species is a brood parasite—we do not need it hijacking real nests."

"Yes, Dr. Perez. Will you require a specific surrogate from Genetics?"

Perez paused and thought for a moment. "*Corvinella corvina* should suffice. Thank you, Athena."

"You are welcome, Dr. Perez."

Her HUD displayed the status of the job requests:

Sanctuary Theta - Animal Revival and Conservation (ARC)

Cloning and Genetics: work order received. Status: pending.
Trapping and Transfer: work order received. Status: en route.

Perez decided to check on a couple of the aviaries before taking the specimen in for necropsy. They contained species known to be vulnerable to the anomaly. Large swaths of netting that contained them prevented them from flying into the panels. Her graduate student, Nedjma Ramdani, was there now, checking on clutches, logging successful hatches for the week. Perez had yet to show her how to perform an avian postmortem.

She glanced again at the specimen bag.

Birds were not the only animals displaying erratic behavior, but they were the most vulnerable, especially migratory species. Perez suspected that a localized electromagnetic disruption was throwing off their ability to navigate the dome safely. To her knowledge, only one thing could cause such a disturbance, and the culprit lay five hundred meters beneath the shimmering desert.

She sealed and labeled the specimen bag with the cuckoo inside, then climbed into the rover and tapped her key badge. She set a nav point for the Acacia aviary, where she would rendezvous with Nedjma and wait for the transfer team.

While en route, Perez made a final request through the comm.

"Athena… schedule a meeting with Lotta Eklund."

$|q_0\rangle$

FIRST POSTULATE
The state of an isolated system is defined by its wave function.

| SUPERCOLLIDER >

Lotta Eklund fidgeted with one of her pearl earrings. Unblinking, she peered through the driver's-side window of the rover. Her fingers ached from picking at her cuticles, which were seeping a clear fluid. The air outside had an ashen quality, the sort of sepia haze that preceded a sandstorm. The blistering Saharan landscape was a far cry from the perpetual winter blanketing Northern Europe. Since the collapse of the Atlantic Ocean's meridional overturning circulation, Earth's northern latitudes had been plunged into another ice age.

But Algeria was a different story.

Snow, perpetual sub-zero temperatures—these things, Lotta thought she would never miss. Not until she experienced the punishing heat of the Sahara.

Up to now, her career had spanned thirty years, the entirety of it with CEPP—the Commission of European Particle Physics, the largest scientific research division of the European Interprovincial Research Organisation, or EIRO.

Before her assignment to Algeria, Lotta worked as a researcher at CEPP's Fermi Circular Collider situated along the Swiss-Franco border.

It was one of the multiple ring-like supercolliders destroyed in the cataclysmic 2112 Geneva quake. After the disaster, the Federation sought a new location for CEPP's headquarters—one far from major population centers. Algeria's annexation and induction into the United European Federation provided such an opportunity, and in 2115, CEPP broke ground five kilometers southwest of the abandoned municipality of Ed Abiodh Sidi Cheikh. Shortly after, Lotta was appointed to Principal Investigator of Quantum Entanglement Studies for CEPP-Algeria, part of EIRO's proposed "Mecca of Science."

And now, her team was on the verge of unlocking the key to faster-than-light travel.

A violent jerk whipped Lotta. The rover swerved to the right, maintaining its specified course. Her heart fluttered. She swept her hair back, her eyes staring intently through the driver's-side window. Outside, a massive Goliath freighter—a frigate on wheels—barreled alongside the rover.

We are way too close, she thought.

She had set the nav to adaptive autopilot. The rover kept pace alongside the towering transport, but it kept over-correcting every few minutes.

"Athena," Lotta said, "widen berth to fifty meters."

The rover eased to the right, maintaining its speed as it pulled away from the Goliath's billowing dust cloud. A crisp white CEPP logo emblazoned on the freighter's graphene-clad hull penetrated the haze. It eased to the left to avoid a rocky pillar jutting out of the sand a hundred meters up ahead. Such stone columns grew denser near the base of the mountains. To Lotta, they resembled cairns.

Like shrines to the gods.

That would be her mother talking.

They were also causing jerky movements and course corrections as the rover attempted to match the freighter's trajectory while maintaining a safe distance. The Goliath passed along the other side of the column and crawled lazily back to center. The rover responded accordingly.

A constellation of white sprites danced across Lotta's vision.

The enormous freighter's chassis bore down on eight wheels—each as tall as a Siberian mammoth—veiled by billowing plumes of earthy grit. The hollow Nitinol tires sifted the coarse sand through their mesh walls, a mechanism that kept the freighter from getting trapped in dunes and undergrowth while providing strength and flexibility over the unforgiving landscape. Terrain that served as a proving ground for the future of Mars.

Lotta bit her lip and glanced at the windshield display. The nav indicated they were halfway to ALICE Command. She wanted to get back to the lab, back to her research.

A little over fifty kilometers to go.

But the way the Goliath's crew navigated caused a lump to settle at the back of her throat. She had already warned the captain to take it slow while the payload was loaded back at the airfield. He seemed indifferent to the fact he was responsible for piloting what equated to a building on wheels.

But *no*, the crew seemed more interested in making good *time*.

"Oy." A raspy male voice from the adjacent seat stole Lotta's focus. "No amount of staring's gonna change how they pilot that thing."

Lotta flashed a callous look toward Edgar Fischer, a burly man of sixty-five who had agreed to accompany her on the run. Fischer was the chief engineer on her research team at ALICE. He stroked a poorly kept gray beard while his other hand fidgeted with the lid of a flask concealed in his pants pocket. A military-style knife, something he always carried, was sheathed at his side. *Liquor and a blade.* He struck her as a survivalist, an ex-military type anxious to relive his glory days—or perhaps unable to escape them.

Lotta turned away, ignoring his remark, and maintained her gaze on the freighter just in time to watch it crash through a large dune in a spectacle of exploding sand and dust. She exhaled sharply and switched on the comm.

"Please lower and maintain your velocity. You are pitching again," she said through cracked lips into the console. The dry desert air permeated the cockpit, settling in the back of her throat. She turned to Fischer. "For what they spend on tech, you would expect the air filtration in here to bloody *work*."

A respirator dangled around her neck. She pulled it over her face, and a stream of stinging oxygen filled her lungs. Even having undergone DNA hardening and mitotransfection, the atmosphere of the Federation's African provinces proved far more difficult for her to breathe. But so far, she hadn't come down with anything, despite a raging pandemic throughout the region amongst the unhardened. So, there was that.

No response came from the Goliath. The freighter rocked smoothly on its suspension, trailing a massive plume of dust in its wake. With each rocking motion, Lotta's heart fluttered. She raised her hand back to her earring, and its backing clacked to the cockpit floor.

"*Shit,*" she hissed, scanning the bottom of the shaking rover. There was no sign of the metal backing, just dancing granules of sand.

Oh, hell. I will get it after we are stopped.

She put the earring into her pants pocket and went back to picking her cuticles, now raw and bleeding—a nervous habit she had adopted as a girl.

She leaned forward again to repeat the message. A moment later, her harness pressed into her shoulders as the rover decelerated to keep pace with the slowing freighter.

"*Thank you,*" she snapped into the comm. The Goliath's crew remained silent.

Fucking idiots.

"Maybe they are trying to beat the storm." Fischer shrugged. He leaned in, peering through her window under a sun-faded outback hat. A brown wall of dust was moving in from the east. The sandstorm was closing fast.

"We will get below the surface before it hits," Lotta said. Her gaze fell back on the Goliath, watching its hulking wheels cut through the land-scape. "Have you ever seen a mammoth?" she asked, changing the subject.

"What?"

"A mammoth. Have you seen one before?"

"In real life? No. Have you?"

Lotta nodded, her eyes still on the spinning wheels. "When I was little. I remember they first passed into Finland, then Old Sweden. Caused quite a stir. Their populations exploded after the Eurasian Cold Snap."

"Aye. We really messed this planet up, eh?" Fischer said, still staring at the approaching storm. Lightning bloomed behind the wall of dust, illuminating it with a dull glow.

Lotta had first met him during the construction of CEPP-Algeria's sixth-generation particle accelerator, the Higgs Circular Collider. He had worked on the superconducting magnets for CEPP's particle accelerators in Geneva and was brought on to spearhead the engineering team in Algeria.

In particular, Lotta worked closely with him on the specifications of the HCC's storage rings. She recalled her first impression of him—unkempt, always smelled of whisky—but the man had a brilliant way about him. For one, he had found a way to generate a magnetic field that could minimize the Heisenberg Uncertainty Principle in the accelerator's beam output, effectively breaking the Heisenberg limit and achieving levels of detection and measurement never obtained by previous colliders. After completing the project, Lotta knew she wanted him to continue with her team and offered him a full-time position with ALICE.

It wasn't until later that his substance abuse bubbled to the surface.

Thud. The rover lurched as it careened over the lip of a dune.

"*Verdammt noch mal!*" Fischer snorted as he clamped a hand down on his thigh.

A potent smoky odor permeated the cabin: the smell of aged whiskey. Lotta looked down and spotted a wet blotch soaking through Fischer's pants. He stiffened and looked up at her.

"Look, I, uh—this—I do not drink on the job, I just thought… for the ride… it'd be good to have in case—"

Disregarding him, Lotta cocked her head. "*Verdammt?*"

"Huh? Er, it's German. 'Verdammt noch mal'—it means 'dammit.' You are from Switzerland—you did not speak Schwiizerdütsch growing up?"

She gave a half-grin. "No, I did. Before the English mandate. I've not heard it in so long. I could not speak it now if I tried."

Fischer's expression turned from concern to one of nervous jest. "*Hoffnungslos,*" he said, shaking his head in feigned disappointment.

Lotta's jaw dropped, and she turned her body toward him. "I am *not* hopeless, you *Schweinehund!* And do not assume you're getting off so easily. If I find you getting pissed on the job, you are *out.* Understood?" There was an odd satisfaction in the way Fischer nodded stupidly as she spoke. "Keep your little juice tin at home."

The engineer sighed and pretended to study the HUD. "The cheese maker *does* speak some Deutsch…" he mumbled as if making some astute observation.

Lotta bristled, folding her arms as she stared out the window. She didn't want him to see her smiling.

He nudged her on the shoulder. "Just takin' the piss outta ya…" he said, peering back out through the windshield into the murky air. "Schönes wetter heute, eh? A day for the beach." Lotta batted him away and stifled what would have been another ear-to-ear smile.

Long shadows darkened the cockpit as the rover accompanied the Goliath through a wide valley between two towering mesas, their sheer chalky faces obscuring the hazy sunlight overhead. The sound of pebbles striking the rover's base reminded Lotta of the hailstorms up north. She peered out at the Goliath, the wall of stone behind it, a dull, sanguine blur. Then, as soon as it had disappeared, sunlight poured back into the cabin, and the mesas fell away like stone curtains. The rover dashed into open desert, and Lotta turned to meet an awe-inspiring view—a sprawling vista dominated by a mountain-sized dome.

"Oy," Fischer whispered. "We are coming up on one of the sanctuaries." He pointed at the enormous structure. A GPS watch partially concealed a deep linear scar on his wrist, which Lotta pretended not to notice.

The windshield's LIDAR outlined the dome's perimeter in red. As they neared its base, the geodesics flashed a dull digital blue overlayed by the display.

"That is something else," Fischer said as he strained to look at the top of the colossal structure. High up, dark clouds coalesced along the dome's windward flank. The HUD indicated they were looking at Sanctuary Theta—the ARC—one of three such domes. "You think the ones on Mars'll be that big?"

Lotta gazed up at it through the glass roof of the cockpit. "Maybe," she said.

The sheer immensity of the dome filled her with awe and wonder. Theta constituted a massive research facility operating as a closed ecological system, fully self-sufficient from the outside environment. The sanctuaries would prove instrumental in the widespread colonisation of Mars, but for now, they had only been built on Earth, usually in areas where harsh conditions prevailed—ideal prerequisites for taking on the Red Planet.

"Wonder if your chum Camila is inside… maybe she's seen a mammoth before. You'd have something in common then, *ja?*" Fischer looked over with a grin.

"Fuck you, Ed." Her bottom lip split open; she tasted blood on her tongue. She regretted telling him earlier about her disdain for ARC's eminent head of animal research. She was not looking forward to their upcoming meeting, the third one in three months.

Fischer smiled. "Rather rude for a Swiss lady, no?"

Lotta feigned indifference to that remark. "I'm not like other Swiss women. Certainly not a *lady.*"

"Right, fair enough. I'll sod off, then." Fischer tipped his frayed brim and returned his attention to the dome.

Lotta wondered if he kept a flask in that mess of a beard. She caught herself studying his weathered face, the red-tipped bulb of his nose, and shifted her gaze back to the view before them.

As the rover drew near, Lotta lost all sense of the dome's shape. From this close, Theta's exterior looked like a vertical wall of hexagonal geodesics that extended toward the horizon. Its curved perimeter began to resemble a straight line the more they closed in, and Lotta could make out enormous windswept dunes along its base. Sand whipped against its surface, rising skyward along convection currents generated by the temperature differential from its interior. Inside, trees and lush greenery flew past. At the center, the faded outline of a mountain rose high from the forest floor.

"Incredible engineering feat," Fischer said. "I talked to a guy that worked on the variable pressure system that keeps these domes from imploding. That mountain in this one keeps the entire structure intact."

"The *mountain?* How?"

"It's called a 'lung.' Technical term is pulmonem—a variable expansion membrane over a kilometer in diameter. It seals the perimeter of a crater inside the mountain."

"The mountain… is *hollow?*"

Fischer nodded. "Aye. The pulmonem is suspended hundreds of meters down, oriented horizontally above an underground flow chamber and tunnel system."

"And those lead to where?"

"They connect her to her two sister domes and a central pulmonem that is open to the outside. As the air volume expands and contracts inside the dome, her pulmonem rises and falls, causing the mountain to 'breathe' through a series of openings—mouths—around the mountain's base. Equalizes the dome's internal pressure with the outside to maintain structural integrity. A complete technological marvel."

Minutes later, the hexagonal array started curving away, and soon, the dome was behind them. Lotta looked back, watching Theta grow smaller as the rover pressed forward. For the first time, she could make out the faint shape of Theta's two sister domes. They dwarfed the mountains in the backdrop.

Around a kilometer to the west of Theta, sunlight glinted off Shin tower, SANCTUM-Algeria's operational headquarters, looming over a small outpost meant to represent a Martian proto-colony. Such research outposts would mark the first phase of large-scale colonisation, preceding construction of the domes on the red planet.

SANCTUM was the other major research division under EIRO.

Another fifteen minutes passed.

Lotta found herself staring blankly at the Goliath once more, her heart rate slower now, Fischer snoring beside her.

A female voice came over the comm, interrupting the droning continuity of the rover's wheelbase. "Entering Sector 18: ALICE," it said. Fischer jolted upright.

Lotta turned to look through the windshield. ALICE Command's LIDAR signature emerged on the veiled horizon. As the rover neared, an enormous loading hangar loomed in the growing haze. It encompassed the eastern wing of a sprawling multi-story compound—a vast command center for what lay five hundred meters beneath the sand. As large as this facility was, it was only underground that its true scale was on full display.

Lotta assumed autonomy over the rover, gripping the steering wheel. She pulled ahead of the Goliath and approached an enormous bay door. A loading crew of synths—synthetic lifeforms—stood by at the entrance in yellow jumpsuits and hard hats, awaiting their arrival.

"They've synths wearing helmets now?" Fischer scoffed. "Bloody *shicks*[1] ... things give me the creeps." He shook his head and folded his arms over his chest. "*Damned helmets*. What next, a paycheck?"

Part biology, part machine, synths were relegated to grunt work. Some were commissioned for other purposes—mostly underground, like the illicit sex trade (although without the proper calibrations, their strength was said to be problematic in the bedroom). Initially used as cannon fodder in wars past, they eventually gained a degree of sovereignty and integrated into human society, but were considered less than human—*less than alive*.

"EIRO protects its investments," Lotta said.

"*Aye*. I guess we are no different in that regard."

Lotta eased forward, the Goliath trailing close behind with dust and sand billowing off its tires. Angled overhead, house-sized fans roared to life, sweeping the grit back out into the desert. A thunderous groan echoed all around as the massive bay door slowly lowered to seal the entrance.

One of the synths, a tall female, signaled for Lotta to steer the rover to the east wing of the hangar toward a docking platform the size of half a city block. Metal catwalks formed a perimeter around its edges, where two synths gestured a team below to clear out while the Goliath approached. A sign affixed to a railing read *SECTOR 18. HARD HAT AREA*, pulsing red with the flashing red lights that dotted the platform's perimeter. The freighter backed in and ground to a halt, and the synths leapt into action, securing all eight wheels to the platform with heavy steel chains. They showed no signs of fatigue.

High overhead, rows of beams and struts lined the flat roof of the hangar. A gantry whirred along a track, ferrying a bipedal loading mech past a lattice of catwalks to the south end of the facility, where rows of aerial construction drones sat idle. Beyond them, a tiny elevator climbed a yellow track, running perpendicular to a column of running platforms that led to various sectors in nearby buildings. People moved like tiny ants across them.

Lotta pulled ahead and parked the rover to the side of the docking zone and unfastened her restraints. She moved to the rear of the cabin,

---

1 Derogatory slur for synths. See appendices for more information.

retrieved two rubbery electrostatic discharge uniforms from a side compartment, and handed one to Fischer. He finished adjusting the straps on his respirator and took it from her.

Lotta suited up and stepped onto the platform with Fischer. One of the personnel, a ginger-haired woman in an ESD uniform, handed them each a hard hat. She stood out in stark contrast to the synths, mainly because she wore a respirator. Her eyes were beet-red from constant exposure to the elements, and her weather-beaten skin aged her—nothing like the pallid, waxy features of her crew.

Their oddly flawless skin.

Lotta watched them work, their purple eyes darting every which way, their bleached whites too perfect to be human. She secured her helmet, catching the eyes of the ginger-haired woman, which were fixated on her mangled fingertips as she clipped the chin strap. The woman's gaze shifted to Lotta's empty earlobe.

Shit. Lotta had forgotten to look for the backing to her earring before leaving the rover. *Too late now, about to descend.*

The woman noticed Lotta catch her stare and quickly looked away before walking over to a flat biometric touch display to activate the lift.

A digitized female voice boomed through the hangar: the same as the one in the rover. It was Athena, EIRO's artificial intelligence.[2] "Welcome to the ALICE facility. The lift is active. Stay within the designated safe zone markings and limit your movement about the platform. The entrance will now close. Please stand clear."

Lotta licked her cracked lips from behind the steamy face shield and scanned her surroundings.

An alarm buzzed, and a metal gate slid up from a recess along the platform's vast perimeter. The buzzing continued as the entire structure began to drop, slowly receding underground. Soon, the opening it had passed into loomed several meters overhead, the synths standing on the staging growing smaller by the second until they disappeared behind the edge of the opening.

The top of the Goliath was the last thing to fall into shadow.

---

2 See appendices for more information on Athena.

A second high-pitched alarm rang, and the screech of metal on metal grated Lotta's ears. The lift lurched, sidling down an inclined shaft like a massive funicular. Lotta watched the overhead bay door crawl shut with a booming metallic clang, and the ringing stopped. The elevator crept to a stop and lingered.

Something sputtered overhead; a torrential downpour of clear solution rained over the entire platform. The liquid coalesced into frothing eddies at Lotta's feet, quickly draining through the grated floor. She looked up at the Goliath, sheets of brown liquid flowing off it like miniature waterfalls, the muddled foam swirling at its base.

Everything underground needed to be sterile, all sources of static discharged.

After several minutes, the downpour ceased. There was an abrupt jolt, and the elevator resumed smoothly down the track. The ginger-haired woman walked to the aft end of the Goliath, inspecting its exterior. It towered four stories above her tiny form. The synths stood idle along its starboard side.

Lotta turned back to Fischer. "This thing always reminds me of riding the Stoosbahn as a girl."

"Maybe not quite as scenic," he said, his voice muffled behind his mask. "Less snow, too."

Lotta looked surprised, "You've been to Schwyz? Big bad German came down to little old Switzerland just to ride the funicular?"

He laughed. "Aye, to ride the funicular. And joint military training… before things got bad with Russia. Before the Cold Snap."

"The Federation conducted military training *in Schwyz?* I don't recall this, a military presence."

"It was classified. We camped in the mountains near Morschach. Visited Schwyz a few times in our civvies." Fischer appeared agitated and changed the topic. "Eklund… this is a Swedish name, no?"

"My father was Swedish, yes. Mum is Swiss." Lotta's gaze was far off as she recounted the story her father had ruminated on many times over. "They decided to move to Schwyz to be close to Mum's family when I was young. Fled Old Sweden to get away from the Russian Buffer Zone."

"Why'd they need to run? Unless they were—"

"Heathens. My father was unapologetically neopagan; my mum converted after they were married."

Her parents had been some of the last to flee south, had seen the writing on the wall after evangelical extremists and pro-Russian separatists had driven the remaining neopagans from neighboring Finland.

The looming threat of a Russian invasion had provided another reason to flee. Lotta's mother often referred to its standing armies as the jötnar—giants—lining Europe's borders, emboldened after the collapse of NATO and the retreat of the Western Allies toward nationalistic policies. She remembered the fear that the jötnar might invade the Scandinavian territories. After the fall of Kyiv in Ukraine, there was speculation the Baltics might be the next to witness Russian aggression.

As she grew older, Lotta had drifted from her heathenistic roots—ultimately denounced religion altogether—but the stories stayed with her. She told Fischer all of this before she realized she had probably overshared, so she consciously omitted the fact she barely knew her father and that her mother fell into a deep depression after he left. That Lotta had spent her childhood raising herself. That she hated both of her parents for it.

Fischer nodded solemnly. "Aye, the RBZ. Glad I got out before things went to shit." His unkempt scruff almost disguised a disdainful grimace.

They continued downward for another twenty minutes before the elevator decelerated and came to a stop. The alarm buzzed again, and the gate retracted back into the platform. A massive bay door groaned open, revealing a sprawling chamber that would have easily housed the hangar back at the surface. It was a labyrinth of ladders and suspended landings. Pipes ran along the walls and ceiling, and cables weaved intricately through mechanical structures, connecting one to the next in a web of circuits. The particle accelerator was sheathed in a colossal metal tube that coursed through the chamber. A maze of catwalks vaulted high overhead, some spanning the accelerator's storage rings to adjoin sections within the extensive underground facility. People in ESD smocks and hard hats walked across them, appearing as distant blue specks overhead.

It was a cathedral of science. And that was precisely what Lotta called it. The Cathedral.

Back on the platform, the synth crew mobilized. A team of engineers in rubbery blue ESD smocks and hard hats descended a metal staircase from one of the labs above. SAM, the Station Analysis Monorail robot, whirred along a suspended track overhead, analyzing the chamber's atmospheric composition, running system checks.

Lotta turned and watched the synths remove the wheel restraints from the Goliath. Smirked at an intrusive thought about synth bedroom antics gone awry.

The shadow of the Goliath swallowed her as it backed into the chamber port, the floor groaning beneath its bulk. It emitted almost no sound despite its size, while the crew guided it like runway attendants toward a yellow dashed line on the chamber floor. Once in position, the vehicle ground to a halt and its lights dimmed.

Along its aft end, white plumes of nitrogen gas poured onto the waiting crew as the rear cargo door lurched open. The suited figures stood, unflinching, heads tipped up toward the payload: a three-story high levitating orb sequestered inside an electromagnetic array. The final piece required for generating a transient singularity.

"That thing make black holes, you reckon?" Fischer chuckled. Playing stupid. It was his team that had fabricated the apparatus—the same team eagerly waiting by the cargo hold.

Lotta smirked, maintaining her gaze on the matte-black geodesic sphere. Her heart pounded in anticipation. Her cracked lips burned. Her ravaged fingers throbbed.

"Something like that."

| AQUILA CHRYSAETOS >

A gloved hand stroked the sedated rabbit's head. The animal remained calm, flaring its nares from atop a steel lab bench that sat like an altar at the center of a cold, desolate room. The hand stopped on its midriff and pulled the white scruff into a bunch. A hypodermic needle containing a translucent solution slid beneath the skin. The rabbit shifted, agitated, pink eyes wide. Its back legs kicked. But the gloved hand held firm, pinning the helpless creature against the cold surface until its struggling ceased.

Basem Bensoussan eased his grip as he removed the needle and massaged the injection site. A moment later, the rabbit calmed.

"Athena, begin dictation," he said.

"Dictation initiated." The AI's response sounded tinny, almost hollow.

The room bore a sterile quality, one conducive to medical experimentation. Clean lines. Bare walls. Not a speck of dust nor stain in sight. Searing white light bathed every surface. A chemical smell lingered, an odor akin to burnt plastic doused in bleach. It settled at the back of Basem's throat, a bitter taste that would persist long after he left for the night. Overhead, the hum of the ventilation system was punctuated by the soft chirping of the rabbit's vitals on a holographic display. To the right, near the edge of the bench, a clear cage sat on a stainless-steel cart.

Basem swallowed hard. Cradling the rabbit in his arms for a moment, he walked over and placed it in the cage. The animal nibbled at the water feeder, its front teeth clacking against the metal nozzle. It lapped with such ferocity that blood seeped down its chin, staining its snowy fur a bright cherry hue.

Basem adjusted his surgical mask and began his dictation. "Subject 0014, Leporidae Entanglement Trial, Phase Two: DNA Hardening. Subcutaneous injection of sirtuin-like nano polymer substrate appears well-tolerated by the subject. Previously, Phase One demonstrated habitual expression of telomerase, catalase, and superoxide dismutase agonists. Close monitoring of all twenty subjects will begin today, followed by Phase Three: Radiation Prevention and Mitigation. Subjects will be vetted for entangled traversal fitness upon completion of all three preparatory phases. I am awaiting ALICE and BOB's time-of-flight data to ensure wormhole stability before Phase Four is deemed safe and humane. Phase Four trials are projected to commence in the coming weeks."

Basem activated the room's sanitation system and wheeled the cage out into the hallway. Atomizing misters sputtered overhead as the door closed behind him. He was on the sixteenth floor of Shin Tower, a sprawling facility, physically large but with a strangely claustrophobic quality inside its research sectors. His footsteps reverberated off the sterile walls like a lumbering death march.

A dozen other examination rooms lined the white corridor—each the same as the next—designed for the evaluation, treatment, and preparation of animals for untold experiments: drug trials, pain tolerance studies, stress tests. Each one served a role in joint cooperatives between SANCTUM and EIRO's other research divisions.

For his part, Basem led the animal studies for CEPP's ALICE sector. And as SANCTUM's Chief of Veterinary Research, he held the highest qualifications for the assignment. The current project involved preparing subjects for Lotta Eklund's studies on a novel method of transport. He still could not wrap his head around the concept, which made his task—subject survival—even more challenging. Subjects were conditioned through genetic manipulation so the rabbits could tolerate the journey. Could *survive* it. That meant a lot of trial and error regarding protocol.

It also meant integrating a genetic kill switch triggered by a predetermined threshold of physiologic adrenaline and cortisol.

In the face of so many unknowns, there was only one thing Basem could be certain of, one thing over which he had control: suffering. If all else failed—the DNA hardening, the physical conditioning, every painstaking measure taken to ensure survival—he could at least pull the plug, eliminate anguish through the merciful gift of death. The kill switch gave him a back door. If a subject reached a certain level of pain or distress, a genetically directed cascade would initiate widespread cell death and organ failure within seconds.

Over the past few months, Basem had attended mock trials at ALICE transporting inanimate organic matter, a prerequisite he insisted on prior to the use of live animals. The results were amazing—they evaded all conventional logic. At least to him. To Lotta Eklund, it all boiled down to Gaussian integrals, Calabai-Yao shapes, Hilbert spaces, Dirac equations, unity matrices. *The list is as long as Planck's length is short*, she had told him. Basem knew none of what it meant. He struggled to understand even basic concepts like the dual nature of matter. Wave? Particle? But never both simultaneously (at the moment of measurement). Perturbing the system forced it into one state or the other, *a collapsing of the wave function*, according to Eklund. The extent of his understanding ended there. The double-slit experiment was as meaningless to him as G-protein coupled receptors or phenotypic plasticity were to her. All he knew was the test subject started in ALICE's lab at the beginning, and in an instant appeared at BOB's. *More than fifty kilometers away.*

At least, that was the idea. His task was to get a live subject to traverse the gap unscathed.

The rabbit stirred.

Basem glanced down at the helpless creature, its back muscles twitching. Each subject responded differently to treatment. This one was agitated, trying to burrow through the hard plexiglass floor of its tiny prison. In a day or two, most of its fur would fall out. Basem studied it for a moment, watching it alternate between hapless digging and voracious drinking. An incessant clacking. Insatiable thirst—*polydipsia*—was a symptom shared by all Phase II subjects.

It was a common side effect of DNA hardening in people, too.

He remembered his own experience with DNA hardening. The procedure was compulsory for all personnel attached to Eklund's research—those who faced potential exposure to extreme physiological stress. An unlikely event, but one well within the realm of possibility. DNA hardening had, until now, been reserved for those assigned to low-G environments or the harsh conditions of the outer colonies.

But as the global crisis on Earth marched on, it became increasingly apparent that the general population would also require some form of mass genetic modification in the coming years to tolerate the altered climate.

Basem had undergone the series of infusions and tests a year ago for CEPP, but it still seemed like yesterday. For almost a week after the treatment, he drank and pissed constantly. Nothing stifled the dry mouth, the gritty, constant longing for hydration. He remembered the sensation that came with each infusion, like his skin was on fire. Electrical shocks on his tongue, in his eyes, his nose, kept him awake at night. It lasted for days. Everything smelled like a chemical fire. Food had an acrid taste. Colors looked washed out or absent altogether. Before the procedure, his hair was deep black—eventually it grew back, patchy at first. He had lost a bit of the pigment in his beard; it grew back with a peppered-gray stripe down the middle. It was weeks before he felt like himself again.

After the recovery phase, he realized he could breathe the air, process it fully for the first time. He had grown more aware, more alert than ever. Felt stronger. Desirable side effects that demonstrated the efficacy of DNA hardening and its potential applications for battling human mortality amid the climate crisis.

But DNA hardening in people was nothing like the novel methods Basem implemented in his subjects. His inner turmoil over the rabbits was unyielding. Their suffering was tenfold that of conventional treatments. But it was necessary.

The hallway was an endless corridor of doors reminiscent of some dream he probably had years ago, an optical illusion, a never-ending conveyer of doorways. At the end sat the animal housing facility—a maze of yet more rooms harboring everything from zebra fish to mice to marmosets. CEPP's rabbit room was just inside to the left. He stepped inside, flanked by rows of stacked cages. The stench of animal excrement trickled through his mask. It provoked within him a stomach-turning affliction. Even after years of experience, he struggled to overcome it.

A chorus of clacking filled his ears like dozens of mini jackhammers.

He placed the rabbit back in its designated location among the other subjects, their cages stacked in neat rows on steel shelves bolted to the wall. He started inspecting each one to elucidate how the other rabbits were faring in their progress. Many subjects were in various stages of losing fur or growing it back. Some trembled, feverish. Others scratched their haunches raw.

Starting at the top left, Basem peered inside each cage, then moved to the next. All subjects appeared stable except for one. It was near the end of the line on the second row—Subject 0218. The rabbit was motionless, its water bottle full. There was an unsettling placidity inside the cage, a silence that drowned out the background frenzy around him. A stillness that he had grown numb to.

He gave the cage a light tap. *No response.* The rabbit's bald skin possessed a bluish pallor. With gloved hands, he pulled the cage off the shelf and placed it on a nearby lab bench. He unlatched the cover and reached inside. His fingers met cold skin.

"Athena," he said, his voice hushed, "Log ALICE Subject zero-two-one-eight as deceased, pending necropsy."

"Subject zero-two-one-eight logged. Postmortem analysis pending." To Basem, Athena's response sounded procedural, indifferent. A collective conscious without conscience.

Free from the trappings of empathy.

He thought it odd how she—the sum aggregate of human cognizance—lacked certain qualities, basic traits considered "human." Emotionless. Unfeeling. Perhaps Athena was programmed that way. But maybe not.

Basem removed the carcass and slid it into a biohazard bag. He walked out and proceeded back down the hall to the walk-in freezer where the bodies were kept, all the while thinking back to his first experience with death.

Algeria was sovereign back then, before its annexation into the United European Federation. Basem was maybe five or six at the time. His home was nestled in a district of the Algiers kasbah, a winding labyrinth of seventeenth-century stone homes dotting a hillside along the Algerian coast.

He had been dribbling a football through the narrow cobblestone streets. A layer of dust covered the ground from the last sandstorm just days prior. The primitive buildings were decrepit, with exposed brick where the outer masonry had crumbled away. Lazy wires sagged overhead between the ramshackle stone structures, and linens dangled from clotheslines strewn across windows. The kasbah clashed with the modern graphene superstructures that loomed within the City Centre just blocks away. There were many rumors circulating as to what resided beyond those sleek gray walls—clean air, green plants, fresh water. Once considered basic human needs, now commodities of the aristocracy.

It was a wonder that anyone outside the City Centre managed to survive. Living in filth and squalor. Suffocating on dust. Drinking contaminated water and parasite-infested food. *When food could be scrounged.* The planet was sick, the people were sick, and though Basem could not comprehend its scope as a boy, he remembered the sense that things had not always been that way. That it was not always typical for a boy to struggle to breathe the air around him. That his lived experience was somehow not normal.

That day, little Basem continued past pillars adjoined by arches, white and embellished with vibrant mosaic tiles ensconced in stone. The structures opened into intricate courtyards, once glamorous in ancient times, now littered with trash and construction materials liberated from decrepit buildings.

Shouting spilled out from a window overhead—a father scolding a child, or maybe a woman. The smell of fresh bagita poured into the street, enveloping Basem's senses. It had been over a day since his last meal, but to him, this was normal. It was all he had ever known.

He pressed on, kicking the worn football across the pitted ground.

It was evening, his favorite time of day, when the sun was low and people were in their homes with their families. When the streets were empty, silent. He dribbled around a corner and came up on the ruins of an ancient mosque. It had collapsed from neglect. A lone carob tree loomed over the loose stone. Mama had always told him not to go beyond the ruins.

He faced the tree and bent forward to steady the ball at his feet, then took several steps back and eyed the center of the trunk. Taking two bounds forward, he swung a leg back and pitched the soccer ball into the pale bark with a satisfying *smack*. After running to collect the ball, he reset it and settled back on his target. As he readied himself for another kick, another sound, a subtle *thud*, came from behind. Startled, he turned.

There, motionless against the cobblestones, lay a mutilated macaque monkey.

The animal's limbs were contorted, twisted like a discarded marionette, a faded red collar around its neck. It was illegal to own them, but this did not stop people. Old World monkeys had been all but wiped out in the wild of their native Morocco, choosing instead to reside in villages, where they were considered pests—most were killed on sight, though some orphans were taken in or sold as pets.

Basem's heart raced. He glanced up at the rooftops. Had it fallen? He crouched and stared at the small black hands. They were tiny, like a baby's. They almost passed as human. He held his palm out and studied it, then looked back at the monkey. At that moment, intuitively, he knew the essence of the monkey had ceased to be.

A hair-raising screech pierced the air. He craned his neck, squinting in the sunlight, and caught the silhouette of a golden eagle circling above.

Then it dove.

With outstretched talons, it bore down on the monkey with incredible speed. Basem leapt back and watched in captivated horror as the little body jerked upward, clutched in the bird's razor-sharp talons. The eagle soared over the rooftops and out of sight.

Basem looked back down at the spot where the monkey had been. There was no trace of it. As if it had never happened. In an instant, a life erased.

The finality of it hit him, left a deep impression that raised more questions than it answered. Questions his mum did not want to hear after he ran home crying. Questions about his father. Why he had never known him. Whether he was alive. Had an eagle gotten him too?

He never did learn about his father. His mother had taken that to her grave. But he did learn about golden eagles. How they lived and hunted. How they dropped their prey from high up to incapacitate them.

Basem's fascination with animals became an outlet. It bloomed in his formative years, leading him to pursue a career in veterinary medicine. He wanted to help animals. Contribute to the waning biodiversity of the planet—the plight of modern ecosystems unable to adapt to the rapid changes imposed by the Anthropocene Thermal Maximum.

But that was a dream. Naive.

The paradigm shift into research was slow. It took years. Even now, in this moment, dead rabbit in hand, he wondered how he had fallen into the business of animal torture in the name of "progress." That it could be somehow justified. A means to an end.

He was now standing inside the walk-in freezer. Plumes of mist billowed from his nose and mouth. He opened a glass door marked *BIOHAZARD* and gazed upon countless bags of tightly packed rabbit corpses—other subjects that had not survived Phase II. He laid Subject 0218 among them with as much care as he could muster.

The door slid shut with a soft hiss.

Long ago, he came to the realization death no longer had the same impact on him as it did that day, back home in Algiers. Even now, that thought, though sad, was nothing more than a dull pinprick to his core.

Conscious without conscience.

Perhaps he and Athena were not so different.

| NAKED I CAME >

"All roads lead to Berlin."

Fischer, staring at the bottom of an empty rocks glass, wasn't sure if he had spoken the words out loud or heard them in his head. The European Special Forces had many sayings. For some reason, that one had always stuck with him.

Fischer often thought of his time in the service. Some days, it was inescapable, set off by some unexpected trigger—a loud noise, a news headline, the words of a stranger. Today, it was initiated by the meanderings of a chatty Lithuanian who planted next to him at the bar, droning on about his harrowing experience as a child trapped in a proxy war between Russia and the EU. Fischer had heard it many times before. He relived it daily. He studied the scars on his left wrist for a moment. They had faded over the years, like the memories of his daughters.

The run with Lotta was a good distraction.

"Fled west after the Three-Day War," the Lithuanian said between swigs of a sweet-smelling spirit he called viryta. Each swash he threw back was followed up with a twisted facial expression. He'd look down and swirl the piss-colored drink, shaking his head. "They never get it right here," he'd mumbled half a dozen times already. Then he'd drone on, reliving the time he faced down an entire Russian brigade as a mere boy. Most of it was fantastical, nonsensical. His speech was slurred, and he didn't seem to mind that Fischer paid him little heed.

The Three-Day War. Three days. That was how long it took—from the Kaliningrad offensive to the fall of Latvia's final stronghold—for the Baltics to be swallowed by the Russian machine. That *did* happen. The dissolution of NATO years prior had set the eventuality of a resurgent Russia in motion. The rise in Russian nationalism solidified it. And after the Russkies claimed Northeast Europe, they wasted no time establishing a beachhead in the Baltic Sea, providing a direct threat to what was then Germany, the de facto leader of the European Union, now Prussia and the heart of the UEF. An armistice that persisted to this day.

"Got out. Got out. Fled west," the Lithuanian stammered, nodding. He turned and faced Fischer. "So, what's your story?"

"Got no story," Fischer said.

"What about that?" The man nodded toward Fischer's knife, sheathed at his waist. "That got a story? Looks like standard EU military issue. Pre-Federation."

"Aye."

"You serve?"

"Used to."

The man nodded. "My brother served. Died serving."

"Sorry for your loss." Fischer glanced down at his watch.

The Lithuanian readied himself for another long-winded monologue, only to be cut off by a figure approaching behind the counter: the barman, a middle-aged Algerian man with a plump, clean-shaven face. He addressed Fischer.

"What you need, sahbi?"

The Lithuanian fell silent, pausing to swirl his piss-drink.

Fischer didn't look up. He had already exceeded his self-imposed limit. The server stood at the edge of his gaze, dark arms folded across a rounded chest, sleeves rolled back. He was tempted to go for another round, but waved the man off instead.

"No alcohol for forty-eight hours ahead of the infusion," the technician had said when calling to confirm the appointment. Something about second-pass metabolism. Interfered with the "prep," a cocktail of pills he had been taking all week that tasted like battery acid. Supposed to stop his cells dividing, keep the genetic code in a state of stasis.

Primed for tinkering.

"The DNA hardening does a number on the liver," the tech had told him.

Lotta made sure he didn't forget that detail. She had been laid up for weeks after her own battery of DNA-hardening infusions. All her hair had fallen out. Everyone's had. *She'd know.* Not that it made a difference. His appointment was in two hours, and here he was in a hotel lobby bar a few blocks from SANCTUM Center, listening to some Easterner go on about his dead brother.

We've all lost something or someone, mate, he was tempted to say. He held his tongue instead.

He thought about the other ALICE personnel. What they had endured to stay on with the study. How he was the last one to get the infusions. He stroked his beard. Imagined what it would be like once all the hair fell out. Hadn't gone clean-shaven in years. The others had shaved their heads, their faces. But Fischer couldn't bring himself to get rid of the beard.

Not since Emma.

He knew very little about how the procedure worked. Lengthened the telomeres on chromosomes so the genes didn't get chewed to shit and mutate into cancers. Or unravel in the vacuum of a singularity. That about summed it up as far as he was concerned. But he was familiar with the sickness that followed. Fevers. Vomiting. Loss of taste.

He nodded to the Lithuanian and pushed himself from the bar. "Best be off. Places to be." He double-tapped the touch screen on the bar and transferred two hundred euros. Amid global crop shortages, drinking was an expensive vice. Especially when it came to aged whiskey. He grabbed his hat and turned to head for the door.

Fischer often imagined existing between realities in a state of quantum entanglement. Maybe *he* was the experiment. Both zero and one. Past and present. Here nor there. One moment staring blankly, off into nothing—the bottom of a glass—the next on his hands and knees, clawing through smoldering rubble, screaming the same three names over and over. *Ellsa. Evi. Emma.* Or aiming down sights under cover of darkness in the Latvian wilderness on some military operation. Or some fucked-up combination of the two.

Sometimes, he could still hear their voices: his girls, now distant, their faces fading with time. An inverse proportion of temporality. Sand through his fingers. Both dead and alive.

Ghosts.

The run was a good distraction.

Sometimes, these thoughts manifested as dreams. Seemed real. He'd wake most nights, sobbing, alone. Memories haunted him. Memories he clung to because they were all he had. He had grown numb to all else, a shell of his former self.

Then there were other times. Moments he found himself wanting to forget everything. To escape the guilt and the grief. To cease to exist. But he didn't want to die. Not really. Not anymore.

Fischer checked the time. He lingered, staring down at his scarred wrist as he walked toward the exit. He recalled the sensation of steel cutting through his flesh, tracking the blade along the bluish venous plexus, bearing through the pain. Determined to end it all when he lost his girls. He remembered the unexpected sensation of cooling blood running down his skin. A moment of weakness. Error in judgement.

No, he didn't want to die anymore. He was past that.

By the time he realized he hadn't been watching where he was going, a jolt to his shoulder sent him stumbling backward. A tall bald figure was standing in the entrance, silhouetted by a corona of white sunlight that bled through the doorway.

Fischer regained his composure. "Shit, sorry, mate. My fault. You okay?"

The man said nothing, only stood and stared back. Arms at his sides. He seemed unruffled by the impact, and it was then that Fischer realized it had been deliberate. He had been shoved.

Footsteps approached from behind, and he turned to face the Lithuanian.

"Rather rude of you, mister, to leave in the middle of my story."

"Nothing personal. I've somewhere I need to—"

"Leichter Speer."

"Beg your pardon?"

"Latvia. August third, 2111. The failed op that launched the Three-Day War. You have the insignia for Erebus Group on your knife handle."

Erebus Group. Erebus Tactical Assault Crew. European Special Operations Team Three. It had many names.

All roads lead to Berlin.

"Got it on the black market," Fischer said. That was a lie.

"Maybe. Stolen valor is a crime, you know this?"

"Yeah? You and your chum here fixing to send me to the gaols?"

The Lithuanian ignored him. "I never told you how my brother died."

"Aye. Didn't ask."

"My brother fought in the resistance after the Baltics fell. After your botched mission in Latvia. The one that triggered the Kaliningrad offensive, the war. He was betrayed by a member of his own squad. Russians got him, tortured him. All because of *you*. My family, my parents—"

"Look, I've no quarrel with you." Fischer pulled out his flask and threw back a mouthful of whiskey.

The man ignored him, his voice low, menacing. "But I managed to get out, and, well, here I am. Face to face with one of the men responsible." He walked up so that his eyes leveled with Fischer's. Breath smelled of lemon and rye. "Must be my lucky day, eh, *mate?*"

"I told you, I—"

Fischer ducked long before his brain registered the Lithuanian's fist coming at his face. The uppercut he planted into the man's diaphragm, though, was premeditated. The Lithuanian's knees buckled, and he dropped to the floor, his mouth gaping, gulping for air.

Special Forces never forgot their training.

Fischer turned just as the man at the door rushed him. His full weight sent them both to the floor. Fischer was pinned.

He took two hits to the face. His vision smeared over.

The man raised a fist and brought it down like a hammer, but Fischer moved to the side. He heard flesh and bone striking tile, and the man shrieked in agony. Fischer threw him off and planted a well-aimed blow into his throat. He collapsed.

There was a tug at Fischer's side. The Lithuanian had crawled over and ripped his knife free. Acting on instinct, he tackled the man and drove his knee into his wrist. *Defang the snake.* The blade clacked to the floor. *Target flexors and tendons.* And without another thought, he picked it up and brought it down on the man's hand. An ear-piercing scream filled the bar. Fischer stood to his feet. He looked down at the Lithuanian, writhing, frothing at the mouth. Gasping, he clawed at the knife with his free hand.

"I wouldn't do that," Fischer said.

"My hand! You f-fucking—pull it out. PULL IT OUT!"

Fischer walked back to the bar and transferred five hundred more euros. He looked over at the server, now crouching behind the bar. "For the trouble," he said.

He walked back over to the Lithuanian, who flinched at his approach. "Please... p-please don—"

"Shut up. Keep quiet, or I'll get your other hand. Make you look like the second coming." Fischer wrenched the knife free, and the man screamed again. "Get up."

"I will fucking kill you!"

"I seriously doubt that, mate." Fischer wiped the blade on the man's pants, then sheathed it. He knelt forward and wrangled the man's good arm over his shoulder, bringing him to his feet.

"You *fucking...* where are you t-taking me?"

Fischer didn't answer.

Choking sounds came from behind them. The other attacker was still on the floor, clutching his throat. Fischer stumbled toward the door, carrying the Lithuanian into the daylight toward a nearby aerial cab stand.

He tasted whiskey and blood.

15:32 Shin Tower
SANCTUM Center – Medical Division
Northwest Algeria, United European Federation

Fischer stepped out of the cab onto the landing platform, hat in hand, and glanced at his watch. He looked skyward, tracking his gaze along Shin Tower, its glass exterior reflecting the rust-tinged haze. Small, house-sized geodesic structures dotted its base, meant to function like a Martian proto-colony. A precursor. The tower, a looming monarch, served as SANCTUM-Algeria's outpost for biodome operations.

A faint putridity hung in the air. It smelled the same everywhere at the surface. But it was good to be topside during daylight for a change. The simulated sunlight throughout CEPP's underground facilities did little to stifle the mood disorders rampant among the ranks. One got used to the monotony beneath the surface, though suicides were not unheard of. Even the post-apocalyptic glow of a sandstorm's aftermath felt cheery by comparison.

Fischer leaned into the cab, its rotors drowning out the surround. He eyed the Lithuanian, cradling his hand, which was wrapped in a blood-soaked piece of bar rag.

"Athena," Fischer said, "take my new friend here to the nearest urgent care clinic. Put it on my tab."

Athena's silky voice spilled out of the driverless cockpit. "Destination set." Aerial cabs were fully autonomous—no driver necessary.

"Don't let me see you again," Fischer said to the man and activated the door.

"F-fuck you," the Lithuanian managed to say before the cabin sealed.

The vehicle rose into the air, drifting lazily toward the tower's upper levels until it docked at a medical ward about halfway up. Fischer coughed, choking on the dust that swirled from the downwash. Everything was covered in a thin layer of it, a fine reddish powder left in the wake of the storm. It was then he realized he had dropped his respirator back at the bar.

The far end of the tower marked the edge of civilization, giving way to a wide stretch of desert that faded into the haze. There was no visible horizon, just a muddled mirage that at first confused him. He craned his neck and caught the outline of a sphere high above, remembering that the entire colony stood in the shadow of one of the domes. Behind it, the orange sun gleamed along the edge of its carapace through a veil of haze. Even this far out, he had to strain to glimpse the top of it.

Masked people streamed in and out of the building's entrance—a glass basilica, a shrine to scientific discovery. The landing platform emptied out onto a sweeping concrete terrace dotted by figures that moved across it in organized chaos. The people marched like automatons, like the unmasked synths moving alongside them, the latter assimilating, acting human in return.

A familiar unrest, an insatiable pit like a singularity, rent Fischer's insides.

He rechecked his watch. *Running late.*

The aftermath of the assault had rooted inside his skull, an incessant throbbing that grew with each step like a tiny drunk Irish man clomping around his brain, singing a jolly tune. He'd been hit harder than he thought.

He slipped his hat over his crown in defiance of the pain. The hyper-loop rumbled on the platform below.

As swiftly as he could manage, he weaved through the crowd toward the building entrance, passing a large sign, a rectangular parapet made of brushed bronze that resembled an altar. He glanced at the engraving as he walked by.

SANCTUM CENTER
S H I N • TOWER
Clinical & Scientific Excellence

He continued up a concrete staircase blanketed in a fine layer of footprint-riddled dust. It opened onto a landing in front of the tall glass vestibule where foot traffic filtered in and out. Through the automatic sliding doors, the entrance opened into a vast atrium. Its glass walls ascended six stories high, interspersed with transparent walkways and landings populated by esteemed dignitaries in white coats. Rows of white columns reached heavenward like an ethereal reincarnation of old-growth sequoias, their arched buttresses joining them beneath an intricate canopy.

There wasn't a speck of dust in sight.

Fischer's lungs ached with the influx of filtered air. He glanced down at his button-up shirt, half-tucked and dappled with droplets of dried blood. He dabbed his nose, which by now had stopped bleeding. Flecks of clumped blood rained from his beard onto the spotless marble floor.

Edgar Fischer. Lead Engineer. Ex-Special Forces. Ex-father. Alcoholic. Thick-bearded, bloodied German limping through a crowd of dignified, clean, functional members of society.

In the middle of the atrium, a bronze statue of a well-dressed man in a lab coat soared to the second story. From Fischer's perspective, he appeared to be Asian, youthful, authoritative. His gaze looking out toward a non-existent horizon through a pair of rectangular spectacles.

Peering through the alabastrine forest entombed within a glass tesseract.

At the statue's base, an inscription read:

"Ad astra"
Dr. Sung-ho Shin
SANCTUM founder
father of molecular eugenics

IN MEMORIAM

Fischer re-tucked his shirt and raked out his beard. He heard a soft whirring approach and narrowly avoided a cleaning robot—a refractile disc that levitated at ankle height—as it passed in front of him. It cleared away the bloody flecks and felled dust, then hovered on.

After slogging up to the second landing, Fischer caught the eye of a beaming young black woman draped in white. She greeted him from behind a guest check-in counter, flanked by half a dozen other agents in identical dress attending to other patrons seeking to navigate the labyrinthine foyer.

"Hello, sir. Welcome to SANCTUM Center. How may I help you?" She smiled, her lipstick the same color as the specks of blood she seemed to avoid glimpsing. *Ba'ala*, her nametag read.

"Have an appointment. Genetics." Fischer's jaw clicked. That was new. The throbbing in his head now approached the threshold of intolerability. He stroked the lid of his flask, resisting the urge to swig whatever back-wash remained to appease the little man stomping around his brainstem.

"Kiosk three." She waved to a row of tinted glass wafers rising as tall as a man from the marbled floor. Biometric scanners. "Please scan in, and someone will be with you shortly."

Fischer nodded his thanks, then turned to walk away.

"Oh, and sir," Ba'ala called after him, her eyes fixed on his knife, "you'll need to leave that."

He glanced at his waist and unfastened the weapon, then handed it over.

He approached the rectangular kiosk, its reflective glass revealing the extent of his injuries. Two black eyes. Busted lip. Torn shirt. He waited, expecting something to happen—for a list of stats or instructions to populate the shiny surface, but there was nothing. He glanced back over at the check-in counter, but all agents were tied up with clients. He glanced back at his reflection and straightened his hat.

Suddenly, Athena's voice bellowed through the glass. Fischer almost leaped out of his skin. "Welcome to SANCTUM, Dr. Fischer. You are checked in. El will escort you to the infusion clinic."

El?

A young-looking synth materialized then. *El*, his nametag read. He was phenotypically male, with a blanched complexion that contrasted sharply against his piercing purple eyes.

Fischer's muscles tensed. The singularity swelled.

Synths were unnatural. An approximation of humanity. An unsettling manifestation of the uncanny valley. Its—*El's*—glassy eyes were evidence of this, projecting a vacant stare devoid of any semblance of a soul.

"Greetings, Dr. Fischer. Welcome to SANCTUM." The synth curled the edges of its—*his*—mouth into what approximated a smile. His creamy skin glistened as light bathed his creaseless face. He wore a white suit, as flawless as his generically handsome physique. "I will lead you to your appointment with Genetics. I have a medical questionnaire for you to fill out on the way." He handed Fischer a holosleeve—a transparent holographic tablet—and extended an arm toward the west end of the atrium. "Right this way. You are right on time."

Cheeky shick.

Fischer was exactly five minutes late.

He gazed down at the holoscreen as they walked. The questionnaire was straightforward enough.

Have you undergone mitotransfection?

Yes.

If yes, at what age? If no, did you inherit it through natural birth?
Age six.

Do you, or have you ever, had cancer?

No.

...autoimmune disease?... diabetes?... heart disease?... reduced libido?
No. No. No... No.

The questions went on like this. In general, Fischer was in good health, despite his appearance. None of the questions seemed problematic until he scrolled to the substance use and mental health sections.

How many alcoholic beverages do you consume per day?
One to two drinks, he lied.

The weeding questions. Fischer needed this procedure if he wanted to recover in time for the first entanglement trials. He had already breached protocol for standing in on the initial test run of ALICE's Penrose core. BOB's would go live later in the week. The first trials were set to begin in a month, and he was the only member of the team left to undergo DNA hardening.

Do you suffer from depression?
He lingered for a moment. *No.*
Do you have thoughts of suicide? A longer pause.
No... Not lately.

"Done." Fischer handed the holosleeve back to El.

"Excellent, right on cue. We are here."

They passed through a set of frosted double doors with the label *HS134 Infusion Center* inscribed in white lettering overhead. Inside, chairs lined the sterile walls, many of them occupied with clients who had no doubt arrived on time. Their eyes fell on Fischer. A young technician stood in the center of the room. *Human.* She had a stiff demeanor, an indifference in her eyes that told him she had been at this job too long.

"Edgar Fischer?" the technician asked. Fischer nodded, gathering the impression it wasn't the first time his name had been called.

El turned to exit, addressing him with another plastic smile. "Have a wonderful day, Doctor."

The singularity swelled yet further. Little Man's stomping intensified.

The technician hadn't yet addressed Fischer directly. She lingered, studying her own holoscreen. He assumed she had pulled up his questionnaire, taking her time to go through it. Making him wait like he'd made her wait. Forcing him to endure the unwavering stares of brooding clients.

When she was finished, her gaze met his.

"I'm Zoe. I will get you ready for—*what happened to your face?*"

"Ran into a wall."

She raised her eyebrows, unconvinced. "Your biometric scan indicates blunt force trauma as recent as one hour ago. Your blood alcohol content is eleven millimoles per liter. Just shy of the upper limit we can accept."

"Forgot to spit out my mouthwash."

"Sir, you filled out that you have one drink per day. How much have you had today?"

Fischer's blood ran cold. "Aye. Says two-to-three—read the file," he said.

"Are you sure?" she asked. "Because I can smell it on you, and you wrote one-to-two."

His anxiety morphed into anger. What followed manifested as a hushed growl, though menace was not his intention. "Just *do* it." He drew more stares. He didn't care anymore. Instead, he leaned into it. "This is the best you assholes will get from me."

Zoe was quiet for a moment. *Strategizing a response.* "Suit yourself. You are clear. Follow me." *Took the diplomatic route.* She turned and led him through another set of doors.

"That reminds me," she said matter-of-factly. "Are you interested in uploading your consciousness in the event you do not survive the procedure?"

"No." The last thing Fischer wanted was to get spun up as some eternal consciousness, roaming Lucid or some other social network, some God-forsaken quantum construct—or worse, wake up in the cold body of a shick. Nothing appealed less to him than enduring his own mind for eternity. Even if it wasn't really *him*. A clone, a copy, whatever. He did not want it to go on. It was his burden, his alone.

Zoe ushered him into a small, featureless room where a reclined infusion chair stood. She pointed to a locker along the back wall. "Take off your clothes. Gown is in there. Put it on and wait here. Dr. Adamczyk will be in shortly to administer your first infusion."

"*First* infusion?"

"Yes. You need a series. Three in total. We will schedule your second after today's visit. Have a seat once you are gowned." Zoe walked out, and the door closed behind her.

Fischer removed his hat. Big mistake. The throbbing exploded forth with such fury that his knees wavered. The singularity accreted an acidic, whiskey-laced bolus into his throat.

Little Man was going to town. Rapping his club feet up and down Fischer's skull. Dancing to a thunderous tune.

"All roads lead to hell," Little Man sang.

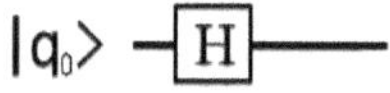

SECOND POSTULATE

Observations of the system are represented by unitary transformations on the wave function.

| LOOKING GLASS >

Entanglement was both the problem and the solution to generating a traversable wormhole. On one hand, it supplied the mechanism required to establish a link—*a bridge*—between two black holes. On the other, it led to unwanted quantum effects on the objects sent through. Up to this point, entanglement had been a mere novelty: the inextricable link between two particles separated by vast distances, whereby an effect on one instantaneously altered the state of the other—what Einstein had referred to as "spooky action at a distance."

In a landmark study,[1] Lotta and her team discovered that this strange connection between particles was formed by a sub-microscopic wormhole linking them together, *warping* the very fabric of spacetime. No matter the distance between them, altering the state of one partner had an *instantaneous* effect on the other. *Faster-than-light travel.* A violation of special relativity.

The quantum background—indeed, all of space itself—consisted of such yoked partners. A cosmic foam of roiling, submicroscopic wormholes entangling photons, neutrinos, quarks. Innumerable, seemingly infinite

1 See appendices for published abstract

marriages, their linkages dynamic, ever-changing, snapping and curling in on themselves like Planckian coronal ejections. Trillions of tendrils writhing in a churning sea.

It was Lotta's co-investigator, Bogdan Kazimierz, who deduced that since observable black holes represented *macroscopic* quantum systems, they, too, could theoretically form entangled pairs. Their singularities, joined by an Einstein-Rosen bridge, could give rise to a *traversable wormhole*.

EIRO's heads latched on to the theoretical possibilities put forth in the study and pushed for a scaled-up apparatus—one that could conceivably transport real-world objects. A wormhole that could be generated by artificially expanding the quantum realm, exploiting the cosmic foam. Bending it to their will.

Until disaster struck.

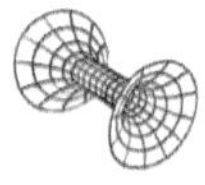

That was over three years prior.

Lotta's bones ached now, her blonde hair streaked with hints of silver. But the flame, the pursuit of that revolutionary concept, was still very much alive.

She looked up from the soft glow of a sprawling console that would have been at home inside a nuclear power plant. Augmented reality displays, blinking lights, auxiliary switches. Behind the console, an expanse of radiation-hardened glass shielded the control room from the Bell chamber, the Cathedral, below. Lotta glanced down at a live feed from inside the chamber, revealing a calm scene within.

But that was the nature of a quantum system, of reality. A bird's-eye view of a placid, featureless ocean. As one drew closer and investigated the hidden reality at the surface—down to the atom, the proton, the quark—it became a boiling sea, a vast mire of frenetic energy. Pure entropy. An orgy of chaos. One dictated by fundamental laws and constants, constrained in their cosmic bedlam by well-defined dimensions.

The bay doors to the freight elevator had been sealed on the far end of the chamber. Along the perimeter walls, rows of steel mesh walkways—

dozens of them, connected by staircases and electric lifts—rose twenty stories high. They faded overhead into shadow, marked only by the dull glimmer of distant path lighting. They were empty, giving the chamber an ethereal quality, like a monument or a ghost town.

Hallowed ground.

All cleared staff now loomed from the safety of the lead-encased control room that doubled as an observation deck on the third story. Its reinforced structure protected them from the weight of gravitational anomalies, the lead and concrete from the poorly understood effects of Hawking radiation.

Behind Lotta, a half-dozen hooded blue uniforms darted about. She watched their reflections in the glass, prepping for what was to come, taking their positions, following protocol. Discussing their theories and calculations. They composed the ALICE crew—leaders in their fields, hand-picked for the project. Flames like her, poised to take the next seismic leap in scientific progress.

But first, Lotta needed live subjects. And for that to happen, she needed to allay the EIRO ethics board. She needed Basem Bensoussan.

She searched for him intermittently among the flurry of rubber suits, but the veterinary scientist was nowhere to be seen. He came to observe the experiments in preparation for animal trials, to collect data and dictate benchmarks for safety standards. Today, it appeared he was running late.

Lotta walked around the console and up to the observation glass overlooking the labyrinthine chamber below. The Cathedral. Her gaze fell on the towering Penrose core—a multi-ton egg nestled in the warmth of its cradle, nourished by buzzing cables, pipes, and circuitry. It sat in the loving embrace of its mother, the Higgs Collider, her colossal storage rings—hydrogen-actuated large oscillating synchrotrons, or HALOS—the source of its lifeblood.

The Penrose formed a perfect sphere that stretched three stories, its crest falling at eye level, flanked by catwalks and semi-permanent main-tenance lifts. In its latent "hardened" state, the shell was opaque, matte black, and composed of a geodesic array that vaguely reminded Lotta of SANCTUM's domes. Yet it was distinct—a network of interlocking triangular electromagnets stitched together to form a spherical cryostat. The lower third of the shell was recessed into a curved concavity within the chamber floor, its rear flank married to the Higgs by a V-shaped beam collider called a Casimir siphon.

Lotta heard laughter behind her and shifted.

At the center of the observation deck, Martin Anderson leaned against the edge of a desk flanked by Fischer and Hassan Kateb. Anderson was the primary operator and consultant on the entanglement project. A renowned astrophysicist, he had made a name for himself decades prior by resolving the equations of eleven-dimensional supergravity. The achievement was a watershed moment in the pursuit of confirming supersymmetry, unifying quantum field theory with general relativity, and ultimately paving the way for the discovery of the graviton. He had joined ALICE as Director of Acceleration in the months following the Geneva quake and quickly proved himself an indispensable asset to the team.

He was smiling, his narrowed eyes darting between the other two as he spoke. As charming a Belgian as ever, a man's man, right at home in his good old boys' club. Clean-shaven, square-jawed, and blue-eyed. A smooth operator with a brilliant mind. Even the suit, with its rubbery bulbosity, could not contain his charisma.

Lotta smirked. She hadn't seen Fischer so enthralled before, that half-grin, the creases at the edges of his narrowed eyes, mirroring Anderson's. His smile widened, the punchline came, and though try as he did, he could not hinder his amusement, letting slip a head-shaking chuckle.

Hassan shook his head from behind a holoscreen. Were it not for his face shield, he would probably be running his hand across that stubbly mustache. Often the quiet one, he was introspective almost to a fault, and when he spoke, it was thought-out, deliberate. An Algerian native, he had been with CEPP almost as long as Lotta, long before Algeria's annexation into the UEF.

Though Hassan's words were generally sparse, they tended to arise when airing a grievance, usually a disagreement with various aspects of entanglement protocol. Most of his tangents revolved around his criticism over the choice of superfluid used in the core and how helium-4 was not an ideal substrate for generating a naked singularity. That, to obtain a pure result, exotic matter was required. Axions, sterile neutrinos, light bosons, and on and on.

Lotta had conceded on many occasions that exotic matter was, theoretically, ideal. Except for the price tag. *Seventy trillion euros per gram.* Helium-4, on the other hand, was abundant and cheap—a mere byproduct of the fusion reactors that generated the nation's energy from lunar helium-3—and it got the job done just fine.

Despite the finality of her decision, she'd been roped into various forms of discourse with Hassan over the preceding months. He argued that he had worked out a way for the Higgs to generate a high enough dark matter yield to establish a wormhole. But the math didn't add up. They couldn't agree on the temperature constants, standard enthalpy formations, chemical equilibria. Her calculations kept spitting out energy input that exceeded output, a recipe for failure. A violation of the laws of thermodynamics. Even if it did work, the process could tie up the Higgs collider for a full six months, bringing every one of CEPP's research sectors to a grinding halt.

Hassan insisted she was mistaken. She reminded him who was in charge. Everyone else stayed out of it.

Lotta returned her attention to the Cathedral. On the other side of the glass, the Higgs's storage rings hummed, priming to fire. The voices, the laughter, the movement of bodies around the observation deck faded into the background, into that bedlam, that cosmic sea. She could taste the electricity on her tongue, hear the static in her earpiece. The quantum foam, now amplified, made manifest to her senses.

In a strange way, the sensation reminded her of her mother. "The Æsir are speaking to you," Sofia Eklund would say. Would have attributed *even a mild static shock* to the gods. In that sense, Sofia had always possessed a unique affinity for the absurd.

Nothing but fables. Myths.

Science was Lotta's god. Her ritual. The algorithms that untangled the web of supersymmetry and quantum gravity. Its inception with Planck's description of discrete quanta, Bohr and the Copenhagen interpretation, Young and the double-slit experiment. They were *her* deities.

From a young age, Lotta had learned to rely on herself. Her father's departure and her mother's negligence ensured that. She didn't mind being alone, at least most of the time, because it meant a life free from distraction. A pure backdrop for seeking truth. Most people clung to the familiar, to rituals. Their routines, relationships, possessions, balanced precariously like ill-conceived cairns guiding them along the path to normalcy. To the familiar.

But Lotta was not afraid of the unknown. She embraced it. Refused to become a victim like Sofia, a misandrist trapped in the rote bastille of tradition. Stunted, small-minded. Living life in the four walls of an echo chamber as she drowned her sorrows with a bottle. Too afraid to see what lay beyond. That there was so much *more*.

There were worse things than being alone. There was nothing *better* than being alone.

Fischer's reflection appeared in the glass beside hers, shattering her momentary hebetude. His facial hair had started to return in patches, eyebrows restored and bushy as ever, cheeks filling out. But he had continued to shave his head, obscured under the thick hood of his suit. She liked the new look.

"Seems you're on the mend," she said, continuing to gaze out into the Cathedral.

He nodded, his Anderson-induced grin fading. Lotta turned to him and forged a smile.

Fischer had experienced a slow recovery after the DNA-hardening infusions. He was out on medical leave on three occasions for treatment-induced hepatitis—something called ascites that required pints of fluid to be drained from his abdomen. She shuddered at the thought of it.

The jaundice had mostly cleared, the whites of his eyes—still somewhat sunken—now an almost imperceptible tinge of yellow. No doubt a consequence of Fischer's inability to stay away from the bottle despite her warnings, the doctor's warnings. But he was here. He had made it. And she was glad for that.

A brief pang of anxiety swelled within her. It was fleeting but traceable. A momentary flashback: the run in the desert, how she might have given away too much about her past. It was the first time she had done so with anyone in a long time. And with Edgar Fischer, of all people.

There were *some* things better than being alone.

"Lattice magnets have been working flawlessly," she said, trying to fill the silence.

"Got a great team," he nodded.

"Insertion magnets in the Casimir siphon, too. Outstanding work."

"Firmware update. You can thank Hassan for that one. Guy's a computing wizard." Deflecting again. Changing the subject, as though unworthy of the praise. "Speaking of, he is getting a bit irritable." Fischer tapped his wrist, his watch concealed beneath the thick lining of his suit. "We about ready?"

She acknowledged him with a nod. "You are being modest. But yes, we are just waiting on Command."

She turned back. Hassan sat alone now, hunched over the Penrose core's control station, fidgeting, obsessing over covariance data. At the far end of the console, Anderson monitored beam dynamics. Next to him, Mattheo Russo, a particle physicist and ALICE's third-in-command, surveyed the core's failsafe—a matrix of green holographic lights superimposed onto the console beneath the words *Summary Fault Unit* in bold lettering.

The static in Lotta's ear intensified, followed by the grainy voice of Bogdan Kazimierz, who was located on the far end of the facility in Sector 23. "Systems are optimal on our end. Ramp seems to be going smoothly. What is your status, ALICE?"

"Ramping" meant increasing the beam energy by accelerating it through the HALOS. It also caused the static noise they experienced with the communications systems, a problem unique to the Higgs that did not plague its weaker predecessors. Once the ramp was complete and the optimal energy level obtained, they'd begin the "squeeze"—narrowing the beams to maximize the number of collisions before diverting them into the core.

Lotta glanced again at the soft glow of the console. The ramp was at eighty percent, climbing steadily.

"Copy, BOB. All systems are a go on our end," she said.

Everything appeared to be in order.

BOB was a mirror image of ALICE, a doppelgänger situated more than fifty kilometers away, at the opposite perimeter of the Higgs. There, Bogdan acted as Lotta's counterpart, overseeing operations at the facility—manifesting the other half of the equation, so to speak. He was a ratty, particular man of around forty-five, his English formal, precise, almost undermined by the weight of his gravelly Slavic accent. Like Lotta, Bogdan had been a fixture at CEPP for decades, and they had worked together at the Fermi Collider before the Geneva quake.

Because of his heritage, Bogdan was often eager to prove his loyalty to the Federation. It was a symptom of a more significant issue along Europe's eastern border—his province of Pol-Polska, formerly Poland, remained divided in its loyalties after the war. Many Poles had been accused of sympathizing, even conspiring, with the Russians to undermine European sovereignty. In general, such accusations fell on the heads of UEF Federalists, especially its Polish constituents, while Unionists were quick to oppose and condemn such "high crimes." This sometimes led to regional violence along the Russian Buffer Zone, warranting a heavy military presence in Pol-Polska. To the south, the provinces of West Ukraine, Romania, Bulgaria, and to an extent, Greece experienced a similar military presence. To the north, New Finland and parts of New Sweden were subjected to the same.

Bogdan hailed from Eastern Pol-Polska—right along the RBZ—exposing him to a higher degree of scrutiny. Lotta suspected this was why she was given the position of Principal Investigator over him after the project was relocated to Algeria, even though Bogdan was more qualified and had been with CEPP an entire decade longer than her. If she suspected him of anything, it was a veiled resentment toward her—*not* of treason or adopting communist apologetics, but of displaying a sort of duplicitous kindness. A dagger poised to plunge into her for nothing more than to advance his own status. *That* was, in her mind, more disqualifying than any perceived caste—even the misfortune of being a Pole.

But she had to believe she got the job because CEPP was after something far greater than stroking the ego of a bitter sycophant.

Command Central, located back at the surface, came in at long last. "This is Command. We are prepping to fire. Take positions."

The screen for the laser interferometer displayed a stable gravitational waveform within the Penrose core, indicating optimal conditions for generating a singularity. The sinusoidal waves danced across the screen, emanating a soft blue glow that entranced Lotta every time without fail.

"HALOS holding stable." Mattheo's voice buzzed in her earpiece. Anderson confirmed with a nod, indicating optimal beam output from the storage rings.

"Bell State initiated," Hassan said.

Lotta raised a thickly gloved hand to the console and flipped the biometrically integrated keyhole cover. "Escape velocity, status?"

"Ninety-nine-point-nine-nine-three percent light speed, and stable," Hassan said.

Anderson chimed in. "Core temperature is zero-point-five-two kelvin and projecting a convergence of one-point-six-seven gigajoules."

"Copy, ALICE," Command buzzed. "Keys in switches. We're starting the squeeze."

Lotta fixated on the luminescent red light, her hand hovering, trembling. She slid the rod into the port. It clicked into place. The light turned green. "Keyed in."

"Keyed in," Bogdan said.

"Copy," Command replied. A second later, the rod receded into the port, and the indicator began flashing. Three tones of the alarm. A moment of silence, a split second that felt like an eternity. Then Command again: "Firing HALOS in three… two… one…"

Lotta's ears popped. She found herself standing in a muted void, a vacuum in which silence prevailed.

Inside the Cathedral, the core's geodesics hummed, imbued with a soft corona, an amethystine glow. A flash of white bloomed from the yolk and washed over the core, consuming it until Lotta found her purview awash with white. Her face shield dampened its intensity, a kaleidoscope of scintillating aurorae, a chromatic fortification like gazing through a revolving prism. The effect persisted for a few seconds, then faded to reveal a soft, orange ring—it too receding, a smoldering ember rotating about the circumference of a massive floating orb where the Penrose core had been just moments prior. An accretion disc of swirling matter at the edge of a naked singularity, the ALICE Gate.

A rotating black hole.

A high-pitched ringing rose back to her senses, and she could hear the whirr of the HALOS once more, except lower in pitch, oscillating like a throbbing heartbeat. There was a momentary doppler shift—a reddish hue endowed on everything inside the Cathedral, leading up to the merger of the singularities.

"Kugelblitz," Fischer whispered in her earpiece, his speech unnaturally slow, distorted through the intense static. *Ball lightning.*

The geodesics had transformed into their ferrofluid state, now a transparent and smooth surface that enabled her to see directly into the core's yolk. It gave off a shimmering effect, rippling in turbulent whorls like hot oil, undulating about the core as it reacted in real-time to the mounting gravitational field containing it.

Most of it.

The accretion continued to fade, its rotation slowed, then ceased as the mouth of the singularity stabilized. As this occurred, Lotta began to discern an even more magnificent spectacle along the orb's perimeter. Gravitational lensing, warped spacetime incarnate, manifest before her like a celestial void plucked from the cosmos. The lensing grew in its intensity, a ring that warped and magnified the Higgs' storage rings behind it. They appeared stretched, smeared like a besmirched oil painting. A visual representation of general relativity.

Cosmic gouache.

Command shattered the moment. "Status?"

Lotta's response was barely a whisper. "Command, we have a visual. Rotation has ceased. I am looking at a magnificent Schwartzchild right now."

Her compression lining tightened around her, reacting to subtle changes in gravitation, still mostly contained within the Cathedral and the Penrose core itself.

Her skin crawled with electricity. She could taste it, smell it. A sensation that defied explanation. She likened it to her time along the Baltic Coast as a girl, the air after a heavy rain, a distant memory from her childhood—before her family fled Sweden, before the cold snap—but amplified a hundredfold.

"It never gets old, does it?" The words were like malt on her tongue. Her compression sleeve loosened around her limbs, her core, as the momentary gravitational field subsided. As a wormhole formed.

"Copy, ALICE." Bogdan came over Lotta's earpiece, breathing slow. "We have a Schwartzchild at the BOB Gate. Radius is seven-point-five meters. Say 'Hi.'"

Out of the inky void, an image began to coalesce. An amorphous refraction that at first looked artifactual—stretched and warped like looking through a crystal ball. She strained, squinting, as it morphed into something more definitive—BOB's Bell chamber as seen from inside *their* core. There were two representations—one image close to the circumference, stretched and warped in an arc, and the other, more recognizable, closer to the center.

Command followed up. "ALICE, what is your radius?"

"Seven-point-five meters and stable," Lotta said.

There was no Doppler shift, no time dilation anymore. Not with a wormhole. It indicated they had formed a stable bridge, that the two singularities had merged.

But then, as soon as it had appeared, the orb evaporated like a burst bubble, ejecting enough Hawking radiation to send Mattheo's detectors into a frenzy. Static stabbed Lotta's ears. She watched the core as its exterior rapidly solidified into the original arrangement of triangular black geodesics.

She exhaled.

Muffled claps erupted throughout the observation deck.

"Time is nine-oh-four. Trial duration: four minutes and thirty-three seconds," Command reported over the comm, the static now absent. "Good work, ALICE and BOB."

In earlier trials, the Gates could only be maintained for a few milliseconds. As trials advanced—diminishing the effects of the Heisenberg uncertainty principle, exceeding its known limits—a wormhole could now be sustained on the order of *minutes*. Almost enough time to send live subjects through. And hopefully enough to convince EIRO that the exorbitantly expensive trials were worthy of continued funding.

Lotta's neck tensed. She was eager to get out of her suit.

Without warning, Basem materialized beside her as if from nothing. *De novo.* His arms were folded against his chest. His immediate presence startled her, giving rise to a momentary sensation that her heart had leaped into her throat.

"Oh, hello! Thought we missed you." Her initial alarm settled into relief. She wanted him to see how far they had come and was glad to learn he had taken in the entire trial. "How are the subjects coming along?"

To her bewilderment, he didn't appear at all thrilled. Quite the opposite.

"We need to lengthen that duration three-fold before we can move to animal studies," he said, disregarding pleasantries, eyes veiled in shadow beneath his hood. His lips pursed behind the reflection in his face shield, framed by a neatly trimmed goatee.

Not the reaction Lotta had expected.

"We will get there," she huffed. Said with confidence despite inner hints of renewed uncertainty.

Hassan, joining them, broke his silence. *Another grievance.* "Dr. Bensoussan, you seem to miss what we have accomplished… what we *will* accomplish. Do you not understand this? We have created, *sustained* a wormhole—harnessed the most *powerful* of forces in the known universe. This is no longer integrals and Greek letters. This is the equations *come to life.* You must see the significance of it, what we have—"

"Hassan…." Lotta shook her head, taken aback that he had come to her defense. She was more accustomed to being the one on the receiving end of his objections.

Basem nodded and raised his hands. "I understand, yeah. Really, I get it. I don't mean to be the bottleneck, but I cannot allow animal trials to proceed until we have met necessary time-of-flight requirements for Phase Four."

"We are close, Dr. Bensoussan," Lotta said. "Let's reconvene over lunch when I get back." She activated her comm. "Command, start the beam dump. Let's power down."

Basem was not the only hang-up stalling the project. In recent months, Camila Perez—SANCTUM-Algeria's eminent animal scientist and ecologist, and a colleague of Basem's—had filed a barrage of formal complaints to the heads of EIRO against CEPP's operations at the Higgs. Most of these grievances had been leveled against Lotta as the head of CEPP's entanglement division, the essence of which involved localized magnetic field anomalies at SANCTUM's domes, and in some cases, tremors. Perez claimed there had even been stress fractures discovered in some of the ARC's geodesics. This in addition to outlandish claims that CEPP's studies were causing erratic avian behavior that threatened to upend the ARC's entire ecosystem, its natural order on the brink of ruin. Similar reports of tremors and a handful of equipment malfunctions had been filed by additional personnel from the other sanctuaries and even SANCTUM Center itself.

This concern was elevated to the heads of state to determine which steps should be taken to investigate the claims. The last thing the government wanted was the perception that another incident like the one in Geneva was imminent, understanding the reality that many people were still on edge, wary of the new facility. Even if the Geneva investigation had vindicated CEPP of any wrongdoing. Even if they'd relocated to middle-of-nowhere-Algeria, far away from any major population centers.

Lotta was scheduled to meet with Perez later that morning to address the matter. Whatever that involved. She hurried out of the observation deck, through the ESD shower, and doffed her protective gear. There was no time to stop at her office, no time to grab a bite. She rushed down a long corridor to the elevator. She needed to be at Shin Tower in six minutes for their meeting.

SANCTUM was situated at the surface, at the center of the Higgs's circumference. The hyperloop ride to Shin Tower was a brief three-minute ride—barely long enough to mentally prepare for her encounter with Perez, but enough time to reflect. To unwind a bit, recharge. Her heart still bounced around her ribcage—a rabid, caged animal—thrilled at the excitement of it all, of being on the bleeding edge of science.

Then, completely unsolicited, her mind shifted back to her mother. Even now, in death, the woman lorded over her, diminishing the weight of that achievement, that joy. Lotta thought back to Sofia's last words to her.

"I did my best," she had said as she wasted away. Stage four pancreatic cancer. It had spread to the bones, the lungs.

"I know, Sofia," Lotta remembered saying.

She had almost felt sorry for her mother. Sofia's glassy stare, her glazed eyes full of regret. The hollowness of unmet potential. Lotta, feeling nothing.

But swallowing her pride, she tried again. "I know, Mamma." *A moment of mercy.*

And what else could she have said? That she *forgave* her? For raising her in fear, taking her from all she knew to flee to Schwyz, to assimilate into a family she had never known, to never again smell the Baltic Coast? Her mother drowning herself in her sorrows, leaving her daughter to neglect? All the while doubling down on a religion she had converted to for a husband, a man who ultimately abandoned her. A ritualistic construct forced on Lotta, solidifying her status as a pariah among her peers.

A loner. That was what Sofia had made her daughter.

Was that what she should have told Sofia? Or that she resented her almost as much as her father?

No, she would *never* forgive. She gave the woman one last moment of validation, a crumb. Spared her from what was really on her mind. And that was more than she deserved.

Forgive her. The voice inside her head. She remembered it more vividly than anything said aloud amid those final breaths. Sometimes, the voice returned, uninvited, but Lotta's answer was always the same.

No.

| IWA >

Perez oriented a pair of surgical shears between the gnarled legs of a dead spur-winged goose. Its gray-tipped wings were folded at its sides, tattered white belly exposed. Its feathers dampened with antiseptic to inhibit airborne dander. Another broken body splayed on cold steel, the latest statistic in a trend of birds colliding into the dome's perimeter.

Of all ARC's facilities, Perez disliked the necropsy lab most. The darkness aroused within her contrasted against the white halide lights, the vast, stale openness. But like the void it instilled, the lab was bare, desolate.

A perpetual odor of formaldehyde lingered, tinged with pine-scented cleaning agents, a vague hint of bleach. Rows of stainless-steel tables were arranged like sacrificial altars, saucer-shaped auxiliary lights hovering above them like parasols at a rainy funeral. Beside them, cleaning hoses dangled, affixed to a high ceiling by spring-arms.

Overhead, a track system led to a large bay door where large specimens—giraffes, rhinos—could be delivered. The far end of the lab led to a walk-in cooler filled with corpses—among them a juvenile lion with leukomyelopathy, a dispatched geriatric boar, a mauled baboon, and a staggering number of birds with crushed skulls and fractured cervical vertebrae.

Perez exhaled over the sound of the downdraft vent, the gentle trickle of blood seeping down the grate. Her warm breath rebounded off a surgical mask as she palpated the cold, damp legs. With delicate precision, she cut away the skin, muscle, and fascia to reveal bone. Each incision brought with it dejection, helplessness, even guilt that she was somehow failing these animals.

Her new PhD student, Nedjma Ramdani, looked on, inquisitive, expectant. A mane of voluminous pitch-black hair draped past her shoulders. Dark skin and intent brown eyes that watched, almost unblinking while Perez instructed her.

"Once we expose the femur, we need to disarticulate the coxofemoral joint," Perez said. A loud pop filled the room as she bent the first leg at a sharp angle to dislocate the hip. She splayed it to the side and started on the second. "This stabilizes the specimen and makes the postmortem easier."

She was training Nedjma to conduct a necropsy, a procedure that had become all too common in recent months. Scalpel in hand, she began an incision along the bird's throat. The neck was broken, bent at an odd angle, the bright red beak shattered and caked with dried blood.

"What do I need to do once I have made the incision?" Perez lingered, still fixed on the specimen.

Nedjma's eyes darted upward, searching for the answer. "Extend it to the base of the neck, then inspect the pectoral muscles for atrophy, bruising, congestion, or discoloration."

"What type of discoloration?"

"Paleness indicating anemia, red for acute hemorrhage, purple blotches for bruising."

"Good." Perez directed Nedjma to examine the area. "What do you see?"

"Multiple red hemorrhages… caused by… blunt trauma to the muscle tissue?"

Perez nodded. "Right. Red hemorrhages are typical of impact injuries. Bruising indicates chronic hemorrhaging, which is why we don't see it here. Okay, let's look at the laryngeal mucosa next. You make the incision just there. Cut longitudinally through the larynx while I collect samples for molecular analysis."

Nedjma, a native Algerian from the Mediterranean port city of Béjaïa, had just graduated from the Swiss Federal Institute of Technology in Zurich. She was only six months into her graduate program in partnership with ARC, but she absorbed knowledge like a sponge. Perez liked her because she had initiative, took personal accountability. In many ways, Nedjma reminded her of a younger version of herself. If Perez's parents had been permitted a second child, she liked to think having a little sister might approximate what she felt around Nedjma.

The student's amber eyes peered out over a blue surgical mask, expressive, eager. But most of all, she appeared nervous, a pair of forceps in one trembling hand, scalpel in the other. Perez gave a nod, ushering her to begin.

The goose's skin was tough, but the blade glided through it with little effort. Perez swiped a collection swab through the fresh incision and placed it into a tube of transfer media. She repeated the process several times until she had six mucosal samples on ice. "These are for sequencing," she said, "so it's critical we properly label each one."

Nedjma set the instruments down and folded back the skin. "Why are we sequencing if we already know the species?" she asked.

"Good question." Perez extended one of the bird's wings, turning it over to reveal a small clawed hand. It was partially obscured by a mound of plumage. "Genetic drift," she said.

Nedjma's head listed inquisitively.

Perez had seen the adaptation all too often in her career. "Atavisms like this have been a problem with dwindling bird populations for decades, but are significantly amplified in the dome, where population sizes are far smaller than in the wild—in captivity, the changes occur more rapidly.

"In small populations, random chance and inbreeding can effectively erase traits from the gene pool. In this case, we are seeing the loss of regulatory genes—so-called 'genetic switches'—that suppress certain traits. This allows the recessive phenotypes—clawed hands, long tails, sometimes even teeth—to be expressed. Both mechanisms—natural selection and genetic drift—seem to be bringing previously suppressed dinosaur alleles to the surface in hybridized avian species."

Nedjma's eyes met hers. "How do we stop it?"

"We can't, really. We've gotten around it somewhat through genetic modification… reinserting genes lost to genetic drift to increase variation. Eventually, though, these processes will undo all our efforts if we do not keep up. After all, we hybridized these birds with ancient DNA to help them adapt to our changing climate, to preserve ecological homeostasis, but it appears this has backfired—undesirable traits we never intended to be expressed are becoming common."

Maybe we should have let it all collapse, Perez thought. *Maybe without us, or at least to our detriment, life would have endured.*

Perez finished writing the last of the labels and placed the final sample on ice. Aside from the obvious trauma, the rest of the examination proved unremarkable. Another data point in the expanding dossier of unnatural avian deaths that brought her no closer to the truth.

Nedjma was now demonstrating the proper inspection, weighing, and logging of organs. The ventriculus, for example, held a sizeable bolus of grass seed and insects, ruling out anorexia at the time of death. Nothing wholly out of the ordinary.

But there *was* something there. Deep in the layers of fascia, inside the cells, the degrading nuclei. Something only revealed by a trend uncovered through careful molecular analyses. On a macro level, the cause of death was clear—skull and cervical fractures, submucosal hemorrhages, breast contusions, cerebral edema—the signs of high-velocity impact. But *why* this behavior was occurring had eluded Perez until recently.

"Nedjma"—Perez watched while Nedjma excised a kidney from the bird's pelvic vault—"what do you think is driving these animals to fly into the geodesics?"

Nedjma took a moment. "Well, these are all migratory birds," she said. "I'd be curious to know the level of CRY4 expression at the time of death."

Perez swelled with pride. "*Exactly*," she said with a nod, "and why CRY4 in particular?"

"Migratory birds contain high levels of cryptochrome 4 in their photoreceptors; it allows them to migrate by detecting and navigating through magnetic fields. I've heard you speak of anomalous fields detected in and around the domes lately. Maybe it's causing this behavior. If we detect up-regulation of magnetoreceptive genes, it will support your hypothesis."

"*Magnetoreception.* Very good. I guess I better show you how to enucleate a bird, then?" Perez reached over to the field of sterling instruments. "We'll need to make a lateral canthotomy to preserve the eyes for histological study."

Nedjma looked on with enthusiasm.

"First, inspect each globe for injury." She pried open the eyelids and carefully gripped the nictitating membrane between a pair of forceps. Gently, she slid it aside to reveal the foggy ocular surface. She turned the mangled head over and inspected the fellow eye. "This is good. Globes are intact. A good specimen for histology and protein analyses."

She oriented a pair of scissors along the outer lid margin, cradling the head in her other hand.

"Next, we make a lateral incision where the upper and lower lids meet to widen the interpalpebral fissure..." She moved aside so Nedjma could observe while she extended the eyelid opening. "This enables easy removal without crushing the scleral ossicle. Then we dissect away the connective tissue and muscle." Once that was complete, she used a pair of forceps to rotate the eye in the socket to demonstrate it was free. "Now all that's left is to sever the optic nerve."

She reached for a pair of curved scissors. Holding them agape, Perez inserted them between the eye and orbital wall until they were fully recessed. Once she found the rigid, cord-like nerve, she closed the scissors around it with a muffled *snip*. With forceps at the ready, she extricated the loosed eyeball and placed it in a freshly labeled container.

"Would you like to do the other one?" She extended the scissors toward Nedjma, who took them eagerly.

Perez glanced at the time displayed on the HUD of her safety goggles. She had a meeting scheduled with Lotta Eklund in a few hours.

Should be enough time to run to the aviary, she thought.

Without warning, a sensation came over her, a sort of unprovoked malaise. But as soon as it had come, so, too, it faded. She swallowed hard and collected herself. Nedjma hadn't seemed to notice.

Need to stop skipping breakfast.

She focused on her breathing, slowed it down. When the sensation passed, she leaned in to assess her student's work. By now, Nedjma was transferring the second eye into the collection container.

"Well done," Perez said, beads of cold sweat erupting across her brow. *Deep breath in, deep breath out.* "Let's… uh… let's clean up. Looks like I have time to run a collection in the moa habitat near the aviary—want to go collect some blood and skin samples?"

Nedjma's eyes lit up. "Absolutely."

"Great, let's transfer our molecular samples to the minus-eighty. Everything else goes in the cooler. Meet me at the decon chamber in ten minutes."

Nedjma's excitement was palpable as she cleared the examination table. She had not yet observed the moa—one of the few remaining de-extinct species left on the planet. The birds had been sent over from New Zealand after the last remaining population fell so low that the species was on the verge of re-extinction. Perez had agreed to house them temporarily at the ARC until a long-term solution could be arranged between SANCTUM and the New Zealand government.

Soon after integrating them into the ARC, Perez had to isolate them to keep them separate from the ostriches. As it turned out, the two species had been hybridized with the same dinosaur DNA—that of *Deltadromeus agilis*—in the early days of avian hybridization. Consequently, the ostriches had wrought mayhem with the newcomers, resulting in a dead male moa—one of five left in existence. In recent months, Perez had studied the effects of genetic drift on the moa—attempting to reverse its impact so the population would survive and hopefully grow. Losing one of the males set the effort back significantly. She could not afford to lose another one if the species were to endure.

"Don't expect them to resemble what you may have seen in books or historical accounts," she said. "Resurrected moa are prime examples of the effects of generations of neglected genetic drift. These moa still resemble their native ancestors in most ways, but do not let that fool you."

Nedjma tore off her surgical gown and tossed it into the biohazard bin. "I know," she said. "That's why I want to see them."

"Good. Let's suit up."

The ride to the moa paddock was around ten minutes by rover. En route, Nedjma brimmed with excitement, the conversation flowing naturally into the nuances of population genetics, what it meant for the ARC, for the outer colonies. For Earth. A hazy Mount Qalil crept past Nedjma's window to the south, then disappeared behind a wooded hillside.

Minutes later, the rover shuddered to a stop in front of an electrified perimeter fence. Its primary purpose: keep ostriches out and moa in.

"Here we are," Perez said.

The moa paddock was situated adjacent to the aviaries housing birds vulnerable to the electromagnetic anomaly. It covered around a hundred hectares with a central stand of trees akin to the moas' native beech-forest habitat. The canopy swayed in the swelling breeze.

Mount Qalil was breathing.

Across the remainder of the enclosure, low-lying shrubs dotted a grassy yellow plain. A narrow stream—a branch off the artificial river along the dome's perimeter—ebbed gently through its middle. Thistles, an invasive species inside the dome, dappled its banks in rows of amethystine orbs.

Nedjma leaned forward, peering through the windshield to try and spot one of the birds. "I try to look for them whenever I come to the aviaries," she said, "but I can never seem to spot one."

"They are wary of open spaces," Perez said. "Evolved to avoid giant prehistoric Haast's eagles, so they stick to tree cover for the most part." She killed the engine and turned to Nedjma, flashing a grin. "Have you ever caught a large animal like this before?"

Nedjma's jaw fell slack. *"...Caught?"*

In the light, a faint scar on her upper lip became visible. It extended to her right nostril, a feature Perez hadn't noticed before. It caught the light in a unique way, or maybe Perez had a unique vantage point. Still, it surprised her she was only now seeing it for the first time. She smiled. It gave Nedjma character.

"How do you expect to retrieve samples if we don't secure the animal first?"

"Don't you have a team for that? Or tranquilizers?"

Perez laughed. "We *are* the team today. And chemical immobilization is out; it's unpredictable and potentially dangerous for both us and the animal. Ratite metabolism is much more complex than other animals. Without a specialized team to place the bird into recumbency, we risk respiratory depression and peroneal neuropathy that could cripple the animal. Here."

She handed Nedjma a black cloth hood that resembled a large stocking, holding a second one for herself in her other hand.

"What's this?"

"You'll see."

Perez raised the driver's-side door and stepped down from the running board into saturated peat moss. She looked around, studied their surroundings for any potential threats. The ARC was home to an array of predators—lions, wild dogs. She shouldered a dart gun for security, then led the way to the enclosure's entrance. The entrance was a reinforced pylon flanked by two electrified entry gates. She scanned her wrist on the access panel, triggering a loud click as the latch unlocked. Nedjma jumped.

Perez turned. "You good?"

She heard the whir of Nedjma's environmental suit's heat mitigation system kicking in.

"Yeah—yeah, I'm good. It's just… they are rather large, yeah?"

"Oh, yes. But don't worry, moa are quite docile. Especially compared to the ostriches—nasty kickers, those ones are." Perez gripped the gate handle. "Ready?"

Nedjma forged a nervous smile and nodded, her bottom lip aquiver. From the top of her helmet, a fine mist poured out—a slurry of artificial pheromones, a scented repellent—another layer of protection to ward off would-be threats. Carried off by the current of Qalil's sighs.

"Right," Perez said. "Here we go."

She swung the gate open and led the way to the second ingress. She badged in once more, then stepped into the enclosure with Nedjma close behind.

They advanced with high knees through the tall grass toward the tree line. As they neared the edge of the wood, Perez spotted a couple of curious brownish heads peering through the shade of the canopy, bobbing in and out of sight.

There was one moa, above all, that held Perez's interest: a female subadult named Iwa. She wanted to run a battery of tests to study recent adaptations in the population—anomalous phenotypes of grave concern—and Iwa was a prime subject.

Perez staggered. Another wave of momentary malaise washed over her, a brief but intense vertigo. She pushed her tongue to the roof of her mouth, keeping low over the swaying grass as they pressed on.

"Oh, my." Nedjma gasped as they drew near. Beneath the canopy loomed majestic forms, blackened beneath the shrouded underbrush. Rounded bodies attached to long necks, intermittently lowering their heads to forage along the moss-shrouded terra firma. Nedjma turned to face Perez. "They are *huge*."

Perez straightened, gave a nod. "We're going for the younger one, toward the middle of the group. She's also due for a booster." She revealed a syringe containing a vaccine affixed to a field pack slung over her shoulder. "Many of the other species in ARC are carriers of avian influenza, which could wipe out the entire moa population. They're prone to a host of other diseases in this environment—pathogens and parasites they've never been exposed to—so we monitor them very closely."

"Do you have to protect the other animals from something the moa might be carrying, too?"

"We screened the moa during processing and administered vaccines. For the rest of ARC's fauna, we release aerosolized vaccines into the air currents. But moa need to be isolated for inoculation, so a more *direct* approach is required." Perez took hold of her field pack. "You can steady her while I administer it. Should be quick and easy."

"How… how are we going to do *that*?"

"Oh, we will just walk right up to her. They're not afraid of people and are quite used to me by now. Just follow my lead."

She felt winded, as if they had sprinted from the rover. She did her best to disregard it.

Nedjma pointed. "Look at the size of their *legs*. And one has a tail? Why don't the others?"

"That's Iwa, our subject. The tail is a Deltadromeus phenotype, a consequence of genetic drift."

"Deltadromeus?"

"Yes, *Deltadromeus agilis*, a species of carnivorous dinosaur that the moa—and many other bird species, including ostriches—were hybridized with in the early days of conservation genetics. Moa numbers have become so critically low that certain alleles responsible for suppressing tail formation have started disappearing from the population. Genetic drift is becoming more common among other species, too. Some of the ostriches display similar mutations, but to a lesser degree."

"They share some of the same dinosaur DNA with ostriches… is that why they tried mating with them ?"

"Partially. I think some of that was a dominance display by the male ostriches. But yes, they do share DNA from an identical genus, although it is unlikely they could produce viable offspring."

From the trees, Perez could hear the hooting, low-frequency warbling of the birds. Their calls were booming, resonant, like the drone of a bassoon.

Nedjma looked on. There was a wavering quality to her voice. "If they were hybridized with a carnivorous animal, aren't you worried they may… you know, *drift* toward an expanded palate?"

"You mean engage in predation?" Perez kept her eyes on the rounded forms. "It doesn't work quite this way, but yes, this is a relevant concern." She rummaged in her field pack and procured another hood. "You ready?"

Nedjma licked her lips and nodded.

"Follow me. No sudden movements. I'm going to bag the head and hold her steady. Just follow my instructions. You'll be fine." Perez began to move.

As they passed into the underbrush, Perez counted eight birds, about half the population in the enclosure. The ground here became springy, thickly layered with a cushion of peat. The moa, indifferent to the approaching women, snorted up shrubs and felled twigs. The largest of them, an adult female named Kaia, stood more than twice Perez's height at the hips. Larger birds like her required a team of at least three well-trained catchers with harnesses. She raised her neck, her cream-colored head swiveling dully in Perez's direction. An empty stare, snapping twigs in her downcurved beak.

Easy does it.

Her muscular legs twitched at flying insects. Robust and columnar, they were far more dinosaurian than an ostrich's—a primal trait no doubt embellished by her prehistoric DNA. They were featherless, thighs shrouded behind long satin strands of plumage from her underbelly. Like ostrich hybrids, moa legs were bare, adorned by the same pattern of mottled green-and-black scales.

Kaia raked the earth with a broad three-toed foot. Though moa were not as inclined to kick as ostriches, a well-positioned strike could be fatal. The suit conferred some protection, but a well-placed kick was sure to break ribs, rupture organs.

Even the subadult, Iwa, could become deadly if spooked. She stood near the middle of the group, dwarfed by the adults. It was her tail that made her easy to spot. The appendage stretched twice her body length, endowing her with an unusual horizontal posture. Usually, birds afflicted by such mutations sported a range of stubby vestigial tails, but none so *complete*, nor with such a drastic effect on gait. Along her rump sprouted a plume of fur-like coverts, yielding wispy filaments that continued to the tail's terminal end. They danced about, shimmered in the dappled sunlight that trickled through the trees, a splotchy pattern of grays, greens, and browns. Iwa possessed an ethereal presence. A mythic, primal quality that commanded attention.

But what Perez found most fascinating about the subadult was something far more conspicuous. Flanking either side of Iwa's breast were two tiny knobs concealed beneath shaggy plumage—*forelimbs*. They were not wings, not really arms, but instead, each resembled a single digit terminating in a claw about the size of a human thumb. It should have been impossible. Moa lacked TBX5, a gene that directed forelimb outgrowth and development. Unlike most other ratites—ostriches, cassowaries—moa had no vestigial wings. Except Iwa.

"She's beautiful," Nedjma whispered. Iwa was raking the ground now, mimicking Kaia.

Perez turned to her student, lips raised into a half-smile. "She is. Though she cannot be allowed to breed. Otherwise, the aboriginal form will be at far greater risk of being lost within a few generations."

Perez turned back and watched. Iwa lowered her head to the ground, rummaging through the thick peat. Her snout was also different—beakless, fleshy, notably toothless—for all intents and purposes, a dinosaur snout. Where the other moa relied on their sharp downcurved beaks to snap twigs, Iwa preferred softer provisions. She had settled on a grove of fruiting bodies, which the other moa seemed to avoid. The gradual disappearance of beak secateurs—a scissor-like morphology optimized for "clipping" and sheering twigs—was rare, even in coelurosaur hybrids. And Iwa had no beak *at all*. She was forced to adapt.

Perez's heart was thrashing against her ribs now. A pressure swelled at the back of her throat, portending a renewed round of malaise. She fought it, pushed it down, swallowed hard. With Nedjma close behind, she crept toward Iwa, arm extended, the black shroud pulled over, pinching the tip between her fingers.

Focus. She lived for this. Pushed the malaise further down, squared her shoulders. Narrowed in on the task. *Just like bagging an ostrich.*

She advanced slowly until she was almost up against Iwa's left flank. At the hip, the young moa stood shoulder-height with her.

Iwa's feathers twitched, suggesting agitation by this sudden proximity. Her head, bulkier than was typical, bobbed for a moment. A large brown eye lingered on Perez, an encrusted substance along its margins. The pupil widened, studied her. A stare that was anything but empty. Head movements that were anything but dull. Bits of lichen and detritus littered her coat, feet caked with dried mud and vegetable matter, swarmed by tiny biting insects. The eye blinked and diverted. She returned to foraging.

The moment her snout touched the earth, Perez exploded into action, leaping forward to grip the base of her neck. Spooked by this burst of activity, the other moa turned and fled into the trees.

Iwa reared back, and for a moment, Perez's feet left the soft earth.

"Dr. Perez!" Nedjma shrieked.

The bird jerked again, but Perez remained steadfast, held firm. Without hesitation, she pinched the shroud over Iwa's beefy snout and slipped it over her head. Immediately, the bird stopped thrashing, head held aloft, darting left to right before finally submitting. Maintaining her hold, Perez turned back to lock eyes with a slack-jawed Nedjma.

"That—was *incredible*," the student shrieked in a half-whisper. "How did you…"

"Lots of practice with ostriches," Perez said. "Now, I need you to come and take my spot—I need you to keep her still while I inoculate and collect blood and tissue samples."

Nedjma fell silent.

"You're going to do fine." Perez placed her free hand on Iwa's breast and began to stroke her soft plumage. "See? Totally mellow. Just come over and place your hands right where mine are. She won't hurt you. Just don't stand in front of her unless you want to risk a kick."

Apprehensive, Nedjma crept forward, leaning back as she approached from the side.

"Just relax," Perez said. "Take your time."

Perez extended a hand and guided Nedjma's palm onto Iwa's breast.

"Oh, wow, I can feel her heart beating through my suit!"

Perez nodded and moved Nedjma over to her position, guiding the student's free hand to the base of Iwa's neck. "Hold here. Be firm. You have her?"

"I-I have her."

"Good, keep her steady." Perez reached around and pulled the syringe from her field pack. "I'll start with the booster."

She affixed a needle to the syringe and carefully removed the cap, tapping out the air bubbles. Gripping the plunger between her fingers and thumb, she placed her free hand on the opposite pectoral and, in one swift motion, poked, pulled back to aspirate, then pushed to inject. Iwa's leg muscles fluttered, but she remained still.

Perez retracted the needle and gently massaged the injection site. "*Good girl. Muy bien, campeona,*" she cooed as she reached into her pack and pulled out a collection kit.

"Now for a blood sample," she said. "Move your hand to the base of her neck and massage here along the jugular, then apply pressure." She placed her finger along the side of Iwa's neck, where the feathers tapered into thin down so that the skin was visible underneath. "This will cause the vein to bulge so I can see it better."

"Won't that choke her?"

"No, it's only for a few seconds. She'll hardly notice, but timing is important." Perez sprayed the area with disinfectant, then picked up a butterfly needle adjoined to a tube that fed into a syringe. She positioned it and met Nedjma's gaze. "On three. One… two… *three.*"

Nedjma's grip tightened. At this, Iwa panicked, lifting Nedjma off the ground and throwing Perez backward as she bucked. But Nedjma held fast. Iwa bent at the knees so that her body lowered to the ground, and with tremendous force, kicked off. Nedjma's hold slipped as she fell to the ground. Perez, collecting herself, looked up just in time to see Iwa flailing and kicking, falling back to the ground. Toward Nedjma.

Time slowed. Before Perez had a chance to lunge for Nedjma, the bird crashed into her. Nedjma let out a blood-curdling shriek. The panicked moa sprang to her feet and, still hooded, darted blindly into the trees, blaring a stuttering distress call.

"Nedjma!" Perez scrambled over to her. She was gripping her calf, wincing. "Are you okay? I'm so sorry, that has *never* happened before. They have never—"

"Yeah… yeah, I think so. I think I can—*ow*—stand on it."

"Okay, let me help you," Perez said. A new darkness filled her, one far more potent and pressing than earlier. One marked by dread, by urgency. Fight or flight.

Perez ran a quick diagnostic and scanned the limb through her HUD. "No fracture. Your suit is intact. Come on, let's get you out of here."

Nedjma slung an arm over Perez's shoulders, and the two rose to their feet. Slowly, Nedjma lifted her arm away and almost immediately placed it back on Perez. "*Ah!* Yeah, I think it's a bad sprain. I'm not sure I can walk all the way back to the rover."

"Okay, you keep your arm right on me, and I'll help you. We need to get you to the nearest med bay."

"No," Nedjma said. "They'll want a report. I'm okay, Dr. Perez. I just need ice and rest. I'll be a hundred percent by tomorrow."

Perez shook her head. "What? You need a medical evaluation. A HUD screening is not a medical diagnosis. You could have a fracture, nerve damage…." Had it not been for the layers of moss and twigs, it was likely Nedjma's leg would have snapped in two.

"Dr. Perez, really, I'm okay. Really. Just bring me back to Sector C so you can get over to your meeting."

Mierda. She had forgotten about the meeting. There was no way she would get there on time now.

"Athena," Perez said, ignoring Nedjma's pleas.

"Yes, Dr. Perez?" The AI chirped over her comm, crackled, distorted.

"Pull the rover up to the entrance of the moa enclosure and get me in contact with the on-call physician. I also need you to contact Lotta Eklund and tell her I will be running a few minutes late. Have her take a shuttle from The Center to Sector C. I will meet her there instead."

There was no response.

"Athena?"

Still nothing.

"You have *got* to be kidding," Perez said. "*Puta*. Every time... it's that *fucking* Higgs." She shifted under Nedjma's weight. "Okay. Let's focus on getting you to the clinic."

"What about the samples?"

"We can worry about that later... let's get you back inside." Perez paused for a moment. "And Nedjma?"

"Yes, Dr. Perez?"

"Call me Cam."

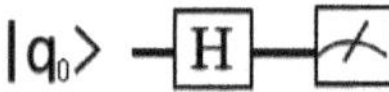

THIRD POSTULATE

Quantum measurements of the system are defined by orthonormal values for the wave function.

May 20, 2147, 10:14 - SANCTUM Hyperloop Station
Center for Off-Earth Ecological Research, Shin Tower
Northwest Algeria - United European Federation (UEF)

| THE ARC >

A cloudless sky was mirrored across Shin Tower, stretching high over a stream of bodies that poured onto SANCTUM Center Station's hyperloop platform. Lotta craned her neck and stared up at the dizzying structure, almost seamlessly blending into the clear blue. It was an illusion, a monolith of seemingly infinite length, stretching perhaps to the cosmos. She turned her head, eyes narrowed, and peered farther off toward the geodesic dome lording impossibly high above. Its presence oppressive, omniscient. An all-seeing eye jutting up from the sand.

This wasn't like Lotta, anthropomorphizing. Projecting. At that moment, a brief but impressionable one, she caught herself becoming the little girl she had left behind long ago. The one who feared the unknown. The one who didn't know any better.

She pulled her UV shroud—a scarf-like shemagh—over her head. A khaki desert shawl flowed from her shoulders down below her knees, further protecting her from the elements. On clear days, the air was breathable, but the sun—and the occasional gust of sand—proved unforgiving even to DNA-hardened skin. Spending most of her time underground certainly didn't help.

The platform led into a crowded vestibule that opened to the main tower lobby. An air quality indicator by the building entrance indicated nominal ozone and particulates.

Lotta wondered to herself how many more of these meetings would be necessary.

"It is a show of good faith," the board had told her. "It will help tip the outcome of the investigation in your favor." *Good faith. For what?* When pressed, the board grew stern. "After Geneva, we are making every effort to convey a level of transparency."

More like the image of transparency.

People and synths streamed in and out in all directions. Vacant faces filtered through the building like drones—no spark, no drive.

Monkeys pulling levers.

It was growing difficult to discern people from synths anymore, not because synths had become more human, but because the living had become less so. With the advent of mind uploading, the lines had blurred.

Instead, life at SANCTUM existed in the architecture—Shin Tower, a sessile, groaning behemoth, carrying the echoes of muted conversations across its sprawling lobby, the belly of the beast. Lotta felt out of her element here—exposed, opened up. A far cry from the close quarters of the ALICE observation deck, the security of CEPP's underground corridors devoid of artifice, of unnecessary polish. Raw, transparent, lying chaste in wait of pure, unadulterated discovery.

The Center also elicited the memory of her DNA-hardening infusions—the ensuing night sweats, the vomiting, the hair loss. Existing as a husk, gutted by her inability to keep food down for weeks. A thought entered her mind: this building, this organization, drew its life from the people within. Sapping the vitality out of those it claimed to serve.

Like a parasite.

The little girl re-emerged inside her, a little older, a little wiser. She sensed oppression, fanaticism within these walls—a pull akin to the paganistic sway of her mother as if her ghost weaved among the high columns, the glass walkways.

A twinge of pain startled Lotta, then a coolness trickled across her fingertips. Blood. She was picking again.

As she passed through the atrium, the shadow of Shin's statue spilled over her. Some dead man, bronze-clad, now an idol to a corporate god. She continued through the crowd of phantoms—scientists, human calculators, philosophers, savants—all united under an ideology a world away from her own, scurrying beneath the shadow of a corporate effigy.

Lotta wondered how Basem did it—shuttling between such vastly different worlds, separated not just by billions of tons of sand and earth but by clashing philosophies and cultures.

Even within a few short years, it was evident that outside interests were slowly eroding the Federation's hold over SANCTUM. EIRO would be well-suited to sell its remaining assets to the off-world investors waiting in the wings. Opportunists. Corporate vultures. Beneath the glamour, it seemed this organization had lost its way. On some level, she thought, Basem must have sensed that.

This is where science comes to die at the hands of shareholders and corrupt bureaucrats.

Lotta crossed the atrium to the help desk, her mangled fingers concealed beneath her shawl, balled tightly into fists so that her nails dug into her palms. Anything to keep from further self-mutilation.

A radiant young Algerian woman draped in white greeted her. She had life. Hope. Lotta yearned for a moment to whisk her away, to keep this place from taking her too. She flashed a wide smile. Her thick arched eyebrows were expressive, innocuous.

"Good morning, madam," the woman said. "Welcome to SANCTUM Center. How may I help you?"

"Camila Perez," Lotta said. "We are supposed to meet here. I've not been able to reach her yet today. Where is she?"

Maintaining a smile, the woman's copper eyes glinted a deep blue as data flashed across her contact lens HUD. "You are Dr. Eklund?"

"Yes."

"Dr. Perez informed me she is meeting you at Sanctuary Theta, the ARC. She is in Sector C. The Blue Line is down for maintenance. Your alternate pickup has been arranged at the transit terminal."

"Wait... what?" Lotta's cheeks flushed. Her patience waned. "She *told* me... to *meet* her *here*."

"I'm sorry, Dr. Eklund. We have been experiencing technical problems this morning. The only information I have is she is meeting you at the ARC. Do you require assistance getting to your transport?"

Lotta reached up and spun one of her earrings on its backing. "No, thank you," she said and turned to leave. She was going back to the hyperloop, back to ALICE. Had no time for this nonsense.

"Thank you, Dr. Eklund, have a wonderful..." The woman's voice trailed off, faded into the droning ensemble of the crowd. The rumblings of lost souls.

"I'm done," she said.

A low voice buzzed in her ear. *"You are getting in that transport."* Tongue tipped with poison, delivered in a thick Greek accent. Dubbed low, distorted to conceal its source, the identity of some lackey on the EIRO audit committee. Lotta reached up to remove the bug, but what came next made her stop cold. *"If you refuse, you know what comes next. We cannot shield you from a wider investigation. At best, your research will be put on hold for months. At worst, well—"*

"I'm *going*."

"Good."

This is bloody ridiculous. Lotta turned back and began to walk toward the transit terminal.

The shuttle was a cramped affair—a two-seated light transport drone, double rotors on starboard and port. Aerial vehicles were only approved for travel across short distances because they were far less reliable than rovers. Their use was further limited by their unpredictability off-world, preventing their use in proof-of-concept applications aimed at SANCTUM's outer colonisation efforts. That ruled out much of their use within EIRO's Algerian division.

The cockpit rattled over the buzzing rotors, hovering mere meters above the whipping sand. The dome now consumed Lotta's visual field, the lines of its geodesics standing in stark relief, superimposed over the sprawling ecosystem shielded within.

It was going to be her first time inside a sanctuary.

She strained, peering up through the glass roof of the cockpit. Inside the dome, faint clouds ebbed. She tracked down the honeycombed carapace, where a ribbon of desaturated green treetops rushed by. A small mountain loomed at the center of this landscape, its peak almost imperceptible through a veil of soft blue haze. The same mountain Fischer had gushed over during the Penrose run—"an engineering marvel," he had said, housed deep inside. *A variable expansion membrane.* A way to regulate the dome's internal pressure.

She glanced through the passenger-side window toward empty desert. In the distance, she made out the faint outline of one of ARC's sister domes, a pearl shimmering above the scorched sand. She guessed perhaps it was Zeta, the most cryptic of the sanctuaries—it was classified, rumored to carry out psychological experiments on human subjects: studying the effects of extreme isolation, of extraordinary environmental stressors. Farther off, the Atlas Mountains receded to the horizon while dust devils danced across the intervening desolation.

The drone veered to port. Lotta's pulse intensified. A waypoint indicator flashed on the windshield below the words *Sector C*, a sprawling outpost situated along the dome's perimeter. Eddies of sand circumscribed its base, generating formations relatively flat compared to the dome's windward side—those colossal sand dunes she had seen during the run.

The low hum of the rotors powering down broke her daze. The air shuttle descended, then came to rest on a square landing pad above the third story of Sector C. Beneath the shade of a covered walkway, Perez stood in wait, head covered, desert shroud whipping from the downwash until the engines fell silent.

Lotta swallowed against the sour taste burning a hole at the back of her throat. She balled her hands again, resisted the urge to pick. *Pick pick pick.* Her cuticles were always raw. Always throbbing. *Seeping.* The restraint drove her mad. She resorted to fiddling with an earring instead. Making enemies was nothing new, but typically, this sort of thing was on her terms—she almost prided herself on it—so the situation was unusual. Even Bogdan knew better than to challenge her authority.

"Dr. Eklund." Perez stepped into the sunlight, her face shielded so that only her green eyes showed. "Thank you for agreeing to meet me here. My apologies for the hiccup. We have—"

"Been having technical problems." Lotta winced.

"Er, yes. Among other setbacks. How was the ride in?"

"Short."

"Right, well… shall we?"

Something seemed off about Perez, like she was rattled, unfocused. Something had happened, and she wasn't being upfront about it. Lotta took note and followed her into the building.

Inside, the air was algid but refreshing, a welcome reprieve from the scorching Saharan sun. They took an elevator to the ground level, opening into a sprawling, brightly lit corridor lined by frosted glass doors. Each branched into large wings, employees donned in scrubs and ESD uniforms filtered in and out. The clean lines of the reflective, smooth surfaces stood in contrast to the snaking concrete pipes and wires that occupied almost every corner of CEPP's facilities. Lotta glimpsed a directory hanging near the elevator lobby.

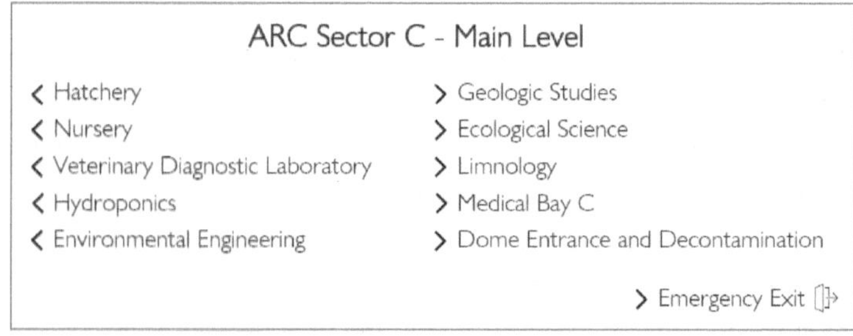

Perez glanced back, her UV hood now draped in a mound around her neck. Lotta considered her quite beautiful—full-lipped and naturally tan, with flowing black hair and high cheek bones. But she was more than a pretty face. She was also a formidable threat, capable of merely *appearing* ill-informed. Lotta understood full well that to underestimate Camila Perez was to do so at her own peril.

"As you can see, there is a lot that goes into maintaining an artificial ecosystem," Perez said. "Sector C is one of three along the dome's perimeter. They function how I imagine the Higgs' above-ground sectors do."

Lotta fought back a grunt. *My work is nothing like yours.* Before she realized what Perez was doing, the emotion had already manifested inside her. The tone was set.

"We house around five hundred SANCTUM staff in each dome."

"Impressive."

"EDEN, our agrarian sanctuary to the northeast, is self-sufficient. It generates enough produce to sustain the entirety of SANCTUM-Algeria—employees and their families." She let out a light chuckle, "We never go hungry here."

Lotta remained silent. She wanted Perez to get on with it.

They stopped in front of a large, reinforced bay door that read *Sector C: Decontamination Chamber, Authorized Personnel Only*. A badge reader was mounted on the wall beside it.

"Here we are," Perez said. "We'll need to don environmental suits and get scrubbed before we go inside the dome." She flashed her badge against the reader, and the door hissed open.

Lotta followed her inside. The room appeared to function as both an airlock and decontamination bay. It was small, able to accommodate a team of six or so. She spotted three sterilization stalls lining either side, each slightly larger than a person. *Like coffins,* she thought.

The door sealed behind them with a loud hiss. Perez pointed to the stall nearest to her. "These stalls add an extra layer of protection from contamination. No person has ever had direct contact with the inside." She turned to Lotta, removing her desert shawl. "Let's get started. Right there, stand on the square and look into the camera."

Overhead, a display jutted from the wall, angled downward. Lotta saw herself staring back through it, the shawl along with her grizzled hair bestowing a nomadic quality, her frame outlined in digitized red—then, a moment later, bright green.

Athena's voice came through the comm. "Welcome to the ARC, Dr. Eklund."

There was a muffled click. A small panel to the right of the door slid open, pouring out steam that cleared to reveal a large sterilization bag holding a hazmat suit.

"Please don your uniform and step inside the decontamination stall."

Lotta reached in and grabbed the bag, then peeled back the seal.

"Just leave the waste in the autoclave," Perez said and walked over to her own stall. She tied her hair into a ponytail, then stepped into the leggings and pulled the garment up over her body. "Remember to pull up your suit's hood before you put the helmet on. You'd be surprised how many people forget. Here, you'll want this, trust me." She reached over and handed Lotta a hair tie.

Lotta was taken aback by the lightness of the material, impressed with how it conformed to her like a glove. She heard a faint whistle and a click as the helmet sealed. A coolness rose against her skin and filtered into her nostrils—oxygen—followed by an electrical smell tinged with lavender.

The stall opened.

"You -ay now ent-r." Athena's words sounded disjointed, almost garbled through the helmet's comm.

She shot a look toward Perez. "What's wrong with her?"

"Like you said, technical problems." Perez gave a sardonic grin and stepped forward.

Inside the stall, Lotta saw markings indicating foot placement. The inner walls were rounded and lined with vertical rows of nozzles.

"-elcome to Sanctuary -eta. -ank you -or following decont-ation -otocol. Please ensure your suit is properly sealed. Place -oth feet firmly on the desig-ed floor-oor markings -nd your hands on the holds."

Lotta planted her feet on the markings and gripped the handles situated shoulder-height at her sides. Her fingertips throbbed, the blood pulsing to the raw self-inflicted wounds. The sting as the oxygen flowed over them.

The door sealed shut, and red light flooded the stall. The nozzles sputtered to life, spraying jets of hot decontamination medium onto her. The liquid streamed down her face shield and coalesced into a frothing vortex at her feet. A tingling sensation mounted in her fingertips, then propagated up her arms as it transformed into numbness.

When the jets finally ceased, the indicator turned green, and the bolt released. The door slid away, and she stepped out. The throbbing in her fingertips returned.

A moment later, Perez emerged, enveloped in a dissipating veil of mist.

"The dec-amination -ocess is complete. Than-ou for protecting bio-ome ecol-gy."

Lotta joined her at the second door, the two of them standing shoulder to shoulder. The door lurched upward, and rays of sunlight bloomed underneath it, growing more intense until Lotta found herself blinded by soft white. The shield's polarizer activated, and, as if a veil had lifted, a stunning vista like nothing she had ever witnessed stretched before her. And for a moment, the stinging, the throbbing faded from awareness. It was only her and the lush expanse.

Just beyond the entrance, the waxy palms of overhanging cycads rattled gently, casting shade across her face as beams of sunlight trickled through. Vast fields of coiled emerald florets circumscribed clusters of shrublike trees aflame with vibrant pink flowers. Further on, swaying grasses stretched over a nearby hillside, where a tufted conifer stood solitary, backlit by golden light. A warden over its domain.

"Saharan cypress." Perez's voice possessed a hollow quality through the comm. She had caught Lotta staring at the tree—its twisted trunk, gnarled limbs stretching skyward—her effort to appear detached betrayed by a brief lapse in focus. "It's one of the last in existence. Would you like to see it up close?"

"I have an hour. We should get on with this."

Perez stared back blankly, appearing wounded by this. "Fair enough."

Lotta considered it a reclamation of her apathy, a momentary win. Except that the longer she peered out across the swaying grasses, the creaking warden, the mountain shrouded in cloud, the more an unsettling sensation came over her. An agoraphobia elicited by the vast expanse that left her feeling even more exposed than earlier. With it came a strong desire to claw her way back to ALICE, to burrow into its depths, back to the familiarity of her lab far underground.

"The rover is just outside. I hope to show you why this ecosystem is under threat."

"You mean under threat *by me*," Lotta shot back. *Careful.*

"Dr. Eklund, this is not personal."

"Show me what it is you want me to see."

Perez closed her eyes. Her eyelashes fluttered. Lotta was getting to her. *Indignant. Another win.*

"*Of course,*" Perez said through a forced smile. The façade was fading.

As they made their way to the rover, Lotta heard Perez in her ear, something mumbled in what sounded like Spanish. Either the woman had forgotten to mute her comm, or it was intentional, meant to be heard. A dig.

They stepped out into the open. Pearls of condensation budded across Lotta's face shield, refracting the sunlight like small magnifying lenses. The distant song of birds, of buzzing insects, of swaying vegetation, filled her surroundings. A soft wind rapped against her suit. She could almost feel it. Almost.

"That breeze is from Mount Qalil. It houses a variab—"

"Variable expansion membrane."

"Yes. Well… our ride is just over here."

Perez led the way to a greenish-brown rover parked and running just outside the entrance. Lotta noticed almost right away how well it bled into the surround, camouflaged against a field of tall bushgrass. The body was outlined yellow by her visor's augmented reality display.

"The adaptive camo helps keep it hidden from animals. We try and interfere as little as possible when we are out," Perez said. "Runs totally silent, too."

Lotta circled to the passenger side as the doors rose like wings.

Overall, it bore many similarities to the rovers used for CEPP's surface operations, with several other modifications that made it better suited to the dome's terrain. Instead of Nitinol, the mud-caked tires were made of thick rubber, grooved with a deep tread. Roll bars reinforced the exterior, and the front bumper was equipped with a steel winch. The versatility and customizability of rovers cemented their employ in EIRO's fleet, both for remote Earth operations and as a staple in the outer colonies.

Lotta stepped up onto the running board and climbed into the passenger seat, arms crossed, casting a disaffected glance out her passenger window. She didn't want Perez to get the sense she was any more intrigued than she had already let on.

"Athena, set a collection route for all tracked avian deaths in the last twenty-four hours," Perez said into the comm. The windshield HUD displayed a waypoint along with the northeastern sector, and she released the steering wheel. As Athena initiated the autopilot, Perez sank back in her seat. "You are joining me on my daily collection."

Great.

Lotta gazed out her window as the rover whipped down a dirt path, past a blur of pink lilies. Neither woman spoke.

The dome's beauty could not be disputed. Lotta looked out across a grassy valley carved by a small river, steam rising from its surface. On the far bank, clusters of animals—wildebeests, zebras, a trio of oryx—drank against the backdrop of Mount Qalil and the dome's honeycombed array.

Then, without warning, Lotta lurched forward. Her lungs voided as the chest restraint halted her forward momentum. The vehicle recoiled on its suspension, and she was thrown back into her seat, sputtering and coughing as she gasped for air. White sprites danced across her vision over a backdrop of billowing dust outside. Something had triggered the vehicle's collision avoidance system.

"Obstacle detected," Athena said over the comm.

Perez, also out of breath, pounded a fist on the steering wheel. "*¡Hija de puta!* Why the hell would she announce that *after* slamming the brakes?" She sat back, heaving, collecting herself. "Athena, run a diagnostic and switch to manual."

"Yes, Dr. Perez."

"*This* is the sort of thing we deal with here," Perez spat. And there it was. Lotta detected the resentment in her voice, still restrained, but there nonetheless. "And Athena is just the tip of the iceberg: the *least* of our worries."

Outside, the dust began to settle. Lotta leaned forward, wincing through the earthy haze. The shape of a large two-legged animal materialized, standing along the edge of the path.

"An ostrich in this part of the dome?" Perez said, nonplussed. "¡Ay! I swear it never *ends*."

Lotta remained silent, watching the bird, studying it. Its neck snaked to the ground, facing the opposite direction. The animal appeared unfazed that it had almost been slammed into by the rover. Sitting atop two featherless scaled legs, the ostrich trotted from one of the pink-flowering trees to another, probing their roots with its beak.

That thing has to be two meters at the hip, Lotta thought.

On each footpad were two toes and two more appendages or dewclaws higher up on the inner ankle joint. The lower of these two digits was especially prominent, extending almost to the ground before curling backward into a fleshy crescent. At first glance, this odd claw appeared useless—a vestigial appendage or mutation—recurved and atrophied from maldevelopment or disuse.

Along its neck, the coloration graded from ash to lighter shades of gray, giving the animal a ghoulish appearance. The eyes—ink-black orbs fixating intently at the tree's base—were angled slightly forward, hooded by prominent bony ridges or crests. But the most alarming aspect of the animal, Lotta found, was a short, featherless tail extending from its hindquarters.

Perez leaned forward. She appeared just as puzzled as Lotta by what was unfolding. The creature began to prod the tree's base with its beak, tearing up bits of ligneous vegetation and tossing them to the side.

"So, *that's* who has been destroying my impala lilies!"

Lotta was shocked but pleased by this outburst. Something to exploit.

Extending a muscular leg forward, the ostrich proceeded to claw at the roots more aggressively. To Lotta's surprise, the recurved claw aided in this activity, providing an effective tool for clearing earth and pulp. This was followed up again with more rapid pecking at the base of the tree.

Lotta, without looking away, broke her silence. "Is this typical behavior?"

"No. No, it is *not*. Not since you started your experiments." Another dig, to be sure. Lotta ignored this.

"Are all of the ARC species acting this strangely?"

"A lot of them. Birds are the most vulnerable. But this… this, I have not seen until now. Impala lilies are host to invasive insects that the ostriches might have developed a liking to. They have been wandering into the forests lately, too, which is unusual."

"What you are saying is you have lost control here." *And that you have no leg to stand on against CEPP.*

"No. We—*humanity*—lost control of Earth's ecosystems *long* ago, Dr. Eklund," Perez snapped. "We thought we could reverse the damage that anthropogenic emissions had caused for centuries, but it's more complicated than we thought."

"And this is *my* fault?"

"This?" Perez laughed. "No, *this* here is *not* CEPP. This is natural selection playing out before our eyes. But, with all due respect, Dr. Eklund, you people at CEPP are not helping. Strange behaviors like *this* become amplified when you do whatever it is you do down there. This is not even what I want to show you today."

Just then, a sharp squeal penetrated the air. The ostrich's bulbous head sprang up with its beak clamped around a wriggling mouse. Lotta looked on in shock and disgust as its mandibles eased up for a moment, then clenched back down, stifling the rodent's cries. The little hind legs kicked and twitched. A futile escape attempt, or perhaps just the nervous system firing away in its final moments. Then, in one swift motion, the ostrich outstretched its neck and swallowed the mouse whole, a lump that glided down in a way that appeared strained, before disappearing altogether.

The ostrich turned and faced the rover—its head cocked to the side as if noticing them for the first time—then darted into the trees. The silence inside the rover was deafening.

Lotta fought back a smile.

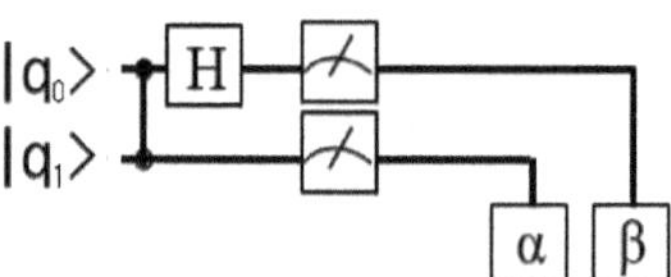

FOURTH POSTULATE

When a quantum measurement is made on the system, the probability of its outcome is determined by the square amplitude of the wave function.

| CAUSALITY >

"I think I've seen enough," Lotta said, staring out with her arms crossed. "You can take me back now, Dr. Perez."

The cryptic voice from the Audit Committee buzzed in her ear. *"What are you doing?"*

Perez, nonplussed, snapped her head toward Lotta. "*What?* You cannot be serious. We haven't even begun."

"I think it's clear what the problem is here—you've no control over your own operation, and you wish to shift responsibility. I am sorry, Dr. Perez, but I cannot be of further assistance to you. I certainly can't be your scapegoat any longer."

"You are making a mistake, Eklund," the earpiece said.

Perez's eyes narrowed. The woman was seething, her cheeks flushed. "Okay, then. If you insist on cutting this short, then I will show you how you—*YOU*, Dr. Eklund—are destroying one of this planet's last remaining ecosystems. I was going to wait to show you this." Perez leaned forward and tapped the console display. "Athena, show us the ARC's electromagnetic readings through the HUD for the last two weeks, ten-times speed. Overlay video feeds of documented impacts registered by geodesic CCTV over the same period, passenger window. And take us back to Sector C."

"Wait, you're having her drive again after what just happened, and this time, you're obscuring the windshield? And you *run* this place?"

"Yes, Dr. Eklund, I am—and yes, I do. Feel free to watch or simply revert to your modus operandi and ignore what is right under your nose. I do not care."

An augmented electromagnetic signature was projected onto the windshield, undulating ribbons that shifted from reds to yellows, then greens, and finally blues, then back again. The augmented reality gave the impression they were riding through vibrant bursts of undulating aurorae superimposed onto the passing landscape.

A time-lapse video of birds crashing into geodesics played on the passenger window to Lotta's right, each strike punctuated by a loud *crunch* that initially jolted her. The tactic was an apparent effort to intimidate her, but she held her ground.

"In the lower right of the windshield is a time stamp," Perez said. "The color changes are cycles showing heightened magnetic fields recorded in this area at that time. When you see red—that's an electromagnetic spike—then, it recedes until it approaches zero Tesla, in the blue—"

"I'm a physicist. I *understand* how electromagnetism works."

Crunch.

"I think you will find these time stamps coincide nicely with your experimental trials. But that is just my suspicion. EIRO's investigation will be enlightening, don't you think?"

Another cycle began. Bursts of red field lines intensified, pulsing upward as if dancing among the cycads and impala lilies all the way to the top of the interior clouds and geodesics above.

Perez pointed. "See? Athena, pause there." The undulating ceased, and all around them, it appeared they were careening through a forest of red peaks and blue troughs. "Look at this timestamp. The magnetic field burst you're seeing right now occurred around nine o'clock this morning, almost two hours before you arrived here." She looked at Lotta, eyebrows raised. "How did your experiment go?"

"I would"—*crunch*—"worry about your own situation." The bitter taste at the back of Lotta's throat returned.

"I am, Dr. Eklund. That is why you are here. It is why we have met three times now, and it is the reason I filed a formal complaint with the Commission. I do not care what you do down there, but I care if it impacts my animals. These bursts are devastating to our birds, as you can see. And SANCTUM would care if it hindered their neo-colonisation efforts. I haven't even mentioned the tremors. We've replaced dozens of panels damaged by seismic activity coinciding with your experiments and these magnetic fields."

Lotta laughed. "You've no evidence. Seismic activity? Are you serious? You don't actually believe the Geneva conspiracy theories, do you?"

"I think it's more than coincidence the same anomalies are beginning to occur here, don't you? Peculiar, to say the least."

Crunch.

"The fact you call yourself a scientist, Dr. Perez, is laughable," Lotta said. Perspiration coalesced on her skin. The cooling system in her suit switched on. "Let's go there. Let's bring Geneva into this. I had good people—friends, colleagues—die in that quake. How *dare* you suggest I had anything to do with that? Second, it is well-established that Geneva lies over a fault line. Do you know another geographic area that does? Western Algeria, right where we are."

Perez's lip began to tremble. She was shaking her head, but appeared to be taken aback by this revelation.

"Oh, you didn't know?" Lotta mocked. "Even your 'professionals' here—your geologists—should be able to tell you that correlation does not equal causation. Perhaps they did, and you simply ignored them."

"That doesn't explain the electromagnetic anomalies," Perez interjected, her voice now rising. "Earth's electromagnetic field does not generate signatures like this, nor at this latitude. The closest natural field is over 6,000 kilometers away in Bangui. These spikes are cyclic, regular."

Lotta's throat burned. She shook her head with a laugh. "Again, as a *phys-i-cist*, allow me to first point out that you clearly have absolutely no clue what you are talking about. I have an alternate theory. Are you familiar with the triboelectric effect, *Doctor?*"

Perez's face had contorted into a scowl, her beige complexion awash with undertones of red.

Lotta didn't wait for an answer. "Of course you aren't. Allow me to *enlighten* you."

"Don't talk to me like—"

"I'm not *finished*. This dome—its internal pressure is regulated by a variable expansion membrane housed inside the mountain. I imagine for a structure this size, such a membrane or diaphragm must be quite expansive—a kilometer or so across." Perez gave an indignant nod, and Lotta continued. "The level of friction generated by this diaphragm's vertical displacement is likely to create a tremendous amount of static electricity. And those clouds above us, don't you think they are undergoing constant friction and charge separation as they swirl around? The clouds, the mountain. Two poles. We are sitting inside a giant Van de Graaff generator."

Crunch.

Lotta flinched. A slight grin materialized at the edge of Perez's mouth. Lotta didn't allow it to phase her, instead regaining her composure.

"Then, there are the dome's convection currents, which I assume are also generating some of your wind. I'd imagine a steady direction and flow pattern that is quite predictable, even cyclical, depending on the temperature differential to the outside. It carries the ambient static and generates a weak electrical current, which in turn carries a localized magnetic field as predicted by Ampère's circuital law. The only points of static discharge are your poor little pets. No wonder they're misbehaving. Your suit grounds you. This rover grounds you. The animals do not have that luxury. I'd be acting up, too, if I was getting constant static shocks. Whatever is happening in here is by design, and a poor one at that."

"Don't patronize me. You have *no*—"

Lotta spoke over her again. Her voice now swelling, agitated. "And how do you know these other anomalous animal behaviors are not something else? Mutations, expressions of previously suppressed dinosaur genes, have been observed for decades. Everyone knows this."

There was a brief pause, and the edges of Perez's lips curled into a full-fledged smile. She erupted into laughter.

"Bullshit. If that were true, other sanctuaries would be experiencing the same issues. They aren't. My scientists would beg to differ with your assessments. I have an entire team working with me on this. No other ecosystem in the entire SANCTUM network spanning the UEF has reported what we observe here. The only relevant variable is your accelerator. Everything else is conjecture."

"I'm amused you want to lecture me on conjecture, Dr. Perez." Lotta scoffed. "And what are your *scientists'* financial disclosures?"

Perez's eyes narrowed. "What is that supposed to mean?"

"I think you know. Funding doesn't just pour into a place like this without outside influences. Anyone can see special interests have their grubby hands all over SANCTUM and its operations."

Crunch.

Lotta didn't shudder this time.

Perez's voice was low, dripping with menace. "I don't like what you're implying about my colleagues. I guess I'm not really surprised. You have operated in bad faith at every turn, so don't worry; this will be our last meeting."

"Last I checked, I invited you no less than three times to visit our lab. Not once have you taken me up on that. So do not lecture *me* on disingenuity," Lotta bit back. "And *I* don't like what you're implying about my research's impact on your oversized terrarium."

"That is a gross miscalculation of the importance of what we do here."

"You don't know as much as you think you do."

"Oh, I think I do!" Perez finally erupted, now yelling. "With all due respect, Dr. Eklund, do *not* tell me what I should *know.*"

And there it was. The response Lotta was after.

Time to go in for the kill. "And what does your supervisor think of all this? I have yet to hear him mention a word… or was he not made aware of all these issues?"

Perez bristled, her face now bright red. "Don't you dare—"

"Don't I dare *what?* He *does* know about the issues you are having, doesn't he?"

"Dr. Bensoussan knows everything I do, but he's also a professional. Don't even think of bringing him into the middle of this."

And there it was, the Achilles heel. Lotta sensed something about her response—defensive posturing. She had struck a nerve. It wasn't much, but it was still leverage, so long as Basem collaborated with ALICE on the animal studies.

"We're done here," Perez said before Lotta could press her further. "I think you need to leave my 'terrarium' *now*."

For the short remainder of the trip, neither woman uttered another word.

When they arrived at Sector C, Perez killed the engine and eased back into her seat. Staring straight ahead through the windshield at the decon chamber entrance, she did not mince words about what came next.

"Now, Dr. Eklund, kindly get the fuck out of my dome."

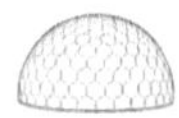

13:40 - Higgs Circular Collider, Sector ALICE
Laboratory Observation Deck
Northwest Algeria, United European Federation (UEF)

Lotta returned to her office and closed the door behind her. She slumped into her chair. She was glad to be back, secure, out of the elements.

Away from Camila Perez.

She leaned over to open a desk drawer and pulled out a holoscreen. The device was quantumly encrypted, untraceable. Unhackable. A favor from Hassan.

She dialed a number she hadn't called in years, surprised she still had it tucked somewhere in the recesses of her brain. After a few rings, there was an answer.

"Eklund?" A gravelly voice greeted her in a rich Greek accent. "My dear friend, it's been what... five y—"

"Cut the shit, Aegis. I know it's you."

"Well, good to hear from you too."

His upbeat demeanor still grated on her after all these years. Underneath the pleasantries, Aegis Galani was a cold-blooded bastard. Admittedly, that was precisely why she was talking to him now.

"I hear you've been causing a shitstorm down in Algeria," he said. "How *is* that new accelerator? I do miss it. Working underground alongside you. Quite a bit, I do. Truly."

"You're the one, Aegis. The contact that's been listening in. Whispering in my ear."

"Oh, Eklund, you haven't changed a bit. What are you on about? Have you gone mad, dear friend?"

"Jesus. Forget it. I know it's you. You know it's you. Let's move past it. I need your help."

A cackling laugh, gruff, like a barking pit bull.

"You? Need my help? This is rich, Eklund." He chuckled again. The sound of a deep drag on a cigarette. "Real rich."

"I need you to call off this investigation."

"What investigation?"

"I said cut the shit. The line is secure."

"Afraid I can't help you. Your friend Perez caused quite a stir with SANCTUM's board of trustees. They want this looked into... a lot of money on the line. You know ho—"

"*You owe me, Aegis.*"

She knew he had always hated being interrupted, recalling it as a point of contention between them in the past.

That's just it, though. He always wanted to insert small talk.

She had no patience for it today.

There was a pause, and the voice grew solemn. A peek from behind the veil. "Let's be clear. I don't owe you a damned thing, understand? Second, would it kill you to say *please*, old friend?"

"Are you going to help me or not?"

Aegis lingered, as if mulling his exit from the conversation. "Look, my hands are tied—we don't have the sway with SANCTUM that we used to, not since the special interests got involved. You know that. You admitted as much to Perez during your little rant. This investigation is going to happen. The board will see to that. However—"

"However what?" Lotta was skeptical.

He would say anything at this point to get me off the line... a bloody bastard through and through.

"Maybe we can keep your friend distracted… keep her from stirring up any more shit for you, make her sorry she ever did in the first place. You got any dirt on her?"

This was something. Perhaps Lotta had underestimated Aegis after all. Maybe he hadn't grown soft. Lotta thought for a moment. "I do, actually. One of her claims is that erratic animal behavior is being caused by electromagnetic disturbances caused by our wormhole experiments."

"Yes, yes… *and?* Is it?"

"I'm not sure. Maybe. Some of what Perez has in there looks like a deeper issue rooted in the hybrids themselves… I fed her some nonsense about the way the domes are engineered."

"So I heard. A good attempt." He chuckled. "Good attempt."

"Right. She didn't buy that, but she did admit to some odd animal behavior, even genetic mutations—I witnessed some of it today with that aberrant ostrich. Seems some previously suppressed dinosaur DNA is being expressed."

"You don't think she's tampering with DNA to cause all this, do you? That would be a shame if it were so…." His tone was insincere, suggestive.

"It certainly would."

"Yes. Such a revelation would perhaps nudge the Committee to attend to *her* instead. My, what a shame that would be. A real damn shame, eh?"

Aegis paused, took another long drag.

"But we need a *motive.* Yes, need a motive. Let me talk to my source on the ground in Algeria. No promises, old friend. You know I do not make promises. As far as this investigation against you: if they *do* find anything linking your research to these events—"

"*If,*" Lotta emphasized.

"Right, *if*—then I will see to it that it doesn't find its way into the 'official' report."

"Just like we did with Geneva?"

"*Just like we did with Geneva.*"

Click.

|OSITO >

Basem stared into the yawn of a portentous void. He did not blink, just stood motionless, arms at his sides, mesmerized by the thing suspended before him—a monstrous obsidian orb. Along its circumference, a faint orange disk smoldered, illuminating his vacant stare.

He saw only emptiness. Felt only emptiness.

Then, a blinding effulgence burst forth, bathing him in white light. He closed his eyes, did not want to see. But no matter how tightly he clenched them, the light pierced through, *made him see.* An invader mining his thoughts, his soul, for anything and everything until it permeated him. Until it displaced all that he had been. Until he was nothing more than a husk, a host, a shell.

A sensation of weightlessness overtook him. *A product of the parasite now entrenched within? Or some exterior force?* The skin of his face now sinking, sloughing down over muscle and bone. His eyes exposed, throbbing. His jaw agape, stretched, cracking, too heavy to close.

The humming grew, a deafening oscillation that drove him to madness. Basem tried to cover his ears, only to realize his hands had become lead, sinking far below into the white depths. He tried to scream, but none came.

At the edge of *nothing*, the light had bent so severely that he could now see the back of his own head. The hum of the accelerator ceased. There was no sound beyond the rupturing of eardrums, the conductance of twisting flesh and snapping tendon through his bones. Hot irons sank into his eyes and ears. The light expanded inside him. Blood seeped from his bulging veins, through his skin like sweat, as if by some grisly osmosis, until a thousand crimson droplets were suspended before him.

He uttered a final gasp, an involuntary voiding, his last breath emptying into a deafening vacuum.

Into nothing.

Basem shot up in bed, drenched in sweat, his heart wrestling to free itself from his ribcage. He wiped his face with his hand and cast the blankets aside, then turned to the edge of the mattress to collect himself. The nightmares were getting worse.

"Nene, ¿estás bien?" a groggy voice mumbled from behind. A hand came to rest on his back, and he turned to meet Camila Perez's slothful gaze.

"Yeah, I'm okay. Just a bad dream." He stood and shuffled to the washroom, rubbing the sleep from his eyes.

"W—wherey'goin?... Okay," Perez mumbled groggily. Her arm fell back to the bed, and she dozed off again.

Basem double-tapped the light panel, setting it to dim, and walked to the sink. The warm water felt good against his cheeks, pulled him back into the present, to reality.

Just a dream.

When he returned to the bedroom, Perez was lying on her side, the curves of her bare shoulders accentuated in the soft light of early morning.

"What did you dream about?" She turned over to look up at him, her eyes now alert, an expression of concern.

"Locura. Chaos." Basem picked up a T-shirt from the floor and pulled it over his head, eager to change the subject. "How is your student doing?"

He really wanted to ask how the investigation with Lotta Eklund and CEPP was going, but he knew better. That was for her to bring up.

"Nedjma?" Perez stretched her arms wide and let out a long sigh. "She's doing okay. Lucky she didn't break her leg."

"She admires you."

"You think so? She's a good egg. Good intentions."

"Yeah? And what about you? What are *your* intentions?" Basem smiled, taunting her playfully. He reached under the sheets to grab her leg.

Perez squirmed. *"Stop!"* she squealed with a wide smile. "I'm ticklish there, you know that."

Basem reached for her again. She leaped from the bed, standing unclothed on the other side. He jumped onto the mattress and lunged for her. Before she could escape, his arms encircled her, and they were falling back onto the bed. He wrestled her onto her back, straddling her while he pinned her wrists above her head. He kissed her on the forehead. She smiled, writhing beneath his weight.

"Osito, let me go!" she shrieked, scrunching her face to suppress a smile.

Basem rolled over onto his back. "Well, are you going to answer me?"

He turned to face her. She was still on her back, panting and grinning.

With a burst of energy, she rolled onto him. "I don't think you want to *know* my intentions, osito."

"Oh, but I do."

She sat up straight, straddling him, and tipped her nose into the air, contemplating her response. "I intend to seduce you into coming with me to the sanctuary today. I still have to inoculate that moa. You are going to come help me."

"Oh, yeah? That so? Is Nedjma going to be there?"

"Why? You interested?" Her eyes narrowed with a smile.

He flashed a mischievous grin, his eyes wandering. "Well… I mean…"

Perez pressed a knee into his ribs.

"Hey! Easy."

"You are *not* funny."

"No? I think so. But really, I was hoping it would just be us today."

She leaned forward, and their lips met. Then she pulled back, her face hovering over him. "You *better*."

Perez sat upright again, raising her hand to her forehead. A shift in her expression suggested something was wrong.

Her smile faded, and her face grew pale.

Basem propped himself onto his elbows and placed a hand on hers. "Hey, you okay? What's wrong?"

"I… I don't know. I felt dizzy just now." As soon as it came, it went, and the color returned to her cheeks. "It's passed. I'm okay."

"Another spell? Maybe we should see a doctor."

"*No!*"

Basem was taken aback by this reaction. *What on Earth?*

Perez seemed to notice his perplexity and softened. "I'm—I'm okay. I just need a shower." She smiled and rolled out of bed. "Will you make coffee?"

"Of course," he said, his voice still tinged with concern. "Are you sure you are okay, habibti?"

She leaned in and kissed him. "You are sweet," she said. "Now get your ass out of this bed and make me coffee."

He watched her leave the room. A moment later, the shower came on, and he made his way to the kitchen.

"Athena, play 'Salut D'Amour,'" Basem said over the sound of boiling water. The pod was filled with the warm tones of a gentle piano accompanied by a violin.

Coffee in hand, he backtracked to the bedroom and peered through the doorway at Perez, her skin backlit by the morning sun. Her hands flowed gracefully in the air as she mimicked the movements of a conductor. Eyes closed, lips curved into a smile of contentment, of safety. As the aroma filled the room, her eyes opened and met his.

"How long have you been standing there?" she asked.

"You'll never know, *mon amour*," he said with his best attempt at a heavy French accent.

Coffee was a luxury, a delicacy in modern times. Basem remembered Mum talking to him as a boy about how it had once been a commodity, as ubiquitous as any other. That was before the global droughts. He held the cup to his mouth and hovered for a moment, taking in the bold smell.

"Thank you, love, it's delicious," Perez said.

He gave a smile. "We'll head out after this, yeah?"

The commute by transit drone was short on a clear day, the perfect weather for Basem to spend his day off with Perez. It had been increasingly difficult to coordinate time together; even when they managed to, there were often still things that came up. Today, it happened to be a moa in need of vaccination. If they were together, though, Basem didn't much care what they did. It was just good to have a day, just them.

Once they emerged from Sector C's decontamination chamber into the dome, he peered off across the landscape as if for the first time. With the CEPP experiments tying him up, he had not been inside the ARC for months. It felt familiar, but also new in a way.

"Let me know if you want me to carry anything." Perez turned toward him. He had her field pack slung over his shoulders.

Basem smiled, sliding his thumbs behind the straps. "I got it, habibti. Lead the way."

He followed her to a nearby rover and got in. About halfway to the destination, they slowed and came to a stop.

Perez turned to him with a wide smile.

"Come with me," she said.

"Why did we stop?"

"You'll see." She handed him a dart gun and secured hers to her waist.

She lifted the driver's-side door and stepped out. Basem's feet found the soft ground. He looked down at his wrist and activated his helmet's pheromone atomizer. He looked up to see Perez's helmet already ejecting a fine white mist into the air.

"You going to tell me where you're taking me?" Basem stumbled playfully. She ignored him and snatched his hand, leading him down a dirt path. He drew the pack's strap over his shoulders, struggling to keep pace with the added bulk. "Did you check the trackers to make sure there are no predators around?"

"Just come. Yallah. Leave the pack behind."

This, he did not abide. Aside from what they required for inoculations and sample collection, the field pack contained a first aid kit and other supplies he had reservations about leaving. Basem often found himself threading the needle between his relationship with Perez and his role as her supervisor. To further complicate matters, they had not disclosed their relationship to EIRO out of fear one of them may be relocated to one of SANCTUM's other locations to the north.

Basem tightened the bag's straps and matched her stride until they walked in lockstep. Despite the challenges, he was content.

Perez pointed to a grassy, flower-dappled knoll straight ahead. A wide smile pushed her soft cheeks up to form two distinct dimples. Basem studied her expression for a moment, admiring her in that ridiculous environmental suit, then turned to look where she was pointing.

On the other side of the elevation, he spotted the silhouette of a narrow head with large ears, joined to a long neck, grazing in the trees. At the end of its snout, a snake-like tongue protruded and wrapped around a branch of leaves, pulling them back toward its mouth.

"Come on!" Perez crouched low to the ground and hurried up the hill. Basem stayed close on her heels.

As soon as the pair arrived at the crest, they slumped together against a large boulder, panting. Perez pointed to a small tower of giraffes grazing peacefully among a zebra herd.

"Those two," she said. "They're my favorite of all of the animals here."

Basem placed his hand on hers, and their fingers intertwined. He wished they hadn't been wearing gloves. She released his hand and stood on the rock.

One of the gentle giants turned and began to saunter in their direction. Even the zebra herd started to make its way closer.

"Not as wild as they used to be," she said. "Despite all our efforts. They have learned the repellants released by our suits drive predators away, so they are drawn to it now. These animals never cease to amaze me."

A light rain started, pecking Basem's face shield.

"They're beautiful, mi cielo." He watched her as she watched them, droplets dancing off her suit, refracting rays of honey-tinged sunlight as they fell.

She looked back at him and gave a playful scoff. "Osito! Stop. Not at me, look at *them*. Mira." She gazed out, eyes full of wonder. "Remember when they were little?"

"I do. You were with those two day and night." Basem grinned and gazed at the giraffe sauntering up the hill, its tail swiping at black flies. He craned his neck to look up at the towering creature, its slender head descending toward Perez as it approached. "They trust you," he said.

She laughed. "Hey, big boy," she cooed, shaking her head as the smooth black tongue probed her outstretched hand. "Sorry, *colega*, I do not have anything for you."

A bulging brown eye studied Basem, its long eyelashes fluttering. A pair of horse-like ears twitched behind two bony, fuzz-covered stalks at the top of its head. The giraffe turned to face him next, arching its velveteen neck—a quilted chestnut patchwork interspersed with white fur. He held out an empty palm. The muscular tongue probed his gloved hand before the giraffe gave up and meandered back toward the trees, beating its tail against its hide in agitation.

"That's Boipelo," Perez said. "The other one is his mate, Akila. She's smarter—lets him come to me first to see if I have food. Only when I need to do a checkup. They haven't produced a calf yet this season. It worries me."

Basem looked over at her. She still seemed to have something else on her mind, but he wasn't sure what. Her demeanor had shifted. She appeared distracted, distant.

"What are you really thinking about, Cam?"

She returned a half-smile, but he saw sadness behind her eyes. Rain droplets had coalesced onto her face shield, which also reflected the dome's lattice-like scaffolding silhouetted prominently in the midday sun. Her smile transformed, twisting into a frown, and the tears followed. She choked and gagged as a torrent of emotion poured out in an incoherent string of sputters and sharp inhales.

Basem, astonished by this sudden outpouring, pulled her into an embrace. "What is it? What's wrong?"

Is it the investigation? Have things taken a turn for her? Something I'm not aware of?

"Basem." She paused, choking on the words. Something difficult for her to spit out. "Basem, I'm pregnant."

Basem, shocked and perplexed, pulled back. His eyes met hers.

"You're... you're... what?"

"Pregnant. At least six weeks, I think." Her eyes, large and expectant, stared into his. A stream of tears stained her cheeks.

"But... that's impossible."

"I-I know... but I *am*. I tested *three times*." She hitched.

"Hey, we're going to be okay. We'll make this work, yeah?" He drew her back toward him, doing his best to console her through their bulky suits. He wasn't sure what to think. His mind was racing. Should he be happy? Upset? Worried?

"People like us—*people like us, Basem*—have disappeared. They could separate us. And do you think they'll let us keep an unauthorized pregnancy? We will be accused of circumventing eugenic policy. They will want to investigate how we got around harvesting, around IVF. You know as well as I do."

Eugenic policy—something he had not thought of much before. It never really applied. They had no intention of having children, at least not anytime soon.

"Cam, you don't really believe that, do you?" he said calmly.

Under the Ministry of Health, human reproduction was carried out exclusively by in-vitro fertilization following a stringent embryoselection process. The Federation's push toward a more perfect society, one free of genetic disease and severe mental illness. An effort to conserve dwindling resources, to reserve them for a physically and mentally fit population. Molecular eugenics was a means to this end. To a more perfect union.

For generations, the Ministry oversaw the eugenics program. Before implantation, the desired embryo underwent a battery of mandated genetic modifications—gender assignment, disease resistance, mitotransfection, and the arrest of gametogenesis. As a result, citizens could not produce viable sperm or egg cells, and instead required specialized and closely monitored in-vitro fertilization to have children.

Natural pregnancy should have been impossible. It *was* impossible. It had been for generations.

But Basem understood he, himself, was a rare exception, born before the annexation of Algeria. Before UEF policies were enforced over its people. He was natural-born—and capable of having children—though still expected to follow the Ministry's contraceptive policies under the law. Perez, on the other hand, *was* a product of embryoselection. She should have been incapable of a natural pregnancy.

"We should have been more careful," she said. Her sobbing became more intense, and the face shield began fogging over.

She was right. Despite this, Basem had confidence that the Ministry of Health would not step in. It was an honest mishap. At worst, EIRO might give him a slap on the wrist for having a nondisclosed relationship with a subordinate. The Federation would not terminate the pregnancy. They would not investigate them. *Would they?*

"We will be okay. This is rare, but it does happen. We can make this work."

"*You...* don't know what it was *like.*"

"What? What was *what* like?"

"They did horrible things to the Spanish, to my family. *My brother*, he was never born. The Federation. If they find out about this...."

She had told him stories before. About her brother, how he had been miscarried, but that she didn't think it was an accident. About growing up in Spain. How the people there had been treated under Federalist rule. How they had been corralled en masse and shuttled into low orbit prison. Some were people she knew and loved.

Basem believed her, even if things were different now. Even if sometimes, on a clear night, he could spot orbiting gaols among the satellites, red lights flashing in the night sky. Beacons of the damned.

He knew little about her parents, though she spoke of them often and with great affection. He knew they still lived in Spain—despite the border security that made it difficult for their daughter to visit, despite her pleas to move them to Algeria to be with her. He knew that, for all its challenges, he'd had a relatively easy childhood growing up in the slums of Algiers amid famine and drought. Basem had endured challenges, but he could not fully grasp the things Perez had experienced, things she concealed from the outside world. From him.

He looked into her eyes. "Cam, look. You're right. I don't know what it was like. I can't begin to imagine—"

"No, you *can't.*"

"I'm on your side." His voice was shaking, betraying the impact of her words. "Things have changed since then. Those laws haven't been enforced in over a decade. At worst, we might get a fine."

Perez shook her head. Her face flushed red, her brow furrowed. "*How can you know that?*"

"All I'm saying," he said, "is maybe we need to think about this."

"*I never should have told you.*"

Her words were like venom. He hated when she said that. Always cut him deep. He glanced at his feet as if to study his dust-covered boots, his mind far off. He wanted to scream, if not for the tightness in his chest.

"Osito?" Perez softened, but the blow had been dealt. Basem looked at her. A river of tears was coursing down her reddened cheeks. "I'm sorry… osito, please talk to me. I-I didn't mean it like that."

Basem wanted to talk, but he was afraid of what he might say. What it might mean. His tongue was knotted and seized up, planting itself against the roof of his mouth. The world began to close in around him.

"Please just tell me what you're thinking," Perez said. "Please. I love you. *Please.*"

He looked off toward the grazing giraffes and then at Perez with welling eyes. His hands were trembling. "Please just think about this."

"I have. We can't have this baby. This is *my* choice. Not the UEF's, not the father's. *Mine.*"

"What are you saying?"

"I am saying I can—I can take care of it."

The void opened again. It started in his stomach. Like his nightmare, brimming with light. It displaced everything he had, everything he was. "You can't be—what if—what if—" Then the tears broke free, incapable of being held back. He tried to form a coherent string of words, stumbling until finally, all that came out was "*I can't lose you.*"

"I will be safe," she sobbed. "Trust me, osito. You have to trust me."

"Please don't… please don't do this. I can't lose you. There must be a better way."

"There isn't."

| RELATIVITY >

Hassan Kateb thumbed through the worn pages of a tattered hardcover book—a volume of philosophical works from the French–Algerian philosopher Albert Camus. He considered the twentieth-century tome an heirloom, a treasured antiquity passed down by his baba before his death.

To Barzakh. In wait of The Day of Judgement. Of eternal life in Jannah.

While Hassan thumbed through the delicate pages, each an artifact to a bygone era, Martin Anderson quietly loomed over a holographic chessboard between them. Garbed in his ESD uniform, his helmet and gloves at his side, Anderson stroked a clean-shaven chin. In the background, the faint hum of the Higgs penetrated even the thick walls of the ALICE observation deck.

Hassan turned another page, the cover's sun-faded leather settling against his fingertips, the title's embossing smoothed over from a century of handling.

The Myth of Sisyphus embodied a masterclass in the doctrine of absurdism, an omnibus of essays arguing that life itself held no fundamental purpose or meaning.

There was no God. There was no *absence* of God. No destiny. No fate. Things just *were*.

Camus considered the search for more profound meaning to life—the notion of a *purpose*—to form the foundation of absurdity. This held true for science—and especially for religion—but one did not have to ascribe to that philosophy to appreciate it. Hassan found freedom in that.

Freedom from indoctrination.

Freedom from subterfuge.

Before Baba, the book had belonged to Hassan's mother, back when they lived in the port city of Oran, along the coast of northwest Algeria. Baba worked as a policy analyst, drafting laws for the Algerian government, and had been a key figure in negotiations leading up to the country's annexation by the European Federation in 2113. As Hassan grew into adulthood, he learned that Algeria's place under European rule was an insidious one—to act as a holding colony for African climate refugees, an effort to stem the flow of migrants northward into continental Europe.

During this time, Hassan's mother worked as a securities lawyer for the Ministry of Finance, where she remained until succumbing to breast cancer a week before his tenth birthday. A year before Yemma's passing, he recalled the walls of book-filled shelves lining the library in their home. Most belonged to her.

Little Hassan had also procured dozens of his own texts, proudly on display in the great room by then.

But during the early days of Algeria's annexation, paper and print texts of all forms were considered contraband. He recalled the emptiness inside that place after the Ministry of Intelligence sent authorities to confiscate everything. Its bare shelves, bones picked clean by vultures. The despair it bestowed upon Yemma. An emptiness that had imprinted from her onto him, as if there had been a death in the family.

The Myth of Sisyphus had been one of Yemma's prized possessions, second only to her Quran. Somehow, she had managed to obfuscate it from the UEF authorities, likely at the risk of disbarment, perhaps even internment. After Yemma's death, Baba had preserved the book as a keepsake, and shortly before he passed, he left it to his only son.

Laws had relaxed since those early days, but there was still a stigma attached to printed texts—not least the works of philosophers. Hassan's defiance extolled his mother's memory and solidified his identity as a denizen among an occupying force. An insurgent in his own home among a populace of interlopers.

"You read that thing more than the Quran," Anderson said.

Hassan looked up from the text, his eyes on Anderson. "Probably true," he replied, "but if for no other reason than to attempt to understand an opposing world view."

Of course, the real reason was more profound, more nuanced. The real meaning was in the act itself. But even the book's contents—often-meandering syntax on the human condition, in and of itself an exercise in the lost art of etymology—held profound significance for him. It was an act of remembrance and one of national—or, rather, *provincial*—pride. Camus was, after all, Algerian.

Anderson raised his eyebrows and returned to the game. He lingered a moment longer, then made his move. "King me."

Hassan quietly placed a worn ribbon in the binding's crease and closed the book. "This isn't checkers," he said, indifferent to the perception that the irony of the joke might have eluded him. "It's 'check.'"

Though he might describe his relationship with Anderson as generally tolerable (if at times contentious, to the delight of his colleague), Hassan supposed that on some level, he regarded the man as an acquaintance. Perhaps a friend.

"I hate to tell you, Hass, but that's checkmate."

Hassan heard footsteps shuffling toward him and turned to see Basem approaching, fully suited, wheeling a small cart carrying a tinted animal cage.

Anderson greeted the approaching animal specialist with a nod. "Hey, look who's on time for the big day." He clapped his hands and rubbed his palms together. "First animal trial, lads. Is this our first subject?"

Basem gave a half nod and looked down at the cage. "Sure is. Ready to make history."

Hassan saw movement inside—a rabbit, barely visible, bobbing its head from side to side. The behavior seemed odd to him. "Why is the cage so dark?"

"She's a New Zealand white. They are very light-sensitive," Basem said. "They contain knockout mutations for tyrosinase, which is needed for melanin production in the skin, fur, and eyes."

"Albinos," Anderson said.

"Yes, oculocutaneous albinism. Her vision is quite poor, so she wobbles her head to induce parallax. Helps her see a little better." Basem looked up at the two men. "So, who's winning?"

"Me," Hassan said.

Basem seemed distracted. Perhaps he was nervous about the trial. After all, a lot was riding on its success. But in the months they had worked together, Hassan had come to know the man to be present, often passionate about protocol, about his role in the project. Today, he appeared off balance.

"Are you *mad?*" Anderson scoffed at Hassan. "That's checkmate."

Hassan turned back. "Sorry, but you are wrong. Look. My king is in a state of superposition—both alive and dead. You just don't understand all the rules yet. You merely collapsed his wave function. In this reality, he is alive." He followed up with this by swapping his rook and king.

"What the—" Anderson bobbed quizzically.

"Castle." Hassan sat back and reopened his book. "My rook and king are in an entangled state."

"You've gotta work on your metaphors, mate." Anderson reached forward and knocked out one of Hassan's bishops. "Your move, Schrödinger."

"Schrödinger was an overrated pedant."

"I know. Seemed fitting."

"You guys lost me." Basem sighed. There was a glassy malaise in his eyes. Hassan was sure of this, though it was not his place to inquire.

Anderson wagged a finger toward him. "There are three types of people in this world, Basem. Those who understand quantum physics, those who do not, and those who *both* do *and* do not."

Hassan rolled his eyes, then looked over at Basem. "Ignore him. You are already more aware of the concept than you may think." He cleared the chess game with a swipe of his hand. "Athena, show me a flock of starlings."

A hologram of thousands of swarming birds materialized.

Anderson smirked at Basem and nodded toward the display. "There you go, biologist. He'll dumb it down for you."

Hassan shot him a look and shook his head. Anderson took the hint. His grin faded, and he fell silent.

The flock of birds undulated in unison, moving collectively like a singular organism.

"A murmuration," Basem said.

Hassan nodded. "Think of each bird as a 'bit' of information, interacting with its immediate neighbors. They, in turn, interact with *their* neighbors. When one moves, the others react. This alteration transmits instantaneously through the entire flock, and in this way, each bird is tied to every other individual. A perturbation from one alters the choreography of the whole. You could say they are *entangled.*

"Quantum systems behave in precisely this way. For example, ALICE's core is like a murmuration—a liquid cloud of supercooled helium atoms—dancing in unison. BOB's as well."

Hassan tapped the hologram again. A schematic of a geodesic sphere—a digital construct of ALICE's Penrose core—appeared. Swiping his hand down the middle, he revealed a cross-section of its inner layers.

"This is also an entangled system. Together, the core's ferrovanadium gel and helium condensate form another layer of entanglement, a dual quantum network called the nucleus. The nucleus of our ALICE gate is, in turn, entangled, in our final and third layer, with BOB's. A bit of an oversimplification, but it gives you an idea."

"Teleportation," Anderson said.

"Quantum networks like this are not new," Hassan said. "They are also the basis for synth AI and Athena's neural network. In our experiments, we have simply co-opted the concept of a quantum network and applied it to transit."

Basem nodded. "That part, I get. It's the nuances that are mind-bending. But thank you."

"Quantum mechanics is all nuance, friend."

Basem shrugged. "I'm just satisfied we have established our time-of-flight benchmarks. Animal safety is my top priority. The mechanistic nature, I'll leave up to you all."

"Appreciate that," Anderson said with a twinge of sardonicism.

"Well, then, good chat," Basem said. "Looks like we are about to prep for the trial. Talk to you lads soon." He turned and piloted the cart toward the loading station.

Hassan spotted Fischer running system checks on the transport cartridge, a containment and delivery apparatus for the subject. The engineering team designed it to be ferried by conveyer into the chamber and remotely loaded into the core. Basem approached, opening the cage to remove the rabbit. Fischer looked up and stepped aside.

The rabbit was a sad-looking thing. Her legs limp, pink eyes aglow, relegated to her fate as her head oscillated erratically. Basem stroked her back as he carried her to the transport cartridge. Once secured, Fischer assisted him in loading the device onto the conveyor.

Overhead, a display provided a live feed of the subject from inside the cartridge.

Command Central came over the comm. "Trial in twenty. Take your positions."

It was around this time that Hassan's focus shifted, that a frantic sort of energy stole over him like the flip of a switch.

He stood up and closed his book. "Right, then."

"Best get to it." Anderson stretched his arms wide before walking over to the console, where Mattheo had started preparing the HALOS for beam ramping. The edges of his suit were outlined by the green glow of the core's failsafe display.

Hassan panned to the far end of the deck. There, Lotta Eklund gazed out into the Bell chamber. She stood inert, hands clasped behind her back, staring. Part of her routine before each trial.

Watching her meditate triggered his own reflections as he turned to his own work. He thought back to Camus, to the absurd.

Simulate logic gates. Monitor magnetic flux. Pursue the abstract, mind-rending world of the quantum. The thirst for knowledge, tightly woven into the fabric of Hassan's consciousness. All of it, absurd. *In the end, what is it all for? To win some never-ending cosmic arms race? And then what?*

A burst of static grated against his ears. The Higgs was ready to fire. The trial had begun.

Anderson's voice cut through the fuzz. "Starting the squeeze now."

A high-pitched howl resonated inside the Bell chamber, muffled by the sound-damping glass and over a meter of concrete and lead. The hissing in Hassan's earpiece intensified.

"This is Command. We are prepped to fire. Take positions."

"HALOS stable," Mattheo said.

Hassan looked back down at his display and opened the bridge channel to establish the gate between BOB and ALICE. The next voice he heard was his own, an utterance that occurred innately, subconsciously. A conditioned response from countless past drills and trials:

"Bell State initiated."

Nearby, Basem analyzed a large display showing the rabbit's vitals. "Test subject appears stable."

The video feed showed the animal—calm, nose twitching, head bobbing stupidly as it approached oblivion. A rabbit with a purpose.

How absurd.

Lotta leaned over the console and inserted the activation rod.

"Keyed in."

"Keyed in." Bogdan's voice whirred distantly.

Three tones of the alarm.

Command, almost inaudible, incoherent: "Firin—HALOS —ee… two…."

The transmission cut out, and a second later, so did the crackling static.

Pressure built behind Hassan's ears, mounting until they finally popped. His compression lining constricted around his limbs, redirecting blood flow to his vitals. All he could hear was his pulse pounding in his head, the air voiding from his lungs. He felt faint.

Something is wrong.

There was a bright flash, pure white, that consumed his surroundings. Almost imperceptible, faster than the blink of an eye. A mere strobe effect. He felt himself levitating in this briefest of moments, lungs deflated, eyes bulging.

Then, like a photo negative, blackness fell, and his body slammed to the ground. He cried out in pain, but no sound came. Only deafening silence.

And as quickly as the moment came, it passed. Hassan's hearing rushed back, his vision returned to behold a scene of chaos, *of entropy.* Muffled groans and screams, coughs as people choked for air.

Something warm ran down his face and over his lips. The taste of blood trickled past his teeth.

Disoriented, he propped himself onto one arm and searched through the dim viridescence of emergency lighting. Bodies were strewn about. Some moving, others still.

His tongue was coated with a metallic taste that would not subside. His ears throbbed. Everything sounded muffled, distant.

Basem sat hunched at the edge of the examination bench, arms resting in his lap, palms face up. His face was speckled with thousands of small purplish blotches—hemorrhages.

"Locura," he muttered.

"My God, Basem. Your *eyes.*"

Hassan heard a groan to his left and turned. Lotta pushed herself up off the floor, tiny droplets of blood, blackened in the green glow, falling from her nose onto the inside of her face shield. Once upright, her expression contorted into a scowl.

"Everyone, take your prophylactics."

Hassan fumbled for his nebulizer—a canister containing a cocktail of sodium iodide and an anticoagulating agent, meant to mitigate the potential environmental effects of core failure, among other things. Pulmonary embolism, radiation poisoning, the bends. His fingers found the small metal cylinder and encircled it. He raised it to a port at the base of his face shield and pressed it into place, turning it clockwise. A fine aerosol sprayed into his suit, and as best as he could manage, he inhaled.

Lotta's eyes darted, searching until they fell on him.

"I thought you said the gravity well was contained to the Bell chamber. What the fuck do you call this?" She held up a hand to present the blood streaming down her face shield. "Only a second longer in that vacuum, and we'd have all boiled to death, or worse."

Behind her, a crumpled Fischer groaned. He propped himself upright, carrying a dazed expression. "Oy, is everyone okay?" A bloody aerosol sprayed from his lips. His speech sounded slurred. *Did he hit his head?*

"Hey, hey. Easy, pal." Mattheo approached Fischer from behind. "We are okay. You rest, take it slow, yeah?" He reached to assist him with his nebulizer.

"M'fine." Fischer batted him away and attempted to rise to his feet, but stumbled.

Mattheo reacted, extending a supportive arm. "*Easy.* Hey, do we have a medic?"

Everyone appeared conscious now, albeit in varying stages of shock. Lotta had now redirected her anger toward Anderson, who had jumped to Hassan's defense. A heated argument over who was at fault ensued.

Hassan pushed himself to his feet and faltered. Searing pain shot up his leg, his skull on the verge of exploding. He felt disconnected from reality, from himself. He mustered the strength to hobble to his desk, leaning hard against it. Around him, lab equipment littered the floor as though a bomb had gone off.

Then he saw his book splayed open on the floor with its cover facing up. He bent down and picked it up. Many of the pages were creased, some torn. For a moment, he forgot about the pain in his leg, the throbbing inside his head.

The absurdity of it all.

"Hey, you good?" Anderson came up beside him.

"Yeah, I think… just a sprain. Not broken."

Lotta said nothing, but Hassan sensed her stare. He felt compelled to say something, anything, to try and defuse the situation. He felt equally inclined to explode into his own rage-filled diatribe, but chose the high road.

"I don't… don't know what happened," he said, drinking in the air. He gently placed the book on the desk. "I scaled the algorithm up from the Planck scale, and in theory, the process is no different at the macro level. There is no reason the Schwarzschild radius should have exceeded the volume of the core."

"You didn't do *anything* wrong, mate." Anderson glared at Lotta, her cheeks flushed, black blood streaming from her nose, down her neck. Hassan knew her anger was misdirected. He was a convenient target. He didn't take it personally—such outbursts were rare, but came with the job.

Basem interjected. "We need to get out of here. We can worry about all this later, but right now, we need to evacuate."

Lotta looked around the room. "*Let's bloody go, then,*" she said, spraying blackened flecks against her face shield.

But before they started for the door, the backup generator kicked in, and the overhead lights flickered back to life. Computer screens glowed blue.

Athena's voice boomed over the comm.

"Welcome to the Commission of European Particle Physics: ALICE Laboratory at the Higgs Circular Collider, a subdivision of the European Interprovincial Research Organization, and the Federation's premier scientific research authority."

"She just rebooted," Hassan said. "Must have been knocked out when all this happened."

"Athena, give me a status report on ALICE," Lotta said. She was looking at the floor, hands on her hips.

"Of course, Dr. Eklund. Preliminary status: control room oxygen is eighty-five percent of optimal. Ambient temperature fifteen degrees Centigrade. Atmospheric pressure is zero-point-seven-six atm. Radiation levels are nominal. System diagnostic status pending. Chamber oxygen, temperature, atmospheric pressure, and radiation levels pending SAM analysis."

Still leaning against Mattheo, his breathing labored, Fischer chimed in. "Athena, we need a… preliminary report on the struc-tural… integrity of ALICE."

"Structural integrity status pending. Finite element analysis suggests decompression of the chamber is subthreshold for structural failure. SAM en route to begin comprehensive analysis. Estimated time of arrival: fifteen minutes and thirteen seconds."

"We need to get out of here," Basem said. "We can run all of this outside the facility once we've gotten back to the surface."

"Athena, outline an evac route from our location," Lotta said.

The comm remained silent.

"Athena, we need an evac."

Still no response.

"Athena…"

"Yes, Dr. Eklund?"

"*Chart* an *evacuation* from our *location.*" A tinge of urgency in her voice.

"I'm afraid I cannot do that at the moment, Dr. Eklund."

Hassan's heart sank. Everyone looked at each other.

"Why not?"

"Per CEPP emergency response protocol, ALICE is under a Phase Two quarantine. Rescue and Recovery will commence in Phase Three."

"How long have we been in Phase Two?"

"Since the power outage—two hours, eleven minutes ago."

"Two hours?" Basem said. "How is that possible? We ran the experiment less than a half-hour ago." He pointed to his watch, which read 14:45, a little over thirty minutes since they had fired into the Penrose core.

"Athena, what time is it?" Lotta asked.

"The time is 16:56."

"Time dilation," Anderson said. His eyes grew wide with the realization of what this meant. "A characteristic of traversing an event horizon relative to an outside observer."

Mattheo chimed in. "That wasn't the full force of the gravity well. We would have been pulled in if it was, regardless of the duration of exposure. The Bell chamber contained most of it, but we must have been exposed to a small fraction of its tidal forces—must have been just within the ergosphere." He looked around at the team, Fischer now resting on the floor beside him. "That was a close call."

"Are you saying the entanglement failed?" Lotta grunted. "That we were just exposed to a pure black hole?"

"I don't know what else would explain what just happened. The entanglement stabilizes the two singularities to form the throat of the wormhole. Whatever the *hell* just happened was anything but stable."

Hassan nodded. "If the throat of the wormhole fails to connect the ALICE and BOB gates the moment they are generated, then it would be unstable. I'll look at the Hadamard and CNOT gates in the computer's quantum circuit to try and zero in on the problem." His eyes darted left and right, envisioning the code in his head.

"You think they're corrupting the tensor product?" Anderson said.

The men fell into technical discussion, debating problems, potential fixes. Hassan lost himself in theory and had begun calculating integrals with Anderson when Lotta interrupted.

"*Just fix it,*" she said.

Hassan nodded with his hands on his hips. "I'll check the calculations, maybe start with the braid operators."

Lotta snapped. "How about you guys cut the Boolean circle jerk until we—"

"Ed! Whoa, come on, mate."

Hassan saw Mattheo guiding Fischer to the ground, his body limp. "Come on. Ed!"

"He just… just passed out," Mattheo said as he began removing Fischer's helmet. "Someone grab a crash cart. We need to find out what's wrong. Ed, stay with me."

In the muddy light, Fischer's face looked blue.

"Did he take his prophylactic?" Lotta said, her voice trembling.

"Yeah, yeah. Help me with him."

A red light blinked on the console's failsafe, and everyone turned except Mattheo. Anderson ran over and began pushing buttons, frantic.

"What is it now?" Lotta demanded.

"The system is ramping again, and I can't stop it. The collimation system, the magnets, nothing is responding. I'm locked out."

"It's restarting the sequence…." She turned to the others. "Put Ed's helmet back on. Now!"

Grinding and popping sounds filled the chamber, and the observation glass began to bow. A thin crack splintered at its base, began to creep upward. Out of Hassan's periphery, Lotta lunged for the activation key, but before she could reach it, everything was once again engulfed by light.

Again came the weightlessness, the blackness, the sensation of his body slamming to the floor.

The mind-numbing silence.

Then, cries for help. People strewn across the deck. Some moving. Some still.

The taste of blood.

Hassan rose to his knees, leaning back on his heels.

His gaze fell on Lotta.

"Everyone, take your prophylactics." She turned to him, blood streaming down her nose.

"I don't… I don't know what happened. I scaled the algor—"

Wait. I've said this before, been here before.

The same conversations repeated.

But with subtle differences:

Lotta raised her hand to interrupt. "There will be time to figure it out later. Let's worry about getting out of here."

A white flash.

Weightlessness.

Blackness.

Crash.

Bodies on the ground.

Blood on the tongue.

"Take your prophylactics."

| RUTH >

Camila Perez walked across acrylic tile to the 37°C incubator at the far end of the genetics lab. She opened the glass door and removed a vial of pink media—immunolabeling antiserum containing markers for cryptochrome 4, the receptor enabling birds to navigate using Earth's magnetic fields. Floating in the liquid were tissue samples, extracted retinal sections from the eyes of yet another spur-winged goose.

Perez set the vial onto the lab bench next to a test tube labeled *rabbit-anti-avian CRY4* and reached for a large flask containing an amber-colored liquid. She removed its seal and was immediately overcome by the smell of formaldehyde percolating through her mask. Before long, the entire lab would smell of it. Sometimes, it lingered for hours. Got into her clothes, her hair, her skin. She poured it out into a glass Petri dish and returned the flask to its place among the other reagents.

Her upper eyelid fluttered. An incessant twitching she had contended with all morning. She fought the urge to remove her goggles and rub it.

One more thing to add to the cramps, the bloating. La mierda de las nauseas mañaneras—the goddamned morning sickness.

"I'm a blimp," she had told Basem that morning before he left for work. He had stayed to hold back her hair while she emptied her guts into the toilet.

He had looked at her with those soft, kind eyes. Sad eyes. Tired eyes. "You're beautiful," he said with a half-smile. Kept the conversation at the surface, though they both knew why she was doubled-over and heaving. Wore it on their faces.

He seemed distracted, had forgotten his shemagh by the door on his way out. She decided to wear it to the lab because it smelled like him. She preferred to push the tension down. Avoid it. Act like everything was okay. She convinced herself it would be selfish not to. After all, today was Basem's big day, the first live animal trial at ALICE. She wondered how things were going down there for him, even if he hadn't been able to tell her much about the experiments.

To be fair, she hadn't filled him in on her altercation with Lotta. It was another point of contention, one she didn't like mentioning. Figured she didn't want Basem caught in the middle, even if she knew it was something he would have wanted to know about.

The reality was she had no idea what was causing the anomalies inside the ARC. The avian deaths. The tremors.

She and Basem hadn't spoken much anyway since she revealed the pregnancy and what she intended to do. Maybe he thought he was giving her space. Instead, she felt alone, guilty, alienated. Could see that he was torn up inside. But in his anguish, he failed to acknowledge what it was doing to *her*. Even if just to say it, that he heard her. Saw her. He was too wrapped up inside himself, and she resented that. A rift had formed between them almost overnight, one she did not know how to bridge.

She pulled out her holosleeve and began an encrypted message to him.

I love you.

Her thumb hovered over "send" for what felt like an eternity. Trembling, she instead deleted the words and tossed the device onto the lab bench.

Reception down there is horrible, anyway.

She pushed it from her mind, turned her attention back to her work.

There's always later.

Once the specimen was fixed, she placed it into a sucrose preparation, then walked to the minus-eighty freezer to store it for cryosectioning. She removed another sample that Nedjma had prepared and sectioned the week prior, then returned to the bench.

Placing one of the slices onto the slide, she pipetted a small amount of solution from the test tube onto it and placed it on the microscope stage. Positioning the oculars, she clicked a 10X objective into place and brought down the coarse focus knob.

When she turned the power on, the effect was immediate. She was astonished, almost blinded, by the intensity of the labelling antibodies—her entire field of view lit up in a nebula of neon green fluorescence.

30X mag.

Ignoring a momentary resurgence of fluttering, she adjusted the fine focus. A constellation of pinpoint dots came into sharp relief.

"Madre mía…"

The level of CRY4 expression far exceeded anything she had ever seen—further evidence the magnetic field anomaly impacted avian physiology. But it still didn't explain *why* they were flying erratically, becoming disoriented. There was something else, something she was missing.

The magnetic field anomalies had only gotten worse since she met with Lotta.

EIRO had yet to circle back on the status of the investigation.

Meanwhile, more birds were dying, and she was no closer to the truth. Just chasing her tail with necropsies and molecular studies that all told the same incomplete story.

She was stuck.

She lifted the next sample, and out of the corner of her eye, she thought she saw the test tube reagent shimmer. Giving in, she removed a glove and rubbed her eye, dismissing it as an artifact. An apparition caused by another twitch. She dipped her pipette into the sample and reached for another reagent. Again, another shimmer, all the liquids, this time more pronounced.

Then a distant rumble.

More tremors.

The effect continued every few minutes. A sensation far subtler than the tremors she was accustomed to.

A light flickered off and on overhead.

She scanned her surroundings.

Nothing.

Perez stood from her chair and reached for a fresh box of pipette tips in the overhead cabinet. As she rose to her feet, her stomach turned. She doubled over, hand gripping the chair's armrest, overcome with vertigo. Pressure mounted in the back of her throat. She began to gag.

Not again. Not now.

She bolted into the hallway, hoping she could make it to the women's room in time.

Once more, she found herself falling to her knees on hard tile, retching over porcelain, her inner voice pleading with her limbic system to make it all stop. And then it came—the apogee, a full-forced projection of bitter-tasting bile.

One round, two rounds, three.

Finally, the contractions subsided. Exhausted and shaking, she slumped to the floor, back against the wall, tears streaming down her face. She waited for the next round of nausea to steal over her.

It always comes again. Always within minutes of the first.

The smell of vomit in her hair. Tongue burning. She sat, wide-eyed, lucid, as she stared at the grout lines in the floor tile. She dared not move her head for fear of triggering a fourth round.

Her mind went back to the moment she told Basem she was pregnant. Replayed it for the millionth time. Racked her brain about all the things she wished she'd said, had yet to say. Fixated on words that she knew cut deep, that should never have left her lips.

A warmth filled her palms, and she realized she had been cradling her abdomen. It struck her as odd, something she'd never done before. *An instinct?* She thought of the concept, how strange life was. The beauty, the brutality. The lack of justice.

She already had a plan—one she kept from Basem because it had the potential to implicate him. But one that he must have suspected nonetheless.

One that was dangerous.

It involved stealing from ARC's animal pharmacy cache. *Misoprostol,* a drug administered to animals for stomach ulcers. It couldn't be given to those that were pregnant because it would induce labor prematurely, leading to miscarriage. She could take a couple doses and terminate the pregnancy.

No one would ever know.

All she needed to do was log it for some made-up veterinary application. A baboon with intractable emesis, perhaps.

Easy enough.

Easy in principle.

But was it? Getting the pills, sure. But taking them? Could she go through with it?

Her hands trembled, head shaking reflexively at the bitter taste on her tongue. Her stomach hurt, her breasts hurt. Joints. Back. Everything railed in protest to even the subtlest of movements.

She propped herself up and rested her hands on her stomach.

No justice.

"Just so you know," she whispered. It felt silly, like she was talking to herself. "Just so you know, Hija…" She paused, choking back an unexpected flurry of emotion. "I am so sorry. I would've *loved* to have been your mamá." And then the tears came, an outpouring of grief.

Of sorrow.

Of regret.

She sobbed, wept harder than she had in years. Felt so alone.

She wasn't sure how she knew, but she was certain it was a girl—*a little chavalita.*

"*Ruth,*" she whispered. "Your name is Ruth."

What kind of monster am I?

No longer able to keep her doubts at bay, she surrendered. Opened the levies and allowed the walls to burst. All the while, welcoming the sting of tears on her cheeks, her lips. The most of anything she had felt in weeks. A spark, a fire.

Maybe I can do this. Maybe Basem is right. We can say it was somatic cell transfer—a clone.

No father.

Maybe another two months, and she would start to show. Maybe she had time. Time to slow down. To think it through a little longer.

You're bargaining. It will never work. Nothing will. You can't have this baby.

The cynic in her returned. Reared its ugly head. Consumed her in shadow. She thought back to something her mother had once said: "Camilita mía, one day you will have children of your own, but you need to be careful. You need to do it right. They can take everything away from you."

This wasn't supposed to happen. I wasn't supposed to be able to get pregnant.

Yet here she was.

The lights flickered. Then came the rattling of the door handle. Perez wiped her eyes and looked around.

Tremors again.

What came next almost rendered her unconscious. A shuddering jolt that wrenched her forward, slamming her into the door. The sound of vomit sloshing in the toilet bowl almost roused another wave of nausea, but she swallowed hard against the lump in her throat, pushed it down.

She inhaled slowly. Counted to three. Exhaled.

The room started to spin.

14:45

When the tremors faded again, it stayed calm for another few minutes. But the vertigo remained. When the rumbling did return, it was so subtle that she thought she might be imagining it, or perhaps it was her nerves. But the sensation grew until it could be heard, could be felt, like thunder through her bones. Everything rattled. The walls groaned and popped. The ground jolted, tossing her body across the floor like a rag doll.

It sounded as though everything was crashing down around her.

I am going to die here. In a washroom. Covered in vomit.

Perez did the only thing she could. She wrapped her hands around her head, tucked herself into a fetal position, and prayed.

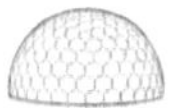

By the time Perez heard the sirens, the shaking had ceased. Disoriented and trembling, she opened her eyes to examine her surroundings. The walls still stood. The floor hadn't fractured to swallow her into the earth. The building held.

The domes and their sectors had been designed to withstand extreme events like this.

But it was the *sounds* that prevented a reprieve from the gnashing jaws of trepidation at her throat—omnipresent moaning and creaking in the walls. The entirety of the ARC, oscillating in the throes of some acute affliction imposed upon it by an unseen force.

I need to get out.

She scrambled to her feet, heart racing. Everything spinning. The creaking, the sirens. A flurry of frantic voices out in the main corridor. Her mind immediately went to Nedjma—*she's still inside the ARC. Alone. Probably afraid.*

When she stumbled back into the corridor, a frenetic scene unfolded. Sunlight filtered in through plumes of kicked-up particulate, and the trill of alarms filled her ears. Most of the glass doors leading to other sectors were blown out. Glass crunched underfoot. Various items lay strewn across the concrete floor—name badges, holosleeves, a toppled cart that had been carrying potted plants.

Panicked employees were fleeing, others tending to injured colleagues. One woman wandered aimlessly. She had a large gash across her forehead, her face shimmering red, clothing caked with dust and blood. She moved through the haze like a specter amid a flurry of white coats running past.

Basem's words from the other day came to Perez.

Locura. Chaos.

And that was when she stopped cold.

Basem.

A nagging sense that something had caused this overcame her, that ALICE was at the center of it. Something had gone wrong down there; this was a mere symptom. The thought seemed absurd, a stretch, but it was one she could not shake.

What if it's not over?

She scrambled past the turmoil and confusion, back toward the lab. She needed to get to her holosleeve and reach him, needed to know he was okay, that she was overanalyzing. That there was no link to the ALICE experiments, and this was all just some freak occurrence of nature.

That Lotta had been right, and she had been wrong.

That this isn't another Geneva.

The lab looked like a bomb had gone off—her reagents had toppled and were now pooling on the bench, seeping to the floor. The smell of formaldehyde stung her nostrils. Shattered beakers and flasks covered her workstation. The microscope had toppled over and fallen onto the chair, which now lay on its side. Pinned beneath it, her lab coat was saturated in pink Tris buffer.

On the far end of the lab, the latch to the minus-eighty freezer had snapped and the door had flung open. Countless tissue and DNA samples—entire generations of priceless cell lines, years of data and research—gone in a matter of minutes.

She walked to the bench. Her holosleeve had migrated to the other end. She picked it up, relieved to find it still functioned. There were two missed calls and a text message from Nedjma.

Nothing from Basem.

She opened the first voice message, which had been left ten minutes prior. Nedjma sounded frightened but okay. She was on her way back to Sector C from inside the dome.

Perez could not shake Basem from her mind. But it had to wait. She dialed Nedjma. All the while, the last thing she had said to Basem played on repeat in her head. Something she had uttered on his way out the door that morning.

Don't forget to stop and pick up drinking water.

It was regular. Mundane. Inconsequential. Not "I love you," not "I can't wait to see you."

Don't forget to stop and pick up drinking water.
Don't forget to stop and pick up drinking water.
Shut up. Shut up. Shut up.

"Hello?" Nedjma's voice cut through the one in her head. "Cam?"

"Nedjma, where are you?"

"I'm in the dome. I can't get into the decon chamber... everything is locked down."

"Okay, just stay put. I will come to you."

How, she didn't know. She hung up and headed back toward the corridor.

15:12

On her way to the decontamination chamber, Perez stopped at the vestibule situated at Sector C's entrance and peered out across the desert. A low-lying dust cloud sat along the surface like fog for as far as she could see.

To the west, Shin Tower rose above the haze into clear blue sky. Toward the northwest, EDEN's carapace was also still visible.

She walked outside to get a better look.

The dust outside possessed an earthy smell, a tinge of sulfur. It stung her eyes, her throat. Soon, she was coughing uncontrollably.

She had turned to retreat to the relative safety of the building when she heard a distant scraping sound. She could not tell from where, only that it was quickly growing louder. Harsher. A horrible screeching and grinding. It seemed to be all around her.

A loud crash erupted to her right. The ground shuddered, sending her staggering backward. Sand sprayed in all directions, forcing her to shield her face from an explosion of stinging granules. Little projectile daggers piercing her skin.

She opened her eyes. One of the dome's hex panels loomed before her, standing upright in the sand, two stories high. Mottled sunlight danced along its edges as it listed toward the open desert and slammed into the sand with a deafening *crunch*, ejecting a billowing dust cloud.

In the distance, toward the dome's northern perimeter, she heard another panel sliding down the dome's carapace. And another.

Panels falling.

Perez got to her feet and dialed Nedjma.

"Cam? I think the perimeter is breached. It's so loud in here."

"Nedjma, listen to me. I need you to take cover. It's the pressure system; I think the quake compromised it. When it's safe to do so, I need you to initiate the containment and recovery protocol."

"I'm on it. Where are you?"

"Outside. I'm going to try and get a better look. I'll head your way soon—I'll track your location."

Perez ended the call. Coughing, she stumbled into an open stretch of desert. She wanted to get a better view of the damage to the dome's structure. At a little over a hundred meters, she turned back and looked up at the looming giant. She huffed against the turbid air as if she had walked a long way, but looking at the dome, it was almost like she hadn't really gone far at all. She had gained enough perspective to make out much of the westward side. She counted around half a dozen panels missing.

At that moment, something inside her snapped. She felt broken, defeated. Tears stinging her cheeks, throat aching with dust, she fell to her knees. Her life's work, her animals, *her entire purpose*, shattered within minutes.

Once again in the throes of grief, Perez didn't notice the sand shifting around her. It was only when she opened her eyes to look back at the dome, shocked to find it obscured behind a wall of brown dust, that she recognized it was happening again. Another aftershock.

The sand jostled and hissed beneath her. More panels slid and crashed to the ground. There was nowhere for her to go. Sand churned, rippling like water at her knees. Over the roaring desert, she heard a deafening, high-pitched screech—the sound of a dome's graphene scaffolding giving way.

"*No.*"

Perez turned toward the sound, watching in horror as EDEN's immense carapace buckled in the distance, collapsing in on itself as though the Earth had opened beneath it. The entire structure pitched down, sinking beneath the dust. An enormous brown cloud surged skyward, swelling until the entirety of the dome was engulfed in a billowing plume that went on to swallow the sun.

Perez choked, pulling her lab smocks over her nose and mouth as she slid beneath the sand. She tried to rise to her feet, only to be tossed onto her back. The dust was so thick she couldn't see her own limbs thrashing about. The loud rumbling in her ears was superseded only by EDEN's twisting and cracking frame.

She felt her legs being pulled downward, then her hips. The sand pressed in against her chest, besieging her lungs. Before long, she was up to her neck, choking for air. Scalded by the sunbaked morass, her scorched skin screaming with pain.

She tried to call for help, but there was no air left in her lungs. Her mind raced, desperate for a way out. Her entire nervous system wailed in protest, urging her into fight or flight, but it was no use. She was trapped.

And then came the calm, almost dream-like. The scent of coffee. Basem's eyes. A feeling of pure bliss.

Everything stopped.

Perez opened her eyes. Coughed against a toxic mire. Mustered what strength she had left to pull herself out up to her stomach, retching, lungs rattling, sucking in the air with little regard for the brown slurry she wasn't sure was even air. She had to get back inside before another aftershock came. Had to get to Nedjma.

In the distance, she could hear pieces of EDEN's edifice crumbling. Sirens blaring. It didn't seem real, didn't seem possible.

The dust thinned. The faint outline of the ARC came into view. From it, a spur-winged goose took to the open sky.

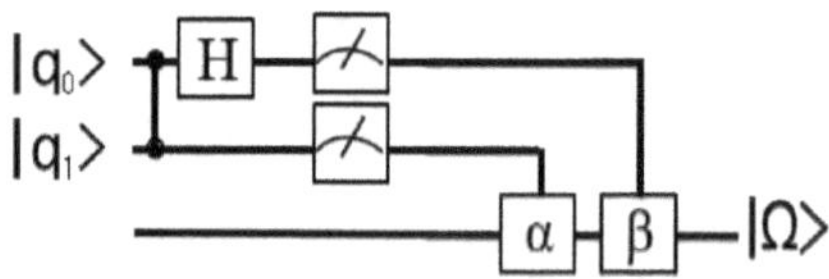

FIFTH POSTULATE

The act of measurement on the system collapses the wave function.

|RABBIT HOLE >

Lotta was around nine when she started questioning the rituals. It marked the beginning of her doubt in paganism, in religion. She began to ask herself if anyone out there—the gods, the fae, anyone at all—was really listening.

Or maybe she had missed something. Some clue. Some natural insight absent, rendering her defective.

One day had always stood out as an inflection point in her fall from grace. A single data point of a troubled childhood. She found it easy to return to it, sense it. The steady, light rain. The bulk of the hand-woven poncho Sofia had made when times were good.

That afternoon, she had followed her mother through a small grove, her rain boots squishing in the saturated peat. They walked for almost an hour, it seemed. The air hummed with electricity and the sweet, static smell of fresh rain. It pattered the leaves overhead, distracted her, made her nervous.

She much preferred the indoors.

After some time, they emerged into a clearing where a moss-covered boulder jutted from a field of cloves. A sun-bleached deadfall leaned against it. A white warden, its limbs gnarled and fractured.

Sofia approached it and spoke. "We're here." From beneath her poncho, she procured a woven sack carrying items for the ritual. Settling to her knees, she pulled out a bottle of amber mead and turned to her daughter. "*Kneel.*"

"But it's wet, Mamma."

Water streamed down Lotta's poncho, her skin clammy and cold, strands of hair plastered against her cheeks.

Sofia continued removing items one at a time—a rune tablet, a blade, a wooden offering mug—and laying them out before of her. "You'll know pain if you do not show the vættir *respect,*" she said in a low voice. "Now, kneel and prepare your offering."

Lotta, pouting, objected. "Blót is for the gods. I want to offer to *Freyja.*"

"Careful, child. Land spirits are ev'ry bit as entitled to offerings as the Æsir." Sofia's speech began to slur. She had been swigging the mead throughout their walk, a habit she had adopted ever since Pappa stopped coming with them to blót.

"I thought you said vættir are *wights.*"

A deep sigh. "They're one an' the same. Now, kneel. I'll not say it again. I bloody won't."

Abiding Sofia's request, Lotta produced an apple and a cluster of white May lily she had picked that morning. She got to her knees and placed the offering in front of her.

Facing the boulder, eyes closed, Sofia raised her hands and spoke. "We are summoning the skogvættir, masters of this wood, seeking protection over this land. May you drive the jötnar from our borders. We bring you this offering in Odin's name."

She bent down and picked up the tablet. A rune was etched into its surface:

Lotta did not know much about the Elder Futhark at that age, but this one she recognized. *Thurisaz.* It meant "giant." *Bringer of misfortune and despair.* A physical representation symbolizing the jötnar, the enemy,

Russia's military machine. Sofia in constant alarm, frightening Lotta. That day, she spoke of the Russki subs in the Baltic Sea, some as far north as Bottenviken.[1]

Picking up the blade, Sofia scraped the tablet over the mug such that the filings fell in. She filled it to the brim with mead, presented it skyward, then placed it at the base of the boulder.

She turned to Lotta. "Put your offering into the blót."

Afraid, Lotta followed her mother's instructions. She did not want to upset the vættir, envisioning them as shapeshifters, indistinguishable from their surroundings. In isolation, she imagined amorphous shadow creatures. Sometimes man. Sometimes beast.

The sweetness in the air grew. First, her nostrils burned, then her throat, and finally, her lungs.

Ozone.

The boulder, the forest, everything fell away as Lotta came to, sprawled on her back against a hard corrugated surface. No longer that little girl, she opened her eyes and peered into blackness.

Her body screamed, relegated to a renewed sense of agony, as if by immolation. She rasped in shallow breaths, the static smell intensifying, somehow penetrating the walls of her suit.

She ran her fingers across her face shield. A gentle trickle of air seeped through a crack running down the middle.

A leak.

Suit still pressurized.

Oxygen still flowing.

You're okay, you're still breathing.

Heaving against sore ribs, the suffocating compression sleeve like a boa constrictor around her chest, she felt around, trying to get her bearings. Despite the mental fog, despite the darkness in which she found herself, Lotta already had a sense of her surroundings.

The only ozone generated in the lab came from the core—*inside* the Bell chamber.

I'm in the Cathedral.

---

1 The Gulf of Bothnia

She could still hear the pattering of rain, but not overhead—something trickling instead to the chamber floor below.

How did I get in here? Was there a breach? Did the barrier wall fail?

She did not remember the moment it happened, her body being wrenched toward a second singularity. But something stopped it, because here she was—picking herself up off the ground once more. Bruised and bloodied, but alive.

No gravitational anomaly this time.

She thought for a moment. Perhaps her limbs *did* feel a little heavy. No more than a mere blip of the subconscious. She glanced at her HUD's accelerometer display, but it was out. No frequency shift data. No doppler. Nothing but a primal whirring within her subconscious telling her that something was ever so slightly amiss. Her orientation, muddled. A rough but potent intuition that her position in space felt off. *Almost normal.* Her equilibrium perturbed as if on the verge of drunkenness. As if the gravitational constant had *shifted.*

Impossible.

After all, it was a *constant.* An elementary principle of the laws of physics. *Unmoving, unchanging. Until now.* But only a nudge of the needle. Not even a Planck length. Unquantifiable, certainly not enough to tear her and her colleagues to shreds, but enough to generate an internal stir. Background noise in the cosmic foam, but still elevated above the basal static.

Or maybe she'd just hit her head. Rattled her brain.

Her thoughts were interrupted by the sensation of the hair standing on her skin. She thought back to her visit with Perez in the domes, how everything she had told her was a lie.

Something moved on the landing beside her. She heard a groan.

"Ed? Ed, is that you?"

"Yeah…"

Behind him, Hassan inhaled sharply, coughing and sputtering. It took a few minutes to adapt to the dark before she recognized the familiar shapes of her colleagues clambering back to their feet.

Hassan placed a hand on Fischer's back, his voice trembling. "Ed, you're… you're okay? You were *dying.* I saw you, saw you—"

Fischer chuckled between coughs. "Must've been another Ed Fischer."

"But you were—you passed out. Your face, it was so *blue*."

"Oy. Don't be ridiculous. Said I'm fine. Feels like I was rolled over by a freighter, though."

Lotta's head throbbed. Every joint, every muscle trembling, aching.

"Everyone, take your prophylactics," she said. *Deja vu.* Her voice hoarse, a sour taste at the back of her tongue. It hurt to speak. Hurt to breathe.

Hassan turned toward her. "And you have repeated that more times now than I can count."

Lotta ignored this. It wasn't relevant. They needed to get their bearings, regroup, and reestablish protocol.

She felt her way to the railing and started toward the observation deck's barrier wall to try to find the point of failure. A quick assessment revealed no apparent breach, no hole, no defect. The wall hadn't failed; she hadn't been *pulled* through.

So how did we end up on the other side?

Her head swiveled, counting bodies, processing the situation. She counted again.

Someone is missing.

"Where's Mattheo?"

No answer. Everyone else looked around.

Lotta turned and walked a little farther to the other end, her feet falling heavy against metal. The trickling sound grew. She perceived a dull pulsing light from above, but it was too far away to discern its source. It intensified gradually as she proceeded toward the sound until a faint crimson glow bloomed over her, growing then fading, cycling between dull luminescence and total darkness.

She took another step, holding fast to the railing, and peered through the hematic scintillation. Toward the chamber's center, the Penrose core stood solitary, plumes of red-tinged nitrogen billowing from its base. A towering blood moon, silent and foreboding.

Lotta's glove grazed something thick and runny. The light came to another crescendo, and the landing in front of her came back into view. She stopped cold.

Pressure mounted in her chest, coinciding with a high-pitched ringing in her ears. The sour taste intensified on her tongue.

In the middle of the catwalk, a blackened mass—viscous, organic in nature—seeped in a thick stream through the grating to the chamber floor below. Bits of what appeared to be clothing and plastic caught the light, glistening red amid the carnage strewn like wet confetti across the walkway. Among the pieces of plastic was part of a photograph—the corner of a mouth curled into a smile—*Mattheo's name badge.*

"Ma—Matheo. He's… he's…"

Lotta could not look away. Nothing about what she saw was recognizable, only hints of a biological form. A biofilm, perhaps. Certainly not a person. Rubbery bits of suit, metal shards from an oxygen generator, and what appeared to be fragments of bone or teeth embedded in the bloody pulp sprayed across the landing.

How? How?

The pressure intensified, rising in her throat, settling at the back of her tongue. She thought she might vomit. The slow thrum of light slowed, and with a *thud*, her knees pounded into the grating.

"Lotta!" A voice behind her, then hurried footsteps, but she could not answer. Could not speak against the vice around her neck. Couldn't breathe.

Hands clasped her shoulders from behind. Fischer's voice came through muffled, distant.

"Hey, *hey*. Are you alright? What happened?"

His grip loosened. She sensed it, sensed his shock, knew he saw it now too.

Her lungs rattled in her chest as she tried to stand.

"Hey, easy." Fischer's hands were on her again. "Jesus Christ, what the fuck is that? Okay, we need to go. C'mon."

His arm encircled her waist, the other hand clasping her wrist, draping her arm over his shoulders. Felt her weight against him as he pulled her to her feet, as he guided her back the way they came.

Away from the pulsing light.

A dark figure approached. "Is she okay?" It was Anderson.

"Yeah. Yeah, just needs to rest for a minute. We need to find a way out. Now."

"Where's Mattheo?"

"Didn't make it."

"What? What the hell do you mean, he didn't *make* it?"

"I mean he bloody didn't make it, and we need to *go*."

"Mattheo!"

Fischer grabbed Anderson by the shoulders, squared up to him. "*I told you. He is bloody dead, mate.*" Anderson tried to pull free, to look away, but Fischer held firm. "If you've any decency, you'll not go anywhere near that end of the landing."

"Don't *fucking* tell *me*—"

"Hey." Hassan stepped in. "Hey, stop. He's right. We cannot stay. We will send a team back for him, Martin. We need to go."

"Yeah? And where are we going to go? We're 500 meters underground."

"The funicular," Hassan said. "Its backup power is linked to a battery system shielded from electromagnetic insult. All we need to do is activate it."

"The *what?*" Basem said.

"The lift we use to get freight in and out of the chamber. Just on the far end, at the main level, beyond the core."

"Okay, so how do we activate it?"

"We have to prime it manually. There is a charging bay we can access below. After that, it's as simple as switching the breaker on. Should take us straight to the surface."

Everyone fell silent. They had all turned, looking to Lotta. This was her call. Her compression sleeve relaxed around her arms and legs, her torso.

Chamber's pressure is normalizing.

With a sigh, she conceded. "We'll take the freight elevator."

Fuck protocol.

Hassan nodded. "I'll go. I know the system."

"Comms are down, but your suit's distress beacon should still work," Fischer said.

Hassan nodded. "If anything happens, I will activate it. Otherwise, expect to see me back in, oh, twenty minutes."

"I'm coming with you," Anderson said, "to keep you on task."

Fischer approached the other two. "Okay, we need to couple our beacons so we can ping you in case we don't hear from you." He pressed in on his wrist. A moment later, Hassan's comm let out a loud chime that reverberated through the stacked landings and decayed into the void above.

"It works," Anderson said.

"Aye." Fischer turned to him and repeated the process. Another chime screeched through the chamber.

Anderson, a good hand's width shorter, looked up at Fischer. "And if we do this, what about Mattheo?"

"Like Hassan said, we'll come back for him."

"It's been thirty minutes." Basem's pacing only made Lotta more nervous, his footsteps clanking loud against the walkway's grating. On the other hand, it masked the incessant dripping noises. She tried to take her mind off Mattheo.

"Aye," Fischer said.

Before he had a chance to activate the call button, a soft chime came from the far end of the chamber, in the direction of the freight elevator.

Basem stopped. "You guys hear that?"

Fischer nodded. "Came from the lift. Wasn't me."

Lotta's throat burned. Her heart tore at her chest. "Can you tell whose beacon that was?"

"I-I don't know. I can try and ping Hassan first." Fischer pressed in on his wrist, but they heard no response. He pressed again, still nothing. "Can't seem to reach him."

"Wait, then where is he?"

The chime came again.

"That has to be Martin," Fischer said.

Fuck. Lotta threw her weight against the railing and leaned over, trying to see the chamber floor below. "Hassan! Martin!" Her voice cracking, throat raw, coated in bile, tinged with the bitter taste of iodine. "Hassan!" She turned to Fischer. "Something is wrong. We need to go to them."

"We don't know the situation. We'd be going in blind."

He was right.

In her frantic state, Lotta felt oddly aware of the dim pulse of the light at the far end of the landing. What lay there, what she had seen. The image of Mattheo burned into her consciousness, no matter how hard she tried to distract herself from it.

Did Hassan and Martin meet a similar fate?

Her mind ran wild. She couldn't contain it, the images evolving into horrific scenes, her colleagues turned inside out, atomized into their constituent parts.

The pulsing light seemed to slow in its rhythm, periods of light and dark now prolonged. Slowing further still.

Anderson's chime again.

"We don't know the situation. We can't just go in blind."

"I know. You said that already."

"Said what?"

The static in her ears rose and fell with the light. A waveform. Rising and falling. Rising and falling. It slowed to the point that the noise and the light seemed constant, blooming into a brilliant effulgence, slowing further until the entire visible spectrum split into its constituent parts—a kaleidoscope of filamentous reds, greens, blues, yellows—undulating strings stretching and snapping free all around her, the pitch of the static now a low rumble in her bones.

She turned to Fischer. His face transformed with the colored light, his demeanor fixed, unmoving. His eyelids crept downward as if entering sleep, then rose again just as slowly. A sluggish blink. And then another.

The others also appeared to be in a suspended state, trapped within a sort of stasis.

What is happening?

Anderson's chime.

The light dissipated, returned to a dull, red glow. Fischer now nothing more than a shadow, his movements, those of the others, regular again.

But the static remained. A constant rumbling inside her.

Do the others not hear this?

Fischer again: "We don't know the situation. We can't just go in blind."

Déjà vu.

Anderson's chime. Slower this time.

"Do you hear that?" Lotta said. The static came in harsh bursts now, a square wave of strobing crunches grinding inside her skull.

"Hear what?"

Then she noticed it. A strong smell hanging in the air, like that of kerosene.

A loud thud filled the Cathedral. Something had fallen weightily to the metallic floor below. Fischer snapped his head in sync with Lotta's. She strained herself, leaning over the railing once more, listening for any sign of Hassan or Anderson.

Another sound, more subtle. Something scratching metal.

"Tell me you're hearing *this*," she said. Her eyes darted aimlessly about toward the source, but all she could make out was the looming silhouette of the core. The faint, almost imperceptible pulse of red light on the far end of the landing. She yelled out. "*Martin?*"

Fischer grabbed her wrist. "Something's off," he whispered.

He pressed the call button again. Another chime came from the direction of the scratching sounds. Then, she heard another sound—much like the radio tone, but cavernous.

Fischer turned and faced Lotta, still gripping her wrist, his hand trembling. "I didn't press it that time."

The chime came again, closer. It possessed an unsettling *gurgling* quality. *A malfunction? An echo?*

Static still in her ears, disorienting her. She wanted to scream out again, but she knew Fischer had been right. Something *was* off.

She didn't want to be in charge. Didn't want to call the shots anymore.

The light changed again, this time *increasing* in frequency, shifting across the color spectrum. The taste of electricity was on her tongue, varying in intensity with each color, a dizzying strobe of variegated hues. They bled and bloomed into one another until all she could see was white; the static flavor now a constant tingling sensation that coated her palate. The sweet smell of ozone once again percolated through her suit's defenses; tiny electrical shocks coursed along her skin.

A warmth washed over her, a strange calm.

This time, the others took notice.

The static in Lotta's ears had also changed, morphing into a painful screech. Eyes squeezed tight, she clamped her hands over the sides of her helmet, trying to press in against her ears. A hand grazed her shoulder, and the sound stopped. Her eyes opened, blinded momentarily by alabaster.

She turned to Fischer, the others. Could see Basem's mouth moving. He seemed to be shouting, but she could not hear over the turbulent static. Realizing this, he pointed, eyes wide, toward the observation deck.

Lotta turned.

Through the barrier glass, she saw a suited figure standing solitary, watching the core, seemingly oblivious to their presence.

As if they were ghosts.

It was *her*.

Streams of blue passed behind this doppelgänger, and she realized they were *people*. Versions of the ALICE crew in their suits, darting in and out at impossible speeds. It was like watching a film at high speed, set to a long exposure, their forms little more than bright blue streamers weaving about. But this other version of her, this impossible presence, remained still, unwavering, staring at the core from her perch.

My perch.

The howling in Lotta's ears morphed into something recognizable, a vibrating hum she had only heard from inside the observation deck—*the Higgs collider.*

She turned back to behold the monstrous core, now aglow, its carapace flowing, undulating and shimmering like hot oil. Along its circumference, light began to smear, encircling it. The entire chamber now warped into a non-Euclidean representation of reality. Straight landings, linear surfaces bending into parabolic distortions of what she had known.

Every physical law shattered. In an instant, her understanding of the universe was cast in doubt.

I shouldn't be here. Should be boiling alive, crushed into atoms, deconstructed.

Anderson's chime cut through the scream of the Higgs. This time, it had come from the base of the core.

Fischer placed his hands on the railing and peered over the edge, down to the chamber floor. Lotta felt a renewed sense of calm and, as if by impulse, she found herself joining him.

Toward the base of the core, through the searing white, a silhouetted figure began to take shape.

"Anderson?" Fischer shouted. The words came out garbled and broken, like listening through a corrupted comms signal.

The figure reacted, moved, its form distorted. As it did, Lotta could decipher some of its qualities. The first thing she noticed was its size, which was far greater than that of a person—she estimated it to be over two meters in height, and three to four in length, half of which appeared to be a horizontal tail or appendage. Its body rested atop two legs, shifting and smearing amid the churning space. From its front end, what appeared to be its head, there dangled a long mass terminating in two appendages that nearly reached the ground. It moved, its form amorphous, changing. It swung to one side, and that was when Lotta caught a fleeting glimpse of something that sent the bile rushing into her mouth.

Legs. Human legs.

Fischer pressed Anderson's call button. The chime echoed throughout the chamber.

It—*the thing*—had Anderson.

Then there was another sound, similar, but muffled and gurgling. It was *mimicking* Anderson's call signal.

The little girl inside Lotta thought back to images of the vættir. Her knees buckled; her nostrils burned with the scent of ozone. She was nine again. Trembling, afraid.

"Basem? What is it?" Fischer screamed over the howling collider.

"*I-I don't know.*"

Lotta's feet grew heavy. In the core, a scene began to coalesce, too distorted for her to decipher. At its center, a swirling nimbus shimmered across a blue backdrop.

It looked like moonlight.

And then, nothing.

THREE

"'And I saw Sisyphus at his endless task raising his prodigious stone with both his hands.... he tried to roll it up to the top of the mountain, but always, just before he could roll it over on to the other side, its weight would be too much for him, and the pitiless stone would come thundering down again on to the plain. Then he would begin trying to push it up the mountain again, and the sweat ran off him and the steam rose after him.'"

—Adapted from *The Odyssey,* Book XI

"Each atom of that stone, each mineral flake of that night filled mountain, in itself forms a world. The struggle itself toward the heights is enough to fill a man's heart. One must imagine Sisyphus happy."

—Albert Camus, *The Myth of Sisyphus*

< ᚠ | DECOHERENCE >

A gentle breeze on the skin, filling the sinuses—musty, humid.

    A scent of pine?

    Respirator torn free. Lungs rattling, taking in the unfamiliar.

The sound of trees, like back home on the coast, whispered in the wind. Speckled rays of sunlight bled through a latticed canopy overhead.

    But still dark. Mostly dark.

Hassan tried to turn his head, to get a better look at his surroundings. The signal was sent. He willed it, every synapse between cortex and striated muscle, firing in unison, commanding momentum. Demanding it. *Begging.* But nothing. No response, not so much as a flinch.

He couldn't move.

The last thing he remembered was priming the power to the freight elevator, then something taking Anderson. *Martin…* A blinding light. The deafening howl of the Higgs through a barrage of static…

    Need to activate my beacon.

The air seemed heavy yet dilute. Beads of sweat coalesced on his skin, ran down his face into his mouth, jaw hanging slack. The taste of salt on his tongue, trickling down his throat. A sputter, a gag. He tried to close his mouth, tried to swallow, clench his teeth. Anything to temporarily allay his desiccated tongue, to ease his tortured, raw throat. Screaming inside his own head, aching for water. But it was no use.

He was paralyzed.

With each breath, Hassan heard a sticky rattling, a sort of crepitus inside his heaving chest. Only it didn't sound like it came from within. That was when the warmth spread over him, swelling into a terrible inferno that blazed through his lungs. He wanted to look down. Wanted to see, but his gaze remained on the dappled sunlight creeping past the trickling shadows.

Hassan tried to swallow again, began to gag. Produced a horrible gurgling sound he could not be sure was his own. His mind raced, images of himself splayed out, ripped open. Inert, nothing more than a husk, screaming to escape.

As he looked around, he realized he had no vision in his right eye. Something protruded from it, long and slender, adorned with pink fruiting bodies. *A tree branch?* His first thought was that maybe he had fallen from high up, had become impaled in the branches of a tree. How he got here didn't matter. Not anymore.

Something inside him shifted. With the mounting fire in his chest, a pain like nothing he had ever experienced, he started to pray it would all end soon.

Allahu Akbar. Qul a'oodhu bi rabbil-falaq. I seek refuge in the lord of the dawn.

Fear gripped him, his pulse throbbing in his temples. An ear-shattering ringing besieged him—the oscillating hum of the Higgs. He wished it would stop.

Allahu Akbar.

Banded fronds of a cycad swayed overhead, a momentary distraction—the tree he had landed in. His tomb. Its leaves were peculiar—not green like the surrounding brush, but deep crimson. The color of blood. Something about their gentle sway brought him an unexpected calm, even euphoria. Inside himself, the inferno faded, the humming ceased. His panic subsided as he lazily studied the long blades. They seemed to pulsate in unison, an almost imperceptible twitching, regular, rhythmic.

The thrum of his pulse in his head, growing, as if synchronized to these odd, arboreal spasms.

Strange, he thought as he began to fall into a beatific daze. *Absurd.* Awash with drunken bliss. The chirping of insects lazing in dark places. Birds chattering beyond his purview, through the ferns and lording columns of monolithic trees. A sort of hypnosis that had stolen over him.

The forest began to fade…

Hassan found himself back in the Bell chamber—what Lotta called the Cathedral—high up, standing on a maintenance lift near the center of ALICE's Penrose core. Though he was suspended almost two stories off the chamber floor, the thing still towered over him. Beyond it, a backdrop of grated landings, dozens of walkways rising high up toward the surface. Hassan peered back down at his work. He had accessed the inner mantle of the colossal sphere, elbows deep in a mess of wires suspended in viscous ferrofluid.

"These damn core failures," he said to an unseen presence behind him. Someone familiar but lost on him in the moment.

There was no response.

He tried to turn his head to see who it was, but couldn't. Something held him there, fixed, unmoving except for his hands, feverishly pushing aside wires, clipping fried Hadamard nodes in the quantum processor. The thick ferrofluid like molasses, a resistance that caused his forearms to burn.

But the movements were not voluntary. Instead, it felt like reliving a memory, or a lucid dream. This had all taken place before.

While Hassan messed about with the guts of the core, algebraic expressions and unity matrices danced around his head. He was always teasing out faults in his designs. Making them better. *More perfect.* "Zero, one, zero, zero," he mumbled to himself, disconnecting another faulty node. He glanced intermittently at his diagnostic display to check his notes.

At their operating temperature—around two Kelvin—the nodes became brittle and could easily fracture during trials. But this seemed to be the case more with the supercooled helium in the device's core. It had been leaking out during recent trials, an inherent quality of a quantum fluid. One that proved extremely problematic for stability because of its tendency to seep into the circuitry.

"One, zero, one, one. Input vector omega. Input vector gamma. Vector zeta Ket zero one plus vector gamma Ket zero zero. It seems right… seems right. The normalization signal appears preserved through the Bell State. This setup is flawless—but we're still losing nodes. It has to be the condensate."

Should have used dark matter. Helium-4 too unstable.

The presence behind him stirred, but remained silent. An uneasy specter.

Who's behind me? Why can't I remember?

Allahu Akbar. Deliver me. Free me from the absurd.

Hassan found himself beneath the inky canopy again. A bluish-green blur had passed his line of sight, pulled him back to trickling sunlight and the gently pulsating fronds overhead. The chirping of insects and birds had ceased; the forest was now smothered in silence.

A rustling in the branches of a nearby tree startled him, sending his pulse into a frenzy. The crimson blades reacted in kind, pumping to the rhythm in his head.

Then, barely out of sight, a brightly colored bird about the size of a crow perched on one of the branches overhead.[1] Something shuddered inside of Hassan then, a pang of alarm. He could *feel* it. *He could feel the little black talons digging into the skin of the branch.* The uneasy warmth in his chest returned, but this was quickly dulled by his lingering intoxication. A strange calm. Knew in the back of his mind that it was odd to feel so unmoved, so indifferent. But he leaned into it, surrendered himself to the mounting euphoria. Suppressed all unease, let go of the questions flitting in and out. *How is this possible? Where am I? Am I going to die?* Allowed it to consume him, to detach from his innate reflexes, from his humanity. Filled their absence with bliss.

The bird flew off again.

He could hear the creature flitting about the other trees, returning a second, third, and fourth time to its newfound perch, the sensation of its cold talons like little knives digging into the tree, into *him*. It was investigating him, coming and going. Curious, but cautious. The pangs pulled him back for a moment, enough to repeat his prayer before fading once more.

I seek refuge in the lord of the dawn. Allahu Akbar. Allahu… Allahu…

---

1 *Confuciusornis indet.*

The next time it returned, the bird landed on a small branch in front of his face. It was beautiful, with an azure crown of long feathers that danced about its bobbing head. The body was equally striking—vivid blues and yellows ablaze against the gloom of the surround. He thought it quite resembled the magpies back home in Oran. But it was brighter, more vivid, and he had never seen a magpie this far south before. Surely not in the Sahara. Then again, there were no forests in the desert, either, at least outside of the sanctuaries.

Another pang.

Little talons digging in again.

It seared down his neck, burrowed into him. But it amused him, *feeling* the tree. *The absurdity of it.* His laughter erupted as more gurgling. More gagging. The bird cocked its head at the sound, chattering its black beak, as inky as its intent little eyes. Ceaseless voids staring back at him, *into* him. Curious, attentive. As if *Hassan* was the anomaly.

Its head turned to the side, one eye on him now. A translucent membrane flitted across its glassy surface. The bird ruffled its feathers and turned its attention to preening, as if it had lost interest in him. He watched the black pincers go to work, digging in, combing as the creature let out an arpeggio of muted chirrups. It extended a wing, beautifully iridescent, and began to primp its flight feathers. As it did so, Hassan let out another amused gurgle, because concealed beneath the wing's terminal joint were three spindly claws, like those of a dinosaur.

A hand. How absurd.

He heard the chirping of more birds—more *things*—once distant, steadily growing louder, nearer. The one in front of him shook out its plumage and turned over, exposing its rear, from which two long tail ribbons flowed prismatically. They felt soft against his skin. Then came an odd percussive sensation in one of his teeth, accompanied by a light clacking—the sound of the bird's beak tapping at it like a seed or insect. One by one, it clicked at each tooth like piano keys. Another gurgle. Hassan was laughing now.

The dappled sunlight started to smear together. The looming columns began to spin.

A prickling on his tongue. The sensation was light at first, then escalated to painful jabs and nips. The little claws sunk deeper, tail feathers pitched up as the bird leaned forward, hanging almost upside down in front of his gaping mouth. The searing pain brought him back again. After a series of rapid jerks—each punctuated by sharp pangs tunneling to the back of his throat—the bird came upright, bits of ragged flesh dangling from its beak.

Hassan tasted blood.

A second set of talons gripped a nearby branch, and then a third and fourth. He felt them, *all of them*. Dozens. And all he could do was froth and gurgle in amusement as the treetops started to sway once more. Something warm splattered onto his forehead, trickled down the side of his face, a putrid smell. But he didn't care.

He watched another creature land beside the first. It scratched at its crown with its funny little hand and, like the first, it studied Hassan. This one appeared piqued by the movements of his eye. Each blink, each saccade, elicited a reaction, a subtle twitch of the head. The bird observed the mechanics of his eyelids, then rapped gently on the bony rim of his upper orbit. Still gurgling, the sound of laughter in his head, Hassan squeezed his eye shut.

Please don't. Please don't. It tickles.

The pain started light, but soon shot to the back of his skull like a hot iron. He saw light again—dappled, watery rays of red-tinged sunlight. Another rush of pain, the blurred form of the bird recoiling, snapping his eyelid away like an elastic band. A bloody ribbon flopping as the little head bobbed, a content warbling from behind the bright plumage.

Tears streamed down Hassan's cheek. His eye burned. He rolled it back, his vision smeared red. Temporary relief. Another twinge. Another roll. When his gaze returned to center, he realized the bird's gaze was back on him, its hazy form almost obscured behind a flowing veil of crimson. Watching, reacting to his movements. He tried to stop, tried to hold off as long as he could, the voice of reason screaming through the bliss not to give in. To keep still.

He rolled his eye back again, and with this came a gentle tap on the white of his globe. The laughter in Hassan's head gave way to screams. Awash with renewed desperation, he snapped out of it in time to realize what was about to happen.

Each jab manifested a colorful explosion of phosphorescence, dazzling bursts like stars raining all around him. Bolts of electricity, a frenzy of nociception, coursed over his brow, down his neck. His facial muscles convulsed, spasmed, desperate to fend off the source of his insurmountable agony. A gelatinous substance spilled out onto his cheek. It cooled as it trickled down, seeped into his gaping mouth. The taste of brine burned his throbbing tongue.

More explosions of light as the prodding continued, each fainter than the last. The pain was unbearable. Worse than what had come before. But the bliss fell on him anew, and soon, he felt far away. Far from the piercing jabs, far from the mounting pressure in his skull. Soon, the flashes ceased altogether, though by now, he had found them quite beautiful. All that remained was blackness. Then the pressure released: a brilliant kaleidoscope of colored sprites erupted before him with such intensity, such brilliance, that he was consumed with light and warmth.

So beautiful.

The luminance faded, gave way to another scene. *A dream?* He found himself back in the observation deck, the hum of the Higgs revived. He was staring at a chess board across from Anderson, whose mouth curled into a grin, lips parting, moving in slow motion as he spoke.

"C-h-e-c-k-m-a-t-e."

Like before, it felt real. But Hassan had no control. He was trapped inside himself, inside a memory, a dream. The chair pushed back up on him, the electricity imparting the air with a chemical smell. He looked on as Anderson moved his queen sluggishly into place. An overwhelming sense of *déjà vu.*

"*My king was in a state of… superposition… collapsed… wave…*" Anderson faded. Hassan found himself lingering over the Penrose core's fried circuitry as if for the first time, the sound of oxygen flowing through his respirator, forearms on fire.

Who is behind me? He replaced another node. His mind was fractured, two simultaneous states of consciousness. At times, he was staring across the chessboard at Anderson, and at others, laboring over quantum circuitry.

"*Zero one. Vector beta Ket zero zero…*" And again back to sitting across from Anderson. "*Castle… collapsed… wave function. Ket… one… one…*"

It was like listening to himself speak from outside his own body, his voice distorted—like that from a radio or comm. But he recognized it. Because it was him. His voice, his thoughts, coming from somewhere distant. Garbled by static. Background noise, a voice in his head.

He heard a ping. The sound of a distress beacon. *His* beacon.

Martin. Something took Martin.

Now, he was poring over the creamy pages of Camus, reading about the suffering of Sisyphus, doomed to repeat his task of rolling a rock up a mountain for eternity. Back to Anderson. Recurrently fidgeting about the core. Everything started to blend together, to become one. Living out multiple realities simultaneously, repeating them over and over, like Sisyphus and his rock, all the while amused by the absurdity of it all.

And then Hassan's essence—his *consciousness*—split. At first, he existed in two states, then four, sixteen, and finally a number unfathomable to classical comprehension. Numbers had no true meaning any longer. One was zero, zero—one. But also two, three, five, eight, every conceivable integer, and combination, and beyond. He was nothing. He was everything. He flowed through each experience, dozens of them, like a phantom, a ghost. Hundreds. Thousands. *Millions*—all at once. All things were possible. All things, malleable, and yet preordained. It consumed him. Kept him safe.

And beneath it all, Hassan still sensed the faint prodding of beaks—distant, gentle, like a light rain. Countless drops falling into a vast sea, seeding infinite states of consciousness, together drowning out the one. An unwitting path to transcendence.

He had conquered the absurd, had gone *through* the mountain, and it was not long before he felt deep gratitude.

For his deliverance.

| CIELO >

The rover felt safe.

Perez saw why Nedjma had chosen to seek shelter here. They had sat in silence for what must have been an hour. The smell of dust inside her environmental suit, hair caked with it. The faint smell of vomit. Cheeks raw and stinging, tears still streaming over her sandblasted skin. She was dehydrated, sore, every muscle in her body aching. Despite her exhaustion, Perez's mind raced, a voice inside urging her to do something, anything, because everything was in peril: ARC's ecology, EDEN reduced to a smoldering caldera, untold numbers of people dead or injured.

Basem among them?

But everything Perez could do had already been done. Most of the ARC's repair systems were automated, tied to Athena. The rapid shift in pressure, changes in atmospheric composition, in ambient temperature: all had triggered the response—ARC's immune system. The AI already had repair drones hovering overhead, sealing off the dome's breaches. Thirteen in all. Other drones outside the dome were actively recapturing escaped animals, primarily birds. Synths had been mobilized in search-and-rescue efforts at EDEN. EIRO and heads of state had been alerted, but communications had been spotty since the quake. Last Perez had heard, the military was en route to aid and begin evacuations. Until then, local orders were to shelter in place. Those who were able carried on. She didn't know what came next—if, by this time tomorrow, she'd be back in Spain.

And what will come of this place? This ecosystem—one of the last and most diverse on the planet? My life's work.

Her mind went back to Basem.

I can't leave without him. I won't.

Inside the ARC, animals were being processed—tracked, vitals assessed by various monitoring systems. The injured and dead ones would be lifted by drone to the decon chamber at Sector C, not far from where she sat. Inside, volunteers from her veterinary team waited to receive the first wave. Perez tried not to think about what this meant, tried not to catastrophize. *But it is a catastrophe, a major fucking catastrophe.* Still, she fought off the mental math, how many populations were in danger—some species the last of their kind, now threatened with extinction. She would try and bring them back, of course. Clone them. But somatic transfer still had problems. It was never the same. *They* were never the same.

She gazed off across the grasslands and wooded hills toward Mount Qalil.

The first wave should arrive any moment now.

My place is here.

She felt many emotions, not the least of which was anger. Anger with Lotta and EIRO, despite all the signs, all she had shown them. Anger with herself for not doing more to stop all of this. Wondering if there really was more she could have done. If there would be more tremors, more destruction.

She became aware of her hands cradling her abdomen again and quickly moved them to her sides. Nedjma didn't seem to have noticed.

Going to start showing soon.

I could lie about Ruth. Say she's a clone.

Her mind was in turmoil. She found herself snapping out of it again and again, trying to stay in the now as she gazed off toward the grassy plains. But her grief remained. Grief for her animals. Grief for Ruth.

It will never work.

In the distance, search drones hovered lazily, silhouetted against the honeycombed backdrop of ARC's geodesics. Perez's thoughts shifted to Basem.

Why couldn't I just fucking say "I love you?"

She remembered the first time he'd laid those words on her. He had been the first to say it, only a few months into their relationship and right on the heels of their first real fight.

She remembered that night being unusually cool, with the first clear sky in months. They were back in Algiers, her first time meeting his mum. After the haze had cleared that day, Basem jumped at the opportunity to take her out stargazing. She already had a sense of unease being in such an unfamiliar place, meeting his mother. She was convinced the woman disapproved.

After almost an hour of cajoling, Basem had managed to get her out into the street. She followed him apprehensively in the dark, but she trusted him. He led her to an outlook—a decrepit ancient fortification overlooking the bay. She recalled rows of cramped stone homes, their lights dotting the hillside. Like thousands of punched-out holes, a speckled white band stretched across the night sky. She couldn't remember the last time she had seen the Milky Way so vividly.

A band tightened around her chest. She had always avoided looking up for fear of spotting a gaol. A reminder of how things had been growing up. But for the first time in what seemed like years, she felt safe, and so she stared into the cosmos from Basem's arms. They were beautiful, the stars were.

And then she spotted one—a gaol. Time had slowed. Peace shattered. The distant prison pulsed lazily through the stars, sending her heart into her throat. She said nothing. Perhaps, she'd thought then, she never would.

Basem hadn't seemed to notice the ominous light blinking across the night sky. Perhaps he couldn't distinguish it from the others—countless satellites, space stations. But Perez could. Her skin was clammy, memories of Uncle Diego flashing by. Wondering if he might still be alive. She closed her eyes, and though she did not pray often, she silently voiced a string of Hail Marys. When she opened her eyes again, the blinking light had passed.

What came next amounted to poor timing on Basem's part.

"Tú eres mi cielo," he said.

Always the hopeless romantic.

At the time, Perez hadn't taken it well. She remembered stepping back, her face running hot, her ratcheted emotions brimming. She said nothing. The silence weighed heavy, her heart pounding in her chest.

"Thanks," she'd said, her arm falling away from his waist.

Basem had stammered. Had seemed to realize it hadn't landed well. "It… it's Spanish. I've been learning… I thought…"

It had been ages since Perez had heard Spanish. It triggered her. Mamá and Papá had stopped speaking it years ago. Aside from the occasional phrase or curse word, Perez rarely spoke it herself. She wasn't sure why, but the nonchalance with which Basem had used her native tongue—had dared to speak anything other than English—troubled her back then.

But it was *what* he said that had made her pull away, grow cold.

You are my sky.

"Don't call me that. Ever." The gaol burned into her consciousness. A lifetime of averting her eyes from the night sky. *Stupid. Why'd I agree to this?* A strong urge to leave. No sense of where, just anywhere but there at that moment, under that sky.

"I-I'm sorry. I didn't mean to upset you."

She'd folded her arms across her chest, feigning a shiver. Had shut down.

A look of total confusion befell Basem. Perez remembered that well. Remembered the shame that came over her when she realized she'd reacted unfairly. But she was too proud, doubling down on her emotions. Basem had said nothing. Only stood, watching her, at a loss for words.

"Cam, I'm sorry, I—"

"Just don't call me that."

"Okay."

She struggled to speak through her emotions, tongue balled in the back of her throat. She choked, tried to force the words out. Tried to convey meaning, make sense of it, make Basem understand, but all that came out was a torrent of tears. A blubbering refrain. "*I don' look—don' look up.*"

And somehow, Basem managed to understand. At least, it seemed that way at the time. "But you did tonight," he said.

It was the first time in years she'd felt heard.

The rest was hazy, but Perez remembered the chilly night air and Basem approaching her, gathering her in those lanky but oddly sturdy arms. There was warmth in that embrace, safety. And that was when he'd said it.

"I love you, Cam."

At that moment, she knew. She loved him, too. But whether by pride or fear, she didn't say it back.

"Can we go back? I'm cold."

But she'd come around eventually, even if it took her almost a year. Had said it in her head more times than she could count. She was sure she'd said it in her sleep once, but when she shuddered awake, Basem was either asleep or pretending to be. He never mentioned it. When it did happen, consciously, with intent, it was strange to hear it out loud. Basem had seemed even more surprised, rendered speechless, as if he had accepted that she might never say it.

"Oh, so *now* I finally say it and you're not going to say it back?" she'd joked.

But what surprised Basem more—and it surprised *her*, too—was the day she asked him to call her *cielo* again.

I love you, cielo.

The words haunted her now.

Perez let out a long sigh and shifted uneasily in the passenger seat.

Nedjma still hadn't spoken. The two of them stared out into the vast dome, engine running idle, now just white noise that felt more comforting than silence.

Nedjma had been fidgeting, one arm across her chest, clasping her right bicep. Her breathing was shallow, her suit's cooling system abuzz. She'd been in shock when Perez found her, sitting alone in the driver's seat of the rover just outside the decon chamber, face pale, engine running.

They both looked on as a wildebeest grazed beneath the solitary Saharan cypress she had pointed out to Lotta. That seemed so long ago to her now. The tree stood solitary, inky black against the setting sun. Ignorant to its peril. The lush landscape looked peaceful, serene, as though nothing had happened, as if this place weren't under threat of annihilation. Despite the precautions. Despite every measure taken. It was an eerie calm. Not a bird in the sky. Branches and leaves littered the ground—casualties of the gale-force winds that had rushed out through the breaches. Aside from that, no indication of anything insidious at play.

But beneath the surface, *everything* in the dome was in flux: the air's composition, atmospheric pressure, ambient temperature. All of it, mired in chaos.

Locura.

The implications were far-reaching, and it would be months or years before they knew the full impact of the breach on ARC's ecosystem.

But for now, it was still. Quiet.

Perez supposed she could be out there, boots on the ground, her sedated footsteps lurching down the long road toward ARC's recovery—or its ultimate demise—picking up detritus, helping track and log animals. Trudging. Crawling. Into the bleak shroud of overwhelming uncertainty. Perhaps she could be in the lab with her veterinary team, preparing supplies and sterile fields, gearing up to triage the first wave of animals. Another part of her was pulled toward ALICE, a strong desire to take a rover out there, try and find Basem.

But right now, at the center of it all, was Nedjma.

She thought back to the moa incident. How three weeks later, Nedjma still walked with a stutter in her step. Not once did she complain. Not once did she slow down. If anything, her student had insisted on *more* autonomy, *more* involvement.

I should have been here. Too soon for her to be out on her own.

Another emotion. Guilt. Perez didn't deserve her. Didn't deserve anyone. Not even Ruth.

She felt helpless for the first time since she was a little girl, when the bad men came to her home to harass her family. Had accused Papá of apostasy, threatened to send them up to those blinking jails far away beyond the stratosphere, never to be seen or heard from again. She felt that way now. Powerless. Held down by something far more powerful than her. That urge to do something, anything, driving every action, every decision, her entire life. And now, burdened with the greatest sense of urgency she had in decades, a multitude of crises pulling her in every direction, she resisted. Because she had nothing left to give.

Perez sighed and broke the silence.

"Thank you," she said.

Nedjma jumped as if waking, and for the first time, she turned to meet Perez's gaze.

"Thank you for coordinating with Athena," Perez continued.

Still quiet, wide-eyed, searching around the cabin, Nedjma nodded.

From the day they met, Perez had sensed a heightened level of restraint from Nedjma. She seemed timid, overly deferential during the interview. *Sensitive.* But something had drawn Perez to her. Nedjma was feeling, perceptive. It was almost like a look inside the most vulnerable parts of herself. The side she walled off from the world, even from Basem. One she displayed openly to her animals and little else. And here, Nedjma laid it all out, allowed herself to be vulnerable, to *feel* things. And though it was apparent now, it had taken almost a lifetime for Perez to understand that sometimes, it was okay to just sit in silence.

"We can stay in here as long as you need." Perez turned back toward the grazing wildebeest, and her mind drifted once more.

Her place, right now, was with Nedjma.

But come morning, she'd rejoin the fray. Find her rhythm.

Night fell.

Drones blinked like those distant gaols in the Algiers sky. Some circled Qalil, where a crew of engineers was probably inside the mountain, repairing ARC's pulmonem. Perez's team of veterinarians had started tending to the first of the wounded animals. She watched with Nedjma from the rover as teams of three came out of Sector C wearing environmental suits to greet each drop. So far, the drones had retrieved an injured boar, three dead wildebeests, and a critical rusty-spotted genet. But these represented the beginning of what was to come. Perez expected an uptick in zoological illnesses in the coming days.

And then there was Basem. She still hadn't heard from him. Communications with ALICE were still out. It would probably be hours before centralized power was restored.

She felt powerless, destitute, grief-stricken.

Angry.

"We should probably go in and help," Nedjma said. "Thank you for coming to find me."

Perez swelled with pride, and for a moment, all her other emotions seemed to fade.

As she turned to place a hand on Nedjma's, she caught a faint bloom of white light through the driver's-side window, northward, off in the distance past the dome's geodesics. Across the intervening desert, stage lighting now dotted the perimeter around EDEN's ruins, occluded by a lingering cloud of dust that still blanketed the earth. It scattered and carried the light cast from the blinking aerials as they searched the wreckage, ebbing, pulsating red. Blood-tinged smoke still billowed, rising high into the night sky.

And higher still, something Perez had never seen before—bands of shimmering aurorae dancing across the sky. Ribbons of green and blue, their margins accentuated by a slight tinge of glowing red that stretched behind the mountainous backdrop. A few wayward bands rippled above the ARC, reminiscent of the magnetic field signatures she had shown Lotta weeks prior. Except these could be seen with the naked eye as they snaked with uneasy majesty. Her spine crawled. It was as if the dancing tendrils had extended from the heavens, a vice of spindly claws reaching out to claim her.

The hand of Death himself.

< ᚱ | LOCURA >

Basem came to on his back, choking and sputtering, head throbbing. His suit's oxygen wasn't flowing. Face shield thick with condensation. It was dim out there, a shimmering, bluish glow: that much, he could decipher. He moved his legs. The ground gave beneath him slightly—not the firm metal grating of a landing or the concrete floor inside the lab. He shifted his weight, turning over to prop himself onto his hands and knees.

Need air.

Without thinking, he leaned upright and fumbled at the base of his helmet. He didn't care about the possibility of contamination. A risky gamble. But the way he saw it, his only option.

A soft hiss erupted. Cool air filled his lungs. An acrid, sweet smell infused his nostrils, like benzene or some other harsh chemical, burning as he sucked it down. He lifted the helmet and tossed it to the ground, where it landed with a crunchy thud. Falling back on all fours, Basem drank the air in exaggerated gulps.

The ground yielded again, his hands sinking slightly, prompting him to open his eyes.

Sand?

He was outside, back at the surface.

How is this possible?

His suit encumbered him, bogged down by a thick fluid smeared all over it. A pool of the tar-like substance coalesced at his knees, mired him to the ground. The smell was awful, strong enough to diffuse through his clogged nostrils. So potent he could *taste* it.

He raised his head and looked toward a horizon draped in undulating aurorae. He craned his neck to the sky, where the subdued cobalt transitioned into deeper red bands that split the night sky like gaping wounds. It felt like he was underwater, his own breathing heavy in his ears. His eyes leveled with the horizon again. ALICE's above-ground facility was nowhere to be seen. He'd probably been dropped somewhere in the middle of the desert, likely kilometers away from the nearest outpost. His mind began to race as panic set in. Temperatures plunged at night in the desert, and if he made it to dawn, he would have limited time to find refuge before the inhospitable heat bore down and cooked him alive. He scanned the horizon for any landmark to guide him, eyes heavy and pulsatile, bulging as they tracked along the smeared landscape. If he could spot the Atlas range, he'd at least have some sense of direction. But all he saw was a sprawling sea of dunes pulsing reflectively beneath the dancing sky. No mountains. Not so much as a hillside.

A gibbous moon bathed the landscape in a soft glow.

Unable to bear the smell any longer, Basem unzipped his suit hastily and let it fall to the ground, where it crumpled onto itself with a wet *plop*. The compression lining alone would not be enough to keep him warm, but the added bulk of his uniform was sure to sap him of energy before he could find his way back. He stood, swaying for a moment, before finding his balance. His legs wavered, almost unable to bear his weight. A tingling sensation pricked at his fingers. Cold air on his skin. He held his hands out and balled them into fists. They felt clammy; his finger joints ached. He opened them again, turned them over, shocked to find his skin covered in dark, purplish blotches—flame-shaped bruises from ruptured capillaries beneath the dermis—evident even in the dim moonlight. He closed his eyes again. They ached in their sockets, accompanied by an intense ringing in his ears and a crushing headache. His chest was on fire. Signs and symptoms familiar to him because he'd been trained to recognize them.

Acute decompression sickness.

He almost certainly would not be here if not for the DNA hardening.

He peered off again, his eyes adjusting to the gloom.

It's early June. There shouldn't be a full moon—

Without warning, Basem's stomach lurched. An onslaught of retching stole over him. Vomit erupted from his nose and mouth, striking the ground with a sickening *smack*. He heaved again. The cool air stifled his rattling lungs, disoriented him further.

And then it passed.

A bitter coalescence dribbled from his lips as he fought to resist another round of retching.

Basem started to remember bits of what had happened, fleeting snapshots of the lab, the Bell chamber. The aftermath of the core's failure. But it was scrambled, as though he'd experienced alternate versions of the same event. They had run the trial in the early afternoon. *That*, he was sure of.

How much time has passed?

Then something in Basem's mind clicked into place, a horrifying realization that coursed through his veins like ice: he was alone.

The others, his mind howled with urgency. *Where are the others?*

Right on cue, he heard a commotion behind him—something scraping along the sand just beyond a shallow dune, maybe forty meters out. He turned toward it and spotted a human form shooting upright and then disappearing again beneath the rim of the sandy peak.

"Lotta? Ed?" he tried to yell, but all he could procure was a raspy moan that was immediately swallowed up by the sand. He waited a few seconds, maybe minutes. Long enough to realize whoever he'd seen probably hadn't heard him. He needed to get closer.

Basem rounded the dune's crest and saw a shadowy figure around twenty meters off. It looked like Lotta. Her back was to him, her hair alight beneath the shifting sky. She was bent over, removing her suit. Behind her, Basem spotted a pair of legs resting flat on the ground. Lotta shifted sideways, revealing a man propped back on his elbows, leaning upright in the sand.

Ed?

Fischer appeared to be hurt, struggling for breath as he spoke. His face looked pale and swollen.

Basem opened his mouth to yell, but all that came out was a hoarse whisper that manifested shooting pains down his throat. He proceeded forward, waving his arms above his head to try and get their attention.

"*Lotta!*"

This time, she heard him. At least, it seemed she had. Her head spun in his direction, hair a tangled mess, helmet at her feet.

"Basem!" Her voice came in a near-whisper. Then, her gaze diverted sharply to his left, a look of confusion on her face.

Basem turned.

In the distance, from behind another dune rose a slender silhouette—a head bouncing rhythmically atop a long, rigid neck. It ascended the moonlit ridge, a gaunt frame resting on four stilted limbs that vaulted effortlessly over the drifts. Basem squinted and studied the thing as it sauntered forward, its blackened form rimmed by the bluish glow.

One of the giraffes? How did it get out?

A jolt ran through him.

Cam. Something happened.

The giraffe appeared to be around fifty meters off now. Basem remembered how tame the gentle giants were, how readily they approached Perez. Her words echoed in his head.

Not as wild as they used to be.

As it approached, Basem noticed a lack of certain characteristic features—no long, pointed ears, nor the signature bony ossicones jutting from its crown. Its muscular shoulders rotated forward preternaturally, rolling a deep chest from side to side, almost like a strutting baboon. But it wasn't until the downturned head listed ever so slightly, breaking away from the silhouette of the neck, that Basem realized this was no giraffe. A long, pointed beak—at least the size of a grown man—caught a tinge of red, then disappeared again into shadow before reemerging on the other side. It was searching, rotating an enormous, stork-like head, eyes glinting white in the gloom.

Basem stood there, horrified, muscles seized up, unable to function.

Lotta shrieked something unintelligible behind him. She sounded muffled, distant against the ceaseless ringing in his ears.

Move, a voice screamed inside his head, but all he could do was tremble and look on in terror.

He had never seen anything like it. Along each flank, a membranous flap of skin—*a wing*—married its wrists and ankles such that its front and hind limb lurched forward in staggered synchrony before those on the other side carried forward in the same manner. It reminded him vaguely of a bat, but more upright, more gracile, like a giant crane, one on four legs, and a gait strikingly reminiscent to that of the giraffe it initially resembled.[1]

A rapid staccato erupted in the distance, beyond the creature, like far-off machine gun fire. Basem shot a look just as a second head crested the dune, then a third. *More of them.* The sound erupted again, coming from the second of the looming giants. Then the third chimed in, the two beasts chattering in unison, such that an odd resonance rippled across the sand.

But the one nearest Basem stayed silent, and soon, the distant mantra of the others faded, leaving a deafening vacuum of silence in the night air. The pit inside of him swelled with an uneasy warmth, expanded into his chest, an unbearable pressure. Blood coursed through his cheeks, through flexing muscle. His arms twitched. Time stood still.

Move.

The hair rose on Basem's arms, his skin awash with crawling maggots. At that moment, he was filled with pure dread.

A sudden movement from the first animal sent Basem's heart into his throat. Chest pounding, his eyes wide with terror, he watched the beast plunge forward into a full-fledged gallop. It was heading straight for him.

MOVE.

His legs shifted unconsciously, spinning his body around.

"Run!" he tried to shout after the other two, his words nothing more than a muffled cry. But they already had started up a nearby dune, Fischer's arm slung over Lotta, hers around his waist. She appeared to struggle under his weight, his legs dragging as he tried his best to pedal through the sand.

---

1 *Alanqa Saharica*

Lotta tripped, and they fell forward, then started sliding back down the slope.

Basem flew down from where he stood, down into the narrow valley between the two drifts, his lungs on fire. Every muscle in his body screamed in protest, his head pounding as each step sent shockwaves through him. It felt as though he were floating, bounding across the sand. He had never run so fast in his life.

Fischer and Lotta had regrouped and now clawed their way desperately up the slope on all fours. Seconds later, they rounded the peak and disappeared to the other side. Basem followed, his legs churning in agony, every muscle firing, sending him careening up the soft slope. When he cleared the ridge, he beheld a spectacle the likes of which he thought he'd never see in his lifetime. A living, sprawling forest of enormous trees had materialized before him, and the other two were heading straight for it.

Where the hell are we?

It made no sense. There were no large forests in North Africa. Not anymore. The last ones had disappeared from coastal Tunisia almost a century ago. *Over a thousand kilometers away.*

But right now, it was *hope*. Another twenty or so meters, and he'd be safe. He could make it. He had to make it. Cold air whistled past as he bounded down the other side.

Fischer and Lotta disappeared into the giant columns, consumed by shadows and thick underbrush.

The faint pattering of galloping limbs striking sand overtook the sound of his toiling lungs, his heavy footfalls. Something moving fast. Growing louder, nearer.

Just as Basem was about to reach the tree line, his legs buckled beneath him.

No. Please, no.

His body rolled forward, sending him tumbling until he came to a stop face down in the sand. The pain hadn't registered immediately, and it was not until he tried to push himself to his knees that it shot through his back like molten steel. He couldn't breathe. Could hardly move. Something had struck him from behind.

He gasped in shallow bursts, each huff generating a crackling sound deep in his chest. *Collapsed my lung.* Dust filled his nose and mouth, burned his eyes. The ringing mounted in his ears, interspersed with the clicking sound he'd heard moments before, only softer, more controlled.

Tk-tk-tk.

It was above him. A clattering beak.

A stench filled his nostrils, like the sickening, sweet smell of stale manure.

Something shifted in the sand behind him—those stilted legs straddling him. He had no strength to gaze up at the thing. He sensed it looming over him, *watching*. It panted in hollow bursts, but with an unsettling calmness that contrasted with his own labored rasps. And the smell. The godawful smell.

Tk-tk-tk-tk.

He raised a trembling hand over his head, a final, desperate attempt to shield himself.

Then, with tremendous force, Basem was wrenched skyward. More stabbing pain, this time in his shoulder, his wrist—a vice squeezing so hard the bones ground against one another—a million hot needles shooting through it as all sensation left. A violent jolt to the right. A loud pop. More intense pain sent adrenaline shooting through his veins. Then left. Alert again, his chest rattling. His vision started to close in, the ground spinning below, where two slender limbs, like down-covered bamboo shoots, met a pair of gnarled, splayed hands.

Without warning, the beast vaulted up with such force that Basem thought his arm might tear free from his body. As he rose and fell, tumbling violently with each thrust, he caught a fleeting glimpse of the monstrous beak clamped around his wrist. His eyes fell back toward the ground. He was higher up now. Airborne. Warmth soaked through his compression lining amid the snapping of joints and sinew. The taste of metal was still heavy in his mouth, now tinged with that of blood. Loud gusts rushed beneath the beast's massive wings, overpowering the incessant ringing in his head.

Soon, the pain passed. A soft warmth stole over him. The air had been squeezed from his lungs, but he was no longer afraid. All fear, all pain had left him. His body had fallen limp, rotating about the axis of his shattered arm, the earth spinning slowly below. He watched the trees recede, the canopy pulsing beneath the soft reddish glow of the shimmering aurorae. Watched the silver crests of dunes anastomose into a luminous river delta alight with the reflected sky. He had never seen anything so beautiful.

When Basem came to again, he was tumbling through the air, the trees rushing back at him, the cold wind rapping his face. His mind was a roaring ocean, a tortured stream of consciousness bordering on hallucination. Nothing was real anymore.

He blinked.

Images flashed before him at lightning speed. Fantasies of fatherhood. A murmuration of starlings. A lone carob tree. The sanguine gaze of a New Zealand White.

He blinked.

Cam's eyes.

Those striking green eyes gazing into him. That smile in the morning sun, curls of hair tossed over the pillow, the scent of lavender on her skin.

Their baby would've had those eyes. That hair.

He blinked.

He was a macaque falling from the sky.

Tears streamed backward. For a brief moment, the pain in his chest returned.

He saw the limbs of trees, the rivulets of snaking dunes, individual grains of sand glistening in the moonlight like distant stars.

I love you.

Basem blinked.

On all sides saw I, Valkyries assemble,
Ready to ride to the ranks of the gods…
—**Poetic Edda**

< ᚺ | VALKYRIES >

Fischer's chest rose and fell under Lotta's weight. Drenched with sweat, she thrust down onto clasped hands, elbows locked, her arms on fire.

Her ribs ached. A high-frequency hum trilled between her ears. She had woken moments prior, suffocating inside her suit. The compression sleeve had done its job reviving her, tightening and releasing around her chest until that first stinging bolus of air expanded in her lungs. But her oxygen compressor had failed, and she'd had no choice but to remove her helmet, to retch against the unknown, taking in the fetid stench of ferrofluid as she gasped.

She realized she had somehow made it back to the surface and that Fischer lay motionless beside her, his face swollen in the ruddy glow. At first, she thought his compression sleeve had failed to revive him, but when she opened his outer uniform, she was shocked to find him wearing *nothing* underneath. Just a bare chest, his skin mottled with hundreds of dark hemorrhages.

Now, she was desperately trying to bring him back.

They were both coated in tar-like ferrofluid. It made compressions almost impossible, causing Lotta to slip at first until she peeled back the top of her suit to free her arms such that it was draped around her waist like shed skin. She dared not stop to remove the rest. Every second, every compression mattered.

The ferrofluid's kerosene smell leeched past her clogged sinuses, burned her eyes. The same intense odor she'd smelled in the Cathedral when she saw the *thing* that got Anderson. *The wraith.* The smell fed the tightness squeezing her head, a vice-like pressure that disoriented her, her eyes on fire with a chemical sting. With each recoil, the pain in her triceps intensified, climbing past her shoulders, traveling down her back. Her trembling arms ready to give out at any moment.

She tried not to look at Fischer's face again. Allowed her disheveled hair to conceal it from view while her hands rebounded on his chest.

Refused to concede that he might already be gone.

He took his prophylactic. I saw him take it. I saw. I watched.

Pop.

Scheisse.

Another rib had cracked. Lotta shook her hair aside as if by reflex and glanced at Fischer's face, but he remained unresponsive. No sign he felt a thing. Blonde wisps fell back over her eyes, and she stared down at her hands. The same blotches covering Fischer's chest seemed to cover the rest of his body, including his neck and head. Lotta had them too, purpuric spiderwebs along her arms, her hands. But his were far worse.

Fischer stirred.

A gurgling sound erupted from his mouth, his jaw gaping open and shut. Lotta pushed him onto his side and delivered several hard blows between his shoulder blades. He coughed violently. The meat of Lotta's palm planted another blow, and dark blood sprayed from his lips. He hacked up a thick black fluid that pooled under his cheek, then sucked at the air in tortured gasps.

"W—where… where…" he mouthed.

Lotta, now sobbing, placed a hand on his shoulder and knelt over him.

"Shhh… Ed, you're okay. Just rest. You're okay."

Fischer rolled onto his back and erupted into a fit of wet coughs, his lips gleaming with blood. He opened his eyes and looked at her, the whites saturated with bright red hemorrhages visible even in the gloom. A pair of shiners rimmed his eyes as if he had lost another of his long string of bar fights.

"I'm okay." He sat upright and wiped his cheek with his sleeve, only to realize his glove was coated in ferrofluid. "Fuck, this shit burns." His voice was raspy, almost a whisper, wheezing with each breath. He pulled his arm free from the sleeve, scraped the tarry substance off with a trembling hand, then turned to look at her. His jaw fell slack.

"*Oy.*" He pointed up at her. "You—you've copped a pair of m—mice, haven't you?"

Lotta raised her hands to her face and palpated the tender swelling around her eyes. She nodded back at him. "You too. Your eyes are redder than a cock's comb."

"Aye." Fischer spat red. "Decompression sickness."

"You're not wearing a compression sleeve."

"Don't fancy 'em."

"We need to get you medical attention. Could be a pulmonary embolism."

"Aye." He spat again, massaging his chest. "Where are we?"

Lotta got to her feet and looked around. "Somewhere back at the surface." But beyond that, she had no idea. The landscape registered as wholly unfamiliar. Alien. Through watering eyes, it shimmered and undulated before her beneath a sky filled with aurorae reminiscent of her ride-along with Perez. *Vision is still shit.* Her foot nudged the helmet at her feet. She turned back to Fischer. "We should ditch these suits. This stuff is toxic to breathe."

"Aye. Guess I'll be going in the nude."

"*Schweinehund.*" She grinned and shook her head as she knelt forward to free her legs. "You're lucky to be alive." Her body ached, but she was relieved to be free of the extra weight—and the smell. A sort of floating sensation swept her.

A distant shuffling penetrated the eerie silence around them. Lotta pivoted, spotting a black form that stumbled along the ridge of a nearby dune in the glowing moonlight, the shifting reds and blues of aurorae, a pair of arms wildly waving about. *A person.* She recognized him almost immediately.

"Basem!" Her voice cracked against the gravelly sensation in her throat. She recoiled slightly as a twinge of pain coursed through her ribcage.

He had seen them, probably before they saw him. He walked parallel to the ridge of the drift for a few meters, looking for a way down. Then, something else caught Lotta's eye. A blackened form off in the distance, a stilted figure rising from the glistening mounds. Noticing her reaction, Basem turned.

The mass in Lotta's throat swelled. The last thing she remembered back in the Cathedral hit her again, a vision that had been momentarily suppressed as she attended to Fischer: Anderson's limp body, dangling in the vice of some horrible wraith, a shadow-being indistinct against the smearing of spacetime. But what now approached was obscured only by the edema ravaging her eyes, stretching and distorting her vision. But this one looked different—a towering form like a wading bird, perhaps a stork, only much, much larger. And it appeared to move on four slender limbs instead of two.

Two more of them emerged in the distance. Stalkers.

Then came the sound, a vibration that erupted from one of the things and decayed across the landscape. A horrible clattering that sent Lotta's spine reeling. And her legs in motion.

"Ed! Ed, we need to go. C'mon, I got you." She ran to Fischer and knelt at his side. "Move your legs, c'mon, Ed, let's go!"

"What? What was that sound?"

"We need to *go.*" She gripped his free wrist and slipped his arm over her shoulders. Her fingertips grazed the scars on his inner wrist, and for a moment, her mind went there. Speculated. A fleeting thought as the sleeve of his suit grazed her back, sandwiched between their bodies. She brought him to his feet, her knees wobbling under the added weight.

"Hey, wait, my suit, I need to—*ow*—what's wrong?"

"No time. Leave it on. Let's *go.*"

She shot a look back toward the ridge, her legs already on fire. Basem was still standing, staring at the approaching things. Could barely see them. But Basem just stood there, watching in shock, maybe wonder.

She tried to yell after him: *"Run, you idiot."* Nothing but a grating whisper.

Everything that followed was a blur.

"Move." She grunted under Fischer's weight, spit and foam spraying from her parched mouth. Her arm around his back, his uniform half off. The loose sleeve pounding her lower back. It took almost all her concentration to keep his wrist from slipping out of her grasp as they kicked through the sandy substrate and started up another nearby drift that pulsed slowly as it reflected the bloody sky. Fischer's legs moved asynchronously, as if he'd forgotten how to walk. Lotta's legs seared and seized, fighting back against her will to press forward. She did not know what lay beyond the crest, only that she had no other choice but to keep moving.

The rattling in Fischer's chest concerned her more and more, but they could not stop, could not rest. Not yet. He coughed up blood.

"Run!" Basem's voice, barely a shriek through the dry desert air.

Lotta and Fischer had almost made it to the top of the drift when her legs quit. Her grip loosened around his clammy wrist, and the combined weight of their bodies pulled them forward into the coarse sand.

No. Nonono.

She slid backward a few meters, clawing at the sand. It was useless, like trying to grasp a fistful of water. Her feet hit a lip, and she came to a stop. Fischer slid limply into her, and they continued down another half meter. He was now bare-chested, both arms free, the top of his suit draped about his waist.

Get. Up.

Lotta pulled herself upright and checked Fischer over.

Still breathing, still conscious.

She tried to bring him back to his feet, but her legs were spent. He was too heavy, the slope too angled to regain purchase. They dragged themselves along on all fours all the way to the top and threw their bodies down the other side, into the unknown. Sand flew all around Lotta, her body rolling and flailing. It hissed around her, stinging her eyes, her nose, her mouth. She gasped for air, trying to take hold of anything to slow her descent, before finally coming to rest on her back. She scrambled to her feet and looked around. Fischer lay face down beside her, his helmet tumbling after them down the drift. She looked up, but there was no sign of Basem.

Fischer groaned. She helped him up again and leveled her gaze. Before them, a forest of colossal conifers stretched in both directions—dark, lording columns rimmed in crimson, their glinting limbs high off the ground, stretching to the heavens.

Trees?

Cover. Refuge. An escape from the horror that might bear down on them at any moment.

Fischer tried to speak, but his speech came in garbled dribbles. His beard stood out in every direction, caked with blood and vomit. A string of spit and blood dangled over his trembling lower lip. Lotta lurched forward, her legs aching in wild protest, oscillating like plucked guitar strings. Fischer did his best to help her, grunting with each step. They pressed forward, slogging desperately, stumbling over low-lying shrubs that rattled in the still night. The smell of ferrofluid hung thick in the air. Each pounding step seemed to bring them no closer to the towering columns. She dared not look back.

Finally, they fell into shadow.

Lotta's lungs were on the verge of exploding, her feet sluggish as they pressed into the underbrush. Ferns grazed her arms, curled around her legs, snaring her momentarily before snapping free. Fischer waivered, and they fell forward again. She landed hard, the air voiding from her lungs in a tortured yelp. She pushed herself onto all fours and ushered a wheezing Fischer deeper into the darkness until they finally slumped against one of the giant trunks. Neither of them spoke, but instead gulped at the air. Fischer's face still looked pale, even in the shadow of the trees.

Lotta leaned over and peered around their cover through rows of trunks, but all she saw was the drift they had climbed, its crest gleaming beneath the undulating ribbons that split the night sky. She strained her ears against silence, punctuated only by Fischer's rattling breaths and her own pulse pounding in her ears.

Soft moonlight percolated the still branches overhead. Lotta found her footing and rose to a crouching position, trying her best to get a view.

"Basem?" she whispered into nothingness.

Silence.

And then, something fell from the sky.

CRUNCH.

A stifled yelp escaped Lotta's lips. She couldn't tell what had registered first—the sound of a body slamming into the ground, or the sight of it. Fischer shifted his weight and leaned around her. A plume of dust billowed out from the impact, and after a moment, it cleared.

It was Basem, lying face up just beyond the tree line.

And again, silence.

Lotta could do nothing but look on in horror. Basem did not move, his limbs splayed awkwardly—one arm pinned beneath him at an impossible angle, a mangled leg forced into a sharp bend toward his side.

The rays of moonlight shimmered, and latticed branches swayed under an unseen force at the forest's edge. The motion swelled until a large form descended over the milky beams, casting everything into shadow. Lotta heard the resonant swoosh of turbulence, the sound of air being compressed beneath thrusting wings. She saw the legs first, dangling, outstretched to receive the earth. Attached just above its spindly feet were a pair of enormous wings, translucent and backlit by the undulating sky. They stretched in an arch, extending horizontally like unfolding switchblades, each about the length of three men. Intricate vascular networks coursed through them like the venous anastomoses of leaves. They rotated downward, scattering divine rays across the forest floor, their downwash rattling the shrubs around Basem's mangled form. The creature descended, body vertical, its flight arms outstretched like a stigmatic deity rimmed in shimmering light.

A crux immissa.

Or an angel of death come to collect its quarry.

The spindly little toes reached for the ground and made contact, folding back and then straightening again as the balls of its feet settled behind a cloud of dust. After one more thrust, the wings folded inward— stowed against its body—and the beast fell forward onto all fours with a muted *thump*. Only then did Lotta catch its true form. Its head, twice the length of its stout body, rotated from side to side, eyeing Basem. Glinting in the moonlight, a pair of glowing eyes flanked a triangular crest, an extension of its beak that protruded from the back of its crown, anchored to a long, robust neck. The neck appeared rigid, with mottled, flaking skin that sprouted a banded pattern of matted filaments. The hind limbs were oddly proportioned—far shorter and lankier than its comparatively robust wing arms. An arrangement that endowed it with an almost chimp-like posture.

Tk-tk-tk.

Soft rattling resonated through the air, the ground, absorbed into ferns and branches. It coursed up Lotta's spine like a thousand spiders, blossoming into her arms and legs. Millions of tiny appendages pattering along nerve endings, mandibles at the ready, prepared to consume her from within. Until nothing remained but a husk.

The thing—*the angel, the stalker*—eyed Basem quizzically, its head bobbing and rotating from one side and then to the other. Towering almost as high as the lower branches of the trees, it rotated forward on stilted limbs, its knobby wing joints segmented like the legs of a praying mantis. Each sprouted a small, knotted hand with three digits splayed out to the side at an odd angle.

Like a bird-ape. A mantis-bird.

Basem dissolved into shadow.

The treetops swirled again, and a second angel emerged. *A chimera of ape and bat and stork. An abomination. A Valkyrie.* And then the third, perching itself before the dancing sky atop the dune's crest, which partially sank under its weight as it landed. Clumps of grit cascaded from its feet, leaving trails in the sand as they snowballed down the smooth slope. The newcomers had rounded heads without crests and were paler in complexion.

The two nearest Basem hissed, bobbing their heads as they danced around his body, beaks engaged in a crescendo of percussive chattering. A resounding, plunky clap came from their chests in tandem with their ballooning throat pouches. A call-and-response pattern.

Oong-oonk. Oong-koon-koon. Gnh gnh gnh.

Tk-tk.

And then the eruption that Lotta had heard carrying across the dunes earlier.

Tk-tk-RATATATATATAT.

The sound ripped through the forest, rolling off the columns. It filled her ears and sent her reeling backward into Fischer. The force of her body slamming into him sent them both falling back.

Lotta's arms flailed for something, anything to hold onto. Unable to regain purchase, her muscles tensed in anticipation as treetops and dapples of moonlight swirled past. Her elbows struck first, a jolt through her bones. The force sent her head whipping back. One of Fischer's boots found her ribcage, voiding her lungs as she was sent rolling over crunching vegetation.

She came to rest in a patch of ferns, pain searing through her abdomen. Fischer lay under her, his chest crackling amid labored breaths. She scrambled off him, staying low as she checked him over. His eyes were open, responsive. He nodded to indicate he was okay.

Disoriented, Lotta looked around until she saw one of the creatures move through a banding of stationary trunks.

Tk-tk.

She saw two pairs of glowing eyes trained on their position, heads bobbing, searching the darkened wood. Her body tensed, every muscle fiber rooting her feet into the earth. Fischer propped himself up and winced, sucking at the air painfully.

Lotta gestured for him to stay still, to keep quiet.

She didn't expect to see him unsheathing his old military knife, which he'd apparently stowed in the lining of his suit.

Oong-koon. Gnh gnh.

Lotta's head swiveled back toward the ecotone, sheets of sweat running down her face. The bobbing heads had turned back on each other, seesawing atop thick, inflexible necks. With Basem between them, their dance had resumed.

The crested individual—and the larger of the two—stretched a mantis arm over Basem and planted a gnarled hand into the dirt. The second reacted, its head moving back, limb joints extending. At this, perhaps a sign of weakness, the first hurdled forward and bellowed another hiss. Its pointed beak, outlined in a soft, cerulean glow, nipped at the neck of its challenger. The second individual recoiled and returned a barb in kind. Both animals pushed off their arms and balanced upright, wings clapping wide, outstretched, their heads wobbling and pitching, beaks clattering into the night sky as if to worship the zenith moon beneath the celestial light show.

Plumes of shed filaments billowed off their bodies, glinting in the shifting light as they swirled around like thousands of threadlike motes. Then, in a startling show of force, the crested individual bore down on the other, forcing it to stumble and lose its balance. The second folded its wings in against its body and fell back on all fours. It shuffled closer to the forest, its head bowed, defeated. The victor rattled its beak and stared the other down, then sidestepped back over to Basem. It crept back into the moonlight, looming over him, casting him once more into shadow.

Lotta's knees pressed against dirt. She was back in the grove with Mamma, a little girl on her knees at the altar. Mamma drunk. But this time, the vættir had come. They were real. *They had come.* Only the prize was not an apple or a flower, but a person.

Put your offering into the blót. I'll not say it again.

Basem.

She had done this. Lotta had killed him. Killed Anderson. Killed Mattheo. Maybe Hassan. Had sacrificed them to… *this.* To her god. To science.

No… I didn't mean to… I didn't…

Around Basem, the sand was black with blood. The beast crouched forward on its mantis arms, its terrible head, angular and narrow, now cantilevered over him. The tip of its beak made contact, then began probing at his compression sleeve. With surgical precision, it nipped and tore away bits of cloth and lining, then ribbons of flesh. Peeled back, snapped free. Strips of skin and muscle cast aside. Lotta's colleague flayed before her eyes. She wanted to look away, but she was frozen, incapable.

Fischer adjusted his position in the undergrowth behind her.

Basem's body jostled as the animal rummaged inside, the tip of its beak struggling against something shifting and slippery. Then it paused for a moment. It tugged up. Basem's body wrenched, almost clearing the ground, then fell again. Another tug. And another, until something inside had been liberated, ripped free.

Dangling from the bloody pincers, it glistened softly in the moonlight, a section of intestine coiled up like a writhing serpent. The beast's massive head rolled, and the slinking organ unwound limply as it tore free.

The other two creatures looked on in silence.

Lotta looked away, her hand clasped over her mouth, fighting against her involuntary gagging, tears streaming down her cheeks. Tears of mourning? Of fear? She wasn't sure which.

Fischer coughed. Lotta shot a glance toward him. His hand was clamped over his mouth, fresh blood trickling between the creases in his fingers. He struggled apologetically against an onslaught of muffled chest spasms.

Tk-tk-tk.

Lotta's head snapped back toward the tree line.

The second creature was gone.

She strained through the blackened rows of trunks with such intensity that her eyes bulged, throbbing to the rhythm of her pulse, the turbulent rush of blood shearing the walls of arteries, her muscles swelling in anticipation of fight or flight. She could still make out the other two creatures. The crested one snapped something wet and glistening to the back of its mouth as the other looked on from its perch—

—waiting for its turn.

And then one of the tree trunks swayed a little.

Lotta's tongue balled into a knot. She lowered herself closer to the clotted earth, her view now broken up by the banding of fern blades. Everything was still again, black against the columns of moonlight filtering in. Her pulsating eyes wide, tears flowing freely, waiting for the blackened thicket to move again. Maybe it had been a breeze, her eyes playing tricks.

Maybe—

More movement.

A bowed appendage crept out from the shadows and into a bar of soft light. The movement was slow, deliberate. She saw the spindly, knotted fingers press silently into a cluster of vegetation not four meters from where she now cowered in the dirt. *Flight.* Her entire body trembled. She fought against herself to keep still, to keep quiet. It was as though the trees had come alive. Her eyes tracked up, tracing along the limb to the rigid neck, where soft downy fibers caught the light. As she strained, the thing started to take shape. The head listed a little, a movement perceptible only in that a pupil caught a twinge of light, a brief flash of green, before falling back into blackness.

Fischer gave another muted spasm.

Tk-tk.

The creature's head tilted to the other side. It was searching. Even with the light at its back, it couldn't see them beneath the ghostly shadows of the canopy. But it was trying. Lotta eased herself closer to the ground, as low as she could manage while still allowing herself the ability to leap up and bolt deeper into the trees if it came to that. *Flight.* She was lying down, almost flat on her stomach, propped on aching elbows. Her view was obscured entirely now, ears shrieking and throbbing against a deafening silence. She turned her head and looked down at her feet, where a darkened Fischer lay on his back, clutching his knife against his chest.

Lotta heard a rustle. Maybe two or three meters off.

It's getting closer.

She could hear it breathing. Thought she might even smell it above the wafts of billowing ferrofluid.

A fecal stench with notes of floral musk. Like May lily and stale shit.

Put your offering into the blót.

More silence. The canopy lay still overhead, pulsing a dull red, needles of dull moonlight trickling through. And then they disappeared behind a darkened form, black like a bottomless void, ready to plunge her body down its horrible maw, to crush her into an infinitesimal point toward a singularity. Into obscurity.

I'll not say it again. I bloody won't. Flight. Flight. Flight.

Her eyes adjusted. The creature towered directly overhead, still searching with slow and deliberate movements. The long, slender beak swept across her field of view and then back again like a languorous windmill blade. She heard the pads of its hands palpating the ground as if trying to detect the faintest of vibrations. Claws scratching dirt, about spitting distance from her head.

It's right on top of us.

Lotta's back pressed painfully into the ground. She was desperate to get away, to recede into the earth, back into the Cathedral or buried alive if only to escape the same fate as Basem. At any moment, with the slightest tilt of the head, that glowing eye would fall on her. She watched as the beak started opening and closing as if to silently mouth a fresh round of rattles. But in her head, she heard it. The horrible vibrating sound. Her eyes connected with the oscillating beak, and her brain filled in the rest. She could hear the *chop chop chop* drumming in her skull like a Gatling gun.

The creature snorted. Seemed agitated. Shook, then snorted again.

Doesn't like the ferrofluid smell.

A glowing pupil flashed. The head fell still.

Now. Run. Now.

But Lotta was frozen in fear. At the edge of her vision, Fischer raised the blade.

Fight.

A muffled cough from Fischer.

Fuck.

Leaves shifted to Lotta's right. A sound that ripped through her, thrust her life out before her. At the mercy of a Valkyrie.

The head shifted, a pupil flashed green.

One of the mantis arms lifted, lurched forward, and pinned the loose sleeve of Fischer's suit against the ground. The knotted fingers palpated it, the creature processing this novel texture. Fischer's blade glinted in the moonlight.

The leaves shifted again.

Before Lotta could squeeze her eyes shut, the beak lunged down like a spear.

There was a horrifying squeal. The stiff neck reared back, the head looming high again. Lotta saw four limbs and a lizard-like tail wriggling in its jaws. Some indistinct creature trying to claw itself free, claws scratching hollowly in vain against the oppressive beak.

The bird-ape pitched its head up and forced the screaming animal down its throat. A lump moved down its neck and disappeared in a manner that invoked Perez's mouse-hunting ostrich.

The towering beast lingered a moment longer. Its fingers caressing Fischer's sleeve. The massive beak swept over them, and the creature turned, sauntering back toward the dunes with ill regard.

Ratatatatatatatat.

Gnh gnh gnh. Tk tk.

Lotta exhaled.

When the creatures finally moved on, back across the dunes, she noticed a searing pain in her fingertips. Soft warmth trickled from them, and she looked down to find herself picking feverishly at her cuticles.

| NEDJMA >

The ostrich had lost a lot of blood.

It pooled at Perez's feet, snaking away across the inclined floor toward a trench grate that spanned the length of the necropsy lab. The space had been converted to a shock-trauma suite, an overflow unit for the inundated veterinary triage wing down the hall. Blue hazmat suits bustled about, comprising a skeleton crew of ARC's veterinary specialists. Techs rushed to assist surgical teams huddled around steel tables performing emergency procedures on dying animals. Over their heads, parasol-shaped auxiliary lights bloomed intensely. Metal trays with sterile fields held an array of bloodied instruments and packaged supplies. Soiled dressings and discarded autoclave bags littered the floor around their feet. Some floated in pools of blood.

They were understaffed and underprepared. Many of the vet staff had been sidelined after sustaining injuries in the quake. The consequences were already proving catastrophic.

The room was filled with animal sounds. The persistent screams of a restrained vervet. The metallic scraping of a wildebeest's hooves. The eerie chirping of painted reed frogs confined to a holding tank along the far wall, nestled among rows of terrariums and freshwater tanks set up over the last two days. These housed hundreds of ARC's most vulnerable species of amphibians, fishes, testudines, and insects—many the last of their kind. Some likely to fall to extinction in the coming days.

But Perez tried not to dwell on it. Just like she tried not to with Basem, especially the fact that he and the ALICE crew were officially missing. She didn't have that luxury.

The military had started filtering in during the night of the disaster and had dispatched search and rescue teams. All she could do was wait. But whatever the outcome, there would be time to process it all later. Right now, her animals needed her. Her student needed her. Everything else was white noise.

Perez redirected her attention to the ostrich's injuries and clamped a metal hemostat over both ends of the gushing femoral artery while Nedjma craned her neck, ready to assist. The artery had been severed, torn in two. From what she could tell, a mother ostrich had gone berserk in the quake's aftermath and savaged her own chicks. This one was female, almost a juvenile. The ostrich lay on her side, legs splayed out in harnesses, neck held aloft in a sling, still covered in speckled down—a camouflage pattern that faded into sexual maturity. A keratinized double crest, V-shaped and almost fully developed, extended from her nares to the bony ridges above her half-open eyes, its craggy peaks like treacherous mountainsides. Her glassy, empty stare bounced lazily through slitted lids, from which rivulets of encrusted tears mattered her tufted lores. A clear intubation tube snaked into her blood-caked beak, a reminder that she'd been at her wounds when the recovery team found her.

Aside from the deep gash on the ostrich's inner thigh, a few shallower lacerations stretched over her neck and chest, consistent with a swiping, high-powered kick from an adult. She had been abandoned, left to die beside her two siblings. Those two now sat in the walk-in freezer, packed in with the other animal corpses, encased in biohazard bags, their entrails bound in polyethylene.

A shudder worked its way through Perez.

Mother ostrich killed her own young.

She'd seen maternal infanticide before in boars and some rodents.

And in humans...

But never ostriches.

...a matter of survival.

"I need another fifty ccs," Perez shouted over the chaos.

"On it," Marceau, one of the vet techs, said. He ran to a nearby row of coolers that served as a makeshift blood bank, dodging a flurry of technicians in hazmat suits as he crossed the blood-smeared tile and almost slipped. He retrieved a milky-colored bag of artificial blood and hurried it over to another expectant tech named Endrik, who was at the ready to swap out the central line that fed into the jugular. They had already gone through four bags.

Under Perez's supervision, Nedjma washed the exposed ends of the ostrich's artery with anticoagulant, leaving them empty and translucent. Sutures at the ready, Perez leaned in and began stitching the severed ends together, her view magnified through her HUD while dozens of fly-sized surgical bots assisted, checking her knots, ligating and crimping ragged tissue with their tiny pincers to direct healing. They moved in and out of the wound like ants.

Dr. Lena Schulz was the veterinary anesthesiologist assigned to the unit. She stopped by and checked the ostrich's holographic monitor, then inspected the vitals. "All good," she said in a nasally South German accent as she tapped the screen. Behind her face shield, she looked as disheveled as anyone else, her eyes sunken from a lack of sleep, creases on her brow indicating her constant state of stress, of grief. Her hair was tied back but untamable, gray locks escaping and falling into her eyes behind the bulge of her suit's face shield.

She turned without another word and moved down the line to the next group.

Perez finished the final suture. Nedjma came around and prodded the artery with forceps to check its integrity, stretching and folding it to ensure no leaks. She released the hemostat, and synthetic blood rushed through the artery, turning it opaque. The milky substance would be replaced by the ostrich's own blood in a few days.

As they began to close the wound, the little ant-bots filed out. They scurried to tend to the less-serious injuries, cleaning them with antiseptic, weaving the ends of ragged tissue together with tiny webs laced with tissue-regenerating cofactors.

Without warning, the cardiac monitor blared. An echocardiogram flashed red in the upper right corner of Perez's face shield.

The ostrich was about to flatline.

"She's going into hypovolemic shock," Perez said, looking up at Nedjma. "She's lost too much blood."

Nedjma's eyes found hers, darkened circles betraying her fatigue under the hood of her suit. Her face flushed, almost ghoulish in the frame of her jet-black hair. She didn't speak. Didn't need to. *We can save her*, those eyes said. *Trust me.*

With a sigh, Perez gave Nedjma a nod and shouted to the team. "I need epi! I have no pulse."

Schulz came running over with a compression halter, a device capable of species-specific pulmonary resuscitation. It consisted of a network of contracting and releasing straps that pumped the animal's chest, freeing the team to focus their efforts elsewhere. She turned off the anesthesia pump, then secured the device around the ostrich's sternum and activated it.

Perez's heart raced, but her hands remained steady as she turned her attention to securing an IPPV bag to the endotracheal tube. She started rescue breaths, squeezing the bag every six seconds, and her eyes met Nedjma's again.

"Ready for the injection?"

Nedjma nodded. "Let's bag the head, secure the legs."

Bag the head.

Perez thought back again to the incident in the moa paddock. That same day, she'd guided Nedjma through her first necropsy in that room, the same table where they now worked. Nedjma had come far in such a short time. The corners of Perez's mouth crept into a meek smile, and she nodded. Pride swelled inside her, pushing aside her anxiety and fear, if for only a fleeting moment.

Marceau slipped a cloth sack quietly over the ostrich's head, minding the tube so as not to pull it out. Nedjma checked the leg harnesses. Endrik pushed epinephrine into the central line.

The ostrich sprang to life and tried to kick herself free of her restraints. The covering over her head did little to stifle her panic, but the bonds held.

Once she calmed down, Endrik and Marceau transferred her to a veterinary gurney and wheeled her into the hall toward the ICU for stabilization.

Perez let out a long sigh and gave Nedjma a nod.

But before they could clean up and move on to the next case, Athena patched through Perez's comm.

· "Dr. Perez, I am sorry to interrupt. A team is approaching the secondary loading bay with another specimen."

"That's an exterior entrance. I thought we'd already accounted for everything that got out."

"My apologies," Athena said. "I will reappraise ARC's logs."

Perez was growing agitated. "What do they have?"

"They did not say. But they requested you specifically."

Leaving Nedjma to continue, Perez walked onto the loading platform and stood before the badge reader adjacent to the ceiling-high bay door. An overhead rail system enabled large animals to be transferred by suspension cables to various areas in the lab—a walk-in freezer, a crematorium, the necropsy benches now serving as operating tables.

The vervet let out another scream.

The reader beeped at the tap of Perez's badge. A green flash, then red lights oscillated along the perimeter. The door shuddered and hissed, opening vertically into a large decontamination chamber that buffered against the outside world. In many ways, it resembled the ones leading into the dome at the far end of the diagnostic wing, but without the sterilization stalls. It was an open, boxy ingress with stippled concrete walls, a floor composed of metal grating, and a ceiling lined with showerheads.

Perez stepped in and raised her badge to the interior reader. The massive door lurched back down, and the chamber sealed with a metallic *clang*.

A loud hiss filled her ears as the exterior door groaned. A sliver of sunlight cut in beneath it, widening into golden columns as the door climbed, opening to a reinforced docking platform that extended toward open desert.

Perez squinted into the vast Saharan expanse. The vista of dunes stretched and faded in the distance, where it bled into the blue sky.

The dust had finally settled.

A colossal shape coalesced on the horizon, emerging from the shimmering eddies that rose from the sand. It was a Goliath—one of the freighters used for CEPP's shipments in and out of its various sectors. She'd occasionally spot one barreling through the desert, heading toward ALICE. Along its flanks, a small convoy of aerial military vehicles escorted it in her direction. They hovered low to the ground, their shadows rippling across eddies of windswept sand, kicking up dust in the downwash of their dual engines. A low buzzing came to her ears as they approached.

The Goliath churned the sand with its octet of mammoth-sized wheels, leaving a billowing brown cloud in its wake. The vehicle's fore resembled a flight deck or the head of some insect, jutting out two stories over the Earth. The sheer size of the thing struck Perez as it turned and backed in toward the loading dock, towering over her. Along its flank, a white insignia flashed in the hot sun:

Warmth trickled into the nape of her neck.

Did they find Basem? Is that why they're here?

A dark veil of dread fell over her. She faltered on trembling legs but regrouped, swallowed against an expanding mass at the back of her throat.

The freighter came to rest, its aft end positioned to receive the docking platform's lift. The military choppers circled around it and roared to the right of the chamber entrance, their engines coming to rest just beyond view as they touched down. Perez heard the hiss of hydraulics, then the sound of muffled yelling. Two soldiers emerged from the platform's right, clad in ash-colored hazmat gear, shouldering automatic weapons.

One of them pointed toward the Goliath. Half a dozen synths came up from behind, then moved out ahead to secure the house-sized wheels with chains.

One of the soldiers remained posted by the entrance as the second started up the docking ramp that led up to the platform. Beneath the rubbery suit and heavy military outfit, Perez saw that the approaching soldier was a woman, her face concealed behind a black breathing apparatus. Her rifle was folded and racked at forty-five degrees against a thick chest plate, freeing her hands. Beneath this, a black vest with thickly padded shoulder straps and a wide waistband added yet more bulk to what already appeared to be a muscular frame. High up on the left strap, a small symbol—a yellow and black trefoil—revealed the vest's purpose.

A radiation vest.

"Dr. Perez?"

A subtle Italian accent. The soldier's voice sounded muffled, almost mechanical through her helmet comm. Around her left bicep, she had a bright blue band with a white emblem at its center—an azimuthal globe encircled by twelve golden stars, the flag of the European Federation. Below this, another band, this one white, sported the letters *MOD* in black typeface, indicating she served in a branch of the European Ministry of Defence. Beneath it, a motto: *We are many. We are one.* Her eyes met Perez's—an intent brown stare from behind her clear face shield. A straight row of short bangs cut across her brow, receding into a bowl-cut fade of jet-black hair. Everything about her appearance was harsh, even her skin. Deep gold, toned, with dark circles around her eyes.

"Yes, that's me," Perez said.

"We have something for you. Follow me." The soldier turned before Perez could respond and started back down the ramp. A crop of tightly fastened hosing fed into the back of her helmet from a back-mounted oxygen generator beneath her suit.

Perez remained in place, hesitant. "What is it? Who are you?"

But the woman kept walking, only turning her head slightly to respond. "We're here on Commission orders; that's all you need to know. Let's go."

Perez followed.

From the ground level, the loading dock stretched a full story overhead. Perez's boots found sand, dragging through it as they sidled past the Goliath's giant mesh wheels one by one. The chalky CEPP logo came into view along its hull, like a huge clock face, and Perez's throat seized. The warmth on her neck intensified. Her heart thrashed against her insides like an animal rattling its cage, looking for a way out. She started to feel winded, her calves burning from walking through the sand.

As they neared the front entrance of the freighter, the crew cabin emerged from the vehicle's hulking flank, vaulting up from the chassis like a polyhedric insectoid head with a trio of facet-angled windshields for eyes. From its angled jowls jutted a boarding ramp that led to the cabin's entrance—a proboscis ready to ensnare them, reel them toward its waiting mandibles. Another suited figure, a man of hardened aspect, greeted them where the ramp met the ground, rifle in hand.

The soldier leading the way stepped aside and gestured Perez toward the entrance, signaling up the ramp.

The world seemed to be coming down around Perez, the anticipation of what awaited her inside. *They found him. They want me to identify the body.* She swallowed, half-choking against the lump in her throat—grief already manifesting, rearing its head. Her subconscious anticipating, preparing her for interminable anguish. After a lifetime of buttressing her emotions, the walls began to crumble, each footfall up the metallic proboscis rocking her foundation, her mental house of cards, bringing her closer to ruin.

She wanted to turn, wanted to run away.

Just like she intended to with Ruth.

Just like she always had.

<h1 style="text-align:center">< ᚻ | DEATH'S SHADOW ></h1>

"She's gone. I'm sorry."

The words dripped like poison from the doctor's slow-moving lips.

Fischer's knees faltered as his wife, Jocelyn, collapsed into his arms.

"Emma!" she wailed, her legs limp as he guided her back into the waiting-room chair. "Oh, no. *No no no*. Not my baby. Not my—m-my sweet bear. Please, God, please, no...."

The memory of Jocelyn's screams still felt vivid, sometimes real. Some nights, Fischer still jerked awake, drenched in sweat, thinking he'd heard her calling out for Emma. Even though he hadn't spoken to his ex-wife in years. Not since the girls died.

Their faces had faded with time because Fischer couldn't bear to keep photographs around. But he wished he could still see them in his mind's eye, choose which memories haunted him. Instead, it was Jocelyn's plaintive wails that endured. Other times, he thought he caught the smell of soot and smoke and rain-soaked plaster. Or dreamed of carrying a tiny, broken body in his arms. Lying limp, draped in blood-stained linen. The rain pounding him as he walked with his little Emma from the smoldering wreckage to a waiting ambulance.

His bear.

Those were the memories that lingered.

Emma. Ellsa. Evi.

They're gone. ›

●

The Forest

"*They're gone. They're gone.*" Lotta chanted the words like a mantra. She was crying. "*Basem… Martin… Mattheo… they're gone.…*"

Fischer was still on his back, staring up at the treetops, knife clenched tightly against his chest. Overhead, the branches swirled about like he'd been on a bender. *Like a bad case of the spins.* Shards of moonlight spilled through the whorled limbs like shimmering water. As if submerged, staring up from the depths, drowning in his own bodily fluids.

Fischer coughed. Lungs rattled, his pulse like a drum roll. He tried to focus, tried to slow his rhythm—*in and out, in and out*—but every time he did, another round of hacking came. He closed his eyes.

They're gone.

He looked over at Lotta. She leaned forward with her hands on her knees, her chest heaving.

"This is my fault," she said. "*This is all my fault.* They're gone, Ed."

They're gone. The words triggered him, but he pushed the memories aside. He had to.

Fischer was not much of a consoler. For years, he'd dampened his own emotions. Had fallen out of practice. Became stunted. Avoided his crushing reality for so long that he didn't really know how to *feel* anymore. Had navigated his despondency through a lens of substance abuse, self-loathing, and, at his lowest, suicidal ideation.

He brushed his fingers over the scars on his wrists.

He was the last person on Earth that Lotta needed.

But he tried.

"Here, slow your breathing," he said as he crawled toward her, his speech slurred owing to his swollen tongue. "Deep breath in, deep breath out."

Lotta inhaled through her nose, exhaled through her mouth.

"Better?"

She nodded and raised her head. "I should be the one coaching *you*. You can barely stand."

"Aye. I'll be alright." Fischer forced a half-smile, tensing his jaw as he stifled another cough. Pain shot through his ribcage.

Lotta got to her feet and wiped her eyes.

"This air seem thin to you?" he asked.

Lotta nodded. "Yeah. Yeah, it is."

Fischer struggled to his feet with Lotta's assistance.

"Best get moving," he grunted. "We need to find shelter."

They were lucky to have moonlight, but they needed to move quickly and get out of the open.

"What about Hassan?" Lotta said. "He could still be out there."

Fischer nodded. "Might be. But right now, we need to find a spot to hole up for the night."

"Ed, we can't just—"

"We'll have a better sense of how to proceed come daybreak."

Lotta said nothing. Fischer knew she was scared, but her suggestions defied logic under the circumstances. It had started to grate on him. He fumbled unconsciously at his left pant leg. His finger and thumb pinched together around—*nothing*—a phantom cap on a phantom flask. Force of habit. By now, he imagined, he'd be back in his dingy flat, three drinks deep. Off to bed. Nurse a hangover the next day before work. Rinse and repeat.

His skin was clammy, sticky with cold sweat. The forest drifted slowly about the axis of his head, as if he were standing in the middle of a carousel. Temples throbbing, hands quivering, his skull in a vice—Little Man was really doing a number up there, clogging away, belting his drunken tune.

Fischer coughed and spit. Focused on his breathing, regrouped.

"Let's take to the woods a bit more," he said. "Those things seem to stick mostly to the open.

And probably for good reason.

"What the hell are they?"

"I don't know." He shook his head and stumbled sideways. *But what I do know is this fucking vertigo won't let up.*

Whatever the creatures were, he wanted as much of a barrier between him and them as possible. No telling if—or when—they might return.

"And that thing that got Martin…." She dug furiously at her cuticles as she spoke. "Where are we, Ed?"

The *click-click-click* of her picking only added to his irritability. He looked down at the ground and shook his head with a shrug. "Can't say."

You're the one in charge—you tell me.

But one thing he felt sure of was that old-growth forests no longer existed in North Africa. And certainly not coniferous woodlands. Those populated the northern latitudes and whatever remained of the tropics. Not Algeria, nor any other part of Africa that he was aware of.

Still, the rich scent of pine felt familiar. A sweet, cloying smell. It broke through the stench leaching from his suit just enough that it conjured memories of his military days, special operations he'd led through the Baltic wilderness.

Leichter Speer.

Fischer's thoughts shifted to the poor bastard he'd stabbed in that dive near Shin Tower. The Latvian bloke and his chum whose larynx he'd readjusted. He remembered the words the foolish bastard had said, clear as day.

"Leichter Speer. The failed op that launched the Three-Day War."

Fischer ran his fingers across the grooved insignia on his knife handle. The same one the Latvian had pointed out before they danced.

"My brother fought in the resistance… Russians got him, tortured him. All because of you."

Fischer breathed as deep as his battered lungs allowed and put the thought out of his mind.

Pine needles and ferns rustled underfoot as they continued farther into the undergrowth. Celestial rays filtered through the canopy, to which rows of mighty conifers rose like ethereal spires. Their curled branches arcing toward the gibbous moon. The antithesis of the colossal white columns lording within the halls of Shin Tower.

The alabastrine forest entombed within a glass tesseract.

Fischer remembered walking into the clinic. Remembered the grueling process he'd gone through, the genetic overhaul. Had it not been for the DNA hardening, he'd already be dead. Prophylactics or not.

Lotta was right. He needed medical attention. They both did.

The winged giants that had killed Basem came up many times as they walked.

"What were those things?"

After a while, Fischer didn't bother giving an answer. It seemed Lotta was asking herself just as much as she was him. She eventually settled on calling them "stalkers." As good an answer as any, he supposed.

Might as well call the fuckers something.

But he preferred to look ahead, not back. Prepare himself for the next thing, whatever it might be. From every shadow lurked unseen denizens of the forest. Fischer heard them move about the branches. Others hooted and moaned deep through the underbrush. He expected the trees to spring to life, morph into something horrible—one of the stalkers. Or something new.

Something worse.

As they pressed forward, he snapped twigs and dropped them in his wake, a trail to keep them from walking in circles. *Might even guide rescuers to us.* He audited landmarks as best he could—rocks, unique root systems, fallen logs. But he could only see so much through swollen eyes amid the veil of night. At any rate, he should have a good mental map back to Basem's body, where they could scavenge anything of utility come daybreak. Then they'd get a move on for a water source. There would be no burial.

Fischer stopped to catch his breath. It came in rattling sighs, required almost constant effort, constant focus. He coughed in his hand and glanced down. Still blood, but less than before.

A good sign.

He studied the splotchy bruises riddling his skin and realized for the first time how swollen his arms and hands had become. His wristwatch constricted around his forearm, the skin imbibed, bulging out from the band like a cinched balloon animal. To his surprise, it didn't hurt. He released the watch's clasp and carefully slid it off. The face was cracked and dark.

Broken.

He dropped it to the ground, where it landed with a soft *thud* atop a bed of fallen pine needles. Another marker. More evidence of their whereabouts. It also served as another guide marker to keep them from retreading trodden ground and wasting precious energy.

Minutes passed. Breathing came a little easier.

Fischer took a moment to glance around at their surroundings. Off to his left, he spotted a downed conifer wedged between two others such that it formed a shallow incline.

"There," he said, pointing at it. "That's shelter. We'll close it in." He stumbled toward the deadfall to inspect it. "We need to work slow and calm to conserve water."

"There has to be water nearby," Lotta said. "Just look at all this vegetation."

Fischer walked around where the large trunk had wedged itself tightly between two other conifers. "Looks can be deceiving," he said and walked back around to the other side, leaning hard against the length of the felled tree every meter or so. He nodded. "It'll hold."

"Okay," Lotta said. "And, so, what about water, then?"

"We'll check first thing."

They worked for over an hour by moonlight. Fischer had built many shelters during his time out on missions. Had learned to use the land, the resources at his disposal. Lotta took his lead.

The shelter was a basic double lean-to, with branches they had set in an A-frame along the length of the trunk, covering the remaining gaps with sticks, twigs, and a modest layer of ferns. The front entrance consisted of two Y-sticks anchored into the coarse soil about a meter from the entrance, with two cross-pieces cantilevered across their notches. This formed a cuboidal crawl space that sealed the structure and helped trap warm air. They closed it in with whatever remaining sticks and debris they could find.

A triplet of low hoots erupted somewhere in the distance. Lotta looked around nervously, rubbing her upper arms. Fischer dismissed the sounds and turned back to their work.

"Not bad," he sighed, giving the final structure a look-over. His swollen hands hung heavy at his sides, throbbing to the beat of Little Man's tune. Another cough. His head and lungs killed, muscles burned, but the vertigo had almost subsided.

"You need to ditch the suit," Lotta said, "or we'll be swimming in fumes."

Without thinking anything of it, Fischer nodded and began to strip down.

Lotta turned away, her gaze shifting to the treetops. "Are you actually *naked* under that thing?"

Fischer nodded. "Told you. I like airflow."

"*No.*" Lotta demurred. "No way in *hell.* I am not getting in that sweatbox with you like *that.*"

"Suit yourself." He gave an apathetic shrug and continued to peel the rubbery suit down his heavily bruised legs. The cold air against his swollen skin. A welcome feeling.

Lotta huffed as she looked at their surroundings, then aimed her eyes squarely at him. "Sleep with your back to me. Understood?"

"Sure thing," Fischer said.

He took his knife, draped his suit on a nearby sapling, and then gestured for the entrance.

Lotta got onto her hands and knees and crawled inside. Fischer followed, backfilling the porthole entrance with a plug of vegetation behind him. Inside, quarters were tight. His shoulders scraped against branches as he probed his way through the dark and came up next to Lotta. She had already claimed her side along a bed of ferns. He eased down beside her, his back against the earth, cramped between her body and the slanted wall of sticks and vegetation.

Fischer stared up into the blackness.

An hour passed, maybe two. Lotta tossed about, butting up against him, sighing heavily. At times, Fischer heard—and felt—her stifled sobs. He did his best to feign sleep, but his head pounded. He longed for a drink. Had broken into a cold sweat, shivering like a wet dog, trying to recount the last time he'd fallen so ill.

Another hour, perhaps. Lotta had eased into a restless slumber. To Fischer, sleep seemed impossible....

Fischer jolted awake with pain in his chest. Felt almost feverish, his skin clammy under a sheet of cold sweat, shivering as if taken by sickness. He felt as desperate as ever for a splash of whiskey under the tongue. Raked his beard with his fingers. Cleared foam from the corners of his mouth. *How long has it been since that last swig? Hours? Days?* He couldn't be sure.

Even now, time slowed. Moments of fleeting wakefulness—elicited by muscle spasms, bouts of nausea—ebbed and flowed, bleeding into lucid fever dreams, each lasting a lifetime. Most consisted of his time in the Special Forces, his last operation—*Leichter Speer*—the flashpoint in the Three-Day War.

"Russians got him, tortured him...."

Trapped between delirium and sleep, dogged by hallucinations of the Latvian wilderness, his men at his side.

"...all because of you."

And then the words of a ghost. His little Emma.

"Daddy! Daddy! Watch me, Daddy!"

Fischer snapped awake again. Smelled decaying wood and pine. Lotta's hand on his shoulder, shaking him.

"Ed!" Her tone came through in a hushed, urgent whisper. "Ed, did you hear that?"

Fischer felt fingers clasp around his wrist, laid over his old scars.

"Hear? Hear what?" he asked through the musty air of the lean-to.

"Shhh! Keep your voice down! There's something outside!"

She trembled furiously. Fischer blinked and wiped the sleep from his eyes. He peered into blackness.

They sat in silence and listened.

All he heard was the soughing treetops.

He turned and whispered, "Just a breeze...."

"Wait."

Another minute passed. Fischer heard something else—light footfalls patting the ground a few meters from his side of the shelter. Then a swell of air, hollow, filling the lungs of something lingering, perhaps watching. A sound like lapping ocean waves. The presence lingered for a time, unmoving. Then more footfalls—dampened thuds atop the fallen pine needles and detritus. Something stalking closer, careful with its approach, determined.

The thing circled to Lotta's side, snuffed along the base of the shelter, then let out a gust of air that sent some of the exterior twigs flying. Lotta's grip tightened around Fischer's arm. A loud snort erupted right beside her head, and Lotta's hand shuddered, her nails digging in.

He gripped the cold handle of his knife.

More snorts tracked upward toward the roof. With each exhale came a faint, oscillating whine. An almost pitiful moan.

Then, the sound of trickling water, followed by a gush of thick liquid splattering against the outer wall directly above Lotta. A putrid stench seeped into the shelter. The cutting sensory assault of ferrofluid couldn't begin to match it. A thickly sour smell.

It took everything Fischer had to stifle his retching through the jolts of pain stabbing through his ribs.

The thing, the creature, lingered for a few more moments and, with a final snort, plodded off into the forest and receded into the rustling trees.

"What the *fuck* was that?" Lotta spat through gritted teeth, her fingernails still digging into Fischer. Her voice muffled behind her other hand clenched over her nose and mouth.

He tensed his jaw through the pain in his arm. "I don't know," he said. "Bear, maybe."

"Is it gone?"

"Don't think so. We're safe in here."

Lotta scoffed.

"Is that supposed to put me at ease?"

"Well, did it?"

"*No.*" She started to sob again. "That thing just… *shit* on us, or something."

Fischer snorted. "Smells that way."

Lotta huffed, then turned away without another word.

Fischer turned on his back, staring into the silent dark once more.

Sleep eluded him.

| JACOBS >

The Goliath's crew cabin far exceeded the size of anything Perez had imagined. At the center of the sprawling interior, an expansive raised platform filled with workstations and holographic displays stretched before her, flanked by meandering passages partitioned by frosted glass. Artificial light beat down from overhead, recessed into a high ceiling that housed an intricate network of pipes and struts.

Along the main deck, a dozen unarmed personnel moved about in hazmat suits, indifferent to her presence. At its fore end, shafts of golden light filtered through the panoramic windshield, silhouetting more hazmat suits against the Saharan backdrop. Workers loomed over a large console from high-backed seats on sliding tracks, dwarfed by the enormous glass panels.

Along the wall nearest her, a soldier stood in front of a large slate door with the words *CARGO HOLD* white across its face.

Perez's sedated footfalls carried her up a set of metal steps as she walked alongside the female soldier toward two other soldiers in identical hazmat suits. Their backs to Perez, they appeared to be conversing as they gazed off toward the open desert. They wore the same armbands as the woman—MOD, the flag of the Federation, the same motto—as well as radiation vests over body armor. A clear liquid fell in streams from their rubbery uniforms, as if they had just come out of the rain. The taller of the two clasped his hands behind his back, cradling a helmet beaded with clear drops that glistened beneath the lights. The second soldier, still wearing his helmet, bounced on his heels, a rifle hugged close to his chest.

"Sir," the female soldier said.

The men turned.

"Kohen." The helmetless one nodded at the woman, then turned his attention to Perez. "And you must be Dr. Perez." He extended his hand toward her. "Oberstleutnant Nikolaj Jacobson. Jacobs, if you prefer."

Perez placed his accent as Scandinavian, possibly Danish. He appeared to be around fifty, hair speckled gray and cropped short into a crew cut fade. Thin-lipped with a long, weather-worn face and gray skin. A thin, straight nose. He looked back at her without expression, aside from the muscles clenching in his clean-shaven cheeks.

Perez kept her arms at her sides.

Jacobs held out his hand a few seconds more, regarding her through piercing blue eyes, then retracted the gesture with a wiry smile.

"Right, then. Welcome aboard," he said.

Perez glanced over at the woman, Kohen, then back at Jacobs. "Is there something I can do for you?"

Her chest ran hot. Fingers trembling. Teeth clicking, doing her best to cope with the utter vagueness of the situation. Military types had a knack for sending her heart into her throat. At the back of her mind, rumblings of her childhood, the maltreatment of her family at the hands of UEF agents. Nightmares of disappearing off to the skies to be swallowed into the penal system, shipped off to the gaols for any offense they might think up. *Like Uncle Diego.*

But at the forefront, what sent Perez reeling, made her want to sink back into the Saharan sands, was the nagging uncertainty of Basem's whereabouts. Of not knowing if he was okay. Of suspecting that maybe these people had an idea, but that she was the last person they would ever tell. Something had happened down there. It nagged at her. Devoured her from within like a parasite.

Like an unwanted pregnancy.

Warmth spread over her cheeks. A pit took root in her stomach.

What an awful thought.

A storm swelling inside her, consuming her. Crushing her.

Forgive me, chavala.

She choked back tears.

Not now. Not here. Please not now.

Her mother's voice cut through: *One day, you will have children of your own. You need to do it right.*

Jacobs drew her back in. "As you know," he said, "we have been conducting a search-and-rescue op over at the Higgs."

A pang in her chest. "Sector ALICE."

"Yes. Sector ALICE. We found something there—*here*—aboard this freighter. Berlin has requested I seek your expertise on the matter, so here we are."

Perez looked around at the crew. Suspected that they were listening, merely pretending to focus on their tasks. Her eyes leveled with Jacobs's again. "My expertise is in veterinary medicine and ornithology." She glanced at the other two, then back to Jacobs. "So, unless you've got some Saharan desert pigeons roosting in your wheel wells, I'd like to know why I'm here."

Jacobs seemed taken by her sardonicism. His eyes narrowed. He lingered there, peering into her, then broke into a trenchant smile and chuckled. "Of course you do!"

"I'm sorry," she said, "but I have many injured animals and a student to attend to…."

Ignoring her, Jacobs turned to the man beside him. It was as if Perez had thought the words instead of uttering them. Then he turned back and looked her up and down. "Your suit will do. Oz, here, will be joining us."

Perez glanced at Oz. Built like an ox, a barrel chest barely concealed behind his body armor. Like Kohen, most of his face was hidden beneath a respirator, but he was obviously younger than Jacobs, maybe early forties. His eyes dark but soft, hooded by a prominent brow that sat straight and low, the skin furrowed in the middle. His square jaw sprouted curled hair from the edge of his respirator, rounding out his grizzled aesthetic.

"We should head in," Jacobs said, nodding behind her toward the aft end of the deck.

Perez turned. The door to the cargo hold peered back at her like some portal into a nightmare.

Her mind kept going to Basem. The thought was irrational, that she might find answers here. But it was one she could not shake.

She turned back to Jacobs, and her skin crawled. She went from clicking her teeth to chewing the inside of her cheek. She knew how these people operated. Knew where it might land her if she continued along the path of resistance. Jacobs didn't need to say anything more to convince her. She knew he knew that.

They can take everything away from you. The words of her mother again.

Face flushed, her pulse drumming behind her eyes, Perez gave a meek nod. Against her instincts. Against all she stood for.

"Good," Jacobs said. He secured his helmet over his head. A loud hiss. A moment later, his suit ballooned around his arms and legs. "Activate your suit's positive pressure before we go in."

Perez toggled a switch on her wrist. A faint whistle came from somewhere at the back of her head. She caught a synthetic chemical smell as her suit inflated. In the upper right of her face shield, lines of green text blinked into view.

Oxygen Status: 100%
Set Pressure: (+)7 kPa
Flow Rate: 379 L/min

Jacobs led the way to the cargo hold entrance. The soldier standing guard moved to the badge reader.

Perez inhaled and closed her eyes. The hum of her suit seemed to block the outside world.

Jacobs patched through her comm. "We activated the onboard cooling system, so it will be cold inside. Your suit's thermoregulation should be enough to keep you comfortable. Just stick with me, and you'll be fine."

Perez's vision narrowed, fixated on the cargo door. A ringing in her ears, a hypnotic dissonance that only furthered the door's—*the portal's*—grip. Her feet had turned leaden, legs groaning, agonizing under burgeoning weight. Resisted the inevitable, that whatever she might find beyond the veil, whatever truth she convinced herself would manifest, was something she was woefully underprepared to confront. If something horrible really had happened to the ALICE crew, to Basem, maybe it was better left unknown.

Turn back.

But something carried her. A competing impulse. An unseen force conducting her advance like a malevolent puppeteer. Instinct. The inescapable impetus to peek behind the curtain, no matter the cost.

Jacobs nodded to the guard. He tapped his badge to the reader, and the door opened.

An opaque barrier with a biohazard sign and the words *BIOCON-TAINMENT: BSL-4 PERSONNEL ONLY* dominated Perez's field of view. It was made of a thin polymer that bowed inward, bisected down the middle by a slit. Jacobs parted it with his hands, wisps of frosty condensation spilling out around him, then stepped inside and out of sight. Perez followed, with Oz close behind.

She emerged on the other side to find herself in a makeshift vestibule the size of a large closet, its frame composed of memory metal draped in the same thick clear material as the entrance barrier. She stared a meter over her head, where a row of metal showerheads loomed.

Oz came up behind her, squeezing through the entrance slit. The walls flexed outward, then sighed back to their original state as the opening resealed behind him.

Perez strained to look out through the dappled barrier. It sealed them off from the interior of the mostly dim cargo hold, where she spotted half a dozen loading mechs standing silently along the nearest wall, their legs chained to the floor beneath rows of suspended walkways and staircases.

She turned her head in the opposite direction and leaned forward. What she could discern of the cargo hold was huge. Cast in darkness, it gave her the illusion of some endless void, its terminal end far beyond her purview. Overhead, what appeared to be a yellow gantry hovered, inert at the end of an enormous steel track that stretched far in the other direction, swallowed by darkness. It looked like a large warehouse more than a vehicle.

From the other end of the structure, she spotted a long, circular tunnel that accordioned out about a dozen meters toward a vague tented unit that glowed a soft white.

Something sputtered overhead. Perez jumped.

"Arms out," Jacobs said.

Streams of the clear liquid rippled across her face shield, the sound of droplets pecking the shell of her suit. Her surroundings reduced to a shimmering smear.

The shower stopped, and Jacobs turned toward another slitted opening on the other end of the vestibule. Perez followed.

The tunnel was a rounded structure—collapsible corrugated piping made of the same material as the entrance. Perez stared down its length, the helical frame stretching out before her like a hypnotic spiral. Overhead, nozzles lined a single flexible hose that ran along its length. A fine mist erupted from them, forming a particulate haze that glowed white from the tunnel's path lighting.

Jacobs led Perez and Oz toward the glowing tent. She strained to see beyond the fine mist, the droplets of clear liquid now speckling her face shield. The light from inside intensified as they drew near, and a third partition materialized through the haze. Jacobs swept it aside with one hand and gestured Perez to move through with the other.

The mist cleared, her vision awash as she stepped through and into the light. Something like a gasp stopped in her throat and settled there as a mass. She stepped backward into Jacobs.

"Unusual, isn't it?" he said.

The thing—an enormous mass of limbs and flesh—lay sprawled on its side atop a steel dissecting table at the center of a large isolation canopy. Stage lighting encircled it—wide dome lights bowing over the creature like contemplative postulants, a religious order of the luminescent. They had come to gather about their cursed altar, a shallow basin, its raised edges tapered to form a rounded lip. It was mounted to a hydraulic lift, bolted to the floor.

Perez noticed the creature's arms first. As long as human legs, they terminated in three black claws—a cage of scythes reaching out in a cold embrace.

Her breathing came in shallow rattles as she processed what she was seeing. Her legs shaking, she stepped forward.

"Is it one of ARC's?" Jacobs said.

Perez's eyes found him. She shook her head, then turned back to the creature. Its head was arched backward, out of sight, obscured behind a body now bloated in death. Its skin—a pattern of greenish-black scales—appeared macerated, sloughing away in areas, dry and flaking in others.

Chemical burns.

A pair of muscular, agile-looking legs almost as tall as her rested limp against the cold steel. Toes with claws the size of her hands splayed from their ends, each locked into rigor mortis like those of some giant lifeless bird. Too long to be contained to the table, they dangled over the edge.

Perez moved in closer.

A viscous ash-colored substance—some type of caustic agent—swathed much of the creature's body, glistening beneath the lights. In some areas, deep ulcerations pocked the animal's pebbled skin, a whitish foam coalescing along their edges.

Liquefactive necrosis.

She rounded the table, her heart thrashing. Off to the races. The mass in her throat, the choked gasp, partially escaped her lips as a whimper at the sight before her: a long striped tail, curled backward and hanging over the edge. The body was arched back into a crescent, with wispy filaments—shimmering greens, grays, and browns—extending the length of its back all the way to the head.

The head.

Perez swallowed hard, approaching the front end now, each step heavier than the last.

She stopped, turned away for a moment. Her gaze fell back on the creature. Clotted blood clung to its downy neck, where ragged flesh and bits of shattered vertebrae dangled from a gaping wound. Atop an elongated, almost reptilian snout protruded a cragged double crest, notched and bony, sheathed in keratin and scales.

She came about. Ropes of semi-dried blood dangled from jaws held slightly ajar, locked in their final throes, gums lined with serrated, blood-stained teeth. A dilated eye stared back at her with an empty gaze. Thick layers of gore caked its face and neck, its chest. Dozens of penetrating wounds pocked its hide.

Bullet holes.

Perez flashed a look at Jacobs.

"What happened to it?"

Jacobs bowed his head as if to consider something. He leveled again with her and narrowed his eyes. "Athena, patch incident log seven to our comms. No video feed."

Perez heard static, then a high-pitched scraping in her ears. The sound of animal claws, maybe hooves, dragging across metal. A loud thud. Then, something wholly alien, distant.

<*Grreelllppp… ellppp.*>

A chill ran down her spine.

"What was that?" she said. "Was that a person?"

Jacobs remained stone-faced, his blue eyes staring into hers.

The strange calls repeated. Gurgling and raspy, muffled as if concealed behind some sort of barrier.

She heard what sounded like guns being shouldered, indistinct movements, light footfalls. Then a voice.

<*Sir, someone's in there,*> a man whispered in a French accent. It sounded like Oz. <*I'm not picking up any movement. Can't get a heat signature.*>

Jacobs: <*Open it.*>

A mechanical sound, a door sliding open. *The entrance to the cargo hold.* More movement. They stopped. Silence.

A soft whimper.

<*Grrreelllppp-p-p-p.*>

<*Oy. The fuck is that?*> Another male voice. *Welsh accent.*

<*Fall back.*> A woman this time. *Kohen.*

A loud hiss.

<*—ellpp-elpp-ellpp.*>

Perez found Jacobs's eyes again. "Is that…" She raised a trembling finger toward the carcass.

Jacobs only stared back.

Another scream clipped through her comm. *<Greelll-ell-ellp.>*

It sounded almost human.

"We have reason to believe it mimicked its victim to draw us in," Jacobs finally said.

Perez felt herself leave her body. "Victim? Who?"

Please, not Basem.

"A man. Remains have yet to be identified."

Nausea overtook her.

"What did he look like?" Before she thought to temper the urgency in her voice, the words had already come out.

Jacobs narrowed his eyes again. "There was not much left to look at, frankly. Pasty fellow, white, by the looks of it. Dead a day or two. Like I said, we couldn't get a positive ID."

Not Basem. Perez sighed quietly. A weight had fallen from her chest.

She returned her attention to the carcass, imagined how it must have moved. How it behaved. Started to think of animals capable of vocal mimicry. Some birds, primates, whales.

Margays—a now-extinct species of wildcat—had been known to mimic the calls of tamarin monkeys to lure them in....

But she was at a loss for what lay before her. She had never seen anything like it.

A loud clang in her ears, claws falling to metal. She jumped at the sound. Another. And another.

<Fire!>

Jacobs gave a thin-lipped smile and cut the feed amid a hail of rapid bangs.

"Hope that answers your question," he said.

Perez bounced her gaze over the animal's bullet wounds, the ulcerations. She looked at Jacobs.

"This *thing* is not coming into my lab. We have strict biocontainment protocols. Our animal populations are extremely vulnerable."

"Not to worry," Jacobs said with an indifference Perez found agitating. "You will be conducting your investigation here."

"The Scientific Council—"

"Has no sway. It takes its marching orders from the Commission, and so do you. You have seventy-two hours to get me a report." He turned to Oz, who straightened.

"Sir?" Oz said.

Jacobs eyed him for a moment. "Stay behind, help get the containment area set to Dr. Perez's specifications. You're going to supervise her for the duration of her investigation. No one else comes in, understood?"

Oz nodded. "Sir."

Perez stepped toward Jacobs. "I need my team for this."

Jacobs mirrored her and leaned in. "Out of the question."

A power play.

"Then I cannot help you, Colonel." A hill she was prepared to die on.

Haz lo que te salga de los cojones. Take me to the gaols if you must. Que os den por saco.

She hoped the suit concealed her trembling hands, her trembling legs, tremors coursing through her. Not because of the creature. Because of him. Jacobs. What she knew he was capable of. What the Federation was capable of.

His eyes seared into her, a flash of anger—almost imperceptible—there and gone in an instant, replaced by an attempt at a warm smile. His jaw clenching, betraying the facade. He glanced at Oz, then back at her. The corners of his papery lips fell.

"One. You get one assistant."

With the thrum of her pulse in her ears, Perez exhaled.

< ᛒ | LILITH >

"ETAC, this is FHQ. What's your status? Over."

Fischer peered through still trees toward a desolate dirt road. His men, a crew of six, lay prone, cloaked beneath densely packed pines near the edge of a moss-covered forest. Mushrooms sprouted up along buttressed trunks. Tinges of brassy sunlight glimmered through needled branches. A musky, sweet smell hung like malt in the air.

Dusk would be on them soon.

"Sir, waiting on our transport. Over," Fischer whispered over his helmet comm.

Their pickup was late.

We should've been en route to Daugavpils by now.

His team was composed of a rag-tag stitchwork of elite European Special Forces known as Erebus Tactical Assault Crew, or ETAC. Team 3 to the suits in Berlin. Erebus to everyone else. After half a decade of serving in the European Maritime Force, Edgar Fischer had climbed to the rank of team leader for naval special operations. A title that carried with it great honor, great responsibility. For the mission, the lives of his men. For a unified Europe.

"Oy," one of his comrades, a poor bloke from Belfast who went by Capp, chimed in. "I'm fuckin' threaders, mate. Let's get this show on the road."

Fischer shot back with a half-grin. "You wouldn't expect any less from such a high-profile op, eh?"

"Guess not." Capp turned and eyed their sniper, Sully. "Almost went to shit, eh, mate?"

Sully was a grizzled Irish man in his early thirties, hair as ginger as a Jack-O-lantern, a long beard jutting from his jowls. "Almost," he said, taking a swig from his canteen.

Erebus's insertion into Latvia had gotten off to a rocky start, and a civilian was dead because of it.

They had crossed by way of a powered submersible from Šalna—a small lake in the Lithuanian border district of Zarasai. After reaching shore, they started on their twelve-kilometer hike through dense Latvian wilderness toward their rendezvous. But two clicks in, Sully had nearly walked up on a man strolling through the thick brush, a dead lynx draped over one shoulder, rifle slung around the other. And not a second later, the hunter spotted them, too, then took off running in the other direction.

Sully was the one to pull the trigger, but Fischer had given the order. FHQ deemed the mission too valuable and had given him full autonomy. The suits took no chances, and neither did he. They were unlikely to get a second shot at capturing Evgeni Dmitriev, head of the Latvian Separatist Militia, a splinter faction of Russian sympathizers. So, Fischer made a calculation.

"One less poacher in the world, at any rate," Capp said.

Fischer paid him no heed and looked toward the road again. Another five minutes passed.

The unrelenting scent of pine. The final bloody rays of daylight. He raised his binoculars. A glint of light—*headlights*—crept around the bend.

"Sunday driver inbound. That's our ride," he said.

"'Bout time the fuckin' mong found his way," Capp mumbled. "Let's pop smoke, lads."

The headlights flickered as the vehicle jostled up the dirt road. Shadows danced over the spindly trees, their limbs curling down claustrophobically as dusk fell. Bits of gravel crackled beneath tire treads. The vehicle jolted to a stop, and the driver killed the engine. Fischer heard a battered door creaking open behind the shroud of white light.

A shadowy figure stepped down onto the running board, but Erebus did not move. Fischer stared, perplexed by what he was seeing.

This... this isn't possible.

It was his wife, thirty-five weeks along and standing barefoot in the middle of the path.

Can't be. It's not real.

She was wearing a thin, flowing nightgown. Mud caked midway up her legs. She rested her hands gently beneath her navel and looked directly at him. Her gaze cut through the darkness, his veil of shadow. Cover blown. She smiled at him, her face pale, black circles around her eyes.

"Jocelyn?" Fischer whispered. Pressure in his chest. Hands trembling, gripping the binoculars. Tears streamed down his cheeks.

She stared back, unblinking. Empty. Her smile fell away. Lips now curling into a grimace. Teeth bared with glowering fury. Her skin blanched white.

The stench of death.

"You were never here," she howled. A shrill, throaty cry. "I needed you, and you were never here." The mud crawled up to her thighs and crept beneath her gown. It consumed her.

"I-I'm sorry, I—"

Fischer stopped cold, his pulse whooshing in his ears.

A crimson spot bloomed between Jocelyn's legs. Slowly, it swelled, cascading as a bright red band down the white linen. Her mouth fell open, stretched to her collar bone. She reached for him with blackened fingers.

Edgar Fischer tried to scream.

Before he could get to his feet—bound toward her through the thicket, take his wife in his arms, make everything okay again—her form faded into the glowing lights. >

Day 1, Dawn - The Forest

"Jocelyn!" Fischer bolted upright, his head striking something hard and ligneous. "*Verdammte Scheisse!*"

Branches.

"What? What is it?!" Lotta's voice to his left. Still on edge, a nervous energy to her tenor. She turned over but quickly diverted her gaze.

Fischer was shivering, naked, drenched in sweat.

"*Fuggin' hell,*" he muttered and wiped his hand across his lips. "Yeah… yeah, just a dream." Sleep in his eyes. Sandman had taken him after all.

He rubbed his forehead and squinted into the dim interior of the shelter. Shards of daylight pierced the latticed walls. The crawl space had partially collapsed, allowing glints of sunlight into his eyes. Judging by its angle, they'd slept well past morning.

The smell of stale animal excrement lingered.

Fischer glanced down at himself—fully exposed, skin clammy. Forgot the purplish hemorrhages that covered his body. Pine needles and detritus plastered all over him. Every muscle ached, trembled. He felt run-down, faint. His insides like mush, as if he'd spent the previous night getting pissed on an empty stomach. Pulse thudding at a snail's pace in his ears, the shelter's interior awhirl.

And Little Man, back with a vengeance. *Heavy jigging on my medulla oblon-fuckin'-gata.*

"How are you shivering? I'm sweltering in here." Lotta batted at a mosquito. Bits of twigs and leaves fell from her tousled hair. Tiny raised welts covered her face, and she appeared to be missing one of her pearl earrings again. Still had two black eyes, but the swelling had gone down. Looked like she'd run into a wall, or a wall ran into her.

Fischer raked his beard. "We need to get going. We're losing daylight."

He rolled forward to the entrance and pulled back the plug of vegetation, causing it to collapse in more. Golden motes swirled about as a gush of fresh air poured in. Lotta coughed behind him. He leaned back on his elbows—unsteady, weak, shaking like mad—and kicked out one side of the crawl space with his remaining strength. It crumbled in on itself; he was momentarily blinded by shafts of bright sunlight.

Fischer shielded his eyes and peered out. A light mist ebbed against the forested backdrop, taunting his thirst. He crawled into the open and got to his feet. *Vertigo.* Faltered. Caught himself. Every muscle in his body twitched, his legs like bungee cords. Lungs heaving. Head pounding. He extended his tremulant arms skyward toward the chirping of birds, stretched his aching limbs. Wiped his lips between finger and thumb.

Shot a' bourbon'd take off the edge.

He tried to push the thought aside. Bury it.

"We need to find water," he said, turning to help Lotta to her feet as she staggered out into the open.

She looked around, then craned her neck to the treetops, a baffled expression painted on her face.

The mosquitos converged.

"Damn bugs. They're bloody everywhere," Lotta snapped.

Fischer smacked his right pec and pulled his hand away. He studied the crushed insect in his palm, eyed his trembling fingers, then fixated again on the mosquito. Its iridescent wings gleamed in the midmorning sun. An insignificant thing.[1]

Before long, he found himself engulfed in a cloud of buzzing insects. He hustled to his suit, knife in hand, the smell of ferrofluid rising in his nostrils. The bugs thinned as hoped, repelled by the chemical fetor. The thought of booze resurfaced, almost came as a reflex. He patted the suit down feverishly. Knew the flask wasn't there, knew he'd stopped bringing it into the lab. But still, he checked. Knew it was implausible. Impossible, even. But so was everything he'd been through the last forty-eight hours. Given the circumstances, the manifestation of a full flask he knew wasn't there didn't seem like such a ridiculous prospect.

But he found nothing. No flask.

He collected himself as if coming out of a trance. Ran his hand across his mouth again. Lips withered, tongue scraping against the roof of his mouth.

He tugged at the suit, yanked it free of the sapling. The tree rebounded, flinging thousands of tiny glinting dewdrops into the air.

Water.

"Ah, shit," he growled, looking the tree over. *Stupid.*

---

1 *Burmaculex antiquus*

"What is it?"

"Nothing," he said, sweeping his gaze across the undergrowth. Knew there had to be more nearby. Then, flecks of light caught his eye, glancing off the leaves in a grouping of ferns a few meters off—a constellation of dew drops.

Naked as the day he was born, Ed Fischer staggered over to its edge and fell to his knees.

"Ed, what are you—"

"Come here." He used the blunt edge of his knife to gently scrape droplets from one of the leaflets. With the blade held level, he collected enough liquid to form a small bead along the spine, then raised it to his tongue and tilted it so the water fell.

He turned and waved for Lotta to come closer. "Water. It's not much, but it'll hold us until we find more. Here…"

He repeated the same sweeping motion on more of the ferns until he had another sparkling bead. He gestured for Lotta to hold her mouth open. She tilted her head back, and he angled the blade. Three drops fell to her tongue.

She closed her eyes, savoring it. "Thank you."

Fischer nodded, then turned back to collect more. "We need to get as much as we can before it evaporates."

With that, Lotta strolled into the ferns, palms out so they brushed against them. She stopped and held her hands out before her, glistening in the sun. One by one, she drew her fingers to her lips and placed them into her mouth. Fischer ditched the knife and did the same.

In all, he figured they each got about a milliliter or two. Not even enough to take off the edge. Before long, his tongue was back to sticking to the roof of his mouth.

He gathered up his knife and hobbled back to his suit, spreading it out before him, then leaned over and inserted the blade into the outer lining. He sliced up along the seams to separate the exterior shell from the inner layers.

Lotta came up behind him. "What are you doing?"

"Cutting out the insulating liner," he said. "The rest is dead weight."

The suit was rugged, but the knife cut through the rubbery exterior with little effort. Within several minutes, he'd separated out the innermost lining.

"You know it's against CEPP protocol to carry weapons into the lab."

"Aye," Fischer said, "and we're not in the lab."

He cut several ribbons from the outer shell, then notched holes in the liner where he'd cut the seams. Here, he threaded the ribbons through, cinching and tying them to rejoin the edges. Soon, the suit's self-healing polymer would form a watertight seal over any cuts or defects.

Stepping into the neckline, he fed his feet through the legs, then pulled the garment up and over himself. It fit loose, but weighed little and was relatively comfortable. He windmilled his arms and took a few steps to test his range of motion, then returned to the suit and began fashioning a pair of moccasins from the boot liners.

"This should do for now," he said.

Lotta walked over to the ragged remains of the suit and turned it over with her foot.

"You're defacing CEPP property," she said.

Fischer raised his brow and bounced her a look that said *piss off.*

He knew Lotta had no control over the situation. Wasn't in charge anymore, and she knew it. No, the *other* her was—her doppelgänger—the one they'd seen before waking up in this hell. She ran the show at CEPP now. Probably always had.

Fischer didn't know what he'd seen before the flash, what was real. Only that now, out here, he was their best shot at survival. Out here, the lab didn't exist. The Federation didn't exist.

They were nobody.

But that didn't keep Lotta from trying to retain her relevance.

Fischer's eyes locked onto hers, held her gaze. Thought for a moment he could understand it. Sort of. Even if her antagonism appeared somewhat juvenile.

No matter; he needed to be the level head. Maybe attempt to bring a little levity to the situation.

"Put it on my tab," he said with a grin.

"Oh, yeah?" she clapped back, arms folded.

He thought he detected a slight upturn at the corner of her lips as he walked over to the heap at her feet. The stench of ferrofluid was something he'd never get used to.

"Anything else we can salvage from it?" she said, her hand over her nose, the rigidity in her voice softening.

"Suppose so." Fischer chewed the inside of his cheek, looking down at the suit. "Portable oxygen generator can be parted. Gloves might come in *handy*."

"Funny."

A sustained hooting erupted in the distance and decayed deeper into the forest. The two of them turned toward the sound. A distant response carried through the trees.

Lotta picked her fingers in the corner of Fischer's eye.

"You injured?" He nodded toward her hands. They looked horrific—swollen, raw, oozing clear yellowish fluid.

Lotta balled them into fists like she had before, her face flushed. "I'm fine. Bad habit."

Fischer studied her expression for a moment. She'd diverted her gaze back to the suit.

"So, are we going to get what we need or just sit here all day?" she said. *Changing the subject.*

Fischer maintained his gaze. Moved to chewing the inside of his lip. "You're gonna want to kick that habit."

"I *said* I'm *fine*."

"Infection sets in out here, and you've really got problems."

"Add it to the list."

Fischer looked around, chest heaving as if he'd just run a kilometer. *This fuckin' air.*

Shadows flitted through the treetops. He snapped his eyes up, peering through the curved boughs. High-pitched chirrups panned through the latticed canopy, then fell silent again.

Beads of sweat erupted on Fischer's forehead. A reminder they were on borrowed time.

He knelt over the suit's rubbery shell and tossed it over, exposing the back, where the POG was nested between the shoulders and concealed within the inner and outer layers. He cut along the perimeter to expose the unit, then cut the tubing and ripped it free. It was an enclosed rectangular device, matte-gray in color. Carbon-fiber shell.

"Here."

Lotta took it from him and tucked it under her arm. Fischer went to work on the gloves next, cutting them free. He scraped away some of the ferrofluid residue that covered the outer shell and smeared some on his clothing. He gestured for Lotta to do the same.

"No way," she said. "Can't stand the smell."

Fischer grunted with a shrug. "Suit yourself. Contend with the mosquitos."

Lotta scowled at him. Reluctantly, she spread a dab of the substance over the leggings of her compression sleeve. Fischer placed more of it into one of the gloves, then cinched it shut with another ribbon he had cut from the suit.

"Let's get going," he said.

He limped over to the shelter, circling around to the back, where the felled tree that formed their lean-to had wedged itself between a pair of conifers. The towering trees looked even more monolithic by day, their rounded branches densely packed with thick, dagger-tipped needles. Strands of sap oozed from their boughs, and cones the size of his head dangled precariously like ethereal viridian orbs. As Fischer came about the other side of the enormous trunks, he spotted globules of hard amber-colored resin sealing off the wounds where the fallen conifer had crashed into them.

Lotta came up beside him.

"What are you doing now?"

"This resin here is good on cuts. Stops the bleeding and makes a great salve—full of polyphenols to stave off infection." Fischer wedged the tip of his blade beneath one of the rounded clods and pried it free. "Just need to melt it down."

He placed several nuggets into the other glove and turned his attention to the tree's outer bark. He cut a section away to expose the fleshy underside, then peeled a small piece up with the blade's tip. It was thin and papery with a distinct pine scent. He placed it into his mouth and began to chew. The stringy texture and sweet flavor were vaguely familiar. Memories of his time in the military came back—situations during Leichter Speer when he and his men relied on it to keep them going.

His dream came back to him. Jocelyn's face. He scrubbed the thought. Refocused on the task at hand. Took up another piece and handed it to Lotta. "Here."

"What is *this?*"

"Cambium. It'll keep our energy up until we find food. Spit it out when the flavor's gone."

Lotta looked at him as if he'd tell her he was joking at any moment. After a brief pause, she placed the pale green chip on her tongue. Her expression contorted to one of disgust.

"Flavor? Tastes like a pine tree's arschloch."

Fischer spat his out and started on another piece. "It's a bit bland." He shrugged and peeled away more for later. "We should get a move on. Daylight's waning."

"Where are we going?"

"Back to Basem—salvage what we can, then head deeper into the forest, stick to tree cover. Land slopes down that way." He pointed off into the thicket where they had heard the hooting. "Probably leads down into a ravine."

Lotta licked her lips. "Water."

"Aye, water."

Her expression shifted. A troubled look fell over her. "What are we going to do with Basem?"

"*Do?*"

"Ed, we can't just leave him."

"We can if you want to get out of here alive."

Lotta fell silent. Started picking again.

Fischer dug his blade into the tree's flesh.

"Hold out your hands." He turned to face her, thick sap oozing from the blade.

"What?" Lotta took a step back. "Why?"

"You're going to get an infection. This'll act as an antiseptic until we can get some resin on those wounds."

With palms facedown, Lotta presented her fingers. They already looked to be festering—swollen, seeping. It wouldn't take long for sepsis to take hold. Fischer applied the amber sap gently to her cuticles. She winced on contact, teeth clenched, face contorted into a grimace.

"Hold still," he said.

"I am." Tears fell onto her cheeks. "Just fucking hurts."

A moment of vulnerability.

"You're okay," Fischer said. "All done. Now, we best be off. Lass uns gehen. Let's go."

Lotta wiped her cheeks and nodded with a meek smile. The first he'd seen in days.

They started in the direction they had come the night before, passing by Lotta's side of the shelter. Fischer took a moment to inspect it.

"Scheisse, the *smell!*" Lotta moaned, her hand shielding her nose and mouth.

Splattered across the wall of the lean-to was a tar-colored substance. Streams of white ran through it. Some type of animal excrement. It had run down the side, had by now dried out, but still gave off a rancid stench that combined sickeningly with that of pine. Fischer's stomach turned.

"What did that?" Lotta said.

Fischer turned from the smell. "Bear, maybe."

"Outside of captivity? And in the Sahara? Didn't sound like a bear, and *that* doesn't look like bear shit."

"Yeah? You ever see bear shit? Didn't sound like one of those giant murder storks, either... 'stalkers,' whatever. Point is, the animal consultant is dead." His head was pounding again, ushering renewed agitation with the situation. "Does it look like we're still in Kansas, Dorothy?"

Lotta said nothing. Her face flushed. In the daylight, the bruising looked much worse, in part because it had settled into her cheekbones, leaving traces of blue and yellow around the blood-tinged whites of her eyes.

"I'm sorry," Fischer said.

A moment of tense repose, Lotta's gaze far off. She muttered something.

Fischer furrowed his brow. "Come again?"

"Oh." Lotta snapped back to attention. "I, uh... I said *'Björn,'* it means—"

"Bear."

"Yeah, bear." Lotta nodded. "But I don't think that's what this was."

"Aye, wasn't a bear, then." Fischer didn't want to argue. He wanted to move on, to find his way out of this hell. "Whatever it is, it's gone now."

He heard voices again.

"She's gone. I'm sorry."

"Not my baby. Not my sweet bear. Please, God, please no."

Ghosts.

"Ed, you good?" Lotta leaned in, eyebrows raised.

Fischer met her gaze, and the thought evaporated. He nodded. "Let's go."

He secured the gloves to his uniform and inserted his knife into a makeshift sheath he'd fashioned.

The air became drier as they retraced their steps to the forest's edge. Fischer inspected his blotched hands, the skin now cracked and flaking. Fingers tingling, almost numb. His throat raw, a scraping sensation whenever he tried to swallow. His desiccated eyes burned, lids heavy, falling sluggishly with each blink. He wiped his lips with a trembling hand and raked his beard.

Something caught the sunlight on the path just ahead. *The wristwatch.* Fischer made his way to it and leaned forward to pick it up. He studied it for a moment. The glass face was warped and discolored as if exposed to flame. The watch had been a gift from his ex-wife, an anniversary present.

The year before the girls…

He held out his wrist and clasped the mesh band around it.

After a few minutes, they came to the edge of the wood. The sun beat down on them as they moved out of the trees and into the clearing where they had last seen Basem. Fischer shielded his eyes. In the daylight, the dune fields glistened, a refractile quality like nothing he'd ever seen. The effect was almost blinding. He swept the ground with his finger and studied the crystalline residue, then pressed it to his tongue.

Salt.

"This isn't desert," he said. "It's a salt flat."

"What? How?"

"Don't know. But this isn't aeolian."

"Doesn't look flat to me."

Fischer ignored her and looked out across the rolling formations. A brownish haze muddied the horizon, bleeding into a clear blue sky.

Squinting, his hand over his eyes, he came to the spot where it happened, where he'd last seen Basem. But he was gone. Nothing but bits of suit and clods of blood-soaked earth. The ground had been disturbed, heavily trodden, and was now littered with dozens of strange footprints. Some appeared to be from birds. A few larger ones looked to be from the stalkers. Most, though, were unrecognizable.

Lotta placed her hand over her mouth.

Fischer searched around, then gazed back at the stained earth. "He's gone."

"You don't think… that *thing* we heard last night… *Björn?*"

"I don't know," he said. "Maybe."

Fischer scrutinized the area. Walked around the perimeter. Saw no evidence Basem had been dragged. No blood trail, no distinct sets of footprints indicating which direction the body had been taken.

Lotta began to wave her hands, to pace, tears welling in her eyes. "*I did this,*" she muttered. "I-I didn't mean for… for *this.*"

"It's not your fault," Fischer said impassively as he looked around.

He grabbed a stick lying amid the toiled earth. Broke off any aberrant twigs, then knelt and forced it upright into the dirt. Picking up a small stone, he placed it at the end of the stick's shadow. Lotta muttered something incoherent behind him.

A distant high-pitched shriek traveled toward them from across the dunes.

Fischer spun around. Lotta had stopped, her attention on something— an indistinct mass a few hundred meters off, near the base of the dunes, partially obscured in the brownish haze. A plume of dust rose up from it and trailed off into the sky. Fischer's eyes were nothing more than slits as he struggled to decipher what he was seeing. An unintelligible mass—a dark, undulating mound obfuscated by the shimmering surface of the withered expanse.

Another screech. Fischer caught a glimpse of something flapping madly along the mound's shifting margins. *Wings.* Lots of them. Creatures of similar build to a stalker, but no taller than a man, with curved, upturned beaks.[2] The mass swarmed with them, like a hive of wasps, their membranous wings sliding over one another. One of the beaks tilted skyward, clapping open and shut with a sharp, hollow *snap.*

---

2 Various sexually dimorphic species, including *Xericeps* and *Nicorhynchus*

Lotta gasped. "Ed… you don't think that's…."

"Basem." Though he couldn't see a body beneath the swarm. Couldn't be sure.

Fischer had never seen anything like these animals. Some had heads adorned with broad crests like oar blades. Others were truncated, more rounded. They walked on all fours, their stilted forelimbs vastly greater in length than those at the rear. Circling high above, more creatures vied for a spot among the clamor against a blue sky.

"Time to go." Fischer turned his attention to the stick and kneeled to where the shadow had moved. He marked this with a second stone and then drew a straight line between the two. "That's east." He pointed out across the dunes.

"So…"

"We're going to head west, back through the forest. Find water. If we get lost, we turn around and come back east, try another direction until we succeed."

"…or until we're rescued," Lotta added.

Fischer looked up at her and nodded. "Or until we're rescued."

But he knew that no one was coming for them.

"So that's it?" Lotta gazed off toward the mound. "We're just going to—to *leave him?*"

"That's it."

"He deserves a little dignity."

"Be my guest." Blood pulsed through Fischer's temples. "I'm headed west, with or without you."

"And what about Hassan? He could be alive, Ed."

"Could be. No way to know. Equally likely, he's back at the lab waiting for us."

"You're a fucking asshole."

"Noted. Let's go."

"I didn't do anything wrong," she muttered. "I did everything I needed to…."

Fischer softened. "Aye, you did."

He had a lingering sense that Lotta was trying to convince herself more than she was him.

He spat out his wad of cambium and started back through the trees. For a moment, he considered thanking Lotta for saving his life.

Then the moment passed.

| DN1451.21 >

Maternal infanticide.

Perez had observed the behavior in nature more times than she could count. But an ostrich savaging her own chicks? Never. A rarity in birds. Never ostriches.

But nature was like that—unpredictable, brutal, unforgiving. Everything came down to survival. Sometimes mothers had to do the unthinkable. Sometimes survival was more important.

Her mind was back at the necropsy lab. With her animals. Back at Basem's pod, the smell of coffee, the sound of music. The warmth of his arms cocooning her.

And she thought of Ruth.

Sometimes mothers must do the unthinkable. Sweet Ruth.

Perez had grown attached. And now, she was trying to distance herself. Revert to when she felt nothing. When Ruth had no name.

The pregnancy would be over in a few days.

Using her assignment aboard the Goliath as cover, Perez had managed to retrieve enough misoprostol from ARC's pharmacy cache. Jacobs and his team didn't know what it was, its intended purpose. No one at ARC knew about the necropsy or the strange carcass, only that she needed equipment, reagents, supplies. No questions asked. She only needed to smuggle the capsules out of the containment area and back to her pod, calculate the right dose, and swallow it down. Then wait. Easy.

For survival. For mercy.

Yet despite all her justifications, all her rationalizing, Perez felt defeated, devastated, lost.

"Get a grip."

Perez flashed a look in the direction of Nedjma's voice. "What did you say?" A rush of heat flushed her cheeks.

"I need your help, Cam. Can you get a grip on that end?"

Nedjma cranked down on a heavy steel device akin to a jack, ratcheting the animal's jaws open. It was slippery with blood, shifting over the creature's swollen tongue. Perez adjusted herself, leaned forward with her full weight to secure the monstrous head. Nedjma gave a few more cranks, prying apart the cage of teeth.

Ideally, Perez would have moved the tongue aside, but it was anchored to the floor of the mouth—a specialized feature she'd seen in crocodilians, owing to their extreme bite forces. A trait evolved to ensure they didn't accidentally sever their own tongues. She stared at the bloated organ, deep blue in coloration, its surface covered in hundreds of barbed papillae. Peered into the gaping maw, a palate of fleshy curtains receding into a blackened void. Teeth enveloped by thick gums, draped with scaled lips. She recalled Jacobs's audio recording. The sounds the animal had made. How it *mimicked.*

Nedjma hadn't said much since Perez brought her to the staging area. Since first laying eyes on the creature. But slowly, she was becoming more inquisitive. More curious. "What is this thing, Cam?" she said.

"I don't know." Perez shook her head. "That's what we're here to figure out."

"Why did they shoot it?"

"It killed someone."

Nedjma's upper lip quivered. Perez noticed a small notch along its lower margin—the only indication of a scar.

"It's not one of ours, is it?" Nedjma said.

"No."

Her nostrils flared. Eyebrows turned in. An expression of confusion, of urgency. "Then why aren't we back inside, helping with ARC's recovery?"

Perez flashed her a look. Tried to convey the weight of the situation without giving too much. Not with Oz in earshot, with Jacobs listening in. "It's important." She didn't tell her they didn't have a choice. That she was afraid. Afraid of the soldiers standing outside. Afraid of the Federation. Of the answers she might find.

Nedjma fell quiet again. Her eyes darted to the entrance. Outside, Oz's slow footfalls paced up and down the tunnel. Receding, then building, then receding again. She glanced back at Perez with a disquieting look about her. Seemed to understand.

Perez had grown to trust her student, to have confidence in her. But the real reason she had brought Nedjma on was so she could keep an eye on her. Protect her. From what, she didn't know. She just *knew*. Knew that she'd dropped the ball in the moa paddock. Knew she was absent when the tremors hit. But not again.

The interior of the containment zone had transformed into a fully equipped field lab overnight. Its translucent walls were now adorned with steel work benches. On one sat a high-speed centrifuge and two inverted microscopes, and between them an array of magnifying objectives and fixing media. Underneath, a CO_2 incubator with a stack of clear cell culture flasks on top was skirted by a compact minus-eighty freezer.

Perez turned her attention back to the middle of the containment tent and scrutinized the creature. It baked under the parasol lamps; they formed a halo of light from which four long pneumatic arms extended like invaders from another dimension. They loomed above the carcass, folded on themselves. Metallic insect legs. Around the table, wheeled trays contained sterile fields, prepped with surgical instruments lying in chaste. Thirsting for first blood.

Only now did Perez get a sense for the animal's sheer size—at least twice the length of an adult moa. The head was no longer arched backward, owing to relaxing incisions she and Nedjma had made along ligaments in the back. With the aid of the pneumatic arms, the body had been reoriented, laid out straight on its right side, its left arm and leg exposed and wrapped in restraints secured to motorized cables. The tail, now held aloft by wired harnesses, extended beyond the table's edge, where it vaulted over the adjoining sink.

"You getting this?" Perez muttered into her comm. A live feed from her suit's camera played on one of the holoscreens, along with shots from more cameras situated around the staging area.

Jacobs's voice cut through her earpiece. "Looking good from here."

"I think we're ready to begin the examination." Perez turned to acknowledge Nedjma, who returned a nod in kind. Her pressure suit bulged around her, the hiss of the positive pressure now nothing but white noise. A capsule that conferred an almost ethereal sensory deprivation to her surroundings. Perez closed her eyes and exhaled. "Athena, begin dictation."

The AI patched through. "Dictation initiated."

Perez faced the animal, her head tilted. With arms at her sides, she started to move around the table. "Thirteen June, twenty-one forty-seven, oh six thirty-three. This is Dr. Camila Perez, joined by doctoral candidate Nedjma Ramdani." She walked around the tail to the animal's dorsal side, with Nedjma trailing close behind. "We are conducting a necropsy on specimen DN1451.21—an indeterminate species of tetrapod."

She activated her HUD's LIDAR to map the creature's dimensions. She started at the tail with her head down and slowly made her way to the head. Hundreds of flame-shaped hemorrhages dappled its body, lying just beneath the skin's surface. "Body length is six meters and twenty-three centimeters from rostrum to tail tip." The exit wound at the back of the neck was in the early stages of decomposition.

One of the holoscreens displayed a three-dimensional reconstruction of the animal, along with markers recommending various approaches for the internal examination.

"What's this stuff on its skin?" Nedjma said. She swiped a gloved finger across the glistening substance and held it in front of her face. "Wow, it's kind of *heavy*."

Perez watched as Nedjma bobbed her hand up and down. The tarry fluid appeared thick and viscous as it conformed to her index finger. "We'll take samples and run it through mass spec to determine its composition."

Her eyes reverted to the carcass, bouncing over the macerated bullet wounds riddling the head and chest.

They must have fired at least thirty rounds into this thing.

The tissue around the wounds had imbibed with fluid, swelled up enough to split the skin in some areas. Many of the bullets hadn't gone all the way through, save for the giant hole at the back of the neck—splintered bone, shredded flesh. They had almost decapitated the thing. She'd need to run a CT to map all the fragments and their trajectories.

Nedjma split off and moved around to the legs. The bottom limb protruded forward from under the body so that nothing above the upper ankle was visible. The other was contorted, sprawled backward, suspended out over the table's edge with toes locked straight. A death pose Perez had seen many times in birds.

"There's a lot of blood on the footpads," Nedjma said. She produced a swabbing kit and took a few samples.

But something else about the feet caught Perez's attention. She rounded the front of the table and came up beside Nedjma. Each digit was dorsally lined with a column of large scutes stacked from claw tip to ankle, where they joined to form a singular stack extending to the joint at the base of the tibia. They were flaking and peeling up along their margins. Ground with grime and dried blood.

Perez leaned in.

"This arrangement is only seen in birds," she said. "The scales on the neck and torso are polygonal like those of lizards and crocodiles, but these here on the feet are characteristic of derived feathers."

"So, which is it—bird or reptile?"

"Birds are reptiles, monophyletically speaking," Perez said. "All compose clades nested within Sauropsida. Birds just don't have scales like lizards do. But this… has both."

"It's something between the two? A hybrid of bird and lizard?"

"I don't know what else it could be."

"A more primitive sauropsid."

"No." Perez gave a dismissive laugh. "That's impossible."

Nedjma doubled down. "Yes, but dinosaur traits have been showing up in the wild, in the domes, right? Genetic drift. Mutation. Natural selection.

What if this is something like that? What else could have seemingly exclusive traits of such disparate taxa?"

"It doesn't work quite this way, not to *this* extent. Not by accident."

Nedjma paused for a moment. Perez could see the gears turning. "You think someone bred this?"

"I don't know. It still doesn't explain how it got here, how it found its way underground into CEPP's labs. Nothing really does."

Perez left Nedjma to continue and made her way back to the front of the examination table. She cracked open a collection tube, slid a swab across the animal's bloodied snout, and placed it in a cooling vessel. The glistening maw, its rows of daggered teeth, was caked with dried foam and blood. An ulcerated lesion appeared to have been in the early stages of infection along the lower jaw, with putrefaction of the surrounding tissues well underway. The wound was almost gelatinous to the touch.

She took more samples.

Nedjma had taken a few punches of skin and several crops of the fur-like down. It was green and brown. The fine wisps shed to the bottom of the basin, all over the floor, into pooled blood. It got on their suits, their instruments. Perez plucked one from the lip of the table and inspected it, a singular bristle extending out from a follicle. Not the down of most birds, which formed tufts—clusters of multiple filaments arising from a single node. Rather, something more primitive.

Out of nowhere, something shifted inside her.

A kick? No, it's too early. Nerves. Just nerves.

Get a grip.

And then it came. A rush of vertigo. It stole over her like a type of weightlessness. Like falling in a dream. She wavered. Her stomach turned.

Not now, Ruth, don't do this to me now.

Nedjma, misting detergent over the skin and feathers with a spray bottle, had noticed. She approached Perez. "You okay?"

Perez inhaled, nodding. Procured a smile.

The vertigo faded.

Focus.

She regrouped. Slowed her breathing.

Nedjma appeared unconvinced. "Are you sure?"

"We all good in there?" Jacobs again. Nedjma snapped her head toward the tunnel, where Oz had stopped pacing.

"I'm okay," Perez said. "Let's start the internal examination."

Oz's footfalls resumed.

Perez stumbled around to the stomach, Nedjma close by, watching her. But Perez brushed it off and continued with her task. "We will start by disarticulating the limbs on the left flank to gain access to the internal organs," she said. She had grown winded, fatigued. "You make an incision along the left coxofemoral and glenohumeral joints and run another from the pubis to the pectoral girdle. Then rig the limbs for dislocation. I will start with the neck."

Nedjma became muted. Took the instruction she was given, but eyed her mentor as she worked in silence.

Perez handled a large pair of surgical shears and made an incision from the middle of the breastbone and up the neck toward the base of the lower jaw. She swallowed against the bulge in her throat. Pushed the nausea down. As she cut, the callused hide dulled the instrument. Her hand ached and cramped until, finally, the incision was complete. She switched to a scalpel and dissected away connective tissue to free the hide, then folded it back like heavy textile—a matrix woven with collagen, keratin, and vascular networks.

As the skin fell away, she was taken aback by the enormity of the jaw muscles. "The adductors are notably robust," she said. *Another anatomic feature suggesting a tremendous bite force.* She made more incisions until the inside of the throat was exposed, securing flaps of tissue with clamps while she dictated her findings. "Esophageal mucosa appears unremarkable. I am now incising the trachea...."

She worked slowly, delicately guiding the blade through the windpipe. She pried it open with gloved fingers. The organ was slippery, rigid, difficult to manipulate. But with the aid of another clamp, she managed to turn it inside out to inspect the inner mucosa.

She paused for a moment. "This is unusual..." she said. In the back of her mind, she heard the animal's raspy wheezing, its tortured gurgling. "There appears to be diffuse necrosis along the proximal lumen that extends distally to the bronchial bifurcation. Blanching of the vascular tissue is also observed, suggesting severe chemical burn. I am collecting a sample for a toxicol—"

Her voice stopped in her throat.

Nedjma looked up from the other end of the carcass. "What is it?" She spoke over the sound of snapping cartilage. One of the robot arms whirred overhead, torquing the enormous leg back while she cut along the inside of the hip joint.

Perez remained fixated, slack-jawed. "It has a syrinx," she said, her voice trembling. "That explains the vocal mimicry."

"It can *mimic?*"

Perez nodded. In her mind, she still heard the distressed cries. The desperate pleas of something almost human. A man screaming for help.

Greellllppp.

Its last victim. A sound convincing enough to draw in a team of experienced soldiers.

Electrical shocks coursed up her back. A back-and-forth ensued inside of her. An argument with herself.

What if Basem…

No… he is okay. They will find him.

But how do you know?

She regarded Nedjma with a nod, then resumed her dictation. "The… typical structures of the vocal organ—tympanum, pessulus, both membrana tympaniformi—all appear to be highly conserved. An exceptionally high density of cartilaginous rings—both proximally and distally—suggests advanced vocalization ability. Everything about its anatomy appears homologous with the vocal organs of talking birds."

He is okay. They will find him.

"Well, it's not a lizard, judging by the orientation of the pubic bone," Nedjma added, pointing to the leg. It was bent in at the knee, the thigh cranked back almost ninety degrees by the robotic arm. "And the pelvis has a perforate acetabulum. This thing walks upright like a bird or mammal." Her charcoal eyebrows turned inward, brow furrowed. "Cam, what is this thing?"

Perez shook her head. "I don't know." She swabbed the mucosal lining, then shifted her focus to the animal's midsection. "Let's disarticulate the arm so we can access the body cavity."

More cracking, popping, tearing of flesh. Once Perez and Nedjma had the arm retracted, they got to work dissecting away the skin along the torso. The hide here was much bulkier, far too heavy for the two of them to lift. It had the thickness of two human hands, its layers visible as it was peeled back by one of the pneumatic arms, exposing bone, fat, and muscle underneath. Nedjma hooked the hide with large clamps that anchored to the underside of the lipped edge of the table across from where they worked. The steady trickle of blood drummed metallically through the grate to a collecting pan below.

Nedjma took up a scalpel and started to deepen the incision along the length of the torso, cutting through muscle and fascia. She leaned into the abdomen to drive the scalpel deeper, but her blade jutted against something rigid. She stepped back, a look of bafflement in her eyes. "What kind of animal has ribs in front of its stomach?" she said. "We'll need loppers to get at the internal organs."

"Not ribs," Perez said. "Gastralia. I'm only aware of this structure existing in extant crocodiles and tuatara. It's a primitive structure that protects the stomach."

"Cam. This animal… it shouldn't be here."

Perez shook her head. "We don't know that. Let's take our time and figure this out. Focus on stating the findings. Not speculation." She sighed and turned back to the specimen. "Athena, strike our last two statements from the record."

Perez traced her index finger along a large muscle extending from the breast to the rib cage. She ran her finger under its margins, strategizing their next approach.

"We'll retract the left pectoral and cut lengthwise along the serratus. Then we can disarticulate and retract the ribcage to inspect the lungs and digestive tract."

Once the ribs were hinged away from the body, the gastralia laying in a flap against the table, the internal organs presented themselves. Perez took a section of the windpipe and cut through it, then fed an air hose into the opening. She eased down on the trigger, and the lungs inflated. A muffled crackling erupted from them. Then, one by one, more organs ballooned down the length of the abdominal cavity, each rattling an ensemble of crepitation.

"The ribs are highly pneumatized and appear continuous with multiple air sacs extending from the neck to the pelvis, a unidirectional respiratory system analogous to that of most birds." Perez heard the hiss of air escaping some of the organs. Some were not inflating fully. "Many connections between the air sacs and ribs have been avulsed or obliterated, in part from expansion due to hemothorax, while others are presumed to result from high-velocity shearing from heavy weapons fire. There are extensive cavitation injuries to the viscera—owing to multiple ballistic wound paths—and extensive hemorrhage and edema in the lungs, as well as pericardial effusion. Several bullet fragments are readily observed."

Perez laid down the hose and moved down to the stomach. Scalpel in hand, she cut through the protective tunic shielding the stomach and intestines. The steady trickle of blood had become background noise against the pulsatile whooshing in her ears, the sound of metal on bone, the smacking of soft tissue against steel. The drone of her own voice in her head as she expatiated her findings.

"The organization of the gastrointestinal tract is unexpected for such a birdlike animal. There is no gizzard or crop, and it's remarkably compact—more akin to that of a highly specialized predator, like a lion." She breathed in through her nose, exhaled through her mouth. Looked up at Nedjma, who was now working to dissect the heart. They had been at it for hours. "I'll take it from here, Nedjma," Perez said. "Why don't you step outside the containment area for a moment and take a break?"

"I'll take a break when you take a break," Nedjma said without looking away from her task.

Perez hesitated for a moment. Her pulse quickened. Her chest couldn't get any tighter. She had no idea what she would find once she proceeded. *Here goes.*

The outer wall of the stomach proved tougher than expected. The fibrous lining had dulled two blades by the time Perez got through. Gases erupted from the opening, and the organ deflated as a black slurry spilled out and pooled into the abdominal cavity. She palpated the outer walls of the stomach to fully expunge its contents, but something was blocking it.

"There is still something in there," she said to Nedjma. *Something big.* "I need your help."

The object was lodged at the apex of the stomach. She leaned in and fed her hand through the incision, inserting her arm into the cavity. She was up to her elbow when something grazed her fingers. She tried to grasp it, but it slipped away, deeper into the stomach. She repositioned herself and leaned in more, her arm buried almost up to the shoulder. Her ears throbbed. The back of her tongue swelled. Legs burned as she held her position.

Then the vertigo returned.

Perez brushed the object again and closed her fingers tightly around it. It slipped. She inhaled, closed her eyes, fought back against the sickness brewing in her core. Once more, she gripped the object and wrenched her arm back. The stomach collapsed inward. Suction fought her, the organ encasing her arm. She couldn't pull herself back out without dropping the object.

"Nedjma, I need you to puncture the stomach so I can free my arm," she said.

Nedjma picked up a fresh scalpel and approached. "Where?"

A sour taste diffused over Perez's tongue. Vertigo claimed her and she broke into a cold sweat. She could not speak, only nod to the location.

Nedjma drove the blade down.

The suction around Perez's arm released, and she pulled herself free, but the object fell from her grip at the last second, splashing into the slurry that had pooled at the bottom of the abdominal cavity. More contents spilled out, but there was still something inside. She had only removed a piece of it. She looked down at the thing, partially submerged in digestive fluids. Nedjma jumped back.

Rising from the tarry ichor, Perez saw four macerated fingertips. They bobbed lazily, then listed, rolling to reveal a translucent, swollen hand sprouting shreds of pearlescent tendon.

Nedjma gasped. Stood speechless. Suit smeared with blood.

Perez's pulse sheared the arteries in her neck. Her heart in her mouth, sour bile burning her tongue. Her vision closing in.

It was a *human hand.*

One of seemingly fair complexion, despite its state of decomposition.
Not dark-skinned.
Not Basem's.

< ʀ | LAMENTATION >

| Emma came fourteen weeks early; 576 grams and small enough to rest in Daddy's palm. Except she couldn't be held. Her skin was too fragile—maldeveloped and translucent, veins showing through like a plexus of purpuric spiderwebs.

Fischer and Jocelyn had been through it before with Evi, but not to this degree.

Emma had to be transferred to an artificial womb seeded with stem cells from failed embryos—the rejects, the ones the Federation had deemed unfit for implantation. They now served a greater purpose, to save their sister. Ectogestation would help Emma's lungs and immune system grow strong. *Grow to the standard.* He'd pulled a favor with the suits in Berlin to save the pregnancy. Keep them from terminating Emma.

For twenty-one days, Jocelyn remained in the NICU with the baby. She had grown pale and weak from countless transfusions—her blood pumped into Emma's umbilical system, Emma hanging on by a thread. The artificial womb was not much to look at—an opaque sac of synthetic amnion cushioning Emma's fragile little body, various catheters piercing the membrane, exchanging vital nutrients and waste. It was housed in an incubator, kept dark, so the only thing visible was a glowing ultrasound feed.

It was the first time Fischer's little girl showed him how much of a fighter she was.[1]

Almost three years later, Emma was thriving. Daddy's miracle girl.

Fischer remembered her watching him, glancing back pensively in the mirror. She'd grown like a weed. Met every developmental milestone and excelled in many. Possessed Mommy's wit and Daddy's blue eyes.

"Daddy, why you shave you bea'd?" Wisps of sandy blonde floated about her round face, catching the light like an angelic aura.

"Because Mommy will like it, little bear." Fischer wrapped her tiny fingers around a pair of scissor handles and guided her to his chin. "Here, go ahead."

She closed the blades around a clump of hair, and her mouth fell open as she watched it fall into the sink.

"Good job, bear!"

"You proud of me, Daddy?"

"I am so proud of you, baby." Fischer picked up a pair of electric clippers and closed her hands around the handle. "Which part do we take off next?"

She pointed to his cheek, hands gripping the clippers tight, face beet red. Her blue eyes wide and serious.

When they had finished, he got down to her level. Let those soft little hands run over his smooth skin. He smiled wide. "How do I look?"

"You... you *Daddy?*"

"I'm Daddy."

"I like bea'd-Daddy."

She was opinionated like her mother, too. >

●

---

1 See appendices for more information on the birth complications of Fischer's daughters.

Day 1, Midday - The Forest

Fischer wasn't sure how long he and Lotta had stumbled through the forest. An hour, maybe longer. He'd caught himself brooding over the dream from the night before. Jocelyn's ghost-white skin, her blood-soaked gown. Same as the day he'd rushed her to the hospital. The day she almost lost the baby. His bear. Found himself lamenting in silence with the weight of each step and not a drop of bourbon to blunt his thoughts.

The monolithic conifers had grown denser, crowding in so that every direction looked the same. From the sagging boughs draped wisps of wolf lichen, like tattered emeraldine cobwebs. Whorled branches nearly blotted out the sun. A welcome reprieve from the heat.

Lotta trailed behind. Had not spoken since they broke camp.

The air grew thicker, muggier as they moved deeper into the wood. Fischer realized he was too dehydrated to sweat, his skin tacky, tingling almost painfully with the slightest graze of his garments. Each movement sapped his remaining energy. Throat raw, lips cracked, tongue grating against the roof of his mouth. Determined nonetheless, he stayed the course, followed the shallow incline—their route to water, to salvation. It had to be.

He raised a trembling hand to his mouth, wiped the corners, matted his beard. There was a subtle but appreciable ache in his temples. Little Man mounting his next offensive.

What I'd do for a sip of bourbon.

Doubt began to chip away at his resolve, the notion of turning back seeding his thoughts.

Then, something bright yellow, tiny, almost insignificant, stood out like a beacon through the gloom. A solitary flower sprouting from a shrub, nestled at the base of an enormous moss-choked conifer. He plodded closer. Underfoot, the ground softened. He dropped to one knee and moved his fingers over the cool, silky earth. *Moisture.* He reached forward and plucked the flower, holding it before him.

"What is it?" Lotta's voice cracked through the stillness like a whip.

Fischer sprang up and rounded the massive tree. "Come on!"

The rows of trunks parted, opening into a clearing of brilliant color— magnolias, speckled yellow and red beneath the prodigious columns. They blanketed the entire area, fading beyond a wedge of soft sunlight. Fischer looked down at the one in his hand, plucked one of its petals, then held out his other forearm and rubbed it into his skin.

"There has to be an underground spring right here," he said.

His tongue was like sandpaper against his stinging lips. He examined his arm after a few minutes. *No reaction.* Plucked another petal and wedged it between lower lip and gum. A subtle hint of ginger diffused through his mouth.

"How do we get to it?" Lotta asked.

"We'll keep moving. Should find an outlet, maybe a stream that it feeds into."

Fischer listened for the sound of water, but heard nothing. Several minutes passed. No swelling, itching, or numbness around his mouth. He swiped the petal with his tongue and swallowed.

"Here," he said, almost choking as he handed the flower to Lotta. Throat so dry he could barely get it down. "The petals are edible if you can manage to swallow 'em. Don't eat too many just yet, to be sure."

Lotta plucked a petal and rested it on her tongue. She closed her lips gently, rolled her jaw, eyes staring off, then swallowed. "Sure beats that cambium shit."

Fischer's facial muscles flexed into a meek smile, and he stumbled into the clearing.

If not for their desperate situation, he might have found solace here. He caught movement overhead—a pair of ribbon-tailed birds, brilliantly colored, weaved among the tangled boughs. They chirped melodically amid a display of intricate acrobatics.

Lotta waded into the field of flowers, sending thousands of yellow pollen granules soaring. A magnificent swarm of bright orange beetles[2] took flight in her wake like specular motes, their tear-shaped wings glinting softly in the sun. It felt like something from a dream.

Hundreds of soft petals grazed Fischer's legs. He began stuffing them into one of the gloves. Imagined himself cooking them over a fire while gorging himself on freshwater.

---

2 *Osteocallis mandibulus*

Then, something else caught his eye—the furled fronds of a fern sprout. He spotted another, and then another. Their clusters dispersed in a distinct linear pattern extending farther into the trees. He redirected his efforts and prioritized harvesting the curled shoots. He knew they packed a far more nutritional—and palatable—punch than any flower.

"Come check this out," he said.

Lotta looked up, clenching fistfuls of flowers, little orange beetles crawling over her fingers. She trudged through the brightly colored vegetation toward him.

"Fiddleheads." Fischer nodded, hands on his hips. "Can only be harvested along upland soils and rivers."

"But that's good, right?"

"Aye. These only grow in early spring, though."

Lotta gave him a puzzled look. "But it's June."

Fischer nodded. He popped a few petals into his mouth and chewed, gathering his thoughts for a moment. "Also means water's nearby. Ground is saturated."

Lotta looked around. "I don't see any. Don't hear any, either."

"We're close." Fischer started pulling up the spiraled green shoots and shoving them into the glove. "These'll be good to eat. Soon as we boil away the toxins, the shikimic acid." He refrained from speaking what was really on his mind—that the more he saw of this place, the more he realized they were far from the desolate, unforgiving Sahara they knew. Sure as shit, fiddleheads didn't grow in North Africa. And Algeria had only two seasons—dry and rainy. He reflected silently. Considered which hemisphere experienced spring this time of year. He wasn't aware of any.

They chewed in silence.

Chirp.

Fischer's head whipped around, the drum of his pulse in his ears.

"You hear that?" Lotta said.

The sound had come from a dense thicket beyond the clearing.

"Aye, I did."

It sounded so faint that had Lotta said nothing, he would have dismissed it altogether.

They waited. Minutes passed with nothing more than the buzzing of insects. Fischer turned to Lotta, his mind swimming, trying to rationalize, to dismiss what they'd heard as some animal. *Probably one of those strange birds.*

Time stood still.

Chirp.

"There. You hear that?" Lotta whispered, wide-eyed. "Sounds like a beacon. Do you think… *Hassan?*"

Fischer rolled a cud of petals with his tongue and forced it down. "Maybe. Maybe not. Sounds a ways off." His mind drifted momentarily. Thought back to what he'd seen before the flash. The creature that had killed Anderson. The *sound* it made.

The sound of a beacon.

"We need to check it out."

Fischer gave a weighty sigh, his facial muscles contorting into a frown. "That thing that got Anderson," he said, gazing off past Lotta toward the trees, weighing his own internal struggle of whether to stay the course or go, "it made that sound."

Lotta looked down at her feet, her head shaking. "That was different. It was raspy." She glanced up at him, eyes still tinged red. She threw a hand behind her toward the darkened underbrush. "But *that* sound, just now, I'm telling you, that's a beacon."

"And if it isn't? If it's that thing we heard last night? Björn?"

"It's a beacon, Ed."

Fischer was hedging his bets. Judging their odds of getting to water before nightfall. They'd need to sanitize it. That meant fire. Then they'd need to eat, build another shelter. Time permitting, treat their wounds. All before dark.

No use in hunting for a dead man.

"You saw our equipment. It's fried, all of it." His voice trembled slightly. "Hassan's will be, too. You're chasing a ghost, and we're running out of time."

"*You don't know that.*" Her face almost purple, jaw slack. Pollen granules in her snarled hair. "We need to check it out."

Another sound. Different. More familiar. *A human voice.* Indecipherable but unmistakable.

"HASSAN?!" Lotta bellowed. She spun around and began to walk with high knees through the magnolias toward the source, a blackened patch of forest.

Fischer stumbled forward and reached for her wrist. *"Have you lost your goddamned mind?"*

Lotta ripped her arm free. Started in on him, almost incoherent, face beet red. Her eyes like blood moons, endowing her with a menacing quality that Fischer had never seen. A brooding, metallic stare. "Asshole. That *is* Hassan. This is on me. We are here because of *me*, don't you get it? I need to make this right. Stay here in your little garden if you're not coming. *I'm going.*"

With tears rolling down her cheeks, she turned again toward the trees.

"Keep your voice down, or you'll get us both killed," Fischer shouted after her.

"Don't tell me what to do," she yelled without looking back.

"Will you just stop? For one minute? Just hang on."

Lotta ignored him and continued forward. She walked with purpose. As reckless as it was, Fischer admired her determination. The same way he always had. A voice inside him screamed to go with her, but his feet were leaden, rooted among the magnolias and fiddleheads. It was pride that kept him there. Pride alone, and he knew it. A battle of the obstinate: one they both might lose. His heart thrashed, almost wrenching itself from his chest, pulling him toward her. But his ego would not relent.

Right up to the moment he thought Lotta might fade headlong into the void of shadow, she stopped. Staring into the underbrush, her chest rising and falling, hands balled into fists. She stood there for a while, head down, then turned to the side.

"It was me, wasn't it?" she said. "That woman standing there behind the glass. Before the flash. Before we ended up *here*. Looking down at us from the lab. It was *me*."

Fischer had won. But somehow, it felt worse than losing. He softened toward her. "Don't know what I saw. Could've been anyone." *A lie.*

"I need to make things right."

"You will. *We* will. Let's just… think this through for a minute."

Lotta wiped away tears and gave him a sidelong glance as he massaged his temples. Little Man was back in full swing, thumping away like a lunatic.

What I'd do for some fuckin' water. A splash of bourbon. Just a splash.

He sighed heavily. Looking around, he spotted a dead bough lying amid the shrubbery. He bent forward to pick it up, and as he did so, an explosion of pain erupted inside his head. His vision dimmed for a moment. He felt almost febrile, every muscle in his body trembling. Wheezing, he lurched forward, both hands pounding the cold soil. Lotta's voice in his ears—muffled, distant, flush with alarm. He waved her off, fumbled for the stick. Wrapped his tremulant fingers around it and stood it upright. Leaned against it and propped himself to his feet, dozens of white sprites flitting before him. He took out his knife and angled the stick away from him, then began carving it into a point with trembling hands.

"Here's the plan...." Spit frothed at the corners of his mouth as he spoke with salt on his tongue. "First—"

"Ed, I can go alone. I'll be right back."

He eyed his work, paying her no heed. "*First*, we'll need protection." He stumbled forward and extended the spear to Lotta. "Here."

"What about you?"

"Got my knife." He waved the blade, then sheathed it.

"Ed, you're in no condition—"

"Second priority is making sure we can find our way back." He looked around at the bright green moss dappling the tree trunks. "Moss on these trees only grows in one spot, probably north-facing. Will orient us when we get back." He searched for more landmarks and stopped on an enormous fallen tree at the edge of the clearing. It was rotting, covered in brightly colored fruiting bodies. "That deadfall will be another indicator. It's oriented east-west."

Lotta trudged back to him and took the spear.

Fischer turned and grabbed a fistful of flowers. "Pick as many as you can carry. We'll drop these behind us so we can retrace our steps."

"Ed—"

"I'm going, and that's the end of it."

Chirp.

Fischer led the way, watching his footing as he maneuvered into the thicket. Thin tendrils of fog feathered from the ground, snaking like vines up the vast trunks. Their lower branches bare, deprived of vital sunlight, devoid of life.

All had fallen still. Silent. Except for Fischer and Lotta's soft footfalls.

An insect whizzed past, buzzed off into a thin veil of mist. But a hum remained in Fischer's ears.

The flowers soon tapered off. In their place, patches of thick moss dappled the ground. It looked ashen in the gloom, a black death spreading over everything, climbing the trees, conspiring with dense webs of lichen to choke its towering hosts.

Fischer dropped a flower, its vibrancy swallowed by the murky shade.

Sound didn't seem to carry far beyond their immediate surroundings. He felt closed in. A sense of being watched, as though the forest had lured them in and was now choking off all routes of escape.

They came upon another giant deadfall. It vaulted high overhead, supported by the weight of its brethren, a bridge to nowhere. Its roots had been ripped up, turned sideways. It leaned against the ground, a tortuous wedge of towering dendrites clotted with earth and moss.

Fischer passed beneath the trunk's shadow and heard a new sound somewhere overhead. A pulsatile buzzing, almost rhythmic. He tilted his head back and winced through rows of arthritic, lichen-choked limbs. The pulse came again, and when it did, he saw movement—an enormous nest swarming with bees. Another pulse of the stirring insects, a choreographed wave that propagated across the colony like rippling water. An entangled hive mind behaving as a singular organism.

And the message was clear: *stay away*.

Something glistened black behind the shifting colony—a tumorous growth. A roiling, wet mass. Too dim to decipher, indistinct through the banded branches, subsumed by the army of vibrating winged thoraces. An inky substance oozed from it like a gaping pestilence. Smelled of rotting flesh. Along its margins sprouted disks of blood-red fungus.

Wet warmth pecked Fischer's cheek. He swiped it with his finger, held it in front of his face. It was dark, sticky, ran thick. Smelled of rust.

"Blood." He looked up again. It had fallen from the hive.[3]

Then something else plummeted to the ground. Pale, indistinct, and small, landing with a light *plunk* at Lotta's feet. Leaning on the spear for support, she picked it up, only to toss it down with an expression of disgust and horror. A whimper escaped her lips as she backed away, her eyes staring back up at the shifting hive.

"That's—that's—" Her breathing hastened, jaw slack. Her face went pale, and for a moment, Fischer thought he was staring back at Jocelyn's ghostly apparition.

He frowned and kneeled over the object. Picked it up and turned it over between thumb and finger.

It was a tooth. Root and all. And it looked human.

SNAP. A branch cracking, crashing to the forest floor through the brush.

"What was that?" Lotta whispered.

Fischer pressed a finger to his lips. They wavered in silence, the oscillating thrum of the hive like a beating heart.

A weighty *thud* came from behind, and another—something moving slowly in their direction, its approach muted by the suffocating thicket. Not the interloper from the night before. Nor a stalker.

Something much bigger.

Fischer waved Lotta over to him and led her away. Dried twigs clawed at his skin, a cage of wooden spears obstructing their advance. Snapping away as they pushed through, each registering like an explosion that sent wave after wave of panic shooting through his searing chest. Through the lazy mist, he spotted a massive nurse log. Hollowed out and crumbling with rot, covered in fungus, smelling of peat.

"There," he said.

He bowed into the entrance and inspected it to ensure it was safe. Turned and ushered Lotta inside, then followed close behind.

The interior was dark and damp, the air musty. Clods of softened wood crumbled underfoot as Fischer walked hunched over, steadying himself with hands out to his sides. Fingers gliding over the slippery, slime-mold-lined walls. He stopped and turned to look out from

---

3 *Melittosphex burmensis*

the scabrous hollow. His joints aching, mouth cottony. Heard the thing approach with a behemothic stride, its breath billowing from great lungs.

He peered through the leaden gloom of the underbrush, the rows of ashen trunks. His view was mostly obscured by the porthole view from the log. Could only make out shadows. A fleeting glimpse of pebbled skin drifted by—three, four meters off the ground—lumbering toward the deadfall. A giant, hulking thing. He tried to get a good look, but the trees were too dense. Nothing but slivers of an indistinct, cobbled bulk, mottled and black, its footfalls coming to rest where Fischer and Lotta had stood just moments before. There was a hollow rumbling of expanding and contracting ribs as it snuffed the air like a bellows.

Another loud crash. The tearing and splintering of wood, then the sound of something else—like bones snapping. The beast gorging itself. Slashing at the riven flesh tree, undeterred by the deafening thrum of swarming carnivorous bees mounting their futile counteroffensive.

After a while, the dank smell of the log no longer registered, and Little Man had caught up with Fischer. His temples throbbed to the tune of the symphony ringing in his ears. Lotta stifled sobs behind him. Outside, the mist had grown thicker, obscured his limited view even more. But he could still hear sounds. Wet snorts. Clapping jaws. Rattling lungs.

Then a distant rumble. Low-frequency, almost inaudible, deep through the trees.

The beast's gnashing ceased, punctuated by a loud exhale. A booming sough like a low wind erupted wetly from the depths of a great chest, rattled twigs, shook Fischer to his core. Lotta's hand gripped his bicep and squeezed. There was a pause, and the sound repeated. Louder this time. A booming *thump-thump*, then a resonant crescendo.

Another distant bellow, a response. After another pause, the beast lurched off toward the sound of its caller, its plodding appendages as large as logs, receding through the trees and into obscurity.

Fischer stepped forward, but Lotta's grip tightened, held him back.

He stopped and turned to her. "S'okay. It's gone."

They crawled back into the open and brushed away wet chips of wood and detritus. Fischer looked around. A fog had settled in around the great columns, ebbing around them, making it seem as though he had been plunged into the abyssal depths of some ancient submerged forest.

They were lost.

Chirp.

The beacon was much closer now. Lotta moved out ahead tentatively at first, then with more confidence once the coast looked clear and her determination was restored.

The intervening silence was deafening as they passed over the springy earth, their feet kicking aside dead branches.

Chirp.

The trees thinned, opening into a narrow glade blanketed in fog. Monolithic conifers leaned into the clearing, snuffing out the sun behind a Stygian dome of vegetation. At the center stood a solitary cycad, ensconced in shadow, its surroundings irradiated, devoid of anything living.

Fischer strained to see through the misty vapors rising from the blackened earth. The columnar trunk of the lone cycad was twice his height, with branches of spiny blood-red blades that fanned out from a rosette atop a ligneous crown of bracts. The palmed branches stretched heavenward, their emaciated leaves thirsting for any wayward photon. A hopeless appeal for mana from a nonexistent sun god.

Lotta, too, appeared stricken by the vividness with which the crimson blades contrasted against the gloom. Fischer moved ahead, edged closer, knife at the ready.

A bee cut through the silence and faded again.

Fischer sensed a palatable unease in the air, a heaviness. As though they were treading on hallowed ground. As he drew closer, a putrid stench overwhelmed him, stopped him cold, sent him retching. He had walked into a wall of rot.

CHIRP.

His eyes moved to the source, where he spotted the twisted remains of a CEPP beacon embedded in the cycad's scaled trunk. Next to it, a partially exposed helmet. The comm inside crackled to life in a fit of static, followed by an unmistakable voice.

"We are one."

I know where Odin's eye is hidden,
Deep in the wide-famed well of Mímir;
Mead from the pledge of Odin...
...does Mímir drink: would you know yet more?
—**POETIC EDDA**

< ♪ | MÍMIR >

Lotta's fingers throbbed to the steady beat of her pulse, the *click-click-click* of her own picking. She gaped through the sting of unblinking eyes, confronted by the fragility of her own sanity. Had fallen into a state of paralytic stasis, her legs like rubber, feet rooted into the earth. Consumed by the insurmountable horror in her midst.

The tree stood solitary, ribbons of mist ebbing through its crimson fronds. A warden over its domain.

"We are one."

The words bled through the helmet comm again. A whisper. Like leaves in the wind, an approximation of human speech. Almost, but not entirely.

Fischer stood in silence, his hand matting his beard, jaw clenching at the stench billowing off the thing, a chimera of root and flesh. A symbiosis. Or perhaps a form of parasitism.

And which then would be the leech? A strange thought. Dark, even. Enough so that a twinge of self-disgust wormed its way into her thoughts.

Fear constricted her.

The arm was the first thing she had noticed. It hung limp against the scaled trunk, shreds of a bloodied CEPP uniform draped around it like vines. It protruded from the middle of the tree at the shoulder, from which horns of pink fruiting bodies sprouted. The skin was pocked with dozens of penetrating wounds. They wept dark tributaries, coalescing into a stream of coagulum that dangled from the tip of the middle finger.

And clasped tightly around its wrist was Hassan's wristwatch.

Lotta's gaze drifted up the scarred trunk. Through its center, the ligneous scutes parted, giving way to a long, vertical fissure. A yawning fleshy maw snaking from a jawless face—or what used to be a face—the head flayed and nestled in a crown of crimson bracts. Smeared with bird droppings, much of the skin and muscle stripped away, steam billowing from its macerated scalp. From one of the eye sockets protruded a frond riddled with fruiting bodies, and the other eye appeared extruded entirely, its surrounding tissue dredged to the bone.

Tufts of black hair—the remains of Hassan's mustache—sprouted from the rim of a sanguineous crater where there had once been a nose. Beneath it, a lipless maw, its teeth exposed. Gaping and jawless, a mucosal lining glistening along its inner walls. A sopping cavitation, wet with blood that seeped from a gnarled bulge of muscle—the remains of a tongue. From here, the fissure stretched a meter down the trunk to a partially exposed chest cavity. It was a damp void, a gaping incision splitting the tree down the middle, with discs of bright red fungi crowded like barnacles along its entrance, some sprouting from tubes that poured from the teeming biomass. A purplish vascular system coursed through it, extending into adjacent plant matter, revealing little distinction between root and flesh. The body and head married only by the gaping maw, a bouquet of vivid fruiting bodies. Warm, damp gusts pulsated from its depths, pumping out a stench of death, of rot.

Except it was *alive*. It was *breathing*.

A warden tree. That was Lotta's mother talking. Whispering in her ear.

She shook the thought.

Her vision fogged over. Ebbed like oil in water. She blinked, unable to look away from the tree. From Hassan. The *thing*.

An abomination.

An impossibility.

Swollen and picked over. His chest protruding as though it had exploded from inside the scabbed trunk. Exposed, unclothed. Skin flaked and mottled with purple hemorrhages. Both dead and alive. Or perhaps neither of those things.

Another noxious gust made Lotta's stomach turn. Her legs trembled; ice filled her veins. Embraced by an unnerving silence—nothing but the languid soughs from the tree's tortured mire. She slipped into a daze, her tongue desiccated and withered, eyelids dragging like sandpaper over her eyes, her body succumbing to thirst.

Kneel.

The forest began to spin. Lotta closed her eyes. Pried them open again.

"But it's wet, Mamma."

Fischer turned to her. "What?"

"One." Hassan's voice again. Leaves in the wind.

Fischer turned back, retched as he held a hand over his nose and mouth. He leaned in, bearing through gritted teeth. "Hassan, this… this is Edgar. Hassan, can you hear me?"

"One."

Lotta wavered as if drunk. Caught herself.

Fischer glanced at her, a growing concern in his eyes, then turned back toward Hassan. "One what?"

"Zero."

Fischer shook his head. "Hassan, it's Edgar. Edgar Fischer. Can you—"

"Fi-s c h e r. One… we are… one…"

Lotta regained momentary lucidity, encompassed by an overwhelming urge to run back through the thicket, to escape, but she was frozen, unable to move. Unable to speak. A prisoner in her own body.

"Hassan, I-I don't understand," Fischer continued.

The comm exploded into a blitz of numbers. *"One. Zero. Zero. One. Zero. One. One. Zero. One."*

Fischer shook his head. He seemed agitated, running his hand over his beard. "Sounds like binary," he said and glanced back to consult with Lotta. His expression fell. His brows drew together, jaw fell slack. "Oy, Eklund, you good?"

"Zero-ro plus o n e … over root two. Z e r o   m i n u s   o n e … root two. Alpha zero plus beta one two alpha times zero plus one over root two…"

"Lotta. *Lotta*." Fischer tilted his head, trying to capture her gaze. He snapped his fingers. "Hey, talk to me."

But all she could do was stare, her pulse pounding in her ears. The vertigo growing more intense.

And then a panicked inhale, as if she'd risen to the surface of a roiling sea.

"It's an algorithm." She gasped. She couldn't tell if the fog was swirling around her now, or if it was in her head. She squeezed her eyes tight, licked her lips. "Dirac notation." Her breaths came in labored rasps. Unable to pull the air deep enough. Each inhale as unsatisfying as the last. "He's reciting… reciting the quantum state… state of the core's… circuitry. Describing a wave function."

The comm crackled again.

Whispers. Leaves in wind. In rain.

"Mmm… c'to l i f e ."

Fischer leaned in, a hand over his nose and mouth. "What? What's that, Hassan? Talk to us, mate."

"Mmm th' e-quation come… l i f e ."

A dense pit swelled in Lotta's chest. She opened her eyes. *"I am the equation come to life."*

"I am… t r a n s c e n d e n c e ."

Lotta was overcome with an urge to flee. She regretted venturing from the grove. Regretted that she had resisted Fischer, endangered both their lives. She was losing her mind. Her essence splitting in two, then four, then eight. An exponential fracturing of her sanity.

Her stomach lurched. Sofia's voice emerged from the recesses of her subconscious.

Kneel. I'll not say it again.

Drunk. Intoxicated. Weak.

Lotta's legs collapsed beneath her, knees plunging into the cold dirt. She leaned back and looked up at Hassan like an effigy through desiccated eyes, hands palm-up against her thighs. Grasping at something soft—her last remaining magnolia.

"Eklund!" Fischer turned from Hassan and shuffled toward her.

Sofia's voice came to Lotta again. Drunk on mead, slurring her speech.

Put your offering into the blót.

Lotta was that little girl again. Fearful. Obedient. She extended her hand and let the flower fall in front of her.

In Odin's name.

The air seemed alive. Electric. Lotta tasted it on her tongue.

Ozone.

A million pins grazing her skin. The warmth of fresh blood cocooning her fingertips.

An ear-shattering shriek consumed her. The sound of the Higgs roaring, tearing through her. Splitting her atoms into their constituent parts. Protons and neutrons. Gluons. Quarks. Electrons. Strings. Reconstituting and dissociating again, a sinusoid, a waveform. Alternate versions of herself built up and broken down again and again. A reality within reality. Within realities.

She pictured the woman she'd seen staring down into the chamber at her from behind the observation glass. The one standing in the exact spot she'd always stood before every trial. Her doppelgänger. Her *other*.

Nothing was real. Everything was real.

"Gods, forgive me," Lotta whispered.

She caught movement just inside the opening of Hassan's chest cavity. A shadowy thing burrowed in the pulsing black pit. A pair of beady eyes glinted. Then another pair. Forms shifting. Inquisitive little embers, glowing, beaming back at her. Shifting to Fischer. Then back again. But Fischer didn't seem to have noticed.

You'll know pain if you do not show the vættir respect.

"Forgive her." Hassan's hushed whispers quenched the inferno inside Lotta's mind. Whispers distorted by an undulating coalescence of static.

Fischer's head snapped back in the tree's direction. "Forgive... forgive who?"

The stench had become overwhelming. Claustrophobia clutched at her throat, panic welling deep within her, a neurosis that manifested without warning. Her breath quickened. Her vision began to fade. Everything spinning faster and faster.

Fischer ran to her. His arm encircled her midriff and pulled. "C'mon, we're getting the fuck out of here," he spat.

But Lotta couldn't stand. Her legs would not allow it. Something held her there. Compelled her to kneel.

Everything she thought she knew—her reality—had come crashing down. Collapsed.

"*Forgive her.*" Hassan's voice again. "*She... did-n't... k n o w. But I k n o w. I can s e e. Con-se-quences. Yo u r fa-mily.*"

Fischer's arm receded from Lotta's flank, and she slumped back to her knees. He turned to face the tree.

Lotta couldn't see his face. Only hear his trembling words. "My-my family?"

"*They are... he-here. One. T h e y are every-whe-w h e r e. T h e y are one. T h e y want you... to know... know they... are. One. T h e y are. One... one...*"

Fischer's voice wavered. "Wh-what?" His grimy hands clenched and balled into fists at his sides. "How... how do you know about my family?"

"*We are one. We are m a n y.*"

"What the *fuck* do you know?"

"*E v i.*"

"No. Stop."

"*E l l s a.*"

"I said *stop.*"

"*L i t t l e E m m a.*"

"NO! Don't say another goddamned word!"

The comm ceased. The forest had fallen deathly still. What little daylight that dripped from the dense canopy to the forest floor had begun to fade.

Then a subtle scraping from the comm. Muffled, like a whisper. A splintering, ligneous crepitation.

Fischer took a step toward Hassan. "Emma?"

The noises grew into rhythmic scuffling, like a snared animal clawing to free itself. Gnashing and gnawing. Then shifting foliage again, its intensity rising as if swept into a frenzy by a rogue gale.

Tears spilled over Lotta's cheeks as her eyes rolled lazily to the canopy. The trees were still. She peered back at Fischer. He took another step forward.

"Emma? Bear, is… is that you?"

No. Ed. Don't. Lotta wanted to jump up, pull him away, but she couldn't move.

Fischer's fists grew tremulant. A low hiss escaped his lips. "No. Nonono. You're… you're something else." Lotta saw him motion for his knife. His hand shaking wildly, feeling for the handle, fingers closing around it, knuckles blanched white. She caught a glimpse of his face, almost purple with rage. His voice rising. "No. Stop. I said stop." Bits of foamy spit sprayed from his lips. He began to scream. "NO! *NO! SHUT UP!*"

Fischer lunged at the unholy chimera, a sinuous fusion of man and vegetation. A corruption of the natural order. He drove his blade into the chest, then ripped it free. A blackened substance gushed from the wound as bits of woody, blood-tinged pulp showered the ground. A barrage of chirrups erupted from the pit from which the eyes had watched. Lotta saw shadows shifting inside.

A brilliant burst of color exploded from the shadows.

Fischer ducked away amid the flurry. Fragments of pink fungus flew out in all directions, kicked up by a barrage of prismatic blue wings and ribboned tails. Strange birds taking flight and receding into the fog toward the canopy above. Fischer looked up again, chest heaving. Lotta could see his face now, glowering with fury, knife gripped tight. He ran a grimy hand across his mouth and matted his beard. Looked around, eyes wide, confused, as if waking from a stupor. He looked down at the knife in his hand, then gazed up at the tree. He stumbled backward, his chest heaving.

Another whisper came from the comm.

"*R u n .*"

Lotta heard the rustling again, but this time, it came from the forest behind Hassan. Shifting sounds—rhythmic, punctuated. Light footfalls moving through the underbrush. Not the giant that had come up on them earlier. Something else, something smaller.

A spectral form materialized through the pale mist behind Hassan. It glided slowly past the towering trunks just beyond the clearing, a mere shadow behind the haze.

Lotta's throat seized. She watched in terror as the thing lingered just inside the edge of the hazy thicket. A searching wraith. A manifestation of all she had feared as a girl. She *was* that girl. Staring in abject horror at the ghastly apparition. A guardian of the land, of the warden tree.

To offend the warden is to invoke the wrath of the vættir.

It had a build similar in many ways to the thing she'd seen in the Cathedral, the thing that got Anderson—a large, reptilian head, striding legs, a long tail—but the similarities ended there. This creature was smaller, about as tall as a man, with a stocky, rugged build. Pure white in coloration. But a gracile form, almost birdlike in its stature.

The creature's boxy snout canted upward and snuffed the air behind a swath of mist. The same snorting Lotta had heard next to her head the night before.

Björn.[1]

But this was no bear.

The ghoulish head was the first to penetrate the haze, swirling eddies of dew-laden mist rippling over its cobbled hide as it stepped into the open. Wrinkle-faced and pure white, with a cloud of flies pulsing about its jagged maw. A ridge of corrugated keratin rose from the top of its head—a rounded double crest—flanked by a pair of horizontal bony ridges that hooded its searching pink eyes.

The haze roiled, spilling over its thickly cobbled hide. An achromatic specter. A pale ghost. Heavy rolls of skin hung from its jowls, giving way to an iguanian dewlap that extended the length of its neck. It creased and folded with each movement, sliding translucently over branching vessels. Met by a deep, noble chest that sprouted a pair of stubby arms—the limbs of a cold fetus—flaking and rugous, each sprouting maldeveloped knobs that writhed like swollen maggots.

But the legs conveyed a preternatural elegance, lean and muscular. Almost beautiful in their lethality, they raked the earth with long, white claws pink at the quick.

Fischer was backing away slowly toward her, knife at the ready. Björn's head wobbled, tremulant in its movements. It rolled to face the warden tree. To face Hassan. Snuffed at the stench of decay that had grown dull to Lotta's senses. She gazed up into its searching

---

1 *Rugops primus*

eyes. Even now, as it loomed dangerously close, it seemed unfazed by their presence.

It doesn't see us.

Lotta tried to break free from her state of paralysis. Willed herself to push off her knees. A voice screaming in her head to run. Her entire body trembled with effort, her muscles seizing and spasming under their own weight.

Flight.

Fischer had reached her now. He got to her level and placed his arm around her waist. Her body seizing, the voice screaming louder. *Run.* He lifted her onto wavering legs. She stumbled. He caught her. But not before they had stirred up a considerable racket.

Björn snapped its head in their direction. Head wobbling, eyes searching. Startled as if noticing them for the first time. The reptilian head tilted to one side, then the other. It was listening.

Two strides on those pearly legs, and she'd be in its jaws.

The beast threw a leg forward and stomped the ground. A false charge. An attempt to startle them, to flush them out. Get them to flinch. It almost worked because, for the first time, the strength in Lotta's legs returned.

Flight.

But Fischer's arm had tightened around her, steadied her. Communicated to remain still, to hold her ground.

Fight.

The beast's midsection swelled and expelled a guttural bawl from its depths—a resonant, oscillating whine that vibrated its folded jowls as it reared up, its embryonic arms splayed. The dewlap expanded into a rigid disc with a loud *snap* and flushed bright red. Head wobbling, nostrils flaring. The snout and crest engorged with crimson as the murky eyes bounced lazily in their direction.

Björn expelled another snort, then turned back toward Hassan.

The tension left Fischer's arm as it guided her toward the tree line. She stumbled again. Fischer caught her. They froze. Watched. Waited. Björn grunted. Continued its advance toward Hassan.

It didn't want them. It wanted *him.*

Flight.

Lotta wanted to look away. But all she could do was look on in horror.

Björn's dewlap shrank back, its crimson hue diminishing back into pale translucence. Nostrils flaring, snuffing at Hassan's exposed limb, nuzzling it.

No no no no. Lotta didn't want to see, didn't want to hear, but it was already too late.

The beast's jaws gaped, its rows of studded teeth closing around Hassan's upper arm with a sickening snap. The horrible head wrenched sideways, sheering away a sleeve of skin and muscle. A wet sound. Then a soft *pop*—the hand disconnecting at the wrist, tearing free, leaving behind tatters of blood-drenched fascia and coiled tendon.

Björn's head snaked, a curtain of flesh jostling from its brutal maw. Black rivulets seeped down its lips and formed tributaries that percolated into its folded scrag. Lotta watched those unseeing pink eyes searching still, indifferent to the sounds she and Fischer made as they backed out of the clearing. Indifferent as they took off, running into the thicket.

Amid her flailing, the drumbeat of her pulse in her ears, her throbbing fingers, Lotta thought she heard the chirps of a beacon receding in her wake.

| EVE >

The sequencer containing the specimen's extracted DNA samples ran quietly on a steel bench as Perez examined a blood smear under a microscope. She was working in a secondary staging area for sample analysis, constructed by Jacobs's team at her request. It was an extension of the biocontainment tent, separated by a translucent partition beyond which the creature lay upon the cold necropsy table.

Eve. They'd named it Eve. The first of her kind known to science.

Nedjma had proposed the moniker after they found dozens of partially expanded follicles in various stages of development along the oviduct. New ovulation suggested the animal was a subadult, sexually mature. Naming the specimen made the necropsy somehow more personal, more intimate. Helped lighten the heaviness punctuated by Oz's pacing footfalls, Jacobs's eyes burning through the CCTV. Provided a little levity to the darkness surrounding them, the darkness within Perez.

Mortui vivos docent. The dead teach the living.

Her eyelid fluttered, had twitched all day. She looked up toward the partition. On the other side, Nedjma hovered over the body cavity, weighing and cataloging organs, her form nothing more than a hazy apparition through the dappled drapery. The thing—Eve—nearly obscured her, an indistinct mound silhouetted beneath the glowing halide lamps. Perez admired Nedjma's work ethic, her fearlessness. Her detachment from such a horrific finding, her ability to see the work through.

Minimize the horror of the thing by giving it a name.

No. Not a horror. An animal. Afraid, dehydrated, trying to survive. Cornered in its final moments.

Perez had experienced a fleeting, misplaced rage toward Jacobs after what she had found in the creature's stomach. Fleeting, because she had known going into the examination that she might find human remains. Knew she bore some responsibility. Jacobs had told her the thing killed a man. She should have assumed. But she hadn't thought ahead to shield Nedjma. Had too much swirling around her head and neglected to account for it until it was too late.

For his part, Jacobs had sent a team in to collect the remains. Gave a disingenuous non-apology, something to the effect of "Sorry if you and your assistant were not prepared for that." *Bastard.* He knew they would find it.

Perez thought she had caught a slight upturn at the corner of his mouth before he turned and walked down the tunnel after his collection team. But he was right. She should have expected it. She *did* expect it. Should have arranged for Nedjma to be out of the containment area long before the GI exam.

Two days had passed since the incident. The picture of the maimed hand had singed itself into some fold recessed deep in Perez's subconscious, somewhere in the primitive lizard brain that stored trauma.

But Perez found intermittent solace that it wasn't Basem. This renewed hope for his survival ran counter to the persistent crushing weight in her chest, the competing voice in her head that assumed the worst. The lizard brain was never far behind. Periodically, it fed her thoughts as she worked, strobing images through her mind like flickering gaols. Her last interaction with Basem. The argument over the pregnancy. The gurgling sounds of a dead man parroted in a hail of gunfire. The image of a hex panel plowing into the sand. A freezer packed with animal corpses.

Her cogitation transitioned to ARC's status, the crushing anxiety brought on by the plight of her animals. Her ecosystem. All she had built.

Injuries. Deaths. Novel illnesses. Algal blooms cropping up in the dome's stagnant waterways. A rapidly collapsing food chain. With each passing day came a new development, another stone laid upon the plank of disquietude. A *peine forte et dure* slowly squeezing the life from her as she stood mute.

Her mind went back to Nedjma. Then to Ruth. Basem. ARC. The cycle repeated.

She had barely slept since the quake. Hadn't even gone back to her pod. Not that she wanted to. Part of her was avoiding it, not because it was probably upended as though a bomb had gone off, but because of the emptiness, the silence waiting to receive her. Instead, she had stayed in the Goliath necropsy lab the night before. Nedjma had stayed close.

Perez shifted in her seat. She leaned forward and moved the microscope stage as she peered through the oculars. Wanted to get this over with and figure out what Eve *was* so she could get back to her animals. The periodic updates from Dr. Schulz—filtered through Jacobs—were insufficient during the day, and by evening, she was so drained that any briefings she received upon retiring to the necropsy wing remained a blur. She just knew she needed to be there, back in the thick of it.

Boots on the ground.

She let out a long sigh. Watched the red blood cells float slowly across a salmon backdrop. Her HUD displayed hemoglobin concentrations as the tiny discs tumbled by, levels exceeding those of any known hybrid. Previous immuno-stains also revealed Eve had exceptionally elevated levels of myoglobin—an oxygen-storing molecule that functioned as a reservoir in hypoxic conditions—concentrated in her striated muscle tissue. This, coupled with her highly efficient respiratory system of air sacs and lungs, demonstrated an animal optimized for a low-oxygen environment, far beyond any known organism engineered to withstand the post-industrial climate. Perez bounced her attention from one red blood cell to the next. Each contained a nucleus—a typical feature of bird and reptile erythrocytes—unlike mammalian red blood cells, which lacked them. But Eve's nuclei were unique—far smaller than anything Perez had seen.

It explained their higher hemoglobin concentrations, because these cells had more room. Yet another adaptation.

Various white blood cells also dotted the slide—granulated immature heterophils indicated active inflammation at the time of death, suggesting oxidative stress, perhaps infection. It lined up with the strange necrotic lesions covering Eve's skin and respiratory tract. But none of it brought Perez any closer to determining *what* the creature was.

She glanced at the DNA sequencer impatiently.

Twenty more minutes.

Perez wondered how the animal might have moved in life. What motivated her to attack? To kill?

Fear? Hunger?

Her eyelid twitched again.

She removed the slide from the stage and placed a glass cover slip over the sample to preserve it. Next to the microscope, she opened a metal cabinet and removed a block of paraffin containing formalin-fixed lung tissue.

"Athena, dissecting loops."

Her visor magnified her view by a factor of two. She placed the block onto a microtome for sectioning, carefully placing each slice into a petri dish of buffered saline with jeweler's forceps.

She caught herself fidgeting, her leg bouncing on the ball of her foot, her heart rate increasing. She tensed her leg muscles to halt the shaking. Tried to keep her trembling hands in check as a lump coalesced at the back of her throat. This was her opportunity, the moment she had planned for. Her foot grazed the bottle of misoprostol she had strategically placed beneath the lab bench. It came in a powdered formulation that made it easy to mix in with the animals' food. Titrating it into the proper dosage for herself should be straightforward. All she needed to do was get it out of the containment zone. She just needed a mechanism by which—

Thud.

Perez snapped her head up, glancing at Nedjma's apparition through the partition, heart thrashing now. Her student had dropped a large, fleshy mound onto the scale, the wet sound of an organ impacting steel. Perez looked down at the blade, fingers gripping it tightly, trembling. She stiffened, acutely aware of the cameras on her, masking some omnipresent sentinel—Jacobs or one of the crew—watching her every move.

Get a grip. Her new mantra. She exhaled, tried to calm her nerves. It had to look unsuspecting. *Has to look like an accident.*

Oz's muffled footfalls paced from inside the tunnel over the whir of her suit's positive pressure.

She hovered over the sections apprehensively. The lump in her throat swelled. She clenched the forceps and tried to still her trembling grip as she rested her free hand along the edge of the dish. She brought the forceps down, its tips catching the index finger of her glove. She applied downward pressure and pulled the instrument.

A loud hiss filled her ears. Her HUD flashed red as her suit's pressure indicator started to fall.

Set Pressure: (+)7kPa
Actual Pressure: (+)6.57kPa ▼

An alarm went off inside the containment area. Jacobs patched through.

"Dr. Perez, what's going on? What's your status?" His accent was almost indiscernible through the whooshing in her ears.

"Shit, sorry," Perez yelled. "Ruptured my suit."

(+)6.28kPa ▼

"Your suit's positive flow should protect you until we can get you to decon. I'm sending Oz in."

"It's okay," she said. "It's my glove. I have more here. I can seal the breach if I slip another one on."

She fumbled for the box of gloves she had set at the edge of the bench and, as planned, sent it tumbling with a rack of polymer test tubes to the floor.

"Jacobs?"

No response. Perez needed to act quickly. Could not tell if Oz was coming to her, but she assumed he was.

She fell to all fours, out of the camera's line of sight, then reached for the misoprostol and one of the test tubes strewn across the floor. She scooped the powder feverishly into the bullet-shaped tube, capped it, fed it through the hole in her suit, then grabbed another.

(+)5.79kPa ▼ <<CRITICAL>>

She thought she heard Oz's footfalls heading her way. Impossible to know if it was just in her head over the roaring hiss that besieged her.

Just a few more.

Her hands were shaking uncontrollably, which made re-capping the tubes challenging. She fed a second, a third, then a fourth into her suit, replaced the lid to the misoprostol, and shoved it out of sight. She fumbled for the gloves, snapped one free, and then pulled it over her hand to seal the breach. Almost immediately, the hissing subsided to the usual dull roar, and her HUD stopped flashing. The pressure indicator started to climb.

(+)6.64kPa ▼ <STABLE>

Perez stood straight, and the test tubes tumbled down to her ankles. She looked back toward the partition, where Nedjma stood with a look of confusion on her face.

Mierda.

Warmth filled Perez's cheeks. Hot pressure burrowed into her chest.

A moment later, Oz emerged. "What's going on?" he said.

Nedjma didn't look away from Perez to acknowledge him.

The DNA sequencer's alarm went off. Perez jumped.

"Everything's fine," she said. "If you'll excuse me—" Trembling like mad, she looked to the sequencer, then back at the entrance.

Oz eyed her for a moment, then gave Nedjma a sidelong glance. He was a mountain of a man; Nedjma looked like a child next to him. He narrowed his eyes and turned without a word. A few seconds later, Perez heard him pacing the tunnel again.

"Glad you're okay," Nedjma said in a cagey tone. The confusion on her face remained as she slipped quietly back through the partition and made her way back to Eve.

Perez's chest was pounding. Her vision narrowed. She closed her eyes and slowed her breathing. The hotness in her chest intensified, working its way into her throat, creeping into her facial muscles. It crawled along her scalp as her eyes brimmed, then spilled over. *Tears for Ruth?* She squeezed them shut, then opened them again. She couldn't stop shaking.

Breathe. Just nerves.

She exhaled. Regrouped. It had worked. She had the misoprostol.

Relief stole over Perez. Salt burned her lips, and an overwhelming desire to wipe her cheeks was thwarted by the barrier of her face shield. The tears flowed without abandon, even as she fought to ossify her emotions. Already, she was letting go of Ruth. Detaching from her. A mother doing what she had to do to survive.

Her focus shifted. Concentrated instead on the itch of saline drying over her skin. Retrained herself on her task. Despite her exhaustion, the lizard brain screaming peril, the urge to rip off her suit and rub her flaring cheeks.

Lizard brain telling her she'd never see Basem again. Lizard brain portending ARC's doom. Lizard brain reinforcing the notion that she could never be a good mother. Screaming murder. Screaming for the lack of justice in it all.

Noise. Distractions.

Perez took up the forceps again. Reactivated her HUD loops. She took a piece of sectioned lung tissue, mounted it onto a slide, and then placed it on the microscope stage. She centered the slide beneath the microscope objective and peered into the oculars. The inner lining of the tissue was coated in a thin film—collagen, fibrin, endothelial abnormalities—signs of respiratory distress.

The sequencer sounded again.

Perez glanced over at the holoscreen. The results from the automated sequencer had started filtering in, the first round of data for Eve. Her tongue balled up at what she beheld. Couldn't believe her eyes. But there it was, plain as day: a positive ID.

DATABASE MATCHES/HOMOLOGOUS SEQUENCES:

TEST SAMPLE (SPECIMEN DN1451.21: "EVE")
[MATCH]...................................*Deltadromeus agilis*, 99.97% homology
[PARTIAL HOMOLOGY].............*Excinereum dinornicus* (MOA[h]) intercombinant sequences
.............*Struthioveritas dinosaurum* (OSTRICH[h]) intercombinant sequences
.............*Botaurus powellus* (AMERICAN BITTERN[h]) intercombinant sequences
.............┬ FIFTY-FOUR MORE RESULTS...
　　　　　　 └ TAP TO EXPAND

Homology of ninety-nine point nine seven percent. Hostia… this is not possible.

Nedjma had been right. The specimen *was* ancient. A near-identical match for the long-extinct *Deltadromeus agilis*—a late-Cretaceous theropod whose genome was used extensively in SANCTUM's hybridization efforts because of its unique adaptations to environmental extremes…

…including low tropospheric oxygen.

She tapped to expand a node labeled *LOCUS AY_241089* and watched sequencing data populate in real time, identifying matches as the machine read the amplified DNA sample. She then selected a string of data within it—a section of a gene encoding a cell-signaling protein—and began to read.

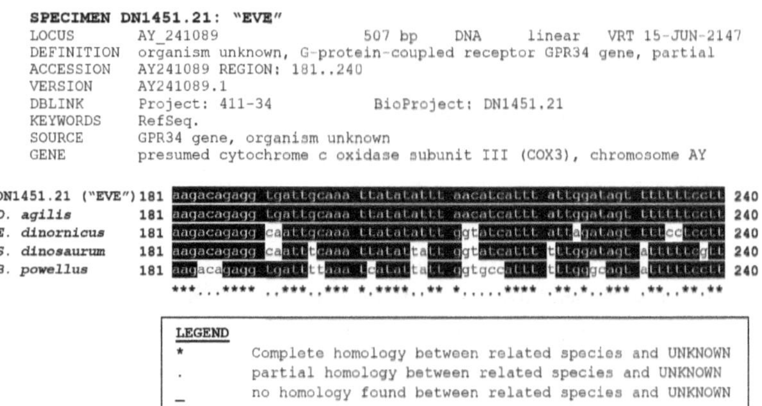

```
SPECIMEN DN1451.21: "EVE"
LOCUS       AY_241089              507 bp    DNA        linear    VRT 15-JUN-2147
DEFINITION  organism unknown, G-protein-coupled receptor GPR34 gene, partial
ACCESSION   AY241089 REGION: 181..240
VERSION     AY241089.1
DBLINK      Project: 411-34          BioProject: DN1451.21
KEYWORDS    RefSeq.
SOURCE      GPR34 gene, organism unknown
GENE        presumed cytochrome c oxidase subunit III (COX3), chromosome AY


DN1451.21 ("EVE") 181 aagacagagg tgattgcaaa ttatatatt aacatcattt attggatagt tttttttcctt 240
D. agilis         181 aagacagagg tgattgcaaa ttatatatt aacatcattt attggatagt tttttttcctt 240
E. dinornicus     181 aagacagagg caattgcaaa ttatatatt ggtatcattt attagatagt tttcctcctt 240
S. dinosaurum     181 aagacagagg caatttcaaa ttatattatt ggtatcattt tttggatagt attttttcgtt 240
B. powellus       181 aagacagagg tgattttaaa tcatattatt ggtgccattt tttgggcagt attttttcctt 240
                      ***..****  .,***,.*** *.****,.** *.....**** .**.*..*** .**..**.**

                  +---------------------------------------------------------------+
                  | LEGEND                                                        |
                  | *        Complete homology between related species and UNKNOWN|
                  | .        partial homology between related species and UNKNOWN |
                  | _        no homology found between related species and UNKNOWN|
                  +---------------------------------------------------------------+
```

Perez filtered through more lines of code. The results were preliminary, but Athena estimated that Eve's genome contained 1.3 billion base pairs.

That's on par with some birds.

Perez shook her head in disbelief.

This can't be right. It has to be engineered. Has to be a clone.

"Athena, search test sample for artificial vector sequences."

If it was a clone or hybrid, the AI would uncover synthetic promoter regions—pieces of engineered DNA embedded in the animal's genetic code, remnants of the molecular tools used during genetic modification. All modified organisms—including people—had these markers. The Federation used the same method to "validate" human pregnancies as part of its eugenic mandate. A dinosaur cloned from ancient DNA would be no different.

"No artificial vector sequences found." Athena's voice grated on Perez. "Would you like to search for viral vectors instead?"

"That can't be right," Perez said. A twinge of agitation shot through her. "There is no way this is a wild-type specimen. This species went extinct *millions* of years ago. It has to be a clone. Search it again."

She waited in silence. Tried to keep the lizard brain at bay.

"No artificial vector sequences found. Would you like to search for vir—"

"No."

Nedjma shuffled through the partition, her suit bulging around her, covered in blood. Still with the same nonplussed look on her face as earlier. A blank visage, but with hints of a tentative reproach behind her eyes.

It made Perez aware of the test tubes rattling behind the walls of her suit, somewhere around her left ankle. With her heart pounding, she took up the impulse to speak first. "Anything new?"

Nedjma hesitated for a moment. "I'm not really sure," she said quietly. "Maybe. The kidneys are really mottled and shriveled. Looks like she was dehydrated when she died. Chronic changes indicating she might have been looking for water for quite some time before her death."

Perez nodded. "Good work."

Nedjma appeared to stumble over what to say next. Skirted around the elephant in the room. "How about you?"

Perez furrowed her brow and turned back toward the holoscreen. "Come see."

Nedjma strolled sheepishly to Perez's side and gazed at the sequencing data.

"The sample is completely homologous with the genome of *Deltadromeus agilis*." It sounded absurd out loud. "It's essentially *identical*."

Nedjma's mouth fell slack. "How—how is that *possible?*"

"I don't know," Perez said, shaking her head. "The matching reference genome in the BLAST[1] database was sequenced in the 2050s by a group of paleontologists under the direction of SANCTUM's founder. But there

---

1 Basic Local Alignment Search Tool (BLAST). See appendices for more information.

was never any attempt to resurrect a pure Deltadromeus, according to historical registration logs. Even if someone wanted to, it would be almost impossible to pull off, let alone conceal it from the system."

"But what if it could be?"

Perez sighed. Reminded herself to remain patient with her student. "If something like this could be achieved—which it can't—Eve doesn't show evidence of genetic tampering. No markers or transcription promoter sequences. No NOS terminators." She kept a measured tone to conceal the growing sense of frustration she was taking care not to project onto Nedjma. Frustration, because it was a problem that had no immediate answer. "This is a wild-type specimen—a genetically *pure* animal. Not engineered or cloned, nor the offspring of a clone. It shouldn't be here." Perez looked away from the screen. "Nedjma, you were right. This is an ancient organism."

"Where did it come from?"

"I don't know."

Among the more salient takeaways was that Eve shared significant sequence overlaps with dozens of modern hybrids. At most, hybridized birds should have contained around thirty percent delta DNA. But because of a high degree of genetic drift in particular species, especially those in captivity, the percentage appeared to have climbed dramatically within just a few generations. And to a far greater degree than Perez had anticipated. At the top of the list were ostriches, moa, and a species of Bittern native to North America, with the most recent data for each indicating greater than *fifty percent* overlap with Eve.

"Athena, display phylogeny for *Deltadromeus agilis*," Perez said. "Specify extant taxa containing fifty percent or greater homology."

"Expanded data set. Please define parameters."

"Specify root Dinosauria through node Neoaves."

"Would you like to further refine?"

"Collapse non-homologous sister nodes. Include autopolyploidal species demonstrating horizontal gene transfer."

"Transgenic species added to search."

Seconds later, a branching tree populated, hovering in space over the holoscreen's sequencing data. Each node on the schematic represented a clade of common ancestors from which distinct species had evolved. Eve was classified as a coelurosaur, the same family that had given rise to *Tyrannosaurus rex* and, eventually, modern birds. As requested, the schematic displayed hybridized species demonstrating considerable sequence overlaps:

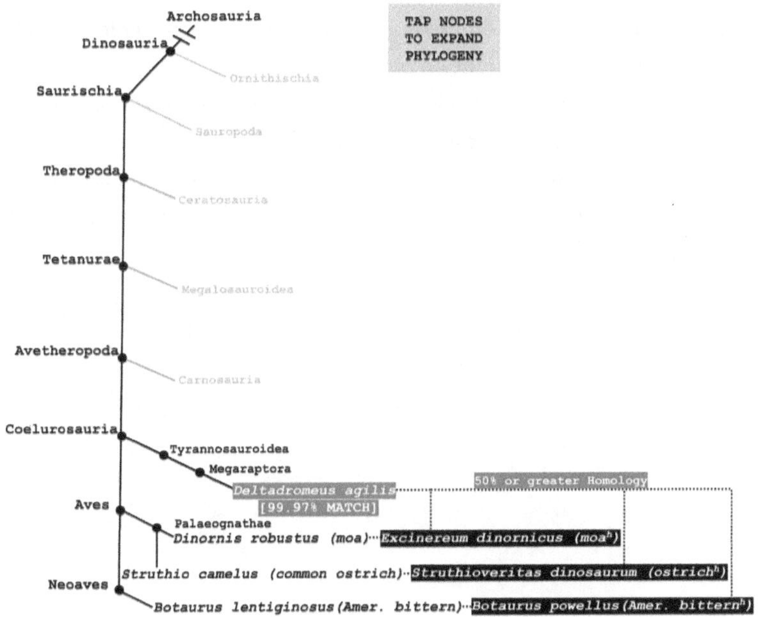

"These hybrids have far more ancient DNA than they should," Perez said. "It makes sense for ARC species because their population sizes are limited."

"Genetic drift," Nedjma said. "That explains some of the atavisms, the regressions towards masked genes."

Perez nodded. "But the American Bittern is the real outlier. It has enjoyed sustained populations in the wild for a century. If this data is correct, this species has been undergoing natural selection for dinosaur phenotypes, regardless of its population dynamics. It is worse than I thought."

"What does that mean?"

"I don't know. Many of these genes were thought to have been suppressed or absent in this species. But it appears the phenomenon isn't as isolated to captive populations as I thought."

"Do you think Eve is a product of evolutionary regression?"

"No. Athena would find a signature if she came from an engineered lineage." Perez's voice rose, her frustration bubbling at having to repeat herself. She took a deep breath and made a renewed effort to modulate her tenor, to explain. "Artificial promoters are passed down from generation to generation the same way native DNA is. Even so, this level of homology with the wild-type Deltadromeus genome would be impossible through reemerging atavisms brought on by genetic drift."

There was a moment of silence, Perez's eyes locked on to Nedjma's.

"This specimen came from somewhere else...."

Oz walked through the partition with his gun drawn, muzzle pointing toward the ground. He approached the two women and loomed over them like a giant.

"Time to go," he said calmly.

"What?" Perez said, perplexed by the abrupt shift in circumstance. "Where are we going?"

"Escorting you back to the loading dock. We have everything we need."

"Wait... we haven't finished—"

"Yes, you have. Let's go."

< ∩ | UZ >

"Oy! I found something! Over here!"

A fatigued Fischer stood and wiped his sweaty hands across his dust-coated jeans. He had toiled ceaselessly among the rubble for days, clutching to hope. And, right now, hope sounded like a middle-aged man shouting from across a mound of twisted steel and concrete.

Fischer sneezed as he glanced up, scanning for the best route to the other side. A particulate cloud hung heavy over the city like a dense fog. The whir of aerial search vehicles hovered somewhere unseen overhead. A few patches of visible sky billowed ominous gray clouds that looked ready to open up and threaten the city's rescue efforts. But seventy-two hours after the Geneva quake—the worst in Europe's history—hope for survivors had started to fade. Still, Fischer held onto hope. The remains of four children and two staff members had already been pulled out. But no survivors. Not yet.

He negotiated shifting debris, heaving against the cloying smell of particulate dust that choked the air. It was a smell one never grew accustomed to. It breached his respirator, an alkaline odor that filled his nose and throat and settled on his tongue. A rancid, almost nauseating taste that sent his throat into periodic spasms.

Something crumbled underfoot, sending bits and chunks raining down into a pocket below the rubble. A five-story building, reduced to four or five meters of pancaked slabs and rebar. One misstep over a sizeable void could send someone plummeting toward a fresh pair of broken legs or a snapped neck. But Fischer didn't care. Hope was calling for him. That was all that mattered.

"Over here!"

Through the haze, Fischer spotted hope's head poking out from behind a mess of snarled pipes—an ash-coated ginger dome, a receding hairline. He was a middle-aged man, his grime-ridden face obscured by a red floral bandana tied over his nose and mouth. The man was hunched forward, yanking a body-length sheet of metal with thickly gloved hands. Several other volunteers had converged and started joining in the effort.

Fischer stumbled down the other side of the rubble pile. His head was heavy, almost as if he had forgotten how to hold it up. His aching limbs locked up sporadically, nearly causing him to slip over a shifting pile of pulverized concrete as he made his way down the other side.

"Think I found something," the man with the red bandana shouted. "Here, look."

"Looks like a dress," a French-sounding woman said.

Crushing pressure clapped against Fischer's lungs, accompanied by weakness in his knees, joints locking up. A warning to turn away and never return.

A red dress.

Fischer had bought Emma a red dress for her birthday. She was turning three in a couple of weeks, but the day the disaster struck was also her last day of daycare, and she wanted to wear that dress so bad. Fischer couldn't say no. She was so proud walking out the door that morning. Before the quake. Before the building came down. Before Geneva had become a smoldering wasteland. A mass grave.

Fischer's world slowed. By now, the crowd had converged, obstructing his view as they feverishly cleared debris. His feet carried him but couldn't cover the ground fast enough. A sensation like floating in a dream. Floating in a nightmare.

A ribbon of red emerged from behind a pair of shifting legs as the volunteers moved about. Fischer stopped and swallowed hard, but his throat had cinched shut. He stumbled forward.

Her tiny legs were crushed, pinned beneath a ton of concrete, fingernail scrapings striping the slab, her head buried beneath a mound of wet ash. The middle-aged man was working frantically to wipe it away. But Fischer did not need to see her face to know...he saw the little red dress in sharp relief against the gray ruins, against the ashen diggers, the toiling phantoms and their weary movements. The little red dress, torn and soiled, but still radiant. Still beautiful. Just like Emma.

But it was the scratches in the concrete that haunted Fischer most of all. In her last moments, Emma had tried to free herself. Tried to claw herself free. His little bear. His little fighter. >

Day 1, Post Meridiem — The Forest

No more pain, Daddy.

The words rang out in Fischer's head as trees whipped past. It was *her* he had talked to, had seen. *It was Emma.* As if she had manifested out of thin air. She was lying still. Legs pinned, fingers raw and bloody. Face covered in soot. Her eyes were far off, empty as they gazed up at him. Those faded, blue eyes. Hassan had made him see. Made him *feel.*

That red dress.

Her body motionless but for her moving lips.

No more pain.

Those blue lips. That pale face. My baby. My bear.

Fischer's chest heaved as he pushed through the underbrush, branches lashing his cheeks, his legs pumping, searing. He heard Lotta panting, hot on his heels. They ran without sense, without purpose beyond the innate impulse to escape, succumbing to the archaic drive for self-preservation. Fight or flight. A reflex so immediate that it subverted awareness until the immediate danger had passed. But Fischer was better than this. Had trained for extreme situations.

At one time.

And yet he convinced himself this was different. That the horrors of war could not begin to compare. The things he heard. The things he *saw.*

As if they had been real. They *were* real. He pumped his arms harder as tears and snot streamed down his face.

But once his higher faculties had wrested control, seeding logic, scrambling the signal, his pace slowed to a light jog.

And that was when Fischer noticed they were lost.

Scheisse.

"Stop." He wheezed, bringing his body to a halt. "Stop...."

"*Stop?* That *thing*—" Lotta nearly slammed into him.

"Isn't after us. It—it want—wanted Hassan."

Fischer drank the air, his hands clasping his knees as if somehow that might help draw the breaths deeper. He was trying to come to grips with what had just happened. He needed a shot. Needed water. He swiped a trembling, grime-covered hand over his cottony lips and closed his eyes.

She was there. Those eyes. Looking at me. Looking through me.

An echo. A ghost. Fischer had tried to reach for her—for Emma—tried to pull her free, and when he did, the voices of his other daughters filled the crackling static emanating from Hassan's comm. Then, as soon as she had appeared, little Emma *vanished.* That was when Fischer heard the screams. When the rage boiled up. The fury. And like a roiling inferno, it sent him lunging at Hassan. At that *thing.*

They were suffering, all three of them. My girls, wailing in their last moments.

Or it had been nothing more than a fugue, an altered state of consciousness brought on by extreme shock.

Maybe just a case of the DTs.

Fischer had heard about delirium tremens before—what sudden withdrawal could do to people—but had never considered the prospect of it happening to him. Never thought he drank enough. But he had also heard most alcoholics didn't realize they were addicts. Not until they hit rock bottom, and usually not even then.

I could stop anytime. I did stop. Not by choice, but stopped nonetheless.

Fischer opened his eyes. Looked down at his open hands in their ceaseless trembling. He raised them to his eyes, buried his face in his palms, and wept.

It wasn't real. Wasn't real.

No. It was.

"Ed, what was that? What happened back there?" Lotta's hand found his shoulder. "Ed?"

"Just… need—need a minute."

Lotta's hand fell away, grazing his back as if to cautiously reassure him. He wiped his eyes and inhaled as deep as he could manage, craning his neck to the treetops. Daylight was wearing thin.

Wasn't real.

He exhaled and leveled his eyes at Lotta. "I'm good."

"Something happened to you."

"Said I'm good."

Every time Fischer blinked, he could still hear, *see, feel* the building crumbling, coming down on his girls. On *him.* The sensation was dull now, but it was still there. He had felt what they felt. Smelled what they smelled. The dust choking his lungs, his flesh singed by an underground blaze. The deafening crash of floors collapsing overhead, one by one. Each boom came louder than the last until nothing but a thunderous roar had swallowed him like a black hole.

It was all fading now.

But the screams remained. As did the fear, the dread that his girls had endured. That *he* endured as he passed into death. Into *their* deaths. Where there was nothing. No happiness. No sorrow. No thirst for water or want for air.

No pain.

Only nothing. An incomprehensible void. Not black, nor empty, nor silent. *Nothing* was a dreamless sleep. *Nothing* was death.

Fischer's breathing slowed. He looked down at his feet. The ground spun about him as his mind drifted in and out.

The voices. The voices wouldn't stop.

"Ed…."

No more pain, Daddy.

"*Ed.*" Lotta waved her hand at him, again pulling him out of his trance. "Hey… what was that back there?"

Fischer looked up at her with a glassy stare. "I think we established it was Hassan. And the thing that attacked him—sounded like what we heard last night outside the shelter. Björn."

A dinosaur. It looked like a goddamned dinosaur.

Fischer grew giddy at the thought, probably because it hadn't even broken third on the *oh, shit* meter. He almost fell into a fit of laughter at the absurdity of it, that it was barely a thought in his mind.

Goddamned dinosaurs. What a goddamned fuckin' hoot.

"That's not what I'm talking about." Lotta was nothing if not persistent. She wasn't going to let it go. "Ed, what happened to *you?*"

Fischer shrugged, lied through gritted teeth. "Nothing. It was nothing. And you? What the bloody hell were *you* doing?" He recalled her falling to her knees at the foot of the blood tree, her longing gaze upon a corrupted Hassan.

That did it. Lotta's face flushed crimson. "Don't know what you're talking about." She changed the subject. "So, then, what now?"

"We get our bearings. Figure this out."

Lotta slumped, and a sunken expression stole over her—adrenaline losing its edge, higher-order processes reclaiming her facial muscles, reviving that crestfallen ghostly appearance she seemed to wear more and more. "We're all that's left." Her voice wavered.

"Aye." Fischer hadn't really thought about that, either. It was farther down on the *oh, shit* meter.

Lotta went quiet, to his relief. *A moment of silence,* he thought, *to try and clear my head.*

It was then that he noticed she no longer had the spear, had probably ditched it in her panic. He grazed a thumb over his knife handle to ensure it was still secured to his waist, then walked forward with his hands on his hips. The fog had started to break, and the moss now grew thick and bright green, spreading uniformly around the massive tree trunks. About a dozen meters off, a large grouping of knee-high ferns sprouted among the endless rows of trees. Nothing about their immediate surroundings seemed familiar, and the flower trail leading back to the grove was long gone.

Fischer stopped and stood in silence. For a moment, he managed to disregard the voices, *the echoes,* long enough to hear it. *Salvation*—the distant sound of flowing water.

He turned back to Lotta. "You hear that?"

Her eyes widened and her body tensed. Ready to break back into a sprint from some unseen threat. "*What?*"

"*Listen.*" Fischer paused, holding a trembling finger to the air. "*That's water.*"

He spun around and bounded into the dense blackened undergrowth. A roiling current soon filled his ears. His throat was too dry to swallow. His lids grated against his eyes. He swiped a frothing tongue over a pair of cracked, salty lips. Legs wobbling, spasms coursing down his calves, he stumbled forward. Tripped on a root but leaned into it and regained his balance. His body wanted to quit, to succumb. But soon, the trees thinned, and the canopy opened enough to permit a glimpse of dim blue sky. He lurched forward, foam coalescing at the corners of his mouth.

And there it was, the most beautiful sight in recent memory: clear, gushing water. It spluttered and churned, carving a crystal stream along the forest floor. He turned back to Lotta, grinning from ear to ear. Felt his bottom lip split down the middle.

Lotta emerged through the thicket, gazing out in wonder. "You… you found it!" She dropped to her knees and dunked her hands in. Fischer's expression fell, and he lunged forward to grab her arm.

"*No.*" He grunted, pulling her back.

"Hey, let go of me! What the hell?"

"We don't know if it's safe. There could be giardia or any number of parasites in that. We need to boil it."

"Oh, sod off." She ripped her arm free and settled back to the ground. "Looks clean to me. I can see through to the bottom."

Lotta's voice sounded far off. Fischer's head was spinning again. The echoes, the voices persisted. Relegated to whispers, but that didn't make it any better than if they had been screams.

No more pain.

Fischer's hand twitched. He stifled the instinct to drive his own fist into his forehead. Anything to silence the voices. He took a deep breath and exhaled slowly.

Fire. We need a fire.

"Well?" Lotta looked up at him, her knees still shoved into the mud.

Fischer ignored her. Surveyed their surroundings and spotted what he was looking for—a rigid branch about arm's length with a slight bend in the middle. He picked it up and turned to Lotta, who stared back at him blankly, defiance behind her eyes, her lips cracked and peeling. Arms glistening-wet up to her elbows as her fingers got to work picking away at themselves. Fischer regarded her with a firm tone. "I'm going to get to work on a fire. I need you to build a ring with any large rocks you can find. And do *not* drink any water."

The voices of his girls started coming in a little louder, and not a lick of something stiff to sequester them. But he figured he could manage well enough to at least get an ember started. There really was no alternative.

Lotta turned and stumbled off to the embankment without a word.

Fischer produced his knife and carefully notched the ends of the stick, then reached down to the gloves at his waist. He loosened the ribbon he had cinched around them and flexed it, then cut it lengthwise into two pieces and braided them tightly into a thin but rigid cord with a loop at each end. When squeezed, the woven sections "healed" into a firm band that was both flexible and strong. He secured one loop over one of the stick's notches, then leaned down to flex it and pulled the other loop into place. Once the cord was secure, he let up on the stick to create tension. It wasn't one of his proudest engineering feats, but for a bow, it was passable.

The remaining tools were much more straightforward to produce: the drill itself—a tapered spindle carved from a straight stick; a flat length of wood with a notch in the middle, pulled from a dried-out deadfall for the bore; and a dimpled rock he'd found along the riverbank to serve as a top piece and save him from shredding his palm.

"*Scheisse!*" Lotta's shriek made Fischer jump.

From the corner of his eye, he saw her leap backward along the water's edge. The stone she had just lifted plunged out of her hands and into the water with a loud *pa-loonk*.

Something long—about the length of her arm—slithered away and into the water. It stopped to rest behind a protruding rock, where an eddy provided a dead zone in the current. The snake floated there, motionless, its flat head breaking the surface. A pattern of banded black-and-gray speckles adorned the length of its body.[1] But something about it appeared unusual. Fischer moved closer to get a better look.

"*Do you see that?*" Lotta said, pointing down at it, her body arched back in disgust. "What kind of snake has *legs?*"

Fischer almost scoffed at this, but as he approached the bank, he realized she was right. It *did* have legs—two of them, at the base of a crested tail—minuscule, almost nonexistent appendages sculling the water just below the surface. The serpent looked comical, its little black eyes locked onto them, ceaseless in their gaze as a forked tongue darted in and out to taste the air. All the while, its pathetic legs fought to keep its shimmering body stable in the water. Fischer grew giddy again. Had to stifle the urge to laugh. He didn't know why he had suddenly adopted such a blithe aspect. Maybe because something as silly as a legged snake paled in comparison to the voices in his head. To the sound of nails scraping against concrete. To watching—*feeling*—his girls' death throes, one by one.

Nor did it stack up to his colleagues assimilating into sentient flora, falling prey to giant pterodactyls, getting consumed by carnivorous bees, or atomized across the Bell chamber's landings like wet confetti.

The snake flitted its tongue once more, dove to the stream bed, and then wriggled out of sight.

"Not the strangest thing we've seen all day," Fischer said and turned his attention back to finishing his bow drill.

"Everything here is strange." Lotta picked up another stone and laid it down, completing a ring. Her eyes drifted back toward the water where the snake had dived.

Fischer watched her try to make sense of it, to somehow reconcile the dissonance of this place in her mind and all that had happened since the incident. Place it all into a neat, logical box. Reduce it to an equation, a symmetry. But there was no making sense of it—not of a snake with legs and, for Fischer, not of experiencing death through the eyes of one's child, one's *children*. Nothing about this place fit form or logic. He saw that on Lotta's face, too. That realization taking root. Almost pitied her, sitting

---

1 *Simoliophis libycus*

there, brow furrowed, hair a tangled mess as she fiddled at her remaining pearl earring with shredded fingers.

"What do you think happened to him?" Lotta's voice came through raspy, her eyes far off, still watching the water. "To Hassan?"

"Don't know." It was the truth. Fischer had his own theories, but saw little benefit in sharing them. Half because they were far-fetched and half because Lotta seemed to be losing her mind just fine on her own.

There was little utility in divulging, for example, how Hassan's demise reminded him of a story he had come across in his formative years, when he was into tinkering with electronics and magnets and reading conspiracy theories about extraterrestrials and spontaneous combustion—an alleged event that occurred in an American naval shipyard around the mid-twentieth century. The so-called Philadelphia Experiment. The U.S. Navy was testing out some new cloaking tech on a destroyer in the middle of the harbor. *Some spooky-action-at-a-distance type shit.* According to the story, the tech was based on Einstein's proposed unified field theory of gravity and electromagnetism. Quantum gravity. Higher dimensions. And it had *worked*, only not entirely as intended. The ship had disappeared, sure. But she also re-emerged with her crew embedded in her hull. Flesh and steel melded into one.

We are one.

But it was just a story. A fiction. It wasn't real. Violated every law of physics. Still, that didn't keep it from infiltrating Fischer's thoughts after what they had seen. Probably because it didn't sound all that far off from what the ALICE experiments attempted to pull off.

"And that hive…." Lotta said, drawing Fischer's gaze from his work. "That thing those bees were swarming. The tooth. That was Anderson, wasn't it?"

"Might have been." The same thought had crossed his mind. Before that enormous creature interrupted them to chow down on what was left. "I just don't know, Lotta."

Lotta's eyes turned glassy and began to brim.

Bow in hand, Fischer walked to the fire ring and nudged one of the rocks along its perimeter, inspecting Lotta's work. "Looks good."

He wavered for a moment, taken by a rush of vertigo, stopped to steady himself. Lotta's eyes rolled to him expectantly as he ruffed his beard and swiped a hand over his lips. The sensation passed, and he forced a smile. "Let's get a fire going."

At the center of the ring, Fischer stacked a cone of kindling, then set up the bow drill to get a starter flame going. He laid the flat wooden bore on the ground and wound the spindle tightly into the bow's cord. Genuflecting with his left foot on the bore, he fit the spindle's pointed end into the notch and pressed down against the other end with the top piece gripped tightly in his fist. With his other hand, he began rocking the bow back and forth in a sawing motion. The spindle spun rapidly like a top—clockwise on the forward thrust, counter-clockwise on the back thrust—generating friction where it contacted the bore.

The ground started to spin again. Fischer's parched tongue scraped the roof of his mouth as he swallowed at the thin air, his entire body shaking. He grew faint, but dismissed the sensation, responding instead by increasing the speed of his thrusts.

The scent of rust invaded his senses, invoking images of the pulsating swarm crawling over the festering pestilence that was presumably Martin Anderson at one time, now nothing but a glistening canker. The buzzing hive droned in Fischer's ears, pulsating to the rhythm of his burning arm as he cranked on the bow harder still. Then he caught a new smell. Sweet and smoky—the smell of burning wood. A few silky wisps rose from the bore, where a fine black powder accumulated at the spindle's base.

He tasted blood.

Just a little more. Can't... stop.

Smoke billowed from the bore and caught him in the face. Fischer sputtered, sending foam flying from his cracked lips. Everything began to blur. A strange prismatic fortification coalesced along his periphery, an undulating shimmer of blues and purples, a scintillating scotoma that resembled the migraine auras he'd sometimes get during a bad hangover.

We are one.

Fischer pushed the voices aside. Cranked harder.

The smoke stung his eyes and provoked an influx of tears. But he couldn't stop to wipe them, had to keep going. He was close now. The sweet carbon smell intensified. A purplish blob invaded the center of his vision, but he pressed, his entire body on fire now, muscles spasming in protest.

His arm had grown numb, tendons seized up so that his movements became stiff and sporadic. The spindle squeaked as it spun in the bore.

Can't stop.

Fischer was falling forward. Thought he heard Lotta's distant voice calling after him. He was in a dream now, tumbling endlessly into a void. Into nothing. Somewhere far below, beneath the rubble of his sins, where the fires raged hot and pure.

| *Nothing is a dreamless sleep.*
Nothing is death. >

●

Day 1, Eventide — The Stream

Flickering oranges and reds penetrated Fischer's slitted eyelids. The cold ground pressed against his cheek, but warmth blanketed his body.

Can't stop.

Everything came rushing back. He jolted, tried to sit upright, but his muscles groaned in protest. Everything ached, and Little Man ripped through his head with renewed fury.

"Easy." Lotta's voice came from beyond the glimmering lights.

Glimmering… fire?

Through smeared vision, Fischer saw her coalesce before him, outlined in the soft glow of the dancing flames. He tried to sit up again, but only managed to tilt his head toward the forest canopy, where shards of pale moonlight pierced a sea of boughs. There was still a hint of light in the sky, enough to know twilight was still on them. Over the crackling fire, he heard a chorus of chirping frogs harmonizing with the babbling stream. Lotta knelt beside him and placed a hand on his shoulder. Startled, he jerked.

"Lotta?"

He recoiled at the pain that shot through his swollen tongue.

"Shhh… drink…."

She hovered over him, her messy hair an angelic corona in the moonlight. She raised something metallic to his lips, and steam kissed his skin. Clean water trickled into his mouth, filling him with warmth as it went down. Felt good on his tongue. He reached with both hands and clutched the vessel away from her, choking and sputtering. Lotta put her hands over his and pulled the canister away from his lips.

"Slow down. Let's sit you up."

Fischer was too weak to resist. Lotta set the water down, walked behind him, and fed her hands under his armpits. She pulled, Fischer pushed, and a moment later, he sat with his back propped up against a tree.

"You're not as heavy as you look," Lotta said, huffing. She handed him the water.

"I like a strong woman." Something Fischer would later forget saying. He was pretty sure she could barely understand him anyway, his injured tongue rendering him almost incoherent.

He kicked his head back and imbibed as much as he could stomach, then let out a long sigh that concluded with a belch. The fire crackled peacefully in the gloam.

But relative solitude had always lingered just beyond Ed Fischer's reach. At best, it was a fleeting perception that inevitably gave rise to a forlorn sense of anguish. That was when the ghosts came. The memories. The voices.

He caught himself fidgeting at his side, subconsciously searching for his flask. Part of him wished Lotta had let him die. His eyes met hers, and she produced a haggard smile, then turned to stir the coals with a stick.

"How long was I out?" He shifted his legs. Tried to distract from the pain of speaking.

"Maybe a few hours."

"Thanks," he said. His best attempt at sincerity.

"Thought I'd lost you. You—" Lotta choked on her words as though they had snagged themselves on the way out. "You had a seizure."

Fischer gave a nod and a grunt.

Maybe got the DTs after all, he thought to himself. *More likely that I've lost my mind.*

He looked down into the canister at the clear liquid, swirled it, then raised it to his lips. Savored it like whiskey. Let it linger on his tongue before swallowing it down. He wiped his mouth and glanced over at Lotta. "Well, I feel splendid now. Mir geht's bestens. Picture of health."

Lotta didn't say anything. She sat on the ground with her legs crossed, facing the fire with her head down, hair in her face. She carved into the dirt with a stick like a pouting child. Her inflamed fingers shined in the soft glow, hands trembling—from pain or fear, Fischer could not be sure. All he knew was that *solitude* had already worn its welcome.

He swirled the canister once more. "You get this from that POG?"

Her head still down, stick dragging in the dirt, Lotta nodded. "One of the sieve cylinders. Dumped the adsorption beads." Fischer couldn't tell if she was sobbing or just withdrawing again.

"Huh. Holds water well." He looked around and spotted the remains of the scavenged oxygen generator by the fire. Ripped apart in a frenzy, gutted, its innards strewn about. "Why didn't I think of that?" He took another swig.

Lotta kept her head down, still carving away as though she hadn't heard him. Maybe she thought it didn't warrant a response. The only sounds were of the popping coals, the stick dragging through the dirt, the warbling of frogs. Fischer tilted his chin up and stretched his neck to try and decipher what she was carving, but couldn't make it out.

Eyesight's shit.

He slumped back down and stared into the smoldering embers. All the while, voices swam in his head. A flat rock sat along the edge of the pit.

Just then, something called out into the night sky—a high-pitched moan. Lotta snapped out of her torpor; just like Fischer, she whipped her head in the direction of the sound. It was long and drawn-out, then, with startling suddenness, it was cut short.

The frogs had fallen silent.

Lotta looked at Fischer, stick in hand, as if thinking the same thing—how there was something deeply unsettling about how it just *stopped*.

Lotta set the stick down and rose back to her feet. Fidgeted at her cuticles anxiously. A solitary frog resumed its song, and soon, the rest joined in.

She paced for a few minutes, then turned to Fischer. "How's your stomach?" she said, her voice cracking.

"Eating itself."

Lotta walked over to the flat rock and brushed something off it into her hand. "Here. Eat this." She dropped three large grubs in Fischer's hand, her fingers cold as they grazed his palm.

He looked down and studied the charred insects tentatively.

"They're safe," Lotta said. "I did the sensitivity test you showed me. They're actually not bad. I would have made your fiddleheads, but didn't know how to get rid of that shackic—"

"Shikimic acid. Where did you find these?"

"Watching hummers." She knelt forward and sat beside him.

"*Hummers?*"

Lotta nodded. "I can't think of a better way to describe them. They're like hummingbirds."

Fischer snorted. "Hummingbirds are extinct."

"I said they're *like* hummingbirds." There was agitation in her voice. ALICE's principal investigator wasn't accustomed to being corrected.

Hassan didn't learn that lesson soon enough, Fischer thought.

Occasionally, Fischer himself got away with a jab here and there. Liked to knock her down a peg, and she usually tolerated it. But this time, he bit his tongue and let her continue.

"They're more like little pterodactyls with hypodermic needles for beaks. And they can hover."[1] Lotta panned her head around, then squared her eyes again with Fischer's. "Don't see any around right now. Sometimes you can hear them flitting about the treetops. They go for the foul-smelling ones." She nodded toward a ginkgo tree at the water's edge.

Then Fischer noticed it—a sour odor. It was faint, like the lingering scent of vomit in his beard after a blackout. "Is that what I smell?"

---

1 *Leptostomia begaaensis*

Lotta nodded.

"Pleasant."

He stared at the tree while she spoke. Its serpentine branches sprouted bright fan-shaped leaves that clustered in shoots at their tips. From the center of each floret bloomed orange stalks, the fire's soft glow playing off them ominously.

"But the bigger hummers walk around and probe for bugs, on all fours like stalkers—" Lotta got quiet. Her expression fell, face went pale. Perhaps the realization she had just alluded to Basem's gruesome death. It was the same expression Fischer saw when she found what was possibly Anderson's tooth. Fischer studied her face. Her eyes far-off. She wasn't there in front of him anymore. Had once again wandered off somewhere into the recesses of her crumbling sanity. She was reliving it, all of it. Basem falling from the sky. Mattheo seeping through a grate to the Bell chamber floor. Hassan… *what the fuck happened to Hassan? Jesus.*

Fischer sighed. "You okay?"

Lotta's eyes snapped to attention, and without missing a beat, she picked up where she had left off with her "hummer" encounter. "I spotted one foraging on a dead log, probing channels with that needle-beak, pulling out grubs. I chased it off and found a whole nest." She pointed at the charred bugs in his hand. "That's the last of them."

It was the strangest thing, Fischer thought, like she'd shut down and rebooted. But everyone dealt with grief and trauma in their own way. He could only imagine what she thought of *his* episode with Hassan. *He* wasn't even sure what to think of it. Something in him had just *snapped.*

"Resourceful," Fischer said and looked down at the blackened grubs, then cupped his hand to his mouth and threw them back. He chased them with water before the taste could set on his tongue.

Lotta's eyes were far off again. Fischer gestured toward her hands, anything to keep her out of her head a little longer. "That looks painful," he said.

"Oh, it, uh…." Fischer could tell she was about to play it down, but instead, she took on a new demeanor. A side he hadn't seen before. *Vulnerability.* The corners of her mouth fell yet further, and she raised her brow like an injured child, her shoulders slumped in a way that conveyed helplessness. "Yeah. It is."

"Let me see." Fischer reached out, and she presented her hands to him. Her fingers were caked in dried blood, their tips swollen, so the skin took on a dull sheen. An image of Emma's little fingers flashed through his mind like a lightning bolt. Her little hands, the fingernails gone. Torn away after clawing at the concrete for God knows how long. *Hours? Days?* Fischer squeezed his eyes shut as if to wipe the image away. Clenched his jaw and inhaled.

Ghosts. Echoes.

Time slowed as he cradled Lotta's hands in his. He probed each finger as gently as he could. Felt for excess warmth, assessed for discharge, signs that might indicate infection. All the while, he pushed the ghosts down. Focused on Lotta's responses, her subtle, painful winces as he examined her. Anything to keep *him* out of *his* own head.

No discharge, just blood. And oddly cold.

"They're inflamed, all right," he said. "But no signs of infection. Let's clean these up before you really have a problem."

"Ed, you don't need to—"

"I know. But I am." *Just shut up and let me do this. I can't deal with the ghosts right now.*

Fischer stumbled like a lame animal over to where he had lost consciousness. The bow drill lay flat on the ground, its spindle still wound into the cord and pitched at an angle. The dimpled rock he had used as a top piece had rolled off a meter or so, and the bore was missing. The gloves were still where he had left them after removing the cord for the bow. He grunted as he bent down to retrieve the gloves, his ribs still sore, knees groaning. He opened one of them, removed a few of the resin nuggets he had stashed, and then limped toward the fire. He stirred the coals, threw on a bundle of sticks before placing Lotta's cooking stone over the flame, and laid the resin on top. The amber chunks softened into a sticky, viscous substance that emitted a sweet aroma. Once it started to bubble, he glommed it on the end of Lotta's discarded stick, then beckoned her over to him.

"This'll seal up those cuts and draw out bacteria," he said. "Nature's antibiotic." He blew on it and let it cool for a minute, then gestured for her to hold her hands out.

He applied the resin thickly over her wounds. The smell was pleasant. Almost masked the ginkgo-vomit smell. It set quick, drying to form a watertight seal.

He sensed Lotta's eyes on him as he slathered more onto another finger. She flinched and drew a sharp breath through gritted teeth. But she didn't look away.

"Sorry," Fischer said. "Just try and hold still." He pretended to be more focused than he was, pretended not to notice her looking at him. Sometimes, Jocelyn would look at him that way when she had something on the tip of her tongue. Testing to see if he noticed her body language, like he was a goddamned mind reader. It always drove him mad. *Out with it, already.*

"What happened to you back there?" Lotta said finally. Taking another stab. "Hassan's comm cut out, and you flew into a rage."

Can't let a sleeping dog lie, can you?

"Did I?" Fischer had a mind to make her wince again, but composed himself.

Lotta nodded, and he looked up into her big blue eyes. The whites had started to show through now that much of the blood had settled.

"You never told me you have a family."

A jolt coursed through Fischer's chest. For a moment, he was convinced his heart had stopped. The corner of his mouth twitched.

"Had."

"Oh… I'm… I'm so sorry." Her brow furrowed, and her eyes glazed over.

Fischer nodded and cleared his throat. "S'okay. Long time ago."

Lotta's eyes again fell to her hands, and she watched silently as Fischer worked.

He stole a glance toward the fire, where Lotta had carved in the dirt. There, he saw a symbol he had never seen before, resembling a 'P' or 'D,' but with severe angles and harsh lines. A rune or pagan symbol of some type.

He felt unsure as to why, but it made him think about Lotta falling to her knees in front of Hassan, something he had attributed to shock—weak knees in the face of insurmountable horror. But the way she had gazed up at that tree, as one might a deity, stuck out as starkly as the wails of his buried daughters.

And the flower. An offering, perhaps?

Now scratching symbols in the dirt, perhaps from the very religion she once claimed to have abandoned when she was a girl.

Clinging to something familiar in a world where nothing is.

Or just a mindless doodle. His gaze fell back to Lotta, her eyes fixed on her fingertips. She was far away again.

And what happened to you *back there, Lotta Eklund?*

| RUPAL >

"Forget what you saw."

Oz's grizzled, square jaw barely moved as he spoke. His words felt unnecessary after the mountain of NDAs Nedjma and Perez had signed, but the tone of his voice crystallized his intent: intimidation.

It was the first time Perez had seen his whole face. An expression of stone, it betrayed no semblance of emotion. Rifle hugged against his chest with brawny arms, his eyes creased slits as they regarded her and Nedjma. He had a broad nose, notched in the middle—likely broken at one time or another—and now wore a beige desert shawl over his uniform. A black-and-white houndstooth shemagh was draped around his neck.

Perez looked past Oz at the Goliath. One level down, soldiers and synths moved about its towering wheelbase, removing chains as they prepared to cast off into the open desert. A loading mech clambered by to return a large container carrying the equipment used for the necropsy. On either side was a large biohazard trefoil; beneath it, the letters *HAZMAT BSL4: STERILISATION REQUIRED* in holographic lettering.

Oz gave the two women a final leering glance and turned without another word to join Kohen, who had been waiting for him at the edge of the loading dock's concrete terrace. Perez felt the woman's cold, silent stare as she waited, those sharp brown eyes encircled by dark rings. The two soldiers then proceeded down the ramp, walking in lockstep as they descended. They passed into daylight and rounded the loading dock entrance, then disappeared to the other side of the bay door.

Just forget, Perez thought. *Forget the animal you examined went extinct almost a hundred million years ago. Forget the fact it's a species whose genome has become ubiquitous in modern hybridization efforts, yet shows no signs of genetic meddling. Forget that it* killed *someone, and that you exposed your student to the aftermath.*

Giddy at the notion of what she'd seen, what she'd verified, she had to fight back laughter, the type that only accompanied crippling self-defeat and almost always ended in tears.

The roar of engines echoed through the entrance, and a plume of brown dust billowed into the loading area as military aircraft took flight. With its personnel back onboard, the Goliath groaned on its chassis, then lurched forward and crawled through the roiling cloud. By the time the dust cleared, Perez watched the hulking freighter move off toward the horizon with the sun at its back, once again flanked by its aerial military escort.

Just forget. She didn't see how it was possible.

But beneath her inner turmoil, Perez was relieved. Glad to wash her hands of Eve, and Jacobs, for that matter, to retrain her focus squarely on ARC's recovery. She was more than happy to move on.

As the sound of engines faded, she turned toward Nedjma, who appeared almost childlike in her suit, now deflated, her shoulders slouched as she stared out.

"Are you okay?" Perez said.

Nedjma nodded without diverting her gaze.

"Listen," Perez said, "about the bottle…."

"What bottle?" Nedjma's eyes drifted to meet hers, then moved back to the horizon. "You heard him. Forget what we saw." One corner of her mouth turned up so that the sun caught the faint line of the scar on her upper lip.

"Do you know how I got my scar?" she said as if having read Perez's mind.

Taken aback by this, Perez shook her head. Her cheeks prickled as she realized she had probably been staring, that Nedjma might have taken notice.

"Cleft palate," Nedjma said. "Me and my sister both."

"You have a sister?" This also came as a shock. "You've never mentioned her."

Nedjma's eyes glossed over, her gaze still far off as she nodded with a plaintive smile. "We're identical twins, both 'defective' under reproductive policy." Her face fell flat, and for a moment, she struggled to speak. "They, uh… they caught her abnormality in the prenatal screenings and not mine…." She choked up, let out a deep sigh. "So they just *took* her."

Nedjma's account invoked the memory of Perez's unborn brother. What Mamá had told her had happened, that she had miscarried, even though Perez had her suspicions that there was more to it than that. Her conclusion was that he had been taken the same way Nedjma's sister had.

Perez had often wondered what genetic imperfection might have led to his termination. Though she'd likely never know, Nedjma's story felt like an affirmation.

And then a more insidious thought entered her mind. *Does Nedjma know about Ruth? Or suspect something?* Her throat seized. Her breathing hastened. She didn't think her student had seen the label on the bottle, not unless she had come across it at some other point. Even then, it would have been a stretch for Nedjma to equate it to evidence that Perez was somehow pregnant, no matter how suspicious things might have appeared in the moment.

Perez was again aware of the test tubes resting against her inner ankle. Mindful of the fact that soon she'd be back at home in her pod calculating the proper dose, that soon this nightmare would come to an end. It seemed almost unreal.

Nedjma continued. "When I was born, the doctors were shocked to find my upper lip, gums, and hard palate split down the middle. Astounded that I had slipped past their screenings. They could have terminated me then if not for one doctor who spoke out, who told my parents she would fix me up pro bono." She started to sniffle as her words ran together.

"Years later, when I was old enough to ask about the scar, my parents told me I had fallen and sliced it open as a toddler. I accepted that. It made sense. Until a few years ago, when the doctor who fixed me reached out. She wanted me to know the truth. Thought I had a right to know. She told me the real story, even sent photos of my mother when she was pregnant with us, sent ultrasounds of me and my… my *sister*." A meniscus now bulged on the margins of each of Nedjma's lower eyelids. "*Rupal.* Rupal was her name—*is* her name."

To Perez's knowledge, her brother never had a name. A whirlwind of emotions swirled inside of her. Part of her wanted to go to Nedjma, to embrace her, but another thought it best not to. And so, she stood there, helpless, as the first tears spilled onto Nedjma's cheeks.

"Nedjma… *I'm so sorry.*" It was all she could manage.

"Sometimes, I feel guilty," Nedjma whispered. "I feel bad that I… that *I* was the one that survived." She closed her eyes.

"No." Perez shook her head. "She would be so proud of you."

Nedjma's lips curled into a frown, her face pinched with grief as tears streamed down her cheeks. "Thank you," she said. "I hope you're right."

After a moment of silence, Nedjma sniffled and, biting her lower lip, stared off in the distance as if reflecting on a fond memory. "I had a good childhood," she said with a nod, "but you want to know the funniest thing?" Her eyes narrowed. Her expression turned into one of regret. "I've *always* wanted a sister."

Perez, too, was now on the verge of tears.

Eyes reflecting the horizon, Nedjma smiled. "I was going to grow up to be a *doctor*, so I could give *every other little girl* a *sister*. Spare them the longing that I had felt. For so long, I had thought that type of pain was normal for a little girl to endure—not a void born of something lost, a severed connection. A loss that, for the longest time, I was unaware I'd endured. But everything changed after I found out the truth."

Perez wanted to confide in Nedjma, tell her everything about her brother, about Ruth, even Basem. She still wasn't sure if Nedjma had caught on, knew somehow that Perez was pregnant. She had no way to be sure without coming clean. Nedjma's story might be a coincidence, a moment of vulnerability that Perez related to on a personal level. But telling Nedjma could come with significant risk. Crippled with indecision, Perez said nothing, and an uncomfortable silence lingered as her mind raced.

"I'm glad you're here, Nedjma," she finally said in a near-whisper. It was all she had.

"Me too." Nedjma looked as exhausted as Perez felt.

"Come on, let's go inside."

The women made their way across the loading dock toward the decon chamber. Perez tapped her badge, and the door climbed upward, then came down behind them with a loud *clang*. Showerheads sputtered to life. Perez closed her eyes and swayed slightly as warm sterilization media trickled over her suit. When the showers stopped, the second door leading into the lab opened.

To her astonishment, the necropsy lab was empty.

The chirping of reed frogs no longer filled the room. Every surface was immaculate. No smeared blood or soiled dressings. No sterile fields or dangling hoses. No IV bags, no beeping machines snarled with tubes and wires.

"Where is everyone?" Nedjma said, looking around.

Just then, Dr. Schulz, the veterinary anesthesiologist, entered the lab from the adjoining corridor with a curious, almost startled look on her face, but her expression changed to relief upon recognizing the two women. She was no longer in her biohazard suit, instead wearing a light blue isolation gown and surgical mask.

"Oh, Cam, it's you," she said. "I thought I heard the decon chamber running in here."

"What's going on here?" Perez said. "Where is everyone? Marceau, Endrik, the other staff?"

"Evacuated. Except for essential personnel."

"*Evacuated?* On whose orders? We're in the middle of a crisis. Every *one* of our staff is essential."

Schulz nodded. "I agree, but we have little sway over EIRO's board of directors. For the time being, SANCTUM has consolidated its resources."

"This is outrageous. We were already stretched thin. Why was I not informed?"

"You weren't getting briefed? The Oberstleutnant himself assured us you knew...."

Jacobs.

"He lied." Perez seethed as pressure mounted in her chest. Nedjma remained quiet, her attentive eyes flitting between the two women.

"Why would he do that?" Schulz said.

"I don't know." Perez already had a couple of theories, the most likely of which seemed to be that if he *had* notified her that he was evacuating most of their staff, she would not have agreed to continue her examination. And he would have been right. "Lena, I need an update on ARC's status. It's clear that whatever information I *was* given is suspect."

Her eyes wide with alarm and confusion, Schulz nodded. "Well, for starters, we've managed to stabilize most of the animals that survived. They are temporarily housed throughout Sector C. As of today, we've downgraded most areas to biosafety level two status. The hazmat suits are no longer necessary."

"And what's the situation inside the dome?"

"Environmental dispatches a skeleton crew into the dome twice daily. Automated tracking has been spotty, but Athena has managed to account for all surviving wildlife, and repair drones have sealed most of the hex breaches. Atmospheric conditions are normalizing enough that we can soon re-release rehabilitated animals—at least as soon as the algal blooms are dealt with and water tests check out with Limnology. In short, the situation is contained."

"*Nothing* about it is contained," Perez snapped. She had a headache now. In fact, everything ached—her feet, her breasts, her back, her bladder. She was fighting another round of nausea. She wanted out of the suit. Needed to pee. Needed to scream. The malaise added to her agitated state, her anger at realizing she had been left in the dark by Jacobs, and she had no idea why. "How can they enforce an evacuation?"

"Some wanted to leave, mainly due to concerns of food and water shortages now that EDEN is in ruins. But most wanted to stay. No one back in Berlin is talking aside from mumblings about vague concerns over biocontainment, which doesn't make sense." Schulz frowned and shook her head. "I can't see how that would even relate to this disaster. The board has stayed largely silent on the matter. We're in a holding pattern for the time being."

Perez found it difficult to contain her anger. "I'm going inside the dome," she said, seething. "I need to check the aviary."

"We have an ecologist checking it daily," Schulz said. "We've had to house most of the birds there for their own safety. We lost several dozen birds in the aftermath of the quake, flying into the hex panels, attacking each other. Some even dive-bombed into the ground. It's as if something drove them mad."

The anomaly, Perez thought. *Lotta fucking Eklund. That's what.* "And the moa paddock?"

"Holding up well," Schulz said with a nod. "They don't seem as susceptible as the ostriches, which are still running amok." She shifted, appearing uncomfortable in her thoughts. "We did lose the juvenile. About a day after you left."

Nedjma gasped. "What? *No.*"

Perez was jarred by an intense pang. Her diaphragm seized, stopping the breath in her lungs. "But she was stable when we—"

"Infection." Schulz bowed her head, her face grave. "A resistant strain of staph we're still investigating." Her eyes fell back on Perez, then shifted to Nedjma. "Both of you should get some rest. You look like hell. If you want to be of any use, go get some sleep first."

Perez's limbs went numb. She wanted to lay into Schulz right then, tell her to fuck off. Tell her she felt fine and that she had no authority. But she knew the woman was right. Perez was not okay. She felt worse than she had in a long while. Dead on her feet. A shell of a person.

More than anything, she wanted to curl into a ball and cry herself into a deep sleep.

"It's good to have you back. Both of you," Schulz added, as if sensing the tension.

Perez softened and regarded this with a nod. She turned to Nedjma. "She's right. Let's go."

Schulz winced behind her mask in acknowledgment and turned to leave. Then, with one hand on the door, she doubled back. "What did they have you doing on that CEPP freighter that was so urgent, anyway?"

Perez looked at her in silence for a few seconds. It was a fair question—one she would have asked if she were Schulz—especially given the controversy around Eklund's Higgs experiments. The military's unexpected and inscrutable interest in Perez. The unexplained evacuation.

"Nothing I'm authorized to discuss."

Schulz acquiesced with a discerning glance, one containing a glint of suspicion, and quietly slipped into the corridor.

Perez dreaded returning home. Had avoided it—the silence that awaited her there. A redolence she couldn't escape. Vestiges of Basem, how things left off between them. But she knew she had to go back sometime. Needed to get some sleep—gather her strength, her mental faculties—prepare for what came next: to completely detach from Ruth. To say goodbye on *her* terms.

Not the Federation's.

Perez thought of Nedjma's sister. Thought of her own brother. Wondered what types of lives they might have led. And Ruth—what kind of woman might she have grown into? Perez liked to think she'd be something like Nedjma. Curious, compassionate. Full of hope, of wonder.

She'd have Basem's smile.

It felt good to change out of the suit and into loose-fitting clothing before leaving Sector C aboard a transport drone. Perez surveyed meandering dunes below as she and Nedjma flew toward the residential zone.

Nedjma had not spoken since they left.

A brown stack of smoke still billowed from EDEN, carried off by a light wind over the mountains. Schulz had told them that the quake didn't extend far beyond the domes. SANCTUM Center had sustained only minor damage. And the adjoining sprawl of residential colonies, the apiaries, had remained largely untouched.

The first of the egg-shaped sandstone dwellings appeared as sepia smudges through the heat haze. There was a spectral quality to the narrow structures, each rising three stories high. Abandoned husks standing like a cortège of urns. Monuments to the dead.

There were dozens of them, regularly interspersed. Still standing, to Perez's relief. Untouched by the quake. They almost blended into the landscape—but by now, Perez had become adept at picking her pod out among the other dwellings. Hers had three reddish bands near the top, owing to variability in the raw materials from the local rock formations used to 3D print the structures.

The transport slowed as it neared and began to circle upon descent.

Perez looked over at Nedjma. "You should stay here tonight," she said. Thought to herself that it would be good to have each other's company after what they'd endured. But that was only half the reason. Perez also wanted her close. After repeated missteps, she felt responsible for Nedjma's safety. She knew it was irrational at best, paternalistic at worst, but that didn't matter.

Nedjma gave a timid smile. "I appreciate that," she said, "but I think I want to be in my own bed tonight."

Perez smiled as the transport settled in front of her pod. She stepped out onto solid ground. "See you tomorrow, then."

With a wave of her hand, Nedjma rose into the sky, and then she was gone.

The condition of Perez's pod was not as bad as she had feared. It seemed odd how such a large temblor had been largely contained to such a small area. How focused its devastation was. Yet less than a kilometer from ground zero, her dwelling showed almost no sign that anything had occurred. A few items knocked off shelves was about the extent of it.

It was the first time Perez found herself alone in days. *Truly* alone. Something she had tried to avoid, because of what must be done, the real reason she had asked Nedjma to stay.

Ruth.

Perez had prepared for days, weeks. Had built herself up to this dreadful moment. Had secured the misoprostol and fortified her justifications. And at the last second, she found herself hesitating, asking Nedjma to stay as a stall tactic—if she was being honest with herself. A way of delaying what she knew she had to do.

But now she had no excuse. Except for exhaustion.

And she needed a shower. The cumulative odor after days spent inside her suit—having removed it only for the occasional meal or trip to the washroom—was less than flattering. Her skin crawled with stale sweat and squalor. She hoped the water still worked in the upstairs washroom, that the vapor compression distiller hadn't sustained any damage.

Perez removed her shawl and hung it by the door. Gripping the tubes of misoprostol in her hand, she walked past the kitchenette and climbed the spiral staircase to the ensuite. As she stepped through the threshold of her bedroom, a whimper escaped her lips, though she swore she had screamed.

She didn't recognize the man sitting on the edge of the bed—not at first—half due to the shock of seeing an intruder in her home, in her *bed*. And half because of his swollen face, his blood-tinged eyes, and the dark blotches riddling his skin.

Perez stumbled backward, placing her hands over her navel, *over Ruth*, as if by reflex or instinct. Or both.

The man didn't move. He wore a form-fitting black suit resembling a unitard. It was peppered with a layer of brownish dust, his hair and skin riddled with grime. It appeared to Perez that he had endured the elements before making his way into her pod. He seemed aware of her presence, yet his eyes appeared placid and faraway where he sat hunched with upturned palms.

Then, the intruder looked up at her. The sunlight spilling through the skylight caught his features, and as his face emerged from shadow, Perez gasped. There was no mistaking the man looking up at her.

That hair. That nose. The gray streak in his goatee.

She almost couldn't say his name, gulping at the air through a torrent of frantic sobs, hyperventilating. She felt like she was drowning. Couldn't breathe. Couldn't move.

But she managed a whisper.

"Basem?"

Over beer the bird of forgetfulness broods,
And steals the minds of men…
—POETIC EDDA

< ✕ | SEIÐR >

Going into the forest is going home. Until Valhalla.

Pappa used to say those words whenever he brought Lotta along for blót. It was his way of conveying the family's roots, reminding his daughter of where she came from.

Before he abandoned us. Then, family ties meant fuck all.

Without Pappa, Lotta was almost as scared of the woods as the vast open spaces—the Baltic's coastal waters obscuring Russian subs, the uncertainty her family faced crossing swathes of land as they fled Sweden. Spaces that accommodated armies of men, monsters. Beneath the trees, it too was the unknown, the looming uncertainty of what may lie ahead that frightened her. But the forest conjured a unique, sinking dread, a silent menacing she feared could swallow her up if not for the spirits that stood watch. Protected them so long as offerings were made. Until she stopped believing and instead embraced the empirical, the experimental, the verifiable—her modus operandi since leaving it all behind. Science. Her guiding light.

Not the gods.

Except now, she found herself in that nightmare. Lost in the woods among monsters, demons, and the knells of the damned. Alone.

I am the equation come to life. Hassan's words haunted her, might always haunt her. At times, she thought she could still hear the sustained chime of his beacon echoing like a tortured soul through the rattling boughs.

Lotta looked up from the fire. The glow of the dying flames played off Fischer's features, casting long shadows over him as his eyes crept shut. For the last hour, he had slurred his speech, mumbled unintelligible strings of words. And now, sleep finally took him. The seizure had drained him, though he had tried to fight fatigue for as long as possible. Had hobbled about the camp, insisting they get a shelter built, even patched up Lotta's hands.

Ed Fischer was built different. An engineer. A builder, a fixer. To him, the situation—the forest, the unknown—presented a puzzle. He almost thrived on it.

But Lotta was relieved to see the exhaustion take hold because Fischer was in no condition to build a shelter. Not tonight.

The shelter.

It was something Lotta had intended to do herself. She knew enough about the basics, and something would be better than nothing. But she hadn't had the time between reviving Fischer, gathering drinkable water and food, and tending the fire.

She gazed again into the dying flames and threw more wood on. It amazed her she had managed to get it going. Chalked that up to dumb luck. The flat piece of timber Fischer was drilling had already been billowing a thick plume of smoke when he collapsed. With thirst clawing at her insides, Lotta had thrown it onto the kindling in a panic. By the time Fischer's seizure had passed, and she had placed him into a recovery position, the pit was alive with flame.

Lotta, too, was exhausted. Her joints groaned, muscles twitched. A dull twinge behind her left eye had steadily swelled into a throbbing headache that wrapped all the way around her head. Still, she convinced herself she would still put up a shelter after a minute's rest. Then minutes became hours. The headache waned, but it had sapped her of almost all remaining energy.

Despite this, her mind refused to tune out, her thoughts racing at the speed of light, driven by a singular question.

Where are we?

She recalled the inky blackness inside the Cathedral. Remembered peering into it from the landing with Fischer at her side, the swirling image of some far-off world manifesting like a prismatic oil slick inside a levitating orb. A cyclopean void. At the last second, turning to see the person gazing from behind the observation glass, seemingly oblivious to her and her team's presence inside the chamber—the woman standing in the same place Lotta stood before every trial. The one who carried herself the same way she did, hands clasped behind her back, legs locked straight, back aligned. Lotta had seen her face in those fleeting moments. She saw through the shield of the woman's helmet, despite the strobing lights' glare.

Saw that the face was her own.

Maybe just a reflection—some quirk of gravitational lensing. Or a trick of the mind.

She recalled smears of blue floating horizontally behind the lone figure, her doppelgänger. Like ribbons of shimmering azure, suits whisked past the woman, appearing almost static, as if photographed on a long exposure.

And then nothing. Whiteness. *Kugelblitz.*

Perhaps she had peered through the looking glass into an alternate reality.

Preposterous. Even if parallel universes *did* exist, it would be impossible to interact with such a construct, let alone be thrust headlong into one. The laws of physics—of space and time—would almost certainly be unrecognizable. A slight shift in one constant, a tweak to a particle's charge or spin, and the entire system would be rewritten. Become inhospitable to life as it was known. The energy requirement to merely *glimpse* it would demand an input approaching the magnitude of the Big Bang—a feat far beyond the capabilities of the Higgs or any other technology.

But that didn't change things. They *had* found themselves somewhere new, somewhere strange. A land of Valkyries, of wights, of giants. Another reality.

"One of the nine realms? Science cannot explain that," Sofia would have said.

Lotta could not help but entertain the thought, despite the shame over her ties to a religion she considered as dead to her as her mother.

She pounded the fleshy part of her palm against her brow and shook her head. *No. There must be a scientific explanation. Something yet to be discovered. Some equation or constant.*

When Lotta realized night had fallen, she had scratched a proof in the dirt, beginning with Maxwell's equations. Then Dirac's. Schrödinger's. And so on. Ran her quantum corrections, canceled the infinites. Accounted for fermions and bosons, every quark, every Yang-Mills particle. Reduced everything to strings, then branes, and further still into hidden, curled-up dimensions and symmetries. Tried to reconcile some formulation, some answer to all of it, but nothing came. All she had were hopeless scrawls in the dirt.

But still, the question persisted.

Where are we?

Had they cracked the quest for a unified field theory? Conquered gravity, broken through the barrier, and ruptured the fabric of reality?

I am the equation come to life.

I am transcendence.

A coal popped, sending an ember into the darkness above.

Lotta thought of Hassan. How he and the tree had become one. Appeared to be assimilated into a singular organism, a chimera. She could still hear his—its—crackling voice.

We are one.

Like rattling leaves in the wind.

His fate evoked in her mind the dual nature of matter. In one instant, existing as a tangible form with defined mass and density, and in the next, an electromagnetic field, a wave function capable of passing through objects unimpeded. *A ghost.* Electrons embodied a rudimentary example, constantly tunneling in and out of existence, violating barriers as they bounced through the quantum foam, perhaps popping up in distant galaxies or the centers of stars—*or tunneling between universes*—and back again. Shifting between wave and particle, interchangeable states of zero or one, or an entanglement of both. Another form of symmetry. Spooky action at a distance.

And what of something as complex and comparably infinite as a person? The entirety of their atoms phasing in perfect synchrony, effectively nullifying the impact of Planck's constant at the macro level? It was one thing for an electron or photon or neutrino, but an entire organism?

One faces greater odds of passing a kidney stone made of gold.

Lotta wondered if Hassan's mind had died when it happened or if some small part of him persisted, still conscious enough to understand. Wondered if he had felt Björn's jaws around his arm, felt the skin and muscle as it tore free. She tried not to imagine what might have come of Hassan after that, after she ran and never looked back. Only hoped that he hadn't suffered.

She shuddered. Her eyes burned and brimmed. Unsure of how long she had stared, unblinking, into the dirt now riddled with integrals, equations, formulaic expressions. And at the center, the rune she had carved earlier: *Thurisaz.* One of the few Elder Futhark she still remembered. Her mother had often invoked it in reference to an increasingly omnipresent Russian threat. *The violent ones,* she had called them. But it also had another meaning, an older meaning: *giant.* She thought of the thing—*the giant*—that had assaulted the beehive in the woods, the sound of its weight bearing down as it approached what might have been Anderson's remains. Its lungs swelling and contracting, a deep rumbling that rattled root and rock and flesh. An oscillation that crept into Lotta's feet, coursed up her legs, and razed her to the bone with rumbling fury.

The call of a giant—a jötunn.

She recalled the Norse legends of the jötnar—myths no more real than those of dragons. Recalled Russia's forces along the Finnish DMZ, Sofia referring to its standing armies as the jötnar. Only those were mere men.

But this *thing… it was a true giant… a true monster.*

She gazed headlong at the rune, and the world around her faded. She found a strange comfort in it, a familiarity she longed for in a place where nothing was. An escape, despite the passage of time—the decades since she had last laid eyes on the Elder Futhark.

Fischer stirred.

Lotta glanced up from her scrawl and watched him. He shifted position, then fell back into a slumber. She tried to picture him as a father. Wondered if he was good. She wanted to believe that. That he was good.

She lowered herself to her side and watched him, weeping silently until her lids grew heavy.

When Lotta's eyes opened again, the fire had dwindled into a constellation of fading embers.

"Shit," she mumbled, wiping the sleep away with aching fingers. Wondered how long she'd been out.

She looked up toward Fischer, and her heart stopped.

He was *gone*.

Lotta jumped to her feet, her heart lurching back into rhythm.

"Ed?" she whispered harshly through the darkened trees, but she only heard the chirping of frogs in reply. "*Ed?*" This time, she gave a muted, groggy shout.

Her pulse throbbed in her fingers, in her hands. The adrenaline provided a reprieve from the pain, though she would have preferred it to the realization she was now alone, exposed, at the mercy of the forest. *The unknown.* Her limbs trembled with electricity, synapses at the ready.

If something took him, it might still be nearby.

Her muscles hummed, prepared to carry her through the looming trees, beneath the gloam of the gibbous moon. Where she would run to, she did not know.

Flight.

The fire pit sputtered a triplet of pops, and Lotta jumped.

No. You need to find him.

She breathed deep and looked around their encampment again.

Fight.

She closed her eyes and exhaled. Scanned the pale forest floor and spotted fresh tracks leading toward the stream.

Walked off? Taking a piss?

But Lotta wasn't satisfied, as plausible as that seemed at first. She looked around for Fischer's knife, but it appeared he had taken it. Instead, she grabbed a stone with some weight to it and started following the tracks toward the embankment. The prints led to the water, then turned and disappeared around a bend along the shore. Lotta tried to see where they went, but her view was obscured by reeds and the bowing fronds of a lone cycad, the sight of which made her stop cold.

For a moment, she thought she had walked up on Hassan again. She stood there, frozen, staring at the sagging blade-shaped leaves in the dappled moonlight. Her heart thrashed in her neck, her ears.

Only a tree.

Then, over the warbling frogs, the gentle flow of water, she thought she heard a moan from the other side of the bend. It sounded like Fischer.

"Ed!" she blurted, again tempering herself so as not to alert the silent creatures that might be lurking in the wood. *The shapeshifters. The giants.*

She heard it again. Mumbling this time. It sounded conversational, like he was talking to someone. She leaned forward, tried to discern what was being said, but all she heard was incoherent muttering. Summoned the courage to press on. Moonlight filtered through the still boughs of the conifer.

"Edgar!"

This time, she thought she had made out a few words.

"Won' happ'n agin...."

She pushed the sagging fronds aside, then slipped, her left foot plunging into the cold water. Ice crawled up her leg. Her grip on the rock wavered, and it tumbled out of her hand and into the water with a loud splash.

Fuck.

She was fully awake now. And so was the forest.

As she turned and rounded the tree, she let out a startled gasp.

Fischer was kneeling at the water's edge, facing away from her, resting on his ankles with his back straight, hands in his lap and his sleeves rolled up. He peered across the water toward the opposite bank. Dappled light filtered through the canopy, peppering him in a patchwork of shadow and light. Lotta's eyes bounced across the water, but she saw nothing but a blackened break in the trees.

"Joce'lyn... din't mean... Please don'... don' go. Y're all I h-have now...." His voice sounded different. Mournful.

There was no one else around.

"Ed?" Lotta whispered. "Ed, it's me... what are you doing out here?" She crept closer, taking care not to startle him.

Fischer didn't seem to hear her. He remained upright, his gaze on the far bank, mumbling incoherently like he had earlier. Lotta stretched her neck and leaned over his shoulder.

She heard the scream, but it took a second to realize it was her own.

One of Fischer's wrists had been sliced open, gushing black with blood. It spilled from his arm in thick ribbons, coalescing into a puddle that trickled toward the water.

He was trying to swap the knife from his good hand, but the fingers of his other hand would not close around the handle. They fumbled at it limply, twitching and bloody, but to no avail. All the while, he gazed, unflinching, into the darkened break in the trees.

He was attempting to cut his other arm.

"Ed! Oh, God, what did you *do*?!" Lotta reached out and grabbed him by the shoulder.

Fischer jumped to his feet and spun around to face her. He gaped, unblinking, with an immediate, lucid intensity that frightened her. With eyes wide, their whites still tinged with blood, he stumbled backward to the water's edge, gripping the knife again in his good hand. His jaw hung slack, mouth hooded by his unkempt mustache.

"Stay… stay away!" He pointed the bloody knife at her, then held it to his throat with clenched teeth. Moonlight glimmered softly along the steel tip as it pressed into his neck. His injured arm flopped at his side, blood streaming from the gash like a spigot.

"*Ed! No! Don't!*"

"It was you! They're gone b'cause… you… *you!*"

Lotta was taken aback by this, at first wondering if she had done something to trigger such anger, then starting to consider whether he recognized her. He had become apoplectic. Seemed to be hallucinating, thinking she was someone else.

"Ed, it's *me*. It's Lotta." She tried to stay calm, keep from shouting, from alarming him further. "Please, just drop the knife. Don't do this. *Please*."

"No… *no*… You! They're gone!"

"Who, Ed? Your girls? Whatever happened to them, they wouldn't… they wouldn't want this. Just… put the knife down. Think of *Emma*…."

"*Emma?*" The anger melted from his face. Now, he looked lost, afraid. His grip loosened around the blade, and it splashed at his feet. "*Emma?*"

He stumbled backward until the water came to his knees. His eyes grew wide, drifting from Lotta to his feet, the water trickling past. He shuddered as if just realizing where he was. Drops of blood fell to the water and disintegrated, drawing his gaze to his wounded arm. He raised his head and squared with Lotta again, his brow furrowed, face sunken and pale in the moonlight.

"Where... what—*what's happening?*" His eyes betrayed a deep inner anguish that Lotta could not begin to imagine. A tear spilled out onto his cheek. "*Lotta?*"

Crying now, too, Lotta rushed to him, clasping both hands firmly around his arm. Searing pain bolted through her fingers and shot up her arms, but she only squeezed harder. Warm blood seeped through the cracks in her fingers, pouring out onto her hands, cooling as it ran down her arms. The wounded limb—limp in her grasp—possessed an unusual heaviness. Slippery with blood, her grip began to wane. The water was frigid, gushing past her knees, imbibing her compression lining. She lifted a leg and trudged forward, pulling gently on Fischer to guide him back to shore. Once they made it to the bank, she helped him to the ground, where he sat shivering, holding his arm above his head.

"I-I didn't mean to... did-didn't m-mean t-to—" he sputtered. Foam frothed and dribbled from his mouth. He was going into shock.

"It's okay, you're okay. We need to stop this bleeding, okay?" Lotta grabbed his good arm and guided it to the wound. "*Squeeze.* Keep the pressure on. I will be *right back.*"

He mumbled something unintelligible, his face pale and glistening with beads of sweat. His voice came through rattled and little more than a faint whisper.

Lotta leaned in, turning her ear to his mouth. A drop of sweat fell from the tip of his nose. "What's that, Ed?"

"*What he showed me... they're one... they're....*" His words fizzled into a woeful whimper.

Nothing he said made sense, but it still struck Lotta to her core because of what it had done to him. He had seen something—real or imagined—and it impacted him in a way that terrified her.

Fischer's words trailed off, and his shaking intensified into full-blown tremors. Lotta rested a hand on his forehead.

"You're burning up."

Foam bubbled from Fischer's lips, and he slumped over. His limbs stiffened, his eyes rolled in their sockets, teeth clenched tight.

"Ed! Stay with me!" Lotta caught him as he fell sideways and laid him flat.

Fischer's convulsions intensified, worse than before. His tongue darted forward, parting his now-blue lips as he snuffed through his nose in tortured rasps. Lotta caught a whiff of urine and glanced down at a puddle spreading out from under his waist.

She didn't know what to do. Could only turn him over and watch, wait for the seizure to subside, keep him from thrashing his head against the rocks. His teeth clenched again, this time coming down on his tongue. Lotta looked on in horror as it turned purple, blood squeezing through the gaps in his teeth and trickling as a bright red foam from the corner of his mouth.

Snap.

A sound from across the water. Lotta's head shot up toward the gap in the trees, but she saw nothing. Only blackness. A gentle breeze soughed through the boughs and died back into stillness. When her gaze returned to Fischer, the jerking had subsided. His muscles relaxed, and his breathing slowed. He sputtered and coughed, then took a sharp breath. Lotta placed a hand on his shoulder and shook him gently.

"Ed? Ed, can you hear me?"

No response. He was still losing blood.

Lotta turned and bounded along the bank back to the campsite, almost slipping again as she rounded the weeping cycad with tears streaming down her cheeks. She came to where Fischer had first lost consciousness, grabbed his bow drill, and turned back, stopping at the fire pit to retrieve a sieve cylinder of clean water she had set aside earlier. When she returned to Fischer, he had rolled onto his back and had foam bubbling from his mouth. She pushed him back to his side, exposing his injured arm.

Pressing one end of the bow into the ground, Lotta bore down on the other end and removed the cord, then wound it tightly around Fischer's upper arm. She tied the ends to the middle of the stick and cranked it clockwise to fashion a tourniquet. Watched as the limb turned purple, its veins bulging like worms, realizing for the first time what it meant if he didn't make it. That she would be alone. Found herself praying to the gods for the first time since she had left home so long ago.

Freyja forgive me.

When the bleeding stopped, Lotta pulled his sleeve down over the tourniquet to secure it in place, then reached for the sieve cylinder and poured water over the wound to clean it. As the blood cleared, she was shocked to find that Fischer had not merely sliced his wrist; he had *carved* something into it. She recoiled at what she saw, dropping his arm. It fell to his side with a meaty *thud.*

"No. *No. Nononono....*" She stumbled backward, catching herself with her hands against the slippery stones. She could hear her sanity crack like a pane of glass flexed beyond its limit.

Vivid in the pale moonlight, Fischer's face deathly still, Lotta saw *Thurisaz.*

Then, something glided across the edge of her vision.

Her head snapped sideways toward the far bank—the same spot Fischer had watched when she found him by the water. She could have sworn a ghoulish form broke from the shadows and sidled quietly off into the trees like a wraith. But now, she saw only blackness. A break in the trees framed by spindly ferns and looming cycads at the edge of an eroded stretch of bank and nothing more. She stared, her pulse throbbing in her ears, her fingers, waiting for more movement, but none came.

And that was when Lotta noticed the frogs had fallen silent.

FOUR

"Canst thou draw out leviathan with a fishhook?
Or press down his tongue with a cord?
Canst thou put a rope into his nose?
Or pierce his jaw through with a hook?...
...Canst thou fill his skin with barbed irons,
Or his head with fish-spears?...
...Will not one be cast down even at the sight of him?"
—Job 41:1-9

"I HAVE BROKEN THE MACHINE AND TOUCHED THE GHOST OF MATTER."
—ERNEST RUTHERFORD

UEF / RD
EYES ONLY

Ministry of Defence
United European Federation

Memorandum of CCTV Interrogation. Partial Transcript.

JUNE 15, 2147, 22:20

Appearances
Oberstleutnant Nikolaj Jacobson (alias: Jacobs)
Jackson Evans (alias: Oz)
Dr. Bogdan Kazimierz
Dr. Aegis Galani (communicating from off-site)

Jacobson	He's coming out of it. Second infusion's almost worn off. Incredible how it turns the blood black, eh? Hell of a drug.
Evans	Sir, we need him alive.
Jacobson	Spurgt? Relax, soldier. Stram ballerne (chuckling). You think he can see under all that swelling? And look at the size of his fucking lip. Split you wide open, didn't we, Dr. Kazimierz?
Kazimierz	[unintelligible]
Jacobson	What was that, Doc?
Kazimierz	Water. Please. [unintelligible]
Jacobson	(laughter) After all that, you want water? Lort. The balls on this guy.
Kazimierz	Please, I am so thirsty... [unintelligible]
Jacobson	'I am so thirsty, sir.'
Kazimierz	I am so thirsty, sir. Please. Please don't kill me.
Jacobson	(laughter) Kill the de facto head of CEPP's Algerian operation? The Commission would have my head. They just want me to talk to you. We're merely having a discussion, Dr. Kazimierz. Words between men. You want to talk with me, don't you?

Kazimierz	Yes, sir.
Jacobson	Good. I want to help you. But I need you to help me, too.
Kazimierz	Anything. I will do anything.
Jacobson	We'll see. You're of Slavic descent, no?
Kazimierz	Yes, Sir.
Jacobson	Untermensch. Are you familiar with this word?
Kazimierz	No, Sir.
Jacobson	Means 'inferior people.' A term the Germans used to describe 'the masses from the East' during World War II. That included the Poles, and especially the Slavs. I'm inclined to agree. Untermensch. Say it.
Kazimierz	Untermensch.
Jacobson	No, no. You need to emphasize the 'øoh.' Again. Unter-mensch.
Kazimierz	Untermensch.
Jacobson	Why the Federation didn't leave Pol-Polska to the Russian dogs will always remain a mystery to me. Bunch of Russian sympathizers. Is that what you are? A damn Russki?
Kazimierz	No, sir.
Jacobson	You sound Russian. You know what they say, if it looks like an orc and grunts like an orc... Oz, restrain his head and start another infusion. (to Kazimierz) We'll give you water.
Kazimierz	No! Please, not again. Please, I can't! No! The water, I can't swim! [unintelligible] Please help me! It's filling the room! Please!
Evans	Does he actually think there's water in here?
Jacobson	La Bête Noire is a hell of a drug, soldier. Now, pour another jug. And hold his fucking head still. I don't want to see that rag come off his face again.

| BASEM >

Perez turned on the bedroom light. Half-asleep and in shock, she stood frozen in the doorway, wondering if she had slipped into a dream.

"Basem?"

His eyes rolled lazily in her direction from where he sat on the edge of the bed. There was no white to them, those bloody, far-off eyes. It looked as though he had cried blood. Now dried and crusted-over, it carved tortuous black trails down his cheeks. More came from his nose, his ears. He gazed through Perez with a dull, unfeeling stare, as though she were invisible. But then his eyebrows cinched, his labored breath coming in clicking rasps, a hint of recognition in his expression. He mouthed something, but no sound came out.

Perez's heart skipped.

With tears in her eyes, she went to the bedside and threw her arms around him, but he remained still with his hands in his lap. His body felt limp, meek in her embrace. A harsh chemical smell billowed off him, almost causing her to gag.

"Osito. Osito." She wept into him, her lungs quickening their pace. "I thought I—*thought I lost you.*"

"Osito," he parroted.

"Basem, it's me. It's Cam." The smell was growing unbearable, inciting a dull ache to take root behind her left eye.

"Cam."

Perez placed a hand on his. He glanced down with a puzzled look—his cheeks puffy and swollen—then locked eyes with her again. Leaning forward, she kissed him, but his cracked lips didn't reciprocate. She pulled back and let her hand fall away. Something horrible had happened. He needed time, that was all. Just time.

Her eyes studied him, looked him over. Hundreds of small violaceous patches riddled his skin, and a gash on the right side of his scalp oozed dark blood. Half-congealed, it had run down his neck and saturated the nape of his uniform.

"You're hurt," Perez choked out, fighting back fresh tears. "We need to get you a doctor."

The military had set up a mobile field hospital near SANCTUM Center. She could take him there. Get him help.

But Basem's eyes widened, bulging where blood had pooled beneath conjunctiva. A flash of lucidity. His lips moved.

Perez leaned in, turning an ear towards his mouth. "What's that?"

"No doctor."

Something about this scared her. He seemed different, seemed afraid. She only nodded, despite the worry gnawing at her. But inside, she was already quietly strategizing how to get him out of there. First, she needed to clean him up, establish trust. She craned her neck toward the ceiling's skylight, which doubled as a reservoir for the pod's water supply. It looked full against the midnight sky.

Perez left him on the bed and walked into the ensuite to check the water. On her way to the shower, she stopped to look in the mirror and almost didn't recognize the woman staring back at her. Dark circles framed her eyes, and reddened, tear-stained cheeks gleamed from behind tangles of oily hair. She looked down at her hand, had forgotten that she still held the tubes of misoprostol. With a sigh, she opened the medicine cabinet, placed them delicately on the shelf, and then closed the door.

The water to the shower worked, ran hot. There was plenty for drinking and bathing so long as the pod's vapor compression distillers were functioning. Such systems were designed to sustain abuse, to endure everything that even the outer colonies could throw at them, but Perez was relieved all the same. Steam grazed her cheeks and put her at ease. It had been days since she felt clean.

She paused, reflecting on the last seventy-two hours. Hadn't begun to process everything that had happened, let alone the thought of never seeing Basem again after how they had left things. She gazed at her abdomen, thought something had shifted inside her. Her hand found its way to her navel.

Am I already that far along?

Thoughts of motherhood came back to her, the responsibility required, the terrifying prospect of nurturing human life, how so much was beyond her control. And there it was, the truth, after she'd lied to everyone, lied to herself.

It was always about control.

And that was precisely what scared her. The ARC, her relationship with Basem, her student—all of it she had control over until she didn't. Until her house of cards had come crashing down. First the dwindling bird populations, then Nedjma's injury, then her failure to protect her animals. Control was an illusion. A fantasy. Perez realized that now.

She met her own gaze again, then leaned through the doorway to make sure Basem was indeed sitting on the bed, that he was real. Watched him as he gazed ahead like a zombie. Shivered at how close she had come to losing him.

She strolled back into the bedroom.

Basem hadn't moved. Even as she undressed him, he remained largely unresponsive. Her breath caught in her chest at the sight of his bare skin. Blotchy hemorrhages and spidery veins covered his entire body, and blood had pooled in his hands and feet, making them purple and swollen. He looked sickly and sullen where he sat, shivering as he gazed into nothingness.

"C'mon, let's get you up." Perez placed his arm across her shoulders and lifted.

Basem's legs wobbled, then collapsed beneath him. Almost losing her balance, Perez righted herself to regain purchase and keep them both from falling over. Slowly, they shuffled toward the ensuite, Basem's feet dragging, meekly pedaling the carpet as Perez carried him. The steam filled the space, swaddling them with ebbing warmth.

She helped him into the shower, laying his trembling body on the floor. His lips opened and closed, lapping up the water as it pattered against his face. Perez was soon drenched, water gushing down her in sheets. She stripped down, threw her sopping clothes in a corner, and then stepped in all the way. Wringing her hair into a cord, she draped it between her shoulder blades and curled up beside Basem as the warmth washed over them. As her eyes grew heavy, she rested a hand over Ruth and thought of second chances.

June 16, 2147, 06:47

Perez opened her eyes and arched her back. A triplet of pops cracked down her spine, and she relaxed back into her original position. Through slitted eyes, she watched the first sliver of sunlight creeping through the water-filled skylight as it cast undulating ribbons over the pallid walls. She was enveloped in warmth, reveling in the sensation of Basem's skin against hers, buried in their cocoon of bedding. Nothing else existed outside of the moment—outside of them. She turned her head to her left, where he lay awake, gazing at the rippling skylight. He was far-off again, tears flowing from the corners of his unblinking eyes. The chemical smell no longer hung on him, but the dull headache over Perez's brow persisted. Some color had returned to his cheeks, and much of the swelling had gone down, but the gash on the side of his head still oozed. Perez wondered in silence if he had slept. Started thinking again about how to get him to a doctor, then considered the alternative of taking him to ARC's medbay and closing the wound herself. He'd need stitches at the very least.

"Hey," she said after a time.

"Cam." Basem's voice was hoarse, faint. He maintained his gaze overhead.

"Did you sleep?"

"Don't know."

Basem still seemed to be in a fog, but he had grown more conversive. At times, Perez was not convinced he fully remembered her, suspecting he had suffered some form of amnesia. But he started to ask questions, which was good. She tried not to inundate him with too many of her own inquiries, but of the ones she did put forward—what happened at ALICE, how he found his way to her pod—he seemed to have no recollection. She thought it best to avoid any mention of the creature Jacobs and his team had recovered. What she had seen. What it might mean.

"I have dreamt of this…" Basem whispered after another period of silence between them. "Of us, here, right now."

Perez tightened her arms around his waist. Held him close. "Me too."

"Is this real?" he said.

"Yes. Yes, it's real."

"I dreamed of falling, of the Earth rushing up at me." His words came slow amid drawn out rasps, his movements sluggish. "I'm falling from the sky. And then… *nothing*." His eyelids fell and opened in slow motion. It was the first time Perez had seen him blink. "Was that real, too?"

"No, Basem."

"How do I tell the difference?"

"Because you are here."

Perez took his hand and guided it to her navel.

Basem looked at her and she felt like he was seeing her again for the first time.

"*This* is real," she said. "*I* am real."

Her mind went to the misoprostol in the medicine cabinet, and she immediately felt ashamed by the gesture.

What are you doing?

But she needed a reaction. Needed to see if he recalled their last interaction, when she had told him about the baby, about what she intended to do. Needed him to remember because the notion of losing him again had become unbearable. Because he wasn't the same.

But Basem returned his gaze skyward.

"I have dreamt of this," he whispered.

Perez rested her head against his chest. His breathing restored her solitude, and she fell into a dreamless sleep.

08:32

Her eyes opened again. The warmth had faded. The bands of dancing caustics projected across the walls now resembled the aurorae over the domes, and a subtle jolt of panic stole over her.

She looked toward the other side of the bed, only to find it empty. "Basem?"

A sound carried from the first floor.

The door.

She jumped up, threw on some clothes, and made for the stairs.

Sunlight slanted through the foyer, where the entryway was open to the outside. A warm breeze filtered through the doorway, but the world beyond was still. Her feet carried her with urgency into the morning air, her eyes searching all around as her panic came to a crescendo. She squinted through the harsh reflection off the ground, spinning and searching as she walked barefoot across hot concrete. But she only saw rows of clay-colored pods devoid of inhabitants. The apiary, now derelict, resembled a ghost town.

"Basem?" she yelled, but her voice didn't seem to carry, the air smothering her attempts as the day's heat started bearing down. *"Basem?"*

She walked around the circumference to the back of her pod and stopped. Basem was standing there in its shadow, naked and battered, his neck craned, unblinking as he gazed skyward. He wavered as if struggling to keep his balance, his chest glistening with sweat as it rose and fell rapidly.

"Basem!" she shouted, but he didn't acknowledge her. Only stared up at the sky.

Then his cheeks puffed out, and his hands started to tremble. They moved up from his sides and clutched his abdomen, at first palpating, then clawing and scratching. Perez looked on in stunned horror as the first trickle of blood fell.

"Basem, no!" Her legs carried her now.

But before she could reach him, a sonic boom sent a concussive pulse of air and sand rushing at her, almost knocking her off her feet.

It took her a moment to realize what had happened. Then she heard the muffled sound of rotor engines through popped eardrums, and the fleeting coolness of a shadow passed over her. A military aerial vehicle like the ones that had accompanied the Goliath to the ARC. It descended from the sky, silhouetted within a corona of sunlight, its twin rotors drawing up plumes of dust.

"*REMAIN WHERE YOU ARE,*" a hardened woman's voice bellowed through a loudspeaker. Perez immediately recognized the tone—and the Italian accent—as Kohen's.

The aircraft circled to the other side of her pod, disappearing momentarily before coming around again on a steeper approach. A hot jet of air blasted down from the exhaust vents lining the base of the fuselage as the hulking thing touched down behind a cloud of brown dust. After a minute, Perez's ears equalized, taking in the full intensity of the screaming engines. She looked over at Basem, who seemed unperturbed, still clawing, his eyes to the sky.

"*Don't move.*" Kohen's voice pierced the shroud of dust. Soon after, she emerged with the unrelenting hum of the rotors at her back. Oz's mountainous form materialized behind her a second later, his shemagh whipping frantically about his neck. Both leered through clear ballistic visors, fully fitted in black tactical gear with their guns raised. "*On your knees,*" Kohen barked over her suit's comm, but Basem still did not react. She walked behind him and struck him between the shoulder blades with the butt of her rifle. His knees buckled, sending him forward into the ground.

"Get away from him!" Perez screamed, and without thinking, she charged.

Oz trained his weapon on her. "Down on your knees, or I shoot."

Perez sneered and raised her hands above her head, her lungs billowing heavily as she coughed at the air. She lowered herself slowly to the ground, her heart in her ears.

Basem lay face down on the hot concrete, his back rising and falling as he gasped for air. He raised a hand behind his head in an apparent attempt to shield himself from another blow as Kohen loomed over him. She produced a pair of restraints, reached down for his wrist, and wrenched him, naked and bleeding, from the ground with surprising efficiency. Perez could only watch in horror and disbelief.

Then movement in her periphery drew her gaze toward another shape walking out from the curtain of dust.

"Take them both," Jacobs said.

Yggdrasil's ash, great evil suffers,
Far more than men do know;
The hart bites its top, its trunk is rotting,
And Níðhöggr gnaws beneath.
　　　　　　　　　—Poetic Edda

< ᛗ | NÍÐHÖGGR >

Lotta shielded her eyes from the glimmer of sunlight filtering through the trees as she crawled out from her shelter. The crammed lean-to represented a crude attempt at replicating the structure she and Fischer had built on their first night in the forest, the night Basem died. This time, there were no deadfalls nearby, but she found she could erect something more compact—enough to accommodate a single person—using felled tree branches to weave a basic frame blanketed with twigs, moss, and pine needles. Then, she smeared the outside with ferrofluid to ward off the denizens of the forest. She had no basis for believing it would work, just a gut feeling. That was enough.

Lotta's shelter had made for good practice—a proof of concept. Proof she could do it herself. Fischer's went a little faster, and she decided the easiest solution was to construct it around him as he lay unconscious in the dead of night. It proved to be a strange experience. Felt like a burial. She imagined the rickety cage of sticks engulfed in flames like a funeral pyre, reducing Fischer to ash. Into atoms.

She shuddered at the thought.

That was three nights ago, after dragging him, unconscious, from the stream, after she had sealed his wounds with resin the same way he had shown her—it was the last time they spoke before she found him by the water. Lotta looked down at her fingers, still coated in resin, throbbing like mad. She had learned to ignore the pain, to live with it.

Just as Fischer had said, the sticky liquid was an effective astringent. Helped stem the bleeding enough to remove the tourniquet. Despite this, his condition had deteriorated over the past twenty-four hours, and he still hadn't regained consciousness.

Lotta bit her lower lip, revived the fading coals with wood scraps and set a few resin nuggets over the flame. She scraped the resulting sticky substance on the spine of Fischer's knife and walked to his shelter. She had examined him periodically through a porthole she had fashioned on one side of the lean-to. It permitted easy access, an innovation she liked to think Fischer would be impressed with, just like the sieve cylinders she had repurposed for carrying water.

"Why didn't I think of that?" he had said. The thought made her smile before it formed a knot in her throat, and she broke down. It felt good to cry. To feel. Most of the time, the emotion was fleeting, but it was a release, a weight falling away.

Lotta pulled away a section of woven twigs that covered the opening and was immediately greeted by a miasma of squalor and urine that enveloped her with an intensity that forced her to turn away with a gag. She took a deep breath and turned back with clenched teeth.

Fischer's arm was purple and swollen twice its normal size, the wound oozing dark blood, old blood. Skin clammy with cold sweat. The symbol he had carved into himself peered up at her, the skin stretched and shining around it.

Thurisaz.

It invoked the sounds of the jötunn, the beast's rumbling calls filling the air with a turbulence that shook leaves and rattled organs. The moaning of its great lungs, muscle and tendon shifting over bone with every plodding footfall. In her mind, she could still hear its great jaws clapping shut around something wet and festering.

Fischer shifted with a shallow moan as she began to treat the wound.

"*Scheisse.*" Trembling, she pulled the knife away. The resin was still too hot. "*I'm sorry.*"

Fischer eased back down, his breathing shallow and rattling. Lotta wanted to cry again. She had no idea what she was doing. Felt helpless and lost and small.

She watched him lying there. Beads of sweat dotted his forehead, eyebrows drawn in and hooding a pair of fluttering eyelids flanked by flushed cheeks wet with grit and earth. Some fever dream amid tortured breaths. Without warning, a hotness spread across her face, an unexpected and explosive anger pulsing through her. The realization that Fischer had almost left her here alone, afraid. Had attempted the easy way out. Abandoned her.

Realizing what she was doing, Lotta tempered her emotions. *These are just stories in your own head. You don't know what really happened.* But it was evident to her that he had tried this sort of thing before. She had seen the scars. Still, it seemed unreal. Impossible. Anger melted away, gave rise to melancholy at the speculation she could not silence.

What had driven him to this? The loss of his family, of his girls? A gut-wrenching prospect. One he seemed to relive after his outburst toward Hassan—or what had once been Hassan. One that made Lotta feel small. Like a petulant child.

Why the rune?

The most likely explanation, Lotta considered, was that he didn't really *know* what he was doing. Simply saw the symbol she had carved in the dirt and, in a state of withdrawal-induced fugue, had cut it into his arm. That was it. Something subconscious. An involuntary act.

His erratic behavior since that first seizure reminded Lotta of Sofia the time she tried quitting the bottle, how it drove her to see things. Demons, monsters. At its peak, her speech had become unintelligible, nothing more than a word salad of paranoid confabulations. And Fischer hadn't exactly tried to hide his substance use. What Lotta did see of his drinking probably scratched the surface, and out here—in this wretched hellscape, devoid of his vice, his source of comfort and sanity—maybe Fischer had simply snapped. That had to be it.

This revelation felt true the same way Lotta knew he'd once been a good father.

More stories. Your stories. Made up. Not true. Not his.

A good parent. Not like Pappa. And certainly not like Sofia.

Forgive her. Hassan's words emerged from the bedlam swirling in her head. Haunted her.

Words meant for me?

Lotta inhaled deeply. The thrum of her pulse faded. Whatever Fischer's reasons for doing what he did, she'd have to wait until he woke. Overanalyzing it wouldn't achieve anything.

She rose to her feet with a long sigh.

As she turned and started back toward the fire, something whizzed by her head. A hum like a giant, buzzing insect. She saw the second one, a tiny blur streaming past her field of view. Tracked it to the ginkgo along the bank, where it came to a halt midair and began to hover, its wings scalloping horizontally. *Hummers.* About a half dozen or so. The small winged things—*little pterodactyls*—came out at dawn to feed on grubs and centipedes. They hovered around the tree's leaves like long-necked hummingbirds or nectar bats, probing fruiting conoids with needly beaks and worm-like prehensile tongues, picking insects out from the orange stocks that glistened with a substance like slime mold or algae.

Along the bank at the base of the tree, Lotta caught more movement—more of them fluttering about clouds of insects above the water, hawking them out of the air with their stringy pink tongues.

A larger individual, about the size of a fledgling magpie, probed the mud along the bank, indifferent to Lotta's presence. It moved on folded wings, little mantis arms like those she'd seen on the stalkers.

It was then that she grew acutely aware of the relative absence of birds, their niches supplanted by these peculiar pterodactyloids, every bit as diverse and specialized. Nightmarish things vaulting atop stilted legs. Able to run you down or ambush you from the air. Death from above. Even the hummers invoked an unsettling sort of dread within her. The largest stood no taller than the distance between thumb and index finger, but that hadn't stopped them from whizzing past her face. She imagined that, at best, they were likely riddled with disease and pestilence.

Lotta's spine crawled and shuddered as she watched the adult from where she stood. It plunged its hypodermic beak—nearly the length of its velutinous body—into the mud. It was darker than the others, mottled brown and gray with white spots and a cream-colored ribbon down the length of its joisted neck. It lowered itself on jointed wing arms, probing deeper into the sodden earth. A few seconds later, its head pulled back to reveal something small wriggling at the tip of its charcoal beak. A prawn or crawfish.

Some of the smaller, less capable hummers descended upon it, landing on all fours, wings snapping tight against their bodies so they appeared nonexistent. The things squeaked and hopped about like ravenous fledglings. Lotta considered that perhaps that was what they were, and this larger individual was their parent. It extended its beak to let the little pink tongues probe its quarry. The little ones worked frantically, dismembering the writhing prawn piece by piece until nothing remained but a gray husk. The adult cast it aside into the water, and it was carried off by the current. Discarded the same way the stalker had tossed pieces of Basem aside like a fussy child at the dinner table. Dismantled him before her eyes, eviscerated him.

Lotta hated them, big or small. Hated this whole fucking place, down to the anemic air filling her lungs.

Icy tendrils plucked her spine, and she swallowed against the knot in her throat. She resisted the urge to break down into grief, or madness, or both.

She leered for a while longer. Watched as they flitted in and out of the bug clouds and ginkgo boughs. Some probing the mud, attempting to mimic the lone parent. Then her gaze turned to Fischer's lean-to as she debated her next steps. They needed food. Pilfered grubs had proven to be inadequate sustenance; digging for prawns seemed unappealing and potentially fruitless, given the state of her hands, not to mention the very real risk of further irritating the hummers that had buzzed her for the second time in two days.

Foraging for fiddleheads was another possibility. Fischer had indicated they grew near waterways, so the banks might be teeming with them. But venturing away from the campsite meant leaving him unattended and vulnerable—at the mercy of the forest, perhaps even his own mind should he wake. If he regained consciousness, he might try and hurt himself again.

Lotta recalled something Sofia had said to her once. After Pappa left. *Always put yourself first.*

And the woman lived by it. Had always put herself first. And second and third. Never her daughter. All the while reminding Lotta that no one was to be trusted, least of all men. Even as a girl, Lotta understood Sofia's sentiment. After all, Pappa had left *her*, too, and she resented him for that. For leaving her alone with her bitch of a mother. Probably would for the rest of her life, the end of which now appeared imminent.

Between her mother's tongue-lashings and her father's rejection—*the coward*—Lotta had never really let anyone in. The superficial companionship between her and Fischer was the closest thing to a meaningful relationship she could recall. Despite having known him for years, she realized they were little more than strangers. Acquaintances at best. She thought it ironic that she felt drawn to him amid this horror. A strange gravitation—buried deep beneath her drive for survival—to a man that reminded her so much of Sofia in some ways and Pappa in others. But she dismissed the notion. Ignored his failings because, until now, no one else had looked out for her except for herself. She had Sofia to thank for that. And thank her she did, as much as she detested the woman, because in the end, it seemed Fischer was destined to abandon her, too.

Maybe her mother was right.

Lotta surveyed the area one last time. Threw more kindling on the fire, hoping it would deter predators and opportunists from coming near the camp.

Her stomach folded in on itself, an unwelcome reminder that time was against her. Without further delay, she broke camp toward the edge of the stream.

Lotta had no set direction other than to keep to the embankment, because it seemed more secure than the dense verdure. It was also the best way she knew to keep from getting turned around. As an added measure, she stopped periodically to stack river rocks into cairns—distinct markers for finding her way back.

One of her few memories with Pappa was of the time she had helped him stack a large cairn as an altar for blót. She recalled him telling her how their ancestors had once built them along coastlines and fjords to navigate waterways. Sometimes, he'd told her, cairns were utilized to form game drivers to help hunters steer reindeer herds off cliffs. Others served as memorials for the dead, a secondary purpose Lotta assigned to hers as she piled the smooth, wet stones.

The first one was for Mattheo.

She wasn't sure how long she stood there, her eyes gazing down at the solitary column. Thinking back to how she had found Mattheo on the landing. Her breathing hastened. She tried to put it from her mind, think instead of his contagious smile, his brilliance in the field. She swallowed hard. Wanted to say something, anything, but couldn't find the words. Supplanted the sentiment instead with a deep sigh to try and alleviate the knot in her chest.

She wiped her muddied hands on her compression sleeve and carried on along the embankment. Moved beyond the overhanging cycad, taking note of her footing, past the spot she had found Fischer the night before. She followed the stream around another bend, where it split into two arteries, forming a V. There, tall ferns sprouted, their long stems buttressed by dozens of spidery rootlets that vaulted them above the water's surface.[1] They stood twice as tall as Lotta, with leaves fanning out radially to form green parasols that shaded their roots from the sun. Horsetails dotted the bank on both sides of the stream.

Here, she erected a second cairn—this one for Anderson.

Still at a loss for words, she took the branch of the stream that forked right.

She turned and glanced back toward the campsite, but a thicket now obscured it from view. Her ears were attuned to the sounds of the forest—nothing but the droning insects and rushing water, the occasional chirrups of now-distant hummer fledglings.

So long as she followed the stream, noted her landmarks, she would be okay. It was what Fischer would do.

As she moved, she thought of the thing she had seen along the far bank the other night—the apparition—gliding past, as if it had lingered there

---

1 Unspecified descendants of *Weichselia,* an extinct genus of fern from the Jurassic and Cretaceous

all along, watching Fischer, *watching her*. A silent phantom in the trees. Perhaps a trick of the moonlight playing off the leaves. Something imagined.

She tried to push it from her mind. Dismiss it as something imagined.

She continued forward slowly and checked her surroundings often, her line of sight shrinking as the parasol ferns grew denser. She eyed each one that she walked past. Their spidery rootlets enclosing placid pools at their base. Potential shelter for things like prawns or fish, maybe turtles.

Lotta's stomach produced an audible rumble. She had yet to spot any fiddleheads. Instead, she had found nothing but the ferns and striped horsetails.

She looked around for a straight stick she could hew into a spear like the one Fischer had made. She snapped a dried branch from a desiccated deadfall and, using the knife, started shaving one end into a sharp point. There was a technique to carving: one that Lotta had no skill in and that Fischer had made look easy. But she managed to get the desired result. It wasn't as clean or sharp as his, but it appeared serviceable. When she finished, she laid the spear down and gathered more stones for the third cairn. This one was for Basem.

As with the others, she lingered there for a time, gazing at the carefully stacked column. Minutes, probably, but it felt longer. Closed her eyes and saw him. Saw Basem falling, cutting through the air out of the night sky. And the *sound* his body made as it hit the earth. *That terrible sound.*

"I'm so sorry," Lotta whispered, her body bowing over the cairn from a kneeling position. "I'm so sorry."

She heard another sound, this time outside her own head—a gentle but sustained hiss from the stream. Her eyes fell on the surface, now churning and roiling with a flurry of splashes. Something erupted from the frothing water—a fish, maybe the size of her forearm.[2] Then another. And another. Dozens of them rushing downstream as if to get away from something. As quickly as it happened, the maelstrom calmed back to a gentle ebb, and the fish were gone.

Before Lotta could process what had occurred, an expulsion of air, as if from a breaching whale, filled her ears. She cast her gaze in its direction and saw something break the surface in the middle of the stream to her

---

2 *Spinocaudichthys oumtkoutensis*

left—a dark hump moving through the water. She thought it might be a turtle, but it appeared too smooth to be a shell. It looked soft and fleshy, the water rippling over its glistening surface, churning eddies in its wake.

A jet of spray billowed about a meter from the hump, and what appeared to be a flat head surfaced. It was adjoined to a serpentine neck, with a half-submerged face that appeared to be of a reptile or eel with rows of interlocking teeth like mangled skewers and inky eyes suspended just above the waterline.

Then another burst of spray. Another breach. A third and fourth. A pod of them, each the length of a man, swam with the current. They glided silently by with nothing but the sound of the water flowing over their smooth bodies. Bobbed over and under the waterline as if to travel between worlds, between realities. Submerged then broke through again, their flippers breaching and clapping against the surface like playful whales.

Lotta watched in stunned silence as they passed. Watched them glide lazily downstream, black-eyed sirens. *Plesiosaurs*, she thought.[3] Watched as they faded into a column of golden sunlight that peered through a distant break in the trees.

An opening.

A flutter of burgeoning excitement swelled in her chest as she peered with a hand over her eyes, squinting past the bloom of daylight cutting through the trees. *A way out.* Without thinking, she began to move toward it, only to stop four paces in as her better judgment took hold. She demurred, unsure of how to proceed. Didn't want to venture too far from Fischer. It was too risky.

Then, in the midst of her hesitation, Lotta heard rustling off to her right. Then a soft warble. Her head snapped toward it, pulse bouncing around her skull, reflexes pulling her into a crouched position. A hot jolt shot through her, electricity coursing over her skin.

She spotted something enormous jutting up from the forest floor through the dense bracken and looming parasol ferns. Ragged and festering, an enormous carcass of some felled beast with cracked, pale skin like dried leather. Gaunt and enveloped in a cloud of flies, buzzing black motes.

---

3 *Leptocleidus indet.*

She studied the great mass for a moment and realized she was looking into an open ribcage, the arched bones vaulting high enough that she'd need to reach up to touch them. They gleamed in the soft daylight filtering through the trees and were flanked at either end by great, weathered legs, their skin shrunken over elephantine bones. But this was no elephant, nor mammoth. It was something bigger. *Longer.* It must have been dead at least a month, picked over by the insects and scavengers of the forest. Subsumed by leaf and loam over time. Back into the earth like all things.

The rustling came again.

Lotta's stomach lurched. She swallowed hard. Swept a hand across her sweaty brow, every muscle in her body loaded upon stretched sinew, hair-trigger synapses poised to send her into desperate retreat. She was aware of every standing hair on her body, every drop of sweat running down her back. Aware of the compression lining chafing the inside of her thighs, of the blisters ready to burst on the soles of her throbbing feet. She stretched her neck above the still ferns and held her position. Waited.

The thistles shook. Something small and gray hopped up from a clump of nettles onto one of the carcass's giant limbs.

Lotta sighed, relieved. Almost laughed at herself.

The little creature resembled a bird, flapping gracefully as it ascended the leathery carcass. Its head darted like a bird, too, with a bright red stripe from head to tail. Next to Lotta, it would have stood halfway to her knee on its rangy, down-covered legs. Each foot, black and devoid of fuzz, sprouted a little sickle claw on the inner phalanx like a raptor's. And when she spotted the hands folded beneath its wings and observed the straight tail counterbalancing its bobbing head, she realized that was *exactly* what it looked like. A tiny raptor.[4] But it was unlike what she had imagined. Felt more ordinary than not, like watching a bird. A familiarity that brought her a sense of ease.

But the carcass troubled Lotta. How it got there. The violence in its arrangement, still evident in its advanced state of decomposition. Its four great limbs, each in varying stages of decay. A long tail, stripped of flesh and half-swallowed by the undergrowth.

---

4 *Rahonavis ostromi*

Around the thing, strange obelisk-shaped trunks sprang up like branchless trees. They resembled tentacles, glistening with water or fungus, and sprouted lush ferns along their knotted lengths.[5] Some loomed a few meters over the felled beast, obscuring what appeared to be a long neck behind a thicket of greenery and several deadfalls.

It looked like a Brontosaurus.

If there was anything to allay Lotta's disquietude, this thing looked like it had been there for some time. If a predator had taken it down, it was likely long gone.

The little raptor-bird preened one of its wings, which looked more like fuzzy arms than anything capable of sustained flight. The hands and tail appeared to contain the most feathers, tipped black with ivory banding. With its back arched, it raised one of its legs to the scruff of its neck and scratched itself with its toe claw. Its back muscles twitched at the swarming bugs, and it turned its head to snap at them. Then the creature froze, its fleshy snout in profile. An inky eye fixed on Lotta. Another soft warble erupted from its puffed chest.

She stared back, frozen, afraid to spook it.

And then she saw the snake.

It sprang from one of the obelisk trees, launching itself toward the raptor, which belted out a blood-curdling squeal. The serpent clamped down on the raptor's neck, sending them both tumbling to the ground.

Lotta heard another squeal, this time muffled and weak. The sound was distressing. It was the sound of panic, of terror. She gripped her spear, then loped in bounding strides across the uneven ground toward the rustling bed of thistles they had fallen into. Retched against the musty smell of rot, moving quickly so as not to lose the element of surprise.

She saw the body of the snake twisting and constricting, squeezing the life from its prey. She tried to spot the head to avoid it, but it was obscured from sight. She made a snap decision, driving the spear as hard as possible into the serpent's bulk. Lifted it and drove it down again. Hard. She felt it give, then collapse under her weight as it penetrated through scales and flesh. More resistance, and again collapse, into the soft abdomen of the kicking raptor. Disoriented, the snake writhed and

5 *Tempskya indet*

hissed, tried to lunge aimlessly for the counterattack, but Lotta kept it impaled, out of reach.

The raptor gave a few more bucks, then fell still.

"I *fucking* hate you," she grunted, bearing as much of her weight down as she could while keeping her distance.

The soft pop of organs and skin traveled up into her fingers as the spear's tip emerged on the other side. Her vision smeared from her brimming eyes. She watched as the checkered body of the serpent coiled in agony around the end of the spear. It was the same type of snake she had seen by the stream days before, with its puny, useless legs, except this one was much bigger—perhaps a meter long. She watched it squirm and hiss, skewered and helpless, until it fell limp over the feathered body and blood-stained thistles.

"Bloody fucker."

Lotta turned to head back, her quarry skewered and in hand. That was when she realized she was turned around. She no longer had sight of the stream, instead finding herself caged in by the strange wooden columns—sopping obelisks glistening in the muddy light—and the stench of carrion and mildew ebbing about the space. The swarming flies fueled her disorientation as panic drove through her chest like a hot dagger.

She tried to remember her orientation, her position, before she had rushed toward the carcass. Her eyes darted in feverish bursts, panic stealing over her like an oily apparition. *Stupid. Stupid.* She fought the urge to bolt aimlessly past the strange woody pillars and peered in desperation for any sign of the stream, of Basem's cairn.

She breathed deeply, localized the sound of flowing water. Turned her head to triangulate it. She moved forward, snagging herself on nettles and horsetails, clawing her way back to the rising babble. Tearing away from the choking ferns and brambles, she pressed on until the sparkling stream materialized. And there was Basem's cairn, shaded beneath the spidery parasol ferns with their pools like smooth glass.

She let out a long sigh, sucking in the air, trying to calm herself.

Fucking stupid.

The fern-pool beside it rippled, drawing her gaze.

She peered into the cage of roots with wincing eyes. Saw something move, coiled tightly in the shallow water. Another snake, its black eyes peering out from shadow, tongue tasting the air. Tasting *her*.

Lotta scowled at it. *That stupid face.* "Fuck you," she spat.

But she stayed where she stood. Didn't have it in her to kill anymore today.

With raptor and serpent speared and in hand, knife in the other, Lotta gazed once more toward the distant opening in the trees. Then turned to head back.

< 4 | SKIN FOR SKIN >

|The driver was late.

Erebus Group moved from cover through the sprigs and brushwood, the moss-addled boughs, and into the waiting headlights. The driver—a European Union loyalist—was a tall, lanky fellow. He greeted them with a terse "Sveiki" and lit a cigarette beneath the mottled shadows. He was middle-aged, clean-shaven, with a long face and a rigid, beady-eyed stare. His hands were rugged, knuckles dense with hair, finger joints knobbed—probably from years of odd jobs and hard labor. His loose-fitting work clothes neatly concealed a 9mm Makarov tucked into the front of his waistband, and he did not waste time presenting it to the soldiers by lifting his shirt to reveal the exposed grip.

"Hope yeh dun mind," he grumbled, then restored his shirt to its previous position.

Fischer racked his own gun and nodded.

"Thought there was six ah yeh on this op," the man said.

"The other guy stayed behind."

The driver snorted, expelling smoke from his nostrils. "Get comfortable. Two hours to Daugavpils."

He waved the soldiers toward the back of the vehicle—a refurbished electric minibus from a bygone era. On the side, a decal read *Путешествие по Латвии*—Russian for Travel Latvia—the red paint smeared by scuffs and scratches, partially obscured behind a layer of dust. It was nothing if not inconspicuous.

The driver slid the backdoor shut and entered the driver's seat, his un-ashed cigarette dangling from his lips. He powered the battery, and they were on the move. The interior stank of burnt tobacco and mold, but Fischer was glad to finally be en route.

The ride out of the Latvian wilderness was quiet. It gave Fischer time to reflect, to check his gear. Sully unclipped his mag to top it off and cleaned his sniper rifle. Capp drew Moreau and Janson into a game of whist. Moreau was the first dealer, but couldn't shuffle to save his life. Something Capp would normally take the piss out of him for. But no one spoke. Their minds were elsewhere.

There was no need for talk. Everyone knew the mission. Fischer tried not to linger on what had already gone wrong—that they were behind schedule, that a civilian was dead for nothing, and on his watch. Wrong place, wrong time, mate. The driver had come late, and their window for bagging Evgeni Dmitriev had narrowed, but they'd baked that possibility into the plan. It changed nothing.

The mood turned tense once they crossed into the slums along the city's outskirts. Many people who lived here were ethnic Russians, some of them separatists. Virtually all were staunch loyalists to the "motherland," though most had never set foot on Russian soil. But that didn't matter. Propaganda mattered. Propaganda was king. And no one was better at infiltrating the hearts and minds of its enemies than Moscow.

Raindrops pecked the windshield. Fischer wiped his steamy passenger window and peered at rows of tents and rundown hovels lining the pothole-ridden road. Heaps of damp trash and human excrement were strewn about the otherwise-empty street. It was dark, quiet. The rain came down light.

The van groaned on its suspension over the rough road, but the driver remained steadfast. A dull orange glow swelled around him as he took a drag from his third cigarette. Fischer caught his ratty eyes in the rearview mirror. They lingered on him through coils of gray smoke, then returned to the road.

The minibus turned sharply into a derelict loading area along the rear entrance of an abandoned warehouse, their point of entry. Dmitriev was meeting with the informant in a nearby structure on the south side of the building. Their inside man had managed to get close to him and become part of his inner circle. The warehouse provided Erebus with the perfect cover to get into position with little risk of detection. The comms were quiet.

The van backed toward the loading platform, and Fischer chambered a round. He switched off the safety.

"Time to go silent," he said and toggled his comm to tactical. "From here, we talk over ARES." He heard a high-pitched ringing in his ears that gave way to mounting pressure. Always reminded him of tinnitus. His ears popped, and the sound faded.

ARES—short for Automated Response and Engagement System—was a mission-based AI and experimental combat assistant that provided situational awareness, neurally integrated tactile aim-assist, and real-time strategic analysis. It also featured a practical method of non-verbal communication via thought transfer between squad mates. Involved quantum entanglement. Spooky action at a distance. One of a battery of genetic modifications Erebus had undergone. Originated from a gene called "cryptochrome" that, when expressed, was integrated with a soldier's neural link. Originally isolated from migratory birds, it helped them navigate magnetic fields. Turned out it also allowed communication within flocks. Explained how so-called murmurations worked.

Bona fide telepathy, perfected by Mother Nature across eons. Fischer's background in electromagnetic simulation and memory interfaces, coupled with his military training, had made him a prime candidate for the program. The rest was history.

<Breacher.> Fischer's simulated voice whirred through his skull as he waved Capp toward their point of entry. Hearing himself this way introduced a sensation he thought he might never get used to. Came almost like a thought, but registered as if spoken from outside his head. A digitized approximation of his own voice trailed by a faint ringing.

<Sir.> Capp stepped onto the loading platform and produced a thermite torch. He uncapped and activated it against the padlock. There was a bright flash and dripping molten steel. Capp turned the padlock with heat-resistant

gloves and removed it, then gently slid the rusty bay door up halfway along its tracks.

Moreau went first, his gun aimed into the dark interior. Fischer followed, and his contact lens HUD transitioned to night vision. The rest of Erebus took up a stack formation behind him, spilling in through the opening with guns raised.

They were inside.

Fischer moved to the front and guided his men into an open corridor. The loading area was flanked by crumbling concrete walls smeared with graffiti and old feces. Most of the scrawl contained anti-European and anti-Latvian propaganda. Every surface wept with condensation, smelled of dirt and mold, the occasional whiff of shit. Along the right wall, a stack of rotting pallets blocked a metal staircase that led to an elevated mesh platform suspended beneath rows of rusted steel girders.

Fischer reached down, unclipped two small drones from his plate carrier, and tossed them into the air. Their rotor blades unfolded and whirred to life, buzzing like insects as they sped away to map the building.

<Sully,> Fischer chirped, <post up on the roof. Get eyes on the target.>

<On it, sir.>

It was strange to hear Sully's digitized voice, devoid of its Irish brogue. He turned right and started up the rusty steps, sniper rifle in hand, his fiery beard obscured beneath a camo shemagh. The platform creaked under each footfall until his movements faded overhead.

Fischer and the others pressed forward.

Standing water rippled underfoot as they moved through the musty corridor. Fischer's HUD indicated they were closing on their waypoint. Their informant's tracking beacon was coming from a rickety compound around fifty meters from the other end of the derelict warehouse. They proceeded in a column along a rounded wall vent until the corridor branched into two narrow hallways lined with rooms, their doors torn from their hinges. Fischer swept his rifle through the first entryway. The room was empty.

<Clear.> He re-emerged and glanced down the split corridor, then turned to his men. <Janson and Capp, go right. Moreau and I will take the left. Clear every room. Drones aren't picking up any biometrics, but we don't want any surprises.>

Capp and Janson split off down the first fork. Moreau moved up the rear and joined Fischer as he quietly proceeded to the second corridor. A few meters in, a sour fecal stench overwhelmed Fischer. Behind him, Moreau cleared his throat.

<God, that smell,> Moreau said, less the French accent.

<Aye. Let's keep moving.>

They had finished clearing the second room when a loud noise erupted into the hallway. Footfalls splashed down the corridor. Someone was inside and was making a run for it.

"Motherfucker," Moreau grunted, turning back to the hallway.

<Use your link, not your voice, comrade,> Fischer clapped.

Fischer trailed him into the hallway, where a shadowy figure sprinted toward the front of the building.

Moreau raised his rifle.

Fischer reached for him. <WAIT—>

Crack.

A silenced tracer round whizzed down the corridor, and pink mist bloomed around the target's head. The person's legs buckled, and their body crumpled with a splash into a turbid puddle.

<God dammit, Moreau. We don't know if that's a bloody hostile.>

<I'm sorry, I thought—the mission, the poacher—>

<I didn't give you a fuckin' order, soldier.>

Sully buzzed somewhere behind Fischer's eyes. <You ladies okay? What's going on down there?>

<Possible tango down,> Fischer said. <We're good. Hold your positions.>

Fischer moved toward the body, Moreau on his left flank, their guns raised, the target unmoving. There was no weapon.

<No....> Moreau said. <Tell me... tell me I didn't just shoot a fucking kid.>

The boy lay face down in the shallow puddle. His hair was dark, cropped short. It curled around the back of his ears, dripping with filthy water. He looked to be around eight or nine. The back of his tattered white shirt was speckled with blood. His head was partially collapsed on one side where the bullet had entered.

Fischer knelt and gently rolled him onto his back. The bullet had gone clean through, and the boy's face had sunken behind his left eye. Dark rivulets gushed from the exit wound—a ragged hole where there had once been a lower jaw. Ribbons of shredded tongue, bits of shattered bone and teeth embedded in macerated flesh. Blood poured from his nose, and the skin around his eyes had turned black and swollen.

Fischer's face went hot as he gazed up at Moreau. <He's gone.>

He lowered his eyes to the boy's face again, but something had changed. It was not a boy anymore, but a girl.

His girl.

His eldest, Ellsa.

Fischer's veins turned to ice. The air stopped in his lungs, swelling into a tempest. Wide-eyed and trembling, he shook his head and stepped away slowly.

<Sunny?>

It couldn't be. But the longer he looked, the more the sunken face resembled his little Ellsa, his sun, her swollen lids ajar. Behind her already-clouding corneas, he caught her vibrant blue irises gazing emptily past him.

His welling eyes—stinging with rage—fell on Moreau, and he raised his gun. His HUD flashed red, warning him he was trained on a friendly. But he didn't care. His finger found the trigger, curled around it. Electric shocks pulsed down his triceps, clamped around his wrists, wresting control over his neural link's aim-assist as it tried to wrench the gun away from a friendly. But Fischer fought against it.

Moreau stepped back, his hands in the air. Let his rifle hang to the side. "Whoa… Sir, I-I'm sorry. It was an accident. It's just some Russki kid—"

Fischer agonized against the targeting system. Felt sinew and tendon seizing and popping against the antagonistic involuntary firing of synapses in his arms. Made his muscles hot. A form of self-immolation. A final, vengeful act.

"You… you killed her. You fucking killed her."

<H-her?>

He fixed his sights between Moreau's eyes, his left arm shredding itself from the inside, struggling against ARES with furious intent.

Then Edgar Fischer pulled the trigger. >

Day 4, Midday — The Stream

Crack.

The sound clapped through Fischer with a suddenness that shook him from dormancy. He drew a sharp breath, gasping and clutching his chest as if he'd been underwater.

His eyes were caked shut. He pried them open with sticky fingers, but the sharp sting of air drove him to squeeze them closed again. With tears gushing down his face, he wondered in darkness how long he'd been out. Realized the smell in his dream had come from his own soiled bedding. And the sound—like a firecracker—had also been real.

He rubbed his eyes vigorously with both hands this time. A searing, stabbing pain coursed down his left arm, and a bleating yelp tore through his throat, past clenched teeth. But the sound didn't carry. He was somewhere confined, enclosed. Panic stole over him, the same fear deep inside all men, the fear of being trapped. But he caught himself before his mind abandoned all logic. Before terror hijacked his motor functions and made him do something rash. He drew a deep breath, focused on his heart rate. Remembered his training. Countless tunnel drills. Drown-proofing tests with wrists and ankles bound. His breathing slowed. His eyes swiveled in their sockets; he tried to open them again. The stinging air took his attention away from his arm for a moment, but he fought through it—his eyes weeping and rolling—until the sensation faded. Body shaking and feverish, Fischer peered with oily vision into a dim cocoon of sticks and vegetation he didn't recognize.

Where am I?

He remembered seeing trees overhead, had gazed at the night sky by the fire while Lotta carved in the dirt. He had passed out. She had cared for him. They spoke, but he didn't remember the substance of their conversation. Didn't recall what she'd scratched in the dirt. At one point, he'd gathered the strength to walk around the campsite. Had flitted in and out of consciousness for a time. Dreamt feverish visions of his final operation in the Special Forces. But it was all wrong. There was no minibus, no chain-smoking driver.

I sure as shit didn't shoot Moreau. But the kid… Jesus, Moreau. He hadn't thought of that Latvian kid—with the curls behind his ears like Evi's—nor

Moreau, not for years, or any of the others from Erebus. Moreau had shot himself shortly after Leichter Speer. Couldn't handle the fallout, what he'd done. Fischer had also come close to killing himself on multiple occasions, botched one attempt to slash his wrists. And then Ellsa and Evi came, and everything changed.

Evi.

Fischer had also dreamt of her and her sisters. Standing on the far bank along the stream. Watching him with eyes blacker than ink, blacker than the emptiest vacuum of space. Not the radiant blue galaxies that had always pierced the darkness, but sunken. Empty. And they watched. Peered into him, through him, in silence.

Silenced. That's what those eyes were. Snuffed out like dead stars.

Just a dream.

His temples throbbed. Little Man had gone full bastard, but next to the pain in his right arm, the stinging in his eyes, a pounding headache was a baseline Fischer found himself wishing he could return to.

Could really use a drink about now. Numb up the gums a bit.

He wiped the foam from the edges of his mouth. Balled his trembling hand and rested it against his chest, then tracked it down to his pelvic bone. Bare skin. *Naked again.* Wondered if everything—the visions, the dreams, the voices—had been just that. Everything he'd seen and heard beneath the rotting remains of Hassan Kateb. All of it, inside his own head. He closed his eyes. Couldn't bear the thought of his girls screaming as the building came down. What would he give to see them alive again? To find them in another reality? He thought of what he and Lotta had seen in the Bell chamber—her *double.* Some other version of her, leering back at them through a cosmic veil. Fischer imagined shattering through that barrier and entering a reality in which his daughters might still be alive.

But would it really be them?

He tried to swallow, but the pain stopped up a lump in his throat. Distracted himself by filtering his beard through his fingers in the stench of his own filth as he pondered his next steps.

Fuck it. Get. Up.

Forgetting about his arm, Fischer propped himself upright and immediately collapsed backward. A hot iron seared through him from palm to shoulder, eliciting mewling whimpers from his cracked lips. He clasped his arm and felt a tight binding covered in something sticky. He gaped down at it, straining to make out more than a blackened silhouette as his fingers probed. He raised his hand to his nose and, through the ammonia-laced fetor, recognized the scent of pine and smoke on his fingertips.

Resin? His mind raced.

A rustling noise from above broke his thoughts. Then came a barrage of clicking and chattering, a quarrel or ritual between wild things.

Fischer's arm throbbed in concert with the renewed pounding in his chest. He leaned against his uninjured arm, then kicked at the twigs and brush of his enclosure until one of the walls collapsed. The rush of air cooled his fiery lungs. Motivated him to push his feet into the ground, to heave against the bilious pit in his throat and slide on his back through the opening. He gazed up, listless and wincing through heavy eyes at shards of blue sky through the nascent canopy.

"Midday," he mouthed.

With great effort, he strained his neck to gaze back at his arm. The movement made him dizzy. His vision steadied, came into brief focus. The lump in his throat swelled at the sight of the injury, despite it being hardly visible beneath what appeared to be a torn-away section of a blood-caked compression sleeve.

Lotta's. His eyes searched for her among the tree trunks, but she was nowhere to be seen.

He propped himself into a sitting position, legs crossed, his wounded limb resting in his naked lap. Winced through tears and snot and dribble as his fingers resumed their probing. A purplish bruise feathered out from underneath the dressing's margins and extended to his palm, where it branched into mottled gray-and-yellow spiderwebs. Fischer tried to make a fist, but could barely curl his fingers before fire erupted through his veins again. He relaxed his hand and was greeted with intense cramps and pinpricks up the length of his arm. The limb was stiff. Unresponsive.

He gazed at the scars on his other wrist. Recalled a similar experience. A distant memory.

But this time was different. It had to be.

What the hell happened? Why can't I remember?

Fischer's head snapped up, his eyes wide and searching. He crawled over the dirt and pine needles, his wounded arm like a dead weight hugged to his chest. He moved with purpose, undeterred by the sharp prickling in his knees. Clambered past a second lean-to closer to the fire pit, his good arm burning under his weight as he clawed forward until it gave out in protest, driving his chest into the dirt and expelling his lungs with an intensity that startled more than hurt him. He got up again. Languished in his movements. Spat dirt.

"Lotta?" He recoiled at the rawness of his throat, his voice little more than a whisper.

Warmth spread over his skin. Real warmth. The fire was still going. *She couldn't have gone far.*

Along the fire pit's perimeter, the gutted POG housed the remaining chunks of resin, along with his gloves. But no knife. Next to the POG lay a neatly stacked bundle of bare twigs and conifer branches, along with the scavenged sleve cylinders standing upright and filled with water. Fischer picked one of the grayish canisters up. The water inside looked clean, so he guzzled it down. It hurt to swallow, but the coolness soothed his throat.

More chattering erupted overhead. His neck craned, eyes rotating skyward. Arboreal shadows moved through the canopy. Twigs snapped.

Maybe something attacked us, Fischer thought. There was nothing to prevent an animal from wandering into the camp. They were exposed on all sides, exposed from above. That had to be it. He had fought something off, but not before it took a chunk out of his arm. Then he'd lost consciousness from shock, blood loss, or both.

He looked down at himself, his skin covered in detritus and excrement. He could not recall a time he had smelled so bad, not even on protracted military assignments. He wiped away what he could and inspected the fading bruises on his body. Tried to remember the last thing he'd done. Recalled feeling a bit feverish the last time he had spoken to Lotta, when he had patched up her fingers....

She must have dressed his wound, built shelter, tended the fire, gathered food. How long had he been out?

Hours? Days?

"Lotta...."

Fischer's lungs labored against the vapid air. He thought of his girls again. *Really* thought of them. Their smiles. Their laughter.

An overwhelming sense of guilt swelled in his chest. After Geneva, he'd taken the job in Algeria to forget them, forget the pain, the loss. To leave their memory in the rubble. At first, the distance, the change in scenery, and the demands of his new position at CEPP helped. For a time. And ultimately, when that wasn't enough, when the isolation and the loneliness consumed him, he drank himself stupid, just like he had before he married Jocelyn. Started to remember why he had the scars on his wrists, how it felt to be hollow and alone. An empty shell.

But now, he didn't have work. Didn't have the bottle. Didn't even have Lotta. Only his thoughts. His girls. Memories he couldn't escape.

Ghosts.

Good or bad, he had tried to erase it all. Bury it. And now, it had all come crashing back.

Fischer hunched forward and wept into himself. A torrent of heaving sobs escaped him. But the moment passed as quickly as it came, because shutting it out meant postponing his suffering. It was easier to render himself inert. Easier to be numb.

He ran his forearm across his grimy face and shook it off. Tried to wrest back control.

Then something moved along the edge of his periphery and disappeared behind a tree.

Fischer shifted to his knees and, bracing himself with his good hand, rose onto the balls of his feet in a crouched position. He searched around for a weapon, anything within reach he could use to defend himself. The pain in his joints and limbs sharpened his presence, his focus. His fingers grazed a flat stone along the fire's perimeter. He smashed it into shards with another rock and picked up the sharpest piece.

He heard noises. Footsteps. Their source emerged from the underbrush.

Fischer breathed a sigh of relief, letting the stone shard fall from his grasp.

"*Lotta….*"

She couldn't hear him. His voice was shot. In one hand, she carried a long spear or walking stick. Something was impaled near its top, with blood running down the side. Some type of bird. And a snake with tiny hind legs like the one they'd seen darting into the stream. Then he saw that the sleeve of her other arm was torn away, and that she gripped his combat knife in that hand.

She still hadn't seen him. Fischer rose slowly to his feet, his joints popping and aching.

Lotta jumped back with the knife raised, her eyes wide. "*Scheisse!*"

"Sorry… I, uh… I'm not sure where my clothes are."

"Scared the *piss* out of me." Her shoulders relaxed, and she breathed a long sigh. Her eyes fell onto his arm, then locked back onto his. Her face had gone white. "How are you feeling?"

Fischer cleared his throat. "*Grottenschlecht*," he managed, his voice still raspy. It hurt like hell to speak.

"You look it." She nodded toward the stream, where his garment dangled from a sapling. "Should be dry by now, though you might want to clean up before you get dressed."

Her eyes searched, fell on the ruins of his lean-to, and her expression fell.

"And you?" Fischer said.

Lotta shot a look back, her eyes narrowed. A little color returned to her cheeks. "What about me?" She'd pulled her tousled hair into a ponytail. Something Fischer had never seen her do before. It drew his eyes to the delicate curves of her neck. She seemed to notice this, and he diverted his gaze down at the fire.

"You good?" he said.

She nodded, regarding him with a look he hadn't seen before. Like she had grown wary of him.

He glanced down at himself, then back at her. "Do I really smell that bad?"

"Pardon?"

"You're acting like I'm a walking plague." He waved her off dismissively, then shook his head as he glanced off into the trees. Felt silly standing there naked. Not like he had the first night. This time was different. This time, he felt exposed. Covered in his own filth and self-loathing. Wondered if she had noticed that he'd been wringing his eyes out like a sniveling babe.

Lotta seemed to soften, though her knuckles had whitened around the knife handle. She dodged Fischer's sentiment and lowered her quarry to the ground, then got to work dressing the snake with his knife. "Clean up, and I'll get these on the fire."

She wasn't particularly proficient at preparing the meat, but Fischer said nothing. He was impressed she had it in her. The physicist that followed protocol, lived by the book, and here she was, improvising while he wallowed. He turned toward the stream, but glanced back when Lotta called after him.

"Stay shallow," she said, her eyes still on her task. "There are… *things* in the water."

Fischer stood there, watching her, processing as she gutted the snake, its pathetic little legs limp at its sides. He glanced down at his useless arm and shuffled toward the stream.

UEF / RD
EYES ONLY

Ministry of Defence
United European Federation

Memorandum of CCTV Interrogation. Partial Transcript.

JUNE 16, 2147, 10:47

Appearances
Subject 001
Dr. Aegis Galani

Galani	Please state your name and date of birth for the record.
S001	Name date of birth for the record.
Galani	Are you Basem Bensoussan?
S001	Basem Bensoussan.
Galani	Dr. Bensoussan, please look at me. There is nothing to see up there. Everything you need to know right now is right in front of you. Can you tell me what happened to you? To the ALICE crew?
S001	Alice?
Galani	What is your relationship to Camila Perez? I see here you are her supervisor, but that does not explain why we found you unclothed at her domicile.
S001	Cam.
Galani	Is that what you call her? Why were you at her home?
S001	Don't know.
Galani	How did you get there?
S001	Don't know. I was falling. But that was a dream.
Galani	What do you know?
S001	This is real. [unintelligible]. Because I am here.
Galani	Okay, Dr. Bensoussan. Athena, I need a medical team.
Athena	Yes, Dr. Galani.
S001	No doctor.

| GALANI >

Pacing steadied Perez's nerves long enough for her to gather her thoughts. Her mind was a roaring ocean, a tortured stream of cogitation that served only to stoke her mounting distress, her anger towards Jacobs. But above all, she was afraid. She didn't know where she was or why she and Basem had been taken. It didn't make sense.

What more do they want from me? From him?

The memory of Uncle Diego's incarceration, his disappearance, claimed her thoughts. At once, the dimly lit room seemed smaller than when she had entered it. It was no longer a room but a cell.

The space was small and square. At the center, a metal chair with its legs bolted to the ground tempted her weary body, but she resisted. Pacing occupied her. Kept her sane. She looked around at the four walls, featureless and bleach-white, her breathing hastening with this momentary pause. Only when vertigo seized her did she take a deep breath and try to slow it down. She stood still and wavered for a moment. Thought of that night with Basem in Algiers, gazing at the stars over the kasbah, how he brought her back from a near-meltdown, his voice like a light in the dark.

Cielo. You are my sky.

The sky. The image of Basem gazing up at it, clawing, naked, at himself terrified her.

By now, she had grown used to the chemical smell of new construction. On one wall, dull blue light spilled through a frosted glass door with no handle, but she could not discern what lay beyond. Mounted next to it, a badge reader glowed a dull red; a service slot contained a cold serving of something thick and gray she couldn't identify and that she had little appetite for exploring. A partition concealed a sink and latrine—which she had only used once to vomit—at the room's far end. Probably nerves, probably Ruth. She didn't know which.

Perez paced again.

She estimated three hours had passed since Oz removed the cloth sack from her head and tossed her in this place. He'd told her to sit in the chair, but she could not remain there long. And so now, she walked. It helped with the cramps that had started an hour prior. Her eyelid was back to twitching again. The pain behind it had transformed into a crushing headache that now radiated up the side of her skull.

There was a shudder, then a subtle rumbling that propagated from the floor and up her legs. After several minutes, the sensation faded into stillness again. It had a regularity to it, once every hour or so, sometimes coming, sometimes going. At first, she thought it might be a nearby hyperloop terminal, but it didn't take long for her to abandon that theory. This seemed different. This was slow and grinding and wholly unfamiliar.

Where am I?

She needed to get back to Basem, back to Nedjma, back to her animals…

…back to the misoprostol in the medicine cabinet.

Mamá occupied a slice of her attention as she shuffled, chewing her cheeks. She thought of the miscarriage. Her brother. Wondered if he had had a name, if Mamá had told the truth, that she had miscarried. Wondered if she also possessed the same flaw, that Ruth might suffer the same fate: a natural death, regardless of outside interference. Perez found an odd comfort in that, a shred of justification. Even a fleeting sense of virtue that termination would be a form of mercy.

But not at the hands of the Federation.

And yet, with Basem's return, she entertained the idea of starting over. Of finding a reality in which they could have this baby. One that might not be possible.

Footfalls emerged from the silence outside, and the vague silhouette of an upright, suited figure appeared on the other side of the door's dappled glass. It appeared to be a man, his body occluding the light in a way that gave him a spectral aura. At first, her mind tricked her into seeing a shadow person, then settled back down as her higher faculties reeled her lizard brain back in. The next thought that came to her was that Jacobs had come to pay her a visit. This sent her pulse into her temples anew, and she was aware of her cheeks flushing with equal parts rage and fear.

What do you want now?

Like death incarnate, the figure raised a spidery hand to the side of the door. She heard the static of an intercom switch being pressed.

"Good afternoon, Dr. Perez," a man's voice said. But it was deep, unfamiliar. Greek accent. "My apologies for disturbing you."

"Do I know you?" she clapped, unable to mask her bewilderment.

"Ah, where are my manners? I do not believe I have yet had the pleasure of introducing myself." He paused as if for effect. "Aegis Galani. I represent EIRO's interests in Berlin and Luxembourg, by extension. At their behest, I am leading a delegation in this region. The board has requested full transparency concerning the recent… *happenings* here in Algeria."

I'm a glorified cog, is what she heard.

We're still in Algeria. That's something.

She saw a murky representation of a mouth opening and closing as he spoke. The smeared hint of a white complexion and slicked-back gray hair resembled an abstract painting more than it did a person. Vacant pits presumably housed eyes. They seemed to burn into her, adding to the ethereal, sphinxlike image that Lizard Brain had conjured from the limited visibility. He looked stiff in his raiment—a tie, collared overcoat, and slacks materialized in her mind, neatly pressed and absent of flaws. No thread out of place, not so much as a speck of dust. The thought bestowed his persona with a tendency toward particularity, perhaps even narcissism. Perez got the sense he liked to hear himself talk, maybe even while gazing longingly in the mirror.

"You mean they want you to clean up their mess," she cracked through desiccated lips. Tried to sound calm, collected. Deep down, she was reeling.

"To put a fine point on it, yes, if you like. But between us, you could say I am doing a favor for an old friend."

"And who's that?"

"That is of no consequence."

"Right. Well, it sounds like you're a long way from home, Commissioner. Sorry, but I can't help you with whatever you are trying to cover up for your friend."

A muffled grunt was returned from the cryptic approximation of a mouth.

"Is that all? Am I under arrest?" Perez said.

A dry laugh. "Of course not, Dr. Perez. You are only under observation. Isolation, to be precise. A mere precaution. You will be discharged upon clearing a medical examination."

Perez's heart stopped. A medical exam meant they would discover the pregnancy. She swallowed against the lump in her throat. "And if I refuse?"

Aegis tilted his head almost imperceptibly. "I am afraid that is not an option."

"There is no need for me to be in isolation and certainly no grounds for a forced medical exam. Tell Jacobs I took the necessary precautions during the necropsy. I'm fine."

"Debatable." He snorted. "I heard about your—er—*accident*. Quite the discovery, too, to be sure. But that is not why you are here."

"Then what is it?"

He sighed as if growing impatient. "Dr. Bensoussan. The report is that you two had direct contact."

"So?"

"*So*, we have been searching for him for days, along with his team. Now that he has been found, containment protocol must be adhered to. Surely you can get behind that, Doctor?"

"What are you not telling me? What's wrong with Basem?"

"I am not at liberty to discuss the matter further, I am afraid. Only to reassure you—and I do assure you—that this is completely necessary for your safety and for his."

"I don't believe you."

"Well, that's fine." He chuckled again. "But enough about me and my burdens. How would you define *your* relationship with Basem Bensoussan?"

"Excuse me?"

"Are you two... close?"

"I don't see how that is any business of yours."

"Mine? None at all, to be sure. I am not one to pry. But EIRO's business, well, that is a different matter."

Perez's cheeks grew hot. "Where is he?"

Aegis paused for a moment. Perez heard him breathe deeply, like he had taken a long drag from a cigarette. "Let me clear something up about our little dynamic here." His voice assumed a saccharine tonality that sounded both disingenuous and vaguely sinister. "As much as I am amused by our chit-chat, I ask the questions, and you answer. That is how this works." His shadowy form straightened, and he spoke slowly, this time sharply enunciating each word. "Are you close with Dr. Bensoussan?" *In five words or less: don't fuck with me.*

Perez was on her heels now, doing her best not to sound defensive. "No. We are work colleagues. I work under his supervision at—"

"Oh, I am sure. I am sure you are under him quite regularly."

"*Excuse* me?"

"My apologies. Clearly a touchy subject," he said with blithe resonance. "Let's switch gears, then, shall we? Tell me more about this supposed... *dinosaur* on our hands. An extraordinary claim, but unless my eyes have deceived me, there is frankly no other way to describe such a monster."

"Animal."

Aegis seemed tickled by this. Amused, toying with her. It occurred to her there was no real purpose to his line of questioning. He was trying to break her down. Get her to crack.

"Of course. An animal through and through," he said passively. "But people... *we* are the *real* monsters, right, Doctor Perez?"

She seethed in silence.

Aegis continued. "This *animal*..." His tone ebbed smoothly from jocosity to firm intent. "Tell me more about it." A soft demand spoken with the inflection of innocent inquiry.

"Everything is in my dictation."

"Oh, I have familiarized myself with your report. I am afraid it is a bit dry for my taste. There is little in the way of speculation."

"That is beyond the scope of my work."

"Humor me." There was the sense of a smile behind the glass. "I am dying to know where you think such an organism originated."

"I don't know."

"Oh, come. You must have considered the possibilities. Perhaps it was made?"

"No. I scrubbed its genome for artificial promoters. The specimen is a wild-type. There are no genetic markers suggesting it was modified or engineered."

"Yes. Yes. Well, you see, *you* know that, and *I* know that. But the board does not, nor do they want to. They just need a good spin for public relations. Plausible deniability, blah-blah, that sort of thing."

So much for transparency, she thought. But with the bureaucrats in Berlin, doublespeak was nothing new. A "request for transparency" meant "tell me what I'd like to hear." *They are a bunch of yes-men living in an echo chamber.*

The floor rumbled, this time swelling as if emerging from deep underground.

Aegis appeared to pull the hem of his sleeve. "And I rather like the rogue-experiment-by-mad-scientist angle," he droned. "Would make for compelling press, don't you think? Certainly more plausible than the thing just popping into existence, like some time-traveling T. rex. Now *there* is a story."

Perez bit her tongue. *Deltadromeus.* She didn't know where he was going with this or what it had to do with her.

"But I must attend to other matters," Aegis said. "I have so enjoyed making your acquaintance, Dr. Perez. It has been absolutely *rapturous.* Always a pleasure getting to know someone new, don't you agree?" He straightened again. "I have grown especially fond of Nedjma... she is quite taken by you. Fiercely protective, that one."

"Is she here? What did you do with her?"

"No need for concern. She is being questioned, just like you. No one is under arrest, Dr. Perez."

"Then let us get back to SANCTUM. I'm sure the board would not be happy that you are obstructing the recovery effort of one of their greatest investments."

He laughed, then sighed deeply, as if he had grown bored of the conversation. "All in good time, friend. You will be escorted to your examination momentarily. Good day, Dr. Perez."

And as suddenly as Aegis Galani had appeared, he was gone.

< ᚼ | BONE AND FLESH >

"Daddy?"

"Yeah, Ev?"

"How did you get your lines?"

"My lines?"

"*Ja. Das Aua.* On your arms."

"Oh, I got these because I was very sad."

"You got so sad that it gave you lines on your arms?"

"I gave them to myself, baby. I wish I never did, but I did."

"Are you still sad, Daddy?"

"No, Ev, I'm not sad anymore."

"But... but what if you *do* get sad?"

"I have you and your sisters and Mama to make me happy."

"But what if we are gone?"

"What do you mean?"

"What if... what if we *die* and you get so sad, and... and you fall into a hole, and it's *so* black and *so* sad... and you get *very* sad that you want to hurt yourself again?"

"Oh, baby, that isn't going to happen. I won't let anything bad happen to you or your sisters. Not ever."

"But *what if?* And if you get so, *so* sad again... What about *then?*"

"Even then."

"Do you promise?"

"I promise."

"I love you, Daddy."

"I love you too, Evi. My strong girl."

"Daddy?"

"Yeah?"

"Does it still hurt?"

"No, Hun, not anymore."

"*No more pain, Daddy?*"

"No more pain." >

Day 4, Midday — The Stream

Evi was Fischer's middle child.

From an early age, he could tell she was perceptive. An empath. She felt things with intensity, felt what others felt. "Sensitive" was how Jocelyn had described her.

It made sense that Evi had been the one to ask if the lines still hurt. Naturally, this transitioned into "healing" her Daddy's scars. Sometimes, she'd bind Fischer's wrists in colorful ribbons—her little hands moving delicately as if bandaging fresh wounds—or she'd decorate them with markers and glitter. And, after that passed, he sometimes still caught her glancing at his arms as if to make sure the wounds had not reopened. To make sure he had kept his promise.

Fischer didn't know why that thought popped into his head right as he submerged his torso into the ebbing stream. "No, not like *that*, Daddy. Like *this*." All ten of her fingers wrapped around his hand, leading his movements over his old scars. He remembered the sensation of the cool ink on uncorrupted skin—how all sensation faded as the tip crossed over cicatrix, where he had cut so deep that the nerve endings never regenerated. A strange sense of déjà vu had come over him, as if the water from the stream were imbibed with that distant memory, one that anchored him to this place in a way he did not understand.

Fischer had been in this place with these thoughts before.

The stink of ginkgo was strong along the embankment. Fischer heeded Lotta's advice and kept to shallow water, but he hadn't spotted any threats. No "things in the water," whatever that meant. Just clouds of gnats hovering above the surface and a strange, eel-like salamander with grubby arms and no legs that scurried away toward a dense stand of reeds.[1]

But no threats.

After Fischer cleaned off, he walked to where Lotta had hung his suit liner. He reached for it and slipped it over his aching limbs, past popping joints. It felt good to be in clean dress again. He never thought he'd feel that way toward his hack job with a suit liner, but it was the closest he'd come to feeling human in days. He rolled the left sleeve past the binding on his wounded arm, which he'd managed to keep dry, and his sense of mental quietude was cut short. A chill rippled upward between his shoulder blades.

No more pain, Daddy.

Fischer stumbled back to the fire. As he neared, a sweet, smoky aroma overtook him, the first time he had smelled anything in days. His mouth watered, teeth grinding together, eager to sink into fresh meat. *Real food.* But an uneasy thought overshadowed his newfound alacrity: If *he* could smell it, so could any animals, probably for three clicks in all directions.

Lotta was sitting by the fire, eyes glazed over, indifferent to Fischer's presence. The meat was skewered at the spear's tip, leaning at an angle over the flames. Fischer tilted his head and studied it. The once-feathered animal—its headless body plucked and dangling—was not a bird at all, but something akin to a small *Velociraptor*. It had a long tail, well-defined arms, distinct toe claws. The snake was splayed open and coiled in a bunch about the spear. An image of Basem's insides dangling from the mouth of a pterosaur flashed in Fischer's mind, and he looked away.

---

1 *Kababisha indet.* – a salamander of the family Sirenidae

Lotta eyed him as he approached. He had grown increasingly aware that she had maintained a minimum distance between them, and didn't know what to make of it. For the time being, he judged it best to give her space and wandered to the other side of the pit.

"Didn't think you'd be back on your feet anytime soon," Lotta said, returning a stolid gaze to the fire. She still clutched the knife in her swollen fingers, which struck Fischer as odd. He hadn't seen her without it since she returned. He gave a sigh.

"Aye."

Lotta reached with her free hand, gripped the spear, and turned it to rotate the meat. "You've got a leech on your hand," she said flatly.

Fischer looked down and shuddered. There it was—glistening and brown, balled up on a yellowing patch of bruised skin. He extended the thumb of his other hand and inserted the nail under the parasite's mouth, then sent it careening into the fire with a flick of his wrist. A high-pitched sizzle came from the pit and died down again. Fischer grunted and took a seat on the cool dirt.

Crack.

The sound rippled like distant gunfire through the trees, nearly sending Fischer tumbling backward. It was the same one that had woken him earlier. The moment it struck his ears, a blinding white light consumed his vision—a muzzle flash. Then he saw the dead Latvian kid from the warehouse—with the curls like Evi's—saw the pink plume blossoming from his skull as it burst like a melon. But before he could fall, he braced his good hand behind him and caught himself.

"The fuck was that?" Fischer barked, righting himself.

Lotta's eyes were on him, wide with surprise. A microexpression Fischer would have missed had he blinked, because in an instant, her face had returned to the cool indifference she had worn all afternoon. She didn't seem startled by the sound, but Fischer's reaction appeared to trigger a fresh round of nail-picking out of her. That was her tell.

"Not sure," she said, plucking rhythmically at the fingers gripping the knife handle, "but it's been going on for a couple days. Right around this time of day. Sometimes at dawn."

"*Days?*" The lump in Fischer's throat rose, and a sour taste crawled over his knotted tongue.

Lotta nodded. "You've been out for three days." She turned the spear over again. The meat had taken on a golden hue and was starting to bubble. She licked her peeling lips. "Dinner's almost ready."

She seemed to be avoiding any discussion over what had happened, why Fischer had apparently been comatose for days after sustaining a serious injury. Every look in his direction registered as almost analytical, and she only looked up when he shifted his weight or moved in any perceptible way. But it was the sparse conversation and the silence between words that had started to grate on Fischer. His only recourse, it seemed, was to change the subject for the time being. Or to shut up altogether.

He tried his hand at the former. "I'll chop some pine needles, make us some tea."

Lotta didn't speak. She glanced down at the blade in her bleeding fingers, then at Fischer. All afternoon, she had acted strange, as though waiting for him to say the right thing, like she was testing him. Only it felt like everything he said was something she didn't want to hear, and it frustrated him to no end.

Fischer sighed, raised his eyebrows. "Can I have the knife?"

Lotta looked down at it again. "I don't think that's a good idea."

"What?" He took a step forward. "Lotta, I'm trying to—"

Lotta jumped to her feet and raised the knife. "Stay... *back*." Her face contorted into a grimace, no longer emotionless and flat.

"*Whoa*." Fischer put his hands up. "What the bloody hell's got into you?"

"I said stay *back!*"

Lotta's eyes flared, glimmering in the firelight, and behind them, Fischer saw fear. Fear toward *him*.

"Okay, let's just... take it easy—" He took a few steps back. "I'm backing up, okay? Tell me what's going on."

"You're *not* getting this fucking knife back just so you can open up your other wrist, *that's* what's 'going on.'"

"I—*what?*" Fischer was stunned. He looked down at his arm. It throbbed to the beat of his pulse.

Lotta's voice trembled. "You did it to yourself, Ed. I saw you do it." Her eyes stayed locked on him, cagey in their expression. "And now, you're acting like it never happened. You're scaring me."

Fischer could not believe what he was hearing. *"I... did this?"* He wavered as the weight of the world bore down on him. Knees swaying, he imagined himself crumpling into a heap like that dead Latvian kid.

Lotta's shoulders dropped. "Yes."

Her feet pointed away from him, toward the stream. She was ready to run, and any desire Fischer might have had to go after her abruptly faded, because he couldn't blame her.

He stared at his arm again and shook his head. It throbbed heavily at his side. "No."

Lotta's voice softened. Wavered. "You did."

Fischer shook his head. Thought he might vomit.

Then he remembered, as if recalling a forgotten dream. Pieces of it had come to him when he cleaned off in the stream, kneeling in the cold water as it gushed and spluttered over his legs, his bruised skin. Memories of Evi.

But now, it all came back in vivid relief, a darkness consuming Fischer from within. He recalled the numbness in his legs as he gazed across the far bank, the same place he'd seen the girls only moments before, except now, it was Jocelyn gaping back at him, her pupils aglow with the murky, opalescent sheen of rapacious intent. She stood there in her white gown, legs blackened with mud. Watched with those glowing, animalistic eyes.

And then Fischer sensed something colder than water, a delicate touch. Dared not look down at the little hand that had come to rest on his. But he didn't pull back. Allowed the cold fingertips to move over his skin while tears slid down his cheeks. Drew a sharp breath when he heard his little girl speak. A child's whisper through papery lips.

Come be with us, Daddy. We are one.

"Evi." Her name had fallen from his driveling mouth.

He became aware of his grip tightening around the knife handle. But still, he did not look. Only gaped in abject horror across the water at Jocelyn's bestial gaze, her eyes glowing and carnal. Insatiable. Complied with the cold little hand guiding the blade to his upturned wrist.

Cold steel pressed against his skin.

No more pain, Daddy.

But that was just a dream.

"Lotta, I don't—" Without thinking, Fischer stepped forward again.

Lotta backed away, raising the knife higher so it was level with his face. Blood oozed from her raw fingertips. "Don't come any closer, Ed."

"I didn't mean to—to scare you." He turned his injured arm inward and inspected it, probed the sticky dressing, then returned a glassy stare. "Lotta, *I swear to God,* I don't remember a thing about this. If you only knew… What I-I've lost… what I've *done. I promised* I would never…."

"Promised you would never *what?*"

"I promised I would never do it again."

"The scars." Lotta's face went white, watching Fischer as he nodded. "You've done it before. Who did you promise?"

Fischer nodded. Hesitated with his daughter's name hanging reluctantly on his lips. As if saying it aloud was like watching her die all over again. "Evi. My…" He stopped short, his voice rising and trembling as he attempted to suppress the mounting emotion rising within.

Lotta seemed to notice his struggle and slowly lowered the knife. "Your daughter."

Fischer nodded. Swallowed hard. "Evi."

Lotta stayed silent. Fischer was looking again at his trembling hands, at the bloodied binding around his wrist. A stabbing pain pulsed up his shoulder, caused the breath to seize up in his throat, and it angered him. Melancholy transformed into self-loathing, a sensation that bled through him like cold ink, mummified him in soft ribbon.

"*And you know what?*" he growled with wincing eyes. "There were times I bloody *wanted* to. Times I came close, when the pain was *so* unbearable and holding that promise was so *fucking* hard. And I *hated* myself for making that goddamned vow to Evi. *Oh, I hated myself.*" His voice rose, and he felt like he was outside of himself. "Do you know what it's like to lose a kid? To lose three?" Fischer's voice wavered again, lowered to a near-whisper. "I wanted to die… wanted to end it *so many* fucking *times* after… after they…." He swallowed against the lump in his throat. But it continued to swell until each breath required tremendous effort.

Lotta started crying.

"Ed, tell me what happened to you…" Her voice had become a hoarse whisper. "What happened back there with Hassan?"

Fischer's vision blurred, his eyes brimming, his chest on fire. He avoided eye contact because he knew that if his eyes met hers, he'd lose it. He wanted to tell her everything and nothing at all. Struggled against an unseen force that kept him there, tortured in perdition, mired in the deafening silence of his personal hell. Whether by obstinance or fear.

Or cowardice.

"I—" he began, then clenched his teeth. Shaking his head, he watched himself try to form a weak fist. "I can't. I *can't.*" His mouth felt cottony and tasted of brine. He attempted to clear his throat. "It's just withdrawals. Haven't had a drink in days. I keep seeing things that… that aren't there."

"Maybe. Maybe not. *Tell me* what you saw."

"He… *showed* me."

"Showed you?"

Fischer nodded. "Showed me how they…" His head fell as he raised a tremulant hand over his eyes. An onslaught of emotion bubbled to the surface again, impeding his efforts to maintain his composure. "When I thought it was over, when I told him to… to *stop*… he made me see—made me *feel* it—*from their eyes.* Each one of my girls in their final moments. *I felt what they felt. Saw what they saw.* Evi and Ellsa… they went almost immediately, *but Emma….*"

The words poured out of Fischer now. He knew there was no use fighting it anymore. His voice rose, his speech slurring, almost unintelligible. But he couldn't stop.

"She'd been trapped for days. Her little *legs… crushed. My little girl.* She knew I was looking for her. She heard me… heard me calling at the surface, but her voice wouldn't carry. Then, the… the shifting debris under the search teams passing overhead, showering down the void on top of her. Buried her alive. And she called for me. Called until she couldn't anymore. Until the dust filled her lungs." Fischer shook his head. "Three years old."

Anger washed over him again. "And how many times had I walked over that spot without care? How many *fucking* times?

"Her voice… it was in my head… *No.* I was… in *her* head. *I was her.* And it was like she knew I was there because she spoke *to* me. *'No more pain,'* she said. *'No more pain, Daddy.'* And it was like she *knew.* She knew Hassan would show me. And Evi had said the same words years before, the same day I made that *stupid* fucking promise that if anything—*oh, God*—if anything ever happened to them, that I wouldn't...." Fischer presented his bandaged arm, his face twisting in self-disgust, then let it fall into his lap. He squeezed his eyes as tight as he could. "I don't know how, but she knew, too. They both *knew*. And when the building came down, and the *pain*. My God, I *felt* it all. And then nothing. Emptiness."

Fischer became aware that dusk had fallen. Time had slipped away. The moon was full, outlining the treetops in a soft white glow. He stared into his lap for a time as tears carved cool trails into his grime-ridden cheeks. It seemed the entire weight of his body had converged behind his eyes to form cracks in his crumbling façade.

"How did it happen?" Lotta said, her voice low and solemn.

Without looking up, Fischer mumbled, "Geneva." He heard a sharp intake of air from Lotta, and nothing more.

They sat in silence for a while.

Then somewhere along the bank, stones clattered, tumbling into the water with a great *splash*.

Fischer snapped his head toward the sound, peering out past silhouetted tree trunks into the shadows of the blue hour. His pulse tore through his neck and ravaged his ears, eyes pulsing as they strained through the blackened underbrush for any sign of movement.

"What was that?" Lotta whispered, her face white with panic.

Fischer raised a finger to his lips and strained his ears into the gloam. Lotta's breathing quickened, her chest rising and falling in his periphery.

They waited for what must have been close to an hour, but the only other sound was the drone of reed frogs signaling the day's transition into night.

Fischer relaxed his shoulders; his body untensed. Lotta followed his lead. They gazed into the fire. Lotta turned the meat again. It was overcooked, but Fischer held his tongue. Allowed her this moment.

Fischer felt content sitting in silence after all that had been said. But Lotta seemed eager to pick up the conversation again, an abrupt change in policy for her, given her demeanor over the preceding hours. Just her way of coping, he supposed. Of putting their situation out of her mind a little longer. An escape.

"Your daughters. They sound lovely," Lotta whispered.

"Aye." Fischer bit the inside of his lip and nodded. "They were."

The taste of blood touched his tongue.

He willed himself to look up at Lotta again, only for his gaze to divert to a pair of glinting, pale eyes shifting just beyond the firelight. He scrambled backward in the dirt and shot to his feet. They were the same eyes that had watched him at the stream, pink and glowing, only they weren't Jocelyn's this time. Amid Fischer's shock, he thought he could just about make out the ghostly snout and dangling jowls of the thing that had confronted them after they had stumbled on Hassan.

And now, it had stalked into their camp undetected.

Lotta jumped up and turned to see what Fischer had reacted to. She bumped the spear, sending the meat into the fire. The flames erupted, flaring almost white as the heat swelled.

To Fischer's shock, the glowing eyes receded, and the reptilian maw recoiled silently. A pale shape turned away and faded like a specter into the night.

"What is it? What did you see?" Lotta shrieked, backing toward Fischer with the knife drawn and aimed at the blackened verdure.

But Björn was gone.

For me a shrine of stones he made,
And now to glass the rock has grown…
— POETIC EDDA

< ᚽ | BLÓT >

Seventy-five thousand and twenty-five.

The number cycled through Lotta's mind as she rotated a bit of charred serpent in her hands. She and Fischer had managed to salvage some of the meat after the close call with Björn. At first, she had thought Fischer was seeing things again. Another suicidal fugue—a notion that mortified her more than the footprints they had discovered afterward. But even in the chaos of the moment, she had known, had heard the cairn fall. Knew that something was out there and that *something* was a predator that had crossed their path on at least three occasions, and whose footprints had stopped and turned mere meters from where she still sat.

And despite the hard evidence corroborating Fischer's account, she could not fully break her suspicion that he was a present danger to them both. He now slept soundly beside her. He had earlier insisted on keeping watch the entire night, but she would not allow it. She didn't trust him. Not yet.

But she listened when he said to keep the fire hot, that it seemed to spook the creature. Standing just over head height to Fischer, Björn couldn't take them both so long as they stuck together.

She chewed off a leathery wad of meat and tossed it over until her jaw stiffened, then pushed it back with her tongue. It was dry, went down slow. What had remained of the raptor—a bit of charred leg, the tail, half the heart and liver—had done little to satiate her nagging hunger. It would have made for the first substantive meal in days. Snake meat, on the other hand, left something to be desired. It was stringy and flavorless, though it did at least take the edge off her ceaseless hunger. She threw more wood on the fire and angled her bleary eyes to the canopy, where cobalt shards of the blue hour glimmered through the gently swaying conifers. Her body swayed with them as the warmth of sleep threatened to sabotage her watch, even as she sat in this strange wilderness under threat from a stalking beast of prey.

Lotta studied Fischer's knife in her hand. Wondered silently whether she could take on Björn by herself if it came to that. Her eyes grew heavy.

A chorus of arboreal chirrups shook her back to attention. She yawned deeply, shook it off. Soon it would be day, and they would set out for a more secure location.

Her thoughts trailed again.

At the forefront was Geneva and its aftermath, which had increasingly filtered into her head after Fischer had opened up about his family. *Three girls.* Lotta struggled to fathom what that might be like, to lose a kid. To lose *three.* Or fifty thousand. To lose anyone at all.

She knew several colleagues who had lost loved ones in Geneva. But she didn't have anyone. She convinced herself that it had made things easier, insulated her from reliving disappointment after disappointment, simplified the move to Algeria. No relationship to maintain, no compromises. Her work, her objectivity—everything she had ever achieved—came with sacrifices, and a life of solitude was a natural byproduct. One that shielded her from something as horrible as losing someone. She was okay with that because she had come to find that people were unreliable and, more often than not, represented obstacles to be overcome.

Seventy-five thousand and twenty-five.

The first shockwaves of the Geneva quake had taken the first nine thousand lives, eradicating the Swiss municipalities of Meyrin and Col-lex-Bossy. In France, Chevry, Segny, Ornex, and Prévessin-Moëns were reduced to rubble, and to the south, Annemasse, Archamps, and Saint-Julien-en-Genevois suffered mass casualties. To the east roared a wall of water from Lake Geneva that swallowed the historic French communes of Thonon-les-Baines and Evian.

But Geneva was the epicenter.

Seventy-five thousand and twenty-five.

Fischer could never know. Lotta shuddered to think what he might do if he found out the truth—that she was complicit, that it had all been covered up long before his involvement in the project. A conspiracy that most CEPP employees were unaware of. One that had destroyed his life and the lives of countless other Europeans.

In the days and weeks that followed the quake, Lotta's team had been transferred to Luxembourg as part of an investigation by the European Court of Justice. The final day of the hearings had always stayed with her. That was when her nail-picking started again.

It was late morning in December. The court had called a recess, and she had found herself slipping quietly into a darkened conference room, where she waited for the hour hand on her watch to strike ten. On cue, she heard a soft click, and Aegis Galani slithered in through the cracked door.

His hair was graying, slicked back with an almost metallic sheen. He was tall and thin, clad in a pressed gray suit with a red tie that brought out the green in his intense, deep-set eyes. Galani had always gone heavy-handed with the cologne. Lotta remembered it well—cedar notes with a hint of citrus—and she found it repulsive.

"We have a few minutes" were his first words. Not *hi, how are you?* Not *everything is going to be okay.* The mask was off. He had dropped the act of feigning concern for anyone but himself.

A pit had dredged itself in Lotta's chest. She remembered that, too, the feeling conjured within her during their encounter. A void approaching critical mass deep inside her, its gravity drawing her folded arms across her chest.

"What's this about, Aegis?"

"Right to business, eh?" Aegis acted disappointed, and for a second at least, the mask was back on. "I'll be brief. I have received an offer for a position at the Commission. They want me to run operations at EIRO, help us rebrand so we can climb out of this mess."

"You're jumping ship?" Heat roiled Lotta's face. "And leaving Bogdan and me to pick up the pieces?"

"I will still be aiding the project, indirectly, of course… canvassing, molding public opinion, that sort of thing. You will be better-positioned if I am pulling strings over in Berlin. It's a *win-win*, Eklund. A 'slam-dunk,' as our American friends might say. Besides, old friend, I am always a phone call away."

"You're expecting me to take the heat for this? Is that it?"

"You're quite good with that, you know. The histrionics. But you can relax. We made a deal with the court. The case is going under seal at the behest of the Commission." He shook his sleeves and shoved his hands into his pockets, moving in closer, his voice lowering. "I want you to take over as Principal Investigator when the operation relocates to Algeria. We have restructured. As of today, CERN is now CEPP—the Commission of European Particle Physics. The French are miffed about the name change, but it falls in line with the Federation's English mandate. Long overdue, if you ask me."

"Algeria?" Lotta had snorted. "It's a refugee holding zone. Why are they sending us there?"

"Oh, you know, the politics of it all. More secrecy. Less regulations. We will build a much larger accelerator out of the public eye. You will love it, dear friend. Our friends at SANCTUM have already established their new venture in the region."

"They're building sanctuaries there, too?"

He gave a silent nod, his eyes flashing with excitement. "Algeria is the new frontier. It will be the *Mecca of science*."

"Seventy-five thousand people are *dead*, Aegis." She had chewed her tongue and run a hand across the nape of her neck. Anything to resist the urge to pick. "I'm thinking of going into the private sector."

Aegis procured a broad grin and removed his hands from his pockets, folding his arms to mirror her. "Of *course* you are." His tone was patronizing, his grin unwavering. "And after the dust has settled, after the vigils and the protests have ceased, I am sure they will accept you with open arms. *Thousands* dead—as you say—and in the court of public opinion, all that blood will still be running through your chapped little fingers." He glanced down at Lotta's balled fists, his eyes narrowing as they returned to hers. "Hardly a good look for prospective employers."

Lotta seethed in the silence between words. "And Bogdan? He's wanted your job for years."

"Dr. Kazimierz will stay on, but he is no *leader*. You are."

"Kozlowski wants to go on the record."

"You need not concern yourself with Ofiara. I have many friends at the Commission, many friends."

Lotta's throat seized. "What is that supposed to mean?"

"Nothing at all. Merely that she has been *handled*."

"Tell me what you did…" She had begun to raise her voice. "Or I walk."

Galani raised an arm and glanced at his watch. "You won't do that, my friend. You are like me. You are a survivor. And out there, they will eat you alive."

"I'm nothing like you. Tell me where the *fuck* she is, Aegis."

"Do keep your voice *down*." His eyes darted toward the door and then back to her. "If you must know, she was transferred to France for processing. The French wanted someone's head, and we gave it to them. In exchange, the Commission has allayed the ECJ. They are calling off this petty charade."

"You *set her up?*"

"Careful, Eklund. She is an enemy of the Federation. She will answer for her malfeasance."

"For what? Telling the truth?"

Lotta recalled the shadow that had fallen over him, and through it burned those green eyes. "I said *careful*." With that, his lips had restored their wry smirk, and his perfectly symmetric eyebrows pulled into arches. He would have appeared almost pleasant to the unsuspecting recipient of his regard were it not for what came next. "I would hate for you to find yourself in a gaol block next to her. You have an extraordinary opportunity before you. Take it and *move the fuck on*."

Galani rarely swore. It had jarred Lotta. Frightened her enough to understand the threat was not an idle one. But as always, her defiance found its way into the open.

"You're a snake."

"We both are, old friend." Galani's smile stayed with Lotta through the years, as did what he said next. "Far better to be the snake than the mouse."

Daylight fell, and the canopy bloomed gold.

I am a snake.

Lotta considered that perhaps this primeval hellscape was her reckoning...

Seventy-five thousand and twenty-five.

...her recompense.

She took up Fischer's knife, cut away a lock of her hair, and then held it over the fire in a tight fist. "Freyja..." she whispered. Her fingers throbbed with her quickening pulse. Blót felt strange, unnatural. Alien. She was out of practice. Could hear her mother's jabbing commands to kneel, to give her offering.

Dappled sunlight filtered into her eyes.

A sign?

She rotated forward so her knees pressed into the tepid dirt at the fire pit's edge, the skin of her hand uncomfortably warm over the dying flame.

"Freyja...." The hair on her arm started to singe. With eyes squeezed tight, she continued through clenched teeth. "Accept this offering of atonement—"

Fischer stirred beside her. Startled, she let the lock fall and rolled back into a sitting position, her heart in her throat. Pain pulsed deep in the fingers of her left hand, and she realized she had gone for the knife, gripping it so that her knuckles blanched white. She looked at Fischer. He breathed heavily, his eyes rolling beneath sallow lids.

Another twenty minutes passed before Fischer rubbed the sleep from his eyes and, with a moan and a stretch, propped himself upright.

"Oy," he said. "See anything?"

"Morning." Lotta's heart slowed a little, and she let up on the knife handle. "No, nothing. Whatever you saw is gone."

"You know what I saw." He nodded toward the fresh set of tracks.

She didn't feel like arguing.

"That time I saw it," Lotta conceded, "it reminded me of Basem's rabbits, the way its head... *wobbled.*"

"Aye, I thought so, too. Explains the aversion to light. Our friend might be an albino."

Fischer's working hypothesis was that Björn stuck to the shadows and was primarily active at night. This corollary gave Lotta a sense of security, of power. A sliver of control to cling to. Each time it was mentioned, said aloud, affirmed, it became truer in her mind. So, with daylight on them, they would set out for greener pastures.

Fischer yawned and reached for the picked-over snake. "Such an odd thing," he said, "a snake with legs." He pointed to the small, almost non-existent hindlimbs. They had withered into charred stalks. "You want one?"

"All you," Lotta said.

She had a hard enough time keeping the other parts down, but Fischer didn't appear to mind the taste. Given that he didn't share her misgivings about cambium, she was not wholly surprised. She watched him pinch one of the charred limbs. It came free with a muffled *click*, and he tossed it into his mouth. The crunching sound was almost too much for Lotta to bear.

"Not bad," Fischer grunted before attacking the second leg and chasing it with a noisy swig of water. He wiped a hand over his mouth and peered through the trees. By now, the chirping had swelled to a high-pitched cacophony of squawks and warbles that welcomed the rising sun. He got to his feet. "We better move." His gaze fell on the knife in Lotta's hand, then leveled with hers. Alarm jolted her senses.

"How're the fingers?" he said.

"Fine," she said in as measured a tone as she could manage, though the petulant vocalization she emitted negated this intent.

The reality was that things hadn't improved since Fischer first treated her. Every morning, her fingertips would be swollen and red, and the pain had become constant. Over the last couple of days, her cuticles bled erratically and with increasing frequency.

Fischer sighed. "Let me see."

"I *said* I'm *fine*."

Fischer frowned, then turned and quietly wandered to the stream's edge with one of the POG canisters. He knelt and dipped it into the water, then turned back, stopping at the ginkgo and picking something off the ground. He dropped it into the canister, then returned to the fire.

Without speaking, he moved past Lotta, placed the concoction on the heating stone and blew on the embers. Once the water boiled, he donned one of his gloves, pulled it off, and tilted it over the empty POG casing.

"This is tannin," he said as he carefully poured the amber liquid. "Full of polyphenols that are both antimicrobial and anti-inflammatory. Also works as a hand cleaner, toothpaste, deodorant. Dip your hands in for a bit before we make tracks. I'll gather our things."

Threads of steam rose from it. Lotta's stomach turned at the smell.

"No, thank you. It's rancid and looks like piss." She leered down at the ginkgo nuts bobbing in the yellow-tinged water with pursed lips. Half of her was genuinely disgusted. The other half didn't want to release the knife still in her grip. Fischer took a few steps back.

"Don't be stubborn," he grunted.

She looked up at him reluctantly, then eased her hands into the concoction. It was still hot, but not scalding. The stench invaded her senses and sat heavily on her tongue. At first, her fingers tingled, then burned with an intensity that made her wince.

"God, this *burns*. And it smells like shit."

"Aye, you'll be quite the stinkend[1] by the end of it."

A smile began percolating on Lotta's lips, but she stifled it before it could surface. It mattered little, as Fischer turned away without expression and got to work packing up and gathering supplies.

An hour had passed when he returned to check on her.

"We're about ready." He loomed over a pile at his feet with an air of accomplishment. He'd salvaged the POG's molecular adsorbers, which they could use for water filtration. They were housed in one of the two canisters, with the second filled with fresh water. Cambium, dried snake jerky, the bow drill, and Fischer's gloves rounded out their provisions.

His gaze fell on Lotta's hands. "How's the pain?"

Like hot knives driving into my bones, what do you think?

She drew breath and forced a half-grin. "Better," she said.

Her attention was drawn to something in Fischer's hand—a fungal disc. By the time she managed to look away, it was too late. An image

---

1 *Stinkend* (German slang)—smelly

of Hassan's flayed face covered in pink fruiting bodies flashed before her, followed by the pulsing hive gorging on Anderson's remains, the same rounded growths framing its margins. And the tooth, falling in slow motion from the throbbing, wet fetor.

Thud.

"Oy, you good?"

Lotta shot Fischer a look and shook her hands dry. "I'm fine." She remained stolid, keeping her eyes off his hand. "What's with the toadstool?"

Fischer glanced down. "Fire carrier. Unless you want to be the one running the bow drill next."

Before they smothered the flames, Fischer mixed a tarry black paste with the remaining resin and ash. "Pitch," he said, glomming it on the end of a stick. "More pliable, longer-lasting than straight resin." He motioned for Lotta to hold out her hands. She acquiesced.

Once she was patched up, she rose to her feet, knife back in hand. Fischer did not ask for it back.

"I'll lead the way," she said.

Fischer raised a hand in protest. His voice swelled. "Oy, hold up 'fore we go running off-piste again."

"I know the route. There's a clearing around a click out. We'll stick to the stream where the most sunlight comes through."

Fischer remained quiet, ponderous. He looked at her with narrowed eyes, chewing his lower lip scrupulously. He gave a heavy sigh and relented with a nod. "Let's go."

Coming up on Lotta's first cairn, the source of the sound from the night before, confirmed her suspicions. The stones lay scattered in the water, a set of tracks leading from them toward the camp. Fischer pointed to the far bank toward another set of tracks leading into the water.

"Bastard crossed from over there."

It was the same spot he had stared at when Lotta found him in his fugue state, bleeding on his knees in the rushing water. Fischer seemed unaware of this as he surveyed the scene. Lotta said nothing.

He kneeled to inspect one of the prints. The weighty depressions—around the length of his forearm—resembled those of a large bird with three deep claw markings. A round hole by the inside ankle indicated a fourth hanging digit, possibly higher up on the leg, which had punched into the mud as the animal walked.

Fischer narrowed his eyes and smelled the air. "Bastard's not far."

"Seems he never is." Lotta's flesh crawled.

Somewhere behind them, deeper into the forest, came a loud *crack* and the sound of a tree crashing to the ground. Lotta spun around and saw Fischer had done the same.

"The fuck was *that?*" she hissed, only to be met with Fischer's hand waving for her to stay quiet.

He looked back again, his eyes wide. Lotta strained through the sound of trickling water, but only heard her heart pounding in her head.

"*Let's go,*" Fischer whispered. "*Quick but quiet.*"

Except she couldn't hear him for her pounding pulse, the swelling tinnitus in her ears.

A familiar rumble found her through the verdure. It vibrated the boughs and tangled bracken. She could almost see it in the air—a shimmering, disembodied vocalization that penetrated everything in its path. It burrowed into flesh, nuzzled past organs, and tunneled up the spinal column to take root in the limbic system. A parasite dictating every bodily function, setting every synapse ablaze. *Flight.* Electricity hummed through her limbs, and the hairs rose from the skin on her neck. She saw herself back inside the nurse log with its slimy walls, listening to the wet, snapping jaws devouring what had remained of Anderson, the swelling lungs of something enormous and inconceivable and horrible.

The only thought in her mind was *survival…*

…and that perhaps she *was* the mouse after all.

June 16, 2147, [time unknown] — ███████████████
██████████████████████████████████
████████████████ – United European Federation (UEF)

|OZ >

Smooth walls. Featureless door. Everything bolted down.

Perez had paced the small room too many times to count, scrutinizing every edge, every surface. Logically, she knew strategizing her escape was pointless. She hadn't spotted any cameras, but surveillance was a certainty—possibly by Jacobs himself. Her stomach turned. The cramps and nausea had killed her appetite over the intervening hours, but hunger had finally stolen over her. She stopped pacing and eyed the service slot, the tray of food resting quietly behind its plexiglass panel.

She walked over and took the tray—*No utensils. Shit.* She carried it into the latrine, where she dumped the dull gray paste into the toilet. Bearing her full weight, both hands gripping either side, she pressed its middle against the metal rim of the toilet bowl. Held her breath and pushed with everything she had, but the tray barely flexed. *Carbon fiber. Of course.* She threw it forcefully against the wall and sat on the cold floor, her back against the partition, panting with her head in her hands. Even if she'd succeeded in shattering it, she had no plan. Maybe she'd attack her escort with a broken-off shard on the way to her medical examination. Make a break for it.

And go where?

She heard footfalls approaching and rose to her feet. Someone stopped at the chamber entrance and activated the comm.

"Face the wall opposite the door, hands where I can see them, your back to me." French brogue. Deep voice. Oz.

"*You* stay the *fuck* away from me," Perez spat. Fear clawed its way up her throat, sank its hooks into the back of her tongue. She tried to swallow, but only managed to ball her tongue to the roof of her mouth. The image of Oz aiming his rifle at her sent fire through her veins anew. It was the first time she'd been held at gunpoint. She had grown accustomed to firearms from a young age, after the authorities had taken Uncle Diego to the gaols. She remembered the times they came to her home to question her family. They had always carried guns. Big ones. But not once had they pointed them at her or her parents.

The door opened, and the broad-shouldered Oz strode in heavily with his rifle drawn, muzzle aimed at the floor. He wore the same uniform he had worn in the containment zone aboard the Goliath, his steely-eyed gaze piercing the dim cell from behind a clear visor. He walked to where Perez stood, racked his weapon to his barreled chest, then pushed her against the wall with a calm ease that shocked more than frightened her.

"Hard way it is," he said in a tone devoid of humanity.

Perez recoiled in his grip, but his fingers formed vices around her arms. He pulled her wrists together behind her back, and a metallic chill encircled them with a soft *click*. She tried to pry the restraints apart, but they held.

Oz gripped her bicep—a little less aggressive this time—turned her around, and guided her to the door. "Let's go."

"Real fucking *man*," Perez jeered. She wrenched her arm again, but Oz held firm. "What, no bag over my head?"

Oz didn't respond.

"I don't consent to a medical evaluation. You hear me, *imbécil?* I'm not going to cooperate. *Que os den por saco.*"

He led her into the corridor, which she found was not really a corridor, but a translucent tunnel like the one that had led to the necropsy suite aboard the Goliath. Lining either side were pearlescent modular containers, their frosted doors labeled with numbers. *004, 006, 008....*

More isolation chambers—prison cells—like hers.

The tunnel was illuminated with white light from above, obscuring much of the view outside. Perez squinted, her vision adapting to the brightness. All she could see was the helical white frame of the collapsible piping spiraling hypnotically before her and its tenement of cell doors.

Galani's voice echoed in her mind. *We are the* real *monsters.* She wanted to spit, as if the very thought of him filled her mouth with poison. Rid herself of the question that had been on her mind since he "stopped by," about what he had meant.

She tugged against Oz's grip as if it achieved anything more than tiring herself. "Tell me where the others are."

Again, he gave no response.

"Basem! Basem, I'm—"

Oz gave her a shake. "Wouldn't do that."

That got a rise out of the fuck.

"Or what? You'll *shoot* me?"

They continued to a fork in the tunnel. At its intersection, an armed guard stood in front of the entrance of a larger structure. This building had no number, no label. Oz and the soldier exchanged a nod, and he guided Perez to the right of the split.

The ground started to vibrate like before. The sensation grew. Perez glanced around and heard a familiar voice in the distance beyond the tunnel's thin walls.

"*—lift is active. For your safety, please clear the loading zone.*"

Athena.

The sensation grew, a tremor that moved through her. A high-pitched alarm blared outside, and a pulsing red light bathed the tunnel in a bloody glow.

Oz nudged her down the spiral to another room-sized cube. He tapped his badge and opened the door into a small decon chamber. He opened a bin recessed in the wall, tore open a bag containing a polyisoprene suit, then removed Perez's restraints and handed it to her.

"Put this on," he said.

"No."

"Alright." He turned with stony indifference and tapped his badge on a small display by the door. "They run the sterilizing reagent at around eighty degrees Celsius. Hot enough to scald. You have just under ten seconds before those shower heads come on."

Perez's heart shot into her throat. She tore the suit from Oz and donned it just as the showers sputtered overhead. She cast daggers at his shimmering bulk until the showers stopped.

Oz closed the restraints around her wrists again and turned her toward a second door. The badge reader beeped. The door opened.

Oz shoved her. "Walk."

The decon chamber opened into a vast open structure resembling an enormous hangar or warehouse, its ceiling lined with struts from which a monstrous gantry dangled. Lines of armed personnel jogged past as if on their way to a conflict zone, their boots drumming in unison. Perez looked around past dozens of light towers forming a perimeter around a sea of modular structures and tents. The place looked like a large military outpost that sprawled like a small city at the foot of a giant bay door towering four—maybe five—stories high.

Oz guided her through rows of tents along the outskirts of the base. Bits of conversations rose and fell as they passed.

A shudder moved up through the floor, then a deafening screech nearly drowned out the alarm: metal grating against metal. It came from the direction of the pulsing lights, where the scaffolding of a towering pylon loomed—some type of communications relay?—surrounded by hovering construction drones aligning large girders along its growing apex.

The rest of Perez's view was blocked by a rounded, burlap-clad truss hangar surrounded by fencing and razor wire. It was open-ended, with crates and storage containers stacked beside columns of pallets and collapsed tubing along its exterior. As Oz moved her along, Perez saw rovers and military vehicles parked beneath the arch of its honeycombed scaffolding. The interior throbbed red.

Once they rounded the structure, the source of the blinking lights materialized through the opposite opening. She had a clear, but fleeting view of what appeared to be an enormous square chasm surrounded by a tall gate with flashing red lights. Various personnel—some in military fatigues, some in hazmat gear, others in streetwear or lab coats—dashed about its outskirts. Overhead, armed figures paced like toy soldiers on elevated catwalks that straddled the gate on three sides. Their lofty positions afforded them a unique perspective, allowing them to steal intermittent glances into the screeching pit as they patrolled. Although the area appeared far-off, the opening was too large to see in its entirety from Perez's vantage point.

Then, Perez saw something climb out from the depths of the yawning blackness—a boxy protuberance that resembled the top of a large building. It crept upward, and Perez realized it *was* a building—one of several—standing nearly three stories high. She saw the bobbing heads of personnel in yellow hazmat suits emerge, then torsos and legs. They shuffled across a platform the size of a city block, the floor of which was the last thing to the surface, sealing off the pit with a ground-shaking jolt. The entire scene was like a bustling post-apocalyptic town square constructed atop a gargantuan lift that led deep underground.

The pulsing red lights ceased, and the perimeter gate retracted into the floor. A brief silence came and went. A vehicle loaded with clear containers carrying what appeared to be exotic vegetation drove off the platform toward the far end of the base. Synths and loading mechs began to board, moving heavy containers from a staging area beneath a burlap canopy near the center of the lift. A group of spectators in white coats emerged from a nearby building and erupted into cheers.

And beyond it all, in the shadow of the pylon and its drones, loomed the Goliath. The one that housed Eve. It had to be. Its ashen fuselage towered over the commotion, the insectoid cockpit surrounded by staging and service lifts populated by workers in hazmat gear. They were easily dwarfed against its hulking form.

A translucent screen cut her view. Her attention turned straight ahead again, and she realized Oz was moving her through another dizzying tunnel. It twisted almost ninety degrees to the right and again to the left. After the second turn, a long stretch of path lighting led to a large red rectangle. *A door?* Like a slow, steady death march, they drew closer to it. Oz placed his badge on the reader.

Perez prepared herself. Thought again of escape. She pondered potential weapons that might be found in an examination room. *Needles. Scissors. Blunt objects.* Ideally, she could menace the doctor with something sharp, then turn it on Oz if needed. *And then what?* She'd find a window of opportunity in the commotion. Make a run for it. *To where?* Anywhere. *You won't get far. Besides, your hands are bound. And Oz has a gun.*

A tingling sensation worked its way up the nape of her neck. Her vision narrowed, the sound of her breath rebounding off her face shield. She had detached from herself, from Ruth. Felt numb. The image of Basem staring, naked, at the open air appeared behind her eyes—the sight of him clawing at his chest, of Kohen burying the butt of her rifle into his back—and for a split second, she felt something. Fear or anger or grief. She didn't know what exactly, but it was something.

The door slid open, and a shaft of dim light spilled into the tunnel. Puzzlement and shock infused Perez as Oz moved her into a light breeze that rapped the shell of her suit.

They were *outside*.

She found herself gazing across an ad hoc airfield where rows of military craft and drones sat idly inside open-ended truss hangars constructed over groomed desert. More modular buildings glowed dully beneath conoids of artificial light, and a perimeter fence adorned with razor wire stretched as far as she could see in either direction. Beyond it, banks of pushed earth gave way to silver-lined dunes stretching toward a distant mountain range crested by a bloody sun. The breeze was picking up.

Storm coming.

Perez glanced back the way they came, sunspots fleeting across her face shield, toward the building they had walked out of. It was a monolithic structure, looming high overhead, its smooth exterior rimmed with harsh light. Her eyes fell on a familiar mark stamped in white and gray across the gargantuan bay door:

A jolt went through her.

"*We're at the Higgs. Something* did *happen here. Lotta Eklund, she lied… she—*"

"Enough," Oz said, nudging her forward. "Let's go."

"Tell me where you're taking me."

Oz tightened his grip, sending shooting pains up her arm, as he led her to the nearest hangar. An autonomous tug ferried a large aircraft out into the waning sunlight. The same type of machine that had intercepted her and Basem at the apiary. Its black fuselage came to rest, cutting a hole against the desert backdrop like an obsidian bird of prey. Behind its tandem rotors jutted a T-shaped tail-wing with a gray azimuthal UEF globe on its side. Below it read *SB1 DEFIANT* in the same shade of gray.

As they neared the *Defiant*, the tug detached from its nose and whirred toward the hangar. Oz led Perez past a missile bay along the craft's starboard flank. They continued beneath the shadow of one of its enormous disc-shaped rotors toward a rear hatch. It lowered into a ramp leading into the cabin.

Another wave of pain shot up Perez's bicep.

"You're *hurting* me." She tugged her arm and tried to pull away, but Oz was too strong. "Let me go!"

"Keep your voice down." He gave her a shake, but loosened his grip a little. "If you want to leave here alive, I suggest you do what I tell you. Now *move*."

Oz was dragging her now, her feet trawling behind her through the groomed sand. He practically carried her up the platform into the dark interior of the cabin, then threw her into a row of collapsible webbed seats lining one of the side walls. The impact drove the air from her lungs.

Perez pulled at her restraints, then tried to stand, but Oz shoved her back down.

"Stay down," he said as the hatch closed behind his brutish physique. He turned toward the cockpit, marked by crowded control panels and blinking displays. Perez looked through the aircraft's curved windshield and saw that night had almost fallen. Oz tapped the glass, and its HUD flickered to life, painting the outside world as it would have appeared by day.

Perez rolled her eyes back into the darkened cabin. She felt dizzy, her vision closing in. Her breath came in labored rasps. At any moment, she thought she'd slip from consciousness.

The scream of engines jolted her. The walls vibrated, and air vents hummed. Path lighting flickered by her feet, casting a dull orange glow over her surroundings.

This is all wrong. Something changed. He's not taking me for a medical evaluation.

Said my life is in danger?

She focused on her breathing. *In. Out.* Slowed it down. She looked around the cabin. More seating lined the opposite wall, interrupted by a gap to accommodate a side hatch with a red lever at its center. A fire extinguisher was mounted next to it. Overhead, another emergency hatch was recessed in the honeycombed ceiling. Her eyes tracked along the wall to her right, then left. Her gaze was drawn to an orange box mounted beside her head with yellow signage across the front:

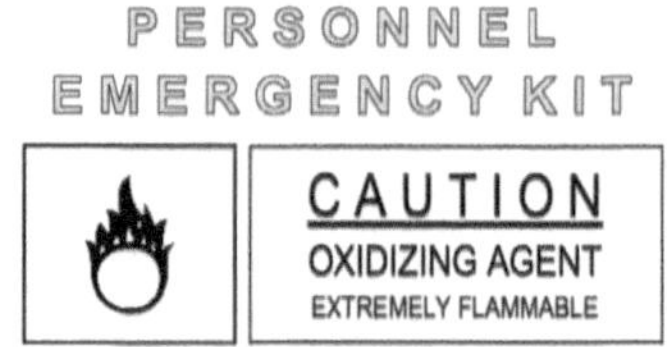

Perez craned her neck and tried to spot Oz in the cockpit, but he was seated out of sight behind a partition separating him from the crew cabin. His houndstooth shemagh was draped over the arm of a partially visible copilot seat, which glowed green from the light of a cartographic display in front of it. She heard Oz speaking over the comm, but couldn't understand what he was saying. It wasn't English. Didn't sound like French, either. She strained to hear over the roaring aircraft, and then it clicked: it was a language rarely heard except in propaganda and on the news. A cold realization washed over her.

Russian. Why is he speaking Russian?

Perez rose to her feet. She was immediately overcome with vertigo, but fought through it and managed to situate herself in front of the orange box.

It was mounted just above waist level, low enough for her to try and open it. She turned her back to the wall and fumbled for the lid. Thousands of pins drove into her fingertips as they fought with the fastening clips for what seemed an eternity. Finally, the first clip released with a *pop* that rang like a gavel throughout the cabin. Her heart skipped, eyes shot to the cockpit entrance, but Oz was still talking over the radio. Perez took a deep breath and worked on the second clip, her fingers numb, practically useless.

The second clip snapped back, and the lid flew open.

Sealed foil bags and medical supplies clanked to the ground. Oz shifted in his seat. Perez glanced back at the box and saw a bright orange flare gun set in foam next to three cartridges. She flexed her fingers, tried to get the blood circulating again. Electric shocks of returning sensation prickled her skin as her trembling fingers closed around the grip. Her other hand found one of the cartridges and miraculously slid it into the barrel, despite her incessant shaking. She heard movement by the cockpit entrance and turned just as Oz's burly form appeared in the doorway. He took a step forward. Perez cocked the hammer back.

"You come any closer," she screamed, her knees buckling, legs shaking as she turned slightly so he could see the loaded flare gun in her hands, "and I'll fucking light this place up." She pointed the muzzle at one of the floor vents. Seemed as good a target as any.

Oz didn't speak. Only stood in front of the cockpit, watching her, sizing her up, knots of muscle clenching in his cheeks.

"Now," Perez continued, "tell me where you're taking me."

"There's no time."

"I swear to God, I'll pull this trigger. You're talking to the Russians."

"You're not safe here."

"*Where* are you *taking* me?"

"Moscow."

Perez froze. Her first instinct was to protest. Russia was the enemy of the Federation, of the Father. Always had been.

Fuck the Father.

And what of her animals, of ARC?

A second thought came to her, a familiar one: one about second chances. For her. For Ruth. She could seek asylum in Russia, become a steward in Siberia's rewilded regions, see a *mammoth* for the first time. Or live off the Russian coast on Sakhalin Island, study revived arboreal bird populations, and contribute to rewilding efforts in the country's other, newer reforested regions. Like the Siberian steppe, Russia's reforestation initiatives were less an act of goodwill and more about claiming carbon neutrality while continuing the Dmitriev regime's exploits in dirty energy. But at least she'd be alive, working with animals again. And if what Oz said held a grain of truth, her days at ARC appeared to be over.

But why?

Oz stepped forward again. Perez backed away in equal measure, her finger tightening around the trigger. Her upper right eyelid fluttered. Something fluttered beneath her navel, and she thought Ruth had shifted, even though it was too early in the pregnancy to feel her. Anger rushed over her, pumped fresh adrenaline through her veins.

"*Don't* come any closer." Her voice cracked as her lips drew into a grimace. Drops of spit struck her visor.

Oz only glowered. His jaw flexed again, his eyes narrow slits.

"If what you're saying is true," Perez said, "why are you helping me?"

"Not doing it for you." The corners of his mouth pulled slightly up into an almost imperceptible sneer. "Tick-tock."

She believed him when he said there was no time. But even if that was true, it had no bearing on what came next. "You're going to go and get Nedjma and Basem. Then we go."

"I can't do that."

"You will, or no one goes anywhere."

She knew a fire might not ground the ship. It might be snuffed out if Oz was quick enough to subdue her and tamp the flames. But it would cause a stir that was likely to draw attention. She knew Oz understood that, knew it was a risk he weighed as he stood there with hatred in his eyes. He glared at her momentarily, then turned to the cockpit and spoke something in Russian over the radio. Without another word, he pulled his respirator back over his head, readied his rifle, and opened the rear hatch. His eyes did not leave Perez's until he descended the ramp into the dwindling eventide, his back to her as he calmly strode out of sight.

The door closed, and the cabin fell into darkness.

An eternity passed in silence before the hatch opened again. A confused-looking Nedjma stumbled up the ramp with Oz trailing her, their rubbery suits still glistening with decontamination medium. Nedjma's hands were secured behind her back.

"I *told* you," Nedjma said, almost losing her balance as she moved inside, "I didn't say a word about what I—*Cam!*" Recognition and relief replaced her fright. Oz dropped her into one of the seats across from Perez. Nedjma shot him a pained look with reddened eyes. Her face looked pale in the glow of the cabin.

But Perez disregarded her, her cheeks hot with the painful realization that Basem was not in tow. Oz's face was perfectly framed at the center of her shrinking tunnel of vision. She was almost blinded by rage, the muscles of her face twisting, her joints locking up. "Where is Basem?"

"Told you," Oz grumbled through a veiled stare, "there's no time, especially for him. He's not who you think...."

You're a fucking liar. You don't know him.

Heat percolated up her cheeks, fury consuming her as memories flashed past, replaying her life over the last few years with Basem. The laughter, the tears, the shouting matches. All of it. The rap of her heart in her head grew until the pounding invoked a hammer striking her skull. And then she saw the night at the kasbah, gazing out at the stars.

You are my sky.

Oz spoke, his voice pulling her back. "You have about thirty seconds to decide where to go from here." His tone possessed an urgency Perez had not previously detected. But his expression remained dull, matter of fact.

He's panicking.

Her mind drifted back to anger, defiance. A heaviness swelled in her chest, drove the air from her lungs. Her eyes swam. Her vision blurred.

"Cam," Nedjma said, her voice wavering through cracked lips. A thin sliver of light lined the faded scar on her upper lip. "What's happening?"

Perez softened a little. A tear fell down her cheek. She tilted her chin up and glowered at Oz as he loomed in the entrance with indifference painted over his face, his gun saddled in his thick hands. Her fingers were numb again, but still clenched the handle of the flare gun. She exhaled and let it fall to the floor.

Oz removed his helmet and respirator—his cropped hair matted with sweat—and looked at her with contempt. His brow knitted in apparent disfavor, then he hulked past a comparatively meek-looking Nedjma and disappeared into the cockpit.

An unfamiliar voice chirped something in Russian over the radio. Oz chirped back.

Nedjma glanced toward the cockpit and then back at Perez, her face drawn with terror. "Where is he taking us?" She sat with her hands tied behind her back, shoulders slumped.

Perez tried to speak, but nothing came out. She swayed on weakened knees, and although Nedjma had started shouting her name, everything now sounded distant in her ears. Her vision closed off as she wilted, then fell to her knees. The floor vibrated, the roaring engines rattling her insides. It felt as though she was floating, though on some level, she understood that she was falling sideways onto the cabin floor.

As her throat tightened, as consciousness faded like the sun over the rim of the mountains, Basem's face flashed before Camila Perez's eyes one more time.

And from Ymir sprang the giants all.
—Poetic Edda

‹ ᚦ | JÖTUNHEIMR ›

Shafts of early morning sunlight spilled onto Lotta's face, blinding her as the cool shade of the canopy fell away. She heard Fischer gasping on her heels. They had made it into the open, out of the forest, away from the loathsome bellowing of an unseen beast. Away from Björn.

Relief.

The ground had turned to muck a few meters from the ecotone, slowing their advance. Then came the stench. *Rotten eggs.* Lotta's stomach lurched. She heaved, covering her mouth with the back of her hand. She swallowed hard, gathered herself, and gazed out through the opening in the trees, where the underbrush had parted to reveal a vast expanse. Her demeanor shifted from urgency to profound disquietude.

Thick, pink-lined clouds swelled across a deep blue sky, and an orange band painted a veiled horizon where the sun loomed bloody above the rim of the Earth. A watchful eye, it gazed upon a sprawling river delta shimmering gold in the morning dew. In the distance, countless pterosaurs spiraled up vaporous columns rising from unseen convection currents.

Lotta's brain adjusted, jolted her back to reality.

Not birds.

They were pterosaurs, their movements unconventional, but efficient and gracile. They sliced through the air with unmatched ease as they soared high above the basin. Some dove into the water to snatch fish. Others performed acrobatic displays against the cerulean backdrop. From all directions, the skies were alive with a chorus of thumping squalls and shrieks. It drowned out her tinnitus, rising and falling with strange unanimity, a bestial ensemble that roared like a swelling and receding ocean.

Lotta lurched into the open. The sour sulfur smell swelled, stinging her nose and throat. The stream snaked from the trees toward a wider rivulet that banked abruptly to the right, disappearing behind a large stand of horsetails and cycads. It re-emerged on the other side, where it carved through a vast mudflat and fed into a network of rivers that fanned beyond the limits of her perception. Gone were the mountains, the whipping Saharan sands. No domes. No ALICE. All that prevailed was a vast landscape sloping gradually into a distant vale speckled by sparse greenery. As the sun climbed, the amber haze on the horizon faded to white and lingered like a far-off ocean.

Lotta was lost on a distant alien world.

She scanned their surroundings, the mudflat a belching mire pocked with what appeared to be footprints and stagnant pools of water stretching beyond her purview. A small prominence covered in a dense copse of cycads rose from the stippled mud about two hundred meters out. A little farther beyond, an old fault scarp pushed out from the forest, bisecting a portion of the mudflat past the copse before ending abruptly in front of a winding river. It formed a craggy mesa atop a bluff with undulating faces of sheer white rock.

Listing along the copse's circumference, Lotta spotted a dozen or more wiry bodies, possibly a meter tall—fat-headed little bird-apes that plucked writhing provisions from the muck under the shade of the trees.[1,2] They were like smaller, bull-necked versions of stalkers. But these had black-and-orange tear-drop heads that plunged toward the ground, their pointed beaks probing as they strode effortlessly through the silt and clay.

---

1 *Apatorhamphus gyrostega*
2 *Kababisha humarensis*

She thought of Basem.

A barrage of caterwauls erupted from above the forest canopy, and half a dozen winged forms emerged from the edge of Lotta's vision.[3] Ice shot through her core as she watched, frozen in terror beside a silent Fischer. The group doubled back, their wings cutting through the air as they began circling something gray protruding from the mud along the opposite bank. They descended on the object, sculling the air to land feet-first. Their wing arms folded, elastic membranes retracting from sight, and they fell forward onto splayed hands that plunged into the mud with little resistance. Familiar forms took shape—slender frames resembling those of the towering stalkers that had taken Basem. These were jerkier in their movements, tentatively rocking fore and aft on stilted limbs. The things were far smaller by comparison, but "small" was relative. Even the lesser of them would have come up to Lotta's midriff. The largest might reach her shoulders. Their chests were puffed, almost aristocratic in aspect, rolling in response to their strange, strutting gaits. But they also displayed a skittish nature that endowed them with a vulpine, almost comical disposition.

From their hindquarters sprouted flocculant wisps that danced about as they moved. Some fanned outward, fibrous plumes shimmering a bright iridescent mauve. Their heads were adorned with large, discoid crests like boat keels striped with helical bands of purple and gray. Those of less pomp displayed tawny bodies with more modest aigrettes and shallower crowns, but looked identical in all other respects. The ornery things surrounded their quarry. Then, one by one, the broad, downturned beaks assaulted it, snapping with hollow *clomps* as each vied for its keep.

"Let's get into cover, keep moving," Fischer whispered, turning toward the thickly walled horsetails that crowded the embankment. "Stay low. I'll lead. Keep your eyes up for threats. I'll keep mine out front."

The vibrant green of the banded reeds disoriented Lotta as she followed. Brush-like leaves sprouted up their lengths, gently combing against her skin, a sensation that gave her gooseflesh. Their spindly stalks grew above eye level and were as dense as grass, but fell away with little effort as they

---

3 *Afrotapejara zouhri*

moved deeper. Through the rustling greenery, she could hear moving water, the squalling banter of the keelheads, and the bestial cantillation that filled the skies.

She kept her eyes up.

"Starting to thin out a bit," Fischer said.

Lotta glanced ahead. He was right, but it wasn't that the density of the reeds had diminished. Instead, they appeared denuded, as though something had stripped them clean.

That was when a new smell hit. It overpowered the sulfuric stench, a putrescence like ammonia and feces. Her throat closed; breathing became difficult. Fischer retched.

She heard the churning of mud, then a deep, slow clicking that swelled like a great gust filling a void, followed by a long rumble. She and Fischer stopped, listened. Time slowed. The background filled her ears once more, and Fischer signaled that it was okay to continue. Lotta nodded and her hand found his. He squeezed, and her fingers throbbed, but she didn't mind. Fear had driven everything else from her.

CRACK.

Lotta's eyes had drifted skyward again when a sudden impact sent her flailing backward into the mud faster than she could process the sound of splitting air. It took her a few seconds to realize Fischer was on her, and a second more to determine that she had been tackled. She panicked. Went for the knife. Her fear was now trained squarely on him.

"Hey! Get *off* me!" she screamed as he pressed her into the mud. "No! No, *please don't hurt me… get away!*"

"*Stay down!*"

Her fingers found the blade, but her arm was trapped between her chest and his. Fischer had her pinned. Pins and needles crawled over her skin, and her fingers started to lose sensation. She tried to scream, but his hand clamped over her mouth. She tasted dirt and grit, jerked her head sideways. But he held firm, his eyes wide and manic, face muddied as he raised a finger to his mouth. "Stop. *STOP.* That sounded like gunfire."

Lotta jerked again and pulled her head free. Her cheek smacked into the muck. She screamed, flashing her eyes up at him. "*Hellllp! Helllp!* Get off me! Let me go. Let me *GO!*"

She cried out, abandoning all logic, hoping someone out there might hear. Or maybe something terrible and hungry would come along and snatch Fischer off her so she could make a run for it.

She pictured him cutting himself, the empty indifference on his face as he traced the blade through his veins. Recalled how he had tried to convince her to hand the knife over. And now, he was taking it by force and might try to hurt her, too.

And just when she had let her guard down.

Fischer's hand found her mouth again. "*Shut up*, or you'll get us both—" *CRACK.*

From the corner of her eye, Lotta caught something ropy sweep over Fischer's head, then retract with alarming speed. The reeds jostled, and Fischer's weight bore down, driving her deeper into the soft mud. An explosion of pulp showered them, producing a cloying, sweet smell, fleeting against the overwhelming stench of sulfur and excrement.

Fischer turned to look up, and Lotta saw her opportunity. She shoved a knee into his groin, and he doubled over. She kicked out, landing another blow that sent him onto his back, then scrambled backward through the reeds, trying to regain purchase. Fischer turned to her, his lips moving, but she could not hear because her right ear had fallen deaf, and the left was packed with mud. All she heard was a high-pitched knell.

The ground shook, and something drew Lotta's gaze above the horsetails.

Like a waking colossus, a proboscidean appendage rose high above the sea of stalks to blot out the ascendant sun. Lotta narrowed her gaze towards its apex and glimpsed a slender wedge-shaped head angled toward the ground, its attention fixed beyond her purview. Clods of earth rained from its bulk as it swayed overhead like a charmed basilisk before the wailing dawn, a king serpent come to cast the Earth into the abyssal depths of Ragnarök.

Down the center of its tightly knit bulk ran a row of dorsal spines that swayed like palm fronds tipped with the blood of the morning bask. They tracked past a pair of broad shoulder blades that rolled with ease beneath a thickly pebbled hide of alternating blacks and browns, and it was then that Lotta realized that the looming monstrosity was a *neck* buttressed upon an enormous body. The bloated flanks of its abdomen swelled, and from the fathoms of its chest resonated a spate of muffled clicks followed by a protracted moan that climbed the column of its serpentine neck with bellowing fury.

A second beast rose to confront it. A pair of columnar forelimbs terminating in fleshy stumps—each with a single horizontal claw on the inner toe—raked the air, windmilling intermittently as they swiped at the flanks of the first creature, which reacted with surprising speed. It listed toward Lotta and Fischer and then righted itself, sending its weight forward into its attacker. The two great chests collided with an impact that rippled through ropes of muscle and flesh. Arteries thicker than a human arm bulged from their jostling gulars, which swelled and moaned in tortured synchrony as the two necks swung into each other with a sickening *slap*. Their wedged snouts sprayed and frothed, venting cavernous sighs like wooden ships in hostile seas.

The creatures resembled the carcass Lotta had seen in the woods.

Brontosaurs.[4]

The rearing beasts recoiled, then plunged headlong into each other again. *Slap.*

Lotta's senses heightened. The ringing in her ears subsided. She heard a sound like an approaching wave, then saw rows of reeds laying down from the force of a fast-approaching bullwhip—a tail the size of a tree, its tip braided in barbs of keratin. It swept past, mere meters from where she lay, spraying splinters through the air as it sliced overhead in an arc with another deafening *CRACK*.

Fischer tried to push himself up, but lost his balance. Lotta scrambled, found her feet, and turned to run through the covert, back toward the forest.

"Lotta! Wait!" Fischer's muffled scream faded behind her.

She plowed through the muck, brushing aside horsetails with fire in her chest, the breath heavy in her lungs. Marshy water beaded from the earth like sweat, the sodden ground belching with acrid putrescence. It moored her within its grasp, and her legs screamed in protest against the suction, every contraction an act of defiance. Then the mud churned with a great shudder—an impact tremor from behind—but Lotta dared not

---

4 *Rebbachisaurus garasbae* – a small diplodocid more closely related to *Diplodocus sp.*

look back. She remained steadfast, toiled in the rising heat, the cool mud squeezing up her legs as she pumped her arms. Wondered if she had taken a wrong turn. This couldn't be the way they had come.

Fischer yelled after her again, sounding closer this time.

She spotted the opening through the trees they had come through, only it was now waterlogged in a pond of turbid water half a meter deep. The stream was now stagnant and brown, and its banks had spilled over, turning the ecotone into a swamp that stretched deep into the thicket. Bits of duff swirled lazily across its surface like desiccated motes.

Perplexed but undeterred, Lotta trudged in up to her ankles, but stopped short when a large ripple moved out toward her across the surface. She winced into the darkened thicket as mud sloughed from her sweat-slicked cheeks and splashed at her feet. The fledgling day's heat bore down.

Another ripple propagated from beyond the shaded bracken, but before Lotta could react, she was yanked by her arm back into the reeds.

"Stay low. Stay quiet," Fischer whispered through heavy rasps.

She wrenched her arm, but his grip held firm. His intense blue eyes were the only recognizable feature beneath the clotted mud concealing him from head to toe.

Another ripple carved across the forest floor's glassy veneer. Their eyes shot to the tree line.

Lotta tampered with her pitch-coated fingers. The pain had returned, along with a tingling sensation and intermittent numbness at the tip of her middle finger.

The thunderous collision of vast bodies behind them broke the silence; the skies, the squabbling keelheads, had fallen mute.

A loud, splintering *pop* tore through the trees. Something heavy crashed into the water, the impact obscured by the thick underbrush. A whitecap billowed forth, gliding across the water's surface toward them.

A tree. Something just knocked down a tree.

Lotta's shoulders tensed. Her breath caught in her throat. She was reminded of Fischer's grip when it pulled her deeper into the reeds, but she no longer resisted. Her mind had left her body—although she sensed her legs wresting through the unrelenting suction, guided by Fischer's slovenly fingers around her bicep, none of it felt real except for the compulsion to look back.

"Over there," Fischer grunted, pointing through a gap in the thicket towards the copse. It was circumscribed by another field of horsetails, the wall of white rock jutting from the earth in the backdrop. The solitary stand of cycads was elevated enough to appear dry, rising from the pitted mudflat, which now mirrored the morning sky beneath a sheen of thin water. Eddies carved through the soft mud, filling the pools and footprints dotting the basin. The area was flooding fast.

They would need to run across.

We can hide there. We can hide and never leave.

Lotta heard a slosh back at the tree line. Fischer stopped and turned, stone-faced, and her gaze followed. He pulled her into a crouching position next to him. They waited.

Trembling, she peered through thin gaps in the still shoots. Saw movement—something massive and black. Strained to see past the green stalks, but the thing went still again, once more obscured under the dappled shadows of the canopy. Lotta hoped whatever it was had not detected them. She had grown deaf to her incessant picking, her attention drawn to the subconscious habit of self-mutilation only once Fischer clamped his hand around her busy fingers. She fell still. But the hum of anxiety would not be silenced, and her body droned with such ferocity that the world around her seemed deafening.

It moved again, an inky, cobbled mass rolling through the banded thicket into the sunlight. A body led by a massive reptilian snout that drifted through the forest's edge, where it hovered low above the turbid water. From shadow emerged two yellow eyes, hooded by crests gilded in blood-red keratin, a cragged comb that tapered to a ridge along the snout. It formed a 'V' that melded with the calloused skin of a black face, one pitted and gouged with the cicatrix of foregone strife. The face of a jötunn.[5]

The yellow orbs peered out, a pair of translucent membranes sliding over them. Bulbous and searching, they embodied the same intensity Lotta had observed in Perez's ostrich an eternity ago.

Slap.

---

5 *Carcharodontosaurus saharicus*

The eyes widened, snapping toward the dueling brontosaurs, their line of sight fixed directly above Lotta and Fischer. Lotta watched, gripped with overwhelming terror as its pupils dilated with an acute fixation that bestowed the animal with a degree of cunning she found deeply unsettling.

For a time, the jötunn remained motionless where it stood. Then its nostrils flared, and its jaws parted to taste the open air, a gaping maw of ivory daggers strung by a muculent web of saliva. It trickled in cords and brimmed at the margin of a sagging lower lip that laid bare tooth and gum. The nostrils flared again as the powerful jaws dipped into the water and scooped a mouthful of brown slurry that cascaded from the gaps in its teeth like the spillways of a dam.

The creature drank. The eyes stared.

Then the beast rolled forward upon great legs, raising more white caps as it strode into the open. The head pitched skyward so that its eyes mirrored the sun, gnats swarming about its flaring nostrils as they grazed the coniferous boughs that moments before had loomed high above Lotta's head. Hugged against its barreled chest, a pair of muscular, short arms stowed three fidgeting digits each, their tips capped in claws that gleamed like obsidian scimitars. From its blackened hide, mottled and patterned such that its form was deconstructed within the shady underbrush, rained twigs and detritus to the water below. Its gray-brown pattern obscured the beast's hulking torso, its size enormous, perhaps rivaling that of the clashing brontosaurs. Lotta beheld a form that exuded raw power and elegant brutality, a mountain of sinew, claws, and teeth.

A jötunn.

Another rumble resonated from the depths of its chest, but deeper, lower in frequency. Felt more than heard. All around Lotta, the reeds seemed to vibrate with a booming *thump thump* that pulsed through the air. Penetrated her. Had she not seen the giant before her, she would have been unable to localize it. Overcome with the swelling hum within, the deafening wail of her own thoughts, Lotta wished for nothing more than to return to the relative safety of the nurse log, with its slick walls, the sweet, cloying smell of rot, and Fischer standing between her and the outside world.

Slap. The brontosaurs collided. Could they not hear—or *feel*—this? Did it not concern them?

The jötunn lingered for what felt like an eternity before it huffed, blasting forth a nebula of septic foam. In one swift motion, it rocked its torso downward, shifting its weight onto its foreleg. The back foot, heavy and clawed, gushed forward through the water, churning up a brown froth in its wake. *Thud.* Mud sprayed as it planted, the rounded belly swaying and settling under its own gravity atop bones forged in steel. The dinosaur inhaled deeply. Again, it paused, its birdlike eyes still glaring beyond Lotta's position toward the dueling beasts.

Then its attention faltered as its pitted snout seemed to be pulled in another direction, toward something new. The eyes resisted. They lingered momentarily before ultimately relenting to the lure of novelty. The head turned away, and the beast's muscular legs followed, carrying it to the overflowing embankment. Lotta looked on as it waded into deeper water, then disappeared behind the thicket, its body trailed by a stiff, swaying tail that counterbalanced its front end.

Lotta's legs seared from crouching, but she resisted her desire to move.

A shriek pierced the air on the other side of the stream. The scavenging keelheads had trained their aggression on the interloper in their midst. Lotta spotted a few through another gap in the banded rows, flaring their gossamer plumes and cavorting madly about the ragged gray mass they had claimed. The jötunn reappeared, approaching with indifference to the pterosaurs' intensifying caterwauls. With each cautious step, its eyes flashed between the carcass and the battling brontosaurs.

CRACK.

Lotta's head jerked involuntarily behind her. The sound decayed across the landscape like thunder. The fighting giants were no longer visible from her vantage point. Her gaze fell on Fischer, who sat on his knees in the mud. But his eyes did not find hers. They only gaped past her, wide with horror.

Lotta snapped back toward the squabbling keelheads, only to be met with the ashen saurian face of the jötunn. Its gaze had been trained over her head toward the brontosaurs, but jerked reflexively in response to her movement. The ghastly head tilted to one side like a giant bird's, its yellow orbs searing into her like roiling suns. A deep pang plunged into Lotta's gut, as if the creature's regard had generated a force with the power to move her. She stumbled backward. Fischer's clotted hands encircled her shoulders, steadied her. She looked back through the reeds, into the eyes of the jötunn.

She forgot Fischer was there.

The beast straightened itself and, with apparent disinterest, returned its attention to the picked-over carrion. It bent down, its fleshy nares expanding and nuzzling the carcass before expelling a loud snort. A clawed foot raked the ragged object, bearing the body's entire weight forward as the horrible jaws clamped down. The thick neck tensed and pulled the head back.

In its vice-like grip, Lotta saw what appeared to be a giant sun-bleached fish. It was the size of a rover, with lobed fins resembling short, rounded legs.[6] Ragged flesh dangled freely from it, the body swollen and distended in the day's rising heat. Then the intumescent mass sloughed free of its bulbous head to expose a spinal column that glistened like a wet ribbon in the midmorning sun. A blackish-green putrescence exuded through the fish's voided eye sockets, and from them oozed tar-tinged blood in long, jostling strings. The jötunn tossed back its head, clamping the ragged meat back with a *clomp* that elicited the wet sounds Lotta had heard from the gloom of the nurse log.

The keelheads stood back and watched, warbling and clicking.

The jötunn's eyes leveled with Lotta again, thick ropes of inky putrescence descending from its creased lips. Its nostrils glistened wetly in the sun, and the remaining vestige of the fish's nervous system dangled from one side of its mouth until it snapped free, falling to the mud with a wet *slap*.

Lotta's stomach lurched. A sour film coated her tongue.

The beast swallowed indifferently, then turned its gaze back to the thundering brontosaurs. There, its attention remained, and it lowered itself into the mud so that it sat upon its haunches with folded arms, its head low to the ground. Even at rest, the jötunn retained a furtive aspect, a guileful, premeditative quality. Its throat swelled, and another resounding *thump thump* moved through Lotta. Something returned the call from a direction she could not determine.

Fischer's hand gripped her arm again, and she almost screamed.

6 *Axelrodichthys lavocati* – a giant coelacanth

"Easy," he whispered, returning her attention to the copse. They were close, maybe a hundred or so meters off.

CRACK.

Lotta glanced back toward the enrapt beast—its great lungs venting through gaping jaws as it scented the fetid air—then turned and slipped deeper into the thicket with renewed ringing in her ears.

Fischer led the way as they slogged past banded rows of horsetails toward the open mudflat. Through the gaps, she saw the copse growing nearer. Her fingers throbbed. Her legs protested with relentless ferocity. The sour stench rising from the mire sat in her throat, where it swelled, refused to dwindle into the background of tolerability. She glanced again across the mudflat through the passing shoots where the stand of cycads beckoned.

Almost there. Can't quit now.

Fischer peered out over the tops of the wispy stalks, then lowered himself with a frown. Lotta attempted to steal a look, but was not tall enough for any meaningful observation.

"Can you swim?" Fischer asked. "We should be fine, but I need to know. We must be in a tidal zone, given how fast the area is flooding."

Lotta nodded.

"Okay. Stay close."

They pressed on, weaving through the green tendrils until they broke into the clearing. In the distance, the vast river system appeared to swell ominously like a network of bulging arteries, and a billowing cloud front was materializing overhead. The shapes of living things big and small toiled and dredged in the gloom of the stagnant vista.

Hell. I'm in Hell.

Fischer crossed into the open first.

CRACK.

Lotta turned. They had covered around twenty meters, and the horsetails had receded so that the sparring brontosaurs were now in plain view. The creatures circled each other on all fours, their flanks exposed, necks pitched as whip-like tails lashed from side to side. Their distended bellies were supported atop four pillars jointed with knobby knees that stomped forcefully into the earth, spraying mud onto their bodies.

Against the backdrop, an entire herd of the long-necked creatures appeared to be gathered along the embankment of the larger rivulet, which churned and roiled as if in retrograde. Their muscular necks were cantilevered over the water, their tails rippling like streamers behind them as they drank. Perched atop their weather-beaten bodies, small pterosaurs plucked parasites from their guano-smeared hides. Others weaved amongst the docile herd. A trio of smaller brontosaurs bathed in the mud nearby.

But the jötunn was nowhere to be seen.

Slap.

The necks of the sparring duo connected with such savagery that blood frothed from their recoiling mouths. Their cavernous moans had grown tortured with depletion, their bedraggled bodies wavering but unrelenting. With an explosion of mud, they reared again on their hind legs and collapsed into one another, then fell back to their feet with a tremendous shudder. The larger of the two recovered first, sweeping its tail back and then driving it forward again. The barbed tip snapped forward to connect with its target, sending thunder across the mire. The smaller brontosaur staggered sideways, and Lotta spotted something protruding from its ribcage. The object bounced and flailed, and she realized it was the barbed tip of the victor's tail, driven deep into the flank of its opponent. From the point of entry bloomed a thick stripe of bright red.

A low, vibrating *thump thump* moved through the ground. Shook Lotta to the marrow.

Then a new sound, a protracted trumpeting moan from the herd along the riverbank.

The necks of the brontosaurs pitched up, and their heads swiveled. The herd moved away from the water and began stampeding in Lotta and Fischer's direction.

Fischer gripped her wrist. "Let's get into cover. Now."

The bouncing necks of the sauropods were elevated high off the ground. They galloped with surprising speed, their striped tails coiling behind as their feet turned up the earth. By the time Lotta had turned to run, some of the herd had split off and headed into the water, while the rest continued along the embankment. The river ahead looped a reasonable distance from the copse, but should the herd decide to move inland, their trajectory would put Lotta and Fischer in its path.

Everything was in motion. Lotta pumped her arms, her legs fighting her every step, lungs exploding, pulse pounding in her head. But she dared not stop. The ground grew more solid beneath her feet, and suddenly, she was running full-tilt up the sloped hill. To her right, clusters of cycads whipped past. More reeds flew past. She followed Fischer into another carpet of horsetails. The shoots lashed her face and arms, but she felt numb. Mud fell away from her like shed skin.

The ground started to shake. Lotta shot a look toward the embankment. The herd had diverted and now headed straight for the copse.

"Almost there," Fischer shouted.

Lotta doubled back, the ground firming up beneath her. The earth here had not taken on as much water. Her pace quickened, though her legs were heavy with mud. Relief started to ease into her aching muscles, and already, she felt a sense of security wash over her. *If we can just get under cover....*

SNAP.

A cycad exploded into shrapnel, sending fronds through the air like spears. A towering monstrosity barreled toward them from the copse, a larger jötunn, its aureolin eyes wide and feral. Its teeth, strung with saliva, caged a black tongue like a chthonic sarcophagus.

Aurgelmir. Mud-yeller. Father of giants.

Without prepense, Lotta whipped around and flew back down the hill. She could hear reeds splintering and snapping behind her, but she dared not look back to verify Fischer's status. Loud bursts of air trailed with growing intensity, interspersed with the pounding of an inconceivable mass of muscle and brute strength. She sank to her ankles in wet clay once more, fighting against the suction of the soft mudflat. Her legs were on fire. Her lungs were exploding. The jötunn was closing in.

The ground jostled beneath her feet. The reeds trembled around her. Her mind screamed at her failing limbs as she trudged with high knees. She spotted the bobbing brontosaur heads again, their mouths producing a refrain of grunts and moans that swelled in her ears. Her heart fell.

A heavy foot plunged into the mud behind her with a viscous *thwuck*. A grunt of exertion soughed from a billowing maw. She heard the slosh of churning silt, then another footfall. Dared not look back to get a visual on Fischer for fear of what she might see. *Thwuck.*

Then, the unthinkable. Her right leg sank to the knee, and panic devolved into dread. She pulled with desperation, muck-blackened tears streaming down her face, so hard her knee popped, but only fell headlong into the thick mud. It packed her mouth and her nose. Made her retch. She couldn't breathe.

"No—"

Lotta's hope faded like a dying flame.

She vomited black and gasped for air as shimmering sprites danced before the constricting sight of the diverting herd. A steady warmth trickled down her thigh and pooled between her toes. Lotta Eklund, the physicist. The Heathen. The incontinent mouse.

She prayed to the gods. To Freyja, the Vaettir. To the entire fucking pantheon. Whoever might listen.

Kneel.

A shadow descended on her, and through the exploding mire, the screaming tinnitus, Sofia's voice rang louder than ever…

We bring you this offering in Odin's name.

…and the world went dark.

UEF / RD
EYES ONLY

Ministry of Defence
United European Federation

Memorandum of CCTV Interrogation. Partial Transcript.

JUNE 16, 2147, 19:34

Appearances
Dr. Aegis Galani
Subject 004

Galani	Please state your name and date of birth for the record.
S004	Lotta Eklund. Twelve September, twenty ninety-six.
Galani	Thank you, Dr. Eklund. Doctors tell me you suffered acute decompression sickness. I see you have been cleared for fluids. Would you like something to drink?
S004	What's this about, Aegis?
Galani	Let's keep this professional. Otherwise, I will need to recuse myself from questioning you further.
S004	That all it would take to get you to fuck off?
Galani	I am here to help.
S004	[laughter] The hell you are. You can help me by letting me out of this hell hole. Help me by telling me how my team is doing.
Galani	Let's talk about your team. In your own words, what do you think happened to Edgar Fischer?
S004	Pulmonary embolism. Wasn't wearing a compression sleeve. We were resuscitating him before the neutrino burst. How is he?

Galani	Tell me more about what led to that situation.
S004	We lost contact with BOB, then Athena. We were exposed to—something... A vacuum. Couldn't breathe. He was the only one that didn't get up when we all came to.
Galani	You'll be relieved to hear that BOB's gate evaporated without incident. Dr. Kazimierz has been instrumental in helping us piece things together, helped us find you.
S004	Give him my thanks. I hope he and his team made it out safe.
Galani	Dr. Kazimierz is... well.
S004	The operation was sabotaged, Aegis.
Galani	Oh? By whom?
S004	Don't be cute. You know who.
Galani	Please state the name of the individual or individuals... for the record.
S004	[laughter] Still, after all these years, you really are a fucking snake, you know that?
Galani	I'm touched, as ever. I need a name.
S004	You really are an asshole. ▮▮▮▮▮▮▮▮, for the record.
Galani	And how did you arrive at this conclusion?
S004	Because she was there.
Galani	In the lab?
S004	Not quite. She was poking around the Cathedral.
Galani	You mean the Bell chamber?
S004	Yes.
Galani	How was she able to get inside?
S004	I don't know, but I have my suspicions. We met at ▮▮▮ to address a matter regarding ▮▮▮▮▮▮▮▮▮▮▮▮▮▮▮▮▮▮▮▮▮▮▮▮▮▮▮▮▮▮▮▮▮▮▮. But you already know that.
Galani	Go on....
S004	▮▮▮▮▮▮▮▮▮▮▮▮▮▮▮▮▮▮▮▮▮▮▮▮▮▮▮▮▮▮▮▮▮▮▮▮ notified IT that he'd lost his access badge. She had taken it, ▮▮▮▮▮▮▮▮▮▮▮▮▮▮▮▮▮▮▮▮▮▮▮▮▮▮▮▮▮. She was there when it happened. I saw her.

Galani	What if I told you that ████████████████████ ████████?
S004	I've suspected it for some time. But you know that, too.
Galani	████████████ has suffered severe head trauma. He has been unable to corroborate this, but I do appreciate your testimony. Let's move on.
S004	Move on? Move on? No. I'm done answering questions. You're telling me ██████ is a vegetable. I still want to know where Edgar is; you haven't answered me. Tell me how he is doing, Aegis.
Galani	Dr. Fischer expired early this morning. The cause of death was, as you said, pulmonary embolism.
S004	No.
Galani	I'm so sorry, Dr. Eklund.
S004	That fucking tree-hugging luddite bitch. She did this. She [unintelligible].
Galani	██ ██ ████████.
S004	And if it hadn't been for [unintelligible]... still be alive, you fucking snake. You [unintelligible].
Galani	I am so sorry to have to do this, old friend. Truly, I am. [unintelligible]. Security, we have a situation. ████████████████. ████████████.

ᚱ | THE GATES OF DEATH

"I'm right here. Focus on my voice. *I'm right here.*"

Elisa had fallen off her new bike and scuffed her knees. She'd been fearless up to that point. Fischer knelt beside her and inspected her legs as tears rolled down her shiny red cheeks. *Skinned 'em good this time*, he thought. Then he looked up into those big blues, and the outside world fell away.

"You remember what I told you?"

She nodded, the edges of her mouth reaching for the ground, her wispy, blonde hair framing her round face.

"And what was that?"

"If something throws me down, I..." Her voice trailed into a mumble.

"You what?"

She gave a big sniffle, her lower lip bulging. "Get right back up."

"That's right." He wiped the tears away, and the cuff of his UEF uniform tugged back as he extended his arm. "So, what are you going to do, Sunny?"

Sunny. Only Daddy called her that, on account her hair was always a blazing corona. A look as wild and free as the little girl tangled up inside it.

Almost six, with a personality as big as life itself. It was moments like these Fischer wished he could stop time, keep her this way a little longer.

He scooped her tiny frame into his arms and kissed her tear-stained cheek. "I'm right here. Daddy will always be right here," he whispered. Her delicate fingers fumbled at the insignia embroidered on the breast of his uniform. Moved over the gold stitching, the letters of the slogan he'd signed his life to.

We are many. We are one.

She had started to learn to read, and in time, she would come to understand the meaning behind the symbols she traced with her fingers. But not today. Not now. Not if time stood still.

Not on his watch. >

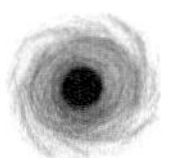

Day 6, Midmorning — Tidal Flat

"I'm right here. Focus on my voice."

Instinct.

That was the only way to describe it. Maybe Fischer's military training had kicked in, or it was the vestiges of PTSD from his days dodging Russian artillery. Perhaps it was the father in him. Or, just as likely, he was *fucking terrified,* and his legs had merely given out. Whatever the reason, his body now shrouded Lotta's in the quaking mud. His fate was sealed. He hoped that she'd make it, continue without him. Hoped for a quick death as he shouted the words and squeezed the tears from his eyes and waited for the charging beast to whisk him away. Edgar Fischer had made peace with death long ago.

He was ready.

"I'm right here!"

Lotta didn't try to push him off. He had gotten to his knees to shield her with his body, the water now up to his thighs.

"I don't want to die," she whimpered. She had sunk to her waist.

"Hey," Fischer shouted, "it's going to be okay. Focus on my voice."

"Please don't leave. Don't leave me."

"I'm right here. Focus on my voice. I'm right here." The pounding footfalls drowned out his voice, but he continued repeating the words. Felt like the right thing to do.

The soft clay shuddered, the charging beast venting a chasmal grunt with each step it took—a terrible, eager panting. The beating sun's heat blanketed Fischer, and a sheen of sweat had spread over his back like a second skin.

"*I'm right here!*" he screamed. His wounded arm pulsated with an intensity that brought him to the verge of passing out. He squeezed his eyes shut, and the world spun. It was as though gravity had shifted. He imagined the flashing lights, the colors dancing before him in the Bell chamber, wondered if death might be something like that. A supernatural experience. Bliss.

The faces of his daughters wheeled past the shifting aura that consumed his thoughts. They beckoned him to the other side. "*I'm right he—*"

THWUCK.

A monstrous foot plowed into the mud on his left flank, and globs of wet earth pelted him like shrapnel. A wave of turbid water crashed into him with almost enough force to throw him. Lotta coughed and spluttered, pushing up to get her face above the swirling alluvium. Fischer fell away with a splash and belched brown water from his lungs. Though it must have occurred in seconds, everything around him seemed to unfold slowly.

THWUCK... *Thwuck... Thwuck... Thwuck... Thwuck....*

To Fischer's astonishment, the footfalls receded. The swaying tail passed overhead—indistinct on account of the slurry seeping into his eyes—as the colossal beast rushed past their position toward the approaching stampede. The lumbering giants held their heads high off the ground, their great necks elevated like giraffes. They resembled the colossal skeletons that captivated Evi during family trips to Geneva's natural history museum. Sauropods like Apatosaurus or Brontosaurus.

He belched up more water. Wiped the mess from his eyes and saw Lotta thrashing in the shallow water beside him.

"My leg. I'm stuck," she cried, coughing and sputtering as she languished.

Fischer crawled to her and placed her arm across his shoulders. He reached into the dusky water to free her leg, which had sunk clear past the knee into the loose mud.

"Here, stay still," he said, sliding his hand over her calf to try and relieve the suction.

"Ow! I think it's twisted."

"Almost got it," he said. Then the negative pressure released with a wet, sucking sound. "Okay. Grab onto me. Up we go."

He prised the limb free and lifted her up with his legs. The added weight made him sink slightly, but he maintained his footing. Lotta let out a painful yelp, sending Fischer's gaze back toward the receding juggernaut. It was the same creature he'd witnessed from the shelter of the nurse log, the one that got at Anderson's remains. He recognized its cobbled hide and the wet clap of its terrible jaws, the thumping call that reverberated from the depths of its great chest. Only now, it was in full view—and more horrible than he had imagined. He watched it barrel through the mire, spraying water with each step, loud gusts pushing out through its slackened maw. The sauropod herd diverted back toward the embankment to avoid it, their tails yawing in tandem, their rounded bellies swaying with each pounding step as they dredged the water-slicked morass. Not far behind, the larger of the dueling pair had abandoned its rut and almost caught back up with the herd, the tip of its tail broken and caked with blood.

In the distance, a second shadowy form came into Fischer's view from the edge of the horsetails lining the stream they had followed out of the forest.

Lotta drew a sharp breath. "There are two of them."

"Aye. Tyrannosaurs or something similar. Allosaur, maybe."

"Dinosaurs."

"Aye. Big ones."

"Jötnar," Lotta said. A sheet of mud covered her from head to toe.

"Huh?" He turned to her, but her eyes—wide and staring—remained fixed across the mudflat.

"Jötnar. Giants," she whispered, her body shaking, arms twitching.

Fischer chewed his tongue. Became aware that he'd lost his bowels, as the smell of his own filth rose through his liner to overcome the rotten-egg stench of their surroundings. He turned and carried Lotta back toward the copse until they found firm ground and collapsed, sending a cast of blue crabs scurrying. She rolled onto her back next to him, their chests rising and falling.

Fischer gathered the strength to sit upright. He watched the herd barrel past, moving along the narrow embankment where the steep wall of rock abutted the river. A thunderous roar of spraying water and churning mud filled his ears, then faded.

Lotta pushed herself into a sitting position beside him.

In the distance, they looked on as another solitary sauropod slogged across the rising floodwaters, with the two beasts—*the yot-nar?*—pacing alongside either flank. The retreating creature plowed heavily through the shallow slick, favoring its left flank as its feet wrenched and toiled against the clinging bedlam. Embedded in the wall of its upper torso, a stiff, rope-like protuberance bounced with each step—the disembodied tip of a barbed tail—while bright blood poured from the point of entry. Below its ribcage, Fischer spotted a large gash where the outer hide had sloughed away so that it hung open, spilling a waterfall of blood that trailed the approaching trine. Winged beasts circled overhead like a cavalcade of vultures, a procession of the damned mirrored by the rising flood.

The sauropod, now prey, grunted with the impact of its front legs, each expulsion producing a pink aerosol from its crimson-smeared snout. Its side ballooned until something sagged over the lip of the wound: a jostling, gelatinous mass. *An organ.* The pursuer along its left flank narrowed its gap and turned in to snap at the exposed viscera—a rust-colored, bulbous mass that appeared to be the sauropod's liver—but pulled back in time to dodge a strike from the bullwhip tail. A dark substance spilled in sheets like hot oil through the gash, intermixing with mud and blood. It glimmered in the dwindling sun while infernal clouds rolled in as if warding off a seraph, a last bastion of hope.

After a few more strides, the glistening mass prolapsed entirely, dangling at the knees of the hapless creature. The animal belted a wet bawl.

Nngraaar ngraar!

From its hindquarters, a geyser of excrement and blood gushed with a wet *smack* into the water, the animal loosing its bowels as lobular sections of gleaming intestine slinked free from the wound. The veering jötunn regrouped, pacing once more along its injured flank.

A web of blood-tinged saliva transited the predator's gaping lips, its lower rows of teeth exposed. Its neck muscles bulged, and the gusting maw clapped shut, the head swinging downward with a sopping *clomp* only to fall short once more. In anticipation of another tail strike, the beast pulled away once again, but maintained its pace, its leg muscles twitching under the weight of its rocking torso. The sauropod's tail thrashed desperately with a blunted *bap*, but fell well short.

Knots of quivering bowels slunk farther toward the churning slurry, bouncing and tossing until, finally, they caught in the splayed toe claws of one of the sauropod's hind feet. In an instant, a coiled mass erupted out onto the soft mud. But the sauropod charged on, making four full strides before slowing. The scaled pillars propping its body faltered, and the animal sidestepped into the overflowing embankment. The loose mud gave way, partially collapsing under its bulk, but it caught its footing and turned, its trembling tail almost striking one of the jötnar across the snout as it readied to counter their advance. It trumpeted again, then pushed off from its front legs, its enormous front end rearing skyward. Its last stand. A torrent of bright red blood poured in sheets from its gash; another glistening mass clapped into the blood-tinged mud, dangled, then broke free. Pterosaurs swarmed like shrieking banshees, picking up bits of entrails from the mire as they swooped past, while the black giants— the jötnar—panted with slackened jaws while they waited. The looming sauropod staggered and convulsed, its eyes torpid and distant, its striped body pale, then attempted another call, only to produce pink foam from the rim of its pendulant maw.

"*Gods,*" Lotta muttered through trembling lips.

The aim of Fischer's focus broke for a moment. He'd never thought of Lotta as religious. Quite the opposite. She had alluded to her upbringing before and had appeared to have shunned her heathenistic roots.

It's all she has now, he thought as he gazed at the towering giant. He massaged his aching forearm through its dressing. *All that is familiar.*

And what about him? Was that why he was seeing—*hearing*—things? Mutilating himself?

One of the jötnar stepped toward its prey, and Fischer's thoughts evaporated. Its yellow eyes tracked the swooping tail, still very much a threat, despite its preoccupation as a third appendage buttressing the sauropod's vertical stance. The watchful predator pitched its torso downward and snatched something glistening and rotund from the turbid water, then threw its head back and swallowed the object whole.

The second beast, the larger of the two, paced toward the left flank of the swaying sauropod. Both predators hung back and watched, their arms hanging, claws twitching. The walls of the sauropod's chest expanded and fell erratically. Then the long neck slumped, the columnar hind legs listed. Like a felled tree, the great body teetered, gaining momentum as it tilted sidelong into the embankment. A tremendous eruption of mud and water rained down in a brown mist, coating the black hides of the jötnar so they glistened like wet obsidian in the waning sunlight. They closed in on their quarry, steering clear of the sauropod's tail and snapping at the flurry of winged intruders. They sheared away chunks of ragged flesh and bone like voracious Komodos.

"Jötnar," Fischer said.

Lotta's eyes fell, and she gave a meek nod. She groaned and stumbled to her feet, shaking the caked mud from her trembling hands, plucking globs from her hair. "I'm sorry," she said. She held her head down, her eyes brimming. "I-I didn't know. You tried to help, and I panicked and—"

"Don't be," Fischer said. He moved in and drew her into a brief embrace. "We're okay. We need to go."

Fischer could still hear them, the herd, wailing and thundering from the far side of the escarpment. He looked down at his shaking hands. Bewildered. Perplexed that he was still alive. The piss down his leg had grown cold. But there was no time to ponder the situation, no time to linger. They were still in danger. Needed to keep moving.

Something shiny and protruding from the mud caught his eye. He knelt to pick it up. Lotta's gaze fell on him as he wiped the object—his knife—against his suit liner. He turned it over in his hand, then extended it to her with the handle facing out.

"Dropped this," he said, and she took it into her trembling fingers.

And then she broke down.

"I din't know. I di-din't know," she sobbed into the back of her hand, her head shaking.

Fischer pulled her to him again, and her arms fell to her sides. "I know. Shhh, it's okay," he whispered. "Let's get you back onto solid ground, okay?"

He looked around. The water had risen almost half a meter, forming banks along the base of the copse.

There was a distant *clomp*, and he looked back at the gorging beasts. *The jötnar.* They appeared oblivious to the water around their ankles, tails pitched to the heavens with bloodied snouts buried in their prize. Amid the lapping waves, Fischer spotted the bulging stomach of the sauropod, a group of winged creatures perched atop it, probing with prodigious beaks. Out of the disarray jutted the barbed end of a broken tail.

"Let's get into cover," he said.

Lotta's eyes turned up at him, then glanced back beyond the bed of horsetails. Together, they gazed through the beaten path laid down by the beast, into the hummocked cycads.

"What if there are more of them?" she said.

Fischer placed his hands upon her shoulders. "I won't let anything happen to you. Do you understand?"

Her eyebrows drew together, and she nodded. Tears carved tributaries down her mud-smeared cheeks, and at that moment, Fischer saw Ellsa. The world around him melted away, and it was only them.

"I'm right here," he said.

| YEMA >

Perez was jolted into consciousness.

Her wrists seared with pain; her knees ached. She lay on her side and gazed through slitted eyes that were met with a dim orange glow. She heard her name, but wasn't sure of the muffled voice's direction.

"Cam, wake up. Please wake up."

Nedjma?

She turned her head, and a gag climbed her throat. There was no time to react before the vomit erupted from her nose and mouth. Her body tensed, the rush of bile from her lips pooling around her head. She retched until her ears popped, then retched some more.

She was jolted again. The sound of groaning steel surrounded her. An alarm shrieked somewhere, or maybe it was just the ringing in her ears. Slowly, she started to recognize things: the red-levered escape hatch, the honeycombed ceiling, the webbed seating along the walls. Her head swiveled toward the cockpit, then to Nedjma's panicked face floating above her. Perez saw that she was on her knees, her hands behind her back, and—like the backdrop that framed her—Nedjma was spinning.

"Cam," Nedjma said, her speech labored. "Cam, I think we're going down. We got caught in a sandstorm."

With this realization came the sharp recollection of a bloody sun falling over the hazy mountains, and a swelling dust cloud in the distance.

The interior of the cabin flashed bright copper, then a clap of thunder drowned out the groaning walls and the droning engines. Another jolt traveled up through the floor. The shaking ceased. The engines powered down, their high-pitched hum fading to give rise to the deafening hiss of sand battering the *Defiant's* exterior.

Footfalls approached. Perez cranked her neck, her cheek sliding through tepid vomit, the smell of which made her retch again. She was turned over, her head swimming. Heightened pain spilled into her wrists, and then the restraints fell away. Her breath caught as her eyes fell on a pair of black boots planted in front of her face.

"We're grounded, need to keep moving."

Oz.

Nedjma straightened. "What? Out *there?* In *that?*"

"Your friend here insisted *you* tag along, so here we are. Could have had a wall of dust between us and them by now."

Nedjma returned to her usual diffidence.

Perez pushed off her elbows into a sitting position. Heat flushed into her cheeks.

He knew about the storm and intended to get out ahead of it to evade pursuit.

"Let's get one thing straight, *pollita,*" Oz said, leaning over her. "You are cargo. Property. And *she* is dead weight. Not in the contract. *¿Comprende?*"

"She comes with us," Perez managed. Her ribs ached, nose, and mouth burned with the acrid flavor of stomach acid. "Why am I so important to the Russians?"

"Doesn't matter," Oz said and turned his gaze on the rear hatch. "We need to go out on foot. Should get to the mountains by morning. Morocco, maybe another day's hike over the Saharan Atlas."

"*Morocco?*" Perez bristled, giving him a once-over. He looked like a gorilla looming over her in the orange light. "The Moroccan government will extradite us straight back to the UEF."

Oz disregarded her and turned back. "Let's go."

Perez pressed. "If we're heading in that direction, we must be close to SANCTUM. We can use the tunnels under the domes. They lead to shipping routes, one of which is in Chellala, near the Moroccan border."

Oz doubled back. "Out of the question. We passed the domes about a click back. All access points in and out of here are being monitored or patrolled."

"*You* didn't seem to know anything about them."

"I'm on a need-to-know brief. There's plenty I don't know. It's a risk."

"So is your plan. We won't survive the journey. And if we're being pursued, what's to keep them sending patrols over the mountains as soon as the storm clears?"

Nedjma's eyes darted anxiously between them.

Oz lingered quietly, his reflective eyes glinting orange. His jaw tightened, and he turned back to the cockpit. Perez heard a back and forth between him and his Russian comrade for a while, the conversation swelling at times into what sounded like a heated argument. He then reached for his shemagh and helmet and moved back into the cabin.

"We'll take the tunnels," he said with indifference. "I've got LIDAR, so stick with me unless you want to get lost. That happens, you're on your own. Do as I say, or the restraints go back on."

Outside the *Defiant*, visibility was about a meter. Even with the visor's headlamp, Oz and Nedjma appeared as dark smudges before Perez. The roar of sand scoring her suit was as deafening as a waterfall, and violent gusts whipped every which way, exacerbating her lingering vertigo. Oz waved them forward, his rifle drawn, just as lightning cast a rusty glow over their hazy surroundings. Perez imagined she was on Mars.

They pushed, hunched-over, trudging through the sand and wind. Arrived at the base of a thinly barrel-shaped structure Perez recognized as a derelict pod.

We landed in the apiary.

She craned her neck toward the top of the structure, but it was mostly veiled in the ruddy haze, where it loomed like a headstone in a dense fog.

She wondered for a moment how far she was from her own pod. Her mind drifted to the medicine cabinet, the misoprostol. The thought was fleeting, inconsequential, no longer relevant. She let it go. And it was then that she realized Basem's final act had saved Ruth. Had saved her.

And now, it's time for me to let you go, too, Osito.

She swallowed hard. There would be time to reflect later. She renewed her focus on Oz's lumbering form and followed. The realization about where they were lent some assurance that he was indeed leading them in the right direction. When they finally arrived at Sector C of the ARC, Perez allowed her mind to approach a modicum of trust in their objective.

"How do we get in?" Nedjma said sheepishly. "Do you have your access badge?"

"No." Perez tried to think when she last had it. "I didn't have it on me when they came for me and Basem." It was somewhere in her pod.

Shit. Too late to go back.

Nedjma's jaw dropped. "Wait, you found *Dr. Bensoussan?*"

"Enough talk," Oz said as he stepped forward and fished around in his plate carrier. He pulled something out and tapped it to the reader, then handed it to Perez. "Here." It was Nedjma's access badge.

Perez went first.

The silence inside the main lobby was as deafening as it was sudden. Somehow, it registered louder than the storm outside, the darkness more suffocating.

"Where is everyone?" Perez's breath quickened. She turned back so the beam of her headlamp fell on Oz.

His eyes remained distant, focused, his rifle at the ready. "Keep moving."

"We had a team in place," Perez said, her voice trembling. "Where are they?"

You didn't want us to see, she thought, her eyes burning into him until she saw nothing but red. *That's why you didn't want to come here. They've taken everyone, and we're not supposed to know about it.*

Along the far wall of the lobby entrance, an access terminal pulsed with soft green light. Perez hurried across the marble floor toward it and tapped the holographic display, which immediately morphed into a blue SANCTUM logo, followed by a line of text.

MANUAL OVERRIDE REQUIRED. ENTER CREDENTIALS TO CONTINUE...

> CPEREZ
> **********

ENTER COMMAND...

CMD> |status report>

[YEMA CONTINGENCY: Sanctuary Theta - Animal Revival and Conservation (ARC), DOME STATUS: latent]

"Someone activated the Yema Protocol," she said through the knot swelling in her throat.

Nedjma broke her silence. "What does that mean?"

"It's the dome's contingency directive, an automation of its constitutive functions. Temperature, barometric pressure, humidity, hydrologic cycling. Everything needed for ecosystem survival for up to three months without oversight. Schulz must have triggered it before... before *they* took her." She shot a glowering gaze at Oz. It took everything she had to choke back tears. "I am going to make it my fucking *purpose* to ensure you bastards pay for this."

"That so?" Oz's nostrils flared.

"*Yes.*"

She quavered with rage. Overcome with apoplexy, imagined herself rushing this mountain of a man—*no, not a man. Not a fucking man at all*—without any plan other than to kill him.

Until he raised his rifle.

"I'll be waiting, then. But right now, you do as I say," he said and turned his gun on Nedjma, "or I'll shoot *her* in the fucking head."

Nedjma's face went ashen, eyes wide with terror. She looked at Oz, then Perez. "*Cam?*"

Perez held her hands out and started backing away. "*Don't...*" she whispered. "Don't."

Nedjma started to plead, shifting her gaze between them. "*Please....*"

Oz narrowed his eyes and rounded his burly shoulders to emphasize his intent. "Shut the fuck up. Now *move.*"

Perez shot a reassuring look at Nedjma, whose brow had creased with panic. Sweat glistened in the glow of Nedjma's visor, her scar a silver line above her trembling lower lip. Wanted to tell her everything would be okay, even though she knew she couldn't promise that. She glowered at Oz and, with her hands balled into fists, turned back to the terminal.

A spasm coursed up her abdomen. Ruth shifted.

"Tell me what you're doing," Oz growled.

"We can't get inside without a manual override."

"Then get on with it."

"I need a damn *minute*." Sweat poured down her cheeks as she worked feverishly with trembling hands. "The best course of action is to pause the protocol so that the dome will go back into lockdown once we're inside"—she cast a glance toward Oz—"in case we're pursued."

And to preserve the ecosystem.

Oz looked at her suspiciously, but conceded with a nod.

She returned her focus to the screen.

```
CMD>    |yema_prot_pause>
        [override y_n?]
  >     |y>
        [specify time parameter]
  >     |20:00>
        [please wait...]

        [YEMA PROTOCOL OVERRIDE: GRANTED. TIME TO
        REACTIVATION: 20:00. AUTH: perez, camila.]
```

Her gaze broke from the screen momentarily. She gave Oz a sidelong glance, but resisted the temptation to turn her head. She heard him shift impatiently over her shoulder while Nedjma quietly sobbed.

"Stop that," Oz said. Nedjma went silent.

"Almost done." Perez's head swirled. Her whole body shook. "I'm activating the dome's occlusion system to block outside surveillance..."

"*Hurry. Up.*"

```
CMD>    |set_occl>
        [activate y_n?]
  >     |y>

        [EXTERIOR OCCLUSION: ACTIVATED. ARTIFICIAL NIGHT
        CYCLE: INITIATED.]
```

"Done."

Oz motioned with his rifle for them to start walking.

Perez led the way down the darkened corridor, lined with its blown-out glass doors leading to the Hatchery on the left, Limnology and Environmental Engineering on the right. She recalled the crunching glass underfoot in the immediate aftermath, the bloodied woman wandering aimlessly with a gash across her head down this same corridor. The breath stopped in her throat with the memory of running out into the open to face another aftershock. Watching EDEN get swallowed into the Earth. Then the sand swallowing her, too, and in that moment, thinking she would die.

Perez closed her eyes for a moment as she approached the chamber door. She held Nedjma's badge to the reader.

ACCESS GRANTED
DON SUIT
TIME TO DECONTAMINATION: 03:00

The door opened. She stepped inside first. Nedjma and Oz followed.

"Our suits will suffice," Oz said.

"No. They won't." Perez scoffed. "For one, ARC's environmental suits are specialized to ward off predators, of which there are many—"

Oz readied his rifle and cut her off. "Our suits will suffice."

Perez glowered at him, but his standing threat—and Nedjma's growing anxiety—made her second-guess any further dissent. It would not introduce any added peril to ARC's already-flailing ecosystem, so she deemed it a battle best left unwaged.

"Okay, then. We'll each need to step into a stall."

Oz let out a grunt. "I'm not going in one of those."

Her frustration grew in equal measure with her fear. She knew what he was thinking. That the moment he stepped into the coffin-sized decon stall, he'd be vulnerable to sabotage. That this was Perez's turf, not his, and if he didn't watch his step, he'd find himself falling victim to subterfuge. *And on some level*, Perez thought, *he's right*. Only that opportunity was not now.

"The system won't permit passage into the dome if we are not cleared," she said, her throat dry.

Oz swept the barrel of his rifle and pointed it at Nedjma. "How about I blow her head off? How's that for clearance?"

A surge of panic stole over Perez as she watched the terror on Nedjma's face heighten, her eyes wide and ringed, her mouth hanging open, cheeks sunken and sallow.

"I don't have any control over it." Her voice wavered. She could hear the fear in it, and she knew Oz could, too. "The system is automated."

"Don't fuck with me."

"I swear to you, I am not lying. Please. Please don't."

Nedjma's sobs swelled uncontrollably. She sucked at the air in frantic gulps.

Oz rammed the butt of his gun against her helmet, and her head whipped backward, almost sending her to the ground. She recoiled and cowered with her hands raised and shaking.

Perez's heart leapt into her head.

"*Please. I don't—don't want to die. Please. I'm sorry. Please, I'm so so sorry. PLEASE.*" Nedjma begged.

"SHUT UP!" roared Oz in response. "Shut the *fuck* up!"

Seeing Nedjma in such distress, and being unable to act on it, brought Perez to her breaking point. It took everything she had not to set Oz off any further. She believed his intent to kill Nedjma was more than hyperbole, and she was helpless to stop him.

But Oz appeared to ponder his next step. He turned his back for a second, then doubled back. Perez wanted nothing more than to get into his head. He seemed conflicted.

He stared emptily at Nedjma. A look of disgust that made Perez hot with rage. His chest heaved as he took aim. He held it for what seemed to be minutes, the entirety of which Nedjma pleaded. This only appeared to enrage him further.

And then he lowered the gun.

"Remember this," he said after a long pause. "And if either of you decide to pull any shit, don't think I won't leave you bleeding in a goddamned gutter." His eyes rolled away from Nedjma, now groveling at his feet, and fell on Perez. "Fuck with me, and *her* blood is on your hands."

Perez was shaking almost too much to manage a nod of understanding.

"Good." Oz racked his rifle and stepped in front of the first stall. "Show me what to do."

Perez helped Nedjma to her feet and held her until her trembling and sobbing subsided. After the decontamination was complete, the three of them watched in silence as the pressure equalized and the entrance to the dome hissed open.

The dome's interior was pitch-black. Silent. Still. It felt strange not being able to see the geodesics overhead. Thick white shafts cut through the darkness from their helmet lamps as they stepped beyond the egress into the open, where conifer fronds loomed just beyond the entrance like silent observers. Perez thought of the sensation of ARC's soft soil underfoot, how this would be the last time she experienced it. How she might never again see fields of flowers like the impala lilies that flitted past as she panned her beam toward the waiting rovers outlined in digital yellow.

"We'll take one of those," she said. "The tunnels are accessible from inside Mt. Qalil. I know the way."

Oz waved his rifle. "You drive."

Perez started forward, her breathing loud inside her suit. Each footfall rang like thunder in her ears. Her hand found the door handle and lifted, pain shooting from her wrist up her arm.

"You." Oz waved Nedjma to the passenger side. "Passenger seat." He followed her around and stepped into the back of the cab.

Perez moved into the driver's seat and secured her restraints. She stole a glance toward Nedjma, who was staring straight ahead with tears streaming down her cheeks. She pushed the ignition, and the headlights bloomed into the inky blackness, illuminating a dirt path hugged by more overhanging cycads. The windshield's LIDAR painted the outside world with a three-dimensional overlay of red, green, and blue grid lines that provided a detailed topography of their surroundings.

Driving through the ARC by night was a strange experience. The dirt road turned and opened to the grassy ridge where the lone Saharan cypress rose from the blackness like a knotted cadaverous hand.

One of the last in existence. A warden over its domain.

Its ashen trunk crossed into the beam of the headlights as the rover rounded a corner, then fell back into darkness.

As they continued down the path, gnarled ironwood trees[1] hugged either side, growing denser until they were surrounded by forest. Gaunt trunks jutted high overhead like arthritic bones, and along the shoulder rose the skeletal branches of shrubs. They cast moving shadows like black claws, only to recede again as the rover charged forward.

"Faster," Oz said.

Trees whipped past, their choking shadows rising and falling away. They were still a few hundred meters away from where they would need to get out and walk the rest of the way to the mountain. The rover started to round a sharp turn. A digital outline of Qalil's peak swelled just beyond the trees, growing larger by the second.

Perez gazed up at it momentarily, returning her eyes in time to catch something large materialize from the darkness in the middle of the path. Something *alive*.

Is that—

"Shit!"

She torqued the steering wheel all the way to the right and slammed the brake, sending the rover into a skid.

"Slow down—" Oz slammed into the back of her seat with a painful groan.

But before Perez could process the thing rushing up at her, she slammed on the brakes and pulled the steering wheel sharply to the left. The rover groaned, then canted onto two wheels. The world rotated just as it had when she woke on the *Defiant*. She was falling sideways. Nedjma screamed.

CRUNCH.

The impact ripped through her. The restraints pulled painfully, digging into her ribs as her body slammed sideways against the passenger door. Pain coursed through her shoulder so intensely that she saw lightning bolts. The sound of collapsing graphene filled her ears. There was a brief sensation of weightlessness. Blood pooled into her head and into her fingertips, which now grazed the ceiling. She was upside down, her weight shifting so the harness dug into her shoulders. A thick metallic taste filled her mouth—the taste of blood. Its warmth rushed over her face, burned her eyes until her

---

1 *Lophira lanceolata* and *Lophira alata*

vision became a swirling nebula. She heard glass shattering, grit scraping the hull's exterior. Heard the sickening *thud* of Oz's body slamming against the cabin's walls—*like the sound of a bird striking a hex panel*—his guttural cries somehow penetrating the deafening carnage unfolding around her. Her body was jerked right-side up again, the deluge of blood now falling in sheets down her neck. She tasted it, choked as it clogged her throat.

Nedjma screamed again, but the scream was cut short.

< | | BENEDICTION >

I'm right here.

Daddy will always be right here.

"Why do you lie to her?"

Fischer pulled out of hugging his eldest daughter. He wiped the dirt from her bloodied knees and looked back into her piercing blues with a smile and a wink. Still kneeling, he turned to face his wife glaring expectantly through the screen door of their military housing unit with her hands on her abdomen. They had decided to name the baby Emma. Hard to believe Joss was already five months along. His eyes met hers.

"*Come again?*" Fischer said.

Even through the shaded doorway, his wife's beet-red cheeks beamed through her tousled blonde hair, every bit as wild as Ellsa's. He always thought she looked beautiful when she was mad. Resented that about her. Made her seem colder somehow. More distant.

As the sun bore down on that clear afternoon, he wondered how long she had stood there.

Did she watch Ellsa fall off her bike and just stand by?

Jocelyn's hands fell to her sides and clenched into fists. "The girls... Why do you fill their heads with rubbish? We both know you'll be off on another mission when they need you most."

If it weren't for the pregnancy, Fischer would have thought Jocelyn was fucking someone else. Hell, maybe she was. Maybe *that* wasn't even a line she wouldn't cross.

He shook the thought, the dark voice that had increasingly tempted him to return to the bottle in recent months.

Not fair. You know that. It's the depression. Happened when Joss was pregnant with the other two. It's always worse when she's expecting.

Aye. Sure. Whatever you say, kamerad.[1]

Fischer ruminated often. Had countless conversations with himself. Found ways to self-soothe. But it wasn't enough to keep him from biting back this time.

He turned to Ellsa, his eyes still level with hers, and smiled warmly. "Hey, Sunny, why don't you show Mama and Papa how brave you are? Show us how good you ride now."

Tears still streaming from her eyes, knees still oozing, his daughter nodded and skulked back to the tiny pink two-wheeler. Fischer stood and turned back to Jocelyn.

"Lie to me if you want," Jocelyn continued, "but don't lie to my daughters. Especially Evi. You *know* how she is."

Your daughters? Fischer sucked air through his teeth. "*Our daughters.*" He paused momentarily, knowing better than to say what came next. But it came all the same. "You off your meds again, Joss?"

"*Fuck* you."

Fischer's regret was instantaneous. He massaged his brow, refusing—against his better judgment—to apologize. "Meine Frau,"[2] he said, seething, "we're not doing this. Not here."

Jocelyn's eyes narrowed. Her cheeks flushed a deeper shade of red. "*Don't* do that."

"Do what?"

---

1 "Comrade" (German)
2 "My wife," German term of endearment.

"Try and get *sweet* after you put me down," she hissed through the screen. "Don't be a fucking shit, Edgar. You scream bloody murder in the middle of the goddamn night, then act like *I'm* crazy?"

"That's not what I—"

"Evi and Ellsa are terrified of you since you got back. *Scared of their own goddamned father.*"

Fischer was about to respond when someone—one of the new neighbors, a serviceman in full military uniform—came walking past with a knowing glance. One that said *I feel you, kamerad.* Fischer greeted him with a nod, then returned his focus on Jocelyn. The corners of his mouth fell. "You done?"

"Oh, *aye,* I'm past being *done,*" she clapped back.

He waved his hand dismissively. "I'm taking Ellsa for a walk, get her mind off her knees. Can't do this right now, Joss."

He knew Jocelyn hated it when he withdrew, but he found it impossible to fight the impulse at times like this. He had already started toward Ellsa when she called after him.

"You know, you've been different since Daugavpils."

There was a slight stutter in Fischer's step, but he continued forward.

"What the hell happened there, anyway? Why don't you just talk about it if it was so bad?"

He kept walking. Watched Ellsa ride in circles near the end of the drive, blood trickling down her shins, then doubled back momentarily.

"Don't go there, Joss. Don't." He returned his attention to Ellsa, who greeted him with a wide, partially toothless smile, and for a moment, all the bullshit faded from his mind. ›

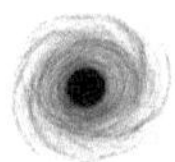

Day 6, Zenith — The Copse

I'm right here.

It happened again. Fischer had lost himself.

God help me.

So, it had come to that. *Prayer.*

He chuckled halfheartedly and opened his eyes to catch Lotta staring at him. She had looked away too late, but it didn't seem to keep her from playing it off, pretending to be distracted by the minutiae of their surroundings. Fischer silently pondered how long she had watched him from beneath a leaning cycad. He raised his soiled hands to massage his eyes.

Thought about how many times he'd drifted, had visions, or dreamed since they found themselves in this alien hellscape. The episodes had grown more frequent, less predictable. Some were just memories, and others wild fabrications. Almost all of them felt real. Especially the hallucinations.

Fischer was propped up against another cycad across from Lotta, sweat soaking him beneath the sticky ESD liner, the smell of his own filth in his nostrils. He glanced down at the binding over his aching arm. The pain had subsided somewhat, enough to make a weak fist. He clenched his hand, and electric bolts shot up his arm. He opened it again just as his fingertips started going numb.

Progress.

His focus shifted toward a plot of scarred earth between where he and Lotta sat. Where an enormous, three-toed foot had raked up the dirt and dross. Another was planted almost two meters away. These led to a cluster of felled trees that now lay testament to their near-death experience.

"Jötnar." Fischer tossed the word out for maybe the fifth time since they took rest. It was an odd term, one he hadn't heard before. He glanced at Lotta expectantly.

She looked intently at her hands, fingers thick with the tarry pitch he'd glommed on before they broke camp. She seemed to avoid gazing at the hellish footprint, instead taking solace in the now-familiar practice of nail-picking. Fischer noticed she'd managed to dig clean through the pitch in some spots, drawing fresh blood.

He sighed. Caught a whiff of sulfur and piss.

They sat silently for a while until finally, Lotta broke the lull. "When I was little, my mother told me tales of giants…" Her voice sounded small, almost childlike. Fischer tried not to be reminded of Ellsa.

"The *jötnar.*"

Lotta nodded, unblinking as she studied her mangled hands. "It's what she called the Russian battalions along Norway's borders. We left

Sweden for Schwyz when I was young, in case they invaded Scandinavia the way they did the Baltics."

Fischer remained silent. Found himself slipping into the Latvian wilderness at the mere mention of the war. Tried not to lose himself again. Instead, he met Lotta's gaze as she looked up, her face drawn, her eyes brimming. It was enough to pull him out of his head a little while longer.

She's reliving her own *hell,* he thought.

Lotta reverted to studying her hands. Examined the weeping cuticles, the swollen fingertips. The tarry pitch gleamed, reflecting the shards of sunlight leaking through the still bracts.

"When I got older, I realized monsters weren't real. *We* were the monsters…." Her voice fell to a near-whisper. "*But I was wrong.*"

Oh, but we are monsters.

The dead Latvian kid's face flashed before Fischer like an overlay onto reality.

Then, with a shudder, Lotta acknowledged the footprint. "Monsters— the jötnar—they *are real.*"

Fischer studied her through narrowed eyes and chewed his lower lip. "They're surviving," he said. "Same as us."

Same as that fucking kid in the Daugavpils slums.

He raked his clotted beard and glanced across the mudflat from the shady cover of the copse. The river's banks were nonexistent, flooded beneath a reflective, murky sheen that mirrored a darkening sky swarming with pterosaurs. They had circled the brontosaur's remains for a couple hours now. The carcass was reduced to a sliver that barely rimmed the waterline, a parcel of flesh reduced to an ever-shrinking plot that teemed with the glistening, wet bodies of more winged beasts. The carcass was bloated in death, the severed tail of its challenger still sprouting above the bevy. The two "jötnar" had since retreated into the forest to escape the rising flood-water, surrendering their prize to the denizens of the sky.

Fischer shifted his weight, and something pressed into his left buttock. *Ow. What the—*

He reached behind himself, rummaged around his waist with his good arm, and pulled out a pair of silvery canisters—the two sieve cylinders. He'd forgotten all about them. He unsealed the first and looked inside.

Water. He took just enough to wet the lips, get a little on the tongue—then extended it toward Lotta. She accepted it with a meek smile.

"Thank you." She took a swig and leaned forward to hand it back. "Take the rest."

Fischer raised his brow and waved her off. "Ah… no, I insist."

"Ed…."

He nodded reassuringly, clenching, then opening his fist several more times. "We'll get more. Go on."

"Thank you." Lotta's smile widened a little. She placed the cylinder at her feet and watched the mottled shadows move along the dirt. Minutes passed.

Fischer opened the second cylinder and immediately smelled a smoky aroma.

"Fire carrier's still lit."

Aside from his knife at Lotta's feet, the rest of their supplies were gone.

Lotta acknowledged this with a nod and raised her gaze. "How's your arm?"

Fischer inspected his binding. It felt tighter. His arm had swollen and was beginning to ache now that the excitement had died down.

"Never better," he grunted.

But Lotta ignored this attempt at levity, her face serious. "We should change that dressing."

She picked up the knife, crawled over to him, and took his arm in her hands. Fischer's immediate instinct was to protest as images of the glowing animalistic eyes came to him. He recalled the cold touch of his little girl's hands guiding the blade. Remembered those eyes watching through the black of night.

No more pain.

"Ed? *Ed.*"

Fischer snapped back to attention to find Lotta gazing deeply into him.

He glanced down at her moving lips as if in a dream.

"Did you hear what I said?"

He nodded with a half-smile, looked down at his arm in Lotta's hands, and found himself calmed by her touch. It was kind, gentle. *Warm.* Gone was his desire to pull free as she cut the binding and began to unravel it.

Air kissed his clammy skin.

More memories flooded in: Evi binding his arms in pink ribbon, making him promise he'd never…

A sharpness swelled within him at the sight of the injury. The skin was dark with bruises, clotted with blood. There appeared to be multiple slices, but his arm was too soiled to fully appreciate their full extent. Lotta, her hands shaking, slowly poured the remaining water over the area and wiped it clean with the dressing, sending fresh bolts of pain through him. He winced and sucked air through his teeth.

"Sorry," Lotta said.

He nodded and looked at the wound. An incoherent whisper escaped his lips.

"How…"

It looked like a symbol carved deep into his flesh. His eyes met hers.

"I don't know," Lotta choked. "I don't—this symbol… it's meant to protect—"

"I saw you carve this into the dirt back at the camp."

"I know. I was trying to—I—n-never meant for…"

Lotta started crying.

"It's not your fault," he whispered, his eyes meeting hers. "It's not your fault."

His mind went numb as he let her fall into him, and he held her as the emotion spilled out. Hoped that she was too congested to detect the stench wafting from him. But she didn't seem phased, her face buried in his chest. What seemed like minutes passed before she relaxed a little, and he eased his embrace.

Lotta swept her hair from her face and wiped away tears. Without a word, she took the knife and cut away her remaining sleeve, then sectioned it into ribbons. Afterward, she stowed the knife and wrapped her makeshift dressing around Fischer's arm while he watched in stunned silence.

Same way Evi used to.

He cleared his throat and rose to his feet. "We best get moving."

He wanted to find shelter before nightfall, preferably on higher ground and somewhere with cover. Threats from the ground, the sky, and allegedly even the water made their existence problematic. Nowhere was safe.

Except maybe…

He peered through swaying cycads toward the ascending headland beyond the opposite edge of the copse. The shady undergrowth opened to a long, flat clearing dotted with peculiar shrubs arranged at regular intervals. The stretch of ground on which the strange plants grew looked continuous with the crop of trees where he and Lotta sat, forming a peninsular bar that bisected the floodwater and extended like an ivory finger from the wall of striated rock he had spotted earlier.

A steady run of translucent fog drifted slowly through the frame of latticed bracts.

"Hey, Ed?" Lotta said behind him.

"Yeah?"

"You had three children. How?"

"Aye. Called in a favor," he said, then cleared his throat. He stepped forward, disturbing a pair of small iguanian lizards that scurried through the undergrowth in a bluish-red blur.[3] "C'mon."

Lotta followed.

The sulfurous odor intensified once they moved into the open. Fischer realized it wasn't fog, but steam pouring up from a large fissure along the bar's edge to their left. The strange shrubs were interspersed at roughly even intervals, their leaves appearing shriveled through the coils of steam.

"What could possibly grow here?" Lotta muttered as they moved past the strange plants.

But Fischer's attention was aimed directly ahead, around fifty meters off, where the wall of rock rose almost straight up from the acrid brume, a brilliant ivory bulwark of sedimentary limestone. It appeared flat at the top, a monolithic table of stone—perhaps a mesa or scarp—standing sentinel above the flooded landscape. About two-thirds of the way up, the formation was bisected by a chalky vein that stretched as a horizontal band along its length. At the base of the wall, a sloped talus of fallen white stones gleamed through the slowly drifting haze.

---

3 *Uromastyx indet.*

Bleached seashells crunched underfoot as Fischer and Lotta advanced. There seemed to be thousands of them, forming the bulk of the bar, piled up over what must have been centuries, perhaps millennia.

Rising heat permeated Fischer's liner with each step. The soles of his feet started to sweat.

"Ground's warm," he said.

"Yeah. Geothermal?"

Fischer nodded. "Probably." His eyes and throat burned.

Fischer swept his head to the left, gazing across the tidal zone where the horizon met the concrete sky. There seemed to be no sign of any immediate threats, and things had grown eerily silent aside from the occasional wave breaking onto the newly formed banks of the bar. Against the backdrop—what was visible of it—flying creatures dove for fish into pockets of deeper water where rivers had flowed hours before. Farther into the distance, he saw thick gray sheets of rain. A trio of strange white cumulonimbus rose from the horizon like mushroom clouds erupting in the distance.

To the right, the coniferous forest continued past an enormous stone monolith jutting from the striated cliff face. The towering trees grazed the lip of the precipice as the canopy continued beyond it into a flooded alcove veiled in a cloud of trapped steam.

"That entire side is shale," Fischer muttered, panning his gaze as he surveyed the wall for viable routes to the top. "Deathtrap."

Lotta scoffed. "You want us to climb *that*?"

"Aye." Fischer's voice trailed to a whisper as his gaze fell.

He felt distracted. Pulled. He peered momentarily into the dark undergrowth of the forest, where the ecotone had flooded and transformed into a turbid marsh. He gazed into it, through coils of steam that drifted along the surface of the intervening floodwater, unsure of *why* he was looking, only that he felt drawn to do so.

For a moment, Fischer thought of Hassan, of the horrific state in which they had found him. He was still out there somewhere, swallowed up by the choking boscage. Likely dead now. Probably hadn't been alive in the first place. Not really.

The thought passed.

Fischer suppressed his sense of prescience and returned his focus to the looming scarp face. He glanced at the whitish band spanning the top. It was cracked and crumbling in sections. Appeared to be the source of the fallen rocks.

"We'll need to be extra careful there," he said, pointing to it. "Looks like it's breaking up, coming loose."

"How, uh, how high is it?" Lotta's voice trembled, cracked.

"Fifteen… twenty meters, tops."

"Oh…."

"You're okay." He tried his hand at reassuring her. It wasn't going well. "Just stick close."

A spasm coursed up his arm. He massaged it through the dressing and returned his attention to the oddly spaced shrubs. But as they got closer, he realized they weren't *plants,* but rounded mounds of loose vegetation— wilted ferns and white lotus petals—each about a meter in diameter. He approached the nearest one to get a better look.

"What are they?" Lotta said.

But before he could respond, his sense of premonition compelled him to steal a final cursory gaze toward the waterlogged forest. This time, he thought he heard a distant sound, like gently lapping water— someone, or something, trudging beneath the undergrowth through the knee-high deluge. He peered deep into the shadows, his heart pounding in his ears, his feet still carrying him forward. His mouth had gone dry, eyelids dragged over his burning corneas. Lotta spoke behind him, but he couldn't make out the words, the entirety of his focus beyond the skirt of the flooded tree line.

Then, something—*someone*—shifted beneath the shadows of the giant conifers. A shape standing in the water, watching them through a waft of drifting steam.

Watching *him.*

She. She was watching *him.*

The water came almost to her knees, her legs black with mud, a flowing white nightgown draped over her emaciated frame. An eldritch face shrouded beneath stringy blonde hair dripped with water, though not even the darkest shadow could conceal its pallor. Through the darkened lines, the vague form, Fischer saw tarry pits where there should have been eyes. Empty black voids, their pull growing by the second.

And, as he stared—as a momentary break in the lazy steam cleared his line of sight—he saw an echo of his former wife. Her papery-thin lips parted, and from her carious mouth bloomed a cluster of pink fluted stalks.

Ed Fischer failed to realize his error until it was too late. Until his foot caught the lip of something jutting up from the ground. Until all he could do was turn his eyes back to meet the pile of greenery rushing up at him through the mist.

UEF / RD
EYES ONLY

Ministry of Defence
United European Federation

Memorandum of CCTV Interrogation. Partial Transcript.

JUNE 17, 2147, 18:21

Appearances
<u>Dr. Bogdan Kazimierz</u>
<u>Dr. Aegis Galani</u>

<u>Galani</u>	My apologies for your treatment, Dr. Kazimierz. Until my arrival, I did not appreciate the magnitude of your... hardship... at the hands of our servicemembers. I assure you, the Oberstleutnant has received a proportionate reprimand. He will not harm you again, you have my word.
<u>Kazimierz</u>	Thank you, Aegis.
<u>Galani</u>	But an apology is not adequate, old friend. Reparations are in order.
<u>Kazimierz</u>	Reparations?
<u>Galani</u>	What would you say if I gave you the entanglement project? Dr. Kazimierz, Principal Investigator of Entanglement Studies. Has a nice ring to it, wouldn't you agree?
<u>Kazimierz</u>	I... what... but Lotta....
<u>Galani</u>	Lotta Eklund no longer exists within this reality, isn't that what we concluded?
<u>Kazimierz</u>	Her doppelgänger is still Lotta Eklund. Still the face of the project.

Galani	Regardless of which manifestation of the Copenhagen interpretation Dr. Eklund enjoys, EIRO's confidence in her leadership has been irrevocably shattered. I assure you she will never witness the inner workings of the Higgs again. So, are you done with the histrionics, or would you like me to consider someone else?

Kazimierz	No... I mean, yes... yes. I'd be honored to continue the work.

Galani	Good. Now, on the matter of these doppelgängers. Tell me everything you have discovered.

< ꕔ | BEHEMOTH >

| "You said things would get better once we got to Geneva, Edgar." The screen door mesh did little to conceal Jocelyn's flushed cheeks, the flash in her eyes. "You're working odd jobs for low pay."

Gravel crunching beneath Elisa's bicycle tires filled the silence as Fischer glared up at his wife from the drive. His vision narrowed.

"It's not *low* pay," he said.

She wants you to drink again.

"Is for an *engineer.*"

Wants to usher you into ruin.

"I'm working on it."

Jocelyn laughed. "We've been *here* six months, and not a fuckin' *thing* has changed."

Wants to take the girls away from you.

Fischer's cheeks rolled. "Would you watch your mouth?" He nodded toward Elisa, riding happily again on her bicycle, knees bloodied without a care in the world. Fischer turned back to his wife.

"Don't tell *me* what to—"

Jocelyn went silent then. Her eyes flashed with something like shock, and her jaw went slack. One hand clutched her abdomen, the other still pointing at Fischer.

He took a step forward. "*Joss?*"

Ellsa's bicycle tires fell silent behind him.

"Mama?"

Fischer could not tear himself free to attend to his daughter, could not look away from his wife.

"*Joss....*"

A red spot appeared between Jocelyn's legs. It grew. Bloomed into a bright red band that cascaded down her white nightgown.

"Jocelyn!" Fischer ran up the porch and threw the screen door open. Made it in time to catch her fall.

Her face had gone pale, her eyes rolling in their sockets.

"Help! Someone help!" He guided her to the ground and swept her hair aside. "Jocelyn, hey... *Jocelyn...*"

No, it's too soon. She's not due for three months. It's too soon....

"Mama!"

Ellsa...

Fischer turned to the sound of his daughter's footfalls pounding up the drive...

...but not before everything was consumed in blinding light. >

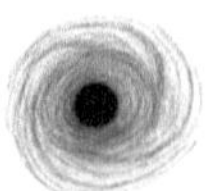

Day 6, Post Meridiem — The Bar

Fischer reacted a split second too late to mitigate the impact.

Crunch.

A flash of white light filled his vision as a bolt of pain exploded through his injured arm. The air left his lungs just as he heard Lotta's shrill voice in his ears.

"Ed!"

Her hands braced his back.

"M'fine," he lied through gritted teeth, his arm searing like a hot blade had plunged into it.

Lotta helped him to his knees.

"Are you okay? Are you hurt?"

"Just lost my balance."

Fischer glanced into the tree line and spotted a solitary ripple pass into the open floodwater.

Jocelyn was gone.

Just another vision, he thought. *Just the DTs. It's all in your head.*

Little Man had started up again, thumping away at his temples.

He was parched. *Ached* with thirst. But not for water. Hadn't had a proper drink in days. It got bad enough that colors seemed washed out, his surroundings desaturated, and the shakes still made an appearance several times a day.

But the visions… he'd thought he had finally moved past those.

"What is it?" Lotta's trembling voice lopped Fischer from his thoughts like a guillotine, her eyes wide. "Did you see something?"

"No," Fischer said. "No… just… lost my footing."

Lotta climbed down and helped him upright. A rush of vertigo befell him, and everything started to spin, his field of view narrowing. He tried to swallow, but his throat was sandpaper. Tried again. Failed. Turned his focus on his breathing.

The world around him became stationary again, and his lungs filled, burning with the acrid air pouring up onto the bar. The vertigo faded.

Once he gathered himself, he realized that he had fallen into a shallow pit, its walls a little over waist height. It appeared rounded, about his body length in diameter. And it was warm. *Very* warm. He leaned forward atop the collapsed leaves and bracken. Something trickled down his hands—a thick, translucent glop—oozing from his fingers like sticky mucus. He brought it to his nose, but it was odorless.

Lotta's jaw fell.

"It's a *nest,*" she said through cracked lips.

Fischer reclaimed enough lucidity to survey their surroundings despite the rising thrum in his skull. He scrutinized the other mounds, his cogent, logical mind at war with the intensifying pulse of Little Man's dance. He fought off a strong urge to lie in the warmth of the wilted greenery, enveloped in its cloying musk, a reprieve from the sulfuric fetor it seemed to somehow escape. Suppressing nausea to ill effect, his eyes darted from one nest to the next. There had to be three dozen or more, each a separate clutch. He returned to the bedding upon which he and Lotta knelt and started brushing it aside. It was warm, covered in more slime.

Then, something round caught his eye. It resembled a softball, milky white, and—aside from the crack in its thick carapace—appeared to be perfectly round. Fischer knelt forward and scooped it up, shocked by how heavy it felt in his hands. And warm, too. He ran his fingers over its surface, a rough texture with fine bumps like brail.

The heat was leaving it.

He inserted his fingernails into the crack and pried back a thickly walled wedge of shell.

"*Don't!*" Lotta hissed. "The parents might be close."

"Maybe. Maybe not."

"*What?* Have you *lost* your—"

"There's plenty of heat here to keep the nests warm. Stench keeps scavengers out. No reason for the parents to stick around."

"Young still need protection."

"Not necessarily. There must be at least six eggs per clutch, so maybe around 200 eggs. It's a numbers game."

"I still don't like it."

Fischer scanned their surroundings and raised his brow to emphasize his point.

"We've already destroyed this clutch, and we could use the protein," he said, removing the remainder of the top shell from the egg. The reddish yolk resembled a bullseye at the center of a translucent albumen sac in which dozens of spidery blood vessels sprouted. Fischer guessed it had probably been laid within the last few days.

A life cut short. He thought of Emma in her artificial womb, reminded of what it was like watching her through the ultrasound.

He nodded toward the empty sieve cylinder. "Hold that up for me, would you?"

"Quickly," Lotta whispered.

He jostled it in his hands, then tilted it against the waiting cylinder.

"Aye, just hold it steady."

Despite his efforts, the yoke ruptured and seeped a pinkish fluid that tinged the sac pink. Jocelyn flashed in his mind.

The blood. There was so much blood.

"Ed."

His vision had smeared over. He blinked. Breathed. The yolk started bleeding into the sac.

"Scrambled it is," he said, grinning at an unflinchingly stoic Lotta. The corners of his mouth fell, and he cleared his aching throat as the slurry filled the cannister. "Anyway, that should do it. Let's seal it and go."

They sealed the cannister and stumbled on wavering legs toward the scarp face, past the nauseating sweetness of the other nests. Fischer's weary feet dragged over the clacking shells, his mind racing, trying to rationalize what he had seen in the shade of the trees. He thought to look back again, but maintained his focus. Resisted the pull of the forest.

Bloody losing it, he thought as he arrived at the foot of the talus and peered up at the looming wall of rock.

Climbing was a skill familiar to Fischer. Was part of his training in the service—those punishing, weeks-long treks up the Alps bordering Schwyz and Morschach—but his joints weren't what they used to be. His knees groaned with each foothold. His fingers pulsed and ached as they gripped the abrasive rock.

But he and Lotta were making good progress. He had taken the lead. Wanted to get a lay of the rock face before subjecting her to an unfamiliar route, what with the state of her fingers. She took to it quick, though, mentioned that she'd taken a few bouldering lessons in college. But it was her injuries—not experience—that limited her ability. Her fingers were the most swollen he'd seen them, and he worried that if the bleeding got any worse, her grip might start to slip. He only hoped they could make it to the top before things got that bad.

Lotta sucked air through her teeth behind him.

Meanwhile, he was trying to keep his mind off his own pain. Easy enough, considering he kept seeing a vestige of his former wife in his mind's eye, her eyes sunken and glimmering behind a curtain of sopping hair. An Eidolon with her white gown and a band of blood running between her legs. And her *mouth*.

God dammit, kamerad. You're really losin' your fuckin' mind.

About a third of the way up, Fischer struggled to catch his breath.

He glimpsed past his legs and saw that Lotta was still doing okay, her face red and wincing. He pushed up, transferred his weight to his feet, and then craned his neck toward the ledge overhead. It blended almost seamlessly into the dull gray clouds, making the remaining distance a challenge to estimate. Sweat stung his eyes and blurred his vision, causing him to squint.

Another five meters or so. Just get to the top so you can get a fire going, make the best fuckin' scrambled eggs you've ever had.

Fischer's arm throbbed with renewed intensity. The compression of the wound dressing had forced all the fluid to his hand, which had swelled up like a balloon. The mounting numbness in his sweaty fingers made gripping the course stone more challenging with each hold. At one point, his right foot cut and slipped free momentarily, but he managed to recover purchase in time to span his good arm and keep from plummeting to his death. He pressed his chest against the jagged rock, his burning forearms groaning in protest, the thrum of his pulse in his ears. He shifted his weight to his right leg, his arms giving out just as he completed a short traverse to a narrow ledge where he could rest. Lotta wasn't far behind, but she seemed unaware of Fischer's close call.

He shouted down to her. "Let's stop here a moment."

They had reached a crumbling recess in the white band of layered stone bisecting the scarp face. It was almost blinding in his eyes. Felt chalky in his grip. Once his feet were under him, he spotted peculiar excavations covering its surface—vertical grooves resembling tilled earth—as if carved in the stone by a rake. The longer Fischer studied them, the more they started to remind him of the fingernail markings he had found in Emma's concrete tomb all those years back. He looked at his own fingers, their abraded tips sprouting beads of blood, and whispered her name. He turned silently and gazed across the flooded tableau.

"Everything okay?" Lotta said, clambering up beside him. She pushed up onto the platform and leaned forward to hug the wall, her chest rising and falling.

Fischer turned his head to speak, but a clatter of falling rock cut his response short. His head whipped to the left.

"*What was that?*"

Lotta's voice startled Fischer. He pressed his back into the wall. Felt high off the ground.

The sound had originated beyond his purview, behind the towering stone monolith that abutted the scarp face. Seconds passed. He heard it again, followed by splashes in the flood waters below. His neck canted toward the surface, where a bulwark of steady steam poured into the open from the obscured inlet. It drifted lazily across the water between the bar and the forest.

Fischer's first thought was that a section of the white band had fallen.

Then came a scraping noise from somewhere high up the rock face, about level with his position. Cyclic, almost rhythmic in cadence, it grew from the far end of the monolith.

Little fingernails clawing to be free. Scratching at the slab pinning her legs.
"Ed...."

He broke free of his momentary lapse. Watched as the backwater sloshed, sending large waves out across the surface.

"*There's something over there,*" Lotta whispered.

Something *was* moving through the water beyond the monolith. Something big, making its way toward them.

"Time to go." Fischer turned and then started to climb.

His fingers seared with pain, the knots in his forearms and thighs building with each pull of his arms, every push off his feet. The scraping sound was below him now.

Get to the top. Almost there. Get to the top.

His hands were now covered in chalky powder, each grip more precarious than the one before. The next hold collapsed in his hand and a jolt of panic shot from his heart to his rectum, which puckered tighter than a singularity. For maybe the fourth time that day, Ed Fischer almost met his end.

The embankment on the forest side of the bar now churned, and a cavernous, rolling *boom* like thunder moved through the rock and into him. *Boom.* He heard as much as felt it the second time: a resonant, orchestral sigh. It was deep and low, vibrating the rock under his pulsing fingertips. Several small pebbles tumbled past his head and added to the rock pile below.

"Almost there," he grunted.

Fischer had turned his attention to his grip when something massive crashed into the embankment at the edge of his periphery. Something that defied explanation. At first, he considered that a large slab of rock had fallen from the side of the stone monolith. But when he saw the thing rise back out of the water—a shadow behind a wall of rising steam—he saw an enormous gray column not of stone, but of *flesh.*

"*Jötunn,*" Lotta whimpered. "*Jötunn.*"

No, Fischer thought, staring wide-eyed toward the undulating water. *It's bigger.*

The column stood perhaps twice his own height. Although it was mostly obscured behind the monolith and the ebbing steam, he noticed that it terminated in a gigantic clubbed foot with a row of recurved claws splayed out to the side. Water fell in sheets as it crashed down again, the force ejecting a torrent of spray into the air. The flesh column pivoted— sinew and tendon shifting like iron pistons over bones of bronze—churning the water into a blackened slurry. Then, something like a mighty deodar swept horizontally above it—past the edge of the rock face—and sliced through the wafting steam.

A tail.

Fischer could do nothing but look on in complete disbelief. A rush of adrenaline filled him with a strange high that left him floating, a sensation heightened by his proximity from the ground. He was no longer afraid of falling, to his bemusement, but rather giddy. His disorientation manifested as tremors, the nerves in his limbs humming like plucked guitar strings.

Might be the willies, he thought. *Might be the DTs.*

The tail receded back into the mist, and it was then that the stone monolith appeared to fall away entirely, transforming before Fischer's eyes into a wall of gray, pebbly flesh.

Lotta shifted below him.

"Ed."

The rolling mass broke through the billowing thermals, strafing along the rock upon four groaning pillars that pushed through the water with ease and indifference. They carried the titanic thing onto the embankment—white coils of mist rolling lazily over flexing muscle—while seashells snapped underfoot like breaking bones.

Fischer was dumbstruck by the sheer enormity, the *size*, of what he beheld. But only once the head materialized did he witness the shifting behemoth in its entirety. And a *behemoth* it was, towering four, maybe five stories high. Its head was nearly level with his position, vaulted upon a long, thickly muscled neck. From its vast throat bulged walls of arteries beneath jostling gulars that slid over a tightly knit bulk down to a hulking—but noble—chest. It stood taller than a Penrose core or Goliath transport and was undoubtedly more massive than anything Fischer had seen in the natural history museums. An inexorable force of nature. Made a brontosaur seem meek by comparison as mist spilled from its enormous frame the way clouds flow over mountains.[1]

A renewed eagerness to get to the top stole over Fischer, panic spilling into his chest for the first time since the cliffside shifted before his eyes. His mind screamed at his muscles to *go*, yet he found himself unable to move, his heart rapping heavily against the walls of his ribcage as rills of stinging sweat traced the creases of his face.

But the behemoth appeared indifferent to their presence, its inky eyes—their corners seeping thick runnels of gummous rheum—focusing instead on the white sedimentary band stretching the scarp face. Its head went still for a moment, hovering close to the rock, then pitched itself forward, beak first. A terrible scraping shattered the momentary silence as snout dragged over stone, and nostrils vented long, slow sighs. And as the beast carved a sheaf of familiar grooves into the cliffside, Fischer could discern a row of strange cylindrical teeth hooded under its beak.

"It's eating *rocks*," Lotta said, her voice cracking.

The behemoth withdrew its prodigious head, leaving a trail of white dust in its path, a chalky scree billowing from its mouth. The dust tumbled

---

1 *Paralititan stromeri*

lazily to the ground like a cloud of chalk as the beast's tongue passed a bolus of stones into its waiting throat.

"What kind of animal eats—"

Another crash cut Lotta short.

Fischer saw another colossal form peel from the monolith and pass through the haze, the banks of the bar roiling in its shadow. A third emerged, and a *fourth*, their skin a reddish-brown mosaic of alternating spots and stripes. Each was coated in a pellicle of mud and guano that was blanketed in patches of bright green moss springing like fur along their backs.

Small pterosaurs clung to their bodies, probing for parasites while a cacophony of warbles erupted from their snapping beaks. Others weaved through legs and around heads, hawking black insects from the periphery, as diminutive to their symbiotic hosts as the bugs on which they dined.

One by one, the behemoths materialized like specters until nearly a dozen crowded the rock face—an assembly line of titans—each a walking biome vying for a position along the crumbling white band. With each quaking step came a deafening refrain of snapping shells as chasmal sighs groaned from rounded bellies, the culmination of which hit Fischer like a cannonade of thunder.

Then a new smell quickly overtook the waning stench of sulfur. Almost rancid, it intensified as the beasts approached. Smelled of spoiled milk. A hint of pine. Made his eyes water and his nose leak. His stomach balled up into his lower chest.

Lotta retched.

Fischer ripped his gaze from the advancing herd and eyed the top of the scarp.

Only a few meters to go.

"Eyes up," he muttered to Lotta. "Don't stop. I'm right behind you." He signaled for her to move ahead.

They scrambled up the scarp face, sending shards of rock careening to the ground below. The remaining strength in Fischer's limbs was waning, his forearms searing with each placement, his footing less precise, his fingertips rubbed raw. He gagged on the bilious tang mounting at the back of his tongue, desperate to escape the intensifying stench. He rolled his eyes, stinging with sweat, and gazed past Lotta toward the looming precipice. They were close, almost to the top. His injured arm had quit on him entirely, and his grip slipped. The pit in his stomach sank to his hips while his legs bellowed and seized, wedged into crags, the only thing keeping him from peeling away and plummeting to his death.

The final push manifested as a primal scream from his cracked lips as he cleared the precipice and fell weightily onto his back beside Lotta. He coughed, then opened his eyes to the gray clouds passing overhead. Terra firma pressed up into his shoulders. He listened to the warbling songs of winged creatures somewhere in the distance, the persistent scraping and popping shells beneath him. Heard the air cycle frantically through his lungs.

Still hacking, Fischer sat up and stretched his neck to peer out over the edge.

He immediately noticed that one of the behemoths had wandered into the nesting site, its head floating upon its great canting neck toward the nest he had fallen into. It hovered for a moment over the corrupted clutch, letting out a wet snort that scattered the top layer of vegetation. Then, a boundless grumble rose from its vibrating throat and its jaws fell, its inky eyes distant and unfeeling. The sound it made transformed into a throaty, gurgling bellow that was soon again muffled as its beak closed over the trampled remains.

Then the behemoth's neck muscles bulged, vaulting its head skyward as long strings of slime dangled from its grinding jaws, and its enormous legs set it in motion towards the water's edge.

The way the animal navigated the bar gave Fischer pause; not only did it disregard the other nests as it approached the embankment, but its movements appeared to be *cautious* and deliberate. It was *side-stepping* the healthy nests, having only disturbed the compromised clutch.

"*They* laid those eggs," Lotta said. "That one's cutting its losses, reclaiming nutrients."

"Could be," Fischer said, turning his attention back to the herd. He watched the Brobdingnagian beasts continue along the scarp face, their beaks scraping along the stone as if on impulse alone.

Reclaiming nutrients…

"It's a mineral lick," he said matter-of-factly. "They're after the calcium in the limestone."

A distant shriek tore Fischer's attention toward a cauldron of pterosaurs circling low over the flooded delta a few hundred meters out. Puzzled, he got to his feet and started along the cliff's edge to get a better vantage point.

"What is it?" Lotta said anxiously, pacing him.

"Don't know." Fischer tried not to stare at her bloodied fingers, which had taken on a concerning purpuric hue.

The winged things moved slowly clockwise on unseen currents. Another shriek split an intermittent silence. Fischer pressed on, past stunted, windswept trees like twisted hands clawing their way east. The world below slowly filled his vision, a new sliver of flood zone revealing itself with each step. Water swirled in bands of turquoise and brown where a brackish slough ebbed into what had been rivers, now a series of sweeping marshlands and swamps where none had existed before. He panned across the vast stretch of shimmering gray toward a horizon veiled in a soft haze and saw the setting sun—barely an orange smudge—over a distant, sprawling sea.

West.

Nearby, a shoal stretching parallel to the scarp rose from the intervening floodwater, where two dozen horizontal forms basked with gaping jaws. Though the island appeared to be a way off, the sheer size of the creatures made them easy to identify: giant crocodiles or gharials, with long, toothy snouts terminating in rounded bulbs, their limbs splayed outward, flat against the ground.[2] Farther in the distance, a chain of small islands dotted the water.

Fischer turned back and continued forward in his original direction—north, he supposed. A light breeze cooled the sweat on his brow. The pterosaurs circled hypnotically.

"Storm coming," he muttered as he approached the cliff's edge. He winced curiously. *More strange plumes in the distance.*

He saw movement in the water a few hundred meters out. His eyes followed, but it was gone before he could pinpoint it. Something directly below the winding aerials. He squinted, trying not to lose the spot where he thought it originated.

There....

---

2 *Elosuchus cherifiensis*

Something bulbous and large bobbed to the surface—a brontosaur—floating belly-up in deep water, its stomach bloated, legs jutting up at odd angles. *Only three legs,* because one was missing, reduced to a ragged stump. Another trill sounded overhead.

The carcass dipped, then rolled. It completed a full rotation, then came to rest again at its original inverted orientation, its legs locked in rigor mortis toward the heavens.

A smooth, glistening mass crested the surface. Fischer squinted harder. Something thrashed along the brontosaur's terminal end—a tail or flipper disturbing the water. Then several more emerged, their slender heads expelling gusts of spray from their snouts. They resembled breaching whales in some respects, except for their jagged, toothy maws, which possessed more reptilian characteristics. One of the glistening heads clamped its jaws around the brontosaur's neck and went into a roll.

A feeding frenzy ensued.

"That's them," Lotta said. "The *things* I saw in the stream. A bit larger, built a little heavier, but that's them."

Another toothy head clamped onto the brontosaur's stomach, twisting its hide like a wrung towel until a wedge of flesh snapped free. The water around it turned dark. The body rotated again. More creatures entered the fray, at least two of which appeared to be sharks.[3]

Then, the pterosaurs plummeted with folded wings, plunging into the water like torpedoes. Unperturbed by the frenzy, they resurfaced and launched skyward again with fresh scraps in tow.

All the while, crimson waves frothed and churned a foam with the color of blood on white linen.

---

3 *Tribodus indet.*

|AKILA>

The river had risen steadily every year since the coming of Spain's great coastal floods, but none compared to the fall of Perez's sixth birthday, shortly after Uncle Diego had gone missing. She recalled the torrential rain that fell from the sky in sheets that year, sometimes for days. It had set records in Benassal, but so had every year prior, spanning the last decade. This contrasted with the desertification of much of Spain and the inevitable water crisis that pitted neighboring towns and cities against one another, sometimes violently. No doubt a pretext for the Federation to mobilize more troops to the troubled province.

Perez remembered the sound of the river. The deluge had sheared away chunks of earth from eroding banks initially, and by the third day of continuous rain, homes had started washing away. And after days of flooding and erosion, caskets started washing away out of the historic Cementerio municipal de Benassal. Dozens had gone downriver from one of the various arteries flanking the cemetery, some washing up as far as the shores of Sant Pau d'Albocàsser—almost twenty kilometers away. Dozens were never found.

The authorities did nothing outside of the modus operandi. No national guard. No humanitarian aid. But UEF authorities did come amid the unrest. They brutalized. Incarcerated.

Murdered.

Perez's nightmares were not of men but of water—a great, churning wall of spume roaring like an ocean as it pursued her relentlessly. And despite how hard she ran, how fiercely she pumped her arms, it seemed that she never advanced, while that monstrous wave closed in with steady, unyielding fury.

The doctor had called it sleep paralysis. After a while, she learned to be aware of when it was happening, at times had woken to find herself unable to move with the walls weeping into her flooding bedroom. Over time, she gained the ability to break the episodes with regularity. Wiggle a big toe, move a finger. An intake of air reactivated her higher faculties—that was unavoidable. Sometimes, she'd jolt upright, urine-soaked and crying.

The bed-wetting persisted for years after the flood, well past puberty, and long after the dreams had altogether ceased.

And here again, Perez found herself running from that roaring tsunami for the first time since she was a girl.

She *was* that girl, the great wave hissing thunderously behind her. Terror coursed through her veins like an oily petulance, her leaden feet carrying her no farther than where she began. Her legs were unresponsive, excruciating in their sluggishness; no matter how hard she tried, there was no escape from the swelling wave. It churned and roiled, pulsing with flickers of light like a menacing cloud, its cold spray kissing the back of her neck.

And as it started to consume her, her eyes ripped open.

She couldn't move. She was upside down, her arms numb, head heavy with pooled blood. The sound of rushing water was still loud in her ears, the scintillating light searing into her skull. But as she looked around—as the cabin of the rover materialized before her—she realized that the sound of water, the flickering lights, were not fabrications of some wild fugue.

The gorge. We're near the gorge. Close to Qalil's entrance.

She had intended to take the service road where it branched and led steeply down the shallow ravine toward the mountain's entrance. She remembered driving, then losing control. Then they were rolling sideways, with the sound of glass and metal collapsing all around her.

The rover had come to land onto its roof. Its front end faced the service road, that much she could decipher. Then, as her vision began to clear, she could start to make out something caught in the rover's malfunctioning headlights, but the beams winked out before she could determine what it was.

The LIDAR display twitched against a stygian backdrop, malfunctioning over what remained of the partially blown-out windshield in its attempt to register the outside world. Shimmering lines of yellow and red crawled across what remained of the passenger side.

Perez searched in the dark. She tried to flex her fingers, get the blood moving. She tilted her head all the way to her right where Nedjma's faint outline dangled motionless in the passenger seat.

Oh, God, please. Please no. Tell me she's not...

"Nedjma?"

No answer.

Perez recollected only fragments of what had happened.

Lost control. Went off the road, then... crashing... and then nothing.

Nedjma had been in front, Oz in the back. If he was still with them, hadn't somehow been thrown from the vehicle, he wasn't making his presence known.

The headlights cut through the darkness again, illuminating the service road. Lying in the middle she saw the thing that she had almost run over, and the air stopped in her throat.

Akila?

The female giraffe's neck was pitched at forty-five degrees, her jaw hanging slack with ropes of spit dangling from her frothing mouth. Her glowing eyes, half-open, appeared distant, and behind her, a dissipating cloud of dust evaporated slowly into nothing.

The lights went out.

A deep chill froze Perez. She didn't remember hitting Akila, but everything had happened so fast.

Had she?

She regrouped. Narrowed her focus.

A tingling sensation spilled into her fingertips, then moved like wildfire up her arms. She made a fist. The sensation in her fingers prickled back to life, her pulse throbbing. She turned to Nedjma again, her throat swollen with panic. *Please don't let her be—* She cut the thought off. Her chest heaved against the restraints as she slowly raised her shaking hands to the harness clip. It went easier than she thought, and the next thing she knew, she was crashing painfully onto the cabin's roof.

The headlights came back on.

Light spilled into the rover. Perez inspected the driver's-side door, which had crumpled inward. The window was blown out, the view outside occluded by the trunk of an ironwood, its coarse bark lined with dim light along its cracks and edges. Perez rolled over, and the shell of her suit caught as she dragged herself over shards of broken glass and bark. Pain coursed down her pulsing arms, her throbbing fingertips.

Perez turned her attention to the cratered windshield. She positioned herself so her feet rested at the center, then brought her legs back and drove them as hard as she could into the glass. It gave a little, but the cost was a painful jolt up her ankles and into her knees. She brought them back again and delivered another blow. The crater bowed out a little more.

Come on.

Perez drew a breath and held it. Pulled her knees again into her chest, then drove her legs forward with everything she had. The windshield collapsed outward, and glass showered the soft earth outside. She peered out at Akila again. The giraffe hadn't moved, her breathing shallow, head swaying through labored breaths. A cloud of flies engulfed her like shimmering motes, her sweat-matted fur glistening in the headlight beams as steam coiled away from her into the encroaching blackness. Her muscles twitched in response to the biting insects, but that encompassed the extent of any resistance from her. Around two meters from where the injured giraffe lay, Perez spotted a pair of skid marks veering off the road into mounds of dredged earth and vegetation that cut a path to the rover. She tried to remember how many times they had rolled. *Two? Three?*

The headlights flickered, then winked out again.

Perez wriggled forward on her stomach, pushed her way out into the open, where she fell with a painful thud onto solid ground. She got to her hands and knees and crawled toward the passenger-side door while the intensifying sound of rushing water roared in her ears. She fumbled meekly with the handle and activated it, but the door didn't budge. Perez panicked. Its vertical opening mechanism was disabled because the rover was lying on its roof. She pounded desperately against the glass, but it had no give.

The headlights bloomed again, illuminating Nedjma's inert form, her face concealed behind her visor. She looked like a dead astronaut, an image Perez struggled to shake as she circled back to the rover's front.

Akila—the giraffe she loved, the giraffe she had raised—shifted in the corner of her periphery.

Overcome with emotion, a forlorn, powerless sense, Perez was aware of her gaze being lured back toward the service road. She watched in drawn despair in time for one of the flies to land on her visor. Only it wasn't a fly.

A bee?

Its wings buzzed, then fell still. Buzzed again. It crawled in front of Perez's face, its striped abdomen pulsing like a blackened heart. Snared in the incurved hairs of its hind legs, she discerned what initially appeared to be pollen granules, only these were perfectly spherical and refractile—little red orbs that resembled crimson dew drops. Then the insect flew off and disappeared into the horde swarming around Akila.

Perez thought it must have been a hallucination, a trick of the light. Bees were functionally extinct. They existed only inside critical care apiaries in the American Pacific Northwest, and those were pollinators that foraged during the day.

She thought of the refractile granules again.

Not pollen. Blood.

These bees collected *flesh*.

Then, from behind the giraffe's rear flank, two reflective eyes flashed white along the edge of the opposite tree line. Whatever it was must have stood three meters off the ground. A low, booming warble came from its direction. It sounded like a bassoon.

A moa outside its enclosure.

A brownish head bobbed into view momentarily before the rover's headlights failed again. But Perez had recognized the fleshy snout almost immediately as Iwa's. And it was smeared with blood.

Akila's breathing hastened. Thick welts, probably bee stings—or bites—riddled her entire body, which had started to swell in some areas. Her hooves scraped the roadway frantically in the blackness. She was trying to stand again.

Perez turned her focus back to Nedjma and felt her way back into the rover, crawling through the windshield and over the broken glass. She reached for Nedjma's restraints, calling her name as tears spilled from her eyes.

"Come on," she said, her speech slurred. "Nedjma, wake up. We have to go. Nedjma… *Nedjma*…."

She probed for the clip and pressed. Nedjma came down with a sickening *crunch*, and—to Perez's shock and relief—a pained groan escaped her lips.

"Nedjma?" Perez nudged her. "Nedjma, can you hear me?"

Nedjma groaned again.

"Hang on, I'm getting you out of here."

The headlights came back on.

Perez's eyes were pulled toward the back of the cab, where Oz's limp arm protruded from behind the driver's seat. She lingered for a moment in anticipation of any hint of consciousness, any tortured moan or twitch of the fingers. But none came.

Glass scraped and crunched beneath Nedjma's dragging body. Sprites flashed before Perez's eyes with each tug, her arms searing from the strain of pulling the weight of a human body. Her suit's heat mitigation whirred in her ears as sweat trickled into her eyes and mouth. She tasted dried blood on her lips. It covered her face so that her skin became tacky, sticking the creases together with every wince. Tears spilled down her cheeks, her vision a blur. She groaned, then pulled again. Nedjma barely budged—no more than a hand's length. Perez's painful mewls rose into primal shrieks, composed of an equal measure of pain and frustration, until she and Nedjma finally clapped to the ground outside the rover.

The headlights beamed into her eyes, blinding her, then went back out again. She activated her headlamp and investigated Nedjma's visor. Her face was covered in blood, but there was no visible wound. Nedjma's eyelids fluttered in the flare of Perez's headlamp, and her throat seized. She leaned forward and placed a hand on her student's shoulder.

"Nedjma, it's me," Perez said through gentle sobs. "I'm going to get you out of here."

She was convinced she saw Nedjma's eyelids flutter in acknowledgment. *She's still in there. She's going to be okay.*

Perez pushed off her knees and wavered onto legs of rubber. A subtle iron taste settled on her tongue as vertigo stole over her, her vision blurring, then narrowing as blood shunted from her head to her feet. Heaviness fell over her, a gravid somnolence that made her want to lie down and sleep. She resisted. Knew she might have a concussion. Or worse. Her mind went briefly to Ruth, wondered how much punishment she could take. She imagined the worst, and a pang of grief struck her, but she pushed the thought aside. Right now, she needed to get Nedjma to safety.

She stumbled forward, and a sharp jolt coursed up her right leg. Sucking air through gritted teeth, she transferred her weight to the other foot while her head swam. Wavering, she glanced toward the sound of water, her beam falling onto the crest of the narrow ravine beyond the rows of ironwood trunks and tangled chaparral.

The gorge had taken almost a decade to form, accelerated via laminar shearing in the early days of ARC's construction. The process mimicked natural erosion by running high-pressure water through the area. Over time, it matured into a sloped vale traversed by a broad stream, its walls now overgrown with vegetation. The steepest section formed a groove in the earth that spanned around 500 meters before flattening out. Perez recognized it because it flowed faster—and louder—than other sections of the watercourse. It also passed by the mouth of Qalil.

They were close.

Iwa bellowed another resonant warble. Then, from somewhere else along the shoulder, came an answering call.

Perez's beam sliced through the gloom back toward the service road and landed on a trembling Akila. She was framed within darkness, the hive a swarming fury around her. Iwa's head bobbed in and out of view, then disappeared altogether.

The answering call came again. It was identifiably moa, but more resonant than anything Perez had heard before. Unique vocalization patterns were characteristic of the large birds, a sort of vocal fingerprint. But this had the same idiosyncratic phrasing of Iwa's, only gravelly, with a muted, percussive click akin to a slowly opening zipper. An approximation.

Sort of like Iwa was being *mimicked.*

And then came a sound Perez had never heard before, but one she knew—one that was rarely observed, but well-documented—the haunting moan of a giraffe in distress.

She panned her flashlight over Akila's twitching hindquarters. The giraffe rocked forward with a punctuated groan, barely lifting onto wavering legs. With this, Iwa's head snapped up from behind the shifting giraffe and backed away, her downy feathers bristling.

Something settled in Perez's chest and swelled there as she gaped in horror at the glistening ribbon of flesh dangling from the tip of Iwa's snout. The moa snapped it up into her toothless mouth and swallowed. Despite the obvious, something in Perez's mind would not allow her to conclude what she could plainly see—that Iwa was *eating* Akila.

Because, well, that would be ludicrous. As absurd as a swarm of carnivorous bees.

Iwa's head bobbed, her fine down shimmering an iridescent silver in the headlights. She looked as though she wanted to move back in on Akila, but was reluctant. Perez recalled how poorly adapted her fleshy snout was for foraging, how she struggled to clip the leaves and twigs like the other moa. But Iwa was equally ill-equipped for carnivory, and the idea of her taking down such a large animal struck Perez as preposterous. More likely, she had found the wounded giraffe and capitalized on the situation. But it still didn't add up. The ARC was full of predatory animals and opportunists. Where were the wild dogs? The big cats?

Except for Akila's haunting moans cutting through the forest, Perez had never seen things so still, so quiet.

The giraffe tried to stand again, her black tongue lolling like a dead slug from her gaping mouth. Muscles all over her body twitched and flexed from repeated assaults by the swarming insects. Blood smeared the ground under her, her coat matted with blackened cruor and clods of bloody vegetation. The giraffe's knobby legs trembled, then wobbled furiously under her body's weight. She managed to raise herself halfway off the ground before her strength gave out and she slumped back down with a loud snort and a fresh plume of dust. The cloud of bees dispersed for a second, then reconvened.

That was when Perez spotted the second pair of eyes floating at the edge of her beam.

Something lurked unseen within the placid undergrowth just beyond the illuminated service road behind Akila. Her first thought was that one of the adult moa had come on the scene, but these eyes possessed a more sinister quality as they gazed back at her with razor-sharp focus.

Like the eyes of a predator.

Perez crouched, maintaining her gaze on the road as the mass in her chest crawled into her throat. Her hand found Nedjma and nudged.

"Nedjma... *Nedjma*, wake up," she whispered, knowing her voice was too low to be heard, her eyes fixed on the glowing orbs shrouded in darkness. Refused to speak louder for fear of drawing further attention to herself, of sparking intensified interest from those eyes. "We've got to go." She prodded a little more aggressively, eliciting a meek groan from Nedjma.

The rover lights bloomed once more, slicing through the dispersing dust, and Perez thought her heart might explode at what she beheld.

It seesawed on two legs—a vague birdlike form at the road's edge. Its head—too large to be that of a moa—bobbed laterally, akin to the optokinetic movements of an eagle locating prey. Then, from somewhere beneath its burning stare came a soft clicking that shattered the tense silence. The thing rocked forward, and through the oily gloom spilled a trine of black claws that tipped a monstrous aquiline foot. A stack of grimy scutes ascended each toe, converging to a fleshy hock of folded skin where a smaller, fourth digit hung suspended from the inner ankle. The foot planted gently and silently onto the dirt road.

Akila let out a panicked snort and kicked her hind legs to no avail.

A familiar dread spilled into Perez's veins. She recalled the thing sprawled before her in the containment tent, the haunting cries from the recording Jacobs had played aboard the Goliath. Distressed mewls that sounded almost human.

Greeellllppp.

DN1451.21—*Eve*—hadn't been alone.

Its head stopped, its reflective eyes hovering motionless at the edge of the service road before tilting curiously to one side. From shadow emerged a snout adorned with rigid crests, jutting like twin cockscombs. They resembled Eve's, except they were larger, their crags forming sets of horn-like peaks tipped with vivid yellows and blues. The structure bore a vague resemblance to the far smaller crests of ostriches and moa—a byproduct of hybridization with ancient DNA—but Perez had never seen one so ornate. The more she stared, the more she suspected this was no hybrid, but something else entirely.

The body of the thing moved into the open. Its head, three times the size of Iwa's, remained level, pivoting on a thickly muscled neck far more robust than any moa's. It tensed as the head resumed its volitant dance, a crown of downy feathers bristling at the base of the skull. Its movements were remarkably avian and, at other times, uncanny and altogether alien. The beast yawped another warble, a near-carbon copy of Iwa's, then cut out with a wet snort. Along one side of its mouth, Perez spotted a festering, full-thickness patch of necrosis that had caused the top row of teeth to become partially open to the air. The skin of its body was covered in more ulcerations, the same chemical burns she had seen on Eve. The beast shook its head and raised one of its legs to scratch at its wounds, belting an eerie yawp akin to an injured lion cub, breathing in rattled wheezes between calls.

Bits of the necropsy flashed through Perez's mind, the panicked voice in her head reciting her findings.

Liquefactive necrosis… chemical burns lining the respiratory tract… a syrinx. It has a syrinx…. it can mimic…. And, of course, the lack of synthetic promoter regions in its DNA, of any sign of genetic meddling.

A genetically pure animal.

Eve had an *Adam.*

UEF / RD
EYES ONLY

Ministry of Defence
United European Federation

Memorandum of CCTV Interrogation. Partial Transcript.

JUNE 17, 2147, 23:57

Appearances
Oberstleutnant Nikolaj Jacobson (alias: Jacobs)
Giana Russo (alias: Kohen)
Dr. Bogdan Kazimierz
Dr. Aegis Galani

Galani	If I am to understand you, these subjects... they are not of this existence?
Kazimierz	Yes.
Galani	A parallel universe?
Kazimierz	That is an oversimplification, but yes.
Galani	And these dinosaurs? The flesh-eating bees?
Kazimierz	Another existence, yes.
Galani	So, a multiverse, then. What do you know about it, this reality we have tapped into?
Kazimierz	As best I can elucidate, these realities are identical to ours, to a point. A fork in the road. One path leads to one reality, the other path to an alternative. But the nature of reality is not binary. Both paths are taken, splitting into two distinct realities. Universes with shared dimensions, identical in every way but one: the relativistic passage

of time. It occurs ad infinitum. Tweaks to the vibrational frequency of macroscopic strings, altering their Calabai-Yao manifolds in a way that alters the arrow of time while leaving other dimensions intact. Every choice we've ever made. Every chemical reaction. Billions of realities budding throughout the cosmic foam.

Kohen   You believe this shit? Are we really listening to this?

Jacobson   Stand down, soldier. You are out of line.

Kohen   Sir.

Galani   Continue, Dr. Kazimierz. These ancient organisms. How do you explain those?

Kazimierz   A reality that split from ours many millions of years ago. Late Cretaceous. Our universes are identical except for the relativistic passage of time.

Galani   This other reality, it is identical to ours, but moving more slowly?

Kazimierz   Yes. It's a window to our own past. Until now. The anomaly has fundamentally altered that reality.

Galani   And what of these doppelgängers?

Kazimierz   From another reality, much closer to our own, one that split months, maybe years ago.

Galani   You may find it interesting to know that we got the autopsy report back on Edgar Fischer.

Kazimierz   What is the significance of that?

Galani   Dr. Fischer served in the military. Neural implants and genetic enhancement have been compulsory for all service members through the ARES program since 2090, before he enlisted.

Kazimierz   I am not sure I understand the implication.

Galani   His mind is linked to Athena's neural net. In our initial attempts to locate the ALICE crew, we enlisted her to tap into his consciousness, and we were successful. Edgar Fischer continues to transmit as we speak. As best we can determine, most of the transmissions are fragments of speech from dreams, perhaps hallucinations.

Kazimierz	What does that mean? That he's still alive?
Galani	Dead men don't dream, Dr. Kazimierz. Dead men don't dream. He's both alive and dead, to put a finer point on it. A superposition of states. Schrödinger's cat incarnate. But what I really want to know is from where—or when—is that signal transmitting?
Kazimierz	His consciousness—it is entangled with Athena's neural net.
Galani	That's correct. At least, any aspect relayed by Broca's area in the frontal cortex.
Kazimierz	He has the capacity to communicate instantaneously across vast distances.
Galani	Again, correct.
Kazimierz	Across continents?
Galani	Across galaxies, in theory.
Kazimierz	Across universes?
Galani	And now, what is it that you are implying, Dr. Kazimierz?
Kazimierz	I think you already know.

*What name has the river that 'twixt the realms
of gods and giants goes?*
—P*OETIC* E*DDA*

ᚴ | NJÖRÐR

I am the mouse.

Lotta sat cross-legged, a silent sentinel framed in stone peering out over a primordial world. But her mind was a crash of rhinos. Worse. Her screams, rising above the thundering march of beasts unknown.

No longer was she Lotta Eklund, Renowned Particle Physicist, Modern Vanguard of Discovery. No, she was Lotta Eklund, the scared little girl inexplicably clinging to a religion she had sworn off decades before, maybe because it was the only thing that felt familiar anymore.

She gazed past the drum of rain upon the blades of a lone stunted cycad from the karst window of a vast subterranean cave. It was one of three portholes that had eroded out of the cliffside, each set into the scarp like garret portholes, overlooking the roiling stormwater that had once been a sprawling river delta. A shiver ran through her as she watched from beneath a poncho of woven pinnate leaves draped over her suit liner.

Weaving, she thought. *A hackneyed skill I thought I'd never actually use.*

But the ponchos she'd made for Fischer and herself held up well enough. They weren't perfect by any stretch, but they were serviceable. The hood contained the bulk of the matted blonde mess swept haphazardly behind her ears, which felt like a small victory in of itself. Her hair always had a mind of its own when it rained.

She wasn't proficient at it, for one, not having woven since childhood. Had hated it then almost as much as blót. Hated the way her fingers bled from the hours-long drills under Sofia's watchful eye. Another in a long list of customs the bitch had forced on her, that she might "better appreciate the notion of Scandinavian convenance." Whatever that meant.

Lotta had started the picking habit around that age. Would do it to fool Sofia into thinking she'd been weaving to avoid her abuse. Somehow, it had evolved into a nervous habit she still carried with her.

At the same time, weaving felt *familiar*. It passed the time. Distracted her from her predicament. And by now, she was used to the pain in her fingers, which had become somewhat constant since scaling the scarp. It had taken a day of recovery after the climb before she could make a fist again, but the residual pain was, by and large, tolerable.

The cave was a vast underground cavern. It provided shelter and afforded Lotta the peace of mind to carry out the mundane. Weaving, carving, even rituals. She and Fischer had discovered it while traversing the roof of the scarp the same day they had climbed to the top. By then, the skies had opened, and rain slammed against the earth in sheets. They had crossed wedges of limestone pavement with grooves like undulating gyri that transformed into a labyrinth of stone pillars erupting from the caprock like nameless headstones. Rivulets of runoff gushed through the gaps between them, rising steadily the farther they pressed.

Lotta had urged Fischer to turn back as the water came to their ankles, her feet numbed by the icy torrent. Yet Fischer had insisted that they continue moving *with* the flow, just as a deafening crack sounded and lightning arched dangerously overhead. The next thing she remembered, she had knocked into him after he stopped abruptly and nearly slipped past the ledge of a black sinkhole.

The pit was around a body length in diameter, its rocky mouth glistening and wet in the deluge as it swallowed the stream gushing through their legs. A plethora of trees flanking the partially obscured opening seemed unprecedented along the otherwise barren plateau.

Lotta still didn't know how Fischer had talked her into climbing down into it. She knew at the time that the growing intensity of the storm had afforded few options. Knew that they were sitting ducks, and at any moment, some beast might spill out of shadow or come down from the sky and take them. Still, at that snapshot in time, the ominous blackness of the gaping earth frightened her more.

But Fischer had spoken with authority, his demeanor almost forceful as water sprayed from his drenched beard, his voice nearly drowned out by a barrage of thunder, and Lotta was reminded then that she was still afraid of *him*, too.

So, she relented. Cowed begrudgingly as she followed him into the pit and down a vertical limestone shaft. She shimmied past slippery rocks, her head pelted by icy ropes of falling water from above. It felt like an eternity before her feet found the solid mossy ground beside a splintered deadfall.

To Lotta's amazement, the passage opened into a cavernous cenote with high walls, at its center a glistening underground reservoir fed by the trickle of countless tiny streams. The pond shimmered placidly beneath stalactites, illuminated by the outside gloom through three portholes that had eroded from the cliffside. A sweet, sour smell filled the damp air—a scent she would grow accustomed to over the coming days. She estimated they had downclimbed the height of a small tree, around five meters or so.

Lotta shivered at the thought of what she had seen then. Her initial inclination was that each opening to the outside had harbored rows of stalagmites arranged like jagged teeth—the tallest about the height of a child—grouped at the edge of rivulets emptying into waterfalls that cascaded out over the scarp face to the crashing waves below.

Then she realized the mounds were *warbling*. Warbling and *moving*.

Pterosaurs. Fat-headed bird-apes. The ones with the tear-drop heads. They had huddled just inside the shelter of the cave, their bristled bodies unusually sluggish. Some swayed slightly, others twitched or nuzzled their strange beaks in their pectorals or under their wing arms. A wall of eyes burned into Lotta from their direction, with pupils like glinting discs inside stoic skulls, displaying little more than indifference to her and Fischer's presence. There was no protest erupting from the rows of bobbing heads. No hint of an impending attack. Only warbling and glinting tapetal reflexes.

Fischer was the first to move without reservation or fear of spooking the creatures. He had started a fire to smoke the loathsome things out, but to little effect. That was, until Lotta uncovered their aversion to the smell of burning spleenwort (or something that resembled it).

The spindly ferns grew thickest between the edge of the pond and the portholes where the bird-apes huddled. Intending it as an accelerant for the dwindling fire, Lotta had picked a sheaf of the waxy fronds, the glinting eyes following her like curious children. She threw the armful onto the smoldering blaze, drawing a shriek of protest from Fischer. Too late. White smoke poured into the cave, filling it with a damp, earthy smell.

Fischer motioned to unmake Lotta's error, but stopped short when a sneeze erupted from the ferine congregation. A growing agitation propagated like a wave among the creatures. They grunted and snorted, some hacked dryly. Without hesitation, they rolled in perfect synchrony onto their jointed wing arms and—as if by some singular command—vaulted forth from the cliffside and into the storm.

When Lotta doubled back, Fischer was already putting the cylinder with their "branchiosaurus"[1] egg on the fire with a childlike enthusiasm she found almost endearing. To her surprise, it turned out to be the best meal she'd had in recent memory.

Three days had passed, and the cave had proven an effective reprieve from the elements and beasts. Lotta's arms were still sore. Her left wrist clicked. But she was okay.

She exhaled through her nose, a spleenwort-induced headache mounting behind her left brow, the sour taste of calcium-tannate toothpaste lingering at the back of her tongue. The latest of Fischer's concoctions, it was composed of calcium carbonate (essentially pulverized limestone, or its common name—*chalk*) and his go-to cure-all, tannic acid. Lotta wondered if letting her teeth rot might be a worthwhile sacrifice as she gazed emptily over the vast expanse of floodwater—a homogenous gray slab—beneath a dark cloak of spitting stratus.

---

1 Uninformed reference to the Brachiosaurus genus with respect to the non-brachiosaurine *Paralititan stromeri*.

Of the three lookouts, this one sat the highest. It was dryer, and—despite the abundance of bird-ape shit—the air here was the freshest in the cave, less polluted by the daily spleenwort burn. She came here mainly to clear her head. That was what she had told Fischer, though it failed to explain the rounded stone salver laid flat before her. The one carved with runes for each of the nine realms. The one intended as an altar for her late-night rituals when sleep proved the most elusive, and when Fischer wasn't around to bear witness.

She also busied her aching hands erecting cairns around the lookout—so far, five and counting. She figured she'd stop at nine. One for each of the nine realms. The stacked piles of limestone stood about waist-high and functioned secondarily as pyres for spleenwort burns. They loomed silently like headstones signifying her previous life. Ushered in a new beginning.

Lotta winced at the sting of dew in her eyes and swallowed hard. Peered pensively over the apocalyptic landscape toward the nearby barrier island where the river crocs still lazed, their sprawled bodies barely visible above a cauldron of foam and spray. The water was high at this time of day, the waves licking the island's banks like voracious tongues. The giant reptiles remained motionless in the punishing deluge while a pair of half-eaten brontosaur carcasses—twisted corpses now neglected by the sated bask—slammed weightily against the island's eroding banks like bloated marionettes.

Every indication was that the stampeding herd had become trapped between wall and water, subsequently drowning in the rising surge. Spray cascaded onto their distended bellies while the lethargic crocs, unmoving and indifferent, endured through the elemental onslaught. The sprawling reptiles reminded Lotta of the crumbling remains of the Crystal Palace statues she had seen as a child, before they were lost. Before London's boroughs were devastated by the great Sydenham Wildfire and the landslides that ensued.

She drew a deep breath. Exhaled.

Three days of unrelenting rain and, on one occasion, hail. Twilight brought on electrical storms that lit the night sky and rallied the tides. Midday introduced sporadic squalls, tapering by dusk to lighter winds and churning concrete skies. By evening, the cycle began anew, casting a continuous rumble that rose and fell like thunder across the cenote's cavernous walls. At their worst, the storms invoked the perpetual supercells that had plagued the United States for a generation, effectively dividing the once-great nation into a fragmented collection of junta-run territories and city-states.

Something like that.

The days were slightly short. Only twenty-three and a half hours. It underscored the sense that Lotta and Fischer had found themselves in an alien world untouched by man. Within the cycle of a solar day, the churning waters rose and fell at regular intervals, almost every twelve hours. Fischer had posited that the river delta emptied into a tidal zone and that the positions of the sun and moon were ripe for generating king tides. His hypothesis was further supported by what appeared to be a distant sea, maybe an ocean, briefly visible before the skies went dark.

But it didn't explain how the flood persisted like a roiling cauldron despite the ebbing tide.

No, Lotta thought, *it's more than the storm or the gravity of a perigean moon.*

The smell of ozone clung to the air. For Lotta, it invoked flashbacks of finding herself suddenly and inexplicably *inside* the ALICE Cathedral, as if she had phased through the observation window of the lab unscathed. Transformed from matter to pure energy and back to matter again, like some Everettian[2] version of Young's double-slit experiment. An impossible feat of macroscopic tunneling, perhaps. The stuff of science fiction. Disallowed by every known law. It defied comprehension, certainly defied the Copenhagen interpretation. Shattered every notion of what was and was not reality.

Heisenberg's rolling in his grave.

But although she, Basem, and Fischer had somehow made it through apparently unscathed, not everyone on her team had defied *uncertainty.* Not entirely.

---

2 Reference to physicist Hugh Everett's proposed many-worlds interpretation of quantum mechanics

The first one they had found was Mattheo. *That sound.* A continuous patter on the chamber floor below. An incessant pecking not unlike the drum of the rain on the cycad leaves or the slow drip of percolating water within the recesses of the vast karstic void in which she now sat.

But Hassan had been the one who made Lotta call into question everything she thought she knew. Neither dead nor alive, or somehow a superposition of both.

I am transcendence.

His voice, like rustling foliage, entombed within his com turned Lotta's stomach with far greater potency than the memory of Mattheo's fate ever could. His words fell on her ears often, as if hearing them for the first time.

Reality had betrayed Lotta and her team that day—some hidden variable they had failed to account for. Constants meant nothing. Bell's theorems, Maxwell and Dirac's equations. Meaningless scrawl. There was no scientific explanation—no calculation, equality, or frame of reference to elucidate what had transpired that day.

And what of the *other* she saw behind the chamber glass as if she had gazed into her reflection just before the light consumed her? What Everettian interpretation could begin to explain *that?*

Her mind had become a tangled web, a Möbius strip of perpetual illusion.

I am going to die here, she thought. Maybe she already had. Perhaps she was an apparition like Fischer's little girls—a ghost, a figment of a tortured imagination—or some discorporate celestial on another plain of existence, some manifold of non-Euclidean spacetime. Another dimension or realm beyond human comprehension.

Gods help us.

And as she tasted the dewy air of the cave, Lotta realized she had traded her Cathedral for a tomb.

She turned and glanced over her shoulder, her elevated position affording a complete view of the pond. Its proximal side was draped in troglodytic flora—hart's-tongue, spleenwort, bracken—interspersed by carpets of moss and loose rock. A few anemic trees leaned toward the gloom diffusing from the portholes, their spindly trunks attenuated like wrung towels, fronds stunted by the limits of their photonic rations.

Plants weren't the only life that thrived here. She and Fischer had already spotted various fishes,[3] a species of frog,[4] and a pair of turtles with strange, swan-like necks.[5] At night, they contended with harmless rat-sized crocs that scurried through their encampment looking for scraps.[6] The things were unusually agile, galloping upright on their lanky limbs, their eyes flashing in and out along the firelight's edge.

While they were indeed nimble, the elusive reptiles weren't sly enough to evade Fischer's drop traps, which he made by balancing a flat rock upon a baited hair-trigger of precisely arranged sticks. These traps had adorned the perimeter of the new encampment by the second night, and by the next dawn, four had been tripped, two with dead crocs. About two days' rations.

But Fischer wasn't the only one capable of securing sustenance. Lotta, too, had spent much of the intervening days developing a novel hunting device of her own design. It was a primitive compound weapon composed of two elements: the first was a throwing stick made from a curved branch notched at one end. The second—a long, thin spear—nested into the notch of the throwing piece, forming a simple, self-releasing hinge mechanism.

The physics of the weapon were rudimentary. In essence, the throwing stick maximized the torque of a throw by extending the moment arm. It achieved this by acting as a lever and increasing the centripetal arc radius of her throw—and thus the angular velocity generated by it—to maximize the power output transferred to the articulated spear. The resultant kinetic force meant dramatically enhanced range, accuracy, and lethality than had she thrown the projectile unaided.

In English: less work, more power.

Body mechanics were also important: she had found a stepping technique that added further power and stability to her throw. Chest at forty-five degrees, eyes level with the target and fixed down the spear like a billiard cue. She hadn't *caught* anything yet, but the trunk of an ill-fated cave tree made for good throwing practice.

---

3 *Spinocaudichthys oumtkoutensis, Arganodus indet., Dentilepisosteus kemkemensis*
4 *Oumtkoutia anae*
5 *Hamadachelys escuilliei*
6 *Araripesuchus rattoides*

And so it went. Calibrate the device. Hone the technique. Rinse and repeat.

Quantum Physicist Abandons All Hope, Defects to Newtonian Mechanics. The thought manifested like a headline in her mind. She almost laughed, but held her composure as she stole another gaze toward the pond, where a thumb-sized Fischer now knelt at the water's edge. He appeared to be building some new feat of primitive engineering.

A little farther along the shore, an angled slab of marbled limestone loomed behind him, vaulting almost to the cave roof from the mouth of an unexplored passage that sloped deeper underground, back in the direction of the forest. Overhead, tangled roots descended from cracks in the ceiling and snaked down either side of the jutting limestone. They looked almost vine-like, veiling a domed "wigwam" of woven bracts and deadfall wood that Lotta and Fischer had erected in the slab's shadow. The new shelter had taken them nearly a full day to construct, and the effort paid off. It was roomy enough for two to sleep separately and still be under one roof.

A shallow slick of water crawled past the wigwam from the stygian passage, trickling from the gaps in the piled rock and petrified boughs piled at its entrance. Lotta peered into it, her gaze met only with blackness, and a chill ran through her.

She redirected her thoughts. Thought about how she had started feeling a semblance of security for the first time in days. She no longer felt exposed, water and food abounded, and the fire burned hot.

And she had Fischer, for better and for worse.

On the one hand, Fischer still unnerved Lotta, his unpredictable nature often putting her on edge. On the other, they had grown close, and she felt an order of magnitude safer with him around. At the very least, she respected him.

And there were times she found herself argumentative toward him for no reason or would revert to avoidance and retreat to her lookout, though she couldn't explain why.

But despite Lotta's fluid disposition, Fischer's remained consistent. He was unfazed. Present, but focused. Always accessible. She was a river, and he was a rock. Her mind often revisited how he had shielded her as the jötunn bore down on them. How he was prepared to sacrifice himself without a second thought. He had done something similar when the brontosaur tail nearly took their heads.

But she also thought of how scared she was of him after what he had done to himself at the stream. How sometimes, she still was.

Her eyes darted briefly to him again before she turned back to face the karst window. A steady flow of refractile mist diffused from outside. Lotta closed her eyes as the cool dampness kissed her cheeks and quietly slipped her hand into her poncho. Her knuckles grazed a sheath of woven palm fronds that stowed Fischer's knife.

She thought of death. Dreamed of it most nights. Thought of Mattheo and Basem and Anderson and Hassan. Thought of Fischer's girls. How they, too, haunted her now. Consumed her and filled her head in the damp dark. Maybe that had something to do with why she distanced herself from Fischer. It was getting harder to look him in the eye. She had experienced her fair share of guilt over the years about what had occurred in Geneva, her complicity in the disaster—the subsequent court dealings, the coverups—but never had it felt so personal.

She built the cairns for them, too.

She imagined Galani's oily voice spilling in through the mist as if to mock her.

Hello again, old friend.

Lotta spat.

"Snake."

"Aye?"

"Scheisse!" She nearly leaped out of her skin as panic coursed through her bones.

"Snake? *Snake?*" Fischer chirped playfully, his growing footfalls crunching at the base of the outcrop. In her abstracted state, Lotta hadn't heard him approaching. "I probably deserve that for dragging you up that rock and down into this dreckslöch, eh?"[7]

Lotta stood, her heart in her throat, and turned to face him. "Don't sneak up on me like that!"

---

7 German for "shithole."

"*Whoa,* I'm *sorry,*" Fischer grunted in a low tone as he ascended. The poncho she had made him glistened in the paleness of the cave, the green leaves woven tightly and beaded with water droplets. His grimy cheeks appeared sunken in the pale light. "But for a basket-weaving heathen, you did climb pretty good."

It was the first time he had ribbed Lotta in a while. The reverberation of his voice off the wet rock seemed to give the dig an added punch. Made her think back to when he found out she was a Swede.

Called me a bloody cheesemaker.

Her fists relaxed a little. Her eyes narrowed.

"*Schweinehund,*" she retorted, her face deadpan.

A glimmer fell over Fischer's eyes, and he tilted his chin to the side. "Hoffnungslos," he said with an expression Lotta hadn't seen before. Subtle creases at the corners of his pale blue eyes, a half-grin. Reminded her of a mischievous little boy.

"Stop that," she said over the ceaseless pounding behind her narrow stare, her mind as conflicted about him as ever.

"Stop what?"

"*That.* You're looking at me strange."

"No idea what you're talking about." He winked quickly and subtly enough to be nearly imperceptible. He looked around at the cairns inquisitively, then his eyes fell on the throwing stick and the spears at her feet. "Been—er—keeping busy, eh?"

Lotta bowed her head, pretending to look so she could conceal the expression bubbling up through her.

"Good…" The corners of her lips curled into a suppressed smile under the shadow of her hood. "It's going good."

But as quickly as it came, Lotta's expression fell when a fresh bolt of pain—the first in days—pulsed through her ring finger and up the middle of her arm. A desperate compulsion to busy her aching hand consumed her with startling suddenness, and her mind went to the knife stowed in her poncho. Something she could squeeze to keep from biting clear through her tongue. Her grinding jaw popped as she traced her restive fingers to the pommel and grasped at… *nothing.*

The knife was gone.

Her heart skipped. Her eyes flashed.

The knife. Where is the fucking knife?

As if to read her mind, Fischer reached into his poncho. "Anyway, sorry I startled you," he said with an air of nonchalance, then presented the knife with its handle extended towards her. "I just came to return this."

Lotta staved off tears as she peered back at him, her mind a whirlwind amid the mounting pain in her arm. Without thinking, she snatched at the handle and almost dropped it. Mystified, a gasp caught in her throat. She couldn't *feel* any of her fingers.

"Hope you don't mind," Fischer said, seemingly oblivious as he procured something else and held it out to her. "I… ah… needed it for this."

Lotta looked at the small, rounded object, then at Fischer, her arm on fire now. He nudged it forward with boyish insistence that contrasted sharply with his demeanor at the sinkhole.

Lotta demurred a moment longer, then held out her palm, and Fischer placed it at the center. She managed to turn it over with wide eyes, her chest fluttering. It was a crude statue carved from wood, humanoid in aspect. The face had a beard, seemed to be missing an eye. She looked at Fischer, puzzled.

"I know you've been… ah… more *spiritual* lately." He glanced down at her trembling hand, still outstretched toward him. "I don't know much, just that heathens sometimes pray to statues."

"We pray to the *gods*," Lotta snapped, immediately regretting her reaction. She softened as she glanced back down at the wooden statue, and her agitation shifted into admiration. "It's Odin, the All-father. You made this?"

Fischer gave a curt nod, his face as expressionless as the statue's.

He's nervous.

"It's not much…."

Why is he so nervous?

Fischer's eyes trailed to her inflamed fingers as if noticing the extent of their disfigurement for the first time. A fresh look of concern fell over him like a shadow, and Lotta knew he wanted to say something. She knew it because it had become impossible to overlook the almost necrotic quality her fingers had taken on, their skin distended and shining with a purple gradation, the tips pocked with pinpoint ulcerations. The nail beds had gone almost black. Some of her fingernails had started coming loose.

Lotta quickly withdrew her hand back into her poncho and manufactured a smile.

"Thank you, Ed."

Fischer gave a single nod, but revealed nothing else through his countenance.

A protracted silence filled the space between them as they stood facing one another. Lotta sensed a renewed disquietude swelling within her. Worried she might drop something, she rushed to sheath the knife.

By the time she realized she had gripped the wrong end, it was too late.

An abrupt, pinpoint pressure built in the tip of her right index finger, then a soft *click* and a release as the blade glided softly into skin and muscle. The sensation sent her heart plummeting from her throat to her bowels, and she reactively pulled the knife back. Warmth trailed down her palm. But she felt nothing else. No pain. No sensation. Only that subtle awareness of pressure.

"You okay?"

Lotta nearly jumped again when Fischer broke the silence. Tight-lipped, her eyes brimming, she nodded.

Fischer eyed her midsection as if trying to see past the veil of her poncho. "Y'sure?"

"Fine." Not one for dissimulation, Lotta deflected. Turned the question back on him. "How about you?" she said in a tone she thought might have unintentionally come off as callous, disingenuous at the least.

Fischer wiped his wrist over his mouth. His lips parted as if to speak, then closed again, his hand trembling.

He didn't just come to check-in. He came to talk. Something on his mind.

"Just thinking more lately," he whispered, bowing his head as the tip of his foot traced figure-eights in the dirt. "Thinking about how much I miss 'em."

Lotta's heart sank past her knees. She feared what he might say next. Hoped with all of her being that he would swallow the words—that he might deem them too unsavory for speech—and bury them deep, just as she buried her own all too often. The weight of the anguish manifesting on his face wrenched her heart downward, ripping it from her body and sending it plummeting to the Earth's core. The droning rain was no longer background noise, but a pelting static so deafening that she wanted to scream.

Coward. Mouse. Tell him. Tell him what you did.

Sweat beaded on her brow. She considered it, pouring her heart out to him then. Laying it all out. Her involvement in the disaster, the coverup, the fact she couldn't wake her fingers, that she was scared. A frightened little girl who needed someone to tell her everything would be okay, despite the terrible things she had done.

Fischer sighed heavily and raised his head. His nostrils flared, eyes gleaming with melancholy reminiscence—far-off, yet still regarding her. "They would've liked you."

Lotta's pulse pounded in sync with the patter of water trickling somewhere in some recess or crag, each *drip* like a dagger plunging into her chest. Gravity seemed heavier, threatening to crush her beneath the weight of what she knew. Collapse her into a singularity until she ceased to exist, her legacy nothing more than an inconsequential fizzle of Hawking radiation or the pathetic squeak of desperation a mouse makes in the crushing grip of a snake.

Her mind went from Fischer to her new injury. *Fingers. Can't feel my goddamned bloody fingers.* She had nicked her finger and had since attempted to wrap it in her suit liner to stem the bleeding. Her body tensed as she worked up the fortitude to try and move her finger, the tip of her tongue running frantically back and forth against her teeth.

It flexed. Seemed to move in all the right places, to her relief, albeit with an unsettling *click.*

"Anyway," Fischer said, clearing his throat as he straightened, "sorry. I, uh… I shouldn't have startled you like that. I should go."

He turned, hunched, and plodded back toward the pond.

Slick with blood, the statue slipped from Lotta's rubbery grip.

Clunk.

Fischer began to double back, but Lotta kicked the bloody idol away before he could look down. She stepped forward.

"It's okay," she said. "I'll come with you. It's getting late, anyway."

His eyes narrowed on her. After a brief pause, his shoulders straightened, and he regarded her with a nod.

"Aye. I'd like that."

In giant-wrath does the serpent writhe;
O'er the waves he twists...
—POETIC EDDA

‹ ◇ | JÖRMUNGANDR ›

Lotta trailed Fischer from the outlook, past rows of stalagmites skirting a narrow passage along the water's edge. To their right, a murky shaft of light filtered through the sinkhole they had downclimbed and bathed the splintered deadfall with an eerie glow. After ten more paces, the stone spires along the embankment fell away to reveal a widening tableau of dew-laden bracken stretching to the edge of their encampment. There, a thin column of smoke rose from a waning fire.

Fischer slowed and moved his arm across Lotta's path. He smelled good. Like pine and tannin.

"Hold up," he whispered, peering into the open from the cover of the last stalagmite.

Lotta craned her neck and tried to get a look. "What is it?"

Her hands were tacky with clotted blood, her fingers still absent of sensation aside from the throbbing pain that had become her baseline, the novel *click* of her oozing index finger.

Fischer turned and pressed a finger to his lips, then pointed to the top of the limestone slab above their wigwam.

Lotta saw only stillness in the gloom. Heard only the subdued hiss of the whispering cave, the rhythm of dripping water in some recess beyond her estimation. She began to doubt if Fischer really saw something. Considered the likelihood he was suffering another bout of delirium.

Until she saw movement. A threshing motion at the apex of the giant slab, then stillness.

The object re-emerged. A long, slender head pulling back slowly. Then, it snapped and rebounded from an unseen quarry, swinging a braid of glistening flesh at the end of an oar-shaped beak. Its jaws parted, revealing rows of needled teeth, then threw back the morsel with a reverberant *clap*.

The creature clicked a throaty warble, then trained its silver eyes over the ledge toward the pond. A pair of spindly limbs slid over the edge like a shadow, jointed mantis arms with probing little fingers that splayed over the stone lip. The body briefly rose into view before rolling forward into a dive, leaving Lotta to watch in stunned silence as the creature torpedoed toward the ground.

But just before impact, its folded mantis arms unfurled, and the *slap* of wing membranes bounced across the cenote's walls. Within a second, the thing was gliding over the pond's surface, disappearing behind the stalagmite rows.

A splash reverberated and decayed. Lotta heard the rush of air beneath its wings, and the soaring creature's silhouette swooped past their location and returned to its perch. A writhing fish glistened in its peculiar beak as it shook a misty spray from its plumed coat.

Lotta estimated that this bird-ape was a little larger than the ones she and Fischer had driven out days before, and the first with *teeth*, as far as she could tell. One clearly not perturbed by the smell of spleenwort.[1]

She reached out and squeezed Fischer's bicep. The pulse in her fingers intensified. He turned.

"I'm going back for my spear thrower," she whispered.

Fischer shook his head.

"I'm going."

---

1 *Nicorhynchus fluviferox*

Lotta pivoted toward the lookout, but was jolted backward. She slipped. Caught herself, though not before the loose grit underfoot filled the cenote with a deafening hiss. Fischer's grasp tightened around her wrist, kept her from falling. Her head turned, not to Fischer, but to the limestone slab, where a pair of glinting discs now probed their position. Her breath stopped in her throat, her muscles tensed, ready for whatever came next.

Bird-ape. Mantis-bird. Fight. Flight. Fight. Flight.

The pterosaur's rounded head tilted curiously. A silent standoff ensued.

The beast broke first, launching itself from its perch, only to glide through the furthest porthole and into the dusk without incident, its quarry in tow.

Lotta relaxed and spilled the air from her lungs. Fischer's physical reaction toward her decision to retrieve the spear thrower distracted her. It made her angry, a little scared. But she thought it best to bite her tongue, to let it go. She knew she had nothing to prove. Knew it deep down.

He means well. He's proven that much.

"Spleenwort burns aren't enough," Fischer said, watching the porthole and shaking his head. "We need to find a better way to keep intruders out." He looked at Lotta, then peered out again. "We should get to securing those entry points sooner rather than later."

Lotta tilted her nose with her brow raised, her eyes directing him to the darkened passage behind their encampment. "And what of *that*?"

"Aye," Fischer said, turning to appraise the tunnel. Water trickled from the gaps in the piled rocks and tree limbs at its base. He spat on the ground as if to underscore the significance of his assessment. "We'll get to work first thing."

Lotta didn't know where to start on such a feat, but she knew he was right.

Fischer shifted focus. Centered his gaze along the water's edge.

"It's just ahead," he muttered.

"What is?"

"You'll see."

He led her into the open, past the bracken, toward a peculiar apparatus standing at the water's edge. It was shaped like a Y pointed inland, a converging lattice of sticks protruding from the shallows and into a rectangular structure shrouded in loose vegetation.

Fischer stood before it and looked back expectantly. "What do you think?"

"What is it?" Lotta's gaze bounced from Fischer to the structure, recognizable only to the extent she had watched him building it from the lookout across the pond.

"Fish corral."

He pulled back a slat of ferns, providing Lotta with a view inside the columnar portion. The construction was simple: a shallow rectangular inlet dredged from the embankment, the V-shaped segment funneling hapless swimmers into cover. Lulled them into a false sense of security beneath its shade, arranged to mimic a natural alcove.

Lotta studied it with an appraising disposition. Tried not to betray any semblance of appreciation for the elegance of its simplicity. "You catch anything yet?"

Fischer's expression fell slightly. He leaned over the structure and stared into it for a few seconds. "Well, I haven't baited it yet...."

But then his face beamed.

"*Hold up.*" His voice pitched up an octave, almost boyish in its excitement, and plunged his good arm into the murky water.

He struggled momentarily, his fingers trailing a black shape darting along the bottom. He lunged, then ripped his hand free. In his white-knuckled grip, Lotta saw a dozen wriggling spidery legs.

"*Prawns,*" Fischer said, his eyes gleaming.

He held the crustacean out to show her. It was monstrous, its thrashing tail almost as long as his forearm. Lotta watched its bulbous eyes, stalked beneath two curved, twitching antennae that brushed Fischer's waist.[2]

Fischer swung the thing, slamming its carapace onto a rock with a sickening *crack*. The tail stopped thrashing. The insectoid limbs ceased.

A twinge of envy manifested as a vinegary taste at the back of Lotta's throat. She swallowed it back down.

---

2 *Cretapenaeus berberus,* a species of shrimp from the Cretaceous.

"Dinner," Fischer said, picking up his catch and walking toward the wigwam, where the fire awaited revival.

Night fell.

Lotta laid her head upon a frigid pile of bracts on her side of the wigwam with a full belly. Savored the sweet taste lingering on her tongue.

Fischer shifted somewhere behind a partition that bisected the hut's interior.

Lotta sensed another sleepless night.

She considered sneaking off to the lookout to retrieve her spear thrower, then maybe some target practice on the rat crocs making the rounds for scraps after dark. Perhaps she'd catch one. Show Fischer he wasn't the only one capable of procuring provisions. Show herself that if anything happened to him, she could carry on.

She squinted—almost longingly—through the veil of night and past the divider, a regrettable concept in retrospect. The dull flicker of distant lightning percolated into the cave, animating the woven twigs with an ensemble of shadowy appendages. There was no thunder. Nothing but the waves filling the cave with their ominous chorus.

"Night, Ed," she said across the short distance between them, though it may as well have been kilometers.

"Night."

Her lids fell to the lull of crashing white noise.

Boom.

Lotta opened her eyes. An unrelenting and inexplicable dread consumed her.

She found herself inexplicably transiting a bower of arched ribs. They curled high overhead like pearlescent talons. Her heels bumped against the knobbed joints of ancient vertebrae, and death's musk cocooned her in a noxious embrace. She peered through the gaps between the bones, the remains of some fallen colossus, where she was greeted by the deepest black.

A low, resonant rumble bellowed like a great horn from the far end of the beast's bowels. Lotta squinted through the whorl of the decaying tunnel toward the source, but saw only mist rising from its depths. The rumble came again, a little higher in pitch. She continued forward and heard a third trill, higher still.

A beacon.

The sinking weight within her deepened. The tunnel flickered white then dimmed again.

"Anderson? Hassan?"

Lotta called their names repeatedly, her pace quickening, the growing mist choking off her view more and more.

And as she readied herself to turn back, two pale eyes flickered at her through the milky void.

Dull and pink and bouncing, she pictured the gaze of a vættir. Or perhaps they encompassed something far worse.

Her heart raced, her mind willing her to double back, to run. But her legs continued forward against her will. She heard the peal of the beacon again, louder this time, and through the haze—framed within the arched bones—she met the ashen stare of an enormous hind-limbed serpent with the head of a jötunn. Coils of steam peeled from its ophidian body, its length partially submerged in a placid pool rimmed within a cage of spidery tree trunks.

A forked tongue tasted the air. Tasted *her*.

The beast appeared increasingly restless at Lotta's approach, coiling, writhing over itself, sending forth waves that disturbed the glassy sheen of the pool.

Without warning, the head lunged at her.

Its septic maw, bearing fangs the length of her arms, crashed into the wall of trees. With a deafening hiss, the beast recoiled within its arboreal cell, its eyes peeling her anatomy like an onion, its tongue mopping up her adrenaline-tainted scent.

It lunged again, rending and gnawing at the trees with abject fury, but to no avail.

Realizing her relative safety, Lotta's attention was drawn to these trees. They were peculiar, like tortuous limbs angled inward along the pool's circumference to fully encase the writhing serpent. She tracked her gaze upward and was shocked to find that they were not tree trunks at all, but the *roots* of a vast ash vaulting above the rotting arcades and high into the stratosphere.

The Ancient One.

It was a silent warden.

The enormity of the tree, its bark like burned flesh, filled her entire field of view. A fissure ran the length of the great trunk, a glistening, wet cavitation that pulsed from root to apex. Lotta's eyes tracked heavenward, where the gaping split stopped at the mouth of a boundless skull, jawless and ravaged, set into the trunk with no clear delineation. Where once there had been a face, she saw only the remnants of muscle, the gnarled dregs of tendon. Its enormous scalp, almost bare, was consecrated beneath a crown of crimson fronds from which prismatic motes descended like helicopter seeds. They bent the space around them as they fell, emitting a growing buzz that invoked a canticle of swarming bees.

Kneel.

Lotta fell to her knees beneath the gallows of the great Fraxinus. The Ancient One. Pale sheaves of light trickled through its boughs and split into kaleidoscopic iridescence. Her neck ached, her eyes piercing past the primordial limbs, a dozen appendages reaching through the entirety of creation. Woven through dimensions. Through space. Through time itself.

The cold earth reached into her at the final peel of the beacon. It shattered her mind like a prism splitting light into an infinite spectrum. Reconstructed it, destroyed it again.

Reconstruct.

Deconstruct.

And just as Lotta's vision failed, as the fruiting bodies erupted from her face, she saw the mind of the All-father, and he spoke to her.

"It's time for blöt."

BOOM.

Lotta woke in a cold sweat. Inhaled sharply. Cool air filled her stinging lungs. The pain in her knees was the next thing to come to the fore. It shot into her thighs, which burned and trembled beneath her weight. She shivered violently, acutely aware of the wet hair plastered to the back of her neck.

The thunder faded in the distance and became lost in the roar of a torrential downpour that hissed all around her.

Questions circled her like territorial bees long before her eyes opened.

Why am I outside? Why am I kneeling?

The rough stone of the cave floor pressed harder into her joints with each passing second, her feet searing like they had endured a kilometer of unforgiving terrain.

Her lids felt heavy as they peeled back. Revealed the Stygian chaos beyond the lookout, a storm raging beyond the porthole.

How… how did I get here?

Thick ropes of runoff bled from the opening and slapped weightily against the smooth stone. Dewy cave air kissed her skin, entreating her to examine herself.

I'm naked. Why am I naked?

She became aware of an undeniable warmth spreading over her hands. Moved her throbbing fingers, and although they still had not recovered sensation, she discerned that there was something slippery in their grasp. Her hands were oriented palm-side down, tightly gripping an object she did not immediately appreciate. She was too distracted by the sticky black substance that covered them, too puzzled by the faint tendrils of steam rising through the gaps between her fingers.

A tinge of iron infused the air.

Lotta's eyes widened.

Blood. It's… it's…

Her shivering intensified. Not from the cold, but from the horror that permeated her as the object slid past her fingertips and struck the damp limestone with a wet *slap*.

The pale eyes of a rat croc's severed head gazed emptily back at her, bulbous and opaque, ceaseless in their empty stare.

Behind it, Lotta spotted the stone altar, upon which the rest of the body appeared to have been arranged belly-up, limbs splayed, tail stiff and trailing over the edge of the unholy salver. Spray lines of blood spatter streaked the checkered mosaic of its abdomen. A thicker, glistening band led directly to where she knelt.

She glanced at the head again, its purpose fully realized, a spent aspergillum drained of its essence. An essence that now speckled a cleansed offering.

Fischer's knife glinted in the pale darkness beside her.

What have I done?

She retched. Turned to vomit and fell onto her side with a pained screech. The taste of bile and pond shrimp coated her mouth, and she retched again. Sobbed naked in her own filth.

Too far. It's gone too far.

She lay there on the stone pavement of the lookout for a time, shivering and feverish, until a white flash shook her from her malaise-induced stupor. The gleaming rock walls flickered, casting shadows like probing tendrils around her.

BOOM.

She shot upright, her heart a bucking gazelle in her chest. She rolled weightily onto her haunches against the cold stone, her gaze falling on the torrent beyond the karst window. She squinted, drawn to a small, rounded object inside the opening. It puzzled her, its features indistinguishable, as it loomed like a black hole punched out of the stormy backdrop.

Another flash of lightning brought the object into stark relief.

Lotta gasped.

How?

It was the statue Fischer had carved for her, standing equidistant from the walls of the porthole as if placed. *Had* to have been placed. There was no other explanation for it.

BOOM.

Lotta struggled to her feet and wavered on buckling knees. She stumbled, shaking and half dazed, nearly numb to the pain in her hands and feet. Too distracted by the chill of the damp air against her skin, by the effigy taunting her from the porthole, she pressed forward, hugging herself, the entirety of her focus on the punched-out silhouette before her.

As she approached, she barely made out the narrow barrier island as a black stain amid the swelling and churning backdrop below. Shivering with an intensity that almost knocked her off balance, she planted a hand against the stone frame to brace herself.

The sound of the runoff drew her attention momentarily. She held her hands beneath the cascading water, surprised at its relative warmth, and watched the blood melt away from her mangled fingers.

Her eyes fell at her feet.

Kneeling, she curled her unfeeling fingers around the statue. Around Odin.

The All-father.

A twinge of grief struck her then, as if coming back to reality, or moving between realities, the lack of sensation in her fingertips increasingly difficult to ignore. She yearned for that sensation, grieved for it. Wanted to feel something, anything. Her face contorted into a scowl, a pressure mounting in her chest.

Hot rage overcame her, and she threw the statue as hard as she could. Watched it disappear into the storm as tears stung her cheeks.

Is this what you want? she thought, speaking directly to the gods whose existence she had railed against her entire life. *A worthy fucking sacrifice?*

She no longer knew what was real.

"Well?" The sound of her own voice startled her, but the rage boiled up again to fortify her anger. "Then take me. Fucking *take* me, you bloody cowards."

One small slip. That was all it would take to send her over the edge. The roiling ebb would carry her away. The gods would be appeased. Her suffering would cease. And Fischer would never know.

He might guess. But he'd never really *know.*

Lotta turned and peered across the cenote toward the wigwam where he slept. The cave was dark, but she was adequately adapted to make out the black stillness of the intervening pond mirroring the three portholes. The shelter was a gray smudge beneath the looming limestone wedge along the far shore. She imagined Fischer—unaware of her absence on his side of the partition—and longed for warmth and parity and sensation.

She heard the knell of a beacon somewhere in the recesses of her mind and shot a cursory glance at the black mouth of the tunnel behind the camp, its gravity beckoning her.

Another flash of lightning arced overhead, and Lotta doubled back.

She saw the giant river crocs still dotting the barrier island for a split second. The tide was at its most violent since the flooding began, the waves like furious daughters of the Ægir. Whitecaps licked the island's banks, spraying foam over the motionless reptiles.

BOOM.

The ground shook beneath her.

Lotta reneged on her reprimand of the gods, apologized for her iconoclastic insult to the All-father, and instead turned to bargaining. Begged Njörðr to calm the sea and Thor to stay his hammer. But the only response she received was the wind howling through the rocks, the rains of Freyr roaring as if to mock her, Mjölnir soaring through the clouds and lighting them up like white phosphorus.

BOOM.

Then, right before the lightning died, something new caught Lotta's eye. An eminence in the shallows at the far end of the barrier island. It rose from the water like a small hill or mound shaped like a shallow, sinusoidal M.

She had no recollection of any such landmarks. Had seen the barrier island on countless occasions. No, this was *new*. She watched for a time, trying to decipher the nature of its form.

A washed-up tree? A brontosaur carcass?

The skies lit up again, outlining the object in a silver glow. Rain danced along its glistening surface, and in the split second that Lotta had a view, the entire thing *shifted*.

BOOM.

Against the infernal backdrop, a photochemical negative of the thing had seared onto her retina. She strained to see past the fading specter and through the reeling tempest to locate the object again. Watched. Waited for her vision to readjust.

Then she saw it.

Through the swirling deluge, the sheets of rain, the eminence rolled forward and rose from the churning waves like an ascendant god. It lurched again, led by an elongate, almost crocodilian head that bobbed upon an unfolding neck.

Lotta's blood ran cold. At that moment, she realized that the eminence she had seen was no landform, but the enormous dorsal sail of some sibylline monstrosity.

Gripped with horror, she gaped as the thing was cast back into darkness amid the howling torrent. She peered through strained eyes, just able to appreciate its nebulous form lumbering through the shallows, away from the encroaching waves chanting their nocturne of howling spume. From the fathoms of its bulk hung a pair of enormous, bouncing arms with claws like scythes. They dragged along the waterline as the colossal body waded onto the embankment of the barrier island. A pair of stout legs bore the weight of the beast, trailed by a long, newt-like tail that carved a wake through the roiling waves. The salamandrian appendage glistened, boundless like the wurms of myth, as it dragged through the mired breach.

For the first time, Lotta saw movement from the river crocs. They dragged their heavy bodies to the island's opposite end, allowing the newcomer a wide berth. A testament to the power of this *thing*, this sea god. She wrapped her arms around her shivering core and took solace, knowing she was high-up, far from its reach. That it was, for the moment, moored within a boiling sea.

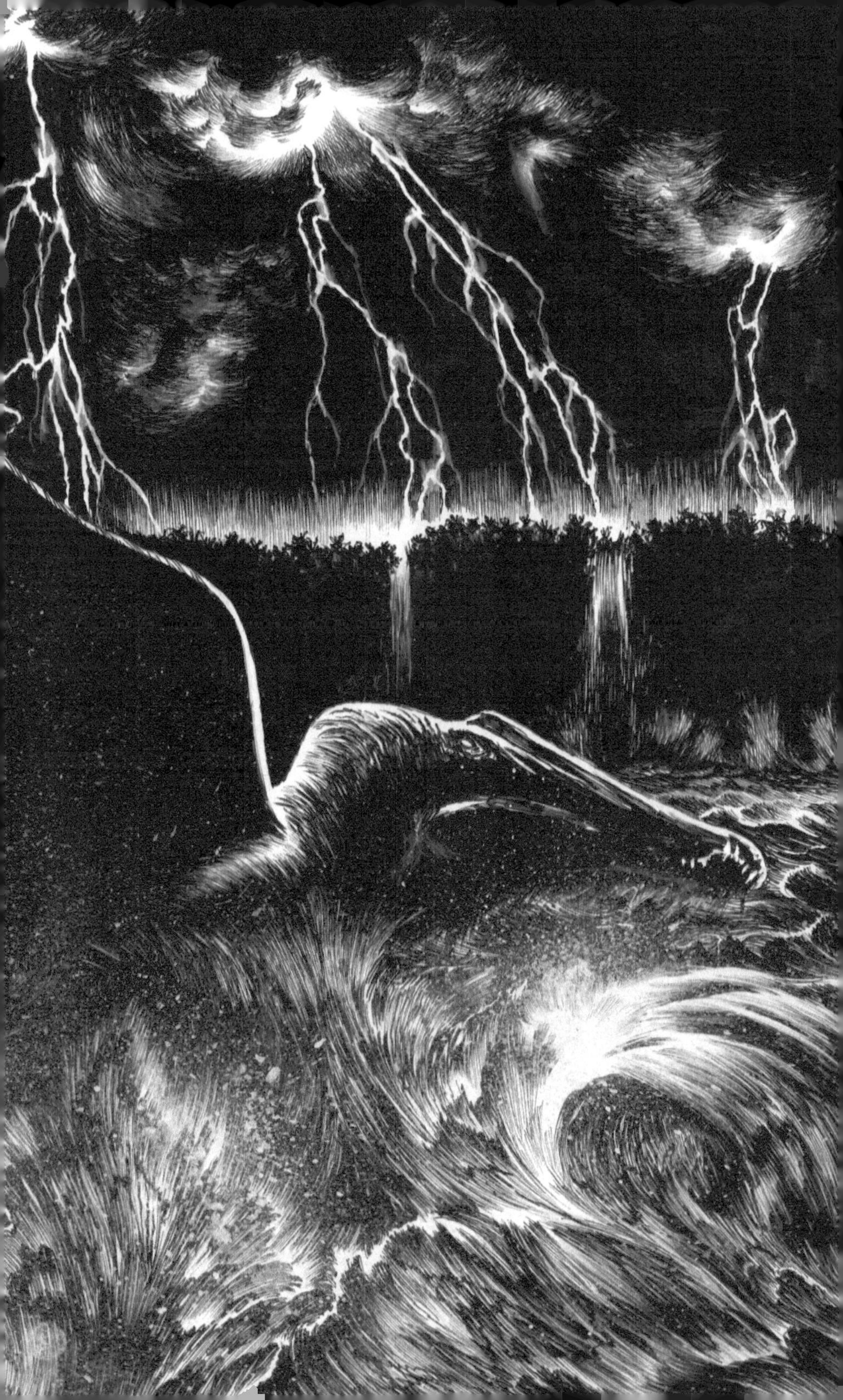

| ADAM >

Akila bellowed into the night.

Her entire body was trembling, muscles twitching under the horde of bees. But Perez's attention was fixed squarely on the thing behind the struggling giraffe, its reflective eyes staring back at her like floating embers in the darkness.

Deltadromeus agilis. Late Cretaceous.

The thing had stood motionless at the edge of the service road for a long time. It appeared cautious, uncertain of Perez's presence. Its arms were long, bent back at the elbows, relaxed wrists oriented in a peculiar clapping posture. Amid the frenetic buzzing, its flexing claws—three on each hand—clacked gently together. All the while, a single thought screamed through Perez's mind: *How did it get into the dome?*

From the delta's neck to the base of its long, striped tail stretched a green-and-brown band of fur-like down that appeared thickest around its shoulders. Thin filaments floated up like silvery strings from the animal's body and drifted to the ground below.

Shedding.

This covering tapered down the delta's flanks, giving rise to a pebbled mosaic of green and black scales that peeled up in patches around weeping sores. The ulcerations covered vast swathes of the animal's hide. It looked almost identical to the areas of necrosis Perez had observed on Eve, only more advanced. Something was making these animals sick.

Then, from the corner of her eye, Perez caught movement.

Iwa re-emerged from darkness and approached the scene warily, her head tilting and rolling from side to side. Next to the delta, it became evident to Perez how much she had grown in recent months. Her legs had filled out, and appeared particularly robust against the delta's leaner, more rangy hind limbs. Trailing her rounded body, Perez spotted a nearly mature tail—almost half the length of the delta's—that gave her a posture that was unique among the moa. She had to stand over two meters now, her head bobbing on its long neck just above the delta's crests.

The delta stretched its neck and greeted her with a nuzzle, then turned its gaze back to Perez. She looked on in stunned horror as its jaws crept open and revealed a blue tongue covered in barbed papillae. And—equally peculiar—a thin,white film coated the soft pallet.

Thrush, Perez thought. *Its immune system is not suited to this environment.*

Perez's mind raced. She recalled the strange number and arrangement of Eve's white blood cells under the microscope, thought of the signs of infection, of poor resilience to garden-variety pathogens that shouldn't have caused illness. It was as though she had dropped into an environment completely alien to her. And now, another individual was presenting before Perez with all the same clinical signs.

But the most concerning question she found herself returning to was how it got *inside*.

And then came an even more unsettling realization.

What if there are more?

Sssssssss-ss-s-ssshhhh.

A brash hiss sent thick gobs of spit from the delta's mouth as a downy corona of bright blue and green filaments stood straight up from its crown. *A warning to stay away*. The beast stepped toward Akila, apparently unde-terred by the frenzied swarm of bees attempting to ward the pair from their prize. All the while, its eyes burned into Perez, its lips lined with thick foam.

Dehydrated.

Perez recalled the appearance of Eve's kidneys. How they had the hallmark features of early failure.

Water. It came here for water.

The delta broke its gaze from her and regarded Iwa again with a soft warble. The young moa did not run from the encroaching beast, but instead *mirrored* it as it turned and strode heavily toward Akila. The two moved as a unit, their movements in perfect synchrony, the same way a mating pair of moa might.

They're courting each other.

Then, with a burst of speed, the delta broke away and lunged at Akila.

Before the injured giraffe could react, a clawed foot drove into the base of her neck. She rolled onto her side, her legs thrashing as a fountain of pulsing blood spilled out onto the service road. She bucked with her remaining strength and struck the delta squarely in the snout with a muted *clop*. The beast recoiled. Snuffed. Shook its head. It reared up, launched a foot into the giraffe's rib cage, and rotated its weight forward. Akila's chest heaved underfoot, the plume of swirling dust and bees intensifying around them.

But the delta appeared impervious to the insects. It drove its cragged head down, its jaws closing around flesh, and sheared away a slab of bloody muscle with a single fluid motion of the neck. The giraffe kicked out again, her hind leg narrowly missing Iwa this time.

Perez gaped in terror. Wanted to look away, but couldn't. Her ears were filled with the drone of water, the competing snorts between predator and prey.

The delta went for Akila's throat next, slicing the air with its striped tail to counterbalance its body. The giraffe choked in its gurgling vice of teeth, her charnel bleating fading into hapless whispers, into nothing.

Her chest shuddered. Slowed. Fell still.

Blood seeped from the corners of the delta's frothing mouth, poured in tributaries down its neck. It released its grip on Akila's throat and, with a *clap* of its reddened snout, turned to face Perez again. Its eyes were cinders, its head painted with glistening blood. From deep within its chest boomed another approximation of Iwa's call. Through crepitant rasps, it stared.

Iwa approached from behind and, with a soft warble, gently nuzzled the delta's snout. The pair dipped their heads to feed.

Sick with fear and confusion, Perez's pulse thrashed in her ears.

Iwa's head resurfaced, her toothless jaws turning over another bloody ribbon as bees swarmed about her head, eliciting in Perez's mind the memory of an ostrich eating a mouse. She heard Lotta's voice pierce the thought like a bullet to the head.

You have lost control here.

Perez breathed deeply. Brought herself back. Needed to get Nedjma out of here, into the tree line, and away from danger.

Her hands found Nedjma's legs, fingers tracing down to ankles. Encircled them. Pulled with everything she had.

But the sound of Nedjma's suit dragging over the coarse ground seemed to agitate the delta. Its head snapped up, its eyes flashing with renewed intensity. The beast circled around its quarry and stepped into full view.

Perez couldn't move. All she could do was fixate on its sibilating form, both familiar and alien.

Its jaws yawned wide, dropping a bloody mass to the ground, then belted a call through bloodied teeth—a gravelly shriek that oscillated as it moved through her.

Her first instinct was to run, but she caught herself. Nedjma needed her.

Stand your ground. Prey runs.

Commotion erupted from inside the rover—movement, then a tortured groan that trailed off. It was Oz.

"Perez?" His voice started with a tremble, then hardened. "Perez!"

At this, the delta pivoted and turned its attention from Perez. It approached the rover, its body floating through the underbrush upon gracile legs. A chimera of bird and lizard, its head held low, bobbing like when it had first emerged from darkness. Its gaze now discerning, curious.

"Shit!" Oz yelped.

Gunfire rang out. A muzzle flash lit up from inside the rover.

Perez threw herself over Nedjma. It seemed like she was down for a long time once the gunfire ceased, though she knew the entire incident couldn't have lasted more than a minute. She lifted her head up and scanned her surroundings. Both Iwa and the delta were gone.

She heard more movement from the rover.

Jumping into action, Perez pulled Nedjma into a sitting position, then pulled again, her legs searing, lungs ablaze. An involuntary scream escaped her lips as she stood with Nedjma over one shoulder and straightened.

Nedjma gave an anemic moan.

"Perez!" Oz wailed from the rover. He was still out of sight, but she could hear him moving to the front of the cabin.

She fled into the tree line. Pumped her legs against insurmountable pain. Within a few paces, Nedjma's weight slowed her to a brisk walk over the moss that blanketed the forest floor. Perez's entire body shook, her lungs blazed. She coughed and spat into her helmet with tears streaming down her cheeks. The darkness of seral undergrowth had swallowed them. The sound of water grew.

The gorge.

Perez knew an artery of ARC's river system meandered around the base of Qalil. It coursed past the mountain's entrance, where the service road led. Once inside the mountain, they could escape into SANCTUM's tunnel system beneath the dome's variable expansion apparatus.

Get to the mountain, to the tunnels.

That was as far as her plan went. What came next was up to chance.

She considered the prospect of Oz smuggling her into Russia, how it had seemed almost idealistic—a way *out* for her and Ruth—until it had become painfully apparent that Oz had intended to kill Nedjma, had leveraged the threat of violence to coerce Perez into submission, to leave Basem behind. And once his use for Nedjma was over, he'd kill her. His proclivity for wanton violence, his callousness toward Nedjma all but confirmed it. They needed to create as much distance between them and Oz as possible.

Basem's blank stare flashed before her eyes.

A pang of guilt pulled at her as if to swallow her into the earth. She longed for him. Knew, in the same way she had intuited Oz's true intentions for Nedjma, that she'd never see Basem again.

Except in Ruth.

Rifle fire pierced the trees.

Shooting at the delta? At us?

Perez quickened her pace. Ferns smacked her thighs, their density choking amid bracts and leaves woven into a wall of vegetation that bordered on impenetrable. Stems hooked her ankles and snapped free. Branches scraped against Nedjma's pendulant limbs. The moss was thick, with a lot of give, causing Perez to almost lose her footing. It felt almost like walking through sand, like she was expelling everything she had but remaining still, unmoving, like in her dream.

Another burst of gunfire clapped through the trees.

Something snagged Perez's ankle, a root or vine. Her legs wavered, then buckled, and her entire body tensed in anticipation as she fell forward. Nedjma went down first, landed hard. Then the ground slammed into her, and a flash of white filled her vision. She went airborne. One of her legs struck something—a tree—sending her body spinning until she struck the ground again. She was careening headlong into the gorge.

Crunch.

Her mind went dark.

When the world came rushing back, Perez was still tumbling headlong through the darkened thicket. The sound of water swelled to a deafening roar, and then… weightlessness. She was falling in slow motion, as if she had plunged into the depths of space.

Clap.

The impact voided her lungs as icy water cocooned her exterior, her shell. But before Perez could process where she was, a churning torrent filled her ears and fell away again. She was crashing through the surface, buoyed by her suit. Had fallen into the stream. Its current wasn't strong, but it had enough power to move her. She did not fight it.

Until…

Nedjma.

Perez gazed with renewed panic across the inky water, its surface an undulating ribbon of shimmering white shards beneath her headlamp's beam. She called out to Nedjma, but there was no answer. Her throat felt raw, her voice little more than a whisper. A sinking feeling stole over her. Then, just as she was about to call out again, the beam fell on something floating a short distance downstream.

Her headlamp flickered, then went dead.

Perez kicked blindly in the dark, in the direction she had spotted Nedjma. Pain shot through her right leg, but she powered through it. Grunted through clenched teeth while searing bolts pulsed up her lower back and sank into her like meat hooks. Despite her shock and pain, she remained determined.

She had almost reached Nedjma when she heard a distant *pop*.

Something struck the water to Nedjma's right, sending a vertical jet of spray overhead. It wasn't until the second struck in front of Nedjma's head that Perez realized they were being fired upon. She flashed a look upstream. A muzzle flashed from high up along the steep edge of the ravine where she had fallen.

Pop.

The bullet whistled over her head and struck the opposite bank into a stand of spidery mangroves.

No!

She kicked harder. Bolts of fiery electricity encircled her leg and coursed up her back. She reached Nedjma, grabbed her, and pulled her close. She kicked again, heard her involuntary scream rebound inside her helmet. She choked back a lungful of air, coughed it back out, then spun her head around to try and spot Oz again, but saw only darkness. They were exposed, powerless, at the mercy of the current.

There was another muzzle flash.

But something was different this time—Oz appeared to be firing in the opposite direction, back toward the service road. *Pop. Pop. Pop.* Several more rounds went off, briefly illuminating the darkened canopy. Then, as the current whisked Perez away, the scene slipped quietly from view.

Perez held Nedjma in one arm and sculled the water with the other. The stream banked, carrying them around a cluster of mangroves and gently swaying banana trees where it widened and fed into a shallow pool. By now, Perez was fully dark-adapted and could see an enormous raft of invasive water hyacinths bobbing quietly at the surface, their round, waxy leaves almost blue under the veil of darkness. Mangroves vaulted upon spidery roots, looming above the floating plants. She gazed past them toward shore, her eyes tracking the water's edge until she spotted a break in the overhanging canopy. There, she spotted the yawning mouth of the cave, the mountain's entrance. It evoked the enormous pit she had seen inside the CEPP hangar, the one that led deep underground.

The one that took Basem, changed him, reclaimed him.

I couldn't save you, Osito. I tried. Please know that I tried.

It was then that a startling revelation stole over Perez.

The pit. The elevator. The Goliath.

The delta came from underground.

A shrill triplet of screeches cut through the ambiance, sending Perez's heart into her throat. A second later, it came again, somewhere behind her. Then from the other side of the stream, an answering call. A branch snapped somewhere over her head.

Vervets.

Something had spooked the monkeys. ARC's vervets produced two known alarm calls when a predator was near—one for baboons, another for pythons—and a third for human interlopers. But although the screams she now heard shared characteristics of those alarms, this one stood apart in its pitch and tempo.

They have a new call.

Perez swallowed hard, hooking her arms under Nedjma's, then kicked as hard as her legs allowed. The current broke as she waded backward into the floating plants toward shore. She gritted her teeth amid the throbbing in her leg. The undulating hyacinths parted to permit her passage with Nedjma in tow, grazing her suit like hundreds of probing fingers, their collective grip providing just enough resistance to nearly immobilize her. When her feet finally found purchase in the soft mud, a fresh bolt of pain exploded into her lower back with an intensity that brought flashing lights before her eyes. She pushed through, each step as agonizing as the last.

An omnipresent drone swelled throughout the encroaching forest, broken only by the sound of her legs sloshing through the water, dredging the waxy hyacinths as she trudged onward.

S-s-s-ssss-s-s-ssss....

Mount Qalil was breathing. Such artificial winds were to be expected near the mouth of the mountain as the dome's internal pressure equalized. That was what Perez heard—the sound of leaves rustling in its breeze, interspersed with the primal call-and-response of overly-agitated vervets.

S-s-s-ssss… s-s-s-sssssshhhh….

That, and nothing more.

S-s-sssshhhh….

Without warning, her arms were wrenched forward. Her grip around Nedjma's armpits tightened, but she had reacted too late. Nedjma slipped away, her arms flailing and sending spray into the air, her body becoming entangled within hyacinths. Perez fell backward and went under.

When she broke back through the waterline, she quickly spotted Nedjma struggling. She was awake, frightened. Perez lunged forward and reached for her.

"Hey, it's me! It's me!" she shrieked. At first, Nedjma tried pulling free again, but she tired quickly, then seemed to recognize Perez's voice as her body went limp.

Perez held onto her and started again toward the embankment. A minute—maybe two—passed before she found herself collapsing beside her student onto a bed of nettles. *Solid ground.* She gazed up at a stand of swaying bamboo, her body ablaze with adrenaline and pain. Her leg throbbed. The bones in her aching wrists felt brittle, almost calcine. A thunderclap split her skull in two.

"*Cam…*" Nedjma groaned beside her. She was hoarse, almost inaudible.

Perez's hand found her shoulder. "You're okay," she said through labored rattles, her voice cracking. The stilted bamboo shoots began smearing together as her eyes brimmed. "You're okay."

Ssshh-h-hssshhhh….

The monkeys had gone quiet.

Perez propped herself into a sitting position and turned back toward the cave. The gaping chasm had been carved into a towering crag stretching almost to the top of the tree line around the mountain's base. Beyond it, Qalil loomed out of sight, obscured by a jutting wall of sheer rock and more trees. Perez spotted the service road. It was overgrown, almost invisible at night, meandering through the trees and descending the sloped ravine through a series of switchbacks. It leveled out as it neared the far end of shore before snaking past the mouth of the cave.

A light breeze kissed Perez's suit.

"*Sss-sshhit!*"

She leapt to her feet. Nedjma gave a startled yelp. There was no ignoring that sound, no dismissing it. It was Oz, just through the trees to her left.

"*Perrrez!*"

But something about his voice sounded off. Deep and gruff, with a hissing quality. It was difficult to hear over the rustling boughs, but it sounded *different*. Like he was choking.

How badly is he hurt?

She toggled her headlamp, but it was dead.

Oz called out again, this time from a completely different direction, farther into the trees.

Impossibly far.

"*Ss-s-s-Ssshit! Prehzz? Brrrez! Ssss-sshhhhh....*"

He sounded drunk.

Unnatural.

Almost *inhuman.*

But Perez's thoughts couldn't go there...

A syrinx. It has a syrinx.

...*wouldn't* go there.

She rolled onto her knees and started to help Nedjma to her feet.

"Quick. Into the mountain," she said.

PARADISE LOST

| Before Erebus, Fischer had led missions in North Africa. Neutralized Cypriot terror cells, infiltrated and dismantled Saudi shadow insurgencies, seized and used Iranian and Russian assets against them. There were no sides, only catalysis, and his purpose was to tip the scales in whatever way Berlin saw fit.

He thought he'd seen it all when he was sent on a peacekeeping mission during Niger's annexation into Europe. Violent crackdowns and uprisings. Soft coups, hard coups.

Child's play.

Niger, though, rooted out the boys from the men. Beheadings were common. Rapes ignored in plain sight. Self-immolations appeared to be a trend.

He remembered the filth littering the streets, the parasite-infested water. The packs of feral dogs, picking at corpses. Usually, women or children that had succumbed to hunger or thirst. Bloated corpses baking in the roiling heat.

But it was the young mother he thought of most. Stuffing her face with dirt while she nursed her dead baby. She was top of mind the day the doctors diagnosed Jocelyn with the same condition.

Pica. A sickness that made some pregnant women crave inedible things. A compulsion driven by mineral deficiencies. For Jocelyn, it was mud, dirt, clay. It was what had led to the anemia. Thinned Jocelyn's blood to the point that bruises riddled her body. She'd almost miscarried because of it, nearly lost Emma.

Bled through that damn gown faster than I could run up that porch—

Jocelyn denied it, of course. At first.

Fischer forgave her eventually after she came to grips with it and got help. Knew it wasn't really her fault. But he never let himself off the hook for missing the signs, despite her proclivity for secrecy and obfuscation.

I didn't know. She hid it from me. Hid it until she couldn't anymore.

He left her after the girls died. Couldn't look at her.

But none of that mattered anymore, because now, she loomed naked before him, framed in black. Regarded him with a carnal smile from the entrance of the wigwam. Her hand traced past her navel, fingers running across maternal scars, continued down between her legs.

<Do you want this?> she crooned in his head.

Fischer nodded.

<Tell me you want this.>

<I want it.>

Her skin was smooth, almost glowing in the tenebrous abyss of night. The whites of her eyes flickered through the gloom.

Fischer held her gaze. His breathing was measured, but his heart raced.

Jocelyn seemed to glide as she closed the distance between them, and her body pressed into his. He welcomed the warmth of her breasts against his chest as she fumbled eagerly at the buckle of his suit liner. Her hand found his, guided it over the scars and slipped it between her thighs.

Her mouth fell.

Fischer did want it. Wanted to start over. A second chance.

Everything moved fast from that point. A strong scent of pine enveloped him, his hands migrating to the backs of her thighs. Her cold arms encircled his neck, her legs opening to straddle him as he hoisted her up and let gravity guide him inside of her. Head spinning, his movements fueled by the rhythmic gasps escaping her lips.

He wanted it.

<I want you, too.> Her voice was a whisper behind his eyes. <I want you.>

He succumbed to his instincts.

Heart tearing from his chest, he lowered her to the ground, her legs clasping his waist, squeezing and releasing him again and again. Her hips pressed him into a crude bed of bracts. Into the black abyss.

He welcomed the pain of the ground digging into his flesh.

<Fuck me,> Jocelyn screamed.

She leaned forward, rising to orgasm, her lips clasping his. Her pace quickened in a frenzy of bestial thrusts. He took her hair in fistfuls. Pulled so that her delicate neck arched back and passed the most beautiful sound into her mouth. He pressed his lips to her throat, felt the vibration of her vocal cords calling his name.

They were one.

His lips trailed to her collarbone, continued down and encircled her left breast. He sucked, her sounds intensifying, exhorting him to escalate to gentle biting. Her nails trailed his back, and she rocked forward with a wonderful scream.

Fischer tasted something then. Something strange—grit—wedged between the gaps in his teeth. It clotted and wedged itself between cheek and gum.

Jocelyn slipped into a low, insidious chuckle.

The woman he saw nursing in Niger flickered through his head.

Dirt.

Fischer spat, pulling himself back.

Jocelyn crowed, her eyes pale like dying stars, and squeezed to pull him deeper inside.

A rattled whisper spilled from her lips. <Wouldn't want any to go to waste, would we, love? Not if we're starting over. Leaving everything else behind.>

Fischer wanted to push her away, but couldn't. Wouldn't. And she squeezed in synchrony to the transient pulses moving out of him and into her.

<That's it. Not one drop, love.>

He gazed up at her with a combination of confusion and dread. Stared into those white eyes. The same ones he'd watched from across the stream and through the tree line the night he cut himself. He gazed into them now as the pulsations between his legs faded.

Jocelyn smiled down at him like an eidolon, her teeth black with loam. >

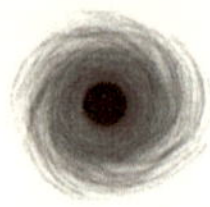

Day 11, First Light — Cenote, Table Rock Karst

Dawn.

Fischer's eyes crept open, beads of sweat erupting on his forehead. He stared up at the thatched roof of the wigwam, his vision blurred. Pale light trickled through the gaps, a reddish gray that signaled the muddied ambience of daybreak.

The cave was silent.

He stretched his arms, then slumped back down with a long sigh.

His inner thigh itched. He brushed his fingernails over the area and encountered a sticky substance smeared across the skin. Pulled his hand away, sat upright.

My clothes. Where are my clothes?

He looked down at himself with foggy bewilderment. Blinked. Fighting off the remaining vestiges of torpor, his vision came into sharper focus as he searched around his side of the shelter. His bedding of bracts was strewn across the floor, his ESD liner tossed against the partition that divided Lotta's side from his. He noticed a musty smell, a faint odor of stale sweat. The leg hair sticking to his inner thigh pulled painfully as he moved.

His gaze fell on the partition again, his senses heightened, listening for any sign of life on the other side.

"Lotta?"

Nothing.

Rolling over, he snagged his poncho, threw it on, and made for the entrance. Couldn't get out of there fast enough.

"*Lotta?*"

Outside, the limestone slab loomed over him like a guardian. Heat radiated from its angled underbelly, swaddling him in warmth, giving him pause. He glanced at the dying bed of coals from the night before, insufficient to be the source of the heat reflecting down at him.

Looking toward the pond, fine threads of mist peeled from the waterline. Beyond the far shore, brass columns of the early morning sun filtered through the two visible portholes, where patchy clouds passed over a crimson sky. The smell of ozone filtered heavily into his sinuses.

"Storm finally broke," he muttered.

The cave was cast in a rusty glow by the fledging dawn, an oxidized quality that made it appear almost Martian. It reaffirmed that he was on another planet, one that did not belong to humankind, certainly not a nude troglodyte who spunked on himself in his sleep.

The third porthole, Lotta's lookout, was partially obscured behind a lip of rounded rock jutting up from the far shoreline. He recalled watching her the day before, periodic glances away from his work on the fish corral. If he moved over there now, he might get a glimpse, see if she had made her way up to catch the sunrise.

But perhaps *not* being seen was the point. Seemed to be part of the reason she liked it up there. Liked her space.

Ellsa was like that. Ever the introvert with a book or a sketch pad, hiding away in her closet or behind a tree somewhere. Smart kid, like her mother.

It was the first time the cave had felt so silent.

He sighed and walked around to the other side of the wigwam, past two husks of smoked rat crocs dangling at head height, their milky eyes unusually bulbous in their shrunken heads. After curing them, he had threaded them through with cordage and secured them to the roots dangling from the flanks of the rock house. Outside of protecting it from spoilage, Fischer found that smoking rations deterred animals from raiding the pantry.

His eyes fell on one of the sieve cylinders set against the outside of the shelter. It contained a new tannin preparation for bathing, made by steeping pine needles from the old campsite. Smelled of pine, something a little more palatable than ginkgo. He had tried various versions of it as a sort of deodorant the last couple of days. Lotta seemed to like it. He hoped to combine it with rendered fat from the rat crocs to make soap, but right now, he just needed to get the dried cum off his leg.

He leaned over the sweet aroma rising from the canister. Smoky pine. Grunted a little as he wet his fingers with it and rubbed his thigh as he attempted to recall the last time he'd had a wet dream. Probably grade school.

A faint chirrup pierced the damp air, and Fischer whipped around. Spotted movement at the corral, a crow-sized form teetering on rangy legs, its head concealed beneath the fern planchments forming the roof. Its striped tail, tipped with a pennaceous ladle of iridescent feathers, shone brilliantly through the morning gloom of the cave.

Fischer immediately recognized the retractable claw on the inner toe of either foot.

Raptor.

A second later, the creature's head emerged, birdlike in its movements. With its inky eyes fixed, its snout dipped to the ground and snatched up something by its feet—a dragonfly or some other insect—and slipped back inside the corral. Fischer watched its plumed arms curl into its chest, its neck extending and then pulling back to hold its head aloft inside the cage of sticks and vegetation.

Its body froze, save for the occasional twitch of eager foot claws.

Little fucker's fishing. In my *corral.*

"*Oye!*" Fischer growled and bolted into the open.

He heard a *plunk,* and the head pulled back, ripping the planchments off the latticed structure. An arc of spray whisked from something glistening in its jaws, an eel-like fish that proved a formidable quarry for the little raptor.[1] The fish writhed and squirmed, jerking its captor's head, and the raptor fumbled it to the wet limestone with a meaty *slap.*

Newly liberated, the fish was on the move. Its body snaked, leveraging its four fins like legs to shimmy away, except it was also moving away from the *pond.* It nudged the ground with its snout as if trying to burrow, but the limestone proved impenetrable. The disoriented raptor zeroed in on it and leaped, pinning it with its sickled toe claws and tearing away a wedge of spine in its jaws. The fish went still.

Fischer gave a mock charge. "I said get on!"

The raptor hopped backward, its head rotating—more quizzical in aspect than afraid—then snatched up its catch and darted into the bracken. Fischer watched its trajectory, marked only by the rustling of ferns until it emerged at the far end near the mouth of the tunnel. It bounded up

---

1 *Argonadus indet.,* a freshwater lungfish

the rock pile, clawed wings scooping at the air so that it floated like a cosmonaut in low gravity. It reached the top of the rock pile and turned in his direction with a final cursory glance, then scurried into blackness with a flick of its tail.

"Little shit." Fischer smoothed his beard through his fingers and turned toward the remnants of the corral.

That was when he spotted the tripped drop trap farther up the bank. The prospect of a fresh snag was enough consolation to cool him off a little. Except when he wandered over to collect his prize, he found nothing but a speckled blood trail leading away from it toward the path snaking up to Lotta's lookout.

Heat filled his cheeks.

"*FUCK.*" The word exploded from him reflexively as he knelt over the flattened stone to investigate. He ran his fingers over it and stood back up. "That palisade's getting started *today.*"

He already knew where to get the wood. Same place they got their kindling. The deadfall. Except they needed all the firewood they could get, and he couldn't be sure that erecting a barrier in front of the tunnel would be sufficient to keep the smaller critters away.

Fischer looked around. Still no sign of Lotta. Called for her, his voice bouncing to the far shore and around the cave's recesses. No way she wouldn't hear him. But only silence greeted him.

He called out again. And still, nothing.

His attention returned to the drop trap. His first thought was that it would take a reasonable amount of strength to flip that stone over to remove the quarry, that something larger than a rat croc or a raptor had gotten in and made off with the carcass. How big had yet to be known, but something with at least the strength to pry away a moderately heavy stone slab.

Fuck. Fuck. Fuck.

His fingers busied themselves, twitching, wringing into fists, hungry for something to grasp. His heart surged, head swiveled, searching his surroundings for more clues. Needed his fucking knife. Needed it *now.*

His mind returned to Lotta. Traced the blood trailing into the stalagmites. Imagined scenarios played out in his head, some of which proved too horrific, too unreal to entertain. He pushed it aside, focused instead on getting to her. She'd be alive, uninjured. Had to be. She was okay, and they'd laugh it off over croc jerky later.

Ha ha ha.

He wiped his cracked lips with the back of his hand and started to follow the blood trail.

Halfway to the lookout, a strange bubbling sound fell on his ears from the pond. It was brief, like the sound of a diver purging a respirator, a churning *glub-glug*. He found a line of sight between gaps in the stalagmites lining the path and scanned the general location of the sound. Steam threaded up from the glassy surface of the pond reflecting the karstic ceiling overhead.

He turned and pressed forward just as a whiff of sulfur incited him to gag, the same rotten-egg stench from the nesting site. Determined, he clenched his spasmodic throat and continued forward. Busied his mind, refocused.

He started to think again about securing the camp, specifically their food. Maybe corrals and drop traps weren't the answer. A trot line might work. He could string a length of cordage across the pond and secure baited hooks whittled from bone or wood at regular intervals just beneath the water's surface.

Could work.

Until another shithead-bird found a way to outsmart that, too. A palisade was the ultimate solution.

Fischer emerged from the path into the warmth of a ruddy daybreak and was met with the silent shapes of around a dozen cairns interspersed around the elevated platform. He squinted past the shapes through a golden effulgence, then almost jumped out of his skin.

It was as though she had popped out of thin air.

Crouched in front of the lookout with her back to him, legs hugged to her chest, Lotta gazed out as if entranced by the alien landscape beyond, her outline rimmed by red efflorescence.

She must have heard him approach, but didn't react.

Fischer hooded his brow with his hand, squinting through the blinding rays, her dim shape visible within a shimmering corona and little more. He caught the outline of the atlatl she had constructed, silhouetted by the sepia backdrop where it leaned against the edge of the outlook.

"There you are." He exhaled, starting toward her, sidestepping two of the stone piles as he moved forward. "Looks like the storm's finally passed…."

He stopped cold. Noticed the rim of her bare breast flattened against the skin of her thigh. He stepped into the column of sunlight, eyebrows cinching as his hand fell to his side. His eyes traced the faint hint of her shoulder blades, the bulge of her spine leading to her dimpled buttocks.

"*Oy*, where are your *clothes*?"

Her gaze remained fixed toward the horizon, past a column of rust-lit steam that bled like ink into a blazing sky. The floodwaters farther on appeared calm, the barrier island a dark band interrupting the bloody sheen of the reflected heavens. It appeared derelict now, the giant crocs having since moved on, the remains of a desiccated brontosaur carcass sloshing against its embankment. Far in the distance, more plumes billowed like belching smokestacks, tinged pink by a sun—an evil orange eye—that straddled a horizon dappled by ruddy cumulonimbus.

The canter of Fischer's pulse intensified as he took another step toward Lotta.

"*Hey*, you okay? What's—"

He lurched unexpectedly. Righted himself from slipping backward as his foot planted into something cold and wet. He staggered backward to regain purchase and was overcome by a putrid stench.

A shudder racked his core as he processed the scene at his feet.

It was a headless rat croc, splayed atop a flat, blood-spattered stone, its entrails exposed, *arranged* circumferentially in a spiral that expanded outward. From the gaping hole in its abdomen peered the pale, cold eyes of its disembodied head, its snout carefully arranged perpendicular to the knife placed at the edge of the stone. Still black with blood, the tip of the blade glinted at him to round out the grisly oblation.

Runes inscribed in crimson fanned out from the altar across the stone pavement, increasingly disordered scrawl that trailed in Lotta's direction, and it was then that Fischer noticed the bloody handprints on her waist. Smeared lines like red ink, almost brown at the edges, dragged by probing fingers across her skin.

Lotta turned to him then, her face drawn and pale, hair tousled. The corners of her lips upturned slightly as though she had emerged from a far-off reverie.

"What happened here?" Fischer muttered, his hands held out at his sides to present the scene. His tone came through as more a demand than an inquiry.

Alertness appeared in her eyes, a hungry, smiling gaze that appraised him up and down. Filled him with unease.

He cleared his throat. "Where are your clothes, Lotta?"

Her eyes snapped up to meet him, and she broke her silence with a playful sigh. "*Funny*," she said, scanning him over again.

Another column of steam climbed beyond the porthole behind her, momentarily blotting out the sun. She turned to shift her weight onto a bloody left hand, then rose to her feet and stepped out from behind a cairn that partially concealed her.

There was much more blood on her front. A semblance of a smeared handprint clasped her left breast. More markings ribbed her inner thighs and snaked between her legs. A half dozen thick crimson smudges lined her navel. Fischer assumed the blood came from the dead rat croc, but couldn't be sure. She didn't seem hurt.

This isn't happening. She's fucking snapped. Verrückt. Gone mad.

He thought of the statue he'd given her and shook his head. The one that was noticeably absent.

Stupid. Never should've entertained the delusion.

But at the time, he had hoped the gesture might get her to let him in a little more, not hide that side of her from him.

You stupid fuck.

His throat burned sour, his mind now entirely fixated on the markings riddling her body.

A strange thought came to him then, stifled the air in his lungs. He recalled how he woke up earlier. Naked. Cock-snot smeared on his inner thigh. Thought of how Lotta looked at him now, her narrowed eyes and upturned lips. Thought of how comfortable she was in front of him without clothes, thought of the bloody handprints on her breast that he tried not to focus on, though now that he thought of it, they looked too big to be her own. *But whose? Are there others besides us?* He thought of the visions, the apparitions he witnessed. *Could they be real? Why would she hide this?*

But this theory was fleeting, eviscerated by Occam's razor as it plunged into his thoughts like a hot knife.

It's just us. Everything else is in your head. Always has been.

But those marks… not her hands….

His face turned hot as bits of his dream came back to him. He made no attempt to hide the fact that despite his growing unease, he was getting hard beneath the poncho. Didn't want the imagery racking his mind to arouse him. That was the *last* thing he wanted.

Jocelyn's black smile taunted him behind his eyes.

He held his hands before his face and turned them over, palms up.

No. No, it can't be….

He curled his fingers and scrutinized his cuticles, his eyes bulging at the clotted substance wedged in the corners and beneath the nails.

Blood.

A dream. It was just a dream.

Lotta strode toward him, passing among the cairns with a steady calm he hadn't seen since before the incident.

She was a different person now, to be sure—not the rigid, methodical scientific purist, but a practitioner of the unknown, the unknowable. Of ritual sacrifice and divination. Of depravity. And were it not for the return of that confident stride, he would not have recognized her.

A camphoric pine scent befell him as she neared, her unclothed frame rimmed in the soft morning Rayleigh.

He closed his eyes. The muscles in his neck had grown weak. The dark figure, the woman in his dream, flashed through his mind, his hands running over her curves, her thighs squeezing his hips. All the while, the smell of pine swelled until it encircled him in a lecherous embrace.

"*No,*" he muttered, horrified at the conclusions he parsed.

He opened his eyes, his head bowed, trembling hands still upturned. How hadn't he noticed the blood until now? *How?*

"Everything okay?" Lotta reached for his hand and grazed it with her index finger. He ripped it away reflexively.

Nothing. Nothing was okay.

"Oh," she said, looking down at herself as if to read his thoughts. "Sorry. I tried to wash up last night, but you woke…" She paused, biting her lower lip.

A dream. It was a fuckin' dream.

"…and we became… *distracted.*"

Pine. The tannin. She used the tannin.

And then what?

He'd had a dream. A terrible dream about his ex-wife.

But was it?

And what of the incident by the stream? That hand guiding the blade through his veins, that hand that had felt so *real?* That, too, just a dream?

He opened and closed his right fist. A dull ache coursed up the belly of his forearm.

No more pain, Daddy.

But *he'd* done this to *himself.* That was the story.

Lotta's story.

He felt numb, his gaze far off. Didn't acknowledge her, instead traced the lines in his clotted palms.

The shaft of light beaming through the porthole dimmed, shrouding everything in pale carmine, and Fischer's gaze bounced briefly to Lotta, whose details were now plain. She smiled at him meekly, her earlier confidence appearing to wane.

His heart skipped, and his gaze darted back to the porthole. He tried to distract himself by fixating on the aftermath of the storm, anything to avoid confronting the unclothed woman before him, but his erection made that almost impossible.

"Tell me what happened last night," he said in a stern tone.

He fixated on the steady plumes rising along the horizon. A dozen fragmented clouds smudged the rust-colored firmament pink as they passed, shimmering, over the rising sun.

"Stop taking the piss," Lotta said in a muffled tone. "You know what happened."

He regarded her again, her expression now serious, searching. Her narrowed eyes lingered on him for a moment, then grew wide.

She stepped back.

"You're being *serious*?"

He gave no response. Denied himself the urge to break eye contact.

She ran her hands through her matted hair; then, as if it had just dawned on her, she turned away, concealing her breasts with her arm. "Shit. *Shit.* So fucking *stupid.*" Her face and chest flushed. "This is *insane*, Ed. How can't you *remember* that we... we—"

She trailed off. Looked to be on the verge of a panic attack.

Don't fall for it. Make her say it.

"We *what*?" he growled.

Lotta snapped out of it and drew a deep breath, her cheeks sunken, face drawn as she procured a sidelong glance.

"Bloody *hell*. You were in your head again...." She threw her hands up as though it didn't matter anymore, started to pace. Stopped to study his expression again, as if to be sure. "That *whole time*?"

His silence betrayed him.

"Right... I should have known." She sneered, her words wavering through stunned laughter. "It wasn't me you were seeing, was it?"

A dark shadow fell over Fischer. "You're way off-piste."

Lotta scoffed and rolled her eyes. "It was *her*, wasn't it? The woman you've been seeing everywhere. Your *wife*."

"You don't know what you're talking about."

"Don't I?"

"Aye. So, you're saying we had a go, that's your story...."

"Sure, Ed. Yes. We had a *go*. A fuck. Shag. Whatever you want to call it."

Fischer nodded. "Aye... aye... so that's your story about *all this* here. Blood and rituals and jacking me off in my sleep."

He looked down at his arm, the wound now scabbed over.

No more pain.

His face hot, he clenched his hand into a fist and pushed it out to present the symbol carved into his flesh. "And *this*? I did *this* to myself, yeah? That's the story, yeah?"

Lotta stepped back. A look of shock and confusion painted her expression. "What? Your *arm*?"

Fischer said nothing, just watched her. Looked for any tell, any sign of deceit.

"I *told you* what happened," she said waveringly.

"Did you?"

"Yes. What's got into you?"

Heat continued to swell in his cheeks. The air in his poncho had grown humid, and sweat trickled down his back. "I'm asking the questions," he said.

"Well, you're scaring me."

"Am I?"

"Yeah, Ed, you are." Lotta's blue eyes started to well up, peering deep into him. "You see things that aren't there, things that didn't really happen. Can't remember things that *did*." She choked up as if wounded.

Fischer wondered what she saw there, behind his eyes, whether she glimpsed the emptiness within the husk of his former self, the tempest within.

"You've lost touch with reality," she said as if concluding this imagined analysis. "And I don't like your *questions*."

"I've—*I've* lost touch?" Fischer spat. "Have you *seen* where we are?" He spread his arms wide and looked around the cave. "Look around, Lotta. *Reality* has lost *us*."

His gaze halted on her profane altar, and the sight of the butchered carcass elicited fresh spasms from his insides.

"And this?" he said. "Mutilating rations for some twisted voodoo bullshit?" He shook his head, sickened by it all. "But go on, enlighten me. Tell me how I've *lost touch*."

Lotta shrunk away, her voice almost inaudible. "I don't need to explain myself to you."

Fischer had her on her heels. Emboldened, he leaned in.

"Aye, well, let me tell you what *I* think…." His voice started to rise, his chest heaving as he presented his forearm again. "I think I'm *not* the one who did *this*."

This elicited a reaction. He read it in her ruby eyes. Her cheeks flared. She took another step back.

"Wh-what are you on about?"

"I think you know."

"No, Ed. I don't have a clue what the *fuck* you're suggesting."

Her sullen face had gone pale, arms trembling, her white-knuckled hands fiddling at her weeping cuticles. Fischer noticed one of her fingers was purple, almost *black*—an affliction he hadn't yet seen. An infection, maybe gangrene. A piece of him became alarmed at this rate of decline, more so by her apparent lack of pain, yet he said nothing of it. Instead, his eyes seared into her, his attention squarely on the notion that something else was on her mind. Something deeper than fear—something meant to keep him in the dark—and he wanted to know what it was.

"I stopped you," she expounded after a prolonged silence, her voice trembling. "Saved your *life*. Brought you back from the brink, so I don't know what else you want from me."

"*Someone's* hand put that knife in me, and it wasn't *mine*. That much I remember." The muscles in his arm burned with fatigue, pain that only fueled the swelling storm within him. "And I never knew what to make of *this* symbol until right here, right now. It's all so clear to me now." He could almost feel those little hands on him again, and his skin prickled. Thought of how sometimes, he saw a sliver of Ellsa in Lotta. Apparently, she had some Jocelyn in there, too. So Evl would be no real stretch. "So, what I *want* from you," he continued in a low voice, "is the *truth*."

Lotta's expression shifted then. Her shimmering eyes narrowed, hooded beneath knitted brows.

"The truth?" she said, her voice finding new strength as a solitary tear streamed down her cheek. "The *truth?* Let's talk about the truth, Ed. The *real* reason *you* did that to yourself. The *real* reason you fucking *hate* yourself. Because I'm tired of living *that* lie."

Her last word cracked the air like a whip, and by the time Fischer noticed her eyes had glazed over, her face was contorting, forcing back a levy of tears. He was caught off guard by this, the lump in his throat preventing little more than a grunt in response, though his anticipation of where this was going was enough to induce madness.

Lotta swallowed and let her jaw go slack. "*Geneva*," she whispered.

"What?" Fischer's mind went blank. "What does *Geneva* have to do with—"

"It wasn't an *earthquake*, Ed." She blurted the words as if she couldn't spit them out fast enough, as if they were poison.

"What?" he managed, barely catching himself from stumbling as the strength left his legs.

It was as though he'd slammed into a brick wall. The haunting memories of searching through endless rubble, of finding the bodies of his daughters one by one among countless others, flooded his consciousness. Time went in reverse from there. Every birthday, every beaming smile. A bemused expression after helping him shave. Thought of tears wiped away after skinned knees and the soft touch of little hands on his scars. Moments he struggled to recapture, decaying like radiation over time. Slipping from him like sand through his fingers.

He couldn't believe what he was hearing.

Lotta had the waterworks on full display now. "The lab," she blubbered. "*My* team. We messed up, Ed. W-we…"

Through his tunneling vision, he glimpsed the old Lotta. For a second, he thought he might even believe her despite the insanity she spewed.

"What—what are you saying?"

"We weren't ready for it… the first singularity," she struggled to say between sobs. "Our AI systems were still too naïve to stabilize… and it… *Geneva*…. W-we covered it up, Ed."

Fischer caught his breath and willed his legs to be still. "You're lying."

"No," Lotta said. "It's the truth. Your girls… they—"

"*Leave* them *out* of *it*." Ed channeled all his menace, glowering at her through slitted eyelids.

"Then I'll make this easy and make it about *me!*" she screamed at him, her words hitching, running together. "The Commission couldn't let it go, that display of raw *power*. They wanted us to continue the program… to expand it. Take it off-site, out of the public eye. So, we blamed Mother Nature and took the operation to Algeria. They offered me the lead in exchange for my silence!" She held his gaze, waiting for a reaction that never came. "How could I say no, Ed?!"

"Stop—*stop* talking."

But Fischer knew she was telling the truth. Everything clicked the moment she strung the words together, and his mind went back to the night of the disaster, to that endless sea of rubble, his daughters somewhere under it all. Remembered the strange aurorae filling the sky over the search crew, a detail he had pushed from his consciousness, buried so deep that the memory of it hadn't even registered as he gazed upon the same lights illuminating the sky on the night they found themselves in this hellscape.

"Ed…"

The sound of his name ripped him from his daze. A swimmy malaise stole over him.

"Ed, you have to believe me, I *never* meant for… for *that*." A drop of blood bloomed on Lotta's bottom lip where she had bitten too hard.

"They're gone." Fischer's vision began to smear. "Gone because of… of *you?*"

"*No.* I didn't know. I promise you I didn't *know.*"

Something like a chime went off inside him then, something as elusive as déjà vu, except he pinpointed it almost immediately. Not a chime, a *beacon.* He had heard those words before.

She didn't know.

The phrase spilled into his thoughts like an invading parasite, a pestilent fungus. That day seemed a world away now, but Hassan's thin whisper came to him as sharply as the day they found his remains in the forest.

No. He couldn't have meant… couldn't have known.…

Warmth filled Fischer's chest, a rediscovered fear that he thought he'd buried, now relentlessly clawing itself free.

It's in your head.

Lotta was silent, sucking her lower lip. She was covering herself with her arms again, her eyes bright red, accentuating their deep blue as tears streamed freely down her cheeks.

"I'm sorry. Ed, you've got to believe me. I'm so sorry."

Forgive her.

He wiped his eyes with a trembling hand.

The beacon tolled once more, and deep inside him something snapped.

No.

"Ed, please—"

"No! Shut UP!"

He strained to articulate a coherent thought, battling against the fear and the anger savaging him, rotting him from the inside out. But it was too much—he was weak—and the slurry of emotion instead manifested as a primal scream, an inhuman sound he never imagined himself procuring.

The fresh wounds of scars reopened, manifesting as an animalistic wail that simultaneously invoked deep mourning and abject wrath.

He leveled a red-hot gaze at Lotta, who backstepped dangerously close to the ledge of the lookout. There was fear in her eyes. *Real* fear. The same fear he had seen many times since the iron fist of misfortune punched a gaping tear in spacetime.

The taste of ozone, the stench of sulfur, of death, swelled at the back of his throat. Warmth settled on his tongue and reached its sticky tendrils down his throat to incite a gag. He retched, doubled over, a stream of acerbic drool snapping away from his bottom lip. Pressure mounted behind his bulging eyes as they fell upon the porous limestone.

Don't let it take you.

Shaking, his hands braced upon tremulant knees, he watched the shadow of another cloud fall over him. Stared hard into the speckled stone until his vision narrowed, until he saw the frantic fingernail markings of his dead baby girl ribboned across the surface. Wanted to cry, to feel something, anything but the crushing weight of blind rage, of helplessness. But he was powerless against it. A broken man.

Maybe he always was.

"You ruined me," he choked. *"Ruined my family."*

Forgive her.

Then, something scuffed the sandstone behind him, and instinct ripped him free of his burdens. Something ascending the corridor to the lookout.

Alarm stifled emotion, and his head swiveled toward the sound, a fresh rope of drivel slinking from his gaping mouth.

But he saw nothing. Heard nothing.

The ensuing silence somehow seemed louder. He lingered on it, then flashed a cursory gaze toward Lotta with a combination of loathing and inquiry. Her shocked expression told him all he needed to know.

Not in your head. She heard it, too. Something on the path.

His senses sharpened, sending him back to his feet as he peered across the pond toward the camp, his surroundings spinning like a carousel. He should have had a view, but was shocked to find it mostly obscured behind a thick wall of vapor rising from the water. Dozens of cigar-shaped objects of varied length floated, motionless, at the surface.

Fish.

Another scrape jolted him. Nails or hooves dragging across stone. He spun to face the path, his eyes bulging, face wet, and through the stone bollards emerged a pale apparition, tinged scarlet by the infernal dawn.

Aghast at its form, Fischer froze, his lungs sucking the anemic air he still struggled against. A pair of shimmering eyes—white holes, charnel and bouncing—encompassed a marriage between the familiar and the alien. Eyes that haunted him.

And only once his rage-induced stupor faded entirely did Fischer fully comprehend the interloper in his midst.

UEF / RD
EYES ONLY

Ministry of Defence
United European Federation

BRIEF

To: House of Commons Committee of Nuclear Research

From: The European Interprovincial Research Organisation (EIRO)

The Commission of European Particle Physics (CEPP)

The Settlement and Advancement of Nature and Colonisation beyond Terrestrial Utilization Modalities (SANCTUM)

Date: June 24, 2147

Introduction

The Department of Entanglement Studies is a research arm of the Commission of European Particle Physics (CEPP), operating primarily out of the Higgs Circular Collider (HCC) in the province of Algeria. Until the recent tragedy in Algeria, CEPP had worked in conjunction with SANCTUM's veterinary arm to study the effects of faster-than-light travel (i.e. traversable wormholes) on biological systems, particularly a specialized breed of New Zealand White, a rabbit commonly utilized in research applications.

Request for Testimony

While EIRO and its subsidiaries, CEPP and SANCTUM, appreciate the need for transparency in animal research, the Committee's request involving the ALICE incident cannot be honored, as it may (1) impede an ongoing investigation and (2) compromise classified information. Therefore, we respectfully decline to provide further details on the Committee's inquiry:

"Recent whistleblower testimony has shed a horrifying spotlight on the happenings within CEPP-Algeria's cryptic experiments involving so-called traversable wormholes. The committee has received a report from an unnamed source who claims to be a former employee within the Department of Entanglement Studies, concerning a matter of animal cruelty. On multiple occasions, our source witnessed healthy animal subjects being sent through the experimental apparatus, only to return at another location in a state that can only be described as cruel and inhumane. Among the most disturbing accounts, a subject was found embedded in a lab bench with little distinction between the transition of living tissue to the surrounding steel construction of the lab equipment. Subsequent studies on nerve conduction, pain tolerance, blood work, and biopsies carried out by your team yielded a result indicating that the living and inanimate had become a singular entity. Disturbing testimony goes on to describe this entity as 'neither dead nor alive, but a superposition of the two—a macro-scale example of quantum tunneling.' In light of this shocking testimony, the Committee is requesting further deposition from all parties involved in this research."

If I can be of further assistance, please do not hesitate to reach out.

Warmest,
Aegis Galani, Directorate-General
The European Interprovincial Research Organisation

ᚦ | NAKED I RETURN

| War was on the horizon.

The dead Latvian kid with the curls behind his ears didn't spark Russia's outcry. Not really. The boy was just a political prop, a poster boy for their proselytism, his death a convenient pretext for a Baltic invasion. And it worked. President Orlov rallied his Baltic sympathizers—disaffected ethno-Russians—and galvanized them to its cause.

Moscow's real motive, though, was more nuanced. It stemmed from the success of Leichter Speer—the "Daugavpils Massacre" to the Russkies—and the trove of information Fischer and his men extracted from it. The entire fucking orc playbook.

Erebus had bagged the treasonous Evgeni. Tortured him in the wilderness. Dispatched him and sunk his body in Lake Salna en route to extraction. Then, there was Pavel Kalashnik, a high-ranking Russian diplomat and oligarch (and an unexpected presence for Fischer and his men). Killing him was a miscalculation, to be sure.

Nebel des Krieges.[1]

But boy, did it fire up the orcs.

Erebus collected DNA samples, which the suits in Berlin seeded into artificial neural nets. Reconstructed Evgeni and Kalashnik's consciousnesses up to their deaths and extracted everything the men knew. Russian state secrets, military plans, the works. The revelations prompted Europe into a wartime economy.

With its hand tipped, Moscow had little time to act.

The Three-Day War started in Narva.

It was Russia's largest offensive since Eastern Ukraine, marking its second violation of the Budapest and Minsk II Agreements. The Russkies invaded under the artifice of separatist "riots" fomented by years of Russian-backed propaganda meant to divide the Baltic populations.

By week's end, the three-nation bloc had fallen.

The annexation triggered a unified Europe, which launched a counter-offensive in Kaliningrad. Forty-eight hours later, an armistice was declared, and in the coming months, the formation of the UEF launched a new cold war between Moscow and the West.

Leading up to the Geneva disaster, Russian operatives had located and taken out two of Erebus's men for their involvement in Leichter Speer. They got to Janson in Bordeaux first. Then Capp in Brussels.

Then Geneva happened.

Fischer's initial instinct was that a bomb had gone off. *The* bomb.

A first strike.

But Fischer was wrong. It wasn't a dirty bomb or ICBM. The Molasse Fault had ruptured. Unleashed the worst natural disaster in Europe's history.

That was the official word.

But none of that mattered anymore. Not after the girls. His beautiful, beautiful girls.

Forgive her. >

---

1 "The fog of war."—German

Day 11, Dawn — The Lookout

Adrenaline overtook the meek, bumbling grief that saddled Fischer as he backed away slowly into Lotta. She whimpered behind him, her hot, sticky fingers clasping his biceps. He resisted the urge to rip himself away. Redirected his ire at the approaching threat.

Björn's overgrown foot claws trawled tentatively up the stone grade toward them.

The pale wraith lowered its keratinous snout, slack-jawed and panting, tasting the air. Its ghostly head bobbed and weaved as if by tremor, a movement that struck Fischer as involuntary, perhaps pathological. Its milky eyes rolled, darting from cairn to cairn.

Fischer recalled how the beast seemed startled after happening upon them in the forest where they found Hassan, how the stupid thing nearly walked on top of them before noticing their presence. And then again by the campfire, drawn by the smell of death, of easy prey. Guided by its other senses. The hypothesis fit, explained previous encounters. Those pale eyes couldn't see well enough to hunt, but the thing knew the forest. Followed its nose.

Fischer leered into those hazy eyes.

Fucker hasn't seen us yet.

The thing's cobbled hide twitched in reaction to the sounds of the cave, the occasional drip of rainwater seeping in from above. Rising again, it carefully planted a weathered, flaking foot forward. Its ghoulish legs were black up to the knee with drying muck, as if it had slogged through muddy terrain.

Shifting its weight, Björn's other leg moved to the fore. Just as slow. Just as quiet.

Its nose pitched down again, tracking the scent of decay until it reached Lotta's altar and—chuffing through wet nostrils—snuffed the disemboweled rat croc.

Doesn't see us. Doesn't know we're here.

Fischer was convinced that the smells broadcasting from the cave over the last few days had lured the beast. *Couldn't resist the bouquet of dead fish and rat crocs.* His eyes darted back in the direction of the tunnel, then fell back to Björn. He swore at himself quietly.

Fuck.

He turned to Lotta. A white-hot slag of rage closed his vision around her haggard face, flashbacks of his daughters cycling through his head like lightning. Entertained the idea of going his own way, of leaving her to her fate. At the same time, he knew she was all he had left.

She peered back at his bridled posture, bleary-eyed, with lines of tears striping her cheeks.

The thought of being alone threatened to consume Fischer with insurmountable dread. He shed his emotion and eyed the outlook. Lotta turned to follow his gaze.

Through there, Fischer mouthed, casting another look past the stacks of rocks toward Björn, then back again. *I'll lead.*

Lotta's face was wan and expressionless, her nostrils flaring. She nodded.

Fischer turned and slipped past her and walked over to the ledge. He gripped the trunk of the lone cycad and leaned out over the precipice through the porthole, peering down at the floodwater below. He judged the distance to the bottom at around three stories. The water level had dropped appreciably from what he recalled days earlier. Thick eddies of mist drifted along its surface like an army of revenants.

To his right and left was nothing but sheer rock. He craned his neck, and against the backdrop of the rusty sky, he noticed a decent hold at the top edge of the rocky opening, taunting him an arm's length beyond his maximum reach. He leaned out again. Saw a route down, but it looked treacherous, mostly shale and loose rock.

May as well jump, he thought, unsure of the water's depth through the steamy veil below.

Then, the unthinkable occurred. An abrupt scuff shattered his focus, and his head snapped to the opening, where Lotta's atlatl clattered to the ground.

Lotta's expression fell, her face white with horror.

Sorry, she mouthed.

A loud *clap* jolted through Fischer like a surge of electrical current. He flashed a look toward the sound and saw Björn's pale eyes searching in their direction, its scaled dewlap now a rigid, veined disc jutting from its throat. A muddled chortle spilled from its chattering maw, from which the tail of the rat croc dangled.

"We need to jump," Fischer said. "*Now*."

Lotta's eyelids peeled back. Her mouth fell. She looked past Fischer out over the edge and stepped back. "That? No, no, no. I-I can't."

Now's your chance, kamerad. Leave her behind.

Mere meters behind Lotta and hedged by two cairns, Björn reared like an evil, hairless bruin, thrusting its barrel chest forward, its cherubic arms flaring out from its flanks. The beast lurched forward with a wet hiss, and its middle toe flung something glinting through the air.

The knife.

Fischer watched desperately as it clattered to the ground and skidded toward him before the hilt came to rest against the base of the nearest cairn, three or four strides from where he stood. He considered lunging to retrieve it, but thought better of it. Retreat seemed the only viable strategy.

Björn's haunting gaze was fixed squarely on their location, but its eyes continued to search. Seemed the beast couldn't discriminate them from the stone mounds, but it was trying. Its jaws gaped wide to reveal rows of pointed teeth embedded in a sanguineous maw. Fischer sensed it knew they were there. Puffed its chest to assert dominion over its quarry, its double crest now flushed scarlet. A threat display. Or just making noise. Trying to flush them out.

Gnarled foot claws raked the ground.

Fucker's going to charge us.

Fischer reached toward the nearest cairn and seized a jagged wedge of limestone. Curled his fingers tightly around its edges until they hurt.

The sun emerged through a break in the clouds, and an opaque shaft of light slanted through the porthole. Fischer shielded his eyes, almost blinded by the debilitating glare bouncing off the limestone, and through slitted eyes, he discerned little more than the outline of the threat before them.

To his surprise, the beast recoiled with a distressed mewl, its spectral form receding toward the shaded declivity from which it came. Its pale head—reddened by the bloody sun—sidled from side to side like a ravening demon as it withdrew into shadow.

Light hurts its eyes.

He recalled Björn's aversion to fire, how it had similarly retreated like a phantom into the darkness the night by the fire. Then he remembered the rabbits from the lab. *Albinos.* They reverted to similar head movements, reactions to bright light. Their albinism had rendered them nearly blind.

Seeing his opportunity, Fischer cocked his arm back and hurled the stone hard so that it lobbed over Björn and struck one of the stalagmites with a *pop*, then tumbled noisily down the path.

The dawn-tinged wraith whipped around with a snort.

"Keep the sun at your back," Fischer whispered to Lotta. "I'm going for the knife."

But the reprieve proved short-lived as the sunlight waned again.

No, no, no.

Fuck it.

He shot Lotta a furtive glance and nodded toward their rear flank. "Find a way out," he said, the balls of his feet like loaded springs. He lifted his poncho over his head and began wrapping it around his good arm.

"*I'm not leaving you!*" Lotta hissed, casting a puzzled expression at his frenzied hands. "What are you doing?"

Fischer raced to secure the poncho, the hair on his bare skin standing up against the dewy cave air. His eyes darted from his arm to the beast.

"Do what I tell you," he growled. "Now *go.*"

Björn pivoted, levied a hot gaze firmly in his direction. The sunlight waned.

Naked except for his bound arm, Fischer lunged full-tilt toward the knife.

Björn charged.

Lotta's scream bought Fischer a second or two. Björn's tremulant head cocked sideways at the sound. Its footfalls slowed.

Fischer seized his opportunity and bounded toward the cairn, mere steps from his stalled attacker. Almost lost his footing, but regained purchase as a guttural hiss flanked him. Holding his wrapped arm up to shield his head, he fumbled with his free hand at the piled rocks until his fingers grazed the knife handle. He plucked it up and spun it in his palm. Reverse grip, edge out. Capped the hilt with his thumb just as the gaping maw closed around his raised arm.

Björn snorted hot gusts laced with the stench of decay, the end of its snout almost touching Fischer's face. Overwhelming pressure engulfed his lower arm like a vice, and the sound of the poncho's splintering bracts flooded his ears. His bones flexed, the sensation leaving his arm in a sea of pins. Suppressing panic, he hooked the blade against the beast's veined throat with his free arm.

Missed.

The blade glanced off Björn's cobbled scrag, grazing the softer skin draping the jugular, and snagged the fleshy dewlap. Fischer pulled, felt the skin pierce, and he dragged it down. The beast reacted with a chuff of gummy mist that coated Fischer's face, then recoiled, ripping the poncho free as it released him. The sensation rushed back into Fischer's arm, the damp, cool air against his sweat-slicked skin. A hot sting trailed down to his hand, and he opened and closed it into a fist to get the blood pumping.

Woosh.

He ducked. A gust tousled his hair as the reptilian tail passed overhead, then he dove for cover behind a nearby cairn. The knife slipped from his grip and struck the cave floor with a metallic dissonance that made his ears ring. He swallowed, the sting of bile scraping down his throat, and stole a cursory glance at his burning forearm. Thin scratches oozed crimson, tracks where small—but sharp—teeth had pierced and dragged along the skin. He realized that, had it not been for the poncho, he'd be staring down at a bloody stump. His chest heaving, he leaned and peered around the edge of his cover to descry Björn savaging the garment in a scud of splintered fronds and blood.

Fischer's eyes bounced between the cairns.

No sign of Lotta.

He slid back behind cover, his shoulders pressing into the piled stones. Caught the lustrous glare of the knife winking at him beside what looked like a glistening mound of worms. He rotated forward and crawled on all fours. Recognized the coiled pink ribbons as the entrails he had seen arranged in a spiral around the altar, now cast aside to rot. Turning his attention to the knife, Fischer brushed his trembling fingers over the Erebus seal stamped into the hilt and curled them around it. Briefly thought of the Lithuanians he'd tussled with in that tiny bar beneath the shadow of Shin Tower.

Then, in what felt like a moment of clarity, he peeled a sticky section of intestine off the stone pavement and folded it over the blade to cut a section free. Pulling the stretchy organ tight, he bound the hilt to his palm with it.

Back to basics. Target flexors and tendons. Cover and slash. Defang the snake, then… and only then… go for the throat.

Death by a thousand cuts.

He tilted his chin and stepped out into the open, his eyes falling on the pale beast and the ribbons of shredded poncho draping its lacertian lips. Björn's torn throat flap—now drenched bright crimson—resembled a rooster's wattle as a steady flow of blood pecked the ground at its mud-caked feet.

That was when Fischer realized the sun was no longer at his back. That Björn could *see* him.

His grip tightened around the knife handle.

Beyond the keratin casque adorning Björn's swaying head, he saw Lotta. She still stood where he had left her, framed within the porthole, naked and in shock.

He considered retreating to the camp and abandoning her to the white demon. Live to fight another day. A miasma of conflicting emotions swelled within his sweat-slicked chest. His vision smeared over, his jaw popping as he clenched his teeth. He glowered against the last memories of his daughters, their broken bodies. At that moment, he hated Lotta more than anything. Wanted her dead but also didn't. She was all he had now on this planet that wasn't theirs. The only two people left in existence.

Forgive her.

He regarded Björn again. Forced the air from his lungs and beat his free fist against his chest. Pumped his arms into a wide boxing stance, the blade clenched tight in his pulsing fingers.

"Come on, y'fucker!"

Björn's eyes, opaque and soulless, oscillated in synchrony with the sinusoidal motion of its pebbled head. Fischer faced those eyes like a matador resigned to his fate. Twisted foot claws raked the rust-tinged limestone.

Björn barreled forward. Closed the distance between them with alarming speed, belting a frothing, guttural noise from its jostling jowls.

Fischer dove a split second too late. A glancing blow from the rugous snout dropped him before he knew he'd been hit. He came down hard on his back in a shallow puddle of tepid rainwater. It sprayed around him as the air vacated his lungs. He choked back air in spasms and sat upright, glancing at his throbbing shoulder. Static coursed through his arm, the skin shredded, sloughed into rolls resembling wet tissue paper. A constellation of red droplets budded and threaded down his biceps.

Motes flitted before him like dancing sparks amid the rising sun's glare, cloaking a reanimated Lotta. Dazed, he watched her right arm cock back.

"Duck!" she shouted right as a wet snort erupted directly behind Fischer's head, enveloping him in a putrid miasma that stank of rancid meat.

He threw himself to the ground more by reflex than by Lotta's instruction. Björn huffed in bursts at his back, compelling him to bear crawl toward the nearest cairn. From the corner of his eye, he caught the rapid motion of Lotta's naked form, red light lining a spear going airborne. Heard the projectile strike somewhere behind him, eliciting a brief surge of hope until it clattered harmlessly to the stone floor.

Move.

He pushed up on his hands into a kneel, then scrambled to his feet. His vision dimmed, narrowed from the rush of standing too quickly. A thick chortle veiled him in another hot gust laced with the fetor of death.

He bobbed, then pivoted on the axis of his heel. Hooked his elbow, the blade passing blindly through free space.

Contact.

Wet warmth gushed over Fischer's hand, and the beast mewled. It pulled away, the studded tail lashing his ribcage. He fell hard onto his back, elbows pounding the rough stone, skin chafed raw. The white wraith stumbled over him, leaning to the right, opposite a fresh gash oozing below its left arm. A thin rope of blood brimmed from the gaps in its teeth while its flapping throat spat specks of blood.

Fischer dragged himself backward on his raw elbows. The pale eyes snapped to his movement, pathologic and rolling as they strained against the rusty dawn, the terrible head wobbling and desperate. He watched in horror as one of the beast's mangled feet kicked out at him. *Crack.* Saw sparks fly before his eyes, his head slamming back against stone, lungs exploding through his chest. As he stared emptily at the cave ceiling, a sharp, searing jolt erupted down his left side. A claw breaking skin. A rib cracking.

Can't breathe.

Lotta screamed somewhere in space. Sounded far away.

Can't... breathe.

The terrible head ascended into Fischer's field of vision like an infernal imp shrouded in the red dawn, the weight of its foot pressing deeper and deeper into his chest. Pressure pushed out behind his eyes. His mouth was coated with brine. Björn's panting mire yawned to greet him, the smell pouring from its face eliciting a gag that further exacerbated Fischer's deflated lungs. He gaped into that pit of sopping flesh, past sanguine teeth that rimmed a scarlet-slicked tongue modulating a gurgling hiss.

Fischer was pinned. Couldn't move. Could only watch in desperate horror as the reptilian jaws sidled to his left shoulder and clamped around it. The pain was unlike anything he'd ever experienced, like his marrow had turned molten. The pop of his breaking ribs sheared through his skull while lightning arced before his eyes. His mouth fell, incapable of procuring the scream lodged in his throat as prickling static coursed down his arm like a brushfire leaving numbness in its wake. Björn tugged, wrenched. Liberated something slick and wet that peeled, then snapped away from Fischer's disabled limb. A glistening, dark mass tossed about in the grip of recoiling jaws.

Fischer's sinuses crawled with the stench of his own urine, its warmth trickling between his thighs as his vision started to fade.

Fireworks.

A fresh explosion erupted down Fischer's side. Another glistening ribbon snapped free of his chest and disappeared with a clap into Björn's gore-smeared snout.

A third rib cracked, and just as the next was ready to give, another spear sliced the air and punched into Björn's midriff. The beast belched a hiss and reared back, wavering from the impact, and the weight eased from Fischer's chest. His lungs swelled painfully, oxygen now an enemy, a raging inferno to his starved tissues. He pulled together enough strength to grip the knife again, his focus turning to the flaking ashen foot that no longer held the beast's weight.

Flexors and tendons.

A starburst fragmented his vision with the exertion required to hook the knife behind Björn's left ankle just above the joint. He pulled the blade through the thickly roped ligament and let his arm collapse back against the stone. The beast belted a dissonant mewl and sidestepped, stumbling as it tried to bear weight on its leg. It faltered and collided with a cairn, then crashed to the ground in a heap of stones and dust.

The ceiling of the cave glared back down at Fischer. Roots from above filled the cracks that veined the crumbling stone roof and appeared to writhe amid his pinwheeling vision. He retched and vomited blood. It filled his mouth and throat, forcing another gag. He tried to draw breath, but the viscid chunder rushed into his lungs faster than he could expel it. Managed to turn over and cough most of it back up. Rasping, he drank the air, his chest convulsing.

His left shoulder was a glistening, hot mass in the corner of his eye. He dared not look directly at it, knew he only had minutes before he bled out. Would lose consciousness long before infection could take hold of him. His inability to feel his arm seemed like its own form of mercy.

Lotta screamed somewhere behind him. Had stupidly drawn the beast away from Fischer instead of heeding his instructions.

Get up.

He couldn't move.

Another scream, this time from within. Fischer managed to roll onto his right side, inviting fresh bolts of pain down his torso. An anguished bawl escaped his lips as he propped himself onto the arm he'd tended for days. Still weak, it trembled furiously under his weight.

Clasping his ribs, he struggled to his feet.

Björn rolled upright and locked a fiery gaze on Lotta. It hissed, its fetal arms flailing like translucent grubs, and limped toward her.

Backing toward the porthole, framed in bronzed sunlight, Lotta swung desperately at the advancing horror with the atlatl. Lamed, trailing a vermillion river from its gaping leg, the loathsome demon snapped blindly, its wobbling head mitered and erratic against the oppressive sunrise.

Each shallow step Fischer took brought agony. His legs shook, feet shuffling painfully across the fluted limestone. His knees bowed, wobbling like the pale head of the reeling monster before him.

"Oy!" he tried to yell, managing little more than a crackling wheeze. "Oy, y-yeh v-vucker!"

Björn was undeterred, and Lotta had edged dangerously close to the cliff. Fischer heaved, spitting up pink foam as he staggered, forgetting about the knife in his hand as he clutched his ribs, his feet painfully slow in the race to intercept the hobbling beast before it got to Lotta. His vision faded again. Vomit and blood clotted his sinuses.

The thought of self-preservation infiltrated his mind again. Turning back was still an option.

Leave the bitch to her fate.

But something in him overcame this nagging desire and drove him headlong into the sun.

Through streaked vision, Björn took a hellish form against the stone skylight that elicited Fischer's last moments in the Bell chamber. He recalled the smeared form against the backdrop of the core, the thing that had taken Anderson, mimicked his beacon. Not Björn, but something else, a different abomination. He heard the faint roar of the Higgs in the recesses of his psyche, and despite how hard he tried to bury it, the hum swelled. Pulsed like a droning swarm of bees rippling their warning, hundreds of mandibles snipping his flesh, extracting their nectar from what remained of his throbbing shoulder.

And through that droning roar, a beacon tolled.

A small hand closed around his, beckoning him toward the light. Toward Björn.

No more pain, Daddy.

Fischer didn't try to stifle the voices anymore. They fueled him. Supplied a fathomless, insatiable rage. Hot blood churned his haggard limbs in motion. Resuscitated his naked, dying flesh. Fed the rivulets of gore dripping from his swollen fingertips.

The beacon tolled.

Its rippling aftershocks fractured Fischer's mind against the pulsing hive, against the hum of the Higgs. Something lying dormant within him welled up, bursting from his sticky lips to cataclysmic effect, and a primal moan exploded from his throat like a raging inferno.

Fear had left him.

Rage.

There was only rage.

Fresh bolts of pain peeled through the marrow of Fischer's left arm with each stumbling lurch. Wincing, he picked up the pace, squeezing his knife hilt with the fist buried in his splintered ribcage.

Ahead, Lotta swung away, but Björn was undeterred.

Fischer shuffled weightily, closing the distance, the thought of how he had failed to save his girls rushing through his flickering thoughts. He watched Lotta back toward the lookout through sticking eyelids, a veil of red accompanying the sting of blood in his eyes. Saw that scared girl again, the one that reminded him of Ellsa.

He suppressed a wave of resurgent nausea and swallowed a cud of breakthrough vomit. Reality had slowed. Imbibed him with an ethereal sense of vertigo he attributed to blood loss. His skin clammy and crawling, Fischer peeled his fist from his shattered ribs and careened headlong into Björn. At the last moment, he pulled the knife back, elbow cocked, his eyes taking aim at the purple veins webbing the beast's neck. Managed to avoid a sweep of the cobbled tail as he came up alongside the left flank and threw his weight forward. The impact voided his lungs.

Björn pitched sideways just as Fischer managed to hook his good arm around its thickly studded neck. The weight of its bulk wrenched him around, his veins coursing with adrenaline, endorphins blunting his throbbing wounds. He pulled the knife, felt it catch on the loose folds of skin draping Björn's throat. Shifted his weight. Pulled harder until a *click* pulsed through the knife and into his fingers.

Björn bucked, but Fischer held fast as the knife sank. Wet warmth gushed out and coated his hand, and a damp, choking sound erupted from the pale creature. He caught intermittent bouncing glimpses of the swaying head in profile. Its keratinous maw—now thickly webbed with blood—snapped shut, spraying flecks from a pinkish bulwark of foam.

A moan intended to be a scream escaped Fischer's cracked lips then, and he pulled with his remaining strength until the blade glided smoothly to the hilt.

Whipping like a rag doll, he tried to free himself, but didn't have the leverage to release the knife. The rat croc binding tightened around his hand, cutting off the circulation. His joints cracked, his skin slamming into the cobbled hide, lips sticky with blood, the metallic taste of iron coating his tongue. A *pop*—both felt and heard—convinced him that his wrist had just broken, but there was no pain. The force of the beast's gait tossed him and spun him around so all he could see was the white cobblestone hide bouncing, the tail yawing in and out of view behind a muscular thigh that pounded his shattered ribs with each stride. His fingers tingled. Pins and needles. Then the sensation left them entirely.

Each time the beast swayed onto its opposing flank, the wigwam across the pond flitted into view, growing smaller and smaller through the rows of cairns.

Fischer didn't know where Björn was taking him, only that he was being dragged, tethered to the white demon by the matrimony of a blade. He heard the *clap* of jaws shutting again, this time at the back of his head. Hot breath infiltrated his tousled hair and spread across his scalp.

"*No!*"

Lotta.

Her voice seemed far-off. An echo.

Forgive h—

An instantaneous searing pressure mounted behind his eyes with the suddenness of lightning, accompanied by a grinding thunder that rolled across his skull. He felt the teeth shortly after, each digging in, the wet stench spurring him to gag. His jaw fell slack, his cheeks and forehead bulging forward, squeezed within the vice of a demonic maw. Felt like his head might explode, and when his ears popped, he thought it had.

Bile dribbled out from the corner of his gaping mouth and trailed down his neck.

Little man pirouetting inside my head, making the entire world spin.

A light chuckle gurgled from his frothing lips. He tugged the knife with the remainder of his waning strength. A violent jolt rent him. The vice released him.

Another jolt, then weightlessness. Ears popped again, whistling as if in a great wind. A dazzling light washed over his vision, and the warmth of a rose-tinged sky kissed his cheeks from behind a receding cliff face whipping past. For a moment, time almost stood still.

Almost.

The impact was sudden.

When Fischer woke, it took him a few seconds to realize he was underwater. Revived by a renewed pulse of stinging pain in his shoulder, he watched his legs trail him through a shimmering sanguine radiance in which clods of ivory rock descended lazily like snow. Cerise whisps coiled around him, leaving a ruddy plume in his wake. A gentle coldness rippled over his skin as he was led by his broken wrist, his body pulled into the depths by something unseen.

Somehow, he'd managed to keep the breath in his lungs.

He tried to turn his head, but an explosion of pain locked up his neck and split his ragged shoulder into atoms. He managed a glimpse of the murky blur leading him into the brackish depths. A pale wraith fluttering lifelessly downward, dragging him into oblivion.

Then his momentum slowed, then stopped. He heard a soft thud, and a silty pall rose from the disturbed bed. Blood coiled up from his wounds in thick ribbons like rubicund fruiting bodies. Burning with brine, his eyes gazed up at the prismatic sky through the rippling surface. Pink and shimmering, it pulsed with the slowing thump drumming his skull. He flitted in and out of lucidity, repeatedly woken by the spasms in his chest.

The surface appeared closer than expected. Two, maybe three meters at the most. A kick or three to open air. He tugged meekly at his tethered hand and gazed up again. The movement sent a dagger of pain through him.

May as well be a hundred *meters.*

Suppressing his panic reflex, he let his training filter into his mind. Closed his eyes. Slowed his heart rate.

No more pain, Daddy.

A shadow veiled the inside of his eyelids, compelling them to snap open.

Cool tendrils enveloped him—a current kicked up by a finned tail gliding past his line of sight. A second dark form skimmed overhead like an angel of death.

Sharks. Circling close enough for him to reach up and touch.[2]

Fischer noticed something else. Something beyond the rippling surface. An enormous, looming form blotting out the fractured firmament.

The sharks continued to wheel, unaware of the monstrous shape descending toward them. The strangely bulbed tip of a snout came into stark relief as it dipped beneath the water and hovered in wait. Dull caustics danced like pink flames over its stippled flesh, the remainder of the head still amorphous beyond the rippling scrim.

All the while, the sharks circled.

Then, an explosive crush of water rammed Fischer's top end into the muddy bed, and a boiling cauldron of bubbles engulfed him as his chest spasmed.

A muffled clap struck his ears, and he glimpsed the shadowy forms of the sharks dashing into the haze of obscurity.

When the swirling beads lifted, the teratoid fore of the colossal thing—like the head of Leviathan—came into vivid relief a mere meter from his feet. Through the roiling maelstrom, he parsed a gigantic snout of interlocking rosettes fringed with conical teeth jutting at harsh angles from a notched jaw. The thing looked part crocodile, part eel, with a slender rust-colored head and forward-facing opalescent eyes that cut through the murk like searchlights in a fog.

The monstrosity lingered underwater for a moment, then canted and rushed upward upon a sinuous neck, its throat ballooning as it breached into the open air. The surface roiled as if lashed by a resurgent storm, and as the shimmering giant reared beyond, a trine of black sickle-tipped digits sprouting from an enormous hand skimmed the waterline.

Fischer's useless limbs tossed around him and then settled again.

---

2 *Tribodus indet*

Once the rippling above him ceased, he peered beyond his floating legs and spotted the long, slender shape of the head coalesce anew against the ruddy sky. It pitched back toward the water and descended, and the ragged-toothed bulbs submerged once more and waited.

With fear exhausted, and any remaining fight Fischer possessed extinguished, came the convulsions in his burning lungs, a reflex referred to as "guppying" in the Special Forces. A sure sign you were thirty seconds from sucking water. His vocal cords yipped involuntarily as his chest heaved. He suppressed panic, a fleeting emotion, as he was lulled into somnolence by a sense of euphoria not unlike the type found at the bottom of a flask. Like an old friend, it wooed him to let go.

Come be with us, Daddy.

So, he let go.

Air mushroomed from his numb lips, eerily beautiful, like an expanding morel against the undulating shards of sky. The world above started to spin. He'd black out soon. Another twenty seconds, and his body would reflexively inhale.

It'd all be over then.

He watched his last remaining essence ascend, framed within a narrowing vignette, until it dissolved against the cage of spikes looming in wait.

A second wall of water rushed down. Another constellation of bubbles swirled. A flash of teeth encircled Fischer's legs and jolted him upward, a force great enough to rend his hand free. A *pop* clapped through him, and a bolt of sharp pain jarred his fading senses. His head whipped backward, his sinuses ready to burst, and as he was lifted toward the surface, he saw *her.*

Jocelyn.

Saw her the way she was before everything fell apart. Before they lost the girls. Piercing blues, lips turned up, her hand reaching, inviting him back to the comfort of the silted floor. A new bed. A new beginning. Golden hair swirled about her high cheekbones, her white gown rippling over her delicate frame. And from her neck billowed a crimson ribbon that formed a fading trail to the knife still bound to his swollen hand.

A mute siren, her lips never parted, but her eyes held him.

Don't go, they mused. A haunting refrain he wanted desperately to heed. *Don't leave again.*

A flurry of bubbles coalesced around her, his woman in white, and constricted until she was choked from view.

Air kissed Fischer's bare skin.

Inverted and spinning in dazzling light, he vomited a pinkish-brown slurry that assumed a bright scarlet toward the end. Cherry-tinged droplets cascaded in slow motion all around him, each refracting a mini-sun below an inverted horizon through the mist of a shimmering rainbow. In them, he saw a billion universes, mere motes within the cosmic foam, glinting like rubies as they rained through his heavy arms and into the inflamed water below. He fixated on the surface, spinning and frothing beneath him amid a hail of hissing foam over the spot where Jocelyn had been.

Then, something flat and shimmering crested the water—a long, compressed body resembling an oarfish.

Not a fish, the engineer's languid mind flickered sluggishly.

It was an enormous, salamander-like tail threshing past, churning the roiling surface like a vat of hot oil. He dangled, mesmerized amid his bewildered state by fractals sprouting from the eddies carved in its wake. An image eerily akin to the sight of an active Penrose core the instant before it punctured spacetime, its whorls of ferrofluid undulating, the void peering back at him like the face of God.

A deafening *crack* coursed through him like rifle fire, wresting him from his stupor. The bones in his legs compressed between a cage of spikes, the *pop-pop* of his splintering femurs rippling across his skull. A new, bottomless pain shot up from his lower half and impelled him to suck air until he vomited red.

Pop.

The kid with the curls behind his ears.

He could see the kid with the curls behind his ears.

Saw his face, split-open and lifeless and staring into the void.

Had he seen the face of God, too?

A renewed sense of weightlessness jarred Fischer, and he saw his limbs flailing skyward, air whistling over his clogged ears as the spikes sank deeper. A rattling screech spilled from his cracked lips, only to be snuffed out by another *crack*. Electricity wormed up his spine, and as if through some form of mercy, all sensation beneath his navel ceased.

No more pain.

Nothing but a semblance of mounting pressure at the base of his spine.

He was jolted to the right.

The world whipped past. A smear of the red horizon. A blanched wedge of the scarp face. His head snapped to the side in time to spot a giant ashen appendage hurtling past, the same black claws he'd watched whisk the watery tomb he had come to accept just moments before. But now, Fischer was airborne, a pit searing his chest. The scaled hand disappeared behind his line of sight, and with dizzying abruptness, the world came to a standstill, and his flailing limbs fell limp. His body was anchored in free space, his vision consumed by swarming motes as he stared blankly down, not at water, but flat, wet stone.

A renewed awareness of the pressure in his lower torso overcame him, and the sound of something tearing and wet behind his head dominated his fading consciousness.

His body lurched forward, then recoiled as the pressure girding his hips released. His purview of the ruddy sky relayed little context, but he knew almost immediately that he was airborne. Falling again.

Crack.

His back clapped hard against stone, and a pink mist plumed from his lips, settling on his face like warm dew. His vision had gone double, two scarps looming above him. The heavens had shifted a subtle yellow ribbed with rust—the birth of a day—as a covey of winged shapes entangled to their corresponding duplicates circled overhead. Fischer tried to laugh at the synchronized pairs. *Ghosts. Doppelgängers.* Managed to gurgle a frothing drivel from the corners of his gaping mouth.

And like a colossal two-headed eel from the fathoms of hell, the glistening, diplopic bulk of Leviathan swept past, its malignant eyes a quartet of cinders burning with the red of dawn. Blood-tinged water drained in runnels through the gaps in its teeth, coursed in a wall down its auburn skin, and pecked Fischer's crawling flesh like rain.

The hulking thing moved off and out of sight.

He coughed blood. Couldn't breathe. Sinuses clogged, limbs inert, his mind reeled at the pressure in his skull, the intractable Little Man with him until the end.

His right eye filled with blood, then went dark.

He tried to move. Nothing. Focused on his big toe with the entirety of his waning faculties. Nothing still. Could only watch vacantly as the switchblades circled against the mottled sky.

At least he wasn't seeing double anymore.

Then, Fischer's head rolled a little to the side and hinged back to its original position. An action not of his volition.

Something had moved him.

His head swiveled again. This time, he caught something out of the corner of his remaining vision. It passed over him, a shadow grazing his cheek and wheeling his head entirely to the left. His eyes leveled with the object as it passed over his open hand and planted itself just beyond his reach, and through the gaps in his bloody fingers, he saw the rear pad of a webbed foot sheathed in iridescent black scales. A cold slurry dribbled from the corner of his mouth while a faint awareness of warmth spilled into his cheek from the slicked sandstone.

He managed to take a shallow breath as a second limb cleared him and settled beside the first.

Fischer watched, frozen, able only to blink. Through his fingers, he saw the feet carry on, thrust by a pair of rangy legs that sprang awkwardly from a clumsy pelvic girdle. And as they receded, he deduced the remainder of the creature. It was a diminutive bipedal thing—a little larger than a mid-sized dog—with an elongated ridge protruding from its spine. A sinuous tadpole tail trailed its cumbersome waddle, dull-red and held low above the ground like a demonic pangolin.

Fischer's purview past his unmoving fingers expanded as the thing moved off, and then he saw *it* in full profile. Leviathan.[3] A rising juggernaut ridged in golden light, looming at the edge of a sandstone slab littered with giant fish bones. Its most striking feature gave rise to its apogee—an imposing dorsal sail composed of two rounded peaks spanned by a shallow saddle. Shaped like a smooth M, the patterned eminence banked steeply down to a sprawling tail.

Not an oarfish.

---

3 *Spinosaurus aegyptiacus*

Almost amphibian in aspect, the tail splayed along the ground, buttressing the bulk of the colossus it partially encircled. It listed lazily, laterally flattened where it tapered to form a glistening, membranous spine.

The little one doubled back, its lithe neck balancing an eely head with a pair of cerulean eyes that regarded Fischer with diminishing intrigue. It panted through a notched snout, a tiny, ruddy version resembling that of the looming giant it did not seem to fear.

Mother.

With a dip of her snout, Leviathan beckoned the fledgling.

Fischer watched her with pulsing eyes, every cell in his body oscillating, desperate for warmth again. Watched her florid throat each time it ballooned. Watched those glimmering opals for eyes. The world outside his head was drowned out by the steady knell of Little Man's cavorting, but he *felt* Leviathan's call. Felt the chortling *thump-thump* pulsing into his cheek through the stone, mesmerized in his state of mounting delirium by its perfect synchrony with her vibrating jowls.

The little one turned back and hobbled into her shadow, where two more of her brood inspected a giant, mangled nautilus that Fischer had initially confused for a dead child in a fetal position.[4]

Leviathan rolled her head back. Something passed toward the rear of her notched jaws against a resurrected sun. Her throat ballooned, then collapsed, and the little ones stopped, their heads snapping to attention as blood-tinged mist snorted from Mother's nostrils like flame against the breaking dawn.

Fischer saw it now—a pair of naked, blood-soaked legs rolling over her tongue. *His* legs. Molded and tenderized to tallow by an antediluvian cage of spikes.

Then they were gone. Tossed backward into her long, congrid snout and passed unceremoniously into her throat.

Her head bobbed on a thick but elegant neck, her lower jaw massaging the new bulge in her crop. A scarlet slurry spilled out between her front teeth in branched rivulets, then coalesced into a dark rill that spouted in

---

4 *Knemiceras indet.*, an ancient cephalopod of subclass Ammonoidea distinct from that of Nautiloidea.

an arc from her ewer-tipped mandible. She pitched her notched jaws down and welcomed her progeny, her eyes aglow as she channeled the slurry down her pulsing tongue and into their fevered mouths.

The little ones plunged headlong into her like hyenas raiding an abattoir, and just before Fischer's vision flickered out completely, he thought he saw one pull out a glistening slab resembling a disembodied foot.

He no longer felt cold, despite his intensified shivering. Felt nothing, really. Little Man had retired. The shrill ringing in his ears had dissipated into deafening silence. Lungs took a final, agonal breath. Expired. But Fischer held onto his fleeting consciousness as long as he could.

Images of his daughters flitted in and out of black.

Skinned knees. Trimmed beards. Wrists gilded in sparkling ribbon.

No more pain, Daddy.

Edgar Fischer's final memory was of Emma. His bear. She ran to him in that red birthday dress, and he swept her off her feet, let those little arms encircle his neck…

Then nothing.

But he reassured himself that sometimes, nothing wasn't *nothing*. Sometimes, it was an incomprehensible void. Not black, nor empty, nor silent. There was no pain. No sorrow. No thirst for water or want for air. For some, nothing was an escape from the vacuum—the sheer *silence* left behind by three little girls, and the only salvation was to let one of their dead little hands bind your wrists in ribbon, to guide that blade through your poisoned veins. Because there were some things far worse than *nothing*.

In the end, nothing was merely a dreamless sleep.

| QALIL >

Scarlet motes danced across the pulsing glow that tinged the cave's entrance, periodically rushing forward along air currents that passed into the void before Perez. Mineral deposits veined its cragged surfaces, glistening in the ruddy light.

Nedjma's arm was slung over Perez's shoulders, the extra weight amplifying the pain in her right leg tenfold. Pulverized rock lay scattered in piles along the edge of the sand-covered path that probed the darkness beyond her purview. A vast tunnel resembling a lava tube, Perez knew that it stretched around half a click into the heart of Qalil.

Something stirred overhead. Perez caught the faint, ruddy outline of a bat.

The path increasingly revealed signs of the cave's inhabitants—droppings, empty scorpion husks denuded and discarded. The insects were the primary draw for the flying mammals, despite the less-than-ideal conditions for this species. Desert long-eared bats tended to prefer dryer conditions. Consequently, the risk of fungal afflictions was markedly elevated within this population, particularly white-nose syndrome. And despite Perez's own peril, it was the reason for a fresh twinge of guilt at the prospect she and Nedjma were tracking lethal spores into an already-fragile ecosystem. It was also why she strained not to drag her injured leg across the packed sand. To tread carefully.

Long, interrupted gusts rapped at their backs as they pressed deeper into the mountain. Qalil was breathing.

Before long, the tunnel fell away and opened into a vast cavern, its far side stretching beyond perception through the oscillating glow. The only light within was generated by an array of slowly blinking lights arranged about the perimeter of a colossal pit resembling a pulsing red caldera. Beyond view, Perez imagined the variable expansion membrane inset around a hundred meters down, rising and falling, sucking air into the mountain, an exhaling crater of colossal dimensions. ARC's lung.

Nedjma raised her head, gazing across its expanse in stunned silence.

"This way," Perez said, nudging her to the right.

She was leading them to the nearest airlock. An elevator ride would bring them deep underground into the dome's tunnel system. From there, they could flee to Morocco, assuming the tunnels hadn't caved. It was the best hope for them. *For Ruth*.

Farther on, the bat droppings had grown so thick that a blanket of guano flaked under each footfall. It seemed thickest along the cave wall that Perez followed, her footing growing more frantic at the anticipation of what lay ahead. The thought of escape, of a new life.

Something snagged Perez's right foot, and she yelped painfully as her leg buckled. She slammed hard onto the ground, her vision flashing white.

"Fuck!" She gripped her throbbing ankle.

She drew a sharp breath. Realized she no longer had hold of Nedjma.

"Nedjma?" she shouted, her vision obscured by her steaming visor. Beads of sweat materialized on her forehead. Her suit's climate control had failed. "*Nedjma!*"

She clawed over the packed sand on her stomach. Then her fingers brushed something solid but moveable. She waited for the red glow of the pulmonem's lights to swell, her fingers probing the object, and through the steamed visor, she saw the mauled, grime-covered leg of a wild dog. Her eyes tracked along its length to the carcass it was connected to. Half-rotted, its ribcage had been opened, exposed, voided of internal organs. But it was not entirely empty.

It swarmed with *bees*.

A reddish blur raced past. Then another. Bats, snatching up one of the insects.

Perez stumbled backward, pushing away with her heels through the sand as everything faded again to black.

Crunch.

Her hindquarters landed on something brittle that collapsed readily under her weight. She turned over, brushing away a loose pile of twigs and vegetation covering a shallow pit that materialized before her in a renewed swell of bloody light.

A nest.

It appeared to contain around half a dozen eggs, each half the length of her forearm. Their carapaces took on an inky quality in the red bloom. Two of them were crushed and seeping.

Perez turned back toward the wild dog as the light faded, and her limbs seized.

There were *more* carcasses. Dozens of them—piled, splayed in tortured poses, displaying various stages of decomposition. Some had been picked clean. She spotted a male moa, a boar, and several ostriches among them. Others were impossible to identify. Most appeared half-eaten.

Not the work of bats or bees.

Beyond the carcasses, the faint outline of the airlock glinted from a recessed slab of earth.

Wings flapped in the gloom. More bats swooped in to claim their quarry.

Perez swallowed the lump in her throat and turned away. She faced darkness once more.

"Nedjma!"

"Here, Cam! I'm here!" Nedjma coughed somewhere to the left, her voice faint amid the fresh gust buffeting Perez's helmet.

Perez got her feet beneath her and tested her weight on her ankle. It throbbed, but held. A fresh bolt pulsed up her other leg.

"Okay, I'm coming toward you." She sucked air through her teeth and hobbled in the direction of Nedjma's voice.

"Cam."

Perez stopped. Nedjma sounded distant, back toward the tunnel leading from the cave entrance.

A little thrown by this, Perez called out again. "Nedjma, follow my voice. I'm over *here.*"

"'Ere, Cammm-m. Mm 'ere."

Her blood went cold. The rubicund hue of the pulmonem's perimeter lighting pulsed again, and she saw Nedjma's face shield reflecting at her. The student stood facing Perez about a dozen paces off, her face barely visible in the light. And just over her shoulder, at the mouth of the tunnel, was a pair of shimmering cinders.

A cragged crest jerked in silhouette atop a birdlike head that bobbed and tilted from side to side.

Searching.

Perez waited for the light to start fading again, then gestured Nedjma to move toward her, nice and slow, as they were cast back into darkness.

"Swee girl-irl-irl. Perrezz? Prezz!"

Perez almost leapt out of her skin. Tears welled in her eyes, and she began to shake. Although mere seconds had passed, there seemed to be a long delay before Nedjma's footfalls tamped the packed sand. Perez had reached out, her hand ready to take Nedjma's, when she heard a harsh scrape before her.

And then silence.

Nothing but the breath inside her helmet and Qalil's drawn sigh.

She dared not speak. Dared not make a sound despite her desperation to call out again. With her hand still outstretched, she gazed straight ahead expectantly as the cave bloomed red.

She saw the eyes first, bouncing nearly an arm's length overhead, their ruddy glow piercing the dark. Heard the delta's crackled panting, the moan of its wheezing lungs.

Nedjma's form materialized next. The outline of her body, her upper torso clasped in those festering jaws, unable to scream. Her left arm was pinned, her hand planted against the hard pallet, biceps speared by the lower row of teeth, blood seeping out through their gaps and pecking the sand. She didn't have long before her arm snapped, before her chest was crushed.

There was no time to think. Perez did the only thing she knew how, and as the light dulled, she launched herself full-tilt at the beast. She knew her best chance was to distract, get it to drop Nedjma, and go for her instead. Moments from the necropsy flitted through her head as she racked her brain for possible weaknesses.

It's in respiratory distress. Go for the ribs, the air sacs.

Perez brushed past Nedjma's limp legs, thrusting herself headlong into the delta's chest. The thick plate of its gastralia deflected her helmet and whipped her head backward. White flashed across her eyes. A muffled cough erupted somewhere overhead. She regained her bearings and swung her fists blindly around the sides of the beast's torso, slamming them with everything she had into its ribs. A hiss ruptured the air and traveled into her as a vibrating tremor. But she was not deterred. She continued to swing as hard as her burning arms would allow.

Thud.

Nedjma crumpled to the ground behind her.

"The airlock, Nedjma!" Perez screamed. "Go! Ru—"

A vice clamped around Perez's arm and wrenched her off her feet. Through the shell of her suit, a barbed tongue scraped her forearm. The pressure mounted rapidly, and a crushing sound clapped through her bones like gunfire. Her body was wrenched sideways. The pain was delayed, but it came on fast once it registered—fire shooting through her arm and down her spine. A complete loss of sensation below her elbow followed almost immediately, and then another *pop* ripped through her.

Perez slammed to the ground. Redness bloomed. Rimmed by the cerise glow, the form of the delta loomed over her, and hanging limp from its crackling maw was the lower half of her arm. A second jolt of pain clapped through her unlike anything she had ever known.

Her suit hissed into action and activated a tourniquet. It cinched the gaping wound, a circumferential cautery that filled her helmet with a sweet, cloying odor. A thousand pins coursed through her shoulder, up her neck—clotting factors, nanomaterials weaving her ragged flesh. She heard the gentle hiss of an adrenaline infusion. The pounding in her ears grew. She slumped backward, laying face up.

She began to fade.

The silhouette of a large head darted down to regard her, its phosphorescent eyes like a demonic apparition. She squeezed her eyes tight. Heard its rattling breath, its nostrils snuffing in deep, resonant bursts.

Perez refused to die in fear. Didn't want the flash of teeth to be the last thing she saw. She cinched her eyes tighter. Imagined the night in the Kasbah, the first time Basem told her he loved her, the warmth of him surrounding her in his arms.

I'm not afraid.

POP. POP.

Bright flashes bloomed beyond her eyelids.

A haunting shriek peeled through the vastness of the cave and echoed into its far reaches.

POP.

She opened her eyes and saw the delta waver. It gurgled and stumbled. A dark, ropey substance slunk from the tip of its mouth and pecked her face shield. *Blood.* The beast swayed. Its legs buckled, and it crashed sidelong into the sand beside her.

Muffled footfalls approached.

A coldness enveloped Perez, her body shivering like mad, cold sweat pouring from her face, tears streaming from her clenched eyes. The smell of singed flesh had grown unbearable.

"And where… the *fuck*… do y'think you're g-going?" Oz's accent echoed throughout the cave, his boots trawling past Perez. His cadence sounded irregular. *A limp.*

Somewhere to the left, Nedjma yelped, then erupted into a series of wet coughs. "Please! Please don't—"

The butt of Oz's rifle struck the sand, and the weapon clattered onto its side.

"I told you not to *fuck* with me."

Perez stretched out her trembling arm, clawed at the flaking guano, and dug her fingers into the packed sand. She managed to turn herself over, head swimming, ears ringing. She clung to the hope that her suit would keep her from bleeding out before she could intervene. That she'd have enough time to claw her way to the sound of Nedjma's thrashing limbs and stifled gasps. Her pulse rapped in her skull; a surge of adrenaline revived her mental faculties. She wavered onto her knees, a rope of drool hanging from her lips. The world spun about the axis of her head.

Oz was on top of Nedjma, his muscular bulk hunched over her, straddling her midsection with his back to Perez. He pulled her up and smashed her head into the ground, then ripped her helmet free and tossed it into darkness. His gun glinted red at his side.

Perez's first thought was to go for the weapon, but she knew it would serve her no purpose. Federation-issued ordinance only registered the bio-signature of its owner. No one else.

But she still had one good arm.

Nedjma's legs kicked from between Oz's, thrashing erratically, but increasingly sluggish.

Perez rolled onto the balls of her feet, her tremulant legs ready to fail. With her remaining strength, she launched herself onto Oz's back. Her fingers grazed something—the hilt of a knife sheathed to his kit—and gripped its hilt. But Oz's reaction was swift. He swung her violently so that her grasp slipped, and the blade tumbled to the ground. She held fast and hooked her arm around his neck before he could throw her off. With everything she had, she squeezed her bicep into his windpipe. He sputtered, and encouraged by this, Perez fought through her searing muscles, her fading lucidity.

A swift jolt traveled into her. Oz had collapsed to one knee.

The momentum was short-lived, however, as Oz launched her backward. Her vision flashed white, her back slamming into the ground, her chest crushed under his weight. She gulped at the air, coughing.

Oz rolled off her, panting. "F-f-fuckin' *bitch*. Don't k-know what's good for you." He reached for his gun.

A melodic shriek erupted over the howling currents.

"*Ssshitt!*"

"What the—" Oz turned toward the sound just as a large shadow overtook him from the darkness. Another came in from his opposite flank.

There are more of them.

The screaming didn't sound like Oz. Almost didn't sound human.

But it was.

There were at least two of them. Deltas. One clamped around each of his shoulders. The sound of their teeth piercing his body armor came first. Then, his second—and final—scream was cut off by the swift tearing of skin, his wails reduced to incoherent, wet gurgling. The glowing eyes on either flank appeared locked on one another as their snouts tugged in synchrony. Twisted. Rent.

Pop.

Oz's right shoulder failed first. A sliver of red light spilled through him as his body bifurcated with a thickly wet release. The deltas met resistance around his waist, but they persisted. Tugged, tugged, tugged, as vicious as wild dogs, and peeled him apart until his remaining connections frayed and failed like snapping rope. His head and legs went one way, half his torso the other. The two beasts recoiled, each with their respective share flopping and spilling Oz's insides onto the blood-soaked guano. They did not cease. Continued to savage their kill. Denuded its armor, its clothing. Exposed the soft parts, red light strobing from the motion of their swaying tails.

Everything around Perez was spinning. Her shivering had grown violent. She was *so cold*.

Then her hearing went. Everything faded.

"Mamá, why do I love patatas so much?"
"Mi Amor, you always have, ever since you were un garbancito chiquitín."
"When I was in your tummy?"
"Yes, when you were in my tummy. You were such a feisty little one."
"I liked patatas even then?"
"Oh, yes. When I was pregnant with you, your poor Papá ran to the market
 every week so I could feed mi garbancito her patatas!"
"But I'm not a little chickpea anymore!"
"No. No, you are not, but you will always be my Camilita."

"Mamá." The word, barely a whisper, escaped Perez's cracked lips. Her eyes might have been open, but it was too dark to know.

One day, you will have a peanut of your own.
Ruth.

"Got you, Cam, c'mon…." Nedjma's voice, barely louder than a whisper, cut through Perez's fugue. Another wet cough erupted from her lips. "Almost there."

Perez's vision was hazy. She peered through slitted lids as she cycled in and out.

Nedjma was helping her move over the carcasses. Grunted and coughed as she helped Perez negotiate the irregular terrain. Perez looked down. Wondered if she was really seeing the body under their feet or if she had slipped again into a dream.

It was Schulz, her eyes drawn and clouded-over in a haunting eternal stare that cut through the glow of the airlock's lighting. Her right leg was gone, half of her midsection missing—now voided and crawling with bees. She was stripped of most clothing, naked below the waist. A few tattered remnants of an isolation gown covered her legs. A soiled surgical mask hung in a wad from one ear. Through smeared vision, Perez thought she saw a bullet wound in the middle of her forehead.

As her vision faded again, Perez heard her name somewhere behind them. *"Cammm. 'Ere Camm-mm."*

She faded again.

When she came to, she found herself leaning against the back wall of the airlock. Nedjma was slumped beside her with her hand clamped over her abdomen. Blood streamed between her fingers.

One of Oz's bullets had found her.

Perez's eyes crept wide. She wanted to go to Nedjma. Wanted to help, but her body failed her. She couldn't move.

No. No. I'm so sorry. Please don't go.

The airlock's lift shuddered.

Perez's pulse had slowed to an impotent thrum. Nedjma, illuminated by the sterile white glow of the lift, stared back at her with unflinching eyes, her lips upturned into a meek smile. Red lines streamed from her mouth, her nostrils, carving a tributary through her scarred upper lip.

Perez's vision narrowed. She sensed herself slumping forward, her body numb. As the muffled drone of the lift faded into obscurity, she felt herself floating in space. Not as a prisoner, but as a bird breaking through the confines of a cage, free to explore the stars.

You are my sky.
Perez had won. *They* would not get her. *They* would not get *Ruth*.
From the pit of a growing emptiness, she crooned a meek lullaby.

Duérmete mi niña, duérmete mi amor
duérmete pedazo de mi corazón.
Esta niña mía que nació de noche…

And, in a moment of capitulation, the first in a long time, Camila
Perez was not afraid.

 *I know of the horn of Heimdall, hidden*
Under the high-reaching holy tree...
—**POETIC EDDA**

‹ ‹ | RAGNARÖK ›

A deep resonance rattled Lotta into consciousness.

A droning wail. A thunderous horn.

A distorted beacon.

The sound swelled.

Through slitted eyes, she saw only darkness.

One. Zero. Zero. One.

She slipped away momentarily, like floating in a dream, enveloped by the sound of leaves in the wind.

I am the equation come to life.

And back again. Jolted awake by a distant clap, a thunderous rumble.

Something solid but movable enfolded her chest, a constriction of loose rock.

Mud.

Her mouth was packed with mud.

A muffled, glottal retching brimmed from her lips, and she expelled a spate of bile-tinged earth. Her throat hitched, her breathing shallow and crackling, bordering on agonal. The air was putrid and dense with particulates. She retched again, coughing through grit-packed teeth as she pushed through a wave of nausea. Her cocoon of earth shifted a little and funneled to her knees.

The stench intensified. Something rotten. Festering.

Lotta put it from her mind. Tried to remember how she got here. She possessed little sense of her surroundings, only that she was positioned at an upright angle, one arm numb and pinned behind her, the other stretched overhead. She wiggled her toes, then tried moving her trapped arm.

Nothing. Need to get the blood moving.

Then, a small victory. One of her fingers twitched, grazed her lower back.

A light breeze kissed the back of her other hand. She shifted her focus there, fluttered her fingers. Or thought maybe she had. Couldn't be sure.

Then, *sensation.* Deep, pressure-like. Below the first knuckle of her middle finger. It sent her heart into her throat and filled her with inexplicable panic. Something probing, pulling. Then a pinch. A peck. A tug.

But no pain.

Lotta managed a muffled scream and tried to wrest her hand beneath the mound.

It worked. Whatever had her finger stopped probing, and the dampened *snap* of expanding wings buffeted the air. Muted squeals of fresh conflict unfolded overhead, a flurry of chirrups, of clapping beaks. She pulled again. Loosed rubble showered over her, infiltrated her hair and crawled down her chest. It worked its way to her hips, then between her legs.

A welcome coolness spread over her forearm, and her lungs hailed a rush of fresh air appended by a sliver of sunlight. Encouraged, she inhaled as deep as she could against the constricting earth, exhaled sharply, and wrenched her shoulder forward. The thrum of a pulse coursed under her armpit, then the familiar static signaling a waking limb. Pushing her feet down, she prised her arm halfway free, a small victory that came at a steep cost. Shifting earth pressed into her chest. Her airway throbbed, her throat sticky and raw. Slicked with sweat, she heaved and trembled against the morass.

"*Heeelllpp...*" A raspy hiss through cracked lips. Tried to swallow, instead choked on the grit lining her throat.

Panic set fire to her heavy limbs, and she pulled harder, the earthen vice compressing her ribcage with each exhale, her pinned arm crawling with white noise. Then, release. She ripped the limb free and vaulted it toward the surface. Toiled and clawed against sliding rock and dirt. With her tactile faculties blunted, she fumbled blindly, desperate to gain hold but unable to verify, through any corporeal sense, what lay ahead.

Muscles wailed. Joints popped.

This is not your grave.

A moan scraped through her throat, and with a final push, she exploded into blinding daylight. Her vision cleared enough to gather that she was still high above the ground, looking out from what appeared to be a large slide of pulverized earth.

A tenebrous form shifted to her right.

Lotta turned to find herself shadowed by a pair of scimitar-beaked bird-apes.[1] They studied her briefly, then pushed off their mantis arms, their pale bodies climbing skyward over a vista of desolation. Gone was the roiling sea, its churning waves reduced to a glassy slick that stretched into the distance. Belching stacks poured from pits of gurgling clay dotting a surface littered by upended trees and floating debris. Overhead, a variety of species of bird-apes moved in synchronized chaos like specters, reflected by the shallow water rimming the carcasses they circled. The winged beasts cackled, weaving between the billowing columns against the backdrop of a towering gray plume that vented into the stratosphere from a smudge of horizon.

Still buried to her waist, Lotta sank a little. She felt powerless against it, her arms limp, sinuses burning with the acridity of sulfur and the unyielding stench of decay. Minutes passed before she mustered the will to rend one leg free. The other came a little easier, but she was too weak to brace against the recoil, and the momentum took her. She tumbled naked down the gentle slope, her skin scraping over crushed rocks and twigs. The world was spinning, intermittently obscured by bursts of white light, when the ground gave way beneath her, and she was in freefall.

Clap.

---

1 *Xericeps curvirostris*

A million pins penetrated her.

She rolled onto her back—her face framed by a shallow slurry—and swallowed a lungful of air. With anesthetized fingers, she scooped clods of muck from her eyes and caught a familiar whiff of putridity. Peering through matted lashes, she regarded her trembling, wet hand through an oily veil, and a sickening warmth swelled within her chest. Her middle finger had turned black from its tip down to the first knuckle, the flesh macerated and damp, shimmering wet beneath the bloody sky. The fingernail was gone, and in its place was a gleaming slick of green pus swirled pink.

It smelled worse than anything in recent memory.

The digit she had sliced with Fischer's knife wasn't faring much better, and every other finger wept a dark substance from painless lacerations she had no recollection of sustaining. A deep purple hue imbued the intervening skin, the flesh pocked with ulcers circumscribed by frothing rings. Fine bubbles pulsed from the center of one of them. She leaned closer to scrutinize it, and something white wriggled out from the coruscated pulp.

A maggot.

The warmth spread up the back of her neck and manifested a familiar pressure at the base of her tongue. Another whiff of rot assailed her, and she ripped her hand away, but not before a pit swelled in her gut, rose into her throat, and snaked to the back of her mouth. She retched against a fresh wave of nausea, her cheeks striped with tears.

Shaking, whimpering, she came to her knees in the shallow water and peered out across the aftermath.

It struck her then—the water was warm. Not *hot*, but almost.

She shifted her weight onto swollen ankles, her strained knees protesting the extension of depleted legs. She managed herself into a wavering stand, but a rush of vertigo threatened to drop her back into the slurry.

The sensation passed.

She looked down at the mud sloughing from her skin, her brow tugged by the sopping hair plastered to the back of her neck. Her bouncing eyes stopped on the remnants of a bloody handprint on her waist, a cue that spawned the realization of a dull ache in her pelvic floor.

Vestiges. Waning tethers to moments in time.

Ed.

Time. Time stood still.

Her mind went to the night before. She was back at the camp, cleaning off with the tannin after blöt. The cave was abuzz with the storm's roar, but Fischer's voice had cut through it, had startled her. His speech was low, almost conversational, but unintelligible from outside the wigwam—so she had slipped inside to investigate. Stood naked and bloody at the entrance for a while, watching his blackened form in the dark, the slow rise and fall of his chest. *Talking in his sleep.* Except that when she had doubled back toward the drone of the lashing rain, he had uttered an unmistakable phrase that stopped her cold.

"I want you."

She had taken it as an affirmation. A reminder of the way she caught him looking at her sometimes. Like he saw her. *Really* saw her.

So, she went to him.

But Fischer *hadn't* seen her, not that time. He'd suffered another bout of delirium and thought she was his *fucking wife.* Lotta felt used upon that realization. Embarrassed. But her instinct to dismiss, to minimize the situation, overcame the emotions welling inside of her.

Was just sex. Not a big deal.

Except Fischer hated her for it.

A large gob slid from her back and into the water.

Plunk.

She studied her trembling hands again. The muscles of her face twisted, and she let the tears spill. She coughed. Split her lower lip, the taste of blood a welcome distraction as she fought to regain her grip.

Just need to find him.

"Ed!" she tried to yell for him, unsure of whether he wanted to *be* found. But all she managed was a whisper and a fresh coughing fit.

Find him. You need to find him.

A deafening *pop* impelled her gaze to the base of the scarp. There, an eruption of exploded rock rained around a point of impact. She craned her neck at the looming cliff face, a trail of dispersing dust indicating the vertical trajectory that a sizeable boulder had taken. Behind it stood the gaping remnants of the outlook, its scarred face weeping runnels of brown water from fissures and newly formed crags. A large span of the scarp seemed on the verge of further collapse, buttressed only by the enormous slide of gutted rock from which she had just emerged.

She recalled the sensation of the ground buckling and giving way beneath her, of being swallowed up by the gored earth, a spiraling singularity of churning dross. Then nothing.

And Fischer. How Björn had husked ribbons of flesh from him with unexacting ease, the pale wraith's shuddering face smothered in bright blood. *Ed's* blood. *Skogvættir. Forest spirit.* A beast detached from its innate drive to maul, to feed. In that moment of inaction, Lotta had become a prisoner within herself, swept by the undertow of an unfolding nightmare, her moment of paralysis only expediting the grisly reality unfolding before her eyes.

It couldn't be real. *Couldn't be.*

But it *was* real, and finding Fischer alive now seemed about as bleak as getting back home.

Reality had lost her.

"Fuck. *Fuck.*" She bit her lower lip amid welling eyes, her breathing erratic, panicked. "Ed!"

Lotta sloshed aimlessly through drifting steam. Doubled back. Reversed again. Her mind was a brooding entanglement of erratic thought, of indecision. Aware of her ambivalence, she stopped, fidgeted with her remaining pearl earring, then reverted to her original path.

Her legs leaden, feet dredging the soft sediment, she followed the margin of the landslide where it tapered along the base of the cliff and abutted an enormous span of ancient sandstone. The sunken slab jutted from the scarp like a toppled monolith of eons past, an imposing altar that filled her with inexplicable reverence and intrigue.

Squinting through drifting mist, she resolved a skirt of rounded boulders along the formation's base. But with each step, their lithic aspect dissolved before her eyes, and the air stopped in her throat. They weren't boulders, but *shells.* Monstrous, spiraled shells that had apparently beached amid the receding waters. Most appeared crushed, all eerily empty. And the *smell*—an acrid putrescence reminiscent of the collective stench of the mass squid beachings during Europe's seasonal red tides.

Lotta tossed her clotted hair and pressed her tongue to the roof of her mouth to keep from vomiting. She looked above the spiraled carapaces, peppered with barnacles and swathed in the soft orange sunlight. Her eyes traced lines of black ink weeping over the sides of the slab and stopped on a tangled mass of tentacles draped over the edge.

She mulled a route up for a better view of the surrounding area, intermittently eyeing the piled shells as she approached. Struck by their size, their strange, coiled shapes, she waded up to the nearest one and gave it a nudge. It didn't move. Felt solid, cold to the touch, the smooth texture of the carapace gripping her palm like cold porcelain.

After sweeping the water off her skin as best she could, Lotta hoisted herself onto the shell and was surprised that it easily took her weight. She aired her feet in the sun until they dried, then found purchase between its corrugated ridges. Without deliberation, she moved toward the slab, clambering to the next shell and the next, her throat hitching from the fetor venting from their voided apertures.

Before long, the precipice was within arm's reach. Lotta extended her arms, her head pounding with anticipation. In her haste, she miscalculated, stumbled and sliced the pad of her heel on a barnacle. Her hands flung forward and gripped the slab's edge just in time to break the fall and—with aching knees and searing arms—she mantled her tremulant body onto the surface and collapsed onto the warm stone.

A half dozen bird-apes wheeled lazily overhead.

No... I'm not dead yet.

She gathered herself and rolled onto her haunches. Her jaw fell.

There was ink *everywhere.*

It pooled beneath the pale gray bulk of a rotting cephalopod crawling with hermit crabs. The mangled carcass appeared to have been ripped free of its savaged carapace. Split down the middle, pried apart, the shell was lined with rows of circular punctures.

Bite marks.

Lotta shuddered to comprehend what possessed the power to wrest such a colossal thing, to *split* it in two. She gazed up at the circling pterosaurs again, perplexed that they hadn't yet descended on such an opportunity.

The soles of her feet stuck to the clotted ink, which, to her surprise, appeared to stifle the bleeding from her foot. Thick like tar, it was smeared in gigantic serpentine arcs, each flanked by a mosaic of black footprints stamped across the stone tableau. The tracks approximated the size of a Jötunn's, but appeared morphologically distinct—flat, webbed like those of waterfowl—their haphazard arrangement across the slab's surface, indicating the area was well-trodden.

Lotta's face swelled with warmth. She wondered if she'd made a serious error. Overcome by a desire to disappear, she started scrutinizing the scarp face for a way back up before whatever had laid the tracks returned.

That was when a reflection caught the corner of her eye. Something beyond the devastated shell's rim, toward the center of the slab. Her chest pounding in sync with her throbbing head, she extended her neck and skirted the carcass to elucidate the source.

Her legs failed her at what she saw, and it wasn't until the pain of her knees striking stone registered that she was ripped from the recesses of her mind—the place she had hidden so often during her youth.

It was Fischer's knife, gleaming within a shallow red pool from which a set of bloody tracks led toward the decaying nautilus to assimilate into the canvas of stygian gore.

With her heart in her throat, Lotta shambled forward, her feet peeling off the sticky surface with each step. She possessed a growing awareness of her left heel. It throbbed, but the bleeding had slowed.

She paid little heed to the pain, her focus fixed entirely on the glimmering blade taunting her from where it lay. She came to the puddle and crouched on wavering knees, her head pounding, then scooped the clotted weapon in her hands. Her swollen fingers managed enough dexterity to inspect it, and through her narrowing vision, the welling tears, Lotta realized that the probability of finding Fischer alive—or at all—had collapsed to zero.

Zero.

Her heart fluttered.

One.

She fixated on the blade's edge, then on her middle finger, its skin stretched and black. Her vision narrowed, and malaise overtook her. She knew what she needed to do. Needed to amputate. She glanced again at her foot and considered coating her fingers with ink to control the bleeding once the deed was done. But she couldn't muster the strength. Not now. Not without Fischer.

Zero… zero… one…

Get out of my head.

Her face swollen with fear, Lotta diverted her gaze to the bloody tracks and discerned that they were not Björn's, but instead resembled the first set, only these were smaller, around the size of her hand.

And the *blood*.

Zero.

She repeatedly struck her forehead with the meat of her palm. Twisted her facial muscles into a grimace and spat at her feet. "Fuck the odds."

She limped to the far end of the slab, where a wall of mist veiled the receding water, and screamed his name.

The silence that answered back was deafening.

Lotta scanned the scene, then stopped on something pale and white vaulting from the shallows. It resembled a thickly muscled ostrich leg bent at the knee, its toe claws curled inward in rigor mortis. Her insides turned molten. Her body tensed. A pall of mist briefly obscured the limb from view and moved away to reveal it again.

"Ed!"

She scrambled off the slab and back into the water.

The waterline had come to mid-thigh by the time she neared the ghostly appendage, and Björn's form materialized as a placid specter beneath the turbid surface. Buzzing insects swarmed the exposed limb, which did not yet give off much of a smell—nothing strong enough to overcome the sulfuric stench, at least. Nevertheless, the absence of bird-apes converging on yet another prize perplexed her.

She saw no sign of Fischer. The tightness in her chest eased a little.

She took a deep breath and plunged face-first. Had to be sure. The visibility beneath the surface was low but good enough to confirm that he wasn't there. That there was still hope.

She breached, drinking the sour air as she waded to the other side of the carcass and dove again. Particulates from the disturbed sediment degraded visibility, forcing her to claw frantically at the soft bottom. But the effort was in vain. The state of her fingers had deteriorated to the point she could no longer intuit what her hands encountered, the ruddy water only further obstructing her view.

She surfaced again and spit out a mouthful of brine.

"Ed!" His name escaped her lips in the form of a prolonged desperate wail.

Something answered. But it wasn't Edgar Fischer.

Lotta's head snapped to the right toward a thick scrim of drifting steam. The sound erupted again, a deep booming click, an eerie crooning. Somehow, the superseding silence seemed far louder.

A faint odor like damp mildew percolated the foul air, and it occurred to Lotta then that she had left the knife behind.

The misty veil ebbed, perturbed by an incomprehensible bulk. White coils peeled from the vast form like a derelict longship materializing from the white emptiness. A dreki unmoored, adrift at sea, its ancient bow sprouting a sinuous neck upon which the slender head of a dragon cut through the haze with eyes like shimmering opals. A looming sail coalesced behind it, crested by the midmorning sun, and it was then that Lotta rendered the genuine form of the thing. Not a vessel or a Jötunn, but the beast that had breached the waves of Njörðr's wrath, defied Freyr's tempest, and repelled Thor's blinding rage. It moved on a hull of bone, rigged in muscle and tendon, armored with strakes of scaled flesh. From the flanks of its bow hung a pair of muscular arms in place of oars, and from stern extended not a rudder but a boundless, glistening tail that trawled lazily through the shallows. No longer sequestered by the roiling storm, it waded on stout legs with an air of triumph and authority, and Lotta now understood why the giant river crocs had withered in its presence.

The musty odor intensified as it sloshed closer. Little more than a pale apparition, the beast appeared unaware of her despite a berth of mere meters between them. It shifted in broadside through a cluster of waterlogged ferns toward a mound of turned mud, its ashen torso ribbed with pearl-string stripes that faded into a mosaic of black spots up the mottled blues and reds of its sail. A pair of eyes—gilded cerulean beneath a black-tipped central crest—flashed from a rust-colored head cleaved by a mouth of interlocking rosettes.

And ink—swathes of it—smeared its terrible face, its arms, its chest.

Its head came about and gently pierced the haze, its snuffing nostrils breaking the eerie silence. The slender maw parted, venting a great sigh through a cage of angled spikes, and pitched toward the mound. A pouch ballooned at the base of its mandible, undulating and vermiform in aspect, and from the fathoms of its tarred orifice bore a glistening mass of writhing appendages that landed with a meaty *plunk*. The mass thrashed, unfurling into distinct parts, each erupting into a cacophony of ravening chirps.

Wincing through the gleaming sunlight, Lotta counted three of them, a trio of glimmering, monstrous progeny about the size of dogs. They flopped upon awkward legs, steam billowing off their bodies as they probed for purchase, their nostrils spouting with the filling and voiding of tiny lungs. Squinting in the light of day, they looked up to greet Mother.

Then, something disturbed the water along the beast's flank, and her knotted jaws swung to port, her body listing slightly, angling her sail toward the water like a tacking yawl. She became motionless with the tip of her snout apeak over the shaded water, her hideous arms grazing the surface to her fore. The squeals of her progeny faded, their heads springing aloft, transfixed on Mother. Again, something perturbed the water in the shadow of her monstrous bulk, and her gaze pitched toward the disturbance with laser focus. Almost imperceptibly, she eased the tip of her snout into the water and waited.

Her next move was explosive and synchronous. Like a great serpent, her crested tail threshed a wall of water and corralled a dark mass. A fin breached the burgeoning wave and glided toward her waiting dentary, and Mother's head speared the churning swell. Coils of steam dispersed around her vast form, the water a flurry of thrashing limbs as she wrested an enormous, shimmering sawfish from the frothing bedlam.[2]

Lotta had little time to react before a second mass retreated through the shallows directly toward her. Amid a hail of spray and foam, she caught sight of another dorsal fin just as its wake pulled her under. A constellation of ruddy bubbles consumed her vision, her dead fingers raking the muddy bed as the water turned crimson. The taste of blood seeped past her lips. Her blood. Had to be.

It had ripped her open.

---

2 *Onchopristis numidus*

She managed to push herself to her knees and get her face above water. Took hold of Björn's leg to steady herself. That was when she spotted a fresh gash in the thigh of the carcass. She exhaled and gave herself a once-over. Found no sign of injury.

With one hand clasped over her mouth to stifle a barrage of sputtering coughs, her attention fell back toward the chaos, and the blood drained from her face.

Mother was looking directly *at* her.

Every fiber of Lotta's being trembled, her breaths devolving into shallow rasps. She wanted to shrink away into nothing, fade from existence. Anything to escape the gaze of those piercing, green eyes.

Flight.

With her impotent quarry dangling from her lips, her chest heaving, Mother chuffed a plume of mist and diverted her gaze with indifference. Her neck folded, pitching her head between her splayed forelimbs, each employing a trine of black scythes as long as human arms. They reached up and skewered the sawfish's gills, procuring a muffled *pop* from within. Then Mother's snout recoiled like a carronade, and the fish's head separated, raining a torrent of bright red blood into the surrounding mire. The disembodied head splashed down, its spiked rostrum bobbing vertically before listing and disappearing beneath the surface.

Mother's throat pouch swelled, and from her mouth vented a wet, pulsing sound. She tossed her head back, vaulting the carcass to the back of her pallet. A spate of popping bone and cartilage drowned out the renewed cries of her sequestered younglings and passed slowly into her pulsing throat.

Shaking, wet, febrile, Lotta clung to Björn and contemplated retreat. The stone outcrop offered the most immediate relative safety, an opportunity to regroup. She tried to imagine what Fischer might do, but all she could think of was that stupid phrase her father had always told her.

Going into the forest is going home.

Until Valhalla.

That was the answer. Probably the only thing Pappa had ever said was worth a damn. She needed to make her way back to the forest. It felt right. Had to be.

Mother's ethereal form came about and lowered onto her bilge, her ink-stained jaws stretching wide as the backwash recoiled from her sprawling bulk. A yawning sphinx, she welcomed a coulee of bird-apes descending from the sky to pluck scraps from her teeth.

Two of her younglings dropped into the water and paddled around the vaulting bracken, their little nares chuffing just above the waterline. The third remained on the mound, pacing, chirping.

Lotta sensed something then. The air had changed, eerily calm but thick. Then something else, a moderate undercurrent, a rending that lightly torqued her ankles. It intensified into a moderate pull around her waist, drawing her attention toward the horizon.

The water was receding.

The youngling chirping from the mound grew more frantic. The bird-apes took flight. Mother's jaws clapped shut.

An undulating cloud of bird-apes approached and passed noisily overhead.

Moving inland.

Lotta tightened her arms around Björn's leg and dug her heels into the mud. The droning hiss of the ebbing water intensified all around her, but above it, she heard a sound that chilled her—a birdlike scream erupting from the mound. She peered through the rolling shroud of mist and saw the runt pacing, its head bobbing as it tracked its siblings being swept away.

Mother shifted, her head snapping to alert. Waves crested from her bulk as she lurched upright and belted a distressed trill. She vaulted after her imperiled offspring, toiling through the clotted dregs, her bellows answered by their fading cries until they slipped from sight.

A violent shudder erupted from the earth. One of Mother's legs sank into the bubbling mud with an audible *snap.*

Lotta splashed onto her elbows. Now less than half its original depth, the water flowed over her midsection. She managed to right herself, planting her feet into the shifting muck. It wormed between her toes, encased her feet. Coughing, she pulled one leg free and lofted her gaze. The shroud of mist had thinned, affording an uninterrupted view of the horizon, where a second massive plume jettisoned into the stratosphere.

Another tremor hit, and she was thrown forward.

She slammed into the mud, the water reduced to a mere slick, and her vision flashed white. The ground crawled, then fell still.

A deafening *BANG* followed, a shockwave that decayed like thunder in all directions, and an eerie silence reigned for a brief time until it was broken by Mother's tortured wails.

Flight.

Lotta pushed herself upright and turned to run. Fought the pull of the soft mud, the odd warmth threatening her with fatigue, with somnolence. Kept her mind sharp, the burn in her lungs rising to the back of her tongue with the metallic taste of dilute blood. Tendrils of sulfur-laced steam rose up around her, rending at her insides.

The forest is home. The forest is home.

The tops of the piled shells—half-sunken fractals, hooded beneath the materializing slab—coalesced through milky white like ghostly congregants before a Hadean altar. The blood-soaked limestone materialized in Lotta's mind, the inky footprints, their connection to the monstrosity she'd just witnessed. The efficiency of Mother's tactics. The way she hungered.

Maimed.

Killed.

Fischer was gone.

A sound like faint static swelled somewhere behind her like a distant but rapidly approaching jet engine. She dared not turn to face what she already knew. That the water had returned. A wave of fury was mobilized by a resurgent Njörðr. Ragnarök was upon her.

She clawed her way over the slippery shells, her lungs heaving against the fetid warmth, her capacity to traverse them a miracle given the state of her ravaged hands. The hiss was now a dull roar. Like leaves in the wind.

Zero. One. One.

Like the screams of the dead.

Two.

All seventy-five thousand and twenty-five of them.

Three.

Three names that a week ago didn't exist in her mind. Three names that had firmly planted inside of her, seeds rooted and growing like a great tree, fighting to break free, tearing her apart atom by atom.

Emma.

Ellsa.

Evi.

And her team. *Five.*

Anderson. Mattheo.

All of them. Gone. *Eight.*

Basem. Hassan. Ed.

The names.

She couldn't silence the names. The voices. Seventy-five thousand and twenty-five leaves squalling from the boughs of a great tree, their anguished cries jettisoning into the heavens within a cloud of ash.

The forest. Need to get to the forest.

No time.

The scarp. The scarp was the only escape. She needed to climb. Needed to try.

She scaled another nautilus shell. It dropped noticeably as she latched onto the side of the slab. The mud roiled like boiling quicksand, and the carapace shifted beneath her just as she cleared it. She managed to hang onto the slab, somehow relying on her footing to facilitate her climb, and mantled herself onto the precipice, where she tripped and fell hard against the ink-slicked stone. She pushed off her hands, got upright again, and eyed the scarp face. Despite her leaden feet, she bounded headlong across the stone span. Tried not to heed the spot where the knife still lay in Fischer's blood.

Another tremor struck.

The stone vibrated beneath her feet. Crushing pops filled her ears. A split threaded through the middle of the slab, and it buckled. She reflexively hopped to one side and pressed forward, her arms pumping, her feet pounding. Craned her neck and peered up at the imposing scarp face, the explosive roar of a great wave crashing into the end of the slab she had just cleared. Her ears popped, and her skin crawled from the cool spray. Salty vapor stung her lips.

She scrambled up a shallow talus and clawed at the crumbling marl. She needed to climb. Needed to try. Needed one more miracle.

She had scaled a few meters when she decided to look down. Frothing water churned below. A tsunami that yielded no signs of slowing, it rose higher and higher as it buffeted the walls of the slab. She turned back to the wall, pressed her body against it, and held on with what little strength remained. The arches of her feet cramped, her knees ached. She couldn't fucking feel her fucking fingers. And despite them, she held on as long as she could.

The swell of the tsunami was a deafening roar. A million leaves. A million voices.

The scarp groaned. Shifted.

Lotta fell.

When she came to, her face was pressed against the shifting slab. Chunks of stone rained around her, a large one narrowly missing her head with an ear-shattering *crack*. The taste of blood filled her mouth, and the stench of sulfur burned her nose. She coughed, and a sticky warmth coated her lips. She was convinced her jaw was broken.

Somewhere in her mind, a beacon tolled.

In her delirium, Lotta mustered enough strength to turn onto her back—to gaze at a darkening sky—and as the water rose around her, a malevolent cloud swallowed the sun like a ravening wolf...

Forgive me.

...and the ash fell like snow.

"Our reason has driven all away. Alone at last, we end up by ruling over a desert."

—Albert Camus

| NIÑA >

You are my sky.

A violin droned softly from somewhere in the ether.

"Salut D'Amour."

Perez couldn't localize it, but the madness started metastasizing inside her long before she woke.

She inhaled sharply as if emerging from underwater. Attempted to sit up, but she was restrained on her back. Her eyes crept open, and she was met with a soft ambient glow. The room was sterile. Familiar. Featureless white walls. Chemical smell. She was on her back in a hospital bed, partitioned off from the rest of the room by a wall of frosted glass. Pale blue light spilled out from the gap on its far end.

Everything rushed back to her all at once. Fleeing into the mountain, the attack. Oz ripped apart like wet tissue.

And Nedjma—the blood pouring from her face, her hand clamped over her abdomen in a vain attempt to stem the bleeding.

Perez tried to yell out for her, but the muscles in her throat collapsed around something rigid, an obstruction—and it was then that she noticed a long tube protruding from her mouth. A breathing machine clicked in concert with a heart monitor at her bedside. An IV drip fed the PICC tubing that snaked up to her arm.

My arm.

She tried to look down at herself, but another restraint held her head. The heart monitor intensified.

How long have I been here?

The music droned on, then faded. Hadn't just been in her head.

Basem?

A door opened somewhere beyond the partition. Perez's eyes darted toward the sound, and she spotted a tall, dark form through the stippled veil. A man garbed in a white hazmat suit emerged. Someone she did not recognize.

The song concluded. Started again.

The individual walked with an upright, rigid posture to the foot of the bed and paused with his arms at his sides. His face seemed both familiar and wholly alien behind the suit's shield. His lips curled into a papery smile, their purplish hue a stark contrast against his sullen white complexion. His hair, thin at the temples, was slicked-back and gray with thin bands of white. But it was his eyes that Perez found the most unsettling. Deep-set, almost sunken, dark circles. They were dark brown, nearly black, and hooded beneath thick eyebrows.

"Good morning, Dr. Perez," the man said with a thick Greek accent. "So good to see you are on the mend. We have eagerly awaited this moment."

A sickening jolt coursed through Perez.

Aegis.

She tensed and pulled against her restraints. The floor shuddered—a sustained trembling from below—and all at once, she realized where she was.

Nonono. NO!

Galani continued with an air of indifference to her malevolent gaze. "We thought we'd lost you there for a bit," he said. "That would have been quite the setback. *Quite* the setback."

Shards of what had transpired in the heart of Qalil spiraled through her mind. It was incomplete, fragmented, hazy. She wondered if half of what she recalled had really occurred. Like Schultz's body, her empty stare. Still in her isolation gown, a bullet to the head.

Galani regarded her, his eyes drawn and glazed—an odd disconnect that betrayed his smile as wholly disingenuous. "But not to fret, my dear… you are safe now. We owe the Oberstleutnant and his team a debt of gratitude for coming to your aid when they did."

Nedjma. Where is Nedjma?

Galani skirted the edge of the bed and leaned over Perez's flank, his hands fumbling with one of the restraints. His brow furrowed, his eyes glistening in the sallow ambiance, and he lifted her arm to his face with morbid curiosity.

"*Remarkable.*"

The heart monitor blared.

Perez had her *arm* back.

She tried to prise the limb free, but her hand remained limp in his grasp, her mind a swarming hive, perplexed—not just by the inability to move the limb—but the total lack of sensation that accompanied it. Neither numb nor brimming with the white noise of a waking limb. More like not *there*.

The disconnect drove her into a frenzy.

Galani turned it over, palm down. "There was a moment when we thought the transplant might not take," he said. "But *look* at *this*. *Truly* remarkable."

He caressed it with his free hand, and Perez watched with wide eyes as the hair on the dead limb stood. The hive inside her swelled into a roiling ocean that drowned out the cycling melody she could still not localize.

"Ah, gooseflesh!" Galani beamed like a giddy boy and leaned closer. "Brilliant! Remarkable! Your autonomic functions are arriving ahead of schedule."

In an apparent attempt at self-regulation, he placed the limb back at her side and gently lifted the tubing of her PICC line. "I do hope the pain has been manageable." He then regarded her directly, but his gaze drifted again to her arm as if compelled by some unseen force.

"I will admit," he uttered without blinking, "I was quite apoplectic when I received word of your abscondence… that Oz had *betrayed* us."

His eyes narrowed, remained fixed, his face sullen. He shook his head, clicked his tongue, and regarded Perez again with a broad smile, as if waking from a trance. "No matter... no matter... he has paid dearly for his traitorous machinations. You see, these things find a way of working out in the end. Call it *fate*."

Galani's eyes trailed into a far-off gaze.

"On the *matter* of *fate*," he said, "I would be remiss if I did not divulge the status of your pupil, Ms. Ramdani...." He paused, clasping his hands. Feigned sorrow in a way that made Perez grow hot with rage. "I regret to inform you that she expired shortly after Jacobs and his team arrived on the scene and dispatched those monst—*animals*."

No. You are a fucking liar!

"Such a shame," he sighed. "I had grown quite fond of her, quite fond."

Perez arched her back, desperate to tear free, to rip out his throat. The bed frame rattled.

Nedjma. No! I will fucking *kill you!*

"Shhh-shh-shh..." Galani waved a hand to appeal for calm. "I recognize that this is a devastating revelation... tragic, really... but *do* mind your current state. We wouldn't want to impede your recovery, *would* we?" He crouched so his eyes leveled with hers, and his voice softened. "Take solace knowing that Ms. Ramdani's selfless actions ensured your survival. And not just *your* survival...."

Tears brimmed and spilled onto Perez's cheeks. Her vision smeared so that the features of his face bled together to resemble that man she remembered on the other side of the frosted glass of an isolation chamber.

"There, there...." Galani's gaze drifted down to her breasts, then her stomach. Perez's heart seized, her eyes bouncing as he slowly extended his hand and rested it below her navel. "All is not *lost*, my dear... There is, in fact, cause for *celebration*. The doctors have informed me that your... *little peanut* is doing *very* well." Galani feigned mercy, but his eyes continued to betray him.

Ruth. Pedazo de mierda—stay the fuck away from her, or I will cut your fucking head off.

"I want you to meet someone," he said, slapping his palms on his thighs as he stood. "*Both* of you."

A brief silence fell. The music began anew. Galani let out a long sigh, humming the melody of the piano as it moved into a crescendo, and walked to the partition. He turned and winked at Perez with his nose tipped up. "Athena, open up the room a bit, would you?"

The opaque surface dissolved away, affording a clear, uninterrupted view of what lay beyond.

Perez tried to scream, but no sound came out.

Against the far wall, cocooned in a hospital bed, a woman slept, her left arm notably absent. And her complexion, her hair, her *face*.

It was *her*.

Perez's mind raced. It didn't make sense. A clone's gestation and development would take *ages*. Would have to have occurred when she was a toddler or child. And what motive would drive such an act? What could propel such a violation of personal autonomy?

"I'm sure you have many questions," Galani said over the droning melody. "I know what you must be thinking. But I assure you the reality of this... *scenario*... defies conventional logic. She is *you*. You are *her*. You are *one*...."

That's not possible. It's not—

"But it is not necessary, nor in anyone's interest, for you to comprehend. Only for you to mend. To prepare. You see, it is incumbent upon you to complete the... transaction."

The pit inside of Perez erupted with violent fury. Tears streamed down her face as Galani again met her piercing stare.

"Ruth," he said. "Such a sweet name."

Don't say her name. Don't you dare *say her name.*

The heart monitor was screeching. Galani reached over and switched it off.

"But, as sweet as she may be," he said, "her existence, of course, violates eugenic protocol...."

No! Don't! Don't you hurt her, you fucking monster! I'll fucking kill you!

"But the *Father* is merciful. Ruth has a higher purpose." He nodded to the other end of the room. "You see, your counterpart here also had a *Ruth* once. Faced with the same decision as you, she embarked on a different path... a decision that has saddled her with incomprehensible grief." He placed a hand on her shoulder and gave a gentle squeeze. "Imagine her elation when she wakes and finds the life she betrayed has been restored. I cannot conceive of a more noble gift."

Galani withdrew his hand.

"You're wondering how I know so many intimate details about your life, your *entanglements*. What other details I am privy to… like what fate has befallen Dr. Bensoussan." He flashed a grin, more expansive this time. "I know a lot of things, Dr. Perez…. The Federation is everywhere. We are *many*, and we are *one*. There is nowhere we are not." He sighed deeply. "Isn't that right, Athena?"

Athena's voice interrupted the music. "Yes, Aegis."

Galani's smile faded. "Every moment. Every interaction. Every… *entanglement*. We have been by your side at every step. Every turn."

Perez fought against the restraints, but it was no use.

"*Ruth.*" Galani went on. "Such a beautiful name. One that conveys loyalty… *innocence*. In the Old Testament, the good Lord rewarded Ruth for her unyielding devotion… her obedience to her *Father*."

Hijo de las mil putas. Don't you touch her.

"Would you say you've been loyal to your *Father*, Dr. Perez?"

His gaze returned to meet hers, and his lips curled back down menacingly. He sighed heavily through his nose.

"I have quite enjoyed our time today," he said, "but the board demands an update, and you require some much-needed rest." He procured another wry smile and tipped his nose at her. "Stimulating conversation, as always."

Galani stopped and turned on his way out. "Dr. Perez, so good to have you here with us." He nodded to the *other*, keeping his gaze on Perez. "*Both* of you."

The door shut behind him.

The music swelled.

UEF / RD
EYES ONLY

Forward Operating Base (FOB)
Ministry of Defence
United European Federation

Memorandum of CCTV Interrogation. Partial Transcript.

JULY 02, 2147, 16:02

Appearances
Oberstleutnant Nikolaj Jacobson (alias: Jacobs)
Dr. Aegis Galani

Galani	The specimens have taken quite well to the new accommodations.
Jacobs	Once acclimated, yes. We lost a handful to illness, but the remaining ones have adapted. Seem to enjoy being at the top of the food chain.
Galani	You're quite perceptive, for a grunt, aren't you? I trust you were discreet.
Jacobs	Of course, sir. Distracting Perez was the easy part. Wasn't easy getting the crates past the security systems, though. We had resistance.
Galani	Your efforts are much appreciated, Oberstleutnant. Unfortunate about Schultz, but you did what had to be done.
Jacobs	Just following orders.
Galani	On another note, I do hope there are no hard feelings over Dr. Kazimierz. You must understand that we need his mental state to remain sharp. He possesses knowledge of the anomaly that is indispensable.

Jacobs   Like I said, just following orders.

Galani   His lucid testimony is equally crucial. Dr. Perez is where we need her in all of this. The media gets its scapegoat. We feed them a story, tell them we have evidence she is behind the creation of these monsters, that she and her cohorts will answer for her role in it while the military secures the dome.

Jacobs   What are you going to do with her? With her double? And the other subjects?

Galani   Above your paygrade, I'm afraid. You just focus on purging your ranks of further Russian meddling. Now, if you'll excuse me, I have other priorities to address. This matter of bees in the dome has proven more disruptive than anticipated.

Jacobs   Best we can determine is they hitched a ride on one of the specimens.

Galani   Also above your pay grade, Oberstleutnant.

"Man is always prey to his truths."
—Albert Camus

Widely I saw over all the worlds.
　　　　　　　　　　—POETIC EDDA

< Ω | VECTOR OMEGA >

"How much farther?"

Dr. Jerome Powell's mess of black hair tossed in the open air as the Benz roared over cracked desert.

Ismail turned away from the parched expanse flying past, squinting in the harsh Saharan sun. "Très proche, maintenant," he said, nodding straight ahead of them. His French was laden with a heavy East Moroccan accent. "La colin, là-bas."

About a kilometer off, a vertical wall of rock loomed above the shimmering sands. The Dugommier formation was far vaster than Jerome had imagined. The escarpment was nestled within a bluish haze, its limestone cap contrasting against the underlying red beds. A pile of felled rocks leaned along the base of the formation at an incline. Despite its height, Jerome figured the team could negotiate it with relative ease—*we'll be at the dig site in twenty minutes, easy.*

Just ahead, another safari wagon led the convoy with Jerome's postdoc, Natalie Favreau, and the eminent Dr. Timas Qasar, another American, bobbing in the back seat.

Timas enjoyed a comfortable tenure at l'Institut Bonaparte in Nouvelle Orléans as Director of Studies for paleontology. He was of Prussian-Moroccan descent, his family having fled to les États-Unis Français from Eastern Eurasia when he was a boy. Timas had gone on to take up the mantle from his late father, the Moroccan-born paleontologist Nadeem Qasar, and now led many expeditions throughout the North African colonies. Almost a decade prior, one of his most notable excursions had unearthed one of the largest sauropod nesting sites ever found—a stretch of *Paralititan stromeri* clutches—not far from where the convoy was currently headed.

Jerome had recently shifted his interest to African dinosaurs after Timas visited as a guest lecturer for his comparative anatomy and zoology course at l'Université de Chigagou. Before that, Jerome's focus had been closer to home, primarily on South American dinosaurs. That was until Timas invited him along for an African dig a year after his talk. Five expeditions later, Jerome could not see himself returning to South America anytime soon. This, though, was his first time visiting the Dugommier formation.

He turned and looked past the vehicle's rear, trailed by three more safari wagons that rounded out the convoy, their shapes little more than specters beyond the plume of brown dust billowing behind the Benz. These transported three of Timas's graduate students and the remaining dig team volunteers from the nearby oasis town of Montesquieu.

Arriving at the escarpment base, Jerome concluded that climbing up to the fossil-rich red beds might prove more challenging than he'd anticipated. The first two hours were spent prospecting the base of the escarpment, wandering clumsily across the sloped talus in search of bone fragments. After around three hours, the most promising find was a partial fragment one of the volunteers had spotted—possibly a length of ulna from a man-sized animal.

"Looks like a mammal," Jerome said, turning the specimen over in the sunlight. He studied it, then passed it off to Timas.

"Unlikely," Timas scoffed. "The region has been prospected and dug for decades. Not *once* has a mammal been unearthed in the Dugommier." He looked the fossil over, conceding that it was indeed old, likely Cenomanian, but a mammal it was not.

Heat rising in his cheeks over that imparted by the roiling desert heat, Jerome pressed him. "Look at the broken end in cross-section. The trabecular bone is not from a dinosaur."

Timas rebuffed him. "There were many other species along this river basin 95 million years ago, Dr. Powell." A gravelly tone came over him.

But Jerome persisted, his tone matter of fact.

"The level of ossification in the epiphysis you're looking at suggests otherwise."

While discord propagated through their ranks over what the find meant, Natalie had split off from the group. Her regard was aimed higher up the rock face at a region that had crumbled away. She yelled over to the squabbling men.

"Looks like it fell from there," she said, pointing up.

Everyone fell silent.

It took over an hour to rig the climbing gear. Another twenty minutes or so to scale the nearly three-story rock face and get equipment up. Jerome was the last to climb. He was almost at the site when he looked down at the buttressed pile of rocks where they had been standing a short while ago, ropes dangling beneath him. Squinting in the sun, his belayer, Ismail, gazed up as he kept the line taught.

Heaving in the unforgiving heat, Jerome turned and accepted a hand from Timas, who pulled him over a sandstone ledge leading to a flat recess beneath the limestone layer. Nearby, Natalie was at work scanning the reddish-brown layers of rock with an optical coherence tomographer, or OCT.

Timas gave Jerome a sweaty clap on the back, and with a smile, he turned away to mark the GPS coordinates on his phone.

"This looks good," Natalie said after a few minutes. "There seems to be something here, maybe three meters into the cliff. It's too far to resolve, but looks like an articulated skeleton. Part of one, anyway."

Timas approached and glanced at the screen. "Interesting," he said. "Doesn't look like anything I've seen yet from this locality."

Jerome bit his tongue. *It's a mammal.* He walked over and looked at the OCT's display. It was *something*, to be sure, but the details were too muddy to determine precisely what.

As they prepared to dig, Natalie gave the area of interest another sweep with the OCT. Jerome had busied himself laying out flag markers when he heard her shout to the group.

"Hey, guys, you're going to want to come see this. I've got something." She stood, her jaw hanging open, her eyes wide and unblinking as she gazed down at the display in her trembling hands.

In the sun's glare, the image on the screen was too faint to decipher, so Jerome reached over and tilted it toward him.

The breath stopped in his lungs. "*Impossible.*"

It had to be an anomaly—an artifact of a new technology with kinks to work out. But the longer Jerome stared, the more he knew this was no glitch. That soon, the specimen would be out of the ground.

"Dr. Powell," Natalie said, her voice quivering, "w-what is this doing *here*? These strata are late Cretaceous."

By now, everyone had gathered around for a look. All, including Timas, had fallen silent and were gazing expectantly at Jerome. But he didn't want to say it. He couldn't. What he was looking at made no sense. It wasn't possible.

Because it *was* a mammal. He was looking at a *human skull.*

And beside it, an area of hyperintensity—a reflective, rounded object embedded in the earth.

How odd, he thought to himself.

Because it almost resembled a pearl earring.

"Einstein, stop telling God what to do!"

—Niels Bohr

Thank you for reading. If you enjoyed *RIFT*, please take a moment to leave a short review:

APPENDIX

Vector Alpha

1. Stromer's Riddle

"Stromer's Riddle" is a term referring to the anomalous faunal assemblage of the Kem Kem beds of Morocco. This ecosystem, dating back approximately 95 million years during the Cretaceous, was home to an unusual abundance of predators. Among them, *Spinosaurus aegyptiacus* and *Carcharodontosaurus saharicus* were some of the largest ever to walk the earth. By comparison, fossils of herbivorous species are relatively sparse, forming the crux of "Stromer's Riddle" and the mystery of how the Kem Kem ecosystem was able to sustain its preponderance of apex predators. Named in honor of Ernst Stromer, a German paleontologist famous for some of the first fossil discoveries in Northern Africa, and the first to observe this phenomenon.

Anthropocene

1. Mitochondria

Mitochondria—the so-called "powerplants of the cell"—are organelles found in the cells of all eukaryotic organisms. Their primary function is cellular respiration and energy production. Mitochondria are unique in that they contain their own set of circular DNA, much like bacteria. Because of this, mitochondria are believed to have evolved around two billion years ago from a common ancestor with bacteria. The theory states that this common ancestor, an ancient intracellular protobacteria, evolved to form a symbiotic relationship that benefited both parasite and host. Indeed, genetic analysis has revealed the closest living relative of mitochondria to be *Rickettsia prowazekii*, the intracellular alpha protobacterium responsible for typhus.

2. Mitotransfection

"Mito-" stemming from "mitochondria."
"Transfection-" refers to the deliberate transfer of DNA into eukaryotic (e.g. animal) cells.

Through a process called conjugation—a bacteria's natural ability to transfer its genetic material to other bacteria—Mitogen's modified *Rickettsia* has been engineered to implant a desired DNA sequence into a host cell's mitochondria. The result is a dramatic boost in cellular function. In all head-to-head studies, mitotransfection was found to be superior to more crude methods like mitochondrial transfer. Mitogen's engineered *Rickettsia* also possesses the ability to assume a mitochondrial role within the cell—an endosymbiotic relationship akin to how mitochondria originally evolved some two billion years ago. This is especially critical in creating hybrids, which require mitochondria that are compatible with their cellular/nuclear (genomic) DNA in order to survive. Because organisms require two sets of DNA (mitochondrial and genomic), and because cloned species do not have parents to inherit mitochondria from, mitotransfection provides a critical step in bestowing first-generation hybrids with the mitonuclear compatibility they require to survive.

During the process, the engineered *Rickettsia* is intravenously infused into the host. Once it enters a host cell, the modified bacteria assumes that cell's mitochondrial functions. Artificial "Rickettsial" mitochondrial DNA can be tailored to suit the nuclear DNA of a host species while enhancing its cellular function.

Later iterations of Mitogen's engineered rickettsial "super mitochondria" possess the ability to replace mitochondrial function completely—with the added benefit of being able to replicate and propagate a limited number of times to neighboring cells. In this way, an organism's entire mitochondrial makeup can be altered in a matter of days. The latest generation can even modify a host cell's genomic DNA. Want blue eyes? No problem. Natural red hair? You got it. It's only a transfusion away.

3. The Cartagena Protocol on Biosafety

An international treatise established in 2003 limiting the transfer and use of living modified organisms (LMOs) across borders in order to protect the biodiversity from the potential harms of genetic engineering and modern biotechnology. For more information, see https://bch.cbd.int/protocol/text/.

PAN AVES

1. Environmental Protection Agency (U.S.) and European Food Safety Authority

Environmental Protection Agency (EPA)
Branch of the United States federal government responsible for enforcing environmental protection and regulation. It also monitors the impact of genetically modified organisms (GMOs) on local ecosystems. Compared to the Cartagena Protocol, biotechnology is loosely regulated in the United States. Most regulations pertain to genetically engineered microorganisms and crops, but the EPA also holds authority over other GMOs and invasive non-native species. Since resurrected animals are technically genetically engineered, and therefore "non-native," the EPA holds authority over the introduction of such species to the wild.

European Food Safety Authority (EFSA)
Regulatory agency of the European Union responsible for the monitoring food and environmental safety as they pertain to the food chain. They investigate and authorize GMO/LMO safety in genetically engineered plants, animals, and microbes, working in conjunction with the European Comission to draft and enforce policy around the potential risks of biotechnology to the food chain.

2. CRISPR-Cas (Figure 5.1)

CRISPR stands for "Clustered Regularly Interspaced Short Palindromic Repeats," unique sequences of DNA code found in the genomes of bacteria and archaea. Bacteria evolved CRISPR as a method for acquiring immunity against invading bacteriophages (viruses that infect bacteria). Once infected, the bacterium would employ a member of the CRISPR-associated Cas family of endonucleases: enzymes capable of unwinding and cutting potentially harmful foreign DNA, rendering it useless. By forming a complex with "guide" RNA encoded by the CRISPR-Cas9 gene, the Cas9 protein complex could zero in on a string of the invading virus's DNA with extreme precision, then inactivate it by cutting it.

These CRISPR sequences compose genes made up of repeating palindromes, like 5'GTTATTG'3, that read the same forward (in the 'five-prime' direction) and backward (in the 'three-prime' direction). Literary palindromes like "racecar" serve as a simple example, as does "do geese see God?" In a given CRISPR sequence, between these clusters of genetic palindromes, chunks of DNA matching short sections of viral DNA are interspaced as in the figure on next page.

These repeats encode "tracer RNA (tracrRNA)," which, when synthesized, helps the CRISPR-Cas complex find the target DNA. The sequence of palindromic repeats is interspaced—or interrupted—by "spacer DNA," which, in nature, is a segment of bacteriophage (viral) DNA that has been incorporated into the bacterial genome. The spacer DNA encodes "CRISPR RNA (crRNA)" that helps the CRISPR-Cas system recognize the invading viral DNA. Cas represents a family of CRISPR-associated genes encoding enzymatic proteins called helicases and nucleases. Helicases unwind the strands of double-stranded DNA, making the nucleotide sequence accessible for manipulation. This occurs naturally in all organisms during DNA replication, because the molecule must be "unwound" before it can be replicated. Nucleases are the enzymes responsible for cutting DNA. Mitogen's CRISPR-Cas17 complex is illustrated below, housed within the circular genome of its engineered *Rickettsia prowazekki*.

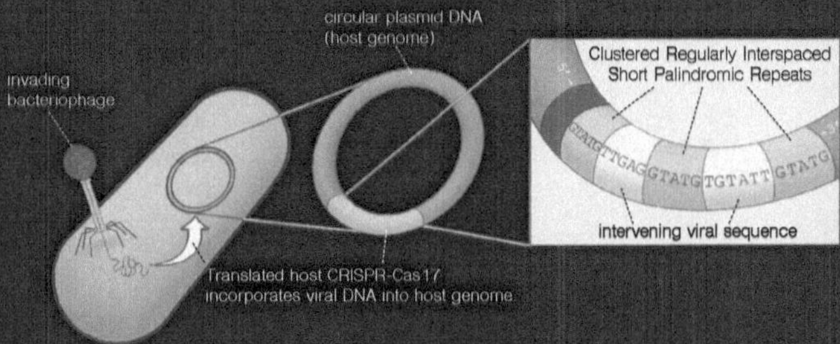

In the case of bacteria, the CRISPR-Cas system behaves as a form of innate immunity: when viral DNA enters the bacterium, the CRISPR-Cas complex recognizes it and cuts it at the specified target site, rendering the virus ineffective. The Cas genes also encode proteins that recognize new viral DNA, even if there is no match within the existing spacer DNA. Sections of this new viral DNA can then be spliced into the CRISPR gene, forming a "history" of past infections that can be used in the future. In genetic engineering, the tracer and spacer DNA is manipulated to form "guide RNA (gRNA)" and can be transfected into a host cell to inactivate a target gene (for example, a gene encoding hair color in a mouse). Since CRISPR-Cas also has the ability to insert new DNA sequences naturally with viral DNA in bacteria, it can also be manipulated to insert a desired gene into a host cell (instead of only turning off a gene for the mouse's hair color, we can replace it with a new gene encoding a different color).

Gene Editing Using CRISPR

The utility of CRISPR-Cas9 as gene-editing "molecular scissors" was first discovered by scientists in 2012. They found that they could engineer Cas9 from *Streptococcus pyogenes* to target a DNA sequence of their choosing by manipulating its guide RNA. After cutting a target sequence in this manner, they could effectively "switch off" a gene of interest the same way bacterial Cas9 could inactivate viral DNA. This modified CRISPR-Cas9 system could then be inserted into a eukaryotic cell where it would inactivate the desired genes. Initial applications switched off genes that inhibited lipid production in the algae *Alaria esculenta*, allowing for greater biofuel yields.

A few years later, out of Harvard, geneticist Jorge de la Iglesia further modified the CRISPR-Cas9 system to insert a new DNA sequence into the cleaved target DNA, effectively providing an organism with an entirely new gene—not silencing, but enhancing. Incidentally, Iglesia also went on to pioneer methods for cloning mammoth DNA, using CRISPR-Cas9, long before Mitogen's mammoths stalked Siberia. He even managed to bring embryos to term in artificial wombs decades before Mitogen's first successful clone. Iglesia's research formed the foundation on which the company developed its own artificial womb technology to facilitate the gestation of its mammalian hybrids.

Cloning Birds

The process of cloning extinct avian species is more complex. Mammals, for example, are relatively straightforward: extract an egg cell from a host species and replace its nuclear DNA with the climate-optimized genome of an extinct species. Then, via mitotransfection, replace the host cell's mitochondrial DNA with compatible engineered mitochondria. Stimulate meiosis and allow the egg to divide in culture until it becomes an embryo. Re-implant the egg into the surrogate of the host species. Or, as is typical at Mitogen, transfer it to an optimized synthetic womb.

But birds require an indirect approach. For one, the nucleus of a bird egg is challenging to identify—let alone extract from behind a hard shell and delicate yolk—and re-implanting it after the genomic transfer poses significant challenges. Instead, paleogeneticist Jerome Powell developed a technique involving modified embryonic germ cells called primordial germ cells, or PGCs for short. In bird development, these cells form in the germinal crescent of the shell before migrating to the yolk. From there, they enter the bloodstream and ultimately become the animal's sperm or egg cells. Because of this, PGCs are far more accessible and easier to extract than the embryonic nucleus.

To harvest PGCs, a small window is cut out of an egg's outer shell. Once extracted, these PGCs can be modified with ancient fDNA using a modified CRISPR protocol that utilizes a protein called Cas17 isolated from a novel species of deep-sea archaea, *Pyrococcus poseidus*. Dr. Powell's CRISPR-Cas17 complex contains the novel Deltadromeus HSP70 gene spliced into the genome of American bittern. Once grown in culture and subjected to mitotransfection, the engineered PGCs are re-implanted into the germinal crescent of the host egg. From there, they will develop further and migrate to the gonads of the growing embryo.

But that is merely the first step. A bittern-Delta hybrid, this hatchling is not., but rather the future *parent* of said hybrid—a chimera containing *two* complete genomes. In this case, this "future" parent is a *Eurasian* bittern surrogate with the sperm or egg cells of an engineered *American* bittern spliced with the heat-tolerant Deltadromeus HSP70 gene. Mating a male with a female chimera is the final step in the process of producing a thoroughbred, climate tolerant, de-extinct American bittern: *Botaurus powellus*. The first ever avian-dinosaur hybrid.

SUPERCOLLIDER

1. "*Shick*" is a derogatory term for synths, and is a phonetic expression of the acronym, SHC, which stands for *Synthetic Human Consciousness*. It has also been joked that it represents the sound made by a fresh synth coming off the production line. "Shick" was initially aimed at synths with uploaded minds—the digitized consciousness of real people, the dead reborn. In time, the word eventually came to include all synths, regardless of autonomy.

2. Athena is an artificial intelligence based on an existing network of collective human consciousness called Lucid. Those that choose to upload their minds into the Lucid platform will "live on" after death. Lucid functions as a vast social network in which friends and relatives of the deceased can continue to communicate with a digitized version of their consciousness. For the deceased, it is a utopian existence, at least for a while.

   The metadata from Lucid represents a collective consciousness that is continuously built upon and curated by Athena to construct and maintain her neural net. Involuntary mind harvesting is also a modus operandi of the UEF, in which those with desirable skill sets and intellect are "wired in" to Athena via neural chip implantation, thereby constantly feeding the system with "high-value" data.

LOOKING GLASS

1. Published abstract

Formation of the first-ever artificial Einstein-Rosen bridge ("wormhole") with implications for future applications in tunneling across space

Lotta Eklund, Bogdan Kazimierz, Hassan Kateb, Norah Van de Berg, and Mathis Devos
The European Organisation for Nuclear Research, 1211 Geneva, Switzerland

Abstract

Once thought to be an impossibility among quantum physicists, we have demonstrated that an Einstein-Rosen bridge is not only allowable by the laws of physics, but is also attainable with the energy resources and technology (i.e. supermassive particle accelerators) at our disposal today. While the traversability of such wormholes appears far off, we have nonetheless demonstrated that a quantumly entangled pair of black holes, referred to as ALICE and BOB, can be transiently merged by implementing the Casimir effect via quantum tunneling within Bose-Einstein condensate pairs. To date, this pair has been separated by a physical distance of 53.31 kilometers. Formation of a transient, scalable wormhole bends spacetime, reducing the traversed distance to mere millimeters within a fourth-order gravitational system. Paradoxically, this appears to violate the Null Energy Condition by avoiding the conventional restraints imposed by the quantum inequalities. Future investigations will attempt to tease apart the underlying mechanisms of this enigma of quantum mechanics.

RABBIT HOLE

1. Bottenviken
   Swedish for The Gulf of Bothnia, the northernmost branch of the Baltic Sea.

   After the cold snap, it disappeared beneath a perpetual sheet of ice.

Death's Shadow

1. Cretaceous mosquito, *Burmaculex antiquus*
2. Various sexually dimorphic species, primarily consisting of *Xericeps* and *Nicorhyncus*. See Bestiary.

Lamentation

1. Two of Fischer's daughters, Evi and Emma, were born with a knockout mutation of EPAS1 at birth, causing prematurity and requiring extensive ectogestational care and gene therapy to include re-insertion of EPAS1 after failure of this genetic modification during embryoselection.

   EPAS1 encodes a class of gene known as a so-called hypoxia-inducible factor. Its product is a protein encoded by a modified gene on chromosome 2 responsible for up-regulating red blood cell and hemoglobin production in a low-oxygen state. The trait is beneficial in environments with low oxygen, as well as low-oxygen states that may arise from anemia, cardiac arrest, plural effusion, and pulmonary embolism. EPAS1 is a unique allele first isolated from a group of Tibetan monks during the twenty-first century, and was an adaptation that had been acquired and passed down through generations of high-altitude living. For survival, wildtype Homo sapiens required an atmospheric oxygen concentration of around twenty percent prior to 2075 when Earth's atmospheric oxygen dipped below seventeen percent. Consequently, EPAS1 was implemented into a growing suite of genetic modifications that gave rise to modern embryonic genetic engineering meant to mitigate the challenges posed by a post-industrial climate.

2. Beetle, *Osteocallis mandibulus*. Beetles were the primary pollinators of the Cretaceous before bees took over. Osteocallis is a form of boring beetle, laying its eggs on rotting carcasses and in some cases festering wounds. Its larvae bore into the bones upon hatching.

3. Bee, *Melittosphex burmensis*. Bees evolved from carnivorous wasps during the mid-Cretaceous, and eventually evolved into pollinators.

Eve

1. Basic Local Alignment Search Tool (BLAST). An algorithm that identifies regions of similarity in DNA, RNA, or protein sequences between organisms, drawing from a centralized database. This aids in species identification, taxonomic stratification, and the evaluation of evolutionary relationships between species.

2. Note on art plate (p. 340): this version has been modified from the original. To view Steve White's original work, please visit www.tomashernovels.com/necropsy.

Article Excerpt from Methods in Molecular Paleontology:

Scientists Have Brought Us Closer to Resurrecting Dinosaurs—an Overview of Molecular Paleontology (opinion)

By Caleb Lynch

The subspeciality of paleogenomics—which combines biochemistry, genetics, and paleontology—got its start after renowned paleontologist Dr. Meridith Schwartz discovered soft tissue remains in an exquisitely preserved *T. rex* femur in 2008. Dr. Schwartz found that such endosteal soft tissues could be preserved through deep time by a natural process involving *iron oxide* formation. This chemical pathway fundamentally alters the native structure of biomolecules—like proteins and lipids—by generating crosslinks that shield soft tissues from degradation. It is, therefore, no small coincidence that most tissues isolated from well-preserved specimens are vascular networks containing iron-rich blood.

Over two decades ago, the torch was passed on to her daughter, also a paleontologist, Dr. Amara Schwartz.

Think "mummification" on a molecular level...
How this type of soft tissue preservation works: iron exists in the hemoglobin molecule as Fe^{2+}, which is thermodynamically unstable. In death, it rapidly oxidizes to the more stable Fe^{3+} configuration by binding to various amino acid residues in proteins, like collagen and elastin. Schwartz et al have found this is also true for histone, an important protein that winds and packages DNA into the nucleus of a cell. Consequently, iron-bound histones shield the DNA from degradation after cell death. Subsequent iron-catalyzed glycation—the fusing of long-chain sugars to these molecules—leads to the formation of advanced glycation end products, or AGEs, which protects the histone-DNA complex further. These chemically-driven processes persist post-mortem, generating a mechanism by which biomolecules can be preserved through deep time. Red blood cells—which contain cell nuclei in dinosaurs just as they do in modern birds—hold the greatest promise for isolating this 'fossil DNA,' or 'fDNA.' Remember, blood vessels are the most commonly preserved tissues found in these fossils.

Despite this fascinating mechanism, fDNA is fundamentally altered. First, it is heavily fragmented, especially in regions not adequately shielded from degradation by DNases (DNA-degrading enzymes) post-mortem. Second, sections of the fDNA phosphate backbone are dimerized—fused—making it difficult to read during sequencing. Over time, cytosine bases spontaneously deaminate into uracil, and methyl groups alter its structure further. Finally, DNA-DNA and DNA-histone crosslinks pose unique challenges for the extraction and sequencing of the sample. In the end, fDNA resembles the original DNA molecule to an extent but is chemically modified in a way that preserves it for *millions* of years. Some of these modifications are easy to work around when sequencing an ancient genome. Others are not. Because of these heavy chemical alterations, fDNA is a mere shadow of its native structure, so the amount of genetic information gleaned from it is often limited.

But Amara Schwartz et al didn't stop there. They asked: is it possible to 'reverse engineer' these modifications and arrive at something resembling the native DNA molecule? And if so, how complete will the genetic sequence be?

"Recent advances in Fourier ptychography enable us to image individual atoms on or within a substrate—a technique that happens to work extremely well with fDNA," Schwartz says. "In conjunction with automated, next-generation quantum computing algorithms, we can rapidly stitch together an entire fDNA molecule imaged this way, repair the errors, and digitally re-assemble it into one continuous DNA strand. High throughput sequencing of this raw data generates the final DNA sequence, which can be synthesized and studied in our highly specialized lab."

While these techniques bridge much of the gap between fDNA and a completed, workable DNA molecule, many errors are still present in the assembled and repaired sequence.

"These gaps are repaired with the genome of a common living ancestor," Schwartz continues. "In our case, extant junglefowl. Using these novel methods, we have attempted to sequence the complete genome of *Deltadromeus agilis*, and I believe we have succeeded."

Deltadromeus, a megaraptoran distantly related to *T. rex*, hails from Cenomanian Morrocco. The species went extinct 95 million years ago and belongs to a lineage that eventually gave rise to modern birds.

Will the dinosaur see the modern era?
Schwartz scoffs. "We are not in the business of generating novelties. This science is geared toward preserving modern-day dinosaurs—birds—who cannot adapt quickly enough to the ongoing climate crisis. *Deltadromeus* endured extreme climate change during the Cenomanian-Turonian oceanic anoxic event in the late Cretaceous and its genetic makeup is already shedding light on how we might genetically alter modern-day birds to do the same amid human-accelerated climate change."

So, no theme park?
She laughs, shakes her head. "No theme park."
Drats.

BESTIARY

THE PLEISTOCENE PROJECT
(Siberia)

Mammuthus asiaticus

LENGTH 7.8 m, HEIGHT 4.3 m (25 x 14 ft). Large proboscid, a hybrid of the extinct *Mammuthus trogontherii* (Steppe mammoth, from the Pleistocene epoch, Eurasia) and *Elephas maximus* (Asian elephant, extirpated as of 2038). Like extant elephants, mammoths are grazers and browsers. Resurrected Steppe mammoths, however, lack a key enzyme for degrading some extant Siberian grasses, opting instead to feed on other plants, like bark from larch trees. Because of their mineral needs, mammoths engage in pica and will eat soils and clays for minerals. This makes them a prime vector for *Mycobacterium tuberculosis.* VOICE trumpeting call, deep-chested roar. HABITAT Siberian steppe FAMILY Elephantidae

Coelodonta excitatur

LENGTH 3.8 m, height 2.1 m (12.5 x 7 ft). Fur-covered rhinoceros, a hybrid of the extinct *Coelodonta antiquitatis* (woolly rhino, from the Pleistocene epoch, Eurasia) and the extirpated *Ceratotherium simum* (southern white rhino, Southern Africa). Like their recently extinct counterparts, woolly rhinos are generally docile graz-ers, though they have been known to be unpredictable. Simi-lar to mammoths, they have some difficulty processing modern grasses, driving them to migrate in search of more palatable fare. VOICE deep-chested bellow, squeal, trumpet HABITAT Siberian steppe FAMILY Rhinocerotidae

Smilodon pardus

LENGTH 1.8 m, HEIGHT 1.3 m (4.9 x 4.2 ft). Large felid, a hybrid of the extinct *Smilodon fatalis* (sabre-toothed cat, from the Pleistocene epoch, North America) and *Panthera uncia* (snow leopard, Central and South Asia). *Smilodons* are very hostile toward humans, an unexpected trait that arises from ancient competition with man for resources. They possess two enormous, recurved canines that deliver a devastatiting, bacteria-ridden bite. Most prey succumb to internal hemorrhaging long before infection sets in. *Smilodon* hybrids also retain many traits of snow leopards, including a long bushy tail, spots, and exceptional cold tolerance. VOICE growl, hiss, sawing roar HABITAT Siberian steppe FAMILY Felidae

PROJECT LAZARUS
(United States of America)

Botaurus powellus

LENGTH 33 cm, HEIGHT 23cm (1.1 x 0.75 ft). Small heron (wading bird). Revived hybrid of the extinct *Botaurus lentiginosus*, in a first for avian species. Its greatest significance, however, is that it is also the first avian-dinosaur hybrid, using the ancient DNA of *Deltadromeus agilis* in an effort to make the species more heat-tolerant amid the changing climate (among other advantages). VOICE ticking, booming "pump-er-lunk" HABITAT North American freshwater wetlands FAMILY Ardeidae

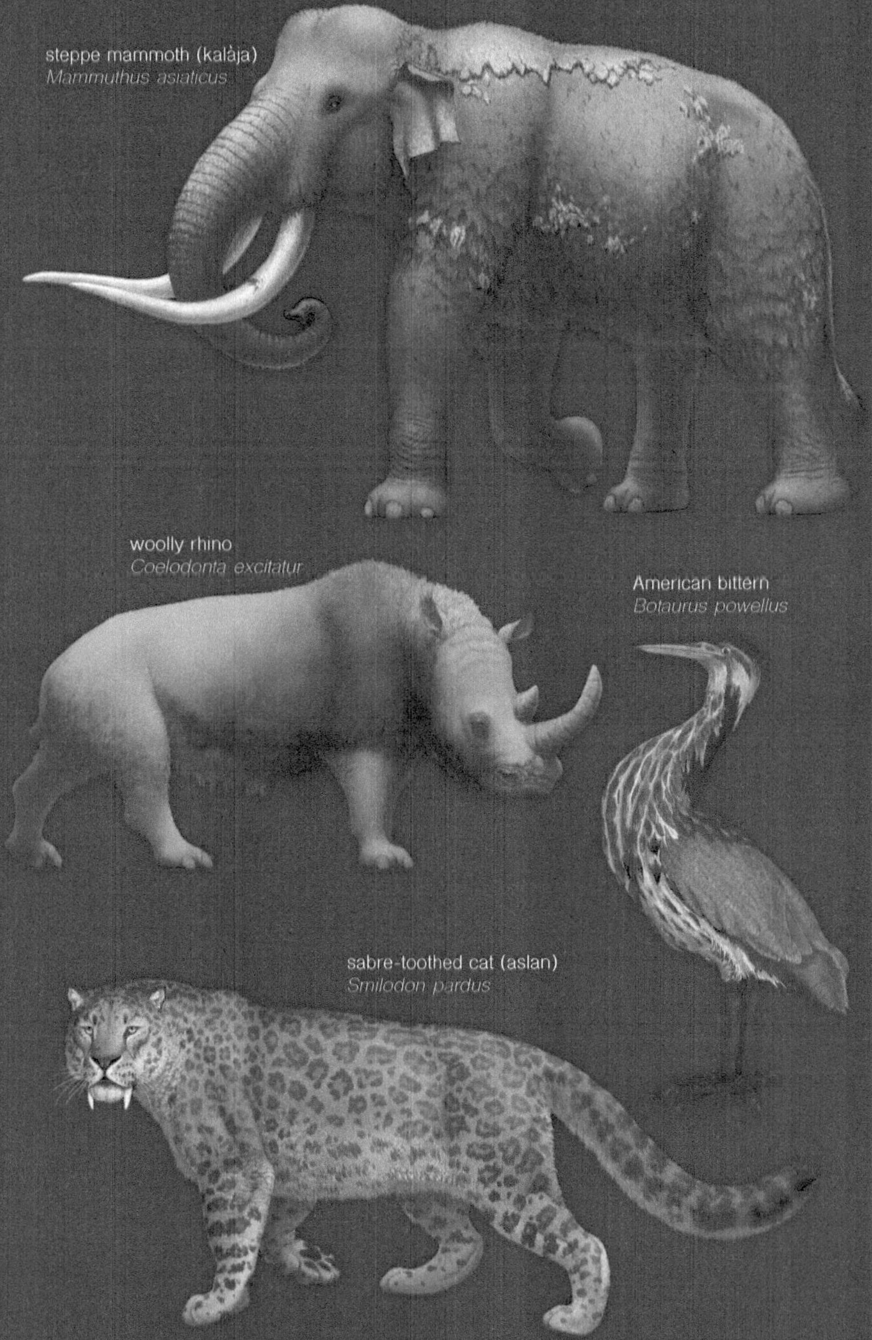

steppe mammoth (kalàja)
Mammuthus asiaticus
woolly rhino
Coelodonta excitatur
American bittern
Botaurus powellus
sabre-toothed cat (aslan)
Smilodon pardus

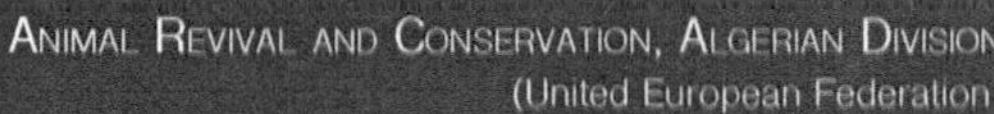

Aenocyon lupus

LENGTH 2.6 m, HEIGHT 1.2 m (8.5 x 4.2 ft). Large canid, a hybrid of the extinct *Aenocyon dirus* (dire wolf, from the Pleistocene epoch, Americas, Eastern Asia) and the extirpated *Canis lupus* (Mackenzie wolf, North America). Contrary to their common name, ancient dire wolves were, in fact, not closely related to wolves and belong to the genus *Aenocyon*. Consequently, the North American dire wolf rewilding initiative was eventually abandoned due to the infertility of resurrected dire wolves. The creation of these hybrids was the result of ignorance on the part of the investigators, though later genetic engineering endeavors would eventually make this possible across genera. VOICE howl, growl, whimper   HABITAT North America FAMILY Canidae

Struthioveritas dinosaurum

LENGTH 1.6 m, HEIGHT 1.8 m to hip (4.8 x 5.4 ft). Large flightless ratite, a hybrid of the once endangered *Struthio camelus* (North African ostrich) and the extinct non-avian theropod *Deltadromeus agilis* (North Africa, 95Ma). Like many avian hybrids containing ancient DNA, ostriches in recent decades have been the subject of intense study due to a propensity toward genetic drift, in which alleles conducive to the changing climate become dominant. As it turns out, previously silenced Deltadromeus phenotypes have proven the most resiliant, and many ratites sport vestigial tails, digits, and crests. VOICE high-pitched screech, mimicry   HABITAT African Savanna, grasslands   ORDER Struthiorniformes

Excinereum dinornicus

LENGTH 2.6 m, HEIGHT 2.4 m to hip (7.8 x 7.2 ft). Large flightless ratite, a hybrid of the extinct *Dinornis robustus* (moa, 1300 BC, New Zealand's South Island) and the extinct non-avian theropod *Deltadromeus agilis* (North Africa, 95Ma). Extirpated from their native New Zealand, moa are once again on the verge of extinction. Where in colonial times, they were hunted by man, modern moa are threatened by rising sea levels that have all but wiped out their native Beech-forest habitat. Conservation efforts have yielded little in the way of preserving this critically re-endangered species. VOICE resonant, low-frequency warble   HABITAT New Zealand beech-forest   ORDER Dinornithiformes   NATURAL PREDATORS Haast's eagle (Ex)

dire wolf
Aenocyon lupus
ostrich
Struthioveritas dinosaurum
"Kaia"
♀ adult
"Iwa"
♀ sub-adult
(aberrant form)
moa
Excinereum dinornicus

DINOSAURIA
[Sauropoda]

Paralititan stromeri

LENGTH 32 m, HEIGHT 11 m (105 x 36.1 ft). Colossal sauropod that feeds primarily on the treetops of auraucarian conifers. These animals are so large that they are themselves mobile ecosystems, harboring a plethora of fauna including pterosaurs, insects, and parasites. They can lay huge clutches, subsequently replacing depleted calcium stores through geophagy. The calcium-rich gastroliths they consume can sustain physiologic Calcium levels through the breeding season. Like other titanosaurs, they are considered poor parents, abandoning their young soon after they hatch. To survive, hatchlings must quickly take to the shelter of nearby forests and, eventually, join a herd. VOICE deep-chested bellow, almost subsonic   HABITAT wooded marshland, fluvial environments   CLADE Titanosauria

Rebbachisaurus garasbae

LENGTH 20 m, HEIGHT 5 m (65.6 x 16.4 ft). "Brontosaurus" is a misnomer, but a common nickname because of its similar morphology to its apatosaurine cousin. These sauropods are low browsers, preferring to graze on ferns, horsetails, and angiosperms. Their barbed tails can break the sound barrier like a whip, a potent and occasionally lethal defense against possible threats. The tail tip is capped with a long cord of keratin capable of breaking away and embedding into its target. Tail tips generally regrow within a month, and the degree of tale-kinking in bulls serves as a visual tally of past ruts and sexual fitness.   VOICE low, rumbling bellow   HABITAT fluvial environments   SUPERFAMILY Diplodocoidea

behemoth
♀ Paralititan stromeri
brontosaurus
♂ Rebbachisaurus garasbae

Dinosauria
[Theropoda]

Rugops primus
LENGTH 4.4 m, HEIGHT 1.8 m (14.4 x 5.8 ft). Opportunistic, often scavenging carrion or taking down weak or injured prey. *Rugops* has a particular affinity for rotting flesh. On occasion, they may resort to cannibalism. HABITAT woodland (Björn exclusively), open tidal flats along fluvial systems (typical morphotype). FAMILY Abelisauridae

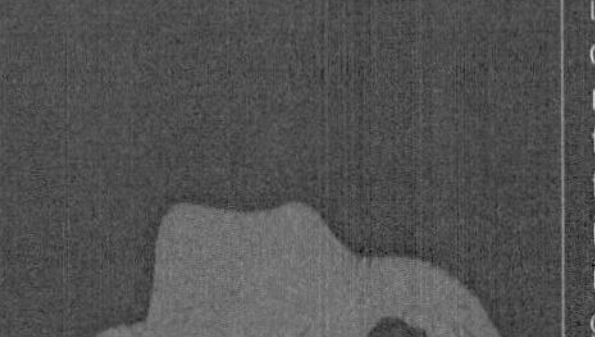

Spinosaurus aegyptiacus
LENGTH 16 m, HEIGHT 5.5 m to sail tip (52.5 x 18 ft). Shoreline specialist feeding primarily on large fish along river deltas or coastal regions. *Spinosaurus's* primary hunting technique involves wading through the shallows, dipping its pressure-sensitive snout beneath the water's surface, and waiting for prey to swim past. Aside from its social function, the sail serves two primary purposes: (1) it aids in attracting prey by creating a shaded region in the water that generates a false sense of refuge, and (2) it reduces glare from the surface, optimizing *Spinosaurus's* view into the water. The tail provides a barrier from escape and can corral prey toward the animal's waiting snout and arms. Once snatched, *Spinosaurus's* prey is immediately incapacitated by way of dismemberment, utilizing its powerful jaws and enormous claws. HABITAT open tidal flats along fluvial systems. FAMILY Spinosauridae

Carcharodontosaurus saharicus
LENGTH 12 m, HEIGHT 4 m (39.4 x 13.1 ft). Apex predator. *Carcharodontosaurus* often hunts in coordinated pairs or groups, using a variety of tactics like ambushing and flanking prey. Once bitten, the anticoagulative properties of *Carcharodontosaurus* saliva lead to accelerated blood loss and internal bleeding in prey. In addition to peptides that inhibit blood clotting, their saliva also contains agents that promote muscle paralysis and hypotension. These properties slow their prey, allowing for energy conservation while stalking and taking down large quarries. HABITAT woodland, open tidal flats along fluvial systems. FAMILY Carcharodontosauridae

LENGTH , HEIGHT

HABITAT
CLADE

Rahonavis indet.
♂ LENGTH ~70cm, HEIGHT ~25cm (2.3 x 0.8 ft). Small, bird-like theropod of enigmatic taxonomy, possibly a basal avialan serving as an evolutionary link between dromaeosaurids and enantiornithes. *Rahonavis* possesses a high degree of intelligence, displaying behaviors like bating fish with insects, tool wielding, and advanced social behavior similar to that of its avian descendants. Like dromaeosaurids, it possesses a sickled toe claw on each foot, which it utilizes for climbing trees and pinning prey. VOICE melodic warble HABITAT coniferous woodlands, karst environments CLADE Maniraptora

specimen DN1451.21 (♀Eve, ♂Adam)
specimen with
anomalous burns
Björn
♂Rugops primus
Leviathan/Mother
♀Spinosaurus aegyptiacus
jötunn (♂Aurgelmir, ♀Ymir)
Carcharodontosaurus saharicus
raptor
♂Rahonavis indet.

Dinosauria
[Theropoda]

Confuciusornis indet.

♂ LENGTH ~40cm, HEIGHT ~15cm (1.3 x 0.5 ft). Primarily arboreal avialan closely related to enantiornithes (North Africa, 95Ma). A beaked, toothless relative of modern birds, they are intelligent and curious. Males are notable for their long, iridescent tail plumage, feathered crowns, and bright coloration. Their diet consists primarily of insects, but they also scavenge whenever the opportunity arises and may even roost in carcasses for weeks or months on end. VOICE shrill chirrup HABITAT coniferous woodlands CLADE Pygostylia

Pterosauria

Nicorhynchus fluviferox

♂ FLIGHT LENGTH 2.7m (9 ft beak tip to toe), GROUND HEIGHT 1.5m (5 ft), WINGSPAN 6m (19.7 ft). Primarily piscivorous, large pterosaur (North Africa, 95Ma) with rows of needle-like teeth ideal for snagging fish by way of skimming its beak beneath water while gliding above the surface. This differentiates *Nicorhynchus* from other pterosaurs, which exhibit diving behavior. Hydrophopic plumage enables this species to easily land and rest on water, enabling prolonged marine habitation. While they are primarily coastal-dwelling, they often make their way inland along river deltas and estuaries to roost and mate. VOICE deep, sustained, sawtooth squall. HABITAT open water, coastal and fluvial environments FAMILY Ornithocheiridae

Afrotapejara zouhri

♂ FLIGHT LENGTH 1.9m (6.2 ft beak tip to toe), GROUND HEIGHT 1.5m (4.9 ft), WINGSPAN 5.3m (17.3 ft). Mid-sized pterosaur with a prominent keel-shaped crest, earning it the "keelhead" moniker. *Afrotapejara* (North Africa, 95Ma) is opportunistic, often scavenging prey or engaging in kleptoparasitism, coordinating in groups to harass other predators into surrendering their quarry. Like other pterosaurs, they are covered in down-like monofilaments, with the more colorful males sporting ornate tale plumage. VOICE vibrating caterwaul HABITAT mudflats, coastal and fluvial environments FAMILY Tapejaridae

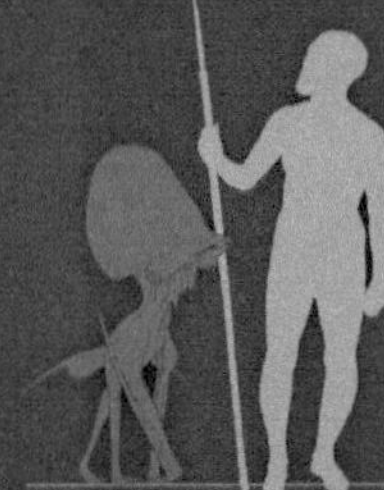

Xericeps curvirostris

♂ FLIGHT LENGTH 6m (19.7 ft beak tip to toe), GROUND HEIGHT 1.6m (5.2 ft), WINGSPAN 5.2m (17.1 ft). Known for its distinctive upturned beak, this species of pterosaur (North Africa, 95Ma) is a fishing specialist, diving into water to snatch its prey. *Xericeps* is also an opportunist, often scavenging carrion along river deltas and mudflats. VOICE deep, sustained trill (often melodic). HABITAT mudflats, river deltas, sabkha environments CLADE Neoazhdarchia

Leptostomia begaaensis

♂ FLIGHT LENGTH 16.5cm (6.5in beak tip to toe), GROUND HEIGHT 12.5cm (5in), WINGSPAN 20cm (7.9in). Small azhdarchoid pterosaur (North Africa, 95Ma). VOICE adults are silent/hatchlings and fledglings produce a high-pitched screech. HABITAT coniferous woodlands, by streams and riverbanks CLADE Azhdarchoidea

fae/ribbon tail
♂ Confuciusornis indet.

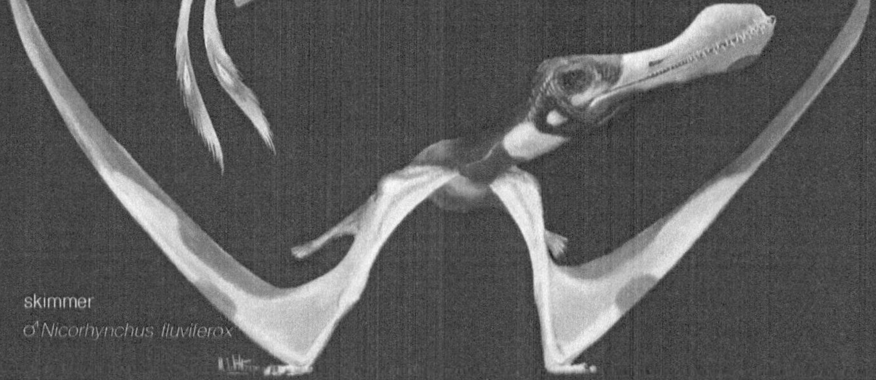

skimmer
♂ Nicorhynchus fluviferox

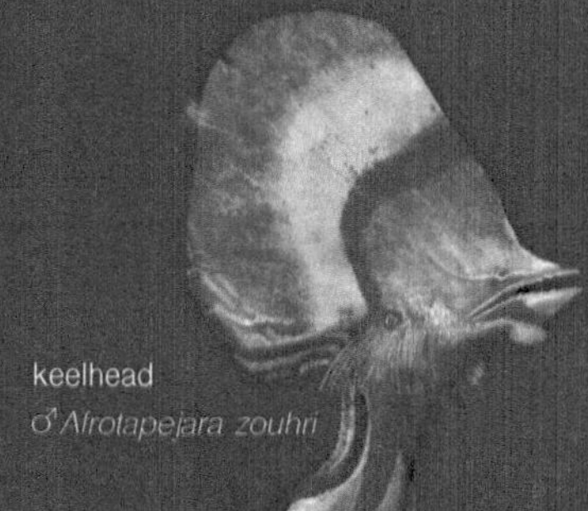

keelhead
♂ Afrotapejara zouhri

scimitar beak
♂ Xericeps curvirostris

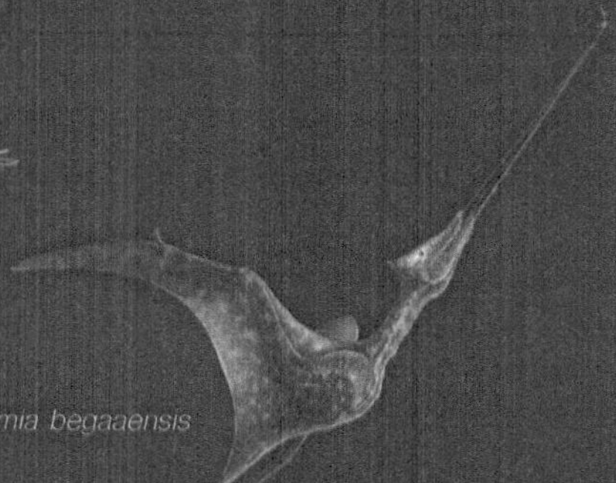

hummer
Leptostomia begaaensis

Pterosauria

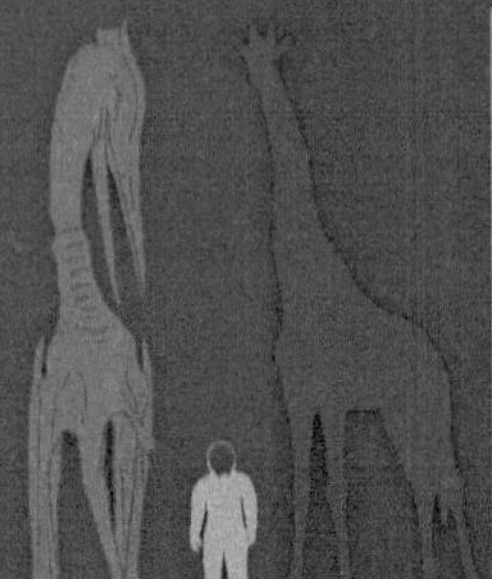

Alanqa saharica

♂ FLIGHT LENGTH 8.5m (27.9 ft beak tip to toe), GROUND HEIGHT 7m (23 ft), WINGSPAN 11m (36 ft). Enormous azhdarchid pterosaur (North Africa, 95Ma). Prior to the discovery of a giant specimen by paleontologist Qadir Nassar in the mid-2030s, *Alanqa* was thought to be a mid-sized pterosaur with a maximum ground height of around 3 m (9 ft). Their bodies are covered in short down-like monofilaments, with longer plumage at the tip of their tails. Males are larger and possess a colorful crest, as well as longer tail plumage. Predatory tactics include foraging for small or injured animals on the ground, and they will occasionally incapacitate large prey by taking to the sky and dropping it from a lethal height. VOICE rapid, clattering beak/throaty, deep hooting. HABITAT grasslands, open plains, sabkha environments CLADE Azhdarchoidea

Apatorhamphus gyrostega

♂ FLIGHT LENGTH 2m (6.6 ft beak tip to toe), GROUND HEIGHT 1.3m (4.3 ft), WINGSPAN 5m (16.4 ft). small to mid-sized azhdarchoid immediately recognizable by its disproportionately large head. These pterosaurs specialize in foraging and fishing for their prey, with a proclivity for hard-shelled provisions (crabs, mollusks). HABITAT mudflats along fluvial systems, karst environments FAMILY Chaoyangopteridae

Pseudosuchia

Elosuchus cherifiensis

LENGTH 6 m (19.7 ft). Large false gharial. This freshwater crocodilian is characterized by its long, slender snout. As a generalist, *Elosuchus* subsists on a variety of provisions, including fish, terrestrial fauna (with an affinity for ambushing slow or sick animals along shoreline regions), water-faring pterosaurs (sub-aquatic ambush), and carrion. HABITAT fluvial environments, swamp forests, marshes FAMILY Pholidosauridae

Araripesuchus rattoides

LENGTH 1 m (3.3 ft). Small notosuchian. These rat-sized crocodyliformes are most active at night, aided in hunting rodents, small reptiles, and insects by their large, dark-adapted eyes. Their long legs and unique, upright posture are optimal for short bursts of speed, enabling them to efficiently take down quick prey. This unique feature among crocodyliformes has enabled their niche as primarily terrestrial, and as a result they spend very little time in or around water. HABITAT karst environments along fluvial systems. FAMILY Uruguaysuchidae

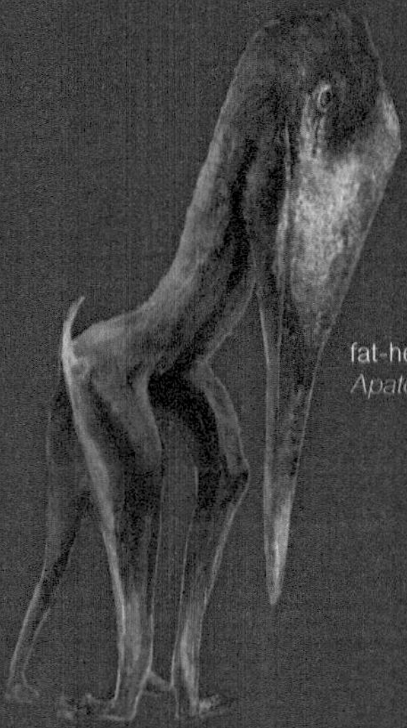

fat-headed bird ape
Apatorhamphus gyrostega

rat croc
Araripesuchus rattoides

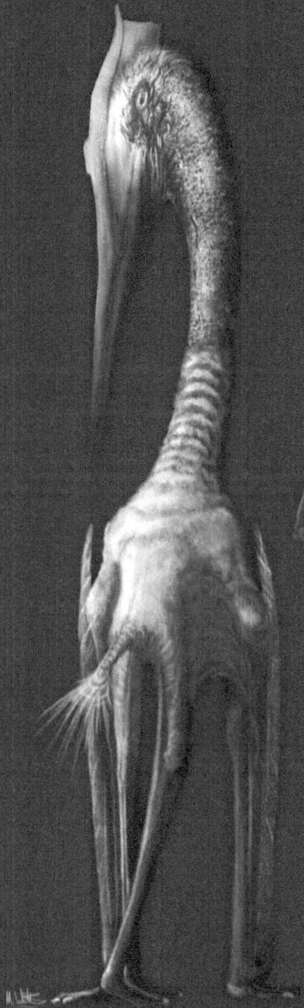

stalker/valkyrie
♂ *Alanqa saharica*

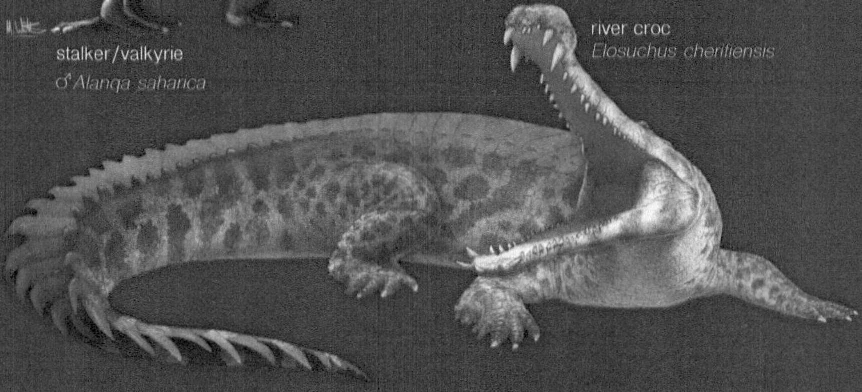

river croc
Elosuchus cherifiensis

LEPIDOSAURIA

Simoliophis libycus
LENGTH 1.5 m (4.9 ft). Venomous hind-limbed snake. A pair of vestigial legs at the caudal region of the body serve little functionality outside of mating in which pairs will interlock with each other to stabilize aquatic coital activity. Males possess brightly colored limbs. Nests are often established under the shelter of mangrove and fern pneumatophores (e.g. Weichselia) HABITAT marine environments, freshwater environments along fluvial systems (breeding, hydration). FAMILY Simoliophiidae

Uromastyx indet.
LENGTH 0.7 m (2.3 ft). Acrodontan lizard. These small iguanians are herbivorous, with a particular affinity for magnolias. They are therefore a keystone species critical to pollination and seed dispersal within a given ecosystem. Nesting sites are typically housed within underground burrows joined by a complex network of tunnel systems. HABITAT woodlands, fluvial environments. FAMILY Agamidae (of the suborder Iguania)

SAUROPTERYGIA

Leptocleidus indet.
LENGTH 3 m (9.8 ft). Small plesiosaur. These fast swimmers possess rows of needle-like teeth that enable them to easily snag fish. As apex predators, they often travel in pairs or small groups, corralling and neutralizing their prey with startling efficiency. HABITAT marine environments (brackish or freshwater for breeding). FAMILY Leptocleididae

TESTUDINIDAE

Hamadachelys escuellei
LENGTH 0.6 m (2.0 ft). 1 m (3.3 ft) with neck extended. Omnivorous, long-necked, freshwater turtle. HABITAT fluvial systems, ponds, marshes CLADE Pan-pleurodira

AMPHIBIA

Oumtkoutia anae
LENGTH 6 cm (2.4 in). Aquatic frog with flattened body and webbed feet. HABITAT ponds, karst environments along fluvial systems. FAMILY Pipidae

Kababisha humarensis
LENGTH 0.3 m (1 ft). omnivorous sirenid salamander with eel-like morphology and possessing a pair of very small forelimbs. Food sources include insects, algae, and snails. They possess gills in their larval stage, but rely on well-developed lungs once mature. HABITAT ponds, mudflats, marshes, karst environments along fluvial systems. FAMILY Sirenidae

iguana
Uromastyx indet.
hindlimbed snake
Simoliophis libycus
pond turtle
Hamadachelys escuellei
plesiosaur/seaserpent/siren
Leptocleidus indet.
salamander
Kababisha humarensis
frog
Oumtkoutia anae

Osteichthyes

Axelrodichthys lavocati
LENGTH 2.4 m (8 ft). Giant coelacanth (lobe-finned fish) that catches its prey through suction and swallows it whole. Both sets of pectoral and pelvic fins are adjoined to the skeleton by bones, forming limb-like stalks with swimming fins situated at their terminus. Similar structures gave rise to the limbs of the first land-dwelling tetrapods, which evolved from a common ancestor during the Devonian era. HABITAT marine, brackish, and fluvial environments. CLADE Sarcopterygii

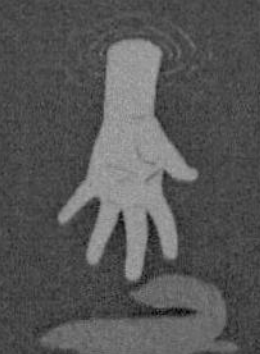

Arganodus indet.
LENGTH 0.3 m (1 ft). mid-sized freshwater lungfish. These fish possess an affinity for enclosed shelter, owing to their burrowing instinct during the dry season. Another adaptation enhancing their survival is the ability to breathe air utilizing a set of lungs, which further prolongs survival during periods of water scarcity, and secondarily to aid their ability to escape predation from land or air. HABITAT karst environments along fluvial systems, ponds. CLASS Dipnoi

Dentilepisosteus kemkemensis
LENGTH 0.2 m (0.7 ft). Gar fish possessing a distinctive ventral spine. Limited ability to respire air via their swim bladders, but to a lesser extent than lungfish. Rows of needle-like teeth are effective at catching passing prey with a lateral swipe of the head. HABITAT primarily freshwater (ponds, lakes), karst environments and brackish water along fluvial systems, marine environments. CLADE Ginglymodi

Spinocaudichthys oumtkoutensis
LENGTH 7.6cm (3 in). teleost fish with collapsable spined ray fins. In particular, the dorsal fin, when dispatched, expands a row of sharp spines that serve as a defensive mechanism against pred-ation. Collapsing these fins also enables for a speedy escape by reducing drag through the water. HABITAT karst environments along fluvial systems, freshwater ponds. CLADE Acanthomorpha

Chondrichthyes

Onchopristis numidus
LENGTH 5 m (16.4 ft). Large sawskate ray with an elongated rostrum adorned with sharp lateral teeth resembling that of modern sawfish. The "saw" apparatus is used primarily in catching small fish by thrashing the head laterally, or as a burrowing tool to conceal the body for the purposes of ambushing prey or evading predation itself. In some instances, the saw may also serve as an effective defense mechanism against predation by animals like Spinosaurus. HABITAT coastal and fluvial environments. CLASS Chondrichthyes

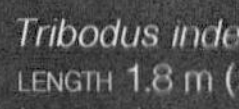

Tribodus indet.
LENGTH 1.8 m (5.9 ft). Shark-like chondrichthyan. While they specialize in preying upon hard-shelled mollusks like small ammonites, they are also opportunistic generalists. HABITAT marine and fluvial environments (both freshwater and brackish). Eggs are laid primarily in freshwater. CLADE Euselachii

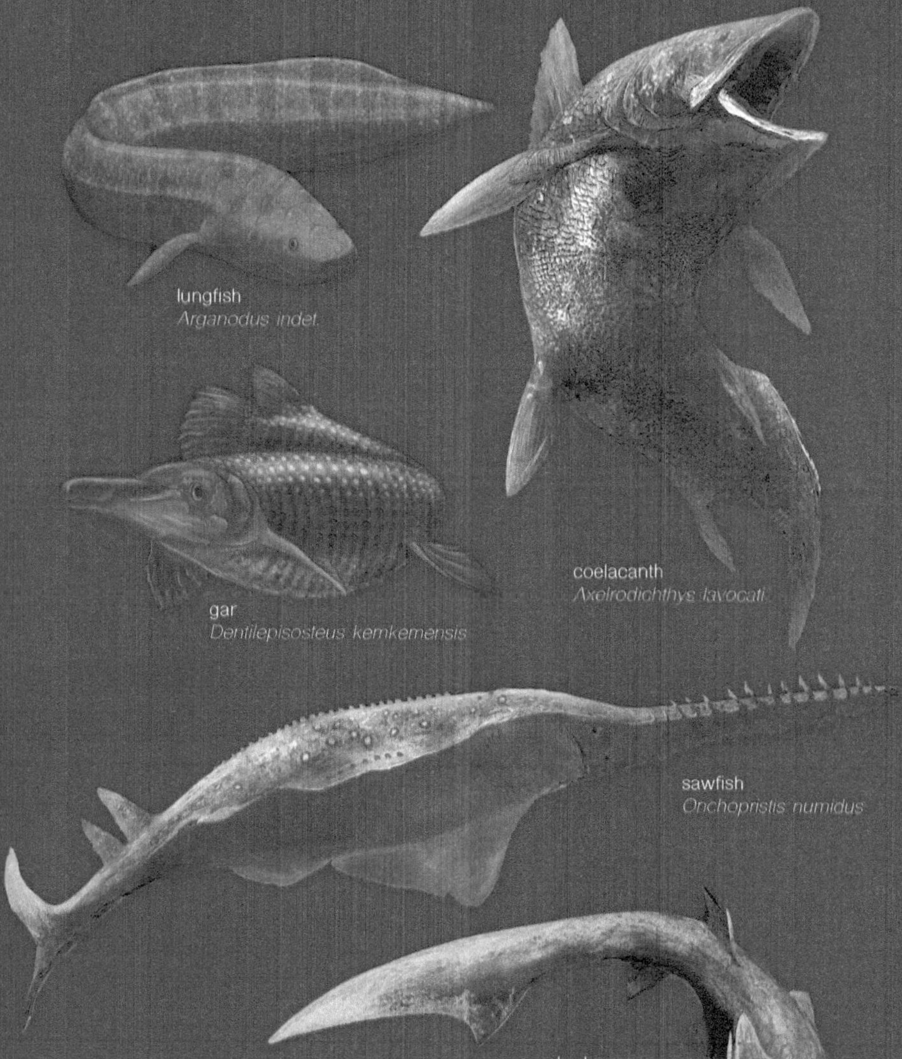

lungfish
Arganodus indet.

coelacanth
Axelrodichthys lavocati

gar
Dentilepisosteus kemkemensis

sawfish
Onchopristis numidus

perch
Spinocaudichthys oumtkoutensis

shark
Tribodus indet.

Arthropoda

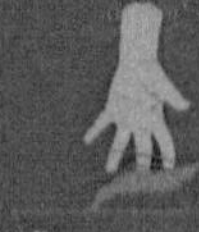

Cretapenaeus berberus
LENGTH 10 cm (3.9 in), excluding antennae. Freshwater prawn.
HABITAT karst environments along fluvial systems. CLASS Malacostraca

Burmaculex antiquus
LENGTH 2.5mm (0.1 in). Mosquito.
HABITAT widespread. FAMILY Culicidae

Osteocallis mandibulus
LENGTH 0.15mm (0.006 in). Osteophagic boring beetle. Nests primarily in the bones of carcasses. Larvae consume the surrounding bone until maturation. Adults are pollinators, with an affinity for the scent of magnolias, which mimic the beetle's natural mating pheromones to draw them in during mating season. HABITAT widespread. CLADE Coleopterida

Melittosphex burmensis
LENGTH 3mm (0.118 in). Primitive carnivorous bee (aculeate wasp) with an affinity for carrion, although it may also engage in predation when encountering injured or dying wildlife. By swarming its quarry, it can easily overcome prey of almost any size. "Meat honey" is a biproduct of its feeding habits (meat instead of nectar), which nourishes the hive's larvae. HABITAT widespread. ORDER Hymenoptera

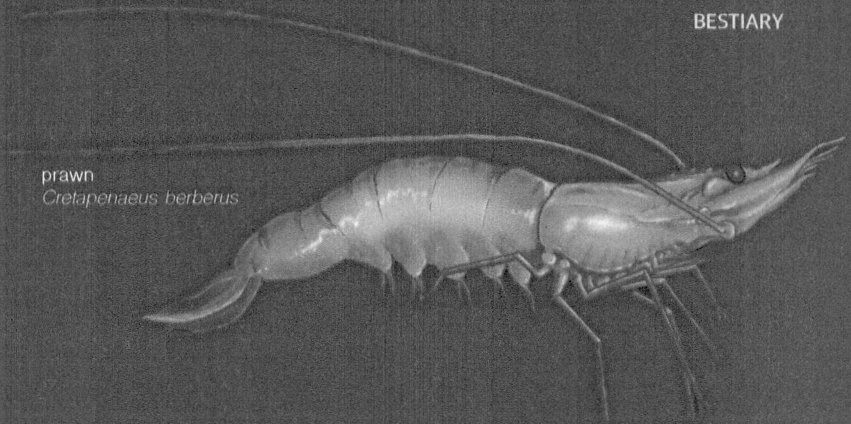

prawn
Cretapenaeus berberus

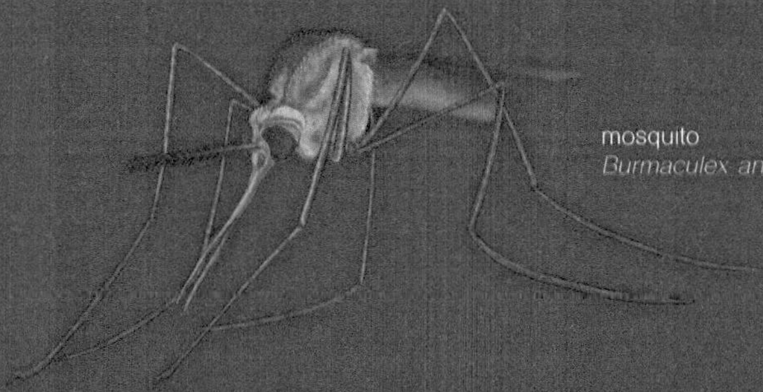

mosquito
Burmaculex antiquus

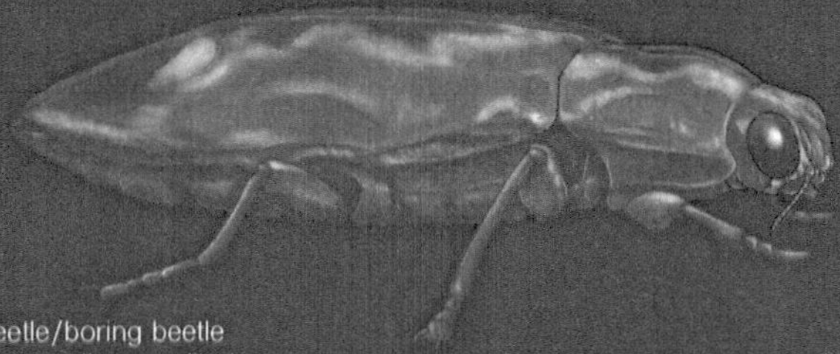

beetle/boring beetle
Osteocallis mandibulus

carnivorous bee/blood wasp
Melittosphex burmensis

May 15, 2025
Sacramento, CA
United States of America

AUTHOR'S NOTE

RIFT was bookended in heartbreak. Its inception was born out of sorrow, and—in the eleventh hour—its completion was nearly a casualty of it. But, in the end, it helped me navigate the tumult of a shattered reality. Got me through the fear of uncertainty, the agony of losing something dear, and the process of letting go. This tome is more than science fiction, more than horror. It grapples with what it means to face loss, so in a way, its completion was timely. That said, I first want to thank everyone who helped me push through. You know who you are, and you know how deeply my love and gratitude for you runs.

I also want to acknowledge anyone experiencing their own loss right now. Thank you for making me a part of your journey. Know that it gets better, that you will get through this, even if it doesn't feel like it right now.

Some losses are a gift. They thrust you on the path toward something far greater and far more meaningful. So, here's to new beginnings and to growth, to letting the past go with love and gratitude.

Don't stop moving forward.

While *RIFT* is something of a magnum opus to the dinosaurs I loved as a child (and still do), it also investigates community, relationships, and partnership. It is no surprise, then, that it is the product of a rich community coming together for a singular purpose. Without the network that has coalesced around the project—this community—it would not be what it is today. In some parallel reality in which I went it alone, in which I didn't choose to rely on anyone, it might not even exist at all. Make no mistake, this book is so much more than the author on its cover, and it is far better for it.

So, thank you, *RIFT* community.

To my friends and family, you are my rock. You have been with me through thick and thin and your support means more than you could ever know.

To my consulting team... my sincere hope is all your brilliance has been represented and honored within these pages, but I am compelled to inform the reader that any inaccuracies in scientific rigor, syntax, translation, or otherwise, are my own. Mark Witton, these prehistoric animals would be a mere shadow of themselves without your paleontological expertise; Antonio Padilla, your insight on "creating" black holes was eye-opening and your blessing to use some of your witty quips in Hassan's dialogue helped bring him to life; J, thank you for the veterinary expertise; Mary Schweitzer, our thought-provoking discussion on your work extracting soft tissue from dinosaur fossils filled in the gaps of the story's resurrection science. For translation, Pedro Salas and Heiko von Drengenberg, you both pulled through in a way that lends authenticity to the book's most memorable characters.

My art team... I still gawk at the work generated by Pablo Dominguez (cover art), Steve White (plates), Mark Witton (appendix), Frederic Wierum (appendix), Jerry Reyes (promotional), Rudolf Hima (appendix, promotional), and Jaroslav Kosmina (promotional). You brought this world to life in ways I could never have imagined. My editing team, Kevin Eddy and Oren Eades, you brought this manuscript to the next level. To my early review and beta readers, Thomas Strimpel, Mariano Canales, MJ Nadeau, Spondon Hazarika, Danny Donahue, Whytnie Martin-Sackett, Marcos Kashiwaya Pinheiro, Nicholi Brown, Pat Savage, MK Mons, Vasileios Ntasis, Justin Roe, Ron Day, and J.R. McEvila, you guys crushed it. Thomas Hebert and the folks at Earth Sciences Foundation: thank you for all of the support and for allowing me to tag along on that Hell Creek dig. My Discord members and social media community, thank you for your unwavering support, for trusting me, and sticking with years of anticipation. My sincere hope is that the wait was worth it. To my street team and early access readership (the Pleistosquad) thank you for spreading the word.

And, to *you*, thank you for taking a chance on me, on us.

Recognizing the seemingly innumerable faces behind a project like this lends itself to the surreal recognition that we are wired to depend on others, grief and loss aside. It is our diversity of talent, thought, and ideas that make something like this book a reality. Sure, we are individuals with autonomy and self-determination who can "go it alone," but we must take caution not to poison our minds in pernicious thought cycles, push intimacy aside in the name of pride and the façade of autonomy, shout deleterious mantras like a badge of honor. *I'm independent. Don't need a man. Don't need a woman. Don't need help, connection, partnership, community.* But when we choose to transcend what it truly means to be self-sufficient, we realize that we also have the freedom to choose *when* to depend on another. We *choose* interdependence in our relationships. We *choose* community. We *choose* love.

RIFT is a product of these principles; behind its brutality is a mirror— one that reveals a deeper truth to our shared inner reality—and that is something I'm deeply proud of.

I hope you've enjoyed the ride as much as I have.

Cheers,
Tom Asher

SELECT REFERENCES

For a complete list, visit www.tomashernovels.com/references

Ackerman J (April 11, 2017). The Genius of Birds. *Penguin Books*.

Ahmad R, Sah A, Ahsan M (2017/01/01). Biochemistry and Pathophysiology of Glycation of DNA: Implications in Diabetes. *Arch Clin Biomed Res* 1(1):32-47. doi:10.26502/acbr.5017004.

Aikio, A. (2002). New and Old Samoyed Etymologies. *Finnisch-Ugrische Forschungen* (57). doi: 10.17613/0DW9-YN79

Albert D, Loewer B (Nov 1988). Interpreting the Many Worlds Interpretation. *Synthese* 77(2):195-213.

Battarra L, Lavrelashvili G, Lehners JL (2016). Wormhole creation by quantum tunnelling. *arXiv e-prints*, 1603.08728. doi:10.48550/arXiv.1603.08728.

Bell JS (Nov 1964). On the Einstein Podolsky Rosen paradox. *Physics Physique Fizika, Amer Phys Soc* 1(3):195-200. doi:10.1103/PhysicsPhysiqueFizika.1.195.

Benton MJ (May 12, 2020). Dinosaurs Rediscovered: The Scientific Revolution in Paleontology. *Thames & Hudson*.

Berlin S, Tomaras D, Charlesworth B (2007). Low mitochondrial variability in birds may indicate Hill–Robertson effects on the W chromosome. *Heredity* 99, 389–396. doi:10.1038/sj.hdy.6801014.

Bousso R, Susskind L (Feb 2012). Multiverse interpretation of quantum mechanics. *Phys Rev D* 85(4). doi:10.1103/PhysRevD.85.045007

Bowman CM, Butler EN, Repine JE (Sep 1983). Hyperoxia damages cultured endothelial cells causing increased neutrophil adherence. *Am Rev Respir Dis* 128(3):469-72. doi:10.1164/arrd.1983.128.3.469.

Brusatte SL (April 30, 2012). Dinosaur Paleobiology. *Wiley-Blackwell*.

Bruun G (Jan 1, 1938). Europe and the French Imperium, 1799-1814. *Harper*.

Camus A, O'Brien J (May 7, 1991). The Myth of Sisyphus and Other Essays. *Vintage*.

Dempster WF (1999). Biosphere 2 Engineering Design. *Ecol Engineering* 13:31-42.

DeWitt BS, Graham N (Eds) (2025). The Many-Worlds Interpretation of Quantum Mechanics: A Fundamental Exposition by Hugh Everett, III, with Papers by JA Wheeler, BS DeWitt, LN Cooper and D. Van Vechten, and N. Graham. *Princeton University Press*.

Donlan C, Berger J, Bock C, Bock J, Burney D, Estes J, Foreman D, Martin P, Roemer G, Smith F, Soulé M, Greene H (2006). Pleistocene Rewilding: An Optimistic Agenda for Twenty-First Century Conservation. *The Amer Nat* 168:660-81. doi:10.1086/508027.

Drozdiak W (Sept 12, 2017). Fractured Continent: Europe's Crises and the Fate of the West. *W. W. Norton & Company*.

Duane G (2018). Tunneling through bridges: Bohmian non-locality from higher-derivative gravity. *Physics Letters A* 383. doi:10.1016/j.physleta.2018.12.015.

Einstein A. (2015). Quantum Theory of a Monoatomic Ideal Gas: A translation of Quantentheorie des einatomigen idealen Gases (Einstein, 1924). Translation by Amendola L.

Einstein A, Podolsky B, Rosen N (May 1935). Can Quantum-Mechanical Description of Physical Reality Be Considered Complete? *Phys Rev* 47:777-780. doi:10.1103/PhysRev.47.777.

Geim AK (June 19, 2009). Graphene: Status and Prospects. *Science* 324(5934):1530-1534. doi:10.1126/science.1158877.

Graziano MSA (September 17, 2019). Rethinking Consciousness: A Scientific Theory of Subjective Experience. *W. W. Norton & Company*.

Greene B (Feb 29, 2020). The Elegant Universe: Superstrings, Hidden Dimensions, and the Quest for the Ultimate Theory. *Vintage Books*.

Gribbin J (Aug 1, 1984). In Search of Schrödinger's Cat: Quantum Physics and Reality. *Bantam*.

Henderson, D.M. and Nicholls, R. (2015), Balance and Strength—Estimating the Maximum Prey-Lifting Potential of the Large Predatory Dinosaur *Carcharodontosaurus saharicus*. *Anat Rec* 298:1367-1375. doi:10.1002/ar.23164.

Herdman C, Roy PN, Melko R *et al* (2017). Entanglement area law in superfluid ^{4}He. *Nature Phys* 13:556–558. doi:10.1038/nphys4075

Hoffman D (Aug 20, 2020). The Case Against Reality: Why Evolution Hid the Truth from Our Eyes. *Penguin*.

Holzer BJ (May 2013). Introduction to Transverse Beam Dynamics. *CERN*:21-40.

Hone D, Holtz T (2021). Evaluating the ecology of Spinosaurus: shoreline generalist or aquatic pursuit specialist?. *Palaeontol Elec* 24. doi:10.26879/1110.

Huynen L, Suzuki T, Ogura T *et al* (2014). Reconstruction and *in vivo* analysis of the extinct *tbx5* gene from ancient wingless moa (Aves: Dinornithiformes). *BMC Evol Biol* 14(75). doi:10.1186/1471-2148-14-75.

Ibrahim N, Sereno PC, Varricchio DJ, Martill DM, Dutheil DB, Unwin DM, Baidder L, Larsson HCE, Zouhri S, Kaoukaya A (2020). Geology and paleontology of the Upper Cretaceous Kem Kem Group of eastern Morocco. *ZooKeys* 928:1-216. doi:10.3897/zookeys.928.47517

Jamail D (Jan 15, 2019). The End of Ice: Bearing Witness and Finding Meaning in the Path of Climate Disruption. *The New Press*.

Jarvie S, Svenning JC (2018). Using species distribution modelling to determine opportunities for trophic rewilding under future scenarios of climate change. *Philosophical transactions of the Royal Society of London. Series B, Biological sciences* 373(1761), 20170446. doi:10.1098/rstb.2017.0446

Kaku M (April 2, 2019). The Future of Humanity: Our Destiny in the Universe. *Anchor*.

Kingma E, Finn S (May 2020). Neonatal incubator or artificial womb? Distinguishing ectogestation and ectogenesis using the metaphysics of pregnancy. *Bioethics* 34(4):354-363. doi:10.1111/bioe.12717.

Law C, Leung P (2002). Entangled quantum tunneling of two-component Bose-Einstein condensates. doi:10.48550/arXiv.cond-mat/0209631.

Leanne D Duffy and Karl van Bibber (2009). Axions as Dark Matter Particles. *New J Phys* 11:105008. doi:10.48550/arXiv.0904.3346.

Maldacena J, Milekhin A, Popov F (2023). Traversable wormholes in four dimensions. *Class Quant Grav* 40(15), 155016. doi:10.1088/1361-6382/acde30.

Marais GA (Oct 2007). The Hill-Robertson effects extend from nucleus to mitochondria. *Heredity (Edinb)*. 99(4):357-8. doi:10.1038/sj.hdy.6801034.

Metzl J (April 23, 2019). Hacking Darwin: Genetic Engineering and the Future of Humanity. *Sourcebooks*.

Myhrvold NP, Baumgart SL, Vidal D, Fish FE, Henderson DM, Saitta ET, Sereno PC (Mar 6, 2024). Diving dinosaurs? Caveats on the use of bone compactness and pFDA for inferring lifestyle. *PLoS One*. 19(3):e0298957. doi:10.1371/journal.pone.0298957.

Ojamaa T. (1997). The Shaman as the Zoomorphic Human. *Folklore (Tartu)* 4. doi:10.7592/FEJF1997.04.triinu.

Osada T, Endo H (2011). Linguistics, Archaeology, and the Human Past. *Research Institute for Humanity and Nature*.

Petranek S (July 7, 2015). How We'll Live on Mars (TED Books). *Simon & Schuster/TED*.

Pimm S, Raven P, Peterson A, Şekercioğlu ÇH, Ehrlich PR (2006). Human impacts on the rates of recent, present, and future bird extinctions. *Proc Natl Acad Sci* 103(29):10941-10946. doi:10.1073/pnas.0604181103 (2006).

Pinzon-Rodriguez A, Muheim R (2021). Cryptochrome expression in avian UV cones: revisiting the role of CRY1 as magnetoreceptor. *Sci Rep* 11, 12683. doi:10.1038/s41598-021-92056-8

Pires M, Souza J. (2012). Galactic cold dark matter as a Bose-Einstein condensate of WISPs. *J Cosmol Astro Phys* 11:024. doi:10.1088/1475-7516/2012/11/024.

Rage J-C, Escuillié F (Feb 2, 2017). The Cenomanian: Stage of hindlimbed snakes. *Carnets de Géologie* 2003(01). doi:10.4267/2042/293

Ramos AP, Cruz MAE, Tovani CB, Ciancaglini P (Apr 2017). Biomedical applications of nanotechnology. *Biophys Rev* 9(2):79-89. doi:10.1007/s12551-016-0246-2. Epub 2017 Jan 13.

Ran FA, Hsu PD, Wright J, Agarwala V, Scott DA, Zhang F (2013). Genome engineering using the CRISPR-Cas9 system. *Nat prot* 8(11):2281–2308. doi:10.1038/nprot.2013.143

Reynolds AR, Seymour KL, Evans DC (2021). *Smilodon fatalis* siblings reveal life history in a saber-toothed cat. *iScience* 24(1). 101916. doi:10.1016/j.isci.2020.101916

Riff D, Kellner A, Mader B, Russel D (2002). On the occurrence of an avian vertebra in Cretaceous strata of Morocco, Africa. *Anais da Academia Brasileira de Ciências*. 74. doi:10.1590/S0001-37652002000200023.

Roberts E, Rogers R, Foreman B (Jan 1, 2007). Continental insect borings in dinosaur bone: Examples from the Late Cretaceous of Madagascar and Utah. *J PALEONTOL* 81:201-208. doi:10.1666/0022-3360(2007)81[201:CIBIDB]2.0.CO;2

Sakamoto M. (2022). Estimating bite force in extinct dinosaurs using phylogenetically predicted physiological cross-sectional areas of jaw adductor muscles. *PeerJ* 10:e13731. doi:10.7717/peerj.13731.

REFERENCES

Sander PM, Christian A, Clauss M, Fechner R, Gee CT, Griebeler EM, Gunga HC, Hummel J, Mallison H, Perry SF, Preuschoft H, Rauhut OW, Remes K, Tütken T, Wings O, Witzel U (Feb 2011). Biology of the sauropod dinosaurs: the evolution of gigantism. *Biol Rev Camb Philos Soc* 86(1):117-55. doi: 10.1111/j.1469-185X.2010.00137.

Shapiro B (April 6, 2015). How to Clone a Mammoth: The Science of De-Extinction. *Princeton University Press.*

Szabo LE (2007). The Einstein-Podolsky-Rosen Argument and the Bell Inequalities. *arXiv: Quantum Physics.* n. pag.

Trimmer JD (1980). The Present Situation in Quantum Mechanics: A Translation of Schrödinger's "Cat Paradox" Paper. *Proceedings of the American Philosophical Society* 124(5):323–338.

Van Haaren KH (December 13, 2019). The Road to European Military Cooperation: Exploring Obstacles and Conditions for Joint Development. *Radboud University Nijmegen, Netherlands Defence Academy.*

Varoufakis Y (July 2, 2024). Adults in The Room: My Battle with the European and American Deep Establishment. *Farrar, Straus and Giroux.*

Veebel V (April 2018). NATO options and dilemmas for deterring Russia in the Baltic States. *Defence Studies*:1-23. doi:10.1080/14702436.2018.1463518

Wang D (June 15, 2019). Traversable Wormholes. *Department of Physics, University of California, Santa Barbara.*

Witton MP (June 12, 2017). Pterosaurs: Natural History, Evolution, Anatomy. *The Crowood Press.*

Witton MP (June 23, 2013). Recreating an Age of Reptiles. *Princeton University Press.*

Zitouni S, Laurent C, Dyke G, Jalil N-E (2019). An abelisaurid (Dinosauria: Theropoda) ilium from the Upper Cretaceous (Cenomanian) of the Kem Kem beds, Morocco. *PLoS ONE* 14(4): e0214055. doi:10.1371/journal.pone.0214055.

www.ingramcontent.com/pod-product-compliance
Lightning Source LLC
Chambersburg PA
CBHW030324010826
48973CB00004B/858